Beloved

Also by Bertrice Small

ADORA
SKYE O'MALLEY
UNCONQUERED

Beloved

BERTRICE SMALL

BALLANTINE BOOKS · NEW YORK

This book is affectionately dedicated to four marvelous men of my acquaintance:

Richard Krinsley, who believed in me when he wasn't even sure why he believed, although I have always suspected that Dick is a romantic at heart.

Marcus Jaffe, who respects all his writers no matter the genre, and has more charm per square inch than any other man I've ever known.

Don Munson, and his good right hand, *Jimmy Harris,* who fantasize my words into absolutely luscious covers.

Thanks, guys!

Love—
Sunny

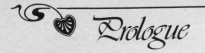

Prologue

The night was black and hot. Not a hint of a breeze stirred the fronds of the tall, stately date palms. The onyx sky was studded diamond-bright with stars, and all was very, very still, as if the earth itself was poised, waiting. On the edge of the great oasis city of Palmyra, the house of the famous Bedawi warrior chief, Zabaai ben Selim, stood alone. Within, a woman labored to bring forth her child.

Her slim white body was tense with the agony of her travail, wet with the perspiration of her effort and the intolerable summer weather. She bore her travail grimly, refusing to cry out, for to do so was a weakness of character in her mind, and she had not won Zabaai by weakness.

In her semidelirium she remembered the day she had first seen him. He had been visiting her father's house in Alexandria on business, and had by mistake wandered into the women's garden. Their glances had met, and her lovely gray-blue eyes had widened at his fierce black gaze. Her soft pink lips slightly parted with surprise, and her young breasts, heaving with emotions she had not known existed, aroused him. No word passed between them. He had not even asked her her name. Instead he had found his way out of the garden, sought out her father, and asked for her to wife. It had been a great impertinence on his part, for her father was not only one of the wealthiest men in Alexandria, he was also a direct descendant of Egypt's last great queen, Cleopatra.

Simon Titus gave his daughter her personal freedom, in the Roman manner. What did she want, he had asked. She had wanted Zabaai ben Selim, that hawk-visaged desert man with his piercing black eyes who in the space of one single moment had captured her soul with his own. It mattered not to her that he was twenty-two years her senior or that he had another legal wife and several concubines. It mattered not that any child she gave him would be unimportant in the line of inheritance. Nothing mattered but her love for this marvelous man, and so Simon Titus had reluctantly given his consent.

They had been married within the month and then she had left the elegant comfort of her father's Alexandrian house to live a life that found her wandering half the year across the Syrian deserts, and living the other half in the beautiful city of Palmyra. It was the custom of the Bedawi to spend the broiling summers in Palmyra, and so part of her dowry had been a fine house and gardens on the city's edge.

A terrible pain, far worse than any previous, ripped through her, and she bit down on her lip. It would soon be over, and her child would at last be born. Zabaai's eldest wife, Tamar, told her to bear down, and she did.

"Push, Iris! Push! Push!" Tamar encouraged her.

"Aiiiiii!" came the collective cry of the other women as the infant began to appear between its mother's legs.

"*Push!*"

"*I am!*" Iris snapped irritably at the older woman.

"Then push harder!" Tamar had no mercy. "The child is but half born, Iris. You must push again!"

Gritting her teeth, Iris pushed down fiercely, and suddenly felt something wet and warm sliding from her body, emptying her out, and miraculously the pain began to subside.

Tamar caught the child, and holding her up announced, "It is a female." She then handed the baby to another woman, and pushed Iris back onto the birthing stool. "You must yet bear the afterbirth. Only then will you be done. One more push will do it."

"I want to see my daughter!"

"Let Rebecca clean the birthing blood from her first. As always, you are too impatient," Tamar scolded, but she understood how it was the first—nay, *every* time.

Within minutes Iris was sponged with cooling rose water, and dressed in a simple white gauze night robe. The baby girl, who had wailed lustily after her birth, was now neatly swaddled, and placed in her mother's arms.

Tamar looked to one of the other women, and commanded sharply, "Fetch my lord Zabaai." As chief wife, she was obeyed and looked upon with fear and respect. It was her son, Akbar, who would one day rule the tribe.

Looking down on Iris, Tamar thought it was no wonder that Zabaai loved her. She was so very beautiful with her milky skin, ash-blond hair, and blue-gray eyes. She was so very different from the rest of them; a woman Zabaai could not only love, but converse with.

He entered the room, a man of medium height and strong

build, his dark eyes sparkling, his dark hair and beard untouched by silver despite his forty-three winters. His handsome face was sharply sculptural with its high cheekbones and hawklike nose. His lips were full and sensuous. His entry brought all the women but Tamar and Iris to their knees. He looked at his two wives, and his black eyes softened. He loved them both. Tamar, the wife of his youth, and Iris, the wife of his old age. The other women might give him variety, and occasional pleasure, but these two he prized.

"The gods have blessed you with a daughter, my lord," Tamar said.

"*A daughter?*" He was surprised.

"Yes, my lord. A daughter."

The kneeling women glanced slyly at each other, and the uncharitable and the jealous among them were hard put not to voice their glee. They were the mothers of sons, and the best the Alexandrian bitch could do was a mere daughter. They watched expectantly for their lord's righteous wrath, wondering if he would deny the brat, and order it exposed.

Instead a smile split his face, and he chuckled with delight. "Iris! Iris!" he said, his deep voice warm with approval. "Once again you have done the unexpected; and you have given me the one thing which, until now, I have lacked. A daughter! Thank you, my beautiful wife! Thank you!"

The kneeling women were aghast. *Praised for having a daughter?* All men wanted sons, the more the better; and Zabaai had never been an exception. He was proud of his thirty-five sons, even remembering all their names and ages. But the more perceptive among the women understood. It was the great love he felt for Iris that would excuse almost any fault. They sighed with resignation.

Iris laughed, and her laughter was soft and filled with mischievous glee. "Have I ever done the expected, my lord?" she asked.

His black eyes laughed back at her. Glancing at the other women Zabaai said curtly, "Leave us!"

"Not Tamar, my lord." Iris would not offend Tamar, who had always been kind to her. She did not forget that if Zabaai died, Tamar's eldest son, Akbar, would hold her fate and her daughter's in his hands.

Zabaai bent to look at his new daughter. Used to large boy babies, he was somewhat awed by the delicate girl child he had sired. The infant slept, dainty dark lashes fluttering slightly against the pale-gold skin. Her dark hair was a small tuft of down upon a well-shaped head. Despite her slumber, her tiny hands moved with a fluttery restlessness, the slender fingers fascinating him with their translucent miniature nails. He regarded her almost warily, for although he knew what one could do with a son, he was not quite sure what one did with a daughter; and this child, of all his children, was the one born out of the great love he felt for its mother.

Looking up, he observed, "She is very small."

Both Iris and Tamar laughed. "Girls," Tamar said, "are usually tinier at birth, my lord."

"Oh." He felt a trifle foolish, but then it was his first daughter. "Where is the Chaldean?" he demanded, suddenly remembering.

"Here, lord." From a dark corner of the room a hunched shape emerged. As it came forward it became an elderly man with sharp eyes and a long, snow white beard, dressed in dark, flowing robes upon which were sewn a pattern of silver-thread stars and moons. The old man bowed low, and Iris held her breath waiting for the slightly askew turban to tumble off his head into her lap. It didn't.

"Did you mark the exact moment of this child's birth in the skies, Chaldean?"

"I did, my lord Zabaai. At the very moment your daughter slipped from her mother's womb, the heavenly bodies of Venus and Mars met in conjunction. Never have I seen the signs so propitious. It portends great things for her."

"What great things, Chaldean?"

"The full natal chart will reveal all, my lord, but I can tell you now that your daughter will be successful in both love and war, for she is already, I can see, beloved of the gods."

Zabaai nodded, satisfied. The Chaldean was the most respected astrologer in the East, noted not only for his accuracy, but his honesty as well.

As the old man backed out of the room Zabaai looked upon his young wife with great affection. "How shall I reward you, my little love, for this marvelous child?" he said.

"Let me name her, my lord," Iris replied.

"Very well," he agreed, pleased. Another woman would have asked him for jewels.

Tamar could not contain her curiosity. "What will you call her?"

"Zenobia," came the answer. "*She who was given life by Jupiter.*"

"Zenobia," Zabaai mused. "It is a good name!"

x

"You must rest now," Tamar said, taking the infant from Iris. "Let your Bab look after Zenobia while you sleep."

Iris nodded, beginning to feel sleepy, now that the immediate excitement of the birth was over. Zabaai arose, bending a moment to kiss his young wife, and then he and Tamar left the room.

Alone, Iris sighed and stretched herself gingerly to find a more comfortable position. How beautiful the baby was! Tomorrow she would have a lamb sacrificed in the Temple of Jupiter to give thanks for her daughter. She wondered about the Chaldean's predictions, not completely understanding them. Then as sleep began to overtake her, her anxieties faded. What did it all really matter as long as Zenobia was blessed and protected? "May you be favored by the gods all your life, my daughter," Iris murmured softly, and then she fell asleep.

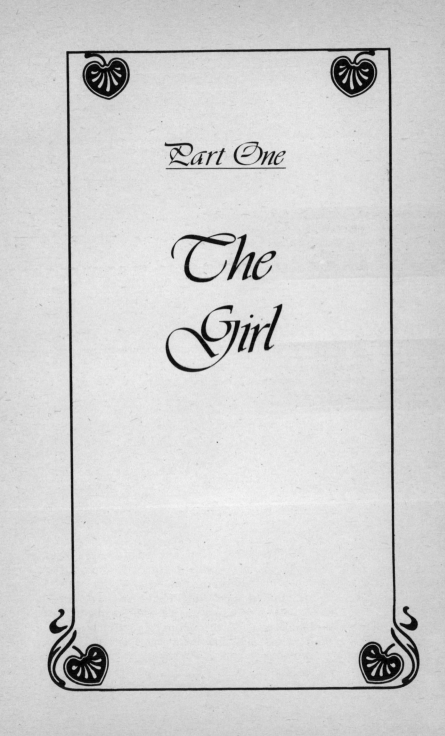

Part One

The Girl

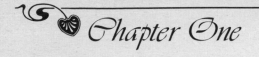

Chapter One

"Happy birthday, Zenobia!"

Zenobia bat Zabaai, now six, smiled happily back at her family. She was a lovely child, tall for her age, with long unruly dark hair that her mother had coaxed into ringlets for this auspicious occasion, and shining silver-gray eyes. Her simply draped white tunic with its pale blue silk rope belt set off her light golden skin.

Zabaai ben Selim swept his only daughter up into his arms, and gave her a resounding kiss. "Don't you want to know what your presents are, my precious one?"

Zenobia giggled and looked mischievously at her adored father. "Of course I do, Papa, but Mama said I must not ask until they were offered."

Zabaai ben Selim was unable to contain himself any longer. "Ali," he roared, "bring in my daughter's birthday gift!"

Into the open courtyard of the house came her father's favorite slave leading a dainty, prancing storm-gray mare, bridled in red leather with tinkling brass bells, and wearing a small matching saddle.

Zenobia was speechless with surprise and delight. More than anything, she had wanted a fine Arab horse for her very own. She had spent the last six months hinting at it none too gently to her father. "Oh, Papa!" she finally whispered.

"Then you like her?" Zabaai ben Selim teased his beloved only daughter.

"Oh, yes! Yes, Papa! Yes!"

"Zabaai, you did not tell me!" Iris looked worried. "A horse? She is far too little."

"Do not worry, my love. The mare has been bred for docility, I promise you."

Tamar put a gentle hand on Iris's shoulder, and said in a low voice, "Don't overprotect her, Iris. You will do her no favor if you do. Bedawi women are bred to be independent."

"I want to ride her now!" Zenobia cried, and Zabaai lifted

his daughter up onto the mare's back. She sat proudly, as if she had been born to sit there. "Come on, Akbar! I'll race you!" Zenobia challenged her father's heir.

"I must get to my horse," he protested, amused.

"Well hurry!" she fussed at him, and was quickly off through the courtyard door.

In the year in which she was eleven Zenobia decided she would not go on the winter trek with her family. Palmyra had suddenly become a fascinating place to her. How she loved the city with its beautiful covered and colonnaded streets, great temples and broad marble avenues, its wonderful shops and open-air markets, each with a different and distinct smell. Leather tanning. Perfumes being blended. Wet wool being readied for weaving and dying. The silk-dyeing vats. The livestock. The spices. Exotic foods of all kinds. She simply couldn't bear to leave it again!

With stubborn resolve she had secreted herself when no one was looking, and now she hugged herself gleefully, convinced she would not be found.

"Zenobia!" Tamar's voice echoed sharply through the virtually empty house. "Zen-o-bia! Where are you, child? Come now, you cannot hide from us any longer! The trek has already begun."

"Zenobia, you are being foolish!" Iris's voice was becoming tinged with annoyance. "Come to us at once!"

Under the great bed in her father's bedchamber the child crouched, chuckling softly. She would *not* spend the winter in the damned desert again this year. The gods only knew she hated it! Miles and miles and miles of endless sand. Long, boring days of blue skies, cloudless and as placid as pap. She sniffed with distaste.

Then there were the goats. While her very best friend, Julia Tullio, got to spend the whole delicious winter season in Palmyra going to the theater and to the games, she, Zenobia bat Zabaai, spent her winters herding a flock of dumb, smelly goats! It was embarrassing! The Bedawi measured a man's wealth in the livestock he owned, which made Zenobia's father an extremely wealthy man; but how she hated chasing those silly, temperamental goats all winter!

Only nights in the desert were interesting. She loved it when the skies grew dark, and filled with crystalline stars, some so bright and so large that they seemed almost touchable. Her father had taught her to read the stars, and she believed that as long as she could see them she would be able to find her way back to Palmyra from Hades itself.

"Ha, Zenobia! There you are!" Tamar reached beneath the bed and pulled her out with strong fingers.

"No!" Zenobia shouted furiously, struggling. "*I will not go!* I hate the months away from Palmyra! I hate the desert!"

"Don't be foolish," Tamar replied patiently. "You are Bedawi, and the desert is our way. Come along now, Zenobia. There's my good girl." Tamar raised her up.

The child pulled defiantly away from the older woman, her strangely adult eyes flashing. "I am only half Bedawi, and even that half does not like the desert!"

Tamar had to laugh, for it was the truth and she could not really blame Zenobia. She was young, and the city was exciting. As Iris joined them, Zenobia flung herself at her pretty parent. "I don't want to go, Mama! Why can we not just stay here? The two of us? Papa will not mind. The theater season is just beginning, and Julia says that a wonderful troupe of dancers and actors from Rome will be performing here this winter."

"Our place is with your father, Zenobia." Iris never raised her soft voice, but there was no arguing with her tone. She stroked her only child's sleek dark head. What a beauty the little one was turning out to be, and how much she loved her!

"Could I not stay with Julia? Her mama says it would be all right. You don't need me to herd the goats!" Zenobia made one last desperate try.

"No, Zenobia," came the firm and quiet reply, but a tiny smile twitched at the corners of Iris's mouth. Poor Zenobia, she thought. She knew just how her daughter felt, but she would say nothing, for she knew sympathy only encouraged rebellion. Iris, too, disliked the desert, but never in all the years she had been Zabaai's wife had she ever admitted it aloud. It was part of her husband's heritage, and when she had married him she had accepted it. She held out her hand to her daughter. "Come now, my dearest, let us go without further ado. The others are already several miles ahead of us, and you know how I dislike galloping a camel. It makes me sick if I must do it for too long. Come along."

"Yes, Mama," Zenobia sighed, defeated.

The three had turned to go when they heard strange footsteps on the stairs outside the bedchamber door. Tamar stiffened,

5

sensing danger. Then, pulling Zenobia from her mother, she pushed the girl down and back under the bed with its bright, red satin hangings.

"Stay there!" she hissed urgently, "and whatever happens do not come out until I tell you! Do you understand? Do not come out until I call you!"

The door to the bedchamber was flung open before Zenobia could protest. She could not see from her hiding place that the room had suddenly been invaded by a small party of Roman soldiers.

Tamar quickly stepped forward, saying, "Good morning, Centurion! How may I help you?"

The centurion eyed her boldly, thinking as he did so that she was a fine figure of a woman with her big, pillowy tits, and that she looked clean, and disease-free. "Whose house is this?" he demanded.

Tamar recognized his look. She prayed she could stay calm. "This is the house of Zabaai ben Selim, warrior chief of the Bedawi, Centurion. Allow me to introduce myself. I am Tamar bat Hammid, senior wife to Zabaai ben Selim. This other lady is my lord's second wife, Iris bat Simon."

"Why are you alone? Where are the servants?" The centurion's tone was arrogant.

"I can see that you are new to Palmyra, Centurion. The Bedawi spend but half the year in Palmyra. The other half we spend in the desert. My husband left but a few minutes ago. Iris and I were checking to be sure that everything was secure. One cannot trust the slaves to see to it." She paused a moment, hoping he would be satisfied and let them go. Seeing his intent still unchanged, she decided to attack. "May I ask why you have entered this house, Centurion? It is not the policy of the Roman Army to enter private houses within a friendly city. My husband is a well-respected citizen of this city, honored by all who know him. He holds Roman citizenship, Centurion, and is personally acquainted with the governor. I would also tell you that Zabaai ben Selim is cousin to this city's ruler, Prince Odenathus."

He did not look at her directly when he said, "The gates were wide open as we rode by, and since we saw that the house appeared to be deserted we came to check that robbers were not stripping the property of a Roman citizen."

He was lying, and both of them knew it. The gates had been firmly locked behind Zabaai when he had left. Tamar was

6

afraid, but she knew that to show fear would encourage these men in whatever mischief they were planning. "As always," she said, her voice heavy with sincerity, "the Romans are the keepers of the peace. I shall tell my lord Zabaai of your concern, Centurion. He will be well pleased."

She turned to Iris, who stood nervously behind her. "Come, Iris. We must hurry to meet our lord Zabaai. Our camels are in the stable, Centurion. Would one of your men be kind enough to fetch them for us?"

"How do I know that you are who you say you are?" the centurion said. "You might be thieves for all I know, and then I should be in trouble with my commanding officer."

The ring of men was closing in about them.

"My lord Zabaai, his wives, and his entire family are well known to the Roman governor of this city," Tamar repeated threateningly. She was very afraid now. These, she realized, were not regular legionnaires. These were auxiliaries, barbarians recruited from Gallic and Germanic tribes, noted for being pitiless, without mercy or respect for anything—including women.

"I am sure that you are both well known in the city," the centurion said insinuatingly, and the men with him laughed, their eyes hot. His gaze bold and cruel, he reached out and pushed Tamar aside. "I want a better look at *you*," he said to Iris, pulling her forward.

At first she looked at him unflinchingly, her blue-gray eyes scornful, but her heart was thumping violently against her ribs. She felt as if she were staring death in the face. The centurion let his hand caress her ash-blond hair almost lingeringly. Slowly the hand wandered downward over her body, fondling her breasts.

"Centurion," she said in a quiet, strained voice, "not only am I wife to Zabaai ben Selim, but I am the only daughter of the great banker, Simon Titus of Alexandria. Do not allow a simple rudeness to escalate into a serious crime."

"You lie," he said pleasantly. "You are a whore of Palmyra."

"Centurion, do not do this thing," Iris said, her voice now trembling. "Do you not have a wife, or a sister? Would you like it if someone did this thing to them?"

He looked at her dispassionately, and she saw no pity or mercy in his ice-blue eyes. "It has been a long time since I have had a fair woman," he said, and then he pushed her back onto the bed.

Her instinct for survival made her attempt to rise, but he

7

shoved her back brutally, and Iris's control left her. She screamed, totally terrified. The centurion slapped her viciously with one hand, while ripping her gown and pushing it up to her belly with the other. His knee jammed between her resisting thighs while she fought him, clawing at his face with her nails, maddened with fear, already ashamed of what was happening to her. She had known no man but her loving, gentle husband. She had known nothing but tenderness and kindness at his hands. Iris had never imagined that a man could do *this* to a woman. Even knowing it was useless, she continued to fight him because something deep within her refused to accept this horror; and the centurion in his fury at being thwarted, continued to strike her into submission. Both her eyes were almost swollen shut when she felt him gain the advantage, and thrust with a cruel, burning pain into her resisting body. Her reason finally left her as he pounded against her again and again, conscious only of his own pleasure in subduing the woman.

"By the gods," he grunted, "this is the best piece of cunt I've fucked in months!"

Beneath the bed, hidden by the coverings, the child Zenobia squeezed her eyes tightly shut. She was terrified by the strange sounds above, trembling and confused at hearing her mother begging in such a frightened voice. Then her mother screamed, and she could no longer hear women's voices, only men's rough laughter, and words she didn't comprehend.

Iris never heard them. She never knew that she was mounted by not only the centurion, but half a dozen other men who patiently waited their turn to violate her now still body. In the end the centurion raped her a second time, cursing when he came too quickly. In his pique he cut her throat as one would butcher a helpless lamb, swiftly, bloodlessly.

Tamar, pulled down onto her back on the cool tile floor, her garments yanked over her head, fared little better than Iris; but Tamar knew enough not to fight back. They left her still body for dead when the last man had finished sodomizing her, not even bothering to use the knife on her. She lay barely breathing while the soldiers stripped the room of the few things left in it for most of its furnishings had gone with Zabaai ben Selim as they always did. Terrified, she held her breath when they ripped the hangings from the bed, along with its coverlets. She prayed to every god she could think of that in their greedy and lustful haste they would not see the child Zenobia. Those fervent prayers were answered. Her eyes met the terrified ones of the

8

girl, and they warned Iris's daughter not to move, to be as silent as the tomb.

It seemed like an eternity that she lay there upon her stomach on the cool tiles, her violated body aching unbearably. She dared not even groan for fear they would realize that she was alive. Finally, after searching through every room for valuables, the soldiers left the house of Zabaai ben Selim. She heard their horses clattering noisily in the courtyard, and wondered why she had not heard them before. Probably because they had led the animals in quietly so as not to surprise anyone left in the house. At least she now knew that they were cavalry, and that would narrow her husband's search for the guilty ones.

Certain that they were now alone, she moaned with pain and tried to sit up. Zenobia scrambled from beneath the bed, her young face wet with tears, as she helped Tamar. The child was pale, and still shaking. She carefully avoided looking at the bed. "Is my mother dead?"

Tamar nodded. "Don't look, child."

"Why, Tamar? Why did they do it? You told them who you were? Why did they hurt you? Why did they kill my mother?"

Tamar spat out a broken tooth. "You cannot tell the Romans anything," she said contemptuously, finally managing to sit up with Zenobia's aid, her back against the bed. Suddenly embarrassed by her disarray, she pulled down the skirts of her dalmatica, which were now ripped, torn, and stained by the soldiers leavings. "I do not believe that they stole the camels, child. Go to the stables, get one, and ride like the wind to your father. Tell him what has happened! I cannot go, Zenobia. I must wait here."

"It is my fault," said Zenobia, tears welling up in her silvery eyes. "My mother is dead! If I had not been such a child, if I had been ready to leave when everyone else was ready instead of hiding like a brat." She began to weep piteously.

Tamar sighed deeply. She ached in every joint, and she wanted to scream at Zenobia that it was indeed her fault for delaying them so that the soldiers caught them unprotected. Then she looked at the child's face, woebegone at the loss of her mother. "No, child," she said firmly, suddenly even believing it, "you must not blame yourself. It was fate, the will of the gods. Go now, and fetch your father."

"Will you be all right?" Zenobia sniffed anxiously.

"Bring me a pitcher of water, and I will survive. Then you must go, but be careful."

"I will leave by the back gate," Zenobia promised.

Tamar nodded wearily. She suddenly felt very tired, and very, very old. She would survive, if only to see those who had done this to her, and so wantonly murdered Iris, punished. She sat in the midday heat after Zenobia left her, watching almost dispassionately as two large horseflies buzzed about Iris's brutalized body.

Zenobia left the house, going by way of the kitchen garden to the stables where three impatient and cranky camels waited, chewing their cuds. She felt nothing. Neither grief, nor anger, nor fear. She was numb with shock remembering her mother's pleas for mercy. Never had Zenobia heard Iris's voice as it had sounded this day—begging and terrified. The echo of it still rang in her ears, and she believed it would haunt her for the rest of her life.

Absently, she patted her own camel, an unusually mild-tempered blond beast. Mounting it, she guided the animal through the back gate of her father's house, after leaning down to unlatch the lock, and out onto the desert road. The camel moved swiftly, taking bigger and bigger strides until it seemed to be flying just above the road.

Zenobia sat atop its back and firmly settled into the red leather saddle, her white linen chiton pulled up to leave her golden legs free to manipulate her mount, her agile mind racing. Why had the men hurt her mother? She did not really understand at all, for she had never known anything but kindness and indulgence from the men in her life. Her father and all of her older brothers spoiled her terribly, as did their close friends. She knew that men sometimes beat their wives, for she was not entirely sheltered; but that was within the realm of the respectable. Everyone said that a woman needed correction occasionally. Still, she had never seen her father beat his wives, and her mother did not even know the men who had attacked her. If Iris did not know them then why were they angry with her, and why did they hurt her, kill her? She simply could not understand.

Was brutality then a trait particular to the Romans alone? Was it some peculiar form of madness that afflicted them that made them turn on innocent strangers?

She goaded the camel to greater speed with her little heels, for ahead she could see the dust of her father's caravan. Soon she was passing the groups of families who made up their tribe. All waved and called out to her in greeting as her camel galloped by them. Their smiles were indulgent, for she was a great favorite with everyone in the tribe, and not simply because she was their leader's daughter. Zenobia bat Zabaai had always been a merry, kindly child. At the head of the group she could see her father, and her eldest brother, Akbar. She began to wave at them, to call out frantically, her young voice sounding hollow in her ears.

"Hola, little one!" Akbar called in a teasing voice. "Want to race that flea-bitten old nag against my champion?" Then he saw her pinched and pale little face, and turning to his father cried out, "Father, something is wrong!"

The entire caravan was stopped and, dismounting his own camel, Zabaai lifted his young daughter down from hers. A crowd began to gather about them.

"What is it, my flower?" the chief of the Bedawi asked. "Where are your mother and Tamar?"

"The Romans," Zenobia began. "The Romans came, and Mother is dead, and Tamar is grievously hurt!"

"*What?!* What is it you say, Zenobia? The Romans are our friends."

"*The Romans have killed my mother!*" she screamed at him, her control finally gone, the hot tears beginning to pour in dirty runnels down her small face. "Tamar hid me beneath the bed. I could not see them, but I could hear them. They did something to my mother that made her scream, and cry, and beg them for mercy! *I never heard my mother beg!* I never heard my mother beg, but they made her beg, and then they killed her! Tamar is so fearfully hurt she cannot even rise from the floor. You must come home, Father! *You must come home!*"

Zabaai ben Selim felt his legs go weak beneath him. He knew what had been done to his wives even if his innocent young daughter did not. His only question was why? With a howl of outrage, pain, and grief he began to tear at his beard and his clothes. Then, when the first onslaught of his anguish passed he began to give orders, and the caravan was quickly turned about. However, Zabaai ben Selim, his elder sons, and his daughter did not wait for the others. Remounting their camels, they quickly rode back along the desert road to the outskirts of Palmyra, where his house stood in the bright midday sun. They rode so hard that the following caravan met their dust, which still hovered in the air, turning it yellow in the heat.

Tamar was but half-conscious when they arrived, and now Zenobia finally dared to look upon her mother's violated body, gasping with horrified shock at what she saw. Iris's body was sprawled grotesquely upon the bed, her pale-blue dalmatic and her snowy interior tunic ripped away to expose her lovely breasts, which were bruised and bleeding. There were great purple blotches on the insides of her milk-white thighs. Her beautiful sweet face with the gray-blue eyes blackened and tightly shut in death, the tender, red mouth viciously savaged and bitten, was barely recognizable. Those who had known her would have been horrified to see how battered her beauty was now.

"*Mama!*" It was a cry torn from deep within Zenobia. She stared in sorrow at her mother's murdered body, unable to fully comprehend, now that she had looked, unwilling to believe that Iris was really dead.

"Take the child out," Zabaai commanded tersely to no one in particular. "She should not have seen this! Take her away!"

"*No!*" Zenobia whirled to defy her father, but she was shaking with shock and grief. "I had to see, and now I will never forget! I will remember what the Romans did!"

Akbar didn't even argue with his small sister. He picked her up with a strong arm, and carried her weeping from the room. She nestled deeply into his arms as if trying to escape the truth, and her bitter sobs tore at his own heart. Wearily, he sat down on the stairs leading to the lower level of the house, and rocked his little half-sister.

Iris had been several years younger than he was when his father had brought her back from Egypt those long years ago. He had imagined himself in love with her for a brief time. He suspected that she had known, but she had never embarrassed him, or played the flirt. She had treated him with respect. A tight sob escaped his own throat.

Zenobia's voice shattered his memories. "Why did they kill her, Akbar? *Why?*" She was looking up at him now, her little heart-shaped face dirty and wet with her tears.

"They killed her because they are Roman pigs," he said angrily. "Everyone not born a Roman they call a barbarian, but it is they who are the real barbarians. They say that Rome was founded by two orphan brothers left on a hillside to die, but rescued and suckled by a she-wolf. I believe it! They are wild animals to this day!"

"What did they do to my mother, Akbar?" she asked fearfully.

He hesitated, not sure he should answer her. She was yet a child. She could even be his own daughter. He had a boy her age. He wasn't sure how much she knew of men and women. Still, he knew from past experience, Zenobia would not be put off.

"Do you know, little flower, how a child is conceived?"

"Yes," she said softly. "Mother had been telling me of these things, for she said that I would one day be a woman in my own body. When a man makes love to his woman a child is the natural result of their union. It is good, my mother said."

"That is correct," he answered her.

He did not elaborate. She understood enough that he might explain, and so he said, "The Romans forced your mother to make love with them, Zenobia. When a woman is forced it is called *rape*. The Romans raped your mother, dishonoring her, dishonoring our father, our family, and the Bedawi. When they had finished with her they then cut her throat so there would be no witnesses against them. My mother they assumed dead without the knife."

Zenobia was silent a moment, and then she said, "Was Tamar raped, too?"

"Yes," he said in a tight voice. "My mother was also raped."

"Is that why she hid me, Akbar?" Zenobia asked. "She did not want me to be raped?"

"Had *you* been raped, my sister, the dishonor would have been the worst of all, for you are a maiden, and have never known a man. Part of your value to your future bridegroom will be in your virginity. A man marrying a maiden does not like to travel a road already well traveled by others." Akbar said solemnly.

She became silent again, and snuggled deeper into his lap. She understood now why her mother had cried, and begged the Romans. She had been attempting to save her virtue, and her husband's honor. What awful beasts the Romans were! Zenobia wanted vengeance!

From her father's bedchamber came the sound of wailing. The other members of the tribe had arrived, and the women going into the room sobbed with sadness, sympathy, and shame. Zabaai ben Selim came out from his room, and said curtly to his eldest son, "Bring Zenobia to her own chamber, Akbar. I would question her."

Akbar arose, and carried his sister to her room in the woman's part of the house. Setting her down upon her bed, he patted her reassuringly and gave her a small smile. Zabaai's own face

13

was grim and forbidding. He looked sternly at his young daughter. "I have heard Tamar's tale, now I want to hear it from your lips."

She gulped, and then told him the story from her child's viewpoint, blaming herself for causing the two women to be delayed. He said nothing. Whatever anger he felt toward his young daughter melted in the face of their shared grief. The Romans would pay! Oh yes! They would pay! A dozen of his sons had already been dispatched into the city with orders to bring the Roman governor back to him, along with Palmyra's young ruler, Prince Odenathus. Only when they saw the horror done his wives would he remove Iris's body from his bedchamber, and bury it with the honor it deserved.

His arm went tenderly around Zenobia and hugged her. "You are not responsible, my child. Rest now, and I will send Bab to you. I regret that you must tell your story a final time to the governor."

Zabaai left the room, his anger now beginning to surface over the shock and the sadness. He had been a citizen of Palmyra for his entire life. He also held Roman citizenship, as did all Palmyrans. It was incredible that imperial soldiers were allowed to get out of hand in a peaceful and nonhostile client city. Suddenly he wanted to be alone so that he might grieve, but it was not yet time for that. First he must beard the Romans, and demand his rightful vengeance.

Returning to the dressing room off his bedchamber he washed the desert dust from his face and changed robes. The slaves removed the basin of rose water that they had brought him. Then they perfumed and combed his beard. He was yet a fine figure of a man, of medium height with his full dark-black beard just beginning to be sprinkled with silver. Only his dark eyes, dull with their pain, betrayed his feelings.

His son entered the room. "They are here, Father."

Zabaai nodded and went out to greet his guests. "Peace be with you, my lord Prince, and you also, Antonius Porcius. You are welcome in my house, though it be a house of sorrow."

"Peace be with you also, my cousin," the prince replied, but before he might say more the Roman governor spoke irritably.

"What is this urgency?" he demanded, his manners gone in the face of his annoyance and the heat headache that pounded in his temples. "I am pulled from my couch by these bearded ruffian sons of yours, Zabaai ben Selim, and forced to come along without explanation! I remind you, chief of the Bedawi,

14

that I am the emperor's governor in Palmyra, and as such I am to be treated with respect!''

"It is in that very capacity, Antonius Porcius, that I have summoned you here.''

"You? You have summoned me?" Antonius Porcius's voice was an outraged squeak. His small double chin quivered angrily.

"Yes!'' came the thunderous reply. *"I,* Zabaai ben Selim, ruler of the Bedawi, have summoned you! You would do well to listen carefully, my lord Governor, to what I am about to tell you. This morning my people and I departed Palmyra for our annual winter trek into the desert. As you well know, we leave this time each year, during the rainy season in the desert, to graze our herds outside Palmyra's boundaries.

"Two of my wives were forced to remain behind, for my only daughter, Zenobia, dislikes this winter wandering, and with a child's logic believed if she hid we would have to leave her in Palmyra. Of course, her mother and Tamar found her. As the women made to leave they heard unfamiliar footsteps on the stairs leading to my bedchamber, and with incredible foresight Tamar hid my little daughter beneath a bed. Praise the gods that she did!

"Roman soldiers had broken into my house, Antonius Porcius. Led by their centurion, they attacked my two wives, raping them, leaving Tamar for dead, cutting my poor Iris's throat. All the while, hidden beneath the bed, my poor little girl cowered, terrified!

"Those men were Roman auxiliaries, Antonius Porcius! Auxiliaries of the Alae! It should not be hard for you to track them down. I want them punished! I will accept nothing less than their deaths, Imperial Governor! Nothing less!''

Prince Odenathus looked distressed at his elder cousin's words. "Your lovely Iris, dead? Zabaai, what can I say to you? How can I comfort you for such a loss?'' Then in a sympathetic gesture he tore his robe. "What of the child, your daughter Zenobia? She was untouched?''

"Yes, the gods be praised! The soldiers did not suspect that my innocent little daughter was also within the room. Had they found my precious child I have no doubt whatsoever that she too would have been viciously attacked! What kind of men are you allowing into the legions these days, Antonius Porcius? Palmyra is not a newly captured city where Romans may rape and loot at will. We are a client kingdom whose citizens are proud to possess Roman citizenship!''

Antonius Porcius, a man in his early middle years, was shocked by what Zabaai ben Selim had told him. He was a fair man who loved Palmyra—indeed, had lived in it most of his adult life. Still he was Rome's governor, and he had to be sure that the Bedawi spoke the truth. "How do I know what you say is true, Zabaai ben Selim? Where are these women you say were attacked? Can they identify their attackers?"

"Come with me!" Zabaai led the way into his bedchamber, where Iris's battered body still lay amid the tangle of her shredded clothing. Tamar, in shock, still sat on the floor, her back against the bed, her eyes staring vacantly. The smell of blood in the hot, closed-up room was now quite apparent, and the flies buzzed noisily about the dead body.

The Roman governor, a small, plump man, looked upon Iris with open horror. He had met her on several occasions and remembered her as beautiful and gracious. The bile rose in his throat, and he gagged it back uncomfortably, ashamed of his entire sex in the face of this tragedy. "Your evidence is irrefutable," he said sadly. "Rome is not at war with Palmyra and her loyal citizens. We are the keepers of the peace. The men involved in this terrible incident will be found immediately, tried, and punished as quickly as possible."

"Today," came the harsh reply. "The sun must not go down upon those criminals unpunished. The soul of my sweet Iris cries out for justice, Antonius Porcius!"

"Be reasonable, Zabaai ben Selim," pleaded Antonius Porcius.

"*I am being reasonable!*" thundered the Bedawi chieftain. "I have not sent my men into the city to cut the throats of every Roman soldier they happen upon. *That* is being reasonable, my lord Governor!"

Suddenly Tamar's eyes refocused, and she spoke. "I can identify the centurion involved, and his men, my lord Governor. I shall never forget his hellish eyes, for they were like blue glass. There was no feeling in them at all. None. They were blank. He had eight men with him, and their faces will haunt my dreams forever. I shall never forget!"

Antonius Porcius turned away, embarrassed. He was often a pompous man, but he was also a good man. The evidence before his shocked eyes was sickening. "My lady Tamar," he said gently, turning back to the woman on the floor. "You say that the men were auxiliaries, and of the Alae. How do you know this?"

16

"They were quite tall," Tamar said, "and very fair with yellow hair, eyes as blue as the skies above, and skin, where it was not brown from the sun, as white as marble. They spoke in guttural accents, as if Latin were not familiar, or easy for them, and they went upon horses, my lord Governor. Their clothing was the clothing of the legions. I am not mistaken, nor am I confused by my ordeal. I remember! I will always remember!"

He nodded, and then asked once more in a gentle tone, "You are quite sure that they understood fully who you were?"

"Both Iris and I explained carefully, slowly, several times. They were bent on mischief, my lord Governor. The centurion said Iris lied, that she was a—a—" Fearfully Tamar glanced toward her husband.

"*A what?*" demanded Zabaai ben Selim.

"A whore of Palmyra," Tamar whispered. Zabaai ben Selim howled his outrage at her words.

Antonius Porcius shuddered. "I must ask you this, my lady Tamar," he said apologetically with a glance of worry toward Zabaai ben Selim. "Who killed the lady Iris? Do you know, or can you remember?"

Beginning to shake with the shock once more, Tamar said, "Iris was taken by the centurion twice. It was he who killed her after he had finished the second time. I pretended to have expired from their attacks, and so they left me for dead."

"What could the child see?" the governor asked.

"She saw nothing, praise the gods!" Tamar replied. "However, she heard everything. The bed coverlets hid her from their lusting eyes. I shall always remember the confused look in little Zenobia's eyes. Those eyes asked a thousand questions I could not answer. What will this have done to her, Antonius Porcius? She has never known anything but kindness from this world."

The governor turned to Zabaai ben Selim. "Can the lady Tamar be made ready to travel? I will have the entire garrison assembled before the city walls. It will not be hard to find the guilty ones with such a witness. Only one of the auxiliary legions is from Gaul. The other one comes from Africa, and its men are as black as ebony."

"I want the centurion," Zabbai said quietly. "Do what you will with his men, but I want the centurion!"

Antonius Porcius agreed quickly, saying, "Only if you punish and execute him before the entire garrison. I want a severe lesson made of him so this will never happen again. We are better off without such scum!''

''I agree,'' Zabaai ben Selim replied.

''I will accompany the governor back into the city, my good cousin,'' the young prince said. ''Will two hours be sufficient time for you to prepare the lady Tamar for her journey to justice?''

Before Zabaai ben Selim might reply Tamar said in a suddenly firm voice, ''I will be ready, my lord Prince! If I live but one moment past the time I testify against those beasts it will be enough!''

Prince Odenathus embraced his cousin, then he and the Roman governor left the room. In the upper hallway they saw the child Zenobia, who had come from her room, her mother's servant, Bab, trailing behind her. Odenathus stopped, greeting her in a kindly voice.

''Do you remember me, my small cousin?''

She stopped, and he was suddenly struck by her beauty. She was but eleven, he knew, but already she showed promise of becoming an incredibly beautiful woman in a city famed for its beautiful women. She had grown tall since he had last seen her some two years ago; but her body was still the flat and rangy one of a child. Her long hair, loose and free of any ribboned restraint, was as black as a clear night sky.

Odenathus reached out and stroked her head as he might his favorite hunting saluki, slipping his hand down to raise up her oval heart of a face. Her hair was soft, as was her pale-gold skin. Her eyes were incredible. Almond-shaped with long, thick black lashes, they were the dark gray of a thundercloud, yet within their depths he could see golden fires banked now by her grief. She had a straight little nose, and such a lovely mouth that he had to restrain himself from bending down to kiss her lips, reminding himself sternly that she was yet a child. Still, he thought regretfully, she was a very tempting nymph of a creature.

''I remember you, my lord Prince,'' Zenobia replied softly.

''I am sorry, Zenobia,'' he said helplessly.

It was then that the silvery thundercloud eyes flashed. ''Why do you tolerate the Roman pigs within Palmyra?'' she burst out angrily at him.

''The Romans are our friends now as they have ever been,

18

my flower. This has been an unfortunate incident," he said smoothly, aware of his companion the imperial governor.

"Friends do not rape and murder innocent women!" she said scornfully. "You have become one of *them,* my lord Prince! A mincing and perfumed fop of a Roman! *I hate them!* I hate them, and I hate you also for allowing them to put a yoke about our necks!"

He could see her eyes were now filled to overflowing with shining tears, but before he could say another word she turned away from him, and ran, followed by her grumbling servant woman.

"Poor little girl," Prince Odenathus said sadly. "She was her mother's only child, and they were very close, Antonius Porcius. I can see how terribly she has been affected by this horrendous crime."

The Roman governor looked after the fleeing child. "Yes," he said. Rome had a bad habit, he thought, of making enemies.

Once the prince and the governor had returned to the city, Antonius Porcius called immediately into his presence the twelve officers who were attached to the two legions at his command. He carefully explained the situation to them, and then asked, "Will the officers of the auxiliary legions stand by us in this matter?"

"I guarantee my Africans," said the tribune of the ninth legion. "They detest the Gauls." His fellow officers nodded in agreement.

"I can see no reason why my Gauls should not see the justice in your punishment, Antonius Porcius," said the tribune of the sixth legion, somewhat stiffly.

"Assemble the entire garrison then," the governor commanded.

Two Roman legions, or twelve thousand foot soldiers plus two hundred forty cavalarymen, and two full auxiliary units, equal in size to the legions, assembled themselves outside Palmyra's main gate. Such a mighty gathering could not help but attract the curious. As word of the soldiers' movement flew throughout the city, the citizenry hurried outside the gates to see what was happening.

On a raised and awninged dais in the hot, late-afternoon sun sat the Roman governor, Antonius Porcius. Resplendent in his purple-bordered white robes, with a wreath of silver-gilt laurel leaves upon his balding head, he waited with Palmyra's princely ruler, Odenathus Septimius. A young man of twenty-two years, the prince set more than one woman in the crowd to dreaming. He was tall with well-formed and muscled arms and legs bronzed by the sun. The short skirt of his white tunic was embroidered in gold. His midnight-black hair was curly, his large eyes velvet-brown. His mouth was wide and sensuous, his cheekbones high, his jaw firm.

He was an intelligent and educated man, who played a waiting game with the Romans. He was not yet strong enough to overcome the invader, but he did have plans. The child Zenobia's angry accusation that he had become one of them had pleased him because it meant that he had succeeded with his ruse. The Romans trusted him.

Reaching up, Odenathus adjusted the crown of Palmyra upon his head. It was a beautiful crown, all gold, formed in the shape of the fronds of the Palmyran palms indigenous to the city. It was, however, hot in weather like this. He sighed, and brushed away a tiny trickle of sweat that attempted to slip down the side of his face.

The governor's trumpeters blew a fanfare, and the noisy crowds grew silent with anticipation. Then Antonius Porcius stood up, and walked to the edge of the dais. Solemnly, with a politician's flair for the dramatic, he let his gaze play over the hushed crowds. Finally he spoke, his nasal voice surprisingly strong.

"Today the glory of Rome was tarnished. It was tarnished not by those who are native to her, but rather by those upon whom she so graciously conferred the prize of her citizenship! Rome will not tolerate this! Rome will not permit those whom we have sworn to protect to be abused by anyone! Rome will punish those who would break her laws—and the laws of Palmyra!"

He paused a moment to allow his words to sink in, and then he continued. "This morning, a wife of Zabaai ben Selim, great chief of the Bedawi, was viciously raped and slain within her very home! Another of this loyal man's wives was also attacked and left for dead!"

A collective gasp arose from the assembled citizens of Palmyra, followed by a low ominous muttering.

Antonius Porcius held up his hands to quiet the anger of Palmyra. "There is more!" he cried loudly, and the crowd grew silent again. "The woman who survived has pushed her shame aside and has come forth to identify those who assaulted her and the poor slain one!"

His words had barely died out when the crowds of Palmyran citizens began to part to allow the camels of Zabaai ben Selim through to the official dais. The sight was both frightening and impressive.

The Bedawi chieftain led the group from atop his own black racing camel. Behind him rode his forty sons from the eldest, Akbar ben Zabaai, to the youngest, a boy of six who sat his own camel proudly and unafraid. Behind the Bedawi chief and his sons rode the other men of his tribe, followed by the walking and mourning women, who wailed a cadence of sorrow.

The camels stopped at the foot of the dais, and knelt in the warm sand to allow their riders to dismount. To everyone's surprise, one of the sons of Zabaai ben Selim turned out to be his only daughter, the beloved child, Zenobia. Flanked on either side by her father and Akbar ben Zabaai, she stood straight and stony-eyed before the Roman governor and Prince Odenathus.

"We have come for Roman justice, Antonius Porcius," Zabaai ben Selim cried. His voice rang clear in the still afternoon.

"Rome hears your plea, and will answer you fairly, Zabaai ben Selim," came the governor's reply. "Lucius Octavius!"

"Sir?" The commanding tribune of the sixth legion stepped forward.

"Assemble your Alae!"

"Yes, sir!" came the brisk reply, and the tribune turned, shouting his commands as he did so. "Gaulish Alae to the front, ho!"

The one hundred twenty men of the cavalry from the Gallic provinces moved slowly forward, finally stopping and lining up in ten rows of twelve men each. Their horses shifted edgily, feeling the men's nervousness. Zabaai ben Selim walked back to where the women of his tribe now stood silent, and led forth his chief wife, Tamar. Together, they moved along the rows of Roman horsemen, and Tamar's strong voice was soon heard as she pointed a short brown finger at the guilty ones.

"That one! And that one! These two!"

Legionnaires of the sixth legion dragged the accused men down from their shying horses, and then before the governor. At the very end of the rows of cavalry Tamar stopped, and Zabaai felt a bone-shattering shudder go through her. Looking

21

up, he encountered a pair of the coldest blue eyes he had ever seen, and a thin, cruel mouth that drew back in a mocking smile.

"It is he, my husband. It is the centurion who raped and killed Iris."

Zabaai, looking into the knowing eyes of the Gaul, understood for a brief minute the terror and the shame that his sweet favorite wife must have felt in her last minutes. A fierce rage welled up within his breast, and with a wild cry of fury he pulled the centurion from his mount. In an instant his knife was at the man's neck, edging a thin red line across his throat. Only Tamar's insistent voice was able to stop her attacker's immediate execution.

"*No, my husband!* He must suffer as our Iris suffered! Do not, I beg you, grant him the blessing of a quick death! He does not deserve it."

Through the red mists of his anger Zabaai felt a hand on his hand, heard the plea of his wife, and lowered his weapon. His black eyes were suddenly filled with tears, and he turned away to hide them, using his sleeve to wipe the evidence of this weakness away so others might not see it. "Is that all of them, Tamar?" he asked her gruffly.

"Yes, my lord," she answered him softly, wanting to take him into her arms and comfort him. If it had been a terrible ordeal for her, so had it been for him. He had lost the thing dearest to him in the entire world. He had lost sweet Iris, and Tamar knew that he would never again be the same. That, more than anything else, saddened her, for she loved him.

She slipped her hand into his and together they walked to the foot of the dais, where Zabaai said quietly, "My wife says that these are all of the guilty ones, Antonius Porcius."

The Roman governor rose from his carved chair and came forward to the edge of the platform. His voice rang out over the crowd. "These men stand accused by their victim, whom they left for dead. Can one of them deny his part?" The governor looked at the guilty eight, who hung their heads, unable to face either Tamar or the others.

Antonius Porcius spoke again. "My judgment is final. These beasts will be crucified. Their centurion is now to be given to the Bedawi for torture and execution. The Roman Peace has prevailed."

A dutiful round of cheers rose from the ranks, a greater cheer from the Palmyrans. Then several legionnaires of the sixth legion dragged forward the wooden crosses that had been brought to the site in anticipation of the punishment to be meted out. The guilty men were divested of their uniforms and stripped naked. They were then bound upon their crosses, which were lifted high and held by one group of soldiers as others pounded them into the sandy ground from atop ladders that had been raised to aid them.

The heat of the late afternoon was barely tolerable, but if the Gauls survived to noon the following day their agony would be exquisite, for spending a morning in the broiling sun of the Syrian desert would swell their tongues black. The wet rawhide strips binding their arms and their legs to the wooden crosses would dry, shrink, and then cut into their flesh, stopping the circulation of blood and bringing incredible pain as, unable to help themselves, the men would sag with their own great weight. Depending upon how physically fit they were, they would begin dying, and they would die by inches.

The cries of their centurion, Vinctus Sextus would follow them into Hell, as he would be kept carefully alive until all of his men were gone. Before their frightened eyes he was even now being stripped preparatory to his torture.

It began simply enough. A stake was driven into the ground, and he was bound to it, his face against the wood, his back to the crowd. Zabaai ben Selim, a slender whip of horsehair in his hand, administered the first five blows. They were not heavy blows, but rather sharp, cutting lashes that gave exquisite pain. Tamar, weakened though she still was, was able to give the prisoner five blows. Then each of the sons of Zabaai ben Selim struck the Roman once. The last five blows were delivered by Zenobia, who wielded the whip surprisingly well for a child, it was thought by the crowd. In all, fifty-five stripes crossed Vinctus Sextus's back, but the Gaul was a tough one, and not once did he cry out, although he remained conscious the entire time.

Zabaai ben Selim smiled grimly. There would be plenty of time for cries, and the Gaul would eventually beg for mercy just as Zabaai's sweet Iris had been forced to beg. It would be many, many hours before Vinctus Sextus expired, and he would wish for death a thousand times before death finally came.

The beating over, the centurion was cut down and dragged across the hot sand to where a block had been set up. Beside the block of marble an open pot bubbled over a neat, leaping fire. Forced to kneel, Vinctus Sextus watched with the first dawning of horror as his hands were swiftly severed from his body before his cry of protest had faded away in the hot afternoon. "Not my hands!" he shrieked. "I am a soldier! I need my hands!" The wolfish faces of his captors grinned mockingly at him, and he realized that even if they should let him live he would be too maimed ever to do battle again.

He watched fascinated as the blood from his severed arteries arced red into the golden sand; but then he was dragged across the small distance to the boiling pot, and his severed stumps were plunged into the bubbling pitch to prevent his death from blood loss. His first real scream of agony tore through the spectators, who sighed with one breath, relieved that the centurion was finally feeling the pain he deserved.

A son of Zabaai gathered up from the sand the two hands, their fingers outstretched in protest, and the chief of the Bedawi smiled once again "Never will those hands again be able to give pain, Gaul," he said. "We will take them into the desert where we will feed them to the jackals."

Vinctus Sextus shuddered. The greatest fear of the men of his northern tribe was to be buried maimed. Without his hands he would be forced to wander in a netherworld that was neither earth nor the paradise of his own woodland gods. He was already condemned by the loss of his hands, yet he still fought on.

He was dragged back across the sand and staked flat upon his back, spread-eagle wide. Two women from the Street of the Prostitutes pushed through the crowd and presented themselves to Zabaai. One of them spoke. "We will help you, chief to the Bedawi, and we will ask nothing in return. Since coming to Palmyra, this man has injured several of our sisterhood, and until now we have had no recourse to justice."

The woman was a tall brunette of mature years, and quite skillfully painted. The beautiful young girl who had come forth with her was no more than fourteen, a blue-eyed golden blonde from northern Greece. With no pretense of modesty the girl stripped off her pale-pink silk robe, and stood naked before the crowd. Her youthful body was pure perfection with marvelous globe-shaped white breasts, a slender waist, and generously shaped hips and thighs. A sigh rippled through the crowd.

With deliberate slowness the girl moved to stand behind

Vinctus Sextus's head. Gracefully she knelt and bent to brush his face first with one of her full breasts, then with the other. The man groaned with pure frustration as Zabaai's deep voice taunted him, "What magnificent fruits, eh Gaul?"

Vinctus Sextus felt his fingers ache and twitch to grasp the tempting flesh rubbing against his face. Instinctively he struggled to move his bound arms. Too late he remembered that he no longer had any hands, and a curse rose to his lips.

Zabaai ben Selim's youngest son, the six-year-old Hassan, had possession of the Gaul's severed hands, and he danced mischievously about the bound man waving his trophies. Taking the hands, he placed them on the prostitute's plump breasts, rubbing them lewdly while the crowd roared with laughter at the boy's impishness. The centurion reverted to his native tongue, screaming, and it was obvious that he cursed the crowd, his fate, and anything else that came into his mind.

"He should be in appalling pain," Antonius Porcius said to Prince Odenathus. "Why is he not?"

"The boiling pitch is mixed with a painkilling narcotic," the prince replied. "They did not wish him to die of the pain, and so they have eased it considerably."

The governor nodded. "They are skillful torturers, the Bedawi. Should I ever need such men, I shall call upon them."

The crowd ohed and ahed at each subtle torture. Fathers held their children on their shoulders for a better look. The two Roman legions and their auxiliaries stood silent, and at attention, but there were many white faces among them, especially those nearest the unfortunate Gaul. Antonius Porcius had already vomited discreetly into a silver basin held by his personal body servant.

As a final torture, Vinctus Sextus was tenderly bathed in warmed water that had been sweetened with honey and orange. Then each of the sons of Zabaai ben Selim emptied a small dish of black ants upon his helpless form. It was too much for even the hardened Gaul. He began to scream frantically, begging for mercy, begging that they kill him now. His big body writhed desperately in an effort to remove the tiny insects feeding upon his sweet-drenched body. Soon his screams grew weaker.

Realizing that the show was now over, the citizens of Palmyra stayed just long enough to see the Roman soldiers break the legs of the eight men who had been crucified, then began straggling back into the city proper, followed by the marching legions. The men of the sixth, and the ninth would consume a great deal of wine in the next several hours in a concerted effort to forget this afternoon.

His legs somewhat shaky, the Roman governor made his way from the dais and walked over to where Zabaai ben Selim stood with his sons and the girl child Zenobia.

"Are you satisfied with Roman justice, Chief of the Bedawi?" he demanded.

"I am satisfied. It will not return my sweet Iris to me, but at least she will be avenged with the deaths of these men."

"Will you now leave on your winter trek?"

"We will stay here until the criminals are finally dead," came the quiet reply. "Only then will justice be done. Their bodies will then accompany us into the desert to become carrion for the jackals and the vultures."

"So be it," said Antonius Porcius, relieved to have the whole messy affair over with. Well, he thought to himself, one good thing came from this. That young blond prostitute was the loveliest creature he had seen in months. He intended buying her from her owners, for he was tired of his current mistress, the wife of a rich Palmyran merchant. Impatiently he signaled to his litter bearers.

"The gods go with you this winter, Zabaai ben Selim. We shall be happy to see you back in Palmyra come the spring." The Roman governor then climbed into the litter and commanded his bearers to hurry back into the city.

Prince Odenathus watched him go, and then he smiled a mischievous smile. "He is as transparent as a crystal vase, our Roman friend," he said to Zabaai ben Selim. "His desire for the blond whore was quite apparent, but he shall not have her. Such a brave girl deserves better than our fat Roman governor."

"She is, I take it, already on her way to the palace," was Zabaai Ben Selim's amused reply.

"Of course, my cousin! The couch of a Bedawi prince is far preferable to that of a mere Roman."

Zabaai ben Selim could not help but smile at his younger cousin. The Prince of Palmyra was a charming young man with not only an intelligent mind, but a keen sense of humor. But like many others in Palmyra, Zabaai still worried that Odenathus was not yet married, and had no heir, for Palmyran law dictated that no illegitimate child might inherit the throne. He looked closely at Odenathus, and asked, "When are you going to wed, my Prince?"

"You sound like my council. It is a question they asks daily."
He sighed. "Life's garden is filled with many beautiful flowers,
my cousin. I have yet, however, to find one sweet bud that
attracts me enough to make my princess. Perhaps," he chuckled, "I shall wait for your little Zenobia to grow up, Zabaai."

It had been said in jest, but no sooner were the words out of
Prince Odenathus's mouth than Zabaai ben Selim realized that
it was the very solution to his problem of a husband for his
daughter. It was something that both he and Iris had worried
about, for none of the young men of his tribe would have been
suitable for their daughter. There was simply no getting around
the fact that Zenobia was different from other girls. Not only
was she far more beautiful than the ordinary Bedawi girl, but
she was highly educated, fearless, and quite outgoing.

She could ride and race both camel and horse as well as any
man. Because she had begged him to do so, he had let her take
arms training with her younger brothers, and he was forced to
admit that she was the best pupil he had taught in years, even
better than her eldest brother, Akbar. She had a natural grace,
and a flair with weapons that was surprising for someone so
young. Strangely, no one gave a second thought to the uncon-
ventional things she did, for she was Zenobia, and unlike any
girl his tribe had ever produced. He was proud of his daughter.

Still no young male Bedawi wanted a wife who not only
rode better than he, but could surpass him in handling a sword,
a spear, and a sling. A woman needed to know how to cook,
how to birth children, how to herd animals, and sew. Zenobia
was definitely not the kind of wife a man of his tribe could
love and cherish, but Odenathus was a different type of man.
Bedawi in his heritage on his father's side, he was yet a man
of the city, and men of the city preferred their women more
educated.

Zabaai ben Selim looked at his young cousin, and said,
"Would you actually consider Zenobia for a wife, Odenathus?
My daughter would make you a magnificent wife, my cousin!
You could have no better. She is more than well born enough
for you, for on my side you share the same great-grandfather,
and on her mother's side she descends from Cleopatra, the last
queen of Egypt. She is not yet a woman, but in a few years she
will be of marriageable age. I will only give her as a wife, not
a concubine, and it must be agreed that her sons be your heirs."

Prince Odenathus was thoughtful for a long moment. It was
certainly not a bad idea, and would solve his problem as well.

27

Zenobia bat Zabaai was dynastically a good match for him. She was also an educated and intelligent girl from what he had seen of her. If a man was to have intelligent sons then he must marry an intelligent wife, Odenathus thought. She might be an interesting woman someday.

"How soon after Zenobia becomes a woman would you be willing to give her to me, Zabaai?" he asked.

"A year at the very least," came the reply. "I will not even broach this matter with her until she has begun her show of blood, and then she will need time to adjust to the idea of marriage. She has lived all her life in the simple surroundings of the tribe, but my daughter is not just any girl, Odenathus. She is a pearl without price."

Palmyra's young ruler looked across the sand to where the girl child Zenobia sat cross-legged upon the desert floor, watching with strangely dispassionate eyes the agony of her mother's killer. She sat very straight, and very still, seemingly carved out of some inanimate material. He had seen young rabbits sit just that way. She seemed not even to be breathing.

He shook his head in wonder. The Gaul was suffering horribly, and yet the child showed no signs of compassion, or even of revulsion. A man could breed up strong sons on the loins of such a woman as this child would one day become; but he wondered fleetingly if such a woman would recognize in her husband a master? Perhaps if he took her to wife early enough, and molded her woman's character himself, it would be possible. Odenathus found that he was willing to take a chance. He found himself inexplicably drawn to Zenobia, for her very strength of character intrigued him greatly.

He smiled at himself. He would not, however, give Zabaai ben Selim too great an advantage, and so he said in what he hoped was a slightly bored and jaded tone, "A match between Zenobia and myself is a possibility, my cousin. Do not give her to anyone else yet, and let us talk on it again when the child becomes a woman if my heart has not become engaged elsewhere."

Zabaai smiled toothily. "It will be as you have said, my lord Prince, and my cousin," he replied smoothly. He was not for one moment fooled by Odenathus's cool attitude, or his nonchalance. He had seen the genuine look of interest in the young man's warm brown eyes when he had gazed so long and so thoughtfully at Zenobia.

"Will you bid my daughter farewell, my Prince?" he asked. "We will not re-enter the city again until late spring. Once the soldiers have died, we will go on our way into the desert as we have planned."

Odenathus nodded, and bade Zabaai ben Selim a safe trip. Then he walked across the desert floor to where Zenobia sat. Seating himself beside her, he took her little hand in his own. It was cold, and instinctively he sought to warm it, holding it tightly in his own.

"The Roman dies well," she said, acknowledging his presense, "but it is early yet, and he will in the end cry to his gods for mercy."

"It is important to you, that he beg for mercy?"

"Yes!" She spat the word out vehemently, and he could see that she was once more going to withdraw into her private thoughts. She hated well for one so young and, until today, so sheltered. More and more this child fascinated him.

"I would bid you good-bye, Zenobia," he said, piercing again into her self-absorption.

Zenobia looked up. How handsome he is, she thought. If only he hadn't given in to the Romans so easily. If only he weren't such a weakling.

"Farewell, my lord Prince," she said coldly, and then she turned back to contemplate the dying man.

"Good-bye, Zenobia," he said softly, lightly touching her soft dark hair with his hand; but she didn't notice. He stood up and walked away.

The sun was close to setting now, and had turned the white marble towers and porticos of Palmyra scarlet and gold with its clear light; but Zenobia saw none of it. Campfires sprang up on the desert floor as she sat silently watching her mother's despoiler. About her the Bedawi went about their own business of the evening. They understood, and waited patiently for the child's thirst for vengeance to be satisfied.

Vinctus Sextus had been unconscious for some time, but then he began to revive slightly, roused by the waves of pain that ate into his body and his soul as the painkillers given him earlier wore off. That he wasn't already in Hades surprised him. Slowly he forced his eyes-open to find a slender girl child sitting by his head, contemplating his misery.

"W-who . . . are . . . you?" he managed to ask through parched and cracked lips.

29

"I am Zenobia bat Zabaai," the child answered him in a Latin far purer than any he had been able to learn. "It was my mother that you slaughtered, pig!"

"Give . . . me . . . a drink," he said weakly.

"We do not waste water here in the desert, Roman. You are a dying man. To give you water would be to waste it." Her eyes were gray stones and totally without feeling as they stared at him.

"You . . . have . . . no . . . mercy?" He was curious.

"Did you show my sweet mother mercy?" The child's eyes blazed intense hatred at him. "You showed her none, and I will show you no mercy, pig! None!"

He managed a wolfish parody of a grin at her, and they understood each other. He had shown her blond beauty of a mother no kindness or mercy. He wondered if, having been given a glimpse of his fate, he would do it all over again, and decided that he would. Death was death, and the blonde had been more than worth it. Men had died for less. He blinked rapidly several times to clear the fog over his blue eyes so he might see the child better. She was a little beauty facially, but she yet had the flat, unformed body of a child.

"All women . . . beg . . . when beneath a man. Didn't . . . your mother . . . ever . . . tell you . . . that?"

Zenobia looked away from him and across the desert, not quite understanding his words. The sun had now set, and the night had come swiftly. About her, the golden campfires blazed merrily, while the stars stared down in their silvery silence. "You will die slowly, Roman," she said quietly, "and I will stay to see it all."

Vinctus Sextus nodded his head slightly. He could certainly understand vengeance. The child was one to be proud of even if she was only a girl. "I will do . . . my best . . . to oblige you," he said with a scornful and defiant sneer. Then he drifted into unconsciousness.

When he opened his eyes again it was pitch black but for the light of the campfires that darted across the sand. The child still sat motionless and totally alert by his side. He drifted off again, returning as dawn came. He watched it creep across the desert floor with tiny slim fingers of violet and apricot and crimson. He could still feel the pain, worse now than it had ever been, and he knew death was near to him.

The narrow stripes upon his back had festered in the night; the thousand ant bites on his body stung and burned unbearably. The rawhide bindings on his arms and legs had now dried, and were cutting painfully into his ankles and his wrists. His throat was so parched that even the simple act of swallowing hurt him. Above, the sun rose higher and higher until it blinded him even when he closed his eyes. He could hear his surviving companions moaning and crying out to their own gods, to their mothers, as they hung upon their crosses. He tried turning his head to look at them, but he could not. He was stretched wide, and tight. Movement was now quite impossible.

"Five are already dead," the child said brutally. "You Romans are not very strong. A Bedawi could last at least three days."

Soon the groans stopped, and the child announced, "You alone are left, Roman, but I can tell that you will not last a great deal longer. Your eyes have a milky haze over them, and your breathing is rough."

He knew that she was right, for already he felt his spirit attempting to leave his body. He closed his eyes wearily, and suddenly he was back in the forests of his native Gaul. The tall trees soared green and graceful toward the sky, their branches waving in the gentle breeze. Ahead was a beautiful and cool blue lake. He almost cried aloud with joy, and then his lips formed the word, *"Water!"*

"No water!" the child's voice cut ruthlessly into his pleasure, and he opened his eyes to face the broiling, blazing sun. It was too much! By the gods it was too much!

Vinctus Sextus opened his mouth, and howled with frustrated outrage and pain. The sound of the child's triumphant laughter was the last thing he heard. It mocked him straight into Hell as he fell back dead upon the desert floor.

Zenobia arose swaying, for her legs were stiff. She had sat by Vinctus Sextus for over eighteen hours, and in all that time she had neither eaten nor drunk anything. Suddenly she was swept up in a pair of strong arms, and she looked into the admiring face of her eldest half-brother, Akbar. His white teeth flashed in his sun-browned face.

"You are Bedawi!" he said. "I am proud of you, my little sister. You are as tough as any warrior! I would fight by your side anytime."

His words gave her pleasure, but she only said, "Where is Father?" Her voice was suddenly very adult.

31

"Our father has gone to bury your mother with the honor and the dignity she deserves. She will be put in the tomb in the garden of the house."

Zenobia nodded, satisfied, and then said, "He begged, Akbar. In the end he begged the same way that he forced my mother to beg." She paused as if considering that, and then she said softly, "I will *never* beg, Akbar! Whatever happens to me in my lifetime, I will never beg! *Never!*"

Akbar hugged the child to his breast. "Never say never, Zenobia," he warned her gently. "Life often plays odd tricks upon us, for the gods are known to be capricious, and not always kind to us mortals."

"*I will never beg,*" she repeated firmly. Then she smiled sweetly at her brother. "Besides, am I not the beloved of the gods, Akbar? They will defend me always!"

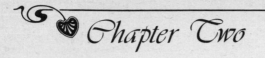

Chapter Two

Odenathus, Prince of Palmyra, sat his horse and watched the maneuvers of a Bedawi camel corps. Its warriors were magnificently trained, and under the direction of their captain they performed extremely well. The prince turned and said to his host, "Well, my cousin Zabaai, if all your troops perform this well; if all your captains are that competent; I foresee a day when I may drive the Romans from my city."

"May the gods grant your wish, my lord Prince. Too long has the golden yoke been about our necks, and each year the Romans take more and more of the riches that come to us from the Indies and Cathay. We are beggared trying to feed their rapacious appetites."

Odenathus nodded in agreement, and then said, "Will you present me to the captain of your camel corps? I should like to congratulate him on his leadership."

Zabaai hid a smile. "Of course, my lord." He raised his hand in a signal, and the camel cavalry whirled away from him, galloped down a stretch of desert, and then turned to come racing furiously back to stop just short of the two men. "The prince would like to present his compliments, Captain," Zabaai said.

The leader of the corps slid from his mount and bowed smartly before the prince.

"You handle your men well, Captain. I hope that someday we may ride together."

"It will be an honor, my lord, although I am not used to sharing my command with anyone." The captain's burnoose was tossed back, and the ruler of Palmyra found himself staring into the face of the most beautiful woman he had ever seen. She laughed at his surprise, and said, "Do you not recognize me, my cousin?"

"*Zenobia?*" He was astounded. This could not be Zenobia! Zenobia was a child. This statuesque goddess could not be the

33

flat and leggy child he remembered. Three and a half years had passed since he had last seen her.

"You're staring," she said.

"What?" He was totally confused.

"You are staring at me, my lord. Is something wrong?"

"You've changed," he managed to say in a somewhat strangled voice.

"I am almost fifteen, my lord."

"Fifteen," he repeated foolishly. By the gods, she was a glorious creature!

"You may go now, Zenobia," Zabaai dismissed her. "We will expect you at the evening meal."

"Yes, Father." Zenobia turned and, grasping her camel's bridle, swung herself back up into the saddle. Raising her hand as signal, she led her camel corps away as the two men re-entered Zabaai ben Selim's tent.

"Did you or did you not propose a match between your daughter and myself several years back, Zabaai?" the Palmyran prince demanded.

"I did."

"The girl was to become my wife a year after she became a woman. Is that not correct?"

"Yes, my lord."

"Has she now reached her maturity?"

"Yes, my lord." It was all that Zabaai ben Selim could do to keep from laughing. Odenathus's desire was so open as to be embarrassing.

"Then why is she not my wife?" came the anguished cry.

"Nothing was formally proposed, my lord. When you did not make formal application for my daughter's hand I was forced to conclude that you were not seriously interested. Besides, your devotion to your favorite, Deliciae, is well known. She has given you two sons, has she not?"

"Deliciae is a concubine," Odenathus protested. "Her sons are not my heirs. Only my wife's sons will hold that distinction."

"You do not have a wife," Zabaai ben Selim reminded.

"Do not toy with me, cousin," Odenathus said. "You know full well that I want Zenobia to wife. You knew that the moment I saw her I would want her. Why did you simply not present her to me? Why that silly charade with the camel corps?"

"It was no charade, my lord. Zenobia commands her own corps, and has for two years now. If I let you marry her it must

34

be with the understanding that she is free to go her own way. She is not an ornament to be housed like a fine jewel in the box of your harem. My daughter descends from the rulers of Egypt, and she is as free as the wind. You cannot pen the wind, Odenathus.''

"I will agree to whatever you wish, Zabaai, but I want Zenobia!'' the prince promised rashly.

"The first thing I want is that you get to know one another. Zenobia may have the body of a woman, but she is yet a child where men are concerned.''

"She is still a virgin?''

Zabaai chuckled. ''Not that the young men of my tribe have not tried, Odenathus, but my daughter is yet a virgin. It is very difficult to make love to a girl who can outwrestle you. Zenobia is, as you undoubtedly noticed, quite tall for a girl. She gets her height from her Greek-Egyptian ancestry, not the Bedawi. She is at least as tall as you, Odenathus. Not at all like your Deliciae, who can look up at you. Zenobia will look you right in the eye.''

"Why did you not offer her to me again, Zabaai? The truth, my cousin.''

Zabaai ben Selim sighed. ''Because I am reluctant to give her up, Odenathus. She is my only daughter; Iris's child; and when she is gone from me I will miss her. If you wed her you will find in her an interesting companion. She will not simper at you like so many of these harem females. She will be your friend as well as your lover. Are you man enough to accept a woman on those terms?''

"Yes,'' came the unwavering reply.

"So be it then,'' the Bedawi chief said. ''If Zenobia has no objections after you two have grown to know one another, then you may have her to wife.''

"May I tell her?'' he asked.

"No, I will tell her, my cousin, and I will tell her immediately so there will be no confusion or restraint between you.''

The two men separated then, the prince returning to his own tent, and the Bedawi chieftain to his daughter's quarters. He found her sponging herself with a small basin of perfumed water, grumbling as she always did over the scarcity of the precious liquid here in the desert. Still she was careful not to waste the water, and reused it several times, storing it in a goatskin bag between her ablutions.

35

"Praise Jupiter that it is almost time to return to Palmyra!" she greeted him. "You have no idea, Father, how I long for a decent bath!"

He chuckled, and sat cross-legged on a carpet. "Odenathus wants to marry you," he said, coming directly to the point.

"Isn't that what you've wanted for me all along, Father?" She took up a small linen towel, and mopped where a few drops of water had spilled on her table.

"You have to marry eventually, Zenobia, but I want you to be happy. Odenathus is a wealthy, pleasant, and intelligent young man. Still, if there is someone you would prefer then it shall be as you desire, my child."

"Only one thing concerns me about the prince," she said. "It distresses me that he gives in to the Romans so easily, and without a fight. I do not understand it."

"It is quite simple, Zenobia," Zabaai replied. "Palmyra, as you know, was founded by Solomon the Great, King of Israel. It has always been a commercial state. We have never been interested in expansion, in taking our neighbors' lands. Our only interest is in making money, and because everyone needed us, and our talents, and because we are located here in the Syrian desert, no one bothered us. We have been friends to the world, but Rome is a conqueror, and has a conqueror's fear of her neighbors. Palmyra is an outpost for Rome against Persia, Cathay, and the Indies.

"But because we are a nation of merchants, and not soldiers, we have never been prepared to defend ourselves. After all, we have never needed to. If Odenathus ever attempts to thwart Rome, they will destroy the city without a thought. He does the next best thing—he welcomes them, and in doing so saves us all. Do not judge him too harshly. When the time is right he will drive them from our land, and we will once again be our own masters."

"If I marry the prince will my children be his heirs? The gossips say he is quite fond of one of his concubines—and her children. I will have no one else's children supplanting mine."

"Your children will be his legal heirs, my daughter."

"Then I will marry him, Father."

"Wait, my child," Zabaai cautioned. "Get to know him before you agree to this match. If you then still wish to wed him, so be it."

"You say that eventually I must marry, Father. The prince has asked for me, and I will agree. If I must wed then at least it will be to a man who lives in Palmyra, so I may at last be free of your desert." She twinkled mischievously at him, and Zabaai chuckled indulgently. How he loved this child. "The prince is handsome," continued Zenobia. "He has always been kind to me, and I have never heard anyone say that he is not a fair or good ruler. There seems to be no malice in him at all." Zenobia knew no matter how fair her father meant to be she could not refuse the prince. Still, she loved Zabaai all the more for pretending the choice was hers.

"You say nothing of love, my child. For a marriage to be successful there must be love between a man and a woman. The moment I saw your mother those long years ago in Alexandria I knew I loved her, and she knew she loved me. Love sustains a man and woman in the hard times."

"You and Mother were unusual, Father. Tamar tells me that love is something that grows between a man and a woman. I believe that, given time, I can love Odenathus, and he already loves me. I can tell. Did you see how foolishly he behaved today? I didn't mean to laugh at him, but he looked so silly with his mouth open." She giggled with the memory.

Zabaai didn't think that this was the time to explain to his daughter the difference between lust and love. Let her believe that Odenathus was already in love with her. It wouldn't hurt to give the prince that small edge. "Make yourself beautiful, my child," he said, and then in a rare show of open affection he kissed her cheek. "You may eat with us instead of the women this evening."

Left alone, Zenobia turned to her mirror, a round of burnished silver. Pensively, she stared into it. Everyone said that she was a beauty, and compared to other girls her age she was. But would she be able to compete with the women of Palmyra? Would Odenathus think that she was beautiful? She knew all about his concubine, Deliciae, and she would have to accept the woman. A slave girl from northern Greece, Deliciae was said to be very beautiful, fair-skinned, azure-eyed, yellow-haired.

Zenobia looked at herself with a critical eye. Pale-gold skin, the cheeks of her oval face touched with apricot; long, thick, straight dark hair, silken to the touch, so perhaps it would be pleasing to him. She seemed to remember that he was always caressing her head.

She looked harder at herself. She was tall for a woman, she knew, but her body was flawless, her limbs well rounded without being fat, thanks to the active life she led. She gently slipped her slender hands beneath her breasts, and looked at them critically. They were round, firm, and full. She knew the value that men put on women's breasts, saw with satisfaction that she would not be found wanting there. Her waist was slender, the hips slim, but pleasingly rounded. Zenobia's gaze moved upward again in the mirror, to her face, and she stared hard.

The cheekbones were high, the nose quite straight and classic, the lips full and generous, the chin small, square, and determined. Her eyes, she decided, were her best feature. Almond-shaped, topped by slender, arched, black brows and thickly fringed with black lashes, they were deep gray with tiny golden flecks, like leaves in a winter pond. The color darkened to almost black when she was angry, remaining a deep gray at other times. They were the kind of eyes a man couldn't resist looking into. Although Zenobia was too young to realize it, her eyes were the mirror of her soul, telling anyone who was wise enough to look deeply into all her secrets.

"If he does not find you the most beautiful woman in the world then he is blind in both eyes, little sister."

Zenobia turned her eyes from the mirror. "It is his favorite concubine I am worried about, Akbar. Men of the desert are susceptible to fair women."

"He has not married her," came the reply.

"She is a slave, Akbar. Men do not marry their slaves. They may love them, but they do not marry them. What if he loves her, but marries me simply for heirs? I have been surrounded by love my whole life, Akbar. I was conceived by a great love. I cannot live without it! What if he does not love me?"

"You do not have to marry him, little sister. Father has said he will not force you to it."

"I am almost fifteen, my brother. Most girls my age have been married for two years, and already have children. What if I never find this love that exists between a man and a woman? If I do not marry Prince Odenathus, who will I marry, Akbar? Who will have an educated woman to wife? I often wonder if Mother and Father did not do me a great disservice educating me. Perhaps I would have been better off if I had learned nothing but woman's ways." She sighed, and flung herself on her couch.

Akbar stared at his half-sister in surprise, and then he began to laugh. "By Jupiter, you are afraid! Never did I think to see the dày when Zenobia bat Zabaai would be afraid, but you are! You are afraid that Odenathus will not like you! You are afraid of a blue-eyed, yellow-haired whore! Zenobia, my sister, the poor Prince of Palmyra is already half in love with you. If you will be but kind to him he will be your devoted slave for the rest of your life. All he desires is a little encouragement. As to the concubine, Deliciae, of course he is fond of her. She is an amiable creature, surely you cannot be afraid of that piece of fluff?''

"She is so . . . so womanly, and I am more at home with a weapon than a perfume bottle!''

"You arc unique, my sister.''

"Would you like a woman like me, Akbar?'' The concern in her young face was so intense that he almost hurt for her.

"Too easy a conquest can be pleasant, but very boring, my sister. Be yourself with Odenathus. He will love you.'' Akbar walked over to where his younger half-sister lounged, and bent to kiss her head. "Stop brooding, foolish child, and make yourself beautiful for the prince. I will come back shortly, and escort you myself to Father's tent for the evening meal.''

When she looked up he was gone, and Bab was entering the tent. Dearest Bab, Zenobia thought affectionately. How she was going to enjoy living in a civilized city again! Bab had been her mother's servant, and had come with Iris from Alexandria. When Iris had died she had simply taken over Zenobia, and continued on with her duties. She was getting on in years now, thought Zenobia, and the traveling was becoming harder for her. She watched with loving eyes as the older woman moved about the tent preparing her mistress's clothing for the evening.

"Ah, your dear mother would be happy with this match,'' Bab commented. "It is your son who will be the next ruler of Palmyra after Odenathus.''

"At least if I do marry him,'' Zenobia teased, "you will spend your declining years within a city instead of out upon the desert.''

"*Declining years?*'' Bab's lined and weathered face registered instant offense. "And who is declining, I should like to know? I served your mother. I serve you, and I expect someday I shall serve your daughter. Declining years! Humph!'' She bent over the cedar chest, and drew forth a soft white cotton chemise and a snow-white tunic. "You'll wear these,'' she said, holding them out.

Zenobia nodded and shrugged off the short black chiton she had been wearing. Bab took a small sea sponge and, dipping it in fragrant oil, smoothed it over her mistress's nude body. The young girl wrinkled her nose with delight. She loved the rich hyacinth fragrance, remembering that Iris had given her a small flacon of the perfume when she was ten. Bab slipped the chemise and then the tunic over Zenobia's head. The tunic was made of fine linen, and Bab belted it with a length of thin leather that had been gilded with silver leaf. There were matching silver sandals for Zenobia's slender feet.

The tunic was sleeveless and its neckline was draped low, revealing the soft perfection of her breasts. Bab sat the girl down while she brushed and brushed the long black hair, finally braiding it and looping it under once to be fastened with a pearl-and-diamond hair ornament. She then offered her young mistress a small jewel case, which Zenobia stared into for a few moments, studying the precious gems and metals. Finally she removed a carved silver bracelet, a smooth ivory one banded with silver, one of carved ivory, and another of polished blue lapis, which she slipped on one of her arms. Into her ears she fitted silver-and-lapis earrings, and upon her fingers went two rings, one a large creamy round pearl, the other a carved scarab of blue lapis that had belonged to her mother.

Bab nodded her approval of Zenobia's choices, and took up a small brush, which she dipped in kohl. Carefully, she painted the girl's eyes to highlight them, but Zenobia's lips and flushed cheeks needed no artifice, having their own color. The girl reached for an ivory scent bottle and, uncorking it, daubed the exotic hyacinth fragrance on herself. She stood and, looking at herself in the mirror, said, "Well, I suppose I am as ready as I'm going to be, Bab."

Bab chuckled. "You will ravish him, my pet."

Zenobia smiled, but it was a smile without enthusiasm.

Zabaai ben Selim might be a Bedawi chief, but he was a man who liked his comfort. His tent was set upon a low platform that could be separated into several sections for easier transport. Inside, the floor was covered with thick wool rugs in reds, blues, golds, and creams. The tent poles were gilded, and the finest brass and silver lamps hung from the tent ceiling, burning perfumed oils. The great tent was divided into two sections, the smaller sleeping area separated from the main part of the tent by woven silk carpets from Persia. The furnishings were simple but rich; low tables of wood and brass, chests of cedar, and many colorful pillows for seats.

There were several men in the room besides the prince and her father. She saw several of her half-brothers besides Akbar. There was Hussein, and Hamid, and Selim, all full brothers to Akbar, all Tamar's sons. They grinned knowingly at her, causing a blush to color her cheeks, which made them chuckle indulgently. For some reason, their smug complacency drove a streak of rebellion into her heart and mind. How dare they presume that all was settled?

"Come, my daughter, and sit between us," Zabaai commanded her gently. He had seen the fire in her eyes, and guessed that she might be feeling a bit fractious.

Zenobia sat down quietly, keeping her eyes lowered, furious with herself for suddenly feeling shy. Silent slaves began to serve the simple meal. A young kid had been roasted, and there was a dish of rice with raisins. Zenobia was delighted to find in the middle of the table an arrangement of fruits the like of which she hadn't seen since they left Palmyra almost six months earlier. There were grapes both purple and green; figs and dates; peaches and apricots. A small smile of delight curved the corners of her mouth, and she reached out to take an apricot.

"You must thank Odenathus for such bounty, Zenobia," her father said.

"You brought the fruit from Palmyra?" She looked up at him with her marvelous eyes, and for a moment the prince thought he was going to drown in the depths of them.

Finally he managed to find his voice. "I remembered how you dislike trekking the desert, and thought by now you must long for fresh fruit."

"*You brought it for me?*" She felt shy again.

"See what an easy woman she is to please, Odenathus?" Akbar teased. "Another woman would have asked for emeralds and rubies; but my little sister is satisfied with apricots. 'Tis an admirable trait in a wife."

"I thank you for the fruit, my lord." She was silent again.

Zabaai was concerned. It was not like Zenobia to be so quiet and shy. He wondered if she were ill, but then he realized that the prince, too, had said very little during the meal. Both he and Zenobia were behaving like two young animals placed in the same cage for the first time. Warily they circled each other, and sniffed the air cautiously for signs of hostility. The Bedawi chieftain smiled to himself, remembering himself in his youn-

41

ger days with each new girl; each girl except Iris. It had always been different with Iris. He was somewhat troubled that Zenobia seemed reluctant about young Prince Odenathus, but then she had never before been exposed to a suitor.

The meal concluded with sweet cakes made of thin layers of dough, honey, and finely chopped nuts. There had been marvelous Greek wine served all during the meal, and the men were feeling relaxed. Zenobia had drunk very little, and seemed unusually sensitive to her half-brothers' teasing. Normally she would have bantered with them.

Finally Zabaai said in what he hoped was an offhand manner, "My daughter, the moon will not rise until quite late tonight. There is a fine display of stars. Take Odenathus and show him your knowledge of astronomy. You could put Zenobia anywhere on this earth, my Prince, and she would be able to find her way back to Palmyra by using the sky to guide her."

"I have a fine observatory in the palace," Odenathus replied. "I hope you will visit it someday." He rose and, holding out his hand, helped Zenobia up.

Together they walked from the tent while behind them Zabaai quelled his sons' ribald humor with a stern look. Silently they strolled through the encampment, and Zenobia stole looks from beneath her long lashes at the prince. He was really a very handsome young man, she had to admit. Unlike her father and half-brothers, who wore the long, enveloping robes of the Bedawi, Odenathus was dressed in a short tunic of natural-colored linen, a painted leather breastplate, and a red military cloak. Zenobia approved this plain and sensible clothing and his sturdy, practical sandals.

As they walked she noticed that his hand was callused and dry and firm. It was a good sign, she thought. "Directly above us is the planet Venus," she said. "When I was born Venus and Mars were in conjunction. The Chaldean astronomer who was present at my birth predicted that I should be fortunate in both love and war."

"And have you been?" he asked.

"I have always been loved by my brothers and my parents. Of war I know naught."

"Has no young man declared his undying affection for you?"

She stopped and pondered a moment. "There have been young men who act silly around me. They behave like young goats when they are trying to attract the attention of a desirable nanny."

42

"You mean they butt heads," he teased.

Zenobia giggled. "They have done everything but that. I do not believe, however, that that is love."

"Perhaps you have not given them a chance to offer you love, just as you have been denying me that chance this evening." He turned her to him and they were face to face, but she shyly turned her head away. "Look at me, Zenobia," he commanded gently.

"I cannot," she whispered.

"What?" He teased her once again. "A girl who can lead a mounted troupe of soldiers cannot look at the man who would love her? I will not eat you up, Zenobia—at least not yet," he amended. "Look at me, my desert flower. Look into the eyes of the prince who would lay his heart at your feet." His hand raised her face up, and their eyes met. Zenobia shivered in the warm night.

Tenderly, Odenathus explored her face with his elegant fingers, outlining her jaw, brushing the tips of his fingers over her high cheekbones, down her nose, across her lips. "Your skin is like the petal of a rose, my flower," he murmured in a deep and passionate voice.

Zenobia was riveted to the ground. She thought she would faint, for she couldn't seem to catch her breath; and when she swayed uncertainly his muscled arm reached out to sweep her next to him. She had no idea how tempting she was to the prince, her moist coral lips slightly parted, her dark gray eyes wide. Her honest innocence was the most tantalizing and provocative spur to his passions; but Odenathus maintained a firm control over his own wants. It would be so easy to make love to her this very minute, he thought. It would be easy to sink onto the sand, drawing her down. How he would enjoy teaching this lovely girl the arts of love! But some deeper instinct warned him that now was not the time.

Instead he held her firmly and said in what he hoped passed for a normal voice, "We will get to know one another, my little flower. You know that I want you for my wife, but because I care for you I want you to be happy. If being my wife would bring you sadness then it cannot be. You would do me honor if you would stay at the palace this summer. Then we may get to know each other within the protective circle of our families."

"I . . . I must ask my father," she replied softly.

"I am sure that Zabaai ben Selim will agree." He let her go then and, taking her hand, again turned back to the encampment. Escorting her to her tent, he bowed politely and bid her a good night.

It was a bemused Zenobia who passed into her quarters. The desert night had grown cool, and Bab sat nodding by the brazier. Zenobia was relieved, for she didn't want to talk at this moment. She wanted time alone in the silence to think. She was quite confused. Prince Odenathus had roused something within her, but she could not be sure if it was the kind of love that grew between a man and a woman. How could she know? She had never felt that kind of love. Zenobia sighed so deeply that Bab awakened with a start.

"You are back, child?" The old woman rose slowly to her feet. "Let me help you get ready for bed. Was the evening a pleasant one for you? Did you walk with the prince? Did he kiss you?"

Zenobia laughed. "So many questions, Bab! Yes, the evening was pleasant and the prince did not kiss me, though I thought once he might."

"You did not hit him the way you have done with the young men of the tribe?" Bab fretted.

"No, I didn't, and had he tried to kiss me I wouldn't have."

The older woman nodded, satisfied. The prince obviously sought to win over her lovely child, and that was good. He was obviously a man of sensitivity, and that, too, was to be commended. Zenobia, little hornet that she was, could be won over by honeyed persuasion. Force would be fatal. Bab helped her young mistress to undress, and settled her in her bed. "Good night, my child," she said and, bending, kissed the girl's forehead.

"He wants me to spend the summer at the palace, Bab. Do you think Father will agree?"

"Of course he will agree! Go to sleep now, my dear, and dream beautiful dreams of your handsome prince."

"Good night, Bab," came the reply.

By noon the next day the camp was struck, and they were on the road back to the great oasis city. The prince rode next to Zenobia, who proved far more talkative in the saddle than she had been the previous evening. By the time the city came in sight two days later they were in the process of becoming friends. The prince left the caravan of Zabaai ben Selim at his home, and rode on to the palace to prepare for Zenobia's visit.

He was greeted by his mother, Al-Zena, who had been a

44

Persian princess. Al-Zena meant "the woman" in the Persian language; a feminine woman who personified beauty, love, and fidelity. Odenathus's elegant mother was all of these things. She was petite in stature, athough quite regal. Her skin was as white as snow, her hair and eyes black as night. Al-Zena loved her son, her only child, above all else; but she was a strong-willed woman who wanted no serious rivals for her son's attention. She held Palmyra in contempt, forever comparing it unfavorably to her beloved Persian cities. As a consequence, she was not popular among Palmyra's citizens, although her son, who loved and championed his city, was.

She knew that Odenathus was back within the palace before he had passed through the gates; but she waited for him to come to her. Pacing the outer chamber of her apartments, she glanced at herself in the silver mirror and was reassured by what she saw. She was still beautiful, her face still virtually unlined at forty; her midnight-black hair unsilvered; her eyes clear. She wore garments in the Parthian fashion, cherry-red trousers, a pale-pink sleeveless blouse, a long-sleeved cherry-red tunic embroidered in gold threads and small fresh-water pearls. Upon her feet were golden leather sandals. Her hair was piled high upon her head in an arrangement of braids and curls, and dressed with twinkling bits of garnet glass.

She saw the admiration in his eyes as he entered the room, and was pleased. "Odenathus, my love," she murmured in her strangely husky voice, a voice that was in direct contrast with her very female appearance. "I have missed you," she said, embracing him. "Where have you been these past few days?"

He smiled broadly at her, and drew her to the cushioned bench. "I have been in the desert, Mother, at the camp of my cousin, Zabaai ben Selim. I have invited his daughter, Zenobia, to spend the summer here at our palace." Al-Zena felt a chill of premonition and, sure enough, her son continued, "I would like to marry Zenobia, but she is young, and hesitant. I thought if she spent her summer here and came to know us she would be less unsure. Although her father can order her to wed with me I should far prefer it if she wanted to do so."

Al-Zena was totally unprepared for her son's news. She needed time to think, but first she would try the obvious. "Odenathus, there is plenty of time for you to marry. Why this haste?"

"Mother, I am twenty-five. I need heirs."

"And what are Deliciae's children?"

45

"They are my sons, but they cannot be my heirs. They are the children of a slave, a concubine. You know all of this, Mother. You know that I must marry one day."

"But a Bedawi girl? Odenathus, surely you can do better than that?"

"Zenobia is but half Bedawi, as am I, Mother." He smiled a bit ruefully. He was more than well aware of her overpossessiveness, although she assumed him ignorant of her feelings. "Her mother was a direct descendant of Queen Cleopatra, and Zenobia is a beautiful and intelligent girl. I want her for my wife, and I shall have her."

Al-Zena tried another tack, one that would give her time to think. "Of course, my son, I am only concerned for your happiness. Poor Deliciae! She will be simply heartbroken to learn that she is to be replaced in your affections."

"Deliciae has no illusions as to her place in my life," Odenathus said sharply. "You will see that Zenobia is made welcome, won't you, Mother?"

"Since you are so determined to have her to wife, my son, I shall treat her as I would my own daughter," came the sweet reply, and Odenathus rose and kissed his mother.

"I ask nothing more of you," he said, and left her, to visit with his favorite concubine, Deliciae.

No sooner had he gone than Al-Zena picked up a porcelain vase and flung it to the floor in a fit of temper. *A wife!* By the gods she had hoped to prevent such a thing. *Heirs!* He wanted heirs for this dung heap of a city! Palmyra, for all its boast of being founded by King Solomon, couldn't compare with her ancient Persian cities of culture and learning. This place to which she had been exiled these past twenty-six years was but a dung heap in a desert! Well, he wasn't married yet. Perhaps if she worked on that stupid little fool, Deliciae . . . If Odenathus wanted the Bedawi girl, let him couple with her. But make her his wife? *Never!*

Deliciae had greeted her master warmly, pressing her ripe body against his in a provocative manner, holding her face up to him for a kiss. "Welcome, my lord. I have missed you greatly, as have your sons."

He kissed her, a fond but passionless kiss. She was a sweet girl, but he had long ago tired of her. "You have all been well?" he said.

"Oh, yes, my lord, although Vernus did fall and give his knee a bad scrape. You know how he must do everything that Linos will do even though his brother is older." Nuzzling at his ear, she drew him over to a couch, and down with her. "The nights are long without you, my lord." The gardenia scent of her perfume overwhelmed him, and he suddenly found it cloying.

He unwound her plump arms from about his neck and sat up. He did not want to make love to her. He realized with surprise that he didn't want to make love to any of the women who peopled his harem. "Deliciae," he said, "I wanted you to know that I will soon be marrying. In a few days, Zenobia bat Zabaai, the only daughter of my cousin, will be coming to visit the palace. She will become my wife, and her children my heirs."

"Her children your heirs? What of my sons? *Your sons!*"

"Surely you knew that the children of a concubine cannot inherit the Kingdom of Palmyra."

"Your mother said that my children were your heirs!"

"It is not for my mother to say. My mother is a Persian. When she married my father she should have become a Palmyran, but she did not. She has spent all her life here belittling my kingdom, never bothering to learn its ways. She might have made me the most hated ruler ever to govern Palmyra had I followed her example. Fortunately, I followed my father's example, and he warned me to wed with no foreigner lest my sons be taught to hate their inheritance.

"The law is clear, Deliciae. The children of a concubine cannot inherit the kingdom of Palmyra."

"You could change the law, my lord, could you not?"

"I will not," he said quietly. "Your sons are good boys, but they are half Greek. Zenobia and I are both Bedawi, and our sons will be, too."

"You are half Persian," she accused, "and your precious bride, as I recall, had an Alexandrian Greek for a mother!"

"But we were raised here in Palmyra, and we are our father's children. Our fathers are Bedawi."

"By that logic *our* sons are Bedawi," she countered.

Odenathus felt a mixture of irritation and sadness. He did not want to hurt Deliciae, but she was leaving him no choice. Silently, he damned his mother for having dared to raise her hopes. Now he fully understood why Al-Zena had encouraged

his liaison with poor Deliciae, though she had always hated the
women of his harem—and, he realized, feared them too. He
sighed and said, "Who were your parents, Deliciae?"

"My parents? What have my parents got to do with this?"

"Answer me! Who were your parents?" His voice was sharp.

"I don't know," she said irritably. "I cannot remember, as I
was quite young when I was taken from them."

"Were they freedmen?"

"I don't know."

"Tell me your earliest memories. Think back, and tell me
what you first remember of your life."

Her brow wrinkled, and for a few minutes she was silent.
Then she said slowly, "The first thing I can remember is passing sweetmeats in an Athenian brothel. I was very small, no
more than four or five. The men used to take me on their laps,
and cuddle me, and call me their good and pretty little girl."

"You were not a virgin when I bought you," he said.

"Of course not," she said. "My virginity was auctioned off
in Damascus when I was eleven. I made my owner very rich,
for no virgin ever brought him a higher price."

"Then you had been a prostitute for three years when I
bought you from the lady Rabi?"

"Yes. Why do you ask me these things? You knew what I
was when you purchased me."

"Yes, Deliciae, I did. You are not a stupid women. Think
on it. You do not know your parents, your antecedents, or even
where you originally came from. Before I purchased you, you
were a professional whore. You performed before the entire
city of Palmyra the day I bought you. How can I make the sons
of such a woman the heirs to my kingdom?

"The laws of this city are the laws of Solomon himself! My
wife will be above reproach, and my sons' antecedents docu-
mented back a hundred generations for all to know and see.
There will never be any doubts. This is as it should be for the
next ruler of Palmyra."

He put an arm around her, and kissed the top of her golden
head. "I know you understand, Deliciae."

"Then you marry only for legitimate heirs?" Her voice held
a note of new hope that he felt obliged to discourage.

"I marry for love, Deliciae. I have always been honest with
you. I bought you to thwart the Roman governor, who would
have satisfied his desires and then sent you back to the lady

48

Rabi where you would have spent the remainder of a very short youth pleasuring many lovers each night. Instead I bought you and made you my concubine. You have all you desire in this world, and more. You are honored and safe. You are free from want, and so you shall remain until the end of your days. Unless, of course, you displease me." The last was a gentle warning.

"What will happen to my sons?" Deliciae demanded. "If they are not your heirs, then what will happen to them?"

"They will be educated to serve Palmyra, to serve me, and to serve my successor. They are lords of the city. Your sons are my sons, and they are safe."

"Even from Zenobia bat Zabaai?" she said spitefully.

"Why would Zenobia want to harm your sons? You are foolish, my pet, and bitter in your disappointment; but remember that it was neither I nor Zenobia who told you that your sons would inherit my kingdom. If you are angry, Deliciae, then direct your anger toward the one who deserves it. Direct it at my mother, for it was she who misled you."

Deliciae's fair skin was mottled red in her anger, and she felt most put out. Odenathus was right. It was Al-Zena who had led her to believe that her children would inherit their father's small kingdom. Deliciae was not a stupid woman, and on reflection she realized that she was indeed fortunate. Not only had she been plucked from what would have been an extremely disagreeable life, but her two sons were her guarantee of remaining in this comfortable position. What a fool she would be to ruin it all because another woman's unborn children were to be the next rulers of Palmyra.

Her master was tired of her, she knew. Very well, Deliciae thought. I am safe, and my sons are safe. I shall even make friends with Zenobia bat Zabaai. *That* will certainly annoy Al-Zena, the old cat! She smiled to herself, her breathing beginning to even out again as the anticipated pleasure of irritating Odenathus's mother swept over her.

"Why do you smile, my pet?"

"Because I realize that you are correct, my lord, and that I am being very foolish. With your permission I will welcome Zenobia bat Zabaai as your wife and my princess."

Odenathus smiled back at Deliciae. "I knew, my pet, that on reflection, your intelligence and inate good sense would surface." He stood, and once again kissed the top of her blond head. "I will see the boys later, my pet. Now I go to give orders so that all may be in readiness for Zenobia when she enters the palace tomorrow. Everything must be perfect!"

Deliciae's beautiful eyebrows lifted delicately as she watched him retreat from her rooms. Odenathus must indeed be in love if he was bothering with household details. Zenobia bat Zabaai must have changed from the skinny, grim-eyed child who sat so dispassionately watching a man die almost four years ago. She shrugged. She was well out of the palace intrigues. Let the little Bedawi girl cope with it all.

In midafternoon of the following day Zenobia entered the palace grounds. Alone, she rode quietly on her camel at an hour when most people were napping in the heat. She had no wish to draw attention to her visit.

As Al-Zena watched stonily, Odenathus leapt forward to aid the cloaked figure from her mount, and her hood fell back, revealing her beautiful face.

"My lord," Zenobia said softly, inclining her head in greeting.

"Welcome to my home, Zenobia," he returned. "I hope you will make it your home soon, my flower."

Zenobia blushed, peach color staining her pale-gold skin. "It will be as the gods will, my lord."

He turned and drew Al-Zena forward. "This is my mother, Zenobia," the prince said.

"My lady, I am honored."

"You are welcome to the palace, my—" Al Zena sought for the correct word. "My child. I hope your stay will be a happy one."

"Thank you, my lady," Zenobia said politely.

A few minutes later she was settled in a comfortable apartment, with Bab busily unpacking her things and chattering away. Bab had come to the palace ahead of her by several hours. "Now this is what a palace should be like!" Bab enthused. "It's big, there are fine gardens, and the rooms are airy. There seem to be plenty of slaves to serve us. I hope the food is decent."

"Hush, Bab! Your tongue runs away with your good sense."

Bab chuckled, and continued with her unpacking, shaking out Zenobia's garments. "I am not sure your clothing is elegant enough for the palace. We should have come later, and taken the time to make you new things."

"You fuss too much, old woman," the girl teased. "Either

the prince likes me, or he does not, and if he does not then no
amount of fine feathers will help me.''

''It is not the prince who concerns me, but his mother.'' Bab
lowered her voice. ''I have heard that she is very unhappy that
he wishes to marry. The gossip is that she hoped he would be
content with the concubine, Deliciae. They say that the Princess Al-Zena is a very headstrong and possessive woman.''

''Is it me she objects to, Bab, or simply any girl?''

''It is both, my baby,'' Bab replied. She and Zenobia had
always been honest with each other.

Zenobia was thoughtful for a moment, then she spoke again.
''The best way to handle the lady, I believe, is for me to be
sweetness itself. How can she find fault with good manners
and a pleasing attitude?'' She chuckled.

''How will you handle the concubine, my child? You cannot
live in the same palace, and not meet.''

''I have no doubt that we shall meet, but when we do I shall
make her my friend.''

''*Zenobia!*'' Bab was shocked.

''I have no choice, Bab. If I marry Odenathus I must be a
help to him, not a hindrance. How can he govern Palmyra
successfully if there is strife within his household? If there is,
he will first worry, and then resent me. No, I must win over
both his mother and Deliciae.'' She smiled at Bab. ''Do not
worry. I am not unmindful of what is involved, but now I
should like a bath. Surely such a simple thing is available to
me in this marvelous place.''

''Of course, child! All is in readiness for you. Come, come!''
Bab took her mistress by the hand and led her into a tiled bath
where Zenobia's hyacinth scent already filled the air. Half a
dozen black slave girls waited to attend the honored guest,
who, looking at the lovely deep bathing pool, delightedly shed
her dusty garments and then stepped into the tepid water. Her
round, full breasts and long legs were noted by two spies
placed in her apartment by Al-Zena and Deliciae.

When Zenobia had bathed, Bab wrapped her in a soft cotton
robe. Then the girl lay down upon her couch to rest until the
evening meal. She was tired from the tension of preparing for
the visit, and not a little apprehensive. Tonight she would meet
with Al-Zena, and she would probably be faced with the beautiful concubine, Deliciae. Yet despite her fears, Zenobia slept
the sleep of the young and the innocent.

When she awoke she found herself alone. Rising, she walked

across the room onto the open portico. Below her was a large walled garden, and beyond, the city of Palmyra was spread like a rich meal upon the table of the desert. Already the lamps were being lit as the blue dusk quickly turned to black night. A faint breeze carried the scent of something so elusive that even Zenobia's sharp nose could not identify it. She felt relaxed, and knew that whatever happened this evening, she would be in total control.

"You are awake?"

Zenobia turned and walked back into the room. "I am awake, Bab."

"You should have called," the older woman grumbled.

"I wanted a moment alone."

"Humph," came the reply, but Bab understood.

Zenobia's sleeveless white tunica with its draped low neckline was a simple garment. She smiled a secret smile. By the very innocence of her dress she would point up the difference between herself and Odenathus's mother. "Leave my hair loose," she said, and Bab nodded, brushing the long thick tresses, containing them only with a simple white ribbon band embroidered with tiny seed pearls.

Zenobia reached for her jewel case. From it she removed a single large cream-gold teardrop-shapped pearl on a thin golden chain. Fastened about her neck, it nestled between her young breasts, a temptation between twin temptations. Matching clusters of pearls on gold wires dangled from her ears; arm bangles of carved pink coral and thin gold wires with pearl bangles braceleted her arms. A single round pearl set in gold adorned one hand, drawing attention to her long, tapering fingers with their polished nails.

Bab nodded her approval as Zenobia daubed on her perfume. "It is perfect, my baby. You will outshine the old witch *and* the Greek concubine!"

The words were scarce out of Bab's mouth when one of the black slave girls hurried in to announce, "A eunuch is here to escort the lady to the banquet hall."

With a faint nod to Bab, Zenobia followed the girl and then the eunuch, hurrying through the vast palace so quickly that she scarce had time to note a thing along her way. The slave girl had been wrong, however, for it was not the banquet hall to which they went, but rather a small family dining room. Dressed in greens and golds, Al-Zena was already there, reclining on a dining sofa. Next to her was an exquisite fair-skinned

52

blonde, dressed also in Parthian fashion; but her colors were sky blue embroidered in silver.

"Zenobia, my child," Al-Zena purred, "this is the lady Deliciae."

"Good evening to you," Zenobia replied sweetly.

Al-Zena was somewhat disconcerted, for the girl showed neither distress nor anger at Deliciae's presence. She was either totally unfeeling, very stupid, or very clever, and the fact that Al-Zena couldn't determine which gave her pause. She eyed Zenobia suspiciously as the girl settled herself upon the dining couch marked for her, then turned to Deliciae, saying, "I understand that you have two sons. How fortunate you are! I hope I shall one day be the mother of sons."

Al-Zena choked on her wine, spilling some of it on her gown, and sending a servant scuttling for water and a cloth. Zenobia cooed solicitously, "Oh, you have spilled your wine. I do hope it will not stain your tunic."

Deliciae eyed Odenathus's prospective wife from beneath her heavily mascaraed lashes, and forced back a chuckle. The little Bedawi girl was wise to Al-Zena, and ready to do battle with her, although Deliciae could see that Al-Zena was not quite sure yet as to the girl's character and intelligence. She took the opportunity to gauge her rival, and sighed. The girl was positively beautiful. She makes me look insipid, thought Deliciae.

A slave was rubbing frantically at Al-Zena's tunic as the Prince of Palmyra walked into the room. His glance swept over the three women, and then he said sharply, "Deliciae, what do you do here?"

"Did you not invite me, my lord? Your mother said that I was to come to supper tonight."

"You were *not* invited," came the icy reply. "Please return to your quarters."

Deliciae rose, stricken, and Zenobia instantly realized that Odenathus's mother was using the woman as a pawn. "Please, my lord Prince," she said, "do not send the lady Deliciae away. I was so enjoying her company."

"It does not distress you, my flower? I would not have you unhappy."

"Deliciae and I are of an age. We will quickly become friends, I know." Zenobia put a hand on his arm. "Please, my lord Prince." Her glance was melting, and Odenathus felt his heartbeat quicken.

"If it pleases you, my flower, Deliciae may remain," he said gruffly, wishing to the gods as he said it that neither Deliciae nor his mother were in the room so he might kiss that adorable mouth that pleaded so prettily with him. Instead he signaled impatiently to a slave to fill his goblet with wine.

"Thank you, my lord Prince," Zenobia said softly.

Al-Zena almost gnashed her teeth with frustration. He was in love! The gods be cursed! Her son was in love, and there would be no reasoning with him. Still, if she could show up the chit for the unsuitable creature she was, then perhaps Odenathus would see reason. A Bedawi girl Princess of Palmyra? *Never!*

The meal was fairly plain, beginning with artichokes in olive oil and tarragon vinegar; followed by baby lamb, broiled thrush on asparagus, green beans, and cabbage sprouts; and finished with a silver bowl of peaches and green grapes. The prince could hardly take his eyes from Zenobia, much to his mother's consternation and Deliciae's resignation. Zenobia ate heartily of the beautifully cooked meal, while the others could only eat sparingly.

After the last of the dishes had been cleared away and the wine goblets refilled, a troupe of dancing girls and a *jongleur* entertained. Deliciae saw how desperately Odenathus longed to be with the beautiful girl he desired for a wife, and so as the dancing girls ran from the dining room she rose, saying, "Would you permit me to withdraw, my lord? I find I am quite fatigued."

The prince smiled gratefully at her, and nodded as Deliciae bowed to Al-Zena and Zenobia and departed the room. For a few more minutes they reclined in silence, Odenathus waiting for his mother to withdraw. When it finally became apparent that she was not going to do so, he stood and, holding his hand out to Zenobia, said "Come! My gardens are justly famous. You will excuse us, Mother? I expect you will want to retire now, for it is quite late."

Zenobia put her hand in the prince's and rose. "I should very much like to see your gardens, my lord Prince."

Without a backward glance at Al-Zena, Odenathus swept Zenobia outdoors into a vast and darkened garden. Here and there torches blazed along the paths, but it was virtually impossible to see. Zenobia could not resist a chuckle. "I hope you know where you are going," she teased him. "I should hate to end up in a fish pond."

He stopped and, swinging her around, looked into her face. "I want to kiss you," he said fiercely. How beautiful she looked with the torchlight flickering molten gold across her features.

"*What?*" Her heart began to hammer wildly, and she felt almost afraid. Looking into his handsome face, her gray eyes widened slightly with surprise.

"I want to kiss you," he repeated. "If you were any other girl I should not even ask."

"*Oh!*" Her voice was suddenly very small, and as he looked at her a slow smile crossed Odenathus's face.

"You are like the fresh breeze that blows across the city at sunset, my flower." One hand moved from her shoulders to encircle her slender waist; to draw her hard against him. The other scalded up her neck and face to tangle in the jet silk of her hair. His dark head dipped, his mouth brushing lightly and swiftly across hers, sending small shock waves racing through her body as she desperately struggled with herself to regain control over her emotions. "*Zenobia.*" His voice caressed her name, and she shivered. What was he doing to her? How could the sound of his voice saying her name render her breathless. "*Zenobia!*" Her legs felt weak, and she fell back slightly against the encircling brace of his arm. His head was poised above hers for a brief moment, and then it came swiftly down and his lips closed over hers.

His mouth was warm, and smooth and hard, but Zenobia, innocent as she was to kisses, felt his restraint. He kissed her gently with great tenderness, his lips drawing the very essence of her from her untutored body. Deep within her core she felt the ache begin. She longed for something, but she knew not what, and when, after what seemed an eternity, he finally lifted his lips from hers she murmured, "More!"

He looked upon her, his brown eyes almost liquid with his passion. "Oh, Zenobia, you have intoxicated me!" he said softly, and then he kissed her again. This time his kiss was less gentle, but she felt no fear, only a desperate longing to know more. He parted her lips, his tongue seeking, learning the velvet softness of her mouth. She wanted—she wanted she knew not what; only that she didn't want him to stop. She shivered deliciously as he sucked for a moment on her little tongue; and then she nestled closer against him, her young breasts taut.

With a groan of impatience he thrust her away from him. "You are so young, my flower," he said softly. It was almost a reproach.

"Have I displeased you?"

She was distressed, he could see. "Come!" He took her hand, and they began to walk again through the darkened garden. "You do not displease me, Zenobia. In fact you please me mightily. At this moment I very much want to make love to you."

"Then let us make love," she said simply. "I have never been with a man before, but both Tamar and Bab say it is a natural and good thing between a man and woman. I am not afraid, my lord Prince."

He smiled in the darkness. "No woman, I believe, should make love to a man for whom she doesn't care, for whom she has no feelings. That, my flower, is immoral. I have never made love to a woman who did not love me a little. Tonight you have barely been awakened to the sensual side of your nature, and you long to know more. You do not yet know me, Zenobia. There is time for us, I promise you."

"You make me feel like a child," she pouted.

"You are a child," he said. "but there will come a night when you and I care for one another, and then, Zenobia, I shall make you a woman, fully aware of her passionate powers."

She sighed. "I must be content with your judgment then, my lord Prince, for I know naught of such matters."

Odenathus laughed softly. "I think I shall enjoy this small submission, for I suspect that you seldom defer to anyone."

"I know that I am not like other women," she said defensively. "If you truly want me, my lord Prince, then you must accept me as I am. I do not know if I can change, nor if I choose to do so."

"I want you as you are, even if I suspect that my desert flower has thorns." He stopped for a moment, tipped her face to his, and kissed her again, sending a pleasurable thrill through her. "Please learn to love me, Zenobia. I ache to love you."

"Love me?" she said. "Or make love to me?"

"Both," he admitted.

She gave him a quick kiss in return. "You are an honest man," she said. "I believe that we can be friends, and friends, I have been told, make the best lovers."

Odenathus was amused. She was quite serious, and he had never met a female who was so delightfully interesting. "Why do you not use my name, Zenobia?" he asked. "You call me 'my lord Prince,' but you never say my name."

"You have not given me permission to use your name, my

lord Prince. I may be naught but a Bedawi girl, but I have manners." She paused, and in the dark he could not see the twinkle in her eyes. "Besides, I do not like your name."

"*You do not like my name?*" He was astounded.

"It is a very serious, almost pompous name, my lord Prince."

"If we are to be married you cannot keep calling me 'my lord Prince.' "

"It is not settled that we are to be married," she said calmly. "Besides, I do not think of you as Odenathus Septimus, my lord Prince."

He could hear the teasing laughter in her voice, and with the same spirit he entered into her little game. "We will be married, my flower, never fear. I am going to teach you to like me, to love me, and to call me by my name." He paused. "If you cannot call me Odenathus, then what will you call me?"

"In public I shall call you 'my lord Prince,' but in private you shall be Hawk, for you look like that bird to me with your long straight nose and your piercing, dark gaze."

He was flattered beyond measure, as she had known he would be. "So I am Hawk to you." He chuckled. "Do you fancy to tame this wild bird, my flower?"

"One should never tame wild things, my Hawk. One should gain their trust and respect, become their friend, as you and I shall do."

Once again she had surprised him, and he grinned to himself. "Hawk I shall be if it pleases you, Zenobia, but now it is late. Come, and I will return you to your quarters."

Taking her hand, he moved through the dark gardens with the surefootedness of a camel traveling a familiar trail. They entered the palace, and she followed him up an almost hidden staircase and found herself in the hallway outside her own rooms. They stopped before the large double doors.

"Can you ride a horse?" he said.

"Yes."

"Be ready at dawn," he said and, turning, strode off down the corridor.

For a moment she watched him go, and then his figure in its long white tunic disappeared around a corner. Zenobia sighed, and stood for a moment before her door. Then one of the soldiers guarding her apartment leaned over and opened the door. With a blush she hurried into her rooms, and closed the door behind her as Bab hurried forward. "It went well, my baby?"

For the first time in her life Zenobia did not want to talk to her dearest servant. What had been between herself and the prince was something she did not choose to share with anyone. "It went well, Bab."

"Good! Good!" the older woman approved.

Sensing that if she did not give Bab something more the servant would continue to pry, Zenobia said, "I am to go riding at dawn with the prince."

Bab was successfully diverted. "Dawn?"

"Yes." Zenobia feigned a yawn.

Within minutes Zenobia found herself undressed and in bed. To her delight, she was alone, for Bab had been allocated a separate small room off her antechamber. She stretched out in the comfortable bed, wiggling her toes in delight beneath the fine silk coverlet, her mind busy with thoughts.

Everyone said she had a choice about this marriage, but the truth was that it was a choice already made. Marriage to Palmyra's prince would make her a woman of property and a person of importance. All she had to do was produce the next ruler of Palmyra. He was a gentle man, the prince. Like her father, he seemed to genuinely care what she felt and what she thought. There was no real choice, and yet was it that terrible a fate? She turned restlessly in her bed, remembering his kisses—and what they had done to her.

In a way those kisses had frightened her, for they had rendered her so helpless. She hadn't known what was expected of her. She had never allowed a man to kiss her before. The young men of her tribe had wanted to often enough, seeking to catch her alone, or entrap her in a tight place; but she had always escaped their seeking mouths, their eager hands, using violence if necessary, for she was no man's toy, and never would be. He had held her gently, tasting of her lips just enough to arouse her curiosity, which, she suspected, was exactly what he had intended. He had touched her nowhere else, and yet she knew from Bab and Tamar's prattle that a man liked to fondle a woman's body. Why hadn't he touched her? Was there something wrong or displeasing about her body?

Wide awake again, Zenobia rose from her bed and walked out onto the portico overlooking the garden and the city. Distracted, she paced back and forth for some minutes. What was wrong with her? To her complete surprise, she was near to tears. Where was her Hawk now? Had he left her at her door only to go to Deliciae's arms? Two tears rolled down her cheeks, and she brushed them away furiously. Why should she care what he did?

"Zenobia?" His voice sounded in her ear and, startled, she cried out. Strong arms wrapped around her, and to her horror she burst into tears, sobbing wildly against his bare chest. He let her cry, and when at last her weeping began to abate he lifted her up in his arms and carried her back into her bedchamber. Sitting on the edge of her couch, he cradled her against him.

"Why do you cry, my little flower? Are you homesick?"

"N-no."

"What is it, then?"

"I thought you had gone to Deliciae."

"I have not sought Deliciae's bed for months. I go to her apartments to see our children. Do not tell on me, though, Zenobia, or you shall ruin my reputation." He was close to laughter—joyous laughter. *She cared!* She cared enough to weep when she thought him with another woman! Still, he must not press her too closely, though her slim hand caressing the back of his neck was maddening.

"Where did you come from?" she asked him.

"My chambers are next to yours, my flower," came the reply. "The portico is mine to walk upon, too, and I also found it difficult to sleep."

She was suddenly aware of his bare chest, of the fact that he wore nothing but a wrap of cloth about his loins; of the fact that she was practically naked herself in her sheer white cotton chemise. It was something that had not escaped the prince's notice, and he could feel his manhood rising to meet the challenge of her beautiful body. He moved to put her away, but her arms tightened about his neck.

"*Zenobia!*" His voice held a plea.

"Love me a little," she said softly.

He shuddered. "Zenobia, my flower, have mercy. I am only a man."

"Love me a little, Hawk," she repeated, and then she moved her body in such a way that her chemise fell open. She shrugged the flimsy garments off her shoulders and it fell to her waist, baring her round full breasts.

The sight was a glorious one, and for a moment he closed his eyes and invoked the gods to aid him. He ached to possess this lovely girl child who taunted him so. His hands itched to caress her, but he tried to practice restraint in the face of incredible temptation. Then her hand reached down, caught at one of his, and lifted it up to one of her breasts. "Zenobia!" he groaned. "Zenobia!" But his hand was already responding to the soft, warm flesh beneath it.

"Oh, Hawk," she murmured against his ear, "do you not want me? Even a little?"

"Do you want me?" he managed to gasp. Her breasts were like young pomegranates, firm and full in his hand.

"I hurt," she responded. "Inside of me there is an awful ache, and I do not understand."

"It is desire you feel, my flower." He let his eyes stray down, catching his breath as he saw the full glory of her breasts. The nipples were large and round, the color of dark honey. He longed to taste the sweetness of her flesh, but now was not the time. He had been quite serious when he had told her he had never made love to a woman who did not care for him.

She would be his wife, but he would give her time to adjust, time to learn to love him. He wanted that love, for he knew that Zenobia had never given her heart, let alone her body, to any man. She was yet a child for all her voluptuousnes of form and facility of mind; and it was the woman he looked forward to knowing, a woman that he would help to shape and mold.

He held the girl child, his own desires successfully under control now as he gently caressed her, crooning soft words of comfort in her little ear. His tenderness had the proper effect, and she quieted, soon falling asleep against his shoulder. When her breathing was calm and even he stood and, turning carefully, placed her upon her bed, drawing the silken coverlet over her. He stood for a long minute looking down on her, drinking in her loveliness, and then with a sigh of regret he blew out the lamp and left the room.

He stood out on the portico, gripping the balustrade, his eyes sightless, not even aware that the desert night had grown cool. How long would he have to wait? He wanted this girl by his side. He wanted to share his whole life with her, the burdens as well as the good things. He somehow believed that Zenobia's shoulders were strong enough to bear some of his load. Treading a path between the Romans and his warlike Persian neighbors to the east was not an easy task, especially when he also had his own commercial community to satisfy. It was up to Palmyra to keep the caravans safe.

Then, too, there was the *other* woman in his life, his mother.

The prince grimaced. The only favor Al-Zena had ever done him was to give him life, and even that had been done grudgingly. He had heard the stories of his birth, and how she had fought against becoming a mother right up to the last minute. It had been said that if she had cooperated his birth would have been an easy one; but she had not, and consequently had injured herself, making it impossible to ever have another child. His father had never forgiven her, but then neither of his parents had loved the other. Theirs had been a political marriage, and it was said his mother had resisted the match, being in love with a prince at the Persian court. It was also said that his father had been forced to rape her on their wedding night, and that he had been conceived then.

Both his parents had loved him, but his father had not allowed him much time with Al-Zena. It was not until his father's death that he had come to know her better, but by then he was eighteen, and a man grown. Still, he had recognized her unhappiness; seen what havoc a loveless marriage could bring; and vowed that never would he touch an unwilling woman.

He had even tried to make friends with her, but she became possessive, and even destructive. Consequently he gave lip service to his filial duty, and kept his own counsel. He was clever, though, and so openly solicitous of his mother that she believed she had won him over, and was constantly advising him, attempting to interfere in the government of Palmyra, a task for which she was singularly unsuited. The hardest part of it all was that he had no one to talk to; to share this burden.

The sudden sound of the water clock dripping the minutes away reminded him of the lateness of the hour. Turning, he walked back into his own bedchamber, lay down, and with habit born of great discipline fell quickly asleep.

When the desert dawn came, reaching across the sands with fingers of molten flame, tinting the land apricot and gold, two figures rode from the city, black silhouettes against the colorful morning sky. Odenathus had personally chosen a spirited Arab mare for Zenobia. The mare was white, as was his own big stallion, and newly broken. Zenobia was her first mistress.

"What is her name?" the girl asked as they rode from Palmyra.

"She has none as yet, my flower. It will be up to you to name her, as she is my first gift to you."

"She is mine?" Her voice was incredulous with delight.

"She is yours," he repeated, letting his eyes stray to her long legs, bare beneath her short chiton. He was going to have to do something about that, for he wanted no man ogling those lovely legs.

"I am going to call her Al-ula," Zenobia said happily.

He smiled, and nodded his approval. Al-ula meant "the first" in the Arabic tongue. "It is a good name, and you're clever to think of it, my flower."

"What is your stallion called?"

"Ashur, the warlike one," he replied.

"And is he warlike?"

"I am unable to keep any other stallions in my stables. He has already killed two. Now I keep but geldings and mares."

"I'll race you," she challenged him.

"Not today, my flower. Al-ula is but newly broken, and will need time to become used to you. Besides, I must return, for I have a full schedule today."

"May I come with you? It will be far more interesting than chatting with the women. I am not used to sitting about doing nothing but painting my toenails and soaking in a perfumed tub."

He chuckled sympathetically. "When you are my wife you may come with me, Zenobia."

"Hades!" She realized she would be forced to remain in the women's quarters, caught between Al-Zena and Deliciae.

He read her thoughts, and chuckled at her discomfiture. "Ah, my poor flower, caught between the wasp and the butterfly."

"How did you know what I was thinking?" she demanded.

"The look on your face was stronger than any words you could have spoken," he replied. "If you become my wife, Zenobia, I will not pen you in a harem, I promise you. You will be free to come and go as you please, for I will do what no Prince of Palmyra has ever done for his princess. I will make you my equal."

"I don't want to live in the women's quarters," she said suddenly. "If I become your wife, I want my own house within the palace. I would choose my own servants, and purchase my own slaves. I want no spies in my household."

She drew her mare to a halt. The sun was now risen, and the sky was bright blue and cloudless for as far as the eye could see. Following her lead, he stopped his stallion, and turned to face her.

"I am unschooled at playing games, Hawk," she said quietly. "Let us be frank with each other. You wish to marry me, and my father has agreed to it, but how soon depends on me for both you and my father have understood my need to accept this marriage. My father believes that you are the right man for me, and because of the great love he bore my mother he would have me happy. I am fortunate. Not many men would understand my feelings.

"I am also fortunate in his choice of a husband for me, for you, too, understand that I cannot be fettered. I must be free! You have been kind to me, and I believe that I am beginning to care for you. The things that I shall ask of you will not be difficult."

"I understand," he answered her, "and you may have anything that is within my power to give you, Zenobia."

"Ah, Hawk, you make very rash promises," she teased. "One should never agree to anything until one has heard all the terms."

"Would you teach me, my flower?"

"Can you not learn from a woman?" came the sharp retort.

"Do you love me a little?" he demanded.

"*Do you love me, Hawk?*"

"I think I fell in love with you on the day your mother was killed. You were so confused, and hurt and frightened. I wanted to reach out then, and hold you in my arms; but I was Prince of Palmyra, and you but the child of my cousin. It was not meet that I comfort you greatly, though I wanted to, Zenobia."

She was very surprised by this confession, and quite pleased as well. Still, he must not be allowed to become sure of her. Both Tamar and Bab said that a woman should never allow a man to become too confident. "I hope you are not going to tell me you spent the three and a half years since my mother's death pining for me, for I shall not believe you, Hawk."

"I forgot completely about you, my flower," he said bluntly, pleased with the outraged gasp that followed his statement. The little minx was suddenly too sure of herself; and had his father not warned him never to let a woman become too confident?

"Then how can you say you love me?!"

"I loved the child that day, and when I saw the lovely girl she had become, I fell in love all over again. I will never lie to you, Zenobia. I love you." He reached out and took her hand in his. "Oh, my flower, I do love you. Have pity on this poor prince who would lay his heart and his kingdom at your feet! When are we to wed?''

"Just a little time," she pleaded.

"I cannot wait long, Zenobia. I am a lonely man, and I long to have you by my side to love, to talk with, to share with.''

He could have said nothing more calculated to win her over. "I will marry you as soon as the priests permit," she answered him, and when his eyebrows lifted in surprise at her sudden decision, she smiled. "You need me, my Hawk. Have you not just said it? Our marriage has been a fact since you and my father agreed upon it. Only the date has remained in doubt. Logic tells me if I was distressed by the thought of your being with Deliciae last night, then I must love you a little, even if I cannot admit it to myself yet.''

"Oh, Zenobia," he said, "I wonder at the woman you will become!''

"Why should you wonder?" she laughed. "You will be here to see.''

He, too, laughed. "So I shall, my flower. So I shall!" Then, turning his horse back toward the city, he said, "It is time we returned, Zenobia. I will not race you, but let us gallop a way so Al-una may show you her paces.''

Before his words had died on the wind she wheeled the mare about and was off. Surprised—she was always surprising him— he put spurs to Ashur and followed her. Together they thundered down the barely visible desert road leading back to Palmyra, the horses' hooves stirring up tiny puffs of yellow dust. He watched her, bent low over her mount, tendrils of her wind-loosened hair blowing about her face. What a glorious creature she was! This girl-woman who was so soon to be his wife.

As they came through the main entry into the large courtyard, the guards at the palace gates were hard pressed not to grin at one another in pure delight. Leaping lightly from her mount, Zenobia cried out triumphantly, "I beat you!''

"We weren't racing," he replied.

"Weren't we?" Her gaze was mocking, but then she turned and, again laughing a soft provocative laugh ran into the building.

He felt a quickening in his loins, and then he chuckled. Their wedding day could not come soon enough to suit him. Despite his crowded day, he intended seeing Zabaai ben Selim before the sun set, and settling with him the details of his betrothal to Zenobia. A public announcement would be made the next day, and then the little minx would be committed. Purposefully he strode across the courtyard to his own section of the palace. Soon, he thought, soon my flower, and then neither of us shall ever be lonely again, for we shall have each other forever. *Forever*. He liked the sound of the word.

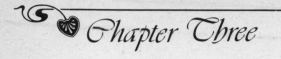

Chapter Three

Palmyra, queen city of the Eastern Empire, lay almost half-way between the equally ancient city of Baghdad and the blue Mediterranean sea. It was said to have been founded by Solomon, a fact of which the Palmyrans were mightily proud. Built upon and around the great oasis where the major caravan routes between east and west crossed, it was the city through which all the riches of the world passed en route west to Europe or east to Persia, Cathay, and the Indies. Greeks and Romans, Syrians and Jews, Arab merchants of all tribes gathered here, building great storehouses and warehouses in which safely to keep the silks, carpets, spices, ivory, jewels, grain, and dates that passed through their hands. They built luxurious villas in which to house their families, as well as their concubines, for as all inanimate valuables arrived in Palmyra so did the choicest of the world's slaves.

The architects of the city had a passion for columns, and all the major buildings were adorned with them. About the central courtyard of one temple were raised three hundred seventy graceful colonnades; and upon projecting stones half way up each column stood statues of Palmyra's most famous men. The city's main avenue was lined on each side with two rows of pillars, seven hundred and fifty to a side; and the Temple of Jupiter had a mile-long colonnade consisting of fifteen hundred Corinthian columns.

The city had been built for merchants by a wise king, and a thousand years later it was still firmly controlled by commercial interests. The main business and shopping streets were all covered over, so even in the heat of a summer noon one could conduct his business in relative comfort. Although not prone to attack due to its inaccessible location, Palmyrans had raised around the city a wall seven miles long, to discourage the boldness of desert raiders.

This was the kingdom over which Zenobia bat Zabaai would soon reign as wife to its prince. Zabaai ben Selim was suddenly and for the first time really considering the serious responsibility he was placing upon his only daughter's shoulders. He sat comfortably in Odenathus's private library, a carved alabaster goblet of fine Cyrenean wine clutched in his hand. Behind him, a deaf-mute black slave plied a large woven palm fan, creating just enough breeze to ease the still heat of the late afternoon.

As he had come into the city today he had looked at it as if for the first time in his entire life. When one is used to something, one sees with dulled eyes, he thought. He had been born here on this oasis, and the city had always been a part of his life. Today he had really looked, and what he had seen made him think. It was not just the magnificent architecture of the city, but the marvelous parks kept green by the oasis's underground springs that suddenly stunned Zabaai. The intellect behind the creation of the city was overwhelming.

Zenobia, he knew, would not be content simply to be an ornament and a broodmare. What part would she play, he wondered, in the government of this city? Palmyran princesses were famed for their beauty, not their administrative abilities. He shook his head wearily. Had his ambition for his beloved child outstripped his good sense?''

"Zabaai, my cousin!" Odenathus hurried into the room, his white robes whirling about him. "Forgive me for keeping you waiting."

"I have been comfortable in these pleasant surroundings, my lord Prince."

"I have asked you here so we may discuss the terms of this marriage before I call in the scribes. What will you give as dowry?"

"I shall give a thousand pure-bred goats, five hundred white and five hundred black. There will be two hundred and fifty fighting camels; and a hundred Arabian horses; not to mention jewelry, clothing, household goods, and the deed to her mother's house."

The prince was astounded by the magnificence of Zenobia's dowry. Never had he suspected that it would be so large; but then her father could easily afford it, for his herds were enormous.

The dowry agreement was drawn up by the prince's scribe, who set his quill flying across the parchment as each point was stated. A transfer of goods between the bride's father and her husband would make Odenathus Zenobia's legal lord according to the Bedawi laws; but the prince was Hellenized, as had been Zenobia's mother and the bride herself. They would be married in the atrium of Zabaai's home, the exact date depending on the omens to be taken this very evening by the temple priests.

Al-Zena was sent for, and she and the prince's Greek secretary witnessed the signing of the document of betrothal and the formal words in which Odenathus said to his future father-in-law, "Do you promise to give me your daughter as wife?"

"May the gods grant their blessing. I promise," Zabaai said.

"May the gods grant their blessing!" Odenathus finished.

"So," Al-Zena said sourly, "you are really going to do it."

"You disapprove of this match, my Princess?"

"Do not be offended, Zabaai ben Selim. I think your daughter a sweet child, but I cannot see the necessity for my son to marry. He already has children."

"Palmyra has never been governed by a bastard line," came the sharp reply. "Surely *you* must know the law."

Odenathus hid a smile as his mother, very discomfited, replied stiffly, "You have always been most outspoken, Zabaai ben Selim. I can only hope your daughter does not take after you."

"Zenobia is herself. She will be a credit to the city."

"Indeed!" Al-Zena snapped, and she turned and abruptly left the library.

Zabaai ben Selim smiled blandly at the prince, and said, "You will want to see Zenobia before we leave." It was a statement.

"*Leave?*" The prince was somewhat taken aback.

"Now that the betrothal is official, my lord, Zenobia must return home. She cannot stay here in the palace under the circumstances. She will return on her wedding day. You may not see each other until then."

"But I thought we might spend this time getting to know one another better," he protested, disappointed.

"Alas, custom demands we be discreet," came the reply.

"Whose customs?" Odenathus demanded.

"Ancient Bedawi customs, my Lord," was the silken answer. "There will be plenty of time for you and my daughter to get to know one another after the wedding."

"I will have the priests from the Temple of Jupiter sacrifice a lamb this very night to determine the date," the prince said. "But first I will go to Zenobia, and bid her farewell."

"I will await your return, my Lord." Settling back in his chair, Zabaai held out his goblet for the slave to refill. He watched with dancing dark eyes as the young man hurried from the room. How very eager he was, and a brief separation would whet his appetite even further for this marriage. Al-Zena might carp and complain, but Zabaai wagered with himself that Odenathus's few sweet memories of Zenobia would spur him eagerly on toward their wedding day.

Odenathus did not go directly to the apartments where Zenobia was housed. First he stopped at his treasury; walking into the roomy jewelry vault, he carefully selected a ring that would be his betrothal gift to his future wife. It was not a hard choice, for he had seen the ring months before when it had been discovered by his treasurer in a rotting leather bag, hidden on a back shelf. The treasurer had been quite excited, saying that the ring was one sent to King Solomon from Sheba's queen as a token of her affection, and was catalogued in the ancient records of the treasury.

Having made his choice, the prince hurried to find Zenobia. He was met, however, in the apartment's anteroom by Bab. The older woman looked him up and down, nodding approvingly. "She is just come from her bath, Highness. If you will wait but a minute my lady will be fit to receive you."

"My thanks, Bab," Odenathus replied courteously. He instinctively liked this small round woman in her simple robe, her graying hair hidden beneath its veil. Her face was brown from the desert sun, and there were deep laugh lines carved about her black eyes and on either side of her mouth.

"You will be good for my child," the woman said with the quiet assurance of a beloved servant.

"I already love her, Bab. I want her to be happy."

"Be firm, my lord. Firm, but gentle."

"Can one be firm with Zenobia?" he teased.

Bab chuckled appreciatively, but before she could answer Zenobia entered the room. Odenathus's eyes were immediately riveted to the girl, oblivious to all else. Smiling, Bab slipped from the room and left the lovers alone.

He could scarce take his eyes from her, flushed and rosy from the bath, the faint hyacinth scent clinging to her unbound hair, her simple white tunic. For a moment he stood powerless to move. Then he heard her voice: "My lord?" The spell broken, he reached out and pulled her almost roughly into his arms. One arm held her firmly against his hungry body, the other hand tangled in her soft hair, drawing her head to his. Bending, he let his lips brush hers lightly, and was satisfied to feel a faint tremor rush through her.

"Oh, Zenobia," he murmured, kissing the corners of her

mouth, her closed and fluttering eyelids. Then his lips found hers, and as his kisses deepened her arms slipped up and about his neck; her lithe young body pressed as hungrily against his. Enchanted by her budding passion, he ran his tongue over her lips, which parted instinctively. Tenderly he explored the fragrant cavity of her mouth; the hand that had earlier held her head now moved to caress her breasts.

The ache that had so mysteriously materialized the night before reappeared to taunt her. It swept over her from out of nowhere, leaving her breathless and confused. His thumb rubbed insistently against the already stiff peaks of her nipples, and she wanted to cry with the strange pleasure that it gave her. It was so new, so wonderful, this marvelous sensation that was called love.

After what seemed the briefest eternity he released her, and for a moment she swayed dangerously, but finally her head cleared and she grew steady once more. She heard his voice coming at her from what seemed a long way off, but the words were clear.

"Your father and I have signed a formal betrothal agreement, my flower; but Zabaai says you must leave the palace before the public announcement is made tomorrow. We cannot see each other until our wedding day."

"But why?!" she burst out, disappointed.

"Custom, he says."

For a minute her lips clamped shut, and then she said, "It must be as my father has decreed."

Her obedience pleased him. "I have brought you the traditional gift," he said, taking her left hand up and placing the ring upon the third finger, whose nerve it was said ran directly to the heart.

Zenobia stared down at the large round black pearl in its simple gold setting. "It is . . . incredible," she said softly. "I have never possessed such a ring."

"My treasurer says that it is listed in a catalogue of gifts sent from the Queen of Sheba to Solomon when he was here in Palmyra overseeing the construction of the city. I knew that it would be perfect for you, my flower. It glows against the warm apricot tint of your skin!" He turned over her hand, which he had yet to relinquish, and placed a tender kiss upon the palm, sending delighted little tingles down Zenobia's spine.

Suddenly shy, she withdrew her hand from his.

His mouth captured hers again in a swift kiss. "Oh, my Zenobia!" he murmured, his breath warm against her ear. "So sure of herself in everything but love. I will teach you to understand those feelings that assail you, and even frighten you a little. I will teach you to love, and be loved in return. There will be no fear or hesitation between us, my flower, and we will trust each other only." His lips caressed hers lightly once more. "I love you, Zenobia. I love you!"

She had never come so close to fainting in her entire life and, clinging to him childlike, she whispered breathlessly, "I love you also, my Hawk. I do!" Saying the words seemed to bring a strange relief.

Neither of them heard the door to the antechamber open.

"And are you ready to leave yet, my daughter?" Zabaai ben Selim stood there, smiling benignly.

Almost guiltily, they sprang apart and, blushing, Zenobia said, "I must change into my chiton, Father."

"No," Odenathus replied. "I will return you to your home in a litter. I would prefer that you did not ride with bare legs for all to see."

To Zabaai ben Selim's surprise, Zenobia bowed her head in assent, and moved to his side. "I am ready then, Father."

The Bedawi chief could only think to say, "Bab will come later with your things, my daughter," but she was already moving past him and out the door.

"I will send you word as to the date of the wedding late tonight, my cousin," the prince said, and the Bedawi chief nodded his assent as he followed his daughter from the room.

Just before sunset in the Temple of Jupiter, the high priest slaughtered a pure white lamb. After gazing at the smoking entrails, he announced that the most propitious time for the nuptials would be but ten days hence. Receiving word from the royal messenger, Zabaai ben Selim smiled to himself, wondering how large a gift Odenathus had donated to the temple in order to receive such a desirable verdict concerning the date of his marriage.

The coming celebration was announced to the public the following day, and the citizens of Palmyra rejoiced.

In the Roman governor's palace, Antonius Porcius Blandus, still the empire's representative, took the news less cheerfully. "Hades!" he said in an annoyed voice to his visitor. "I had

hoped he would remain satisfied with his little Greek concubine. Had he died without a legitimate heir, Rome might have
the city completely and unopposed."

"We have the city," the governor's visitor said.

"As long as Palmyra has a legitimate ruler there is always a
chance of uprising," Antonius Porcius retorted.

"I had been led to believe that Odenathus is totally loyal to
Rome," was the reply.

"Oh, he is loyal. It is his bride that I fear. What a vixen he
has picked, Marcus Alexander! Zenobia bat Zabaai; half Alexandrian Greek and Egyptian; half Bedawi savage. Some Gaulish
auxiliary Alae murdered her mother four years ago, and she
has hated the Romans with a passion ever since."

"Small wonder," the other man murmured.

"You do not know this girl!" the governor protested. "She
sat in the midst of the men who were responsible, and for over
eighteen hours she watched them die. She was but a child, and
yet she sat as still and as cold as a statue as she watched their
agony. There was no pity in her! A man in love is a fickle
creature, and Odenathus is, I am told, totally enamored. She
could influence him against us."

"I think you put too much importance on the marriage of a
petty princeling and a half-caste girl, Antonius Porcius. No girl
will defeat and destroy the empire. There have been men who
tried, and they have all failed. Rome is, and will always be,
invincible."

The governor sighed. Why was it that Romans never understood? Antonius Porcius thought bitterly. I know the East and
its peoples. Unless love has softened that hard-eyed child I
remember, she will bear watching.

He turned his attention to his dinner guest, Marcus Alexander Britainus, the wealthy son of a Roman patrician and his
British wife. Lucius Alexander Britainus had been a Roman
governor in Britain who had married a powerful local chieftain's daughter. Marcus Alexander was their eldest son. A
younger son, Aulus, had already inherited his maternal grandfather's estates and responsibilities in Britain. There were two
sisters, Lucia and Eusebia, who were married to prominent
Romans, and already settled matrons.

Marcus Alexander was not married. He had already served
in the army; and now he was coming to Palmyra to set up a
trading business that would bring the goods of the East to
Britain, where his younger brother would market them. A strange

business for the son of an eminent Roman. Patricians usually amused themselves in lighter pursuits. Still, the early Romans had been diligent and industrious. The governor could not help but wonder if, in addition to his business, Marcus Alexander would be the government's unofficial eyes and ears.

There had been talk of allowing Prince Odenathus to govern for Rome when he, Antonius, retired in a few years. Although the prince still ran the city, with the exception of minor judicial matters it was all done under the governor's direction. The young Palmyran ruler had proved extremely friendly and trustworthy, and why not, thought Antonius Porcius. Roman legions kept the Persians at bay. Rome, however, was not apt to allow Odenathus totally free rein. There would be someone sent to watch, and the governor suspected that Marcus Alexander was that person. By the time Odenathus was given alleged control, Marcus Alexander would be a part of Palmyran life, and no one would suspect him at all. Never in all the history of Rome— either as republic or empire—had the Alexander family been implicated in any kind of disloyalty. They were Romans first and always.

Marcus was an attractive man, thought the governor, although he had inherited his British mother's coloring and height. He was tall by any standards, measuring several inches over six feet. His hair was the warm, burnished color of a chestnut; his eyes a bright, almost startling blue, rimmed in outrageously thick lashes of the same color as his hair. He had a firm and well-muscled body, in proportion with his great height. He was obviously not a man who lolled about the banquet table, his only exercise the lifting of a wine goblet. Antonius Porcius could not help but notice Marcus Alexander's hands. They were large and square, yet the fingers were slender and tapering. The hands bespoke power, but at the same time gentleness.

The governor had not a moment's doubt that the women of Palmyra would flock to the newcomer's bed, for the attractive body was topped by a handsome face of classic elegance. Marcus Alexander might have his British antecedents' size and coloring, but he had his father's features. The face was oval with a squared-off chin and jawline. The forehead was high, the nose pure Roman, long and aquiline; the piercing blue eyes were set well apart; the mouth was sensuously big and yet the lips were narrow, their expression faintly mocking, faintly amused.

Those lips now spoke. "You are staring, Antonius Porcius. Is there something amiss?"

"What? No, no, Marcus Alexander! Nothing is wrong. I was simply thinking how like your father you are in features. I served with him for a time in Britain. Wretched climate, Britain! I could never get warm there."

"And here in Palmyra I'll wager you can never get cool," came the teasing reply.

The governor chuckled drily. "These old bones of mine prefer the heat of the East to the damp of Britain and Gaul."

Marcus Alexander swished the Falernian wine about in his goblet. "Do you really think this marriage will be a dangerous thing for Rome?" He paused, then said quietly, "Perhaps the girl should be eliminated before the event even takes place."

Antonius Porcius felt an icy chill sweep over him. He chose his words carefully. "Zenobia bat Zabaai does not like Rome, or Romans, it is true; but I suspect that you are correct. She is but a slip of a girl. What real harm can she do an empire? She will be kept busy in her husband's bed, and in the nursery for many years to come; and then she will be so busy with her grandchildren that her life will be gone before she has time to think of revenging against Rome for her mother's death. I am growing old, Marcus Alexander, and sometimes see shadows where none exist." And, thought the governor, I certainly do not want that girl's death on *my* conscience.

"Better you are too cautious, than not cautious enough. Will you be going to the wedding?"

"Oh, yes! The Palmyrans have long been Hellenized. It will be a traditional Confarreate ceremony celebrated in the atrium of Zabaai ben Selim's house, and after the banquet the bridal procession will wind back through the city to the bride's new home at the palace. It's really no different from Rome."

"Perhaps I shall stand with the crowd outside the bride's house to see her when she leaves," was the reply.

"She is very beautiful," the governor said.

"Perhaps by Eastern standards," Marcus Alexander said. "I, myself, prefer blondes."

"So did Odenathus," Antonius Porcius said, "until he saw Zenobia."

"Indeed?" The governor's guest was thoughtful. "I shall most certainly then want to see the bride, although girls on their wedding day have a glow about them that gives beauty even to the most unattractive of females."

"Then see her before her wedding day," the governor said mischievously. "She has returned to her father's house, and is in the habit of riding in the desert early each morning. Perhaps if you, too, ride early you will see her.''

Marcus Alexander *was* curious, and so the next morning he rose before dawn and followed the caravan road a small distance into the desert. Waiting behind a dune, he watched as the sun began to color the sky and reflect onto the vast sands. His patience was finally rewarded, and his ears pricked at the sound of drumming hoofbeats. Into sight came a magnificent white Arabian, galloping flat-out, along the track; and on the horse's back, low and almost at one with it, was a rider who slowly drew the sweating animal to a halt, then straightened.

Marcus Alexander caught his breath. It was a girl, but what a girl! Long, bare legs; full breasts; and a face that could only be described as the most beautiful he had ever seen. He had never imagined that a woman could be *that* lovely. When he moved his horse out into view from behind the dune, she turned slowly to gaze at him haughtily. "Good morning," he said.

Zenobia nodded silently to the giant of a man who had so suddenly materialized before her.

"I am Marcus Alexander Britainus, lately come to Palmyra."

"I am Zenobia bat Zabaai."

"Do you always ride alone, Zenobia bat Zabaai?"

"Don't you, Marcus Alexander?" was the disconcerting reply.

"I am a man."

"So I have noted. Good morning, Marcus Alexander." She urged her horse forward.

"Wait!" he caught at the white mare's bridle, but Zenobia was faster, and yanked the horse's head away, causing the animal to rear up.

Bringing her mount under control, Zenobia turned her full attention on the man before her. Her gray eyes were almost black in their fury, and her voice, though controlled, was filled with anger. "*Never* touch an animal I'm riding again, Marcus Alexander! *Never!* You greeted me, and the laws of hospitality demanded that I do so in return; but I do not like Romans. I especially do not like blue-eyed Romans. Blue-eyed Romans murdered my mother four years ago after they had broken into our home and used her for their pleasure. I ride alone through choice. Now, get out of my way! I wish to ride on.''

"Your pardon, Zenobia bat Zabaai. I regret that my personal appearance brings back painful memories for you. I meant no offense, but I am new to Palmyra and, although I enjoy riding, I am not certain I would not get lost in your desert. I merely sought the privilege of riding with you so I might grow familiar with the track.''

She felt guilty for her outburst, but she had no intention of either backing down from her stand, or of letting the Roman know that her conscience had been pricked. "It is best that you not ride in the desert without an escort, Marcus Alexander. There are always marauding Persians, or a renegade Bedawi or two looking for a foolish traveler to rob and murder. They do not distinguish between Romans and other peoples, for it makes no difference to them whose throat they slit or whose purse they cut." As she sat stiffly, proudly staring at him, the thought flitted through her mind that he was a very attractive man, perhaps the most handsome man she'd ever seen. Instantly she felt contrite. It was her Hawk who was the most handsome man in the world.

Marcus Alexander had the most incredible urge to lift Zenobia from her horse and kiss that scornful mouth until it softened, but he did not. He could not jeopardize his position in Palmyra, and making love to the prince's bride-to-be would certainly do that. Instead he nodded, and said, "You are probably correct, Zenobia bat Zabaai. I would do well to return to the city immediately." And then, because he could not resist it, he said, "For all I know you are one of those women used to lure the unsuspecting traveler to his doom." It gave him great satisfaction to hear the furious gasp of outrage behind him as he rode off.

A beautiful girl, he thought; a bitter girl—but who could blame her? Antonius Porcius had simply said that Zenobia's mother had been killed by Roman legionnaires. He had said nothing of rape. Poor girl. This was certainly not the time to explain the differences to her between renegade Gauls and Romanized Britons like himself.

He rode a short distance, then turned his head to look back. She had whipped her horse into a gallop, and was tearing across the desert at an incredible speed. Marcus Alexander chuckled to himself. He liked a woman with real spirit.

He worked hard during the next few days, driven by the ex-slave who was to be his right-hand man. Severus had been his tutor as a boy, but when his father offered to free the man, Severus had asked to remain in the service of the Alexander family. It was a request they could not deny, and from that day on, Severus had learned from Lucius Alexander the ways of business. He had arrived in Palmyra two months before Marcus Alexander to purchase a villa and warehouse.

Now Marcus Alexander had to take the reins. Though he strove to concentrate, his mind was constantly being interrupted by visions of a long-legged girl as spirited as the white mare she rode. It came as something of a shock to him to realize that he wanted her, because he could not have her. Marcus Alexander, son of Lucius, wealthy, handsome, and since birth denied nothing within reason, had fallen in love seriously for the first time in his twenty-five years.

As the appointed day for the wedding grew closer, the excitement within the house of Zabaai ben Selim rose to a fever pitch. Though none of Zabaai's women except Tamar had ever paid the slightest attention to Zenobia, all now wanted to help, wanted to take the place of the bride's mother. Each advised her as many times daily as they could get near her; each attempted to choose her manner of dress; and each bitterly resented the *interference* of the others. Zenobia became as a choice piece of meat to be haggled over by the women in the market. She was finally forced to beg her father to tell his women that she wanted only Tamar to help her. Tamar, who was her friend, would be the bride's mother, and no other. Zenobia was finally left in peace.

On the evening before the marriage Zenobia took the small locket that her mother had given her when she was born, and laid it on the altar of the household gods. These gods had watched over her childhood, but tomorrow that childhood would be gone, never to return, and so she laid upon the altar in solemn sacrifice the last vestige of her early years. Had she been younger she would also have brought her toys, but those had long since been discarded. As she stood quietly in the little family garden that enclosed the altar she prayed for her mother, and wished that by some miracle known only to the gods themselves that Iris would be by her side tomorrow.

Tamar and Bab were both so good to her that she almost felt guilty, but for the first time in many months she missed her mother terribly. It was not so much Iris's golden beauty she recalled, but rather the sweet smell of her perfume; the gentle touch of her hand; the swish of her long skirts when she left Zenobia's room at night. She remembered the beautiful woman who always had time to explain, who hugged easily and without the least hint of embarrassment, who laughed happily to see her daughter and her husband together playing. A tear slipped down Zenobia's cheek, and then another, until her face was wet with sorrow.

Across the garden Bab saw the girl's shoulders shaking with her grief, and made to go to her; but Tamar held her back. "No," said Zabaai ben Selim's surviving wife. "She has never really cried since Iris's death, and she needs to weep. Let her leave her sorrow behind with the rest of her childhood things."

Bab nodded. "You are right, of course, but how I hate to see her hurt. If I could I would shield her from all the evil in life."

"You would do her no favor then, Bab. Zenobia must face everything that comes her way by herself. If she does not know evil when she encounters it, how will she deal with it?"

"I know, I know. Besides, I babble foolishness. Who has ever been able to shield Zenobia from anything?" Bab replied.

"Let us go inside," Tamar replied. "Soon our child will come to try on her wedding garment for luck. She must not know that we have observed her in a private moment."

The two women returned to their quarters and awaited the girl whom they both loved, so they might share this traditional time with her that her own mother could not. Both believed, however, that Iris watched from the paradise within the underworld to which the just are confined.

Sleep was elusive for Zenobia that night. Like any young bride-to-be, she was both fearful and excited about the morrow's events. The tantalizing moments that she had had with the prince those two weeks back had only increased her curiosity. When she finally dozed it was only to awaken with a start, remembering a confused jumble of a dream in which a Roman had gazed upon her with mocking blue eyes. Zenobia sat up trembing, wondering if the shade of her mother's murderer had come to haunt her on this the night before her marriage. Then she remembered the Roman, Marcus Alexander Britainus, whom she had met in the desert a few days earlier. He had been the man in her dream. Puzzled, she wondered why she had dreamed of *him*. With a confused little shake of her head she lay back down to rest, and fell into a light sleep.

In the hour before dawn the public augur arrived, and a young ewe was sacrificed. The omens were considered most favorable. The house of Zabaai ben Selim was decorated with a multitude of flowers; the boughs of palm trees; colorful bands of wool that had been entwined about the pillars; and exquisite tapestries hung all about the atrium, where the ceremony would take place. Before first light, the guests began arriving.

In her bedchamber, aided by Tamar and Bab, Zenobia completed the final preparations. She had already bathed and washed her lovely black hair, which was now divided into six locks with a spear-shaped comb. This was an ancient custom dating from the time when marriage by capture was the rule rather than the exception. These locks were carefully coiled, and held in place with ribbons of silver lamé.

The wedding gown was a white tunic of gossamer silk, woven by Tamar and Bab. The straight garment was made from a single piece of cloth, and fell to Zenobia's feet which were shod in silver sandals. The tunic was fastened around the waist with a band of wool tied in the knot of Hercules, for Hercules was the guardian of wedded life. When he became Zenobia's husband only Odenathus would be privileged to untie this knot. Over her tunic the bride wore a flame-colored veil; atop her head was a wreath of sweet, white freesia.

Downstairs, the groom had arrived with his mother and friends. He wore a silver-bordered white togo, and was given a wreath of white freesia, matching his bride's, for his head. The augur formally pronounced the omens as favorable, the wedding was ready to begin.

Zenobia was brought forward by Tamar, who had been chosen as pronuba for the ceremony. Zabaai's wife then joined the bride and groom's hands before the guests, and Zenobia spoke the words of her consent to this marriage. She spoke them three times, once in Latin, once in Greek, and once in the Aramaic dialect of her tribe, so that everyone in the room might understand:

"When and where you are Gaius; I then and there am Gaia."

Now the high priest from the Temple of Jupiter led the couple to the left of the household altar and, facing it, they were seated on stools covered with the skin of the sheep sacrificed earlier. Then a bloodless offering of a wheat cake was made to Jupiter by the high priest. A second cake was eaten by the bride and groom. Next the high priest recited prayers to Juno, goddess of marriage, and to the gods of the countryside and its fruits. The utensils necessary for the offering were carried in a covered basket by a boy called a *camillus,* whose parents were both living. Zenobia had chosen for this important role her young nephew, Zabaai ben Akbar.

As the ceremony concluded the guests cried *"Feliciter!"* meaning good luck and happiness. Odenathus turned Zenobia to face him. Seeing him for the first time since she had left the palace almost two weeks ago, she felt shy and blushed. There was a hum of approval by those close enough to see.

Gently he kissed her on the forehead. "I have missed you, my flower," he said so only she might hear.

"I have missed you, Hawk."

It was the only private moment they would get for many hours to come. A lavish wedding feast had been planned, and it would last until evening. Knowing what was expected of her, Zenobia took her new husband's hand, and together they led the guests into Zabaai's magnificent outdoor dining room in the back garden of the villa. Here, dining couches and tables had been set up around a tiled court with a center fountain that shot a spray of water from the mouth of a marvelous golden sea dragon who writhed in the center of the fountain. The bride and groom shared a couch at the center table while the other guests were seated according to the order of their importance.

The meal was divided into three parts. The appetizers consisted of asparagus in oil and vinegar, tuna and sliced egg on beds of lettuce, oysters that had been brought overland packed in snow, and thrushes, roasted a golden brown and set upon beds of cress, all on silver platters decorated with apricots and ripe olives. The second course offered loin of goat, legs of baby lamb, roasted chickens, ducks both domestic and wild, hare, great bowls of vegetables such as green beans, young cabbage sprouts, cauliflower imported from Europe, lettuce and onions, radishes and cucumbers, olives both green and ripe. There were loaves of bread, round and hot from the ovens.

When the main part of the meal had been cleared away crystal bowls of almonds and pistachios were set upon all the tables along with platters of green and golden pears, red and purple plums, peaches, apricots, cherries, pomegranates, grapes black, purple, and green. There were sticky honey cakes shaped like butterflies and wrapped about chopped nuts and poppy seeds. A wedding cake filled with raisins and currants was served, and pieces of this cake were distributed to all the guests to take home for luck.

Throughout the meal a mixture of water and wine had been served, but as the desserts were being offered rich red wine was poured and repoured into eager goblets. As the diners became more boisterous the entertainers appeared. There were wrestlers, jugglers, dancing dogs, and dancing girls who were very well received indeed. The late morning had melted into afternoon, and now suddenly evening had come. The most important part of the wedding was about to take place. It was essential to the validity of a marriage that the bride be escorted publicly to her husband's house with much ceremony and pomp.

All afternoon the crowds had been gathering outside of Zabaai ben Selim's house, and along the route that would be taken by the couple on their way back to the prince's palace. Now with the arrival of the torchbearers and the flute players the procession began to form. Bab had already gone on ahead to the palace, and Zenobia had earlier bid the rest of her father's household a proper farewell. The marriage hymn was sung by all the guests, and Odenathus pretended to take Zenobia by force from Tamar's protective embrace. The bride then took her place of honor in the procession, attended by her three youngest brothers, two of whom walked beside her, holding her hands. The eldest of the three lit the way ahead with the wedding torch of hawthorn.

Before the procession moved off into the street Zabaai ben Selim spoke low to his daughter: "Remember we are your family. If you need us, Zenobia, you have but to call."

She smiled a radiant smile at him. "I will remember, and pray the gods I never have need of your offer, my father."

"It is best to be prepared," was his reply.

"Come, my flower." Odenathus was by her side, smiling. She smiled back happily, and the procession was off. Across the street in the crowd of well-wishers Marcus Alexander watched as Zenobia moved away. She was as beautiful as he had remembered, and for the first time in his life he felt envy for another man, envy for the Prince of Palmyra who would soon untie the knot of Hercules on Zenobia's wedding dress and then spend the rest of the night making love to that exquisite creature. Would he be gentle, or would he fall on the girl like a beast and frighten her? He sighed. He would be gentle. He would caress that softer-than-silk skin—somehow Marcus Alexander knew Zenobia's skin would be soft—until a fire raged within that beautiful body. A fire to be possessed, and to possess.

Seeing the look of longing on Marcus Alexander's face, Severus realized with shock that his master had fallen in love with the new Princess of Palmyra.

There was no time to ponder it, for the crowd was joining in the procession, already beginning to sing songs full of coarse jests and double entendres as they accompanied the bride through the city to her new home. It was the same everywhere, Severus thought, not at all shocked. Princess, patrician, or commoner were all escorted with the same vulgar songs. At the first crossroads they came to, Zenobia dropped a coin in offering to the gods of that place. A second coin she presented to Odenathus as symbol of the dowry she brought him, and a third she kept to put upon the altar of her new home's household gods. As they moved along, the crowds scrambled to obtain some of the sweetmeats, sesame cakes, and nuts that the prince scattered along his route, a traditional prayer for his wife's fertility.

It seemed as if the entire city had joined in the procession by the time they reached the palace. At the main gate Zenobia stopped and wound the doorposts with wool, symbol of her duties as mistress of the house; and anointed the door with oil and fat, emblems of plenty. Odenathus then picked her up and carefully carried her across the threshold, gently setting her back on her feet within the great atrium of the palace. A final time Zenobia said, "When and where you are Gaius; I then and there am Gaia." The doors were then closed.

Before the invited guests, Odenathus offered Zenobia fire and water in token of their new life together. Taking the marriage torch from him, Zenobia put it to the wood laid upon the atrium hearth, and then tossed the now dead torch among her guests, who scrambled eagerly for the lucky item. She then recited a prayer to the gods thanking them for her good fortune, and begging them that she be fruitful. Tamar, still in her role as pronuba, led Zenobia to the marriage couch, an ornamental piece of furniture that was always placed in the atrium on the night of the marriage and remained there afterward. This was the signal for all guests to leave, and shortly the bridal couple were alone.

For a few moments they stood in silence. Then the prince said, "Are you tired, my flower?"

"Yes."

"Then we shall go to bed."

"*Here?*" He heard the panic in her voice as her gaze swept the large, open atrium, finally lighting on the large and gilded marriage couch.

"No, not here, Zenobia." He kept his voice steady and even to reassure her. "You have your own house within the palace grounds. We will go there now, for it is there you and I shall live together."

"Is Bab there?"

"Not tonight, my flower. Tonight we will be alone."

"Oh." Her voice was very small, and her hand very cold when he took it to lead her off.

"I hope you will be pleased with your house, my flower. It is not overly large, for I did not think you would want a large home. Every workman, craftsman, and artisan in the city has worked for the last two weeks to build you your house."

"It is new? Oh, Hawk! I did not mean for you to go to so much trouble."

"I wanted you to have a house that was your very own, my love. The structure is of sun-dried brick sheathed on the outside with white marble. It is a simple house, but it is two stories. There is an atrium in the front so you may receive guests, a library for me to work in, a dining room facing south that we will use in winter, and one facing north for the summer. We need no banquet hall, for the palace has several of those. There is also a kitchen on the main floor, and one good-sized room I thought you might enjoy using for yourself as well as a comfortable chamber for Bab. I thought she might enjoy being on the ground floor with not so many stairs to climb.

"The bedchambers are on the second floor along with the baths. I have chosen only a minimum amount of furniture because I thought that you might enjoy choosing your own things from the bazaars. As for slaves, you will choose your own; but for the next few days it is only necessary that Bab serve us."

They had exited the main palace, and now walked through vast gardens, already moonlit and filled with small night creatures tuning up with song. They turned onto a graveled path lined in Palmyran palms, and at its end she saw a lovely small palace. As they reached its open doors he once more picked her up, and carried her over the threshold. But once inside, he did not put her down. Instead he walked through the atrium to the passageway that hid the stairs, and carried her up to a bedchamber, where he deposited her in the middle of the floor.

"Help me with this damned toga," he said quietly. Surprised, she obeyed. "I hate togas, but high state occasions demand I wear them."

Silently she took the garment and laid it carefully on a chair, as she was unfamiliar with the room and did not know where the storage chests were kept. He sat down and bent to unlace his sandals. Quickly she hurried over, and knelt to aid him, sliding the sandals off, quietly admiring his graceful feet. She started at the touch of his hand on her head.

"You don't have to take my sandals off, my flower."

"I want to," she replied. "I will not always be the sort of wife you want, my Hawk, but these small things I will do for you, and as long as I do, you will know that I love you."

His hand reached down to cup her chin and raise her head up. For a long moment he stared into those beautiful, calm gray eyes, and then his lips but brushed hers, sending a little tingle through her. She lowered her eyes shyly only to become suddenly aware that he now wore only a short tunica interior. Zenobia stared fascinated at her husband's muscled and shapely legs. They were long and smooth and tanned. Amused, he watched her for a moment. He could almost sense that she wanted to touch him, but was yet afraid.

He stood up, drawing her with him, his hands going to the knot of Hercules that was tied about the waist of her wedding dress. For several moments he struggled with it, muttering under his breath as the knot's puzzle eluded him, "Who in Hades tied this thing?"

Zenobia giggled. "Tamar."

"She obviously didn't want me to unfasten it. Ah, there!" He drew the wool band off, and the tunic hung loose. Wordlessly he drew it over her head, and put it on the same chair that held his toga, adding her tunica interior before she realized he was taking it. She stood, stunned, as he knelt and drew off her silver sandals. Standing back up, he carefully undid the ribbons that held her long curls, reaching out to take up her brush, which lay set out on a nearby table. He turned her about, and slowly brushed her hair free of its tangles, admiring its sheen and its length, which ended at the base of her spine.

Turning her about again, he set her back from him and stood gazing upon her nude beauty. Surprised by his firm action, and stunned to find herself naked before a man, Zenobia stood quietly under his inspection for several long moments. She had absolutely no idea what he expected of her—if indeed he expected anything other than compliance. Having studied her quite thoroughly from the front, the prince walked slowly around his new wife, viewing her from every possible angle.

"My lord," Zenobia whispered, half-afraid. "What do you want of me?"

Roused from his reverie, he realized her discomfort and gently drew her into his arms. "Zenobia," he said softly, his voice strangely thick to her ear, "I have seen many beautiful women in my time, but never have I seen a woman as perfect, as flawless as you, my flower."

"Then you want me?"

"*Want you?!*" The words were almost strangled in his throat. "I have wanted you for weeks now, you little idiot!"

"I think I want you," she said softly, and he laughed.

"How can you know what you want, my little virgin bride? I am the only man who has ever touched you, but you liked it, Zenobia. Oh yes, my flower, you liked it. Just now when you knelt to take my sandals off you wanted to touch me."

She blushed. "How could you know that?"

"Because I am a man, and I know women." He smoothed his hand down her back beneath her hair to caress and fondle a buttock. Surprised, she jumped, and he murmured against her ear, "No, my flower, don't be frightened. I know how innocent you are, and we will go slowly. There should never be haste between a man and a woman, only time to enjoy." His hand tipped her face up to his, and he tenderly kissed her. "I love you, Zenobia, Princess of Palmyra." He kissed the tip of her nose. "I love your pride and your independence." He kissed her eyelids, which had closed at his first sweet assault. "I love your beauty and your innocence, but most of all I love just you, my little desert flower. I should not have married you had I not loved you." Bending slightly, he swung her up in his arms and carried her across the room to lay her on their marriage bed.

Her heart was hammering wildly in her ears and her eyes were shut tight; but she heard his voice teasingly say, "I have studied you most carefully, my darling, and now I offer you the same opportunity." She heard the rustle of cloth as he drew off his interior tunic. "Open your eyes, Zenobia," he commanded her, and there was laughter in his voice. "A man's body is nothing to fear. If anything it is amusing, for it has not the beauty of form that a woman's has. I, however, think I am rather pretty as far as men go."

A small giggle escaped her, but her eyes remained closed.

"Zenobia!" His voice was mock-stern. "Open your eyes! I command it!"

Her eyes flew open, and she sat up. "I will not be commanded, Hawk!" And then her gray eyes widened, and she gasped. "Ohh!"

Mischievously he grinned down at her. "Am I not pleasing

to your eye, my flower?'' He posed himself, parodying the athletes in the arena.

She was unable to take her eyes from his body. He was an inch or two taller than she was, and he was beautifully formed. His legs were long, the calves and thighs firm and shapely. He had a narrow waist that fanned upward into a broad chest and wide shoulders. His arms were long and muscled and he had slender hands and long fingers. His body was tanned and smooth, and looking at it now, she was again overcome by the desire to caress him as he had caressed her two weeks earlier. She had carefully kept her eyes averted from his sex, but now she let her eyes slide downward, color flooding her cheeks at her daring. To her surprise, the beast she had been half fearful of was nothing more than a gentle creature nestling small and soft upon its dark, furred bed.

Again he sensed her thoughts. ''It only grows large when I desire you.''

''You *said* you wanted me!'' she accused.

''I do want you, my flower, but wanting and desiring are two different things. The wanting is in my head and my heart. The desire comes from my body.''

He stretched out next to her on the bed. ''There has been no time for desire this day.'' Reaching out, he drew her to him. ''No time until now, Zenobia,'' and then his mouth was covering hers, tasting and possessing until with a great shudder she gave herself up to his building passion.

She had never expected a man's mouth to be so tender. It gently commanded her, and she obeyed, parting her lips to receive his velvety tongue, which stroked hers until suddenly she felt a fire beginning to build deep within her. Pulling her head away from his, she tried to clear the dizziness with several breaths of air, but he only laughed and captured her mouth again in a torrid embrace. Finally satisfied that her sweet lips had received their due, his mouth scorched a path down the side of her face, his slender fingers moving ahead along her slim neck. Pressing a hot kiss against her ear, he murmured, ''Can you feel your own desire rising, my love?'' and he gently bit on her earlobe, before moving on to the soft curve of her silken throat.

Zenobia was beginning to tremble, and when her husband's hands found her round full breasts she gasped softly with longing. She wanted his touch! She craved it, for then perhaps the terrible ache that was filling her entire being would dissolve and go away. Reverently he fondled each tender globe, and then without warning his head dipped down to capture within his warm mouth a quivering and already taut nipple. Hungrily he drew on her virgin breast, and she cried out, surprised not only by his action but the corresponding tightness in the hidden place between her legs.

He raised his head, and his voice soothed her. "Don't be afraid, my flower. Is it not sweet?"

Her answer was to draw his head back down to her breasts, where he resumed his pleasing dalliance; but soon he sought to explore further. One arm encircled her waist, while his other hand brushed across her belly, which fluttered wildly beneath his touch. His head dipped and his tongue teased her navel, causing her to writhe beneath him. The hand moved lower yet, to her smoothly plucked Venus mound, and now he could feel her beginning to resist him. She tensed beneath his fingers, and he could hear the nervousness in her voice.

"Please, Hawk! Please, no!"

"Why are you suddenly afraid of me?" He sought to touch her again, but she caught defensively at his hand.

"*Please!*"

It suddenly occurred to him that perhaps she did not know the way between a man and a woman. "Did Tamar tell you how it should be between us, between a husband and his wife?" he asked her.

"No," came the reply, "but I know it is the same as with the animals. The male mounts the female; is that not correct?"

"People are not animals, Zenobia. Animals feel need and they satisfy that need without any thought. A man with a woman is a different thing, my flower." He firmly moved her hand away, and gently caressed her. "I have always believed that the gods created woman to be worshiped by her lover. When I touch you with love I worship at the shrine of your perfection. You must not be afraid of me, or of my touch."

"I have never been touched there before," she said low, trembling beneath his fingers.

In answer he kissed her again, murmuring against her mouth, "Don't be afraid, my darling. Don't be afraid," and she felt him very carefully exploring her more intimately.

A strange languor was spreading over her, leaving her limbs weak and helpless. He was her husband, and yet should he be touching her like that? His finger gently penetrated her body, and she cried out, struggling to escape him, but the prince quickly shifted her so she lay completely beneath him. Atop her, he whispered soft love words into her ear. "No, Zenobia, no, my darling. Don't be afraid. Don't fight me, my flower."

She could feel every inch of his very masculine body. His smooth chest pressed against her full breasts; his flat belly pushed against her gently rounded one; his thighs met hers with a heat that brought a moan to her lips. All this time her hands had never sought to touch him, but now she could no longer control the wild desire that he was awakening in her. When he buried his face in her soft throat, his kisses seemingly endless, her arms wound about his neck and then, palms flat, she caressed the line of his back, ending as she cupped his hard buttocks in a gentle grasp.

"Oh, Hawk," she whispered, "your skin is so soft for a man."

"What do you know of men, Zenobia?" was the reply. His voice was strangely harsh, his lips burning against the tender flesh of her throat.

"I know nothing but what you would teach me, my husband," came the soft reply, and her hands moved back up again to clasp about his neck.

"I would teach you to be a woman, my flower. Are you brave enough?" he demanded, his dark eyes burning into hers.

She trembled against him, but her gaze was unwavering as she said, "Yes, my Hawk, yes, I am brave enough now."

His mouth covered hers in a sweet kiss, and she felt him slide his hands beneath her to raise her hips up just a little. Her blood was racing wildly through her veins and she couldn't control her trembling. Now, suddenly, she felt something hard probing insistently between her shaking thighs. "Hawk! Oh, my lord, I want to be a woman, but I am afraid again!" She squirmed away from him, and huddled in a corner of the bed.

The prince groaned with frustration. He had never wanted any woman so desperately in his life. He was tempted to force her beneath him, and take what he wanted of her. She would forgive him afterward; but when he lifted his head up she was staring with large, terrified eyes at his manhood.

"*You cannot!*" she cried. "You will tear me asunder!"

For a moment he enjoyed the flattery of her innocence. "You will birth our children there, my darling," he explained patiently. "If a whole baby can fit, then I can." Wordlessly she shook her head in the negative, but he drew her firmly back into his arms, kissing her tenderly, gently stroking her until the fire-storm began to build within her again.

She felt so strange, as she had never felt before. Her body was honeyed fire that leapt and flowed under his orchestration; the pleasure-pain building until she believed she could bear it no longer. She was vaguely aware that he was once more cover-ing her burning flesh with his own, but suddenly it didn't matter. She wanted it! She wanted him!

He felt her body relax beneath him, and in that instant his shaft entered the portals of her femininity, gently easing into her incredibly tight sheath. Her virginity was tightly lodged, and he stopped a moment, kissing her closed eyelids, tenderly brushing back a stray lock of hair from her forehead. She whimpered, a half-passionate, half-fearful sound, and he could feel her heart pounding beneath his chest.

Zenobia felt as if he was tearing her apart. His manhood filled her, gorged her, and the pain was fierce. She tried to lay still, keeping her eyes tightly shut so he might not know and have his pleasure spoiled. When he stopped momentarily, lying atop her, attempting to soothe her, she felt a slight relief; but then he drew back and plunged swiftly through her maiden barrier. She shrieked with the hurt, and fought to escape him, but he was firmly in control, pushing deeper into her resisting sweetness.

"No! No!" she sobbed, the tears beginning to come, and then suddenly she became aware that his manhood, which just moments ago had seemed like a red-hot poker, was suddenly the source of the most marvelous sweetness; yet the ache was increasing. She no longer seemed able to fight him off. His shaft moved back and forth within her, and the world about her seemed to pulse and spin with a myriad of sensations. Zenobia had never imagined that anything could be as magnificent as this joining of bodies. She was as lost within him as he was in her. The pleasure built higher until the ache dissolved without warning, and she was falling, falling into a warm and welcom-ing blackness.

She clung to him, lost within her private world, and the prince was ravished by her response to his passion. Tenderly he gathered her into his arms, so that when once more she became herself, she would feel cherished—for indeed she was. Pressing soft little kisses upon her face, he murmured reassur-ingly to her, "I love you, my darling! My adorable wife, I love you so!'' He said the words over and over until she finally opened her eyes and looked up at him.

"Oh, my Hawk, I love you too! I want to please you, but will it always hurt like that?''

"Never again,'' he promised her. "It was only because you were a virgin, Zenobia. I cannot understand Tamar not telling you.''

"Tamar has had only sons,'' Zenobia replied, "and perhaps she did not wish to frighten me.''

"Then why not your Bab?''

"It was not Bab's place to tell me those things,'' she said primly.

Odenathus sighed with exasperation. "Then I suppose it must be my place to school you, my flower.''

"Yes, my lord,'' came the demure reply.

He looked sharply at her, then laughed, for her eyes were mischievous. "Do you laugh at me, my wife?'' he demanded in a teasingly threatening tone.

"Yes, my lord.'' Her look was melting.

He could feel his desire rising once more, and wondered if he dare take her again. It had been a hard breach of her maidenhead, and he had not a doubt that she was sore.

"I want you again, my Hawk.'' She punctuated her remark by turning her head to gently bite at his forearm.

A shiver ran through him as he realized that his bride was a passionate woman. Reaching out, he rubbed her nipple until it stood tall, a tough little soldier upon the rise of her delicious flesh. She pulled his head down, kissing his mouth, whispering against his lips, "Take me now, my darling! I burn!''

Mounting her, he slipped into her sweet sheath, feeling her wince slightly. Slowly he moved within her, pushing deep, then pulling himself completely out, only to plunge once again into her burning body. He felt her nails rake his back, and heard her cry, "No! I want the sweetness, my Hawk! Do not deny me the sweetness!''

He laughed as he sat straddling her. "Do not be in a hurry, my flower. There is much pleasure to be gained by taking time to enjoy each other,'' and then he commenced a tantalizingly slow movement that would drive her to the brink of madness.

Zenobia found herself helpless before the delicious sensations that began to assail her. There had been pain the first time, but then it had been good, and she had liked it. Now, though here had been a moment's discomfort when he had begun again, it was different, yet still good. She didn't believe it could be any better, but each moment brought new delights until she was spinning away, lost in time and not caring. All she could think was that she had been a fool to fear him. Above her the prince groaned with his own pleasure, falling across her breasts, but Zenobia was totally unaware.

Both fell into a deep sleep, but with the resilience of a healthy young animal Zenobia awoke after a few hours. It was the middle of the night, black and so very still. The lamps still burned, for neither she nor the prince had thought to snuff them out. A slight wind came through the portico and the lamps flickered, casting odd, red-gold shadows against the wall. She lay on her back, quietly observing the room in which she had become a woman. It was, she realized, a woman's room; it was her room, the room in which she would share tender, sweet intimacies with Hawk; the room in which she would birth her children; the room in which as an old woman, she would probably breathe her last.

It was a simple place, she thought as her eyes slowly swept the chamber; but then he had said that it had not been decorated because he thought she might enjoy planning the decor of their home. Here was something new and challenging.

"Are you awake?" His voice tore at the stillness.

"Yes."

"What are you pondering, my flower?"

An honest reply sprang to her lips only to be swallowed back. He would hardly think it complimentary that on their wedding night she was thinking of how to decorate their home. "I was thinking of you, Hawk," she said.

"What were you thinking?"

"That I love you," she replied.

He raised himself up on his elbow, and looked down into her face, smiling. "We will be friends as well as lovers, as well as husband and wife. Oh, Zenobia, I am so glad that I have you! I have been so alone since my father died. Neither my mother nor Deliciae can be a friend to me, for they do not understand my feelings for Palmyra; but you understand, my flower, don't you? This is a great city, and we shall make it greater so that our son will be an even greater lord than his father and grandfather!"

"How can we be great as long as the Romans rule us?" she demanded.

"Soon Antonius Porcius will retire," he explained to her,

"and he has told me that the emperor will send no one to take his place. The Romans trust us, Zenobia. I will shortly rule the city in my own right as the princes of Palmyra did before me."

"How can you rule in your own right when the Romans still garrison troups within our city?" Zenobia demanded.

"My wedding gift from the emperor is command of those troops, my beautiful wife!"

She sat up, startled. "You are to command Roman troops?"

"I am. Now what do you think, my flower?"

"I wonder why, after years of occupation, the Romans suddenly decided to let you rule without a Roman governor. I wonder why you have been put in charge of *their* troops."

"Because the Romans know that they can trust me, Zenobia."

"And once you have total control will you overthrow them?" Her gray eyes shown with pride.

"No, Zenobia. I need Rome's soldiers for Palmyra. The world is no longer what it once was. We are surrounded by dangers not even dreamed of in my grandfather's time. I need an army to protect this city."

"Why Romans?!"

"Rome is the central power in the world. If I use her troops then I do not have to force my own people into the military service. Rome's troops cost me nothing. The tribute we pay to the empire comes from the caravans; and not from my people."

"I cannot believe that you have bent your neck to their yoke," she cried. "Tell me you have been but jesting with me, my Hawk."

"Zenobia, you are yet a child, and do not understand these matters," he said gently. "When you see how the government is run, the monies involved, then you will understand why it is necessary for us to cooperate with Rome. Come now, my flower, why are we discussing such weighty matters in the midst of our wedding night." He leaned over and kissed her mouth.

She pulled back, her gray eyes serious. "You once promised to share your responsibilities with me, Hawk. Have you now changed your mind?"

"I do not make promises I do not intend to keep, my flower. There is, however, a time for everything, and this is not the time to be discussing my government."

"When *is* the right time?" she demanded angrily. "Must I make an appointment with you, as do your ministers? Shall I tell your secretary in the morning that the Princess of Palmyra wishes an appointment with the Prince of Palmyra so she may discuss the government with him?''

"By the gods!'' he exclaimed. "We are having our first fight, Zenobia!'' He reached out a hand, and stroked her shoulder. How beautiful she was with her midnight-black hair swirling about her shoulders.

"You must take the good with the bad,'' she muttered, not easily placated, and shocked by the revelation that she *was* quarreling with him.

"I will share everything with you, my darling,'' he promised, "but we are just married; this is our honeymoon; and I do not want to speak of politics or finances with you at this moment. What bride would choose these things over love in her marriage bed?''

Her resistance began to melt, and he reached out and drew her into his arms. "Oh, Hawk,'' she murmured. "I have so much to learn that I am impatient.''

"It is as I have said, my flower. You are yet a child in many ways, but I will teach you.'' He nibbled at the corners of her mouth, and delicious little tingles of excitement ran through her. The prince smiled down at her, and then his lips took full possession of hers. There was no gentleness this time, only a fierce and burning demand that Zenobia found impossible not to answer. She returned his kisses passionately until her mouth was bruised and aching, but to his surprise she did not yield herself entirely. His hands moved to caress her marvelous breasts; his lips moved from her lips downward along a trail of soft, perfumed flesh that quivered beneath his touch.

She knew what to expect this time, or at least she thought she did, but the warm and softly breathing mouth that murmured love words into her ear, the mouth that moved teasingly along the straining muscle on the side of her neck to bury itself in the tender hollow of her shoulder shook her to the quick. He stayed but a moment in that sweet nook only to move onward to cover the swelling tops of her breasts with quick kisses before beginning his assault upon her nipples, which stood at attention eagerly awaiting him.

"Zenobia,'' he murmured, then his tongue began a slow, teasingly sweet encirclement of a nipple. Round and round it moved, sending waves of heat through her veins until she wanted to scream, for the pleasure left her weak and breathless. It occurred to her suddenly that he was diverting her from the discussion she had been trying to conduct with him. Her first reaction to this thought was outrage that he held her opinion so lightly; but then, as his mouth closed over a nipple and he began to suckle upon her sensitive breast, all coherent thought vanished. She gave herself up to the delights of his lovemaking.

"Oh, my Hawk," she whispered, afraid to break the lovely spell that seemed to surround them, "I love you!"

Slowly he raised his head so he might look upon her beautiful face, and for a moment Zenobia thought she would drown in the dark, dark liquid pool of his eyes. His voice had an intensity that gave her the eerie feeling that he had divined her very thoughts. "And I love you, my exquisite bride. I will share all with you, my love. We have an eternity of sharing before us."

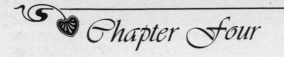
Chapter Four

Marcus Britainus looked up from his inventory sheets. "Yes, Severus, what is it?"

"The Princess of Palmyra is here, sir."

"*Here?*" His heart leapt within his chest. Then he realized that she probably did not remember him.

"She wishes to purchase furniture and see our fabrics and accessories, sir."

"Help her then, Severus." He lowered his head again to the scrolls.

"Marcus Britainus!" Severus's voice was severe. "You cannot avoid Princess Zenobia. If you continue to shun her, this fascination will increase until no other woman can match the woman you have created in your imagination. This is the ruler of Palmyra's wife. You *must* greet her."

"How old must I get before you will realize that I am no longer a green boy?" Marcus grumbled.

"There is something of the boy in every man, Marcus Britainus," came the quiet reply.

Marcus left his office and stopped for a moment to gather his thoughts. *She is here!* Had she sought him out? *Fool!* His practical nature reared its head. Why in the name of all the gods would she remember him? She hated blue-eyed Romans. Besides, from all he could gather, her marriage to Odenathus was a love match. Shaking his head at his own foolishness, he straightened the folds of his toga pura and entered the atrium of his warehouse with a firm step.

Zenobia rose from the bench upon which she had been seated, and watched him come toward her. *The blue-eyed Roman!* Of course! She vaguely remembered that he had introduced himself at their brief first meeting. Merchants were supposed to be old men, she thought irritably, but this was certainly no old man. He topped her by at least eight inches, and Zenobia knew few men to whom she must look up. It gave her a vaguely uncomfortable sensation, made her feel at a disadvantage with him.

Around her, her maidens giggled and made rather pointed and suggestive remarks about the handsome merchant. Zenobia felt her cheeks flushing slightly. Newly awakened to sensuality, she could not help but look upon Marcus Alexander with a woman's eye, and somehow, she thought, that must be disloyal to her Hawk.

Reaching her, he knelt and paid her homage. "Highness."

"Rise, Marcus Alexander Britainus," she said, and before she realized it the words were out. "Why are you so tall? Are you a giant?"

"No, your Highness," he answered her in an even voice, although he was tempted to laugh. "I take my height from my mother's people, the Dobunni. My grandfather was their prince. He smiled down at her. "If I may say it, you are tall for a woman, Highness."

"I take my height from my mother's people too, Marcus Alexander Britainus. My mother was an Alexandrian Greek descended from Queen Cleopatra." Zenobia was openly proud.

"How fitting that Queen Cleopatra's beautiful young descendant should be the Princess of Palmyra, Highness," came the reply.

Zenobia looked up at the Roman, but the deep blue eyes held no trace of mockery, only the deepest respect. "This is a better beginning, Marcus Alexander Britainus," she answered him.

That, he was amused to note to himself, was the only reference she made to their first meeting.

"Severus tells me that you seek to purchase furniture, Highness; yet I have heard Palmyra's palace is most beautifully decorated."

"Palmyra's palace is, but the house that my husband and I share within the palace gardens is but newly built."

"My warehouses are full, your Highness, and I, myself, will escort you."

"Remain here," Zenobia commanded her half-dozen maidens. For the first time he noticed the women who accompanied her; fluttering butterflies, all of whom admired him openly.

"Please follow me, your Highness," he said, leading her from the bright atrium, through a corridor, and finally into a huge room filled with furnishings of every description; great bolts of multicolored silks, linens, and wools; and decorations of every type.

Stunned, Zenobia stood looking at it all. This gave him a moment to feast his eyes upon her perfect beauty. She was even fairer than he remembered. Her skin glowed with a radiance that told him she was well loved. His envy of Odenathus was tinged with sadness. She was wearing a sleeveless, low-necked pale-lavender-colored stola that had been belted at the waist with three narrow strips of gilded leather. Her long dark hair was no longer loose and flowing as he remembered it. Instead, it was parted in the middle and drawn into a heavy coil at the nape of her neck, affixed with amethyst-studded gold combs and long matching pins.

"It is so much," her awed voice brought him out of his daydream.

"The shipment arrived but yesterday," he answered.

"I have visited several other warehouses, Marcus Alexander Britainus, but I have seen nothing to compare with your merchandise." She paused a moment, and then looked up at him. "Marcus Alexander Britainus, I need your help."

"*My help?*" He felt his heartbeat accelerate.

"Can you keep a secret? You must, for I should die of embarrassment if anyone knew. For some reason I trust you although you are a Roman; a blue-eyed Roman at that. Yet my instinct tells me to trust you. Will you keep my secret?"

He nodded.

"Thank you." She drew a deep breath. "I know nothing about furnishing a home, Marcus Alexander Britainus. Nothing at all! All my life has been spent either in a tent trekking the desert, or in my mother's house here in Palmyra. Mother's house was a part of her dowry, and she furnished it before I was born. She never had any need to purchase things, and she died before she might teach me that which a good wife should know.

"Can you help me; tell me what I will need?"

He knew what that speech had cost her, for she was very proud; and he had an almost uncontrollable urge to reach out and take her into his arms to soothe her. Instead he mastered himself, and said quietly, "I am honored, my Princess, that you have entrusted me with your confidence. I will endeavour not to fail you."

"You are a diplomat as well as a businessman, Marcus Alexander Britainus." Her gray eyes regarded him carefully. "The empire has lost a valuable servant in you."

"Part of being a businessman is being a diplomat, Highness," he replied smoothly. "Shall we begin with the couches?"

Zenobia laughed, and nodded. "By all means let us begin with the couches," she agreed.

He led her into a section of the warehouse that was completely filled with couches, carefully lined up side by side, row upon row. They were extremely ornamental, made of finely grained and finished woods, the arms and legs carved ornately or inlaid with tortoiseshell, ivory, even precious metals. Several couches had frames of solid silver and legs inlaid with jewels, or carved in high relief to depict scenes of the gods in various attitudes of play. There was a couch with a rather graphic scene of Jupiter as the swan seducing the maiden, Leda. Zenobia, Marcus noted, quickly turned away from that particular piece of furniture. For some reason her modesty pleased him.

"There are no cushions or coverings for the couches?" she asked.

"Most merchants have such items already made and on the couches, Highness. I, however, prefer to allow my customer a choice of fabric, for I should hate to lose a sale because you disliked the color of the cushions."

"That is very clever of you, Marcus Alexander Britainus."

He chuckled with delight, for it gave him great pleasure to be complimented by this girl. Quietly he listened to her needs, and then suggested several possibilities, always explaining why he chose one couch over another so she might learn, but leaving the final decision to her.

They next moved on to chairs. They were not upholstered, but they did have fabric cushions. The tables were elegant with supports and tops of marble, solid or veneered woods, or thin sheets of precious metals such as gold or silver. The most beautiful and the most expensive table in the warehouse was a round one made form cross sections of exquisitely marked, perfectly matched African cedar. Zenobia reverently rubbed her hand over the surface of the table, almost purring her pleasure.

"Do not tell me," Marcus teased her. "You *must* have it."

"Am I wrong to choose it?" she inquired hesitantly.

"No. It is a fine piece; in fact, to my mind, it is one of the best tables ever done. It will be fearfuly expensive though, Highness."

Her winged brows raised themselves slightly. "I do not recall asking you the price, Marcus Alexander Britainus."

Just the faint hint of a smile touched the corners of his mouth. "Shall we move on to chests and cabinets, your Highness?"

Zenobia followed him into another section of the warehouse with what she hoped was a regal step. There, with Marcus's aid she picked several wooden cabinets, each one more beautifully decorated than the last. The cabinets were compartmented, but had no sliding drawers, locks, or hinges. She chose a dozen iron-bound wooden chests with ornamental locks and hinges of dark bronze, then moved on to purchase footed charcoal-burning iron floor stoves, to heat the rooms on chilly evenings and winter days.

Next Zenobia bought lamps to light her home, exclaiming with delight at the variety available to her. Following Marcus's advice, she chose only lamps made of metals, for they, he assured her, would last a lifetime. There were lamps with handles that could be carried from room to room; some that would be suspended from the ceilings by chains; and others that would be kept on stands or tripods. The lamps were graceful in form, and all had been finely crafted, precious and semiprecious stones set within the gold and silver.

It had taken over two hours for Zenobia to make her purchases, and now she must choose fabrics for her couches and pillows. "I am exhausted," she complained to Marcus. "I think I should rather lead my camel corps in a desert drill than shop."

"Your camel corps?" He kept his voice curious but impersonal.

"The Bedawi are great fighters when they have to be, Marcus Alexander Britainus. When I was thirteen my father began to train me, as he had trained all my brothers in the art of desert warfare; as even today he trains his youngest sons."

"Whom do you fight, my Princess?"

"The Bedawi have few enemies," came the reply, "but, as my father has said, we must never grow soft."

"So all your brothers lead camel corps."

"Oh no, Marcus Alexander Britainus! To lead a Bedawi camel corps you must be the best. Only three of my older brothers and I have our own troupe, although one of my younger brothers appears promising." She smiled a shy smile at him. "You have been so kind, Marcus Alexander Britainus. Now I must choose fabrics. Lead on, please."

The conversation was closed, and he knew that he could not reopen it. She was young and she was inexperienced. He would question Antonius Porcius. The whole idea of this slender and delicate-looking creature being a warrior fascinated him. He smiled in return and said, "I will have a chair brought so you may sit, your Highness. The slaves will bring the fabrics to you.''

He gave several sharp orders, and Zenobia quickly found herself comfortably seated, an alabaster goblet of cool juice in her hand. Another terse command from Marcus Alexander Britainus, and the slaves began to bring great bolts of fabric, unrolling several lengths of silks so she might see them properly. Zenobia's eyes widened at the glorious colors that were spread before her like a thousand sunrises and sunsets rolled into one. There were solid colors; and brocades and silks shot through with gold and silver threads.

The delicately woven wools were both local and imported, and there were many shades ranging from dark red to black. The best linen was from Egypt, he informed her, and cotton was grown only in the eastern provinces.

''I don't know where to begin,'' she said, and so he advised her as to which fabrics were best, showing her how to match colors and textures to make a pleasing effect. Bending over her, he breathed the subtle scent of hyacinths that she always wore; tortured himself with quick glimpses of her pale-gold breasts rising and falling calmly above her stola's low neckline. With superhuman effort he restrained the emotion that encouraged him to turn her to him and cover those luscious breasts with hot kisses.

''You have been so wonderfully kind, Marcus Alexander Britainus.'' Her voice came at him from a million miles away. ''I did not, until today, believe there was any kindness in the Romans. I see now that I was wrong.''

''There is good as well as evil in all peoples, your Highness. If I have taught you not to make quick judgments then I may count it a victory for Palmyra and her peoples.''

''My husband rules Palmyra, not I.''

''All women rule their husbands, your Highness. I have that on the best authority, for my mother and my sisters have often told me so.''

Zenobia laughed. ''I am rebuked,'' she said, rising from her chair. ''Tell me now, Marcus Alexander Britainus, when will all these wonderful things I have purchased be delivered to the palace?''

''I will have them sent tomorrow, your Highness. They might come today, but we will need time to upholster your couches. If you will permit it I will escort you to your litter now.''

He stood outside his warehouse and watched as the large

litter, filled to overflowing with Zenobia and her maidens, disappeared down the street, escorted not, he noticed, by Palmyran soldiers, but Bedawi warriors. He knew now more than ever that this exquisite woman was the only woman for him. Whatever happened he must remain near her. He wasn't sure quite yet how he was going to do it, but somehow he would.

As if Venus herself had heard his wish and taken pity on him, the opportunity presented itself the following day, when he personally oversaw the delivery of Zenobia's purchases to the palace.

She greeted him gaily, then began to direct the slaves as to where they might put each article. Then Odenathus joined them, kissing his young wife's cheek, and smiling indulgently at her explanations.

"I should not have been able to do any of this, my Hawk, had it not been for Marcus Alexander Britainus."

"Then we owe you a debt, Marcus Alexander Britainus," Odenathus said. "Indeed, you are not in the mold of our average merchant. You seem more educated, a patrician I would swear."

"My family is patrician, your Highness. The Alexander family dates back to the earliest days of Rome. The key to our survival, I suspect, is that we have never involved ourselves in political intrigues. Each generation has been taught that only by hard work will they profit. The family estate, which is located in the hills outside of Rome near Tiber, was given to us in the first days of the republic. My grandfather, who is the current head of the Alexander family, still oversees the farm and the vineyards."

"Yet you are a merchant, Marcus Alexander Britainus. Why is that?" Palmyra's prince demanded.

"My father was a younger son, your Highness. Unlike others in his family, he chose to serve the government. Eventually he was sent to Britain as governor. There, he met and married my mother; and there, he began, in order to finance his growing family, to purchase and send back to Rome rare articles of beauty. When he was finally recalled to Rome he discovered that he had a burgeoning business. My grandfather allowed my father to start his own branch of the family. He continued to pursue his business, finding it preferable to life in the country. My younger brother, Aulus, resides in Britain, where he purchases goods to send back to Italy. I was sent here to obtain the magnificent goods of the Far East, and to send the luxuries of the West, east.

Odenathus eyed the tall Roman. "You have served with the army?"

"Yes, your Highness. With the Praetorian under the young Emperor Gordianus, in Africa."

Odenathus was impressed. "My wedding gift from the emperor is that I am to be made commander of Rome's legions here in Palmyra."

"A magnificent gift, Highness, I have no doubt you will bring glory to the region," replied Marcus.

"I think that Marcus Alexander Britainus should stay for the evening meal, my Hawk," Zenobia said. She turned to Marcus. "You will stay, won't you?"

The prince smiled. "I'm afraid you cannot refuse us, Marcus Alexander Britainus."

There was no way Marcus could decline gracefully. The truth was that he did not want to, for though it pained him to see the prince being so affectionate with Zenobia, at least he, Marcus, was with her also.

The winter dining room of the little palace faced south, and its walls were overlaid with thin slabs of pale yellow marble, its cornices and baseboards of carved and gilded wood matching the latticework that covered the windows. The east and west walls of the room had magnificent frescoes, bright with gold leaf, brilliant colors, and mosaic work. One showed a party of hunters after hippopotami and crocodiles on the Nile; the other offered mounted hunters with their sleek, fleet dogs chasing down gazelles in the desert. The floor was done in tiny pieces of blue, green, and yellow mosaic. Three dining couches, each one sectioned to seat three people, were set about a square dining table.

The prince took the center couch, Zenobia sat to his left, and Marcus was placed on his right in the place of honor. Marcus ate automatically, not even noticing the food served to him on silver plates. He was far too busy answering the many questions Zenobia fired at him.

He spoke of different philosophies for a time, then she looked shrewdly at him, saying, "Do you believe in these things, Marcus Alexander Britainus?"

He smiled at her. "I am a realist. I believe in that which I can see."

"I do not mean to offend. I am simply curious. There is so much I do not know of this world, and I want to learn!"

"The most beautiful woman in Palmyra," the prince remarked, "and she is not satisfied with all she has."

"It is not enough to be beautiful, my Hawk. If you had wanted a fluffy kitten of a wife, you would have been married long since."

"What is it you want to know, my Princess? I will gladly share my little knowledge with you."

The prince nodded, and Zenobia said bleakly, "Marcus Alexander Britainus, I do not even know what the sea looks like, and that, my Roman friend, is but the beginning of my ignorance."

He began to speak, and in his eloquence he made wonderful word pictures that allowed them to see the sea and the ships upon it. He told of Rome set upon her seven green hills; and Britain, the land of his birth, with its misty wet weather and even greener hills. He spoke of his service in Africa, that primitive land of fierce contrasts; and all the while Zenobia sat motionless, absorbing his every word like a sponge. The night darkened beyond the dining room windows, and the servants cleared away the fruit and honeyed nut cakes. The goblets were refilled with aromatic red wine, and Marcus spoke on until, out of the corner of his eye, he saw the prince yawning behind his hand.

"It is late," he said, "and I have been droning on like a schoolmaster."

"You have barely begun to tell me what I seek to know," Zenobia murmured.

"Perhaps then Marcus Alexander Britainus will come again and tell us of his experiences," the prince said politely.

"Tomorrow," Zenobia replied.

"*Tomorrow?*" Both men looked startled.

"Yes, tomorrow. You must command him, my Hawk, to come each day for an hour, and teach me of the world beyond our city."

Odenathus seemed annoyed, and glanced somewhat irritably at the Roman. "Marcus Alexander Britainus is a busy man, my flower."

"Is he so busy that he cannot spare an hour each day?" she protested.

Marcus could see that the prince was beginning to eye him with something akin to jealousy, yet he desperately wanted to

103

be with Zenobia. "Perhaps," he said, looking directly at the prince, "you would allow me to visit with her Highness twice a week, my lord. By rearranging my schedule I could manage it."

Zenobia had risen, and now she twined herself about her husband provocatively. "I do not ask you for jewels or other baubles, my Hawk. All I seek is knowledge. How can you object? You spend your days meeting with your councillors. The slaves care for the house, and I am left to the pursuits of boredom. Of course I might visit with your dear mother, or perhaps Deliciae." She smiled up at him with false sweetness.

"I do not want you in the company of another man," the prince hissed.

"Surely you are not jealous, my Hawk?" Zenobia's voice was a whisper now, but Marcus, always sharp of ear, could make out every word, and winced at her next statement. "He is practically old enough to be my father. Besides, I shall have Bab with me, and if you insist, my maidens also. I care not how many people are with me as long as I may learn!" Teasingly, she blew into his ear. *"Please."*

Marcus turned his eyes away from them. He could not bear to see her affectionate with the prince. He drew a deep breath, and made an attempt to control his emotions. Zenobia was married to Odenathus. They were obviously very much in love.

"Would you mind coming to teach my wife, Marcus Alexander Britainus?"

"No, my lord, I should consider it an honor." He kept both his face and his voice grave.

"Very well then, so be it. And I thank you, Marcus Alexander Britainus."

The Roman rose from the table. "I have overstayed the bounds of good hospitality," he said. "With your Highness's permission I shall take my leave."

"You have my permission, Marcus Alexander Britainus."

He bowed from his waist, and exited the room, hearing behind him Zenobia's little cry of glee.

"Oh, my Hawk, thank you! Thank you! Thank you!" She flung herself upon him, and kissed him quite vigorously.

He protested faintly. "Zenobia! We are in the dining room!"

"The couch is big enough for both of us, my Hawk," she murmured, loosening his robe and nuzzling at his nipples.

He groaned, all thoughts of the Roman driven from his mind,

and wrapped his arms about her, burying his face in her soft shoulder. "Zenobia, Zenobia! What am I to do with you?"

"Make love to me, my Hawk," she answered him boldly.

He untangled her arms from about his neck, and stood, pulling her up with him. "A fine idea, my flower, but not here for some poor slave to stumble upon us." He brushed a kiss across her pouting mouth, and with a faint smile led her through their house and upstairs to their bedchamber. "Leave us! Go to your beds!" was his curt order to the slave girls who awaited their young mistress.

As on their wedding night two months earlier they quickly undressed each other, shivering in the cool air of a desert summer night. They stood for a few moments, and his hands caressed the marvelous mounds of her breasts, moving downward to smooth along her firm thighs and hips. He pushed her away from him and stood back, admiring her nudity in the flickering light of the perfumed lamps.

"You are like a golden goddess, to be worshiped and adored. I never tire of looking at you," he said.

She stood quietly, no longer afraid or shy of him, and when he knelt before her she stroked the dark head that pressed itself into her soft belly. She was beginning to feel languorous as she always did when he began to make love to her, but as always he sensed the moment when her legs began to weaken, and stood to pull her atop him as he fell back upon the bed. For a long moment their mouths met in a fiery embrace, and then Zenobia drew away. She sat upon him, and wetting her finger in her mouth began to encircle his nipple teasingly. He watched her through slitted eyes, a faint smile upon his face. In just two months the virgin he had married had become the most sensuous woman he had ever known. She was wonderfully passionate and constantly inventive. In one sense it was fortunate that her mother had died before she might pass on to her daughter those inhibitions that invariably divided a married couple's sexual life into the acceptable and the unacceptable.

Pushing himself into a sitting position, he pulled her forward and impaled her on his ready lance. Reaching out, he grasped one full breast and pulled it to his open mouth, sucking hard on the sensitive nipple while his other hand slipped under her to caress her buttocks. Zenobia moaned, and sought for the wonderful motion that always eventually brought her relief. He, however, would not allow it, holding her still between iron thighs while his mouth and hands wreaked delicious havoc and her desire became more frantic. His lips captured her in a deep kiss, his tongue driving into her mouth, his hands clutching her tightly, holding her still while her ardor mounted, until finally she was tearing her mouth away from his and begging him to give her release.

Swiftly he rolled over, pinning her beneath him, and began the thrusting motion that would give them the pure pleasure they both sought. With a wild cry Zenobia wrapped her arms and legs about her husband, and within moments was lost within a shining splendor that finally dissolved in a tumultuous, all-engulfing explosion of passion. Too quickly it was over, and they both lay exhausted and panting amid the tangled bedclothes.

"By the gods," Odenathus half-whispered, "Venus has blessed us both, my flower. You are all the woman a man could ever want!"

"And you all the man a woman could want, my Hawk!" she replied admiringly.

The same words were spoken that very night to Marcus Alexander by a beautiful and famed courtesan in Palmyra's Street of the Prostitutes. He looked down on the woman, a rather magnificent amber-eyed blonde with a marvelous figure. "Do you mean in all your vast experience, Sadira, no man has pleased you as I have?" His blue gaze was somewhat disbelieving, his voice mocking.

"Why do you find that so hard to believe, Marcus?" she quickly countered him, not in the least disconcerted by his manner.

"I came to make love," he said, "not to talk."

He reached for her, but she eluded his grasp. "You want a whore tonight, Marcus Alexander. I am not a whore, but a courtesan. There is more to me than a pair of open legs, a ready sheath. I can see, however, that your mood is not conducive to my company."

"I am sorry, Sadira," he groaned. "There is a black mood upon me tonight, and I can't seem to rid myself of it."

"I will listen if you choose to speak, Marcus. Where were you before you came to me?"

"I had dinner at the palace," was the answer.

"The gods! No wonder you're in a bad mood. Having to sit through a state dinner would make anyone out of sorts. Was that old bitch, Al-Zena, there? How her nose must have been put out of joint by the prince's marriage to that lovely little Bedawi. Our new princess has a way of holding her head that leads me to believe the prince's mother will not rule Zenobia of Palmyra.'' Sadira chuckled. "How very much in love those two are, and they make no attempt to hide their passion for each other.'' Her eyes grew mellow, and then amorous. "Come, my big and passionate Roman. Let Sadira take your evil humor and turn it into one of joy.''

She pulled his head down and kissed him with superb skill. Marcus let her believe she was succeeding, but his mind had already fled back to contemplate Zenobia, Zenobia and her husband whose passion for each other could not be a secret thing.

No one in Palmyra was particularly surprised when their beautiful princess began to thicken about the waist and formal and official announcement was made that an heir to the desert throne was expected. A year and a day exactly after his parents' marriage, a son, to be named Vaballathus, was born to Palmyra's princess. A brother, Demetrius, followed but fifteen months later.

The government in Rome had been wracked with internal strife for several years; there was no real imperial family left. Soldier-emperor after soldier-emperor rose with the support of one faction of the army, only to fall when another faction raised its own choice.

The current emperor, Valerian, had been called by his troops from Raetia in Gaul. He had marched on Rome, taken the government in hand, and given it the first stability it had known in many years. He made his twenty-one-year-old son, already a tough, battle-hardened general, his co-emperor. Valerian had said it plainly. He might be a man in his sixties, but if he was assassinated as were some of his predecessors, his son, Gallienus, would not only avenge him, but take over.

The emperor then turned an eye to see where he had honest allies. To the east in the city of Palmyra, he noted, the young prince, Odenathus, was well thought of by the Roman governor, Antonius Porcius Blandus. The prince had been given command of the legion in Palmyra, and had been successfully holding the Persians at bay. He had a wife and two young sons, both possible hostages in the event he should prove difficult at a later date.

Now the Roman governor had made application for retirement, and as he had served fifteen years in Palmyra, it was a request that could not be denied. The governor suggested that no new Roman be sent out to the city, but rather that Odenathus be made king, a client king of the empire. His loyalty was certainly unquestioned, and it seemed to Valerian a perfect solution. How could he clean up matters here in Rome if he had to worry about the eastern provinces? The order went out. Odenathus Septimus was to be King of Palmyra.

The city went wild at the news, and the celebration that followed lasted nine days before the populace fell into a drunken stupor that lasted another two days. In the palace Al-Zena preened. "I am now Queen of Palmyra," she purred. "*Queen!*"

"Zenobia is Queen," Deliciae said. "You are not Odenathus's wife. You are his mother."

"If the girl is Queen why should I not be? Is she worthy? No! I am worthy. Have I not served this city all these years?"

Deliciae laughed harshly. "*You?* You serve Palmyra? For almost thirty years you have done nothing but complain about Palmyra. The people hate you! Your name is a curse! The only thing you ever did for Palmyra was to birth a good king. In the three years since Odenathus married Zenobia she has produced two healthy sons for the dynasty, and worked unceasingly for the good of the city. Everyone loves her."

"Does that include the Roman, Marcus Alexander Britainus?" Al-Zena asked slyly. "Why is he always here, and alone with her?"

"By the gods.you are a wicked woman, Al-Zena! You know very well that the Roman comes but twice a week, and that Zenobia is never alone with him. She learns from him about the world outside of Palmyra."

"And this makes her fit to be queen of this desert dung heap? Bah! It is an excuse to be with her lover."

"Oh, you are an evil creature," Deliciae cried. "Your son and his wife love each other deeply. Your nasty tongue will never part them, Al-Zena. Beware lest you become your own victim."

"What a stupid creature you are, Deliciae," the older woman said, her voice dripping with scorn. "How many Bedawi shepherds do you suppose mounted Zenobia before her marriage to my son? Even her brothers, especially the eldest, Akbar who dotes on her so, did not deny themselves, I'll wager. Those savages do not think of incest as a sin."

"Zenobia was a virgin, and you know it! You saw the bloody bedclothes the morning after their wedding night, as did I. I well remember your torturing me with the fact that she was purity to my filth, as you so charmingly put it, Al-Zena."

"What will happen to your sons, Deliciae, when Zenobia's eldest becomes King of Palmyra? Think on it, you little fool!"

"My sons will serve the family as they are being taught to serve it. A king's mantle is a heavy burden, and it is one I would prefer be left to another, to the rightful heir, Vaballathus."

"Sluttish idiot!" was Al-Zena's parting remark as the two women went their separate ways.

Al-Zena's attitude toward her daughter-in-law was not particularly improved on hearing that she, the King's mother, was to be created princess dowager, a title thought of by Zenobia. "As my wife has so carefully pointed out, Mother," Odenathus explained, "you cannot be known as Princess of Palmyra, for if we should have a daughter that would be her rightful title."

"Then why was I not created the dowager queen?" Al-Zena demanded furiously.

"There can only be one Queen of Palmyra," said Zenobia quietly. "Throughout the ages there has been much trouble when a kingdom had an old queen and a young queen."

"I am most certainly not old!" snapped Al-Zena, outraged more by the word old than anything else.

"There can be only one queen," Zenobia repeated, and her gray eyes, their golden lights dancing, met the furious black-eyed gaze of her mother-in-law.

"*How dare you!*" Al-Zena hissed venomously. "*You!* A little desert savage! How dare you attempt to lord it over me. I was a princess born! I am royal by birth not marriage. Do you think a few mumbled words by a priest of Jupiter can make you royal!?"

"You have accepted your royalty as a right," Zenobia shot back. "You believe that having been born royal is merely enough; but I tell you, Al-Zena, it is not! Being royal bears with it many and great responsibilities. When have you ever thought of anything except yourself? Have you ever thought of your people? Worried about their welfare not just today, but in the years to come when you shall not be here, and someone else reigns in your stead? Being royal means knowing the world about us so we may best judge this city's course so our people will always, even in the centuries to come, be prosperous and happy. They are not responsibilities lightly taken, but I gladly help my lord husband, Odenathus, to carry his burden!''

"And you approve of this?" Al-Zena's voice was almost a shriek. "You approve of this mannish attitude on the part of your wife?"

"She is exactly the kind of woman Father would have chosen for me," came the devastating reply.

"And what am I?" Al-Zena was outraged.

The young king smiled. "Why, you are what you have always been. You are a supreme bitch." There was a furious gasp from the older woman, but Odenathus put a friendly arm about his mother and continued with his speech. "Do not be offended, Mother. I actually admire you, for in a strange way you are admirable. You took your position those many years ago when you came to Palmyra, and you have never deviated from it. Such strength of will is to be commended." He gave her a gentle hug. "Be content, Mother, with your lot. You have little to complain of, for all of your wants are most generously met."

"You have made her your enemy," Zenobia later told her husband.

"She was never my friend," was his reply.

"She is your mother, and although you have never been allowed to feel any love for her—although you were never close as a mother and a son should be—in her own strange way she has been proud of you and she has loved you. You were cruel, my Hawk, and that is not like you. You hurt her, and Al-Zena's memory for an offense, real or imagined, is a long one."

"Why do you defend her, my flower? She has never been your friend. She undermines you at every opportunity she gets."

"She cannot hurt me while you love and trust me, Hawk. And I shall never give you cause not to love or trust me. We are as one."

"Perhaps it would be better if you discontinued your lessons for the time being."

"Are you jealous?" she teased him, then grew serious. "Oh, Hawk, he knows so much. He has taught me philosophy, poetry, history, and Western music and art. I am learning how the Roman Empire grew, and that has already taught me that power, especially the vast power that the Romans have gained, is dangerous, for it corrupts completely.

"Marcus says that from the time the Roman Empire began its eventual destruction was inevitable. They are weak now, my

Hawk. Marcus tells me that the emperor is far too busy persecuting the Christians to care about the Eastern empire. That is why he made you king, my Hawk! Be a king, and throw off the golden shackles with which Rome binds us!''

"No, Zenobia. If we revolt, the Emperor Valerian will be here in the twinkling of an eye. We will be free one day, but now is not the time. Besides, the Persians have become bold again. I cannot fight Rome face to face while I have another enemy at my back."

"The Persians will never be Rome's allies," Zenobia replied scornfully.

"No, you are right, but if I leave Palmyra to fight the Romans, how long do you think it would be before King Shapur and his armies would march into Palmyra. They have always coveted this city and its riches. I will not destroy Vaballathus's inheritance."

"What kind of inheritance is it when it can be taken away? The Romans made you king, they can just as easily unmake you."

"No. They need me, and it is little enough that they call me *king* in order to gain my aid. Wait and see, my flower. One day we will throw off the yoke that has bound us all these years; but first I must remove the Persian threat from my rear flank. The Romans do me a favor, Zenobia. They have given me the troops with which to deal with King Shapur."

"And while you do battle with King Shapur, I will hold the city for you, my Hawk. My mounted camel corps and my mounted archers will hold back any attacker," she promised.

He swept her into his arms, and with one swift motion loosed her long black hair. It swirled about them like a storm cloud, and his mouth met hers in a long and burning kiss. Zenobia felt herself melt body and soul into him, but at the same time she was filled with great strength. She slipped her arms about his neck, and when he freed her lips she looked adoringly up at him. "Oh, Zenobia, you are a wife to be proud of, my darling!''

"Was I not blest by Mars at my birth?" she replied.

The retired governor Antonius Porcius Blandus, who had so often threatened to retire to Antioch or Damascus, remained in Palmyra upon his release from the imperial civil service.

"And where would I go?" he had demanded irritably when Zenobia teased him about it. "I have grown old in Rome's service, and I have spent most of my life here in the East. I could not stand Italy's climate any longer. Did you know that it can sometimes snow in the imperial city? Bah! Why do I bother to tell you that? You know nothing of snow! Besides, all the family that I knew is gone. Oh, I have an older brother who writes me every year to tell me of the family, but it means little to me. Perhaps now that I have retired I shall marry. I never before had time for a wife."

"Indeed, Antonius Porcius, you must marry," Zenobia said. "I can recommend the state of matrimony quite highly." She fully expected him to choose some proper widow who would provide him with an instant family in his old age. Instead, to her great surprise, the former governor's choice was Zenobia's childhood friend, Julia Tullio, who at nineteen was still unwed. The young queen was shocked.

"You do not have to marry that old man if you do not want to, Julia! How could your family allow such a thing? He is older than your father!"

"As a matter of fact he is five years younger than my father," came the amused reply. "Dearest Zenobia, I want to marry Antonius. I have known him all my life, and I care for him. I am honored he has chosen me."

"But you do not love him!" Zenobia protested.

"You did not love King Odenathus when you married him— and do not shake your head at me, for you didn't! You have fallen in love with him since your marriage, and now you cannot remember a time when you didn't love him. Zenobia, be sensible. I am almost twenty, and I very much want to be a wife and a mother. Antonius is a kind and good man. He is tender and generous, and we have much in common; in fact I have more in common with him than with any young man I have ever met. Besides, a husband should be older than his wife. Is not the king older than you by some years?"

"Only ten," was the reply. "Oh, Julia, isn't there some younger man you would prefer? What of Marcus Alexander Britainus? He is much younger than Antonius Porcius."

"Marcus Alexander?" Julia shuddered delicately, then looked searchingly at Zenobia. "His heart is occupied, and besides, he terrifies me."

"His heart is occupied elsewhere? Oh, Julia, do tell! I have heard no gossip of it. Who is she?"

So she doesn't know, Julia thought. Am I the only one who

sees that he loves her? Then she said, "It is not a woman, Zenobia, but his business that is his wife, his mistress, his everything."

"Oh." To her puzzlement, Zenobia found herself rather relieved that Marcus Alexander had no lover.

Julia smiled. "Do not fret yourself, Zenobia. I am not being forced into this marriage."

"I still believe that you could do better," Zenobia said.

Now Julia laughed. "No, I could not." She paused for a moment as if debating with herself, then she said, "Most important of all, my dearest friend . . . I shall be loved."

"*Loved?*" Zenobia looked puzzled.

"Yes, loved. Only when I accepted his proposal did Antonius admit that he loved me. He said he had loved me since I was a child, but that he dared not speak until he was sure that my heart was not engaged elsewhere, for he did fret in his mind over the vast difference in our ages."

"But what of children, Julia? Will you be able to have them?"

"It will be as the gods allow," came the reply.

"No, no! I mean—well, do you think he can?"

"Can what?" Then Julia's face grew pink. "Oh!" she said.

"Can he?" Zenobia repeated.

"I expect so," Julia said slowly. "My father still does, and for that matter so does your father. Age, I have been told, is no deterrent."

"Deterrent to what?" Marcus Alexander Britainus entered the room.

The two women giggled, and Zenobia, catching her breath, said, "Nothing that should concern you, Marcus, but come and wish Julia good fortune, for she is to be married."

"Indeed?" He came forward, and smilingly planted a kiss upon Julia's blushing cheek. "And who is the fortunate man if I may ask?"

"It is I who am fortunate, Marcus Alexander. I am to wed with Antonius Porcius."

"I will not be corrected in this, Julia Tullio. It is Antonius Porcius who is the lucky one," Marcus said firmly. "May the gods smile upon you both, and I hope that I am to be invited to the wedding."

Julia colored prettily again, and said breathlessly, "But of course you are to be invited, Marcus Alexander." She then turned to Zenobia. "I must go now. I have already stayed overlong, and I only came to tell you my news.'' She rose, as did Zenobia, and the two women embraced before Julia hurried out the door.

Zenobia watched her go, and then, turning back to Marcus, said, ''I pray the gods she will be happy. He is so much older than she is, and if they have children she will spend all her time nursing her babes *and* her elderly husband.''

''You do not think that a husband should be older than his wife, Highness?''

''Older, yes, but not thirty-two years older! Julia's father is his contemporary.''

''And how does Julia feel?''

''She says he loves her, and that she cares for him.''

''Then you should not worry, Highness.''

Suddenly the door opened, and Deliciae hurried in, followed by Bab. ''Al-Zena is coming,'' Deliciae said, ''and she has the king with her. She wants to make trouble between you, and has told him that you are alone with Marcus Alexander.''

''Why on earth should that matter?'' Zenobia demanded, but Marcus instantly understood, and nodded at Deliciae who then said:

''Bab and I have been with you the whole time, Highness!''

''Julia Tullio is to marry Antonius Porcius,'' Zenobia said, quickly comprehending the urgency of their mission if not the reason behind it.

The two other women had barely settled themselves in a corner when the door to the room again opened and Al-Zena hurried in, followed by Odenathus.

''*There!*'' She pointed a long, bony finger at Zenobia. ''Did I not tell you, my son!? Did I not say it was so!? This wicked creature is alone with another man! It is as I have suspected all along. She is betraying you!''

Before either Odenathus or Zenobia could say a word, old Bab sprang from her corner seat. ''How dare you accuse my innocent mistress of such perfidy!'' she shrieked. ''It is you who is the wicked creature!''

''*Really,* Al-Zena,'' came Deliciae's amused voice from another part of the room, and they all turned to look at her. ''Your obsession is beginning to do strange things to you. Ah, well, 'tis but a sign of age, I expect.''

Al-Zena's mouth fell open in surprise. ''She was alone, I tell you! The Tullio girl left, and she was alone with him! Ala, my maid, told me she was alone with him, and she would not lie to me!''

"Perhaps she was not aware that both Bab and the lady Deliciae were in the room with her Highness when I arrived,'' Marcus said, finally finding his voice. Al-Zena's viciousness had surprised him.

Odenathus's mother looked for someone to attack, and as Bab was too far beneath her she chose Deliciae. "If you were here as you say you were,'' she snarled, "then what did you speak of, tell me that!''

"We spoke of Julia's forthcoming marriage,'' Deliciae said sweetly. "She is shortly to marry Antonius Porcius.''

"I think, Mother, that this must be the end of it. You have made an error, and you owe both my wife and my friend, Marcus Alexander, an apology.''

"*Never!*'' Her face contorted with fury, Al-Zena stormed from the room.

"I will leave you to your lessons, Zenobia,'' the king said. "I must return to the council from which I was dragged.'' He bowed to her, turned, and left the room.

For a moment a heavy silence hung in the room, and then Marcus said quietly, "Am I to be told what this is all about?''

"Al-Zena is angry because she is not to be known as Queen of Palmyra. She simply seeks to make trouble,'' Zenobia said wearily.

"She accused us of being lovers, Highness. A dangerous accusation for you—and for me.''

"An untruth from the mouth of a bitter woman. It is as noisy bird chatter.''

"Do not underestimate her hatred, Zenobia,'' Deliciae said. "Had I not overheard that old bitch, Ala, chortling her story, you would have indeed been alone with Marcus Alexander, and even if the king had believed you, a suspicion would always exist in some dark corner of his mind.''

"Odenathus would never distrust me, Deliciae.''

"Odenathus is simply a mortal man, Zenobia.''

"Listen to her, my baby,'' Bab said urgently.

Zenobia sighed irritably. "Come, Marcus, let us get on with our lesson of the day. I apologize to you for Al-Zena's behavior. It must be her time of life.''

"Humph,'' Bab said with a sniff. "It is her nature, and that is as sour as a lemon!''

"The old woman speaks a truth," Deliciae murmured.

Zenobia ignored them both, and looked to Marcus. He forced back a smile that threatened to turn up the corners of his mouth. "Today," he said, "we shall discuss your illustrious ancestress, Cleopatra, Queen of Egypt." Even Deliciae and Bab now turned interested faces to him, and listened as Marcus began to unfold the fascinating tale of the woman who had ruled Egypt and captured the hearts of two illustrious Romans of the day.

Zenobia, however, was not listening. There was little Marcus could tell her of Cleopatra that she did not already know. Al-Zena's unfounded accusation disturbed her in a way far different than anyone would have thought. Suddenly Zenobia found herself looking upon Marcus Alexander not just as a friend, or a Roman, or her teacher, but as a man. Had his eyes always been *that* blue, and the lashes so long and thick? The gods, he was so handsome! With a guilty start she lowered her eyes from his features, afraid her thoughts would be as plain to him as they were to her. What was the matter with her that her thoughts took such a path? Then the wicked worm of curiosity reared itself, and Zenobia found herself wondering what it would be like to be held tightly against his broad chest by those strong arms, to feel that mocking mouth upon her mouth. Shamed color flooded her face, and with a little cry she rose and fled from the room.

"Poor Zenobia," Deliciae said with genuine sympathy. "That wretched Al-Zena has obviously upset her greatly. I wonder the gods don't strike the old witch dead with one of their thunderbolts. It would be a great justice."

"Aye," Bab muttered. "I pray for it nightly."

He said nothing. What had caused her to flee the room he didn't know, but it was not Odenathus's mother, of that he was certain.

It was not in Zenobia's character to be dishonest, so that night as she and Odenathus lay side by side, fingers intertwined, sated with pleasure, she said quietly, "Ala told Al-Zena the truth today. I was alone with Marcus, but 'twas only a few minutes, my Hawk. He arrived while Julia was with me, and when she left we stood talking. It did not occur to me that we were being indiscreet. Suddenly Deliciae and Bab were there saying that your mother had set her slave to spy on me, and that you were both coming. They begged me to pretend that they had been with me the entire time. I regret that I did so, for now I have lied to you without meaning to."

He stroked the silken head that lay upon his chest, smiling to himself in the darkness. He had known that she was alone with the Roman, for he had set his own spies upon her weeks ago. It was not that he distrusted her, or that she had given him any cause to doubt her love; but his mother's barbs had set the worm of uncertainty gnawing at him in the dark part of the night when he awoke, and he was suddenly afraid of losing her. He had known there was no harm in the little time she and Marcus had been alone. He knew that the Roman treated Zenobia with great respect, and perhaps a little bit of affection; the kind of affection that one might give a younger sister. They were friends, Marcus Alexander Britainus, and his wife, and Zenobia had few friends, for who would dare to be friends with a queen. He would not spoil that friendship for her despite his mother's constant suspicion. They were simply the ravings of a sick and bitter woman.

"Thank you for telling me this, my flower," he said quietly, "but I have never doubted that your relationship with Marcus Alexander is anything more than friendship between teacher and pupil." She sighed with relief, and again he smiled to himself. Never again would his mother's words have the power to distress him. He and Zenobia were as one now, as they had ever been. "You will be regent for me when I go to war against the Persians," he said.

"When will you go?"

"Within the month," he replied. "King Shapur again harasses Antioch."

"I cannot help but notice that every time he does so he carefully bypasses Palmyra in his march to the coast," Zenobia said.

Odenathus chuckled. "He knows that I shall eventually beat him, my flower. He wishes to retain the illusion of invincibility as long as possible."

She laughed. "Neither of you lacks for pride, my Hawk."

"I shall probably miss Antonius Porcius's wedding, but you will go, and then you shall write me all about it."

"Oh," she said, "I had almost forgotten. My secretary has arrived! Just today."

"Who?"

"Dionysius Cassius Longinus. I told you that I had sent for him to come from Athens, where he has been teaching rhetoric. If I am to govern for you while you play the soldier I must have someone of my own whom I can trust. Do not forget that I have watched your council meetings, and I know how difficult your councillors can be. There is not one of them who wouldn't forward his own interests before Palmyra's. You, my Hawk, have the patience of a Christian, but I am not sure that I do."

"Speaking of the Christians, beware of my councillor, Publius. He has a serious quarrel with the Christian merchant, Paulus Quintus, and he will play the outraged moralist in order to gain his way."

"I will remember," she answered him. "Is there anything else you think I should know?"

"Only that I adore you, my flower," he said, and she murmured softly against his chest, sending tiny icy shivers up and down his spine. "I do not think I want to go off and play soldier," he said, "if it means I shall be parted from you. We have never been separated before, my flower."

"Come back either with your shield, or upon it," she teased him, quoting the saying of ancient Spartan women to their men.

"Are you so anxious for me to go?"

"You have proved yourself many times, my Hawk, but I have never been given that chance. With you away I shall rule the city in my own right, and I will at last know what I can do."

He winced. "You are as painfully honest as ever, my flower."

"Oh, Hawk!" She was instantly contrite. "I shall miss you. I shall! But I do want to know what I can do."

"I know, Zenobia, I know that. Go to sleep now, my flower. You will not get much rest once you become ruler."

She was quickly asleep, her even breathing a warm puff against his bare chest. He held her protectively, enjoying her softness, her scent of hyacinth. He would, he suspected, miss her a great deal more than she would miss him, for everything she was to do while he was gone was new to her and she looked forward to it with enthusiasm. Indeed, he wondered if she would miss him at all. For a brief moment he regretted marrying such an intelligent and independent woman; but then he had known what she was like, and still he had wanted her. He wanted her now. The world was full of compliant bodies, but

118

interesting women were a rarity. Whenever she surrendered to him he felt a sense of victory. It was never with others the way it was with her. He smiled at his fancies. It was really very simple, Odenathus thought. He loved her.

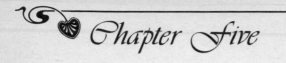

Chapter Five

"Do not hide behind false piety with me, Publius Cato!"

"Your Majesty misunderstands me," came the oily reply.

"I misunderstand nothing, Publius Cato."

"The emperor has shown us the direction to take. Do you say he is wrong?"

The collective intake of breath was quite audible. *Be careful,* Longinus mouthed at Zenobia. Her nod was barely perceptible. "The emperor is correct in all things, Publius Cato. If he persecutes the Christians in Rome then surely in Rome they deserve it; but here in Palmyra our few Christians are honest citizens who obey our laws and meet their obligations promptly. I suspect that your zeal for a persecution stems from the fact that you owe a rather large debt to Paulus Quintus, the merchant, who by coincidence is a Christian."

"The goods he sold me were inferior!"

"Then it is a matter for the courts, isn't it, Publius Cato?"

"The court ruled yesterday, Majesty," Zenobia's secretary said.

"*Did it?*" Zenobia was more than aware of the verdict, but she wanted the rest of the council to know, too. "And what was the court's decision, Longinus?"

"The court ruled in favor of Paulus Quintus, Majesty. The goods were not shoddy, as claimed by Publius Cato. He was ordered to pay Paulus Quintus for the merchandise."

"I see." The look Zenobia sent the rest of her councillors was one of patient tolerance. "Is there anyone else here who feels that the Christians are a danger to this government, or to the city itself? I will listen to anyone who wishes to speak."

Eloquent silence followed. Publius Cato rose angrily from his seat and made for the door.

"This council is not dismissed!" Zenobia's voice was icy.

"I will not stay here and be insulted by a woman!"

"That a woman bore you, Publius Cato, is certainly not a

point in our favor," Zenobia replied, "but if you leave this chamber without my permission you will forever be dismissed from the council. I am Queen of Palmyra, and *I will be Queen.*" She smiled faintly. "Come now, Publius Cato. You have given many years to this government, and have rendered it valuable service on any number of occasions. I can understand your desire for revenge, but whatever is between you and Paulus Quintus, you must not bring your wishes for vengeance into our government. When you have calmed down you will see that I am right. Come now, and sit. We have much business to dispose of before I dismiss you all."

Two other councillors had gotten up, and now spoke urgently and softly to Publius Cato, who, red-faced, shook his head in the negative.

"You can do no more, Majesty," Longinus said. "The man is impossible."

"It would be better not to make enemies."

"Whether he returns to his seat or not he will be your enemy. At least you have made a public attempt at reconciliation. If he is rash enough to leave, he will look the churl he is, and you may appoint one of your own people."

"And if he returns? What then?" She cocked her head to one side.

"He will attempt to block everything you do, for he is a petty man," Longinus replied. Then his eyes widened slightly and he said gleefully, "The gods have heard my prayers! The fool is leaving!"

Zenobia's face was regretful, but she gained immediate sympathy from everyone in the room. "I mourn the loss of Publius Cato," she said, "but if I did not serve the interests of Palmyra first, I could not serve the interests of Palmyra at all." For a moment she looked saddened, then her gray eyes grew bright and alert again. "With Publius Cato's departure we lack a quorum. Unless I immediately appoint someone to take his place we must disband; and there is so much to be done. I do not feel we can afford to lose the time. Are there any objections to my appointing, at least temporarily, Cassius Longinus, my secretary, to fill the place left by Publius Cato? Although he has been away several years, he is a native son of this city."

"I can see no impediment to such an appointment," said Marius Gracchus, the eldest and senior member of the council. After a brief moment all the others nodded their heads in agreement. "It is settled then, Majesty. Welcome Dionysius Cassius Longinus. You are not the first member of your family to serve this council. I remember your illustrious grandfather quite well."

Several hours later, after the council had been dismissed, Longinus said to his mistress, "I am not sure that you did not plan that whole thing."

"Actually, I did not expect Publius Cato to resign his post, but when he did it was only natural that I appoint you in his place, and I'm sure Odenathus will approve my choice, Longinus."

"You do not know me."

Zenobia turned her gray eyes on him, and smiled faintly. "I know you, Longinus. When we first met I instantly knew the kind of man you are—intelligent, honest and shrewd. You will be loyal to me, and therefore to Palmyra."

"You have neglected to say that I prefer men for lovers," Longinus replied wickedly.

Zenobia laughed. "Have you ever made love to a woman, Longinus? But you need not tell me. I shall grant that your private life be your own." Her eyes sparkled mischievously at him, and he was forced to laugh with her.

"I suspect that you are not going to be an easy person to work with, Majesty."

"Why, Longinus, I am simply a woman," she answered with mock humility. Longinus arched an elegant eyebrow in amusement, but Zenobia chose to ignore him, and continued, "You are to escort me to Antonius Porcius's wedding tomorrow. Be here in the hour before dawn."

"The hour before dawn?" He looked anguished. "I do not think my blood courses through my veins at such an hour, Majesty."

"I do not need your blood, Longinus, just your body," Zenobia answered drily.

"Well," he answered, "I think we shall make a handsome couple. Good night, Majesty."

Zenobia chuckled softly and poured herself some wine before seating herself in a chair. Thoughtfully she sipped the sweet red liquid. She had faced her first great challenge today, and she believed that she had acquitted herself quite well. As Longinus had said, whatever had happened Publius Cato would have been her enemy. By using his own weakness against him she had removed him from the council and replaced him with one who would be loyal to Palmyra. She did not think Odenathus would disapprove her choice when he returned from his war.

Cassius Longinus. She smiled to herself. She liked him. He was a man of wit and culture, and, given his reputation, no one could accuse her of infidelity with him. She wondered briefly what made him prefer men over women as lovers, then shrugged. It mattered not, for he was already a friend, and she knew he would be a good servant of Palmyra. He was attractive, though: tall and lean, his gray hair close-cropped, his brown eyes lively and interested. His nose was long, and he had an intimidating way of looking down it that made most people nervous. Both his manners and his dress were elegant; his nature was generous, although he could become impatient with what he called the "general stupidity" of the populace. He was a tireless worker, she had discovered in the few months he had been with her, and this pleased her, for she disliked being idle, especially with her husband away.

A faint scratching at the door caught her attention, and she called, "Come in."

"I thought you might be lonely," Deliciae said, entering the room.

"I am glad for your company," Zenobia answered, although nothing was further from the truth. She had been enjoying her solitude.

"The council met almost the entire day—you must be exhausted."

"I thrive on hard work, Deliciae. Idleness is anathema to me."

"Is it true that you removed Publius Cato from the council? The city is abuzz with rumors."

"Already?" She was amused. "Publius Cato made an error in judgment when he attempted to use the government to pursue a personal grudge."

"Al-Zena says women do not belong in government."

"Al-Zena would quickly change her mind if Odenathus had left her as regent instead of me," Zenobia laughed. "Let us not speak of her, though, Deliciae. Instead, tell me how you spent your day."

"In idleness, Zenobia. The very idleness you so abhor. I spent most of my time beautifying myself, although for what or whom I do not know. I spent an hour with my sons, but alas, they are at an appalling age and speak only of weapons and horses.''

"Are you happy, Deliciae?"

"No, but then what is there for me? I am Odenathus's concubine, although he has not used me as such in five years. I am the mother of sons who no longer need me. I have not the mind of weighty matters, as do you. I am as nothing.''

"What do you want then?" Zenobia asked.

"If I tell you will you keep it a secret? I cannot have what I desire, but I can dream.''

"I will keep it secret.''

"I want a husband, Zenobia. Being a wife and a mother is what I am best suited for in this life. I know it is not possible, but still I dream.''

"Why is it not possible? You have been beloved of a king, and should that king decide to reward your devotion by giving you to some worthy man as a wife, who is to tell him nay? If you wish it I will speak to Odenathus myself when he returns. You are still young enough to have more children.''

"You would do that for me?" Deliciae's hopeful face brought Zenobia close to tears.

What a fool I have been! she thought. I have been so wrapped up in my own happiness that I did not see how miserable poor Deliciae has been. I shall never be a worthy queen if I can only speak of the people's needs, but do not see to them. "I will speak to the king, Deliciae, but once I have then you must be honest with him. I do not believe that you ever loved each other, but you have been friends. When I have paved the way for you, speak openly to Odenathus of your feelings.''

"I am not sure I can, Zenobia.''

"You must, Deliciae. In the end only you can gain your own happiness.''

"What will happen to my sons if I leave the palace?''

"I do not know, Deliciae. However, I believe it would be best if they went with you rather than remain at the palace. They are as yet young, and need their mother.'' While they live here in the palace, thought Zenobia, Deliciae's sons are made to feel like royal princes, which they most certainly are not, and they also are old enough to be troublesome should anything happen to Odenathus. Indeed, for everyone's sake, Linos and Vernus would be better off elsewhere. She focused upon Deliciae again. "I will see that you are not separated from your sons, Deliciae. I could not bear it if I were separated from mine, and I understand a mother's feelings.''

Deliciae fell to her knees and kissed the hem of Zenobia's gown. Her blue eyes were wet with tears. "Thank you, Majesty! Thank you!''

"Do not thank me yet, Deliciae. We have yet to speak to the king.''

"He will listen to you,'' Deliciae said. "I know he will!''

"Come now,'' Zenobia said. "Join me for the evening meal. I must retire early, for tomorrow my friend, Julia Tullio, is to be married, and I have been invited for the augurs at dawn.''

The next morning Zenobia wore a queenly flame-colored stola cinched with a wide gold belt inlaid with rubies and pearls. About her throat was a magnificent necklace of hundreds of small pearls and rubies that dangled from cobweb thin gold wires and glittered upon the pale-gold skin of her chest. Great barbaric ruby ovals hung from her ears. On her upper right arm was a golden snake with ruby eyes, and beneath it were a carved gold bangle and a smooth bangle of pink coral. On her left arm were three gold-wire bracelets, two studded with fresh-water pearls flanking one encrusted with small rubies. Her slender fingers were dressed with but three rings, her wedding band, a great pink pearl, and a square-cut pink sapphire.

Zenobia's heavy black hair was parted in the center, and wound into a thick coil at the base of her neck. An exquisitely wrought diadem of filigreed gold vines and pink-sapphire flowers was set upon her head. On her feet she wore gilt leather sandals. Looking at herself in the polished-silver mirror held up by a slave, she was surprised at how regal she looked. Of course, she thought, my height is finally proving an advantage.

Longinus, shivering in the predawn cold, but elegant in a finely spun long, white wool tunic and a purple-bordered toga trabea of white and red stripes, awaited her in the courtyard of the palace. His gray hair was beautifully curled and smelled of a fragrant pomade. Giving her a wan smile, he helped her into the litter, and climbed in to seat himself opposite her. The slaves lifted them and moved off and out through the palace gate.

"If you are not too cold, Longinus, I should prefer to leave the curtains open. The sky before dawn is particularly lovely.''

He sighed, nodded and as he huddled down into the pillows. She smiled to herself, and for a few minutes they rode in silence, Zenobia watching the starry sky, now beginning to lighten faintly at the edges of the horizon. "Name me an unmarried man of good family whom we might wish to honor," she said.

Her question brought instant interest in Longinus's brown eyes. He sat up, and she could see his subtle brain mulling over the matter while at the same time wondering what she was up to this time. Finally he said, "The man who comes to mind is Rufus Acilius Curius. His father was a Roman centurion who married the daughter of a wealthy Palmyran merchant about thirty years ago. I remember it because it caused a great scandal. The family was at that time untainted by Roman blood, and the father a fanatic on the subject, but the girl got pregnant by her lover, and there was no choice but to marry. The centurion, however, proved a good husband, and when he retired from the army settled here in Palmyra. Rufus Curius is the third son, and he chose to make the army his career. He is the first Palmyran-born commander of Qasr-al-Hêr. He's very loyal to Odenathus."

"Qasr-al-Hêr? The border fortress?"

"Yes."

"The gods! It is perfect! You are sure he has no wife? What of a betrothal? A mistress?"

"None that I have heard."

"Find out for certain, Longinus. I must know immediately!"

"Why?" No one else would have dared to ask the question, but Zenobia was not offended by Longinus. He had become her close confident.

"Deliciae is Odenathus's concubine in name only. She is unhappy, Longinus. Odenathus does not need her. Frankly, she bores him, but he would not dismiss her, for she and her sons would suffer great shame if he did. She longs to be a wife, and to have other children. I have promised her that I would speak to Odenathus. She is young enough to begin a new life. I thought if he gave her in marriage to someone he wished to honor, it would solve the problem."

"Yes," Longinus mused, "and now that you tell me what you want to do I can tell you that Rufus Curius is indeed the right man. I expect you want her sons to go with her, and Rufus Curius would be an excellent foster father for them. He will see they grow up to be loyal citizens and honest men." He gave her a wicked look. "I know that your intentions toward the lady Deliciae are good ones, but I cannot help but think you will not be sorry to see Linos and Vernus go."

"For their own sakes, and for the sake of my son, Vaballathus, it is better that Deliciae's sons not grow up thinking that they are princes."

The litter arrived at the home of Manlius Tullio Syrius. Longinus descended from the vehicle, then reached back in to help her out.

Manlius Tullio Syrius knelt and touched the hem of Zenobia's skirts to his forehead. "You do us incredible honor, my Queen. The humble house of Tullio is made great by your presence."

"Rise, father of my dearest friend, Julia. I should ill repay your daughter's friendship of many years if I did not come to wish her and her betrothed good fortune."

The elder Tullio rose, and then each member of his family beginning with his wife, Filomena, paid homage to Zenobia. It was a large family, and afterward Longinus murmured softly to Zenobia, "If you had come a half-hour earlier I would have been frozen in my tracks by the time they all kissed your hem."

Zenobia stifled a chuckle as the bride's mother spoke.

"Julia would like you to serve as pronuba, your Majesty," Filomena said.

"I should be honored, Aunt Filomena," was the reply.

Zenobia was led to the place of honor, and as the sun slipped over the horizon the public augur slit the throat of a young sheep, catching its blood in a silver basin. For some minutes the augur carefully viewed the young ram's smoking innards, and then he said, "The omens are most favorable."

Now Antonius Porcius Blandus and Julia Tullio both appeared in the atrium, and the wedding began. Zenobia stepped forward, smiling at her friend, and before the many witnesses joined the hands of the bride and the groom. Shyly Julia repeated the traditional words, "When—and where—you are Gaius, I then—and there—am Gaia." The words of consent given, the ceremony continued, now led by the high priest of Jupiter and his assistants.

For a moment Zenobia let her mind wander back to the happy day when she married Odenathus, and she sighed softly. She missed him so very much. If the damned Romans wanted the Persians subdued, why didn't they send their own generals instead of the King of Palmyra? The empire is too big, murmured a little voice in her head, and they can no longer control it all themselves. She pushed away the thought, and glanced about at the other guests. Marcus Alexander Britainus was staring at her, and for some reason that she didn't understand she blushed. She was instantly furious at herself, and shot him a withering look, but to her surprise he was no longer looking at her. What on earth was the matter with her? she wondered.

"*Feliciter!*" the guests shouted, and Zenobia realized that the ceremony was over. She watched as Antonius Porcius vigorously kissed his rosy-cheeked bride.

"Are you satisfied now?" asked Marcus, suddenly at her side. "It is obvious that he loves her."

"Yes," Zenobia answered slowly, "It will be a good marriage, and I am glad for Julia." She took a goblet of wine offered by a slave, as did Marcus.

"Would I offend you, Majesty, if I told you that you were the most beautiful woman in this room, the most beautiful woman I have ever seen in my entire life, in all my travels."

For a moment her heart beat so quickly that she could not catch her breath to speak. Finally she managed to say, "Why do you say such a thing to me, Marcus Britainus?"

"Why should it embarrass you that I speak a truth," he said. "Are we not good enough friends after all these years that I may say what I feel to you, offer a compliment?"

"You have never said such things to me, Marcus Britainus. I am merely surprised."

"The wine makes me bold," he teased gently, and then he said softly so only she might hear, "Zenobia, look at me."

Surprised, she raised her eyes to him. Never before had he dared to use her name. His blue eyes, seeming to devour her, held her prisoner, and she was mesmerized while a strange heat swept over her body, rendering her almost helpless.

"Are you a sorcerer too, Marcus Britainus?" she finally said, very shaken.

"Only a man, Majesty," was the reply. "I am only a man."

She thought about the incident later that night after all the festivities were over. Longinus, who had observed the little encounter between his mistress and Marcus Britainus, had not left her side for the rest of the day; but he said nothing, for he could see that she was disturbed.

She was restless that night. Each time she drifted off she would see his face with its high cheekbones, strong jaw, long nose, and those blue eyes that caressed and blazed down at her until she awoke, drenched in her own sweat, her heart pounding. I have been too long without my Hawk, she thought with strangely clear logic. I seem to be a woman who cannot get along without a man.

It would have disturbed Zenobia even more had she known that Marcus also lay awake that night. His passion for her had not abated, but rather grown over the years. Often he questioned himself as to whether it was simply because he could not possess her, but the answer was always the same. He loved her.

He had chided himself even as he had said the provocative words that risked his entire relationship with her. It had been a rash thing to do, but for once he had longed for Zenobia to look at him like a man, and not a teacher. When his eyes had held hers in thrall that morning he had yearned to sweep her into his arms, to kiss her marvelous ripe mouth, to caress her beautiful body until she swooned with rapture. Then he had seen her frightened eyes, and he had released his hold upon her. Why had she feared him? Was it possible that she was finally realizing that there was more to him than just history lessons?

Marcus stretched his long body as he sought to find a more comfortable position. He smiled ruefully. How unlike the bold and licentious women of Rome Zenobia was. She was still an innocent, and it was his misfortune to have fallen in love with her. A man of less character might have attempted to seduce her, but it was not in his nature to entrap or force a woman. The men he knew in Rome, men who practiced their new morality with lustful gusto, would have laughed at him for a fool.

Zenobia did not see Marcus for several days, and then she was only momentarily uncomfortable. He, however, seemed not to notice as he intently described Roman Britain to her. She would never know the effort it took him to appear so totally impersonal.

Odenathus returned home victorious over the Persians, who had fled back across their borders to lick their wounds. It was autumn, and the Bedawi again left the oasis city to wander the desert while the great caravans traveled in and out of Palmyra with their varied goods. The king confirmed his wife's temporary appointment of Cassius Longinus as a member of the council. The government ran smoothly.

"I have long wanted to get rid of Publius Cato, but there was simply no reason for me to dismiss him.'' He chuckled. "The gossip tells me that Publius Cato had bragged that I would reappoint him when I returned to Palmyra.''

"He will not thank you for making him a laughingstock, my Hawk. It might be wise to offer him some harmless, but seemingly important post.''

He hugged her lovingly. "I shall take your suggestion, Zenobia. The man who collects the taxes upon the silk from Cathay has recently died. We shall offer Publius Cato this post, although I doubt that those who import the silk thread to dye will thank us.''

"I have a feeling that they will cope a great deal more easily with Publius Cato than the government has been able to do,'' Zenobia replied.

"You have done so well while I was gone,'' he complimented her. "Marius Gracchus himself told me—and compliments from that old fox do not come easily or often. Although the council was fearful of my departure, now they feel that I may meet my obligations as Rome's commander of the eastern legions without endangering Palmyra.'' He grimaced. "I am not sure that I should not be worried, Zenobia, for if you prove a more adept ruler than I they could depose me.''

"I could do nothing if I did not know you were coming home to me, my Hawk!'' she answered fervently.

"There might come a time when you have to, my flower. Oh, I do not mean to frighten you, but no man, even a king, is impervious to an opponent's spear, an enemy's arrow. If I should die before Vaballathus is old enough to rule in his own right, you would be regent of this city, its ruler.''

"You will not die in battle. It is not your fate, I know it!''

He kissed her slowly. "Sorceress,'' he murmured against her mouth. "What spells do you weave to keep me safe?'' His hands slipped beneath her robes to caress her silky skin.

"No Hawk!'' she protested. "I yet have something to discuss with you.''

"Is it more important than our love?'' he said, fondling a ripe breast.

She squirmed away reluctantly. "It concerns our love, my Hawk. I love you with all my heart, and you, I know, love me. Still, Deliciae remains your concubine although you have not favored her in several years. Have you any idea how unhappy she is?''

He looked curiously at her. "Are you suggesting that I return to her bed?"

"If you do I shall scratch both your eyes out!" Zenobia said with mock anger. "No, my Hawk, that is not the answer. While you were away, Deliciae and I were much together, and one night she confided to me how unhappy she is. She is grateful to you, of course, but she longs for what we have. She wants a husband, and she wants other children. She has been loyal many years, and she deserves to be rewarded."

"Deliciae really wants this?" he asked.

"Yes."

"And have you chosen a candidate for her hand?"

"Rufus Curius, the commander of Qasr-al-Hêr."

"How did you arrive at that choice?" His voice was somewhat strained.

"It was Longinus's suggestion. He tells me that Rufus Curius is the first Palmyran-born centurion to command our border fortress. He says that Rufus Curius is a good man who will be a model husband for Deliciae and a fine foster father for Linos and Vernus."

"How can you ask me to relinquish my sons?" he demanded of her, and Zenobia was truly shocked by the anguish in his voice.

"I know how you love Linos and Vernus," she answered him, "but you do them no kindness by keeping them here in Palmyra at the palace. They have already begun asking why their half-brother, Vaballathus, is your heir instead of one of them. Your mother does not help, either, for she encourages this attitude in them. Reason cannot aid us, for logic will not prevail over emotion."

"I want no other man raising my sons," Odenathus said stubbornly.

Zenobia lost her temper. "And what of *my* sons!?" she demanded furiously. "If you were killed in battle what is to stop a dissident group from pressing a claim on Linos's part? No bastard has ever sat on Palmyra's throne, but by keeping your sons by Deliciae here in the palace you appear to favor them. There are those who might even assume that you favor them over your legitimate sons! You cannot control the situation if you are not here, my lord King."

Now it was he who was shocked. Never had he heard her voice drip so with scorn and venom. She had always been truthful, even to the point of bluntness, but never had he heard her so fierce. Had her time as ruler of Palmyra given her a taste of power that she was reluctant to relinquish now that he had returned?

The truth of the matter was that Deliciae's presence had become something of a burden. Still, he had never thought of sending his older sons away. "I must think on it, my flower," he said.

"Think well, and do not think overlong," she replied, getting up and moving away from him.

"Do you threaten me, my flower?" His voice held a dangerous note.

She was neither afraid nor impressed, for although she loved him she was suddenly seeing him through different eyes. "I merely ask that you not delay in your decision, my lord," she replied coldly, and walked from the room.

He felt strangely bereft, for in their six years of marriage they had never had a serious quarrel. Odenathus sensed that things between himself and Zenobia would never be the same. He had somehow failed her, failed her in an unforgivable way. Was she correct? Was it possible that his open affection for his two older sons might lead people to think that he favored his illegitimate children over his legitimate ones? He loved all his boys. Still, should he fall in battle before his sons were grown . . . He shuddered at the thought of the civil war that could follow, for Zenobia would not sit quietly by and allow her own sons' inheritance to be usurped. And if Rome involved itself? His whole line could be wiped out.

He shouted for his secretary, and was dictating almost before the unfortunate scribe could ink his pen and put it to parchment. He ordered Rufus Acilius Curius to report to him immediately, no matter the time of day or night. *Immediately!* He realized now that Zenobia was right, and he would brook no delay. If Rufus Curius was not contracted, or in love, he was going to find himself married before week's end.

It was a confused commander of Qasr-al-Hêr who arrived at the palace several hours later. Rufus Curius could not imagine why he had been summoned. Had he somehow offended the king? Was there to be a war? He was justifiably nervous as he was hurriedly escorted before his lord, and Odenathus's piercing appraisal of his person did nothing to put him at his ease. The king noted that Rufus Curius had his Roman father's height, and a reddish cast to his curly hair; but his eyes were brown, and his features very much Palmyran. He stood properly at attention before his ruler.

Odenathus grinned, and the man before him relaxed somewhat.

"Rufus Curius," said the king, his black eyes sparkling with amusement, "you are to be married. I think tomorrow would be a good day."

Rufus Curius's mouth gaped. "*Married?*"

"Married," his king replied. "Your bride is to be the lady Deliciae, who has for many years been in my favor. She is a good and beautiful woman, Rufus Curius. She will bring to your house my two sons, Linos and Vernus. I entrust you with their care and upbringing, for I am told that you are a loyal and virtuous man. These children cannot remain in my house lest others believe I favor them over my heir, Prince Vaballathus. I know that you will be a good foster father to my natural sons."

"Sire, I am not unmindful of the honor you would do me," Rufus Curius said, "but I would have children of my own."

"The lady Deliciae is a good breeder and an excellent mother," Odenathus said.

"Yet she has only given you two children in all the years she has been with you."

"It takes two people to breed, Rufus Curius," was the reply.

Immediate understanding flooded the centurion's face. "I am grateful for this opportunity to serve you further, my lord."

Clapping his hands, the king commanded the summoned slave to fetch Deliciae.

She arrived wearing a pale blue stola, and her lovely milk-white bosom rose rather provocatively above the low neckline. Her beautiful blond hair was braided and looped gracefully on either side of her head. Her only jewelry was a thin gold chain about her neck. The whole effect was of purity and innocence. Rufus Curius looked once, his eyes glazing over, and Deliciae smiled sweetly. The centurion was lost.

The wedding was set for two days later. It was agreed that Deliciae's sons would not go immediately with their mother, but follow her a month later so she might have some private time with her new husband.

The day following their wedding, Deliciae and her new husband left for Qasr-al-Hêr; but in the royal palace of Palmyra Deliciae's sons found themselves in great trouble. With typical eight- and nine-year-old logic, Linos and Vernus had decided that if their younger half-brothers were not around, their father would not send *them* away. They had taken their four- and five-year-old half-brothers to the slave market, and attempted to sell them to a merchant whose caravan was shortly traveling to Cathay. The merchant was enchanted by the two golden-skinned, gray-eyed little boys who spoke so well, and were obviously quite intelligent; but he was equally suspicious of Linos and Vernus. They were a trifle young to be selling slaves. It was fortunate that he was an honest man. Taking the two younger boys aside, he asked them their names. He didn't doubt the answers he received. "I am Prince Vaballathus," lisped the older of the two. "My papa is the king. This is my brother, Demi. He is a prince, too."

"And who are the other boys?" asked the merchant.

"They are Linos and Vernus. Their mama—her name is Deliciae—was married yesterday and we were given sugared almonds." Vaba smiled up at the merchant. "I like sugared almonds, don't you?"

"Yes," the merchant replied. "I like sugared almonds, too. I will give you some to eat while I take you and your brother back to the palace."

No one in the palace had ever seen Zenobia angry, but that day her rage consumed everything in her path. She had to be physically restrained from attacking Linos and Vernus. "Get them out of my sight!" she shrieked. "If I ever see them again I will strangle them with my bare hands!" She ordered her sons' nurses beheaded, an order countermanded by Odenathus.

"You cannot blame them," he attempted to reason with her. "The children have always played together. How could the nurses know what Linos and Vernus planned?"

Weeping, she heaped rewards upon the merchant, invoking the gods' blessings upon him. Odenathus absolved the stunned merchant of all future taxes for himself and his heirs unto the tenth generation.

Zenobia's rage would not abate. "This is all your mother's doing!" she accused. "You would not listen to me when I warned you that she was filling their heads"—she could not bear even to say their names—"with ideas above their station! My sons, my beautiful babies, could have been lost to us forever, and it would have been *your* fault!" The shock and fear had made her unreasonable. "You would not have cared, though, would you?! If my sons had been lost to you then you could have simply done what that bitch from Hades, your mother, has always wanted! You could have made Deliciae's brats your heirs! I will never forgive you! *Never!*" There was no reasoning with her for several days, although she did forgive the nurses for the sake of her children.

Linos and Vernus were confined to their apartment in deep disgrace. They were not malicious children, but the sudden change in their lives had made them unsure of their own future. They very much needed to know who they were and where they belonged in this frightening world. Their father told them in no uncertain terms that although they were his sons, he had not been married to their mother. This meant that in the eyes of the law they could inherit nothing of his. That privilege belonged to his wife's sons, their half-brothers. Whatever ideas their grandmother had given them, they must forget, for she was nothing but a foolish old woman.

Al-Zena, however, was a changed woman as she desperately tried to explain to Zenobia. "I did not mean them to harm Vaba and Demi," she wept, her proud face crumbled and suddenly old.

"If they had I would have torn your throat out with my bare teeth," Zenobia snarled.

"I love Vaba and Demi too, Zenobia," Al-Zena sobbed. "*I do!*"

"You have never loved anyone or anything in your life!" was the cruel reply.

Al-Zena mastered herself. "You have the intolerance of the very young, Zenobia," she said. "I have loved. Oh yes, I have loved!" Sighing, she began to pace, and as she did she spoke. "When I was ten I fell in love, and my whole life I have loved this man, although he is dead almost twenty years now. His name was Ardashir, and he was the King of Persia. His son, Shapur, now reigns. Ah, how I loved him. And from the first he loved me, though I was but a child. It was he who sent me here to Palmyra to be wife to Odenathus's father. I fought against leaving. I begged him to let me be his concubine, to be his slave, anything but to leave him. I might have swayed him, but my older sister was Ardashir's wife. She did not object to Ardashir having concubines as long I was not one of them. So despite my protests, I was sent to Palmyra, and all might have been well if only Odenathus's father had been understanding of my girlish heartbreak; but all he wanted was an heir.

"You have undoubtedly heard the story of how he raped me on our wedding night. Well, it is true, for he did, and every night after that until he was sure I was pregnant. When my son was born he was taken immediately from me. I was not even allowed to nurse him. I remember begging my husband to let me have my baby back, but he only laughed and said that he knew of Ardashir's plan to make my son sympathetic to the Persians, and that I would never be allowed to taint him.

"Each day after that the child was brought to me for one hour, but I was never left alone with him. I begged my husband for another child that might be mine, but he refused. Then too, he said, I was not to his taste. I was too skinny, and he preferred plump women.

"I grew bitter, Zenobia, and is it any wonder? My son was growing up without knowing me. I had a husband in name only, and I was separated from the only man I had ever loved. When Odenathus's father died I tried to regain my son's love so I might have some small comfort in my old age; but you came, and Odenathus had no time for me again.

"Do you blame me that I have hated you, that I have tried to make your life the hell that mine has been? Why should you have been loved and I not? Believe me, though, I would never intentionally hurt my grandsons!"

"*Which ones?*" Zenobia asked harshly.

"None of them. Neither Linos nor Vernus; nor Vaballathus nor Demetrius. I love them, Zenobia! They are all I have, and they love me!"

"I do not know if I can ever forgive you," Zenobia said.

"I do not know if I can forgive myself," was the sad reply. "In my bitterness and jealousy I may have done Deliciae's sons great harm. If you will let me I will try and undo it. Whatever I have said in the past, I know that Palmyra can have only one heir and it must be my son's legitimate heir, your son, Vaballathus."

Zenobia looked closely at her husband's mother. What she saw convinced her that Al-Zena was being honest. "I do not know if we will ever be friends, Al-Zena, but whatever you can do to convince *those two* of the error of their ways, I will appreciate."

"And you will not take Vaba and Demi from me?"

"No."

"And you will forgive my Odenathus? You cannot fault him for loving all his sons."

"His love is not the cause of my anger. I am angry with him because he refused to see the danger until it was almost too late."

"You must forgive him, Zenobia! You are his joy! You have

been surrounded your entire life by love, and cannot know how terrible it is to be without it.''

Afterward, as she sat alone, Zenobia began to question if she had ever really loved her husband. She enjoyed his love-making, and she certainly enjoyed his company. He was her friend and companion, and she respected him, but was that love? Was that all that had bound her parents together? She thought not, yet she did not know for certain, and wondered if she ever would.

For the first time her life was not simple and clear-cut. When she was a child, her father and Akbar had been her gods. When she had married, she had turned to Odenathus. It had never occurred to her that things would someday be different. She could not erase all the good years with him simply because he had disappointed her, but neither could she ever completely trust in him again. She knew that she was being unreasonable, yet the feeling was there and could not be denied. Men, it seemed, were fallible. Why had that thought never occurred to her before? If Odenathus had put her on a pedestal to be worshiped, then so too had she put him on a pedestal.

''Majesty.''

Zenobia turned to see a slave girl. ''Yes?''

''Marcus Alexander is here for your lesson, Majesty.''

Zenobia nodded at the slave girl, and hurried out into the garden of her little palace where lessons were held on pleasant days. When he turned to greet her something within her quivered, and for a moment she looked searchingly at him.

''Good morning, Majesty.''

''Good day, Marcus Britainus. I have decided it is far too lovely a day for lessons. Will you ride with me?''

''Are you certain you are not one of those women sent to lure hapless travelers to their doom?'' he teased her, and she chuckled as she remembered their first meeting in the desert.

''You will have to take your chances, Roman,'' she teased back, feeling more lighthearted than she had in days.

Marcus Alexander rode a large-boned Arab gelding, gold in color with a creamy white mane and tail; Zenobia, a big gray stallion. She was dressed as he first remembered seeing her, in a short white tunic and gold sandals. Although they were both recognized as they rode through the city, they were not stopped by the queen's adoring admirers, and once through the gates of Palmyra Zenobia let her stallion have his head.

They rode without stopping and without speech for several

miles. Marcus Alexander was content to follow, for although he had lived in the desert for some years now one sand dune looked the same as another to him. It always amazed him that the native-born of Palmyra seemed to know exactly where they were going.

Zenobia watched him from beneath her lashes as they cantered along. She was conscious of the long, muscled legs that guided his mount so easily, and suddenly Zenobia was painfully aware of him as a male being. There was an auburn down on his shapely legs, and his feet were much longer than her husband's.

Unexpectedly, Zenobia's mount reared up, and caught daydreaming, she found herself pitched from his back into a small dune. Marcus instantly dismounted and was by her side, gathering her into his arms, and calling frantically to her. She was momentarily stunned, but as her vision cleared she became aware of his mouth but inches from hers. Zenobia stared, momentarily frozen. *He wanted to kiss her, and she knew it!* Instinctively her lips softened and parted as she found to her shock that she wanted to kiss him.

"*Zenobia,*" he whispered.

Hearing the hunger in his voice was enough to bring her back to her senses. With a little sob she turned her head away from him, and hot tears slid down her cheeks. She didn't know why she was crying, but she couldn't seem to stop.

With a deep sigh Marcus held her close to his heart, and crooned to her as he might have to an injured child. "Are you all right, Majesty?" he asked, forcing away any thought of what might have been.

Her tears now controlled, Zenobia replied softly, "I think that I have only injured my pride, Marcus Britainus. I have never been thrown from my horse before. I cannot understand what caused the beast to rear up like that." Her mount was now standing quietly, although he quivered nervously.

"I will see to the animal. He seems yet agitated." Marcus rose and walked over to the queen's gray stallion. "Easy, my beauty," he said gently to the horse, and took his bridle. Scanning the ground around the animal for a few minutes, Marcus finally found what he sought. "Scorpion," he said to Zenobia, "and a huge one at that. No wonder this big beauty of yours panicked."

Zenobia rose to her feet. "Is he all right?" she asked.

Marcus ran a swift and knowledgeable hand over the horse's

138

legs and, looking up, said, "He appears to be perfect, Majesty. He just needs the reassurance of you upon his back again."

"Help me up," she commanded softly, and he bent, cupping his hands so she might have a mounting place. Zenobia vaulted lightly back onto the gray, and then said, "Come, Marcus Britainus, we have not finished our ride." Kicking the beast, she started off again, this time more careful to keep her mind on the horse and her surroundings.

Later, however, in the privacy of her own rooms, she began to think over the incident in the desert. During her whole adult life her beauty and sensuality had been directed toward Odenathus. She had been taught that a woman cleaved unto her husband only. But Zenobia had always been honest with herself, and she was being honest now when she admitted to herself that she had wanted to kiss Marcus; had very much wanted to feel his mouth possessing hers in a burning and passionate kiss. Did she really desire Marcus, or was it that she was still angry at Odenathus? What had made her turn away from the Roman at the last moment? With an angry sound she pushed the disturbing thoughts away. She was a grown woman and the king's beloved wife, not a silly young girl who gave in to her desires.

The Roman Emperor Valerian came east from Italy, and engaged the Persian King Shapur in a pitched battle at the ancient city of Edessa in Mesopotamia, just north of Palmyra. The Romans were defeated, and driven back while their emperor was led into a shameful captivity from which he would never escape. No one could understand why Valerian had come east, especially when Odenathus and his Palmyran legions had successfully driven the Persians out of the Eastern empire the previous autumn.

Shapur now felt invincible, and taunted the Romans with the imperial captive. He used Valerian as a human footstool when mounting his horse. Finally beheading the emperor, he presented his tanned skin to the horrified Roman delegation sent to negotiate Valerian's release.

Valerian's son was wild with grief and thoughts of revenge. He was now emperor, and in their outrage over their defeat his army never considered replacing him which was fortunate, for Gallienus faced usurpations almost immediately on three fronts. While Gallienus took on two of his own challengers, Odenathus defeated the third at Emesa and was reconfirmed king by the grateful Gallienus.

Odenathus returned from his defense of the empire a changed man. Zenobia had greeted him coolly, but he seemed not to notice. "The time is close," he told her, "when we may throw off the chains that have bound us all these years."

"What has changed?" she asked.

"The government in Rome is worse off than ever, my flower. Every legion has a candidate for emperor, although only a few have dared to rebel so far. Gallienus is beset by too many problems both internal and external. He may be resolute, but he cannot possibly solve the empire's difficulties. The silver coinage is being debased, and he has already incurred the enmity of the senate. He has taken away perquisites from the politicians, and the majority of the senate is far more interested in its social position and its privileges than in good government."

"So we will take advantage of their weaknesses," Zenobia mused. "We will attack them and free ourselves!"

"Not quite yet, my Queen. You must learn patience, Zenobia. Never make a move until you can be sure of success. Rome trusts us and, having gained an alliance with us, will not look often in our direction. We will now begin to rebuild our armies, and in a few years we will free ourselves as well as expand our own territories."

She smiled a smile of genuine delight as she finally fully understood his intentions. "In other words, my husband, we shall expand our own empire under the guise of keeping the Roman peace. It is brilliant!"

"Exactly!" was his reply.

"Oh, Hawk! I am so proud of you," she cried, kissing him with the first genuine affection she had shown him in months.

He returned her ardor, wanting it to go on forever but knowing that he must clear the air between them. Gently he disengaged her, and set her back from him. "Zenobia," he said in a serious tone, "do not make the mistake with me that you made before. I could not bear it if you withdrew your love from me again. You must understand that I am only a mortal man. I am not invincible, or infallible, my flower." Reaching out, he cupped her chin in his hand for a moment. "What a paradox you are! You are intelligent enough to run a government, yet emotionally you are still a child in many ways. I erred, Zenobia, and you must learn to forgive those who err."

"Am I so intolerant then?" she asked, troubled.

"Only of those you love," he said, a hint of amusement in his voice, then he drew her into his arms.

It was better between Zenobia and Odenathus then, but the relationship that they had once had was gone forever. Perhaps if they had had the time they might have regained it, but there was no time. Palmyra's king moved to annex Syria, Palestine, Mesopotamia, and eastern Asia Minor, finally breaking the back of the Persian ruler. King Shapur retreated a final time over his own borders, never to return.

In Palmyra Zenobia ruled wisely in her husband's frequent absences. Driving her golden chariot around the city, she became a familiar sight to her people. In an unruly world Palmyra was a safe haven of green in the middle of a sandy sea. Each day Zenobia drilled her own troops, a special guard that had been formed in addition to her own camel corps.

At first the young men recruited for her guard would not believe that a woman could lead a command. At their first meeting, Zenobia quickly disabused them of that notion, fighting the largest of their group and beating him soundly with her broadsword. She could throw a spear farther than any of them, and she taught them to use a bow and arrow while moving at a full gallop. They were quickly devoted to her, for she was patient with their errors and generous with her praise. The queen's guard would have died for her, and on one of his rare visits home Odenathus teased her about it, wondering if he should be jealous of all those strong young men who were so loyal to his wife.

Marcus Britainus waited for he knew not what. Zenobia had never mentioned or even vaguely referred to the incident in the desert when they had both come so close to indiscretion. When they had returned to Palmyra that day he had sought out the beautiful courtesan, Sadira, and used her almost savagely.

"It is obvious that you love a woman you cannot have, Marcus Alexander," Sadira had said, "but I cannot suffer each time you visit me because I am not that woman. Do not return to me unless you exorcise the devils within you."

Marcus might have bought himself a beautiful slave girl in Palmyra's famous slave markets, but he wanted no woman if he could not have Zenobia. Often his thoughts were black, but these thoughts he kept to himself. Sometimes in the night he would awaken and wonder what would happen if Odenathus were killed in battle. Then he would despise himself for having fallen so low in his desperate love for Zenobia that he wished the king, his friend, dead. With an eye to marriage, he made a serious effort to look over the available women within his class, but no one captured his heart. He reconciled himself to bachelorhood.

He saw Zenobia frequently, for from the beginning he had always been included in her social life. He and Longinus were her frequent escorts whenever Odenathus was away. They would stand on either side of her at the games, or at the theater, or amuse her with witty conversation at dull state dinners. It was not a great deal, he thought, somewhat sadly, but at least he was with her. Despite his family's constant pleas from Rome, he could not marry. True, most marriages were things of convenience, but Marcus Alexander Britainus would not marry without love. And there would never be anyone for him but Zenobia of Palmyra, wife to Odenathus.

The Persians were finally beaten, and Odenathus would at last be home for good, barring another war. Palmyra had never been so prosperous, so strong, so invincible. It had a warrior king, a wise and beautiful queen, and two healthy princes, Vaballathus who would soon be twelve, and his younger brother, Demetrius, now almost eleven. There was great celebration in honor of the royal family.

The city was filled to overflowing with dignitaries from as far east as Cathay and the lands beyond the Indus River. There wasn't a family whose house didn't accommodate relatives and other guests. Antonius Porcius and his wife, Julia, were playing hosts to Rufus Curius, Deliciae, and their children. In addition to Linos and Vernus, they had produced six children in the ten years of their marriage.

Julia and Deliciae had both become plump with age. Both were dedicated wives and mothers. The pampered daughter of one of Palmyra's most distinguished families and the former concubine of nameless parentage found that they had a great deal in common, and were fast friends.

Rufus Curius had been a good foster father to Deliciae's two oldest sons. He had never favored his own sons over them, offering equal love and equal discipline to all the children in his family. Unfortunately, Al-Zena had rooted the bitter seed of discontent deep within their hearts, and although they outwardly seemed to adjust to their new life, Linos and Vernus never forgot that they were Odenathus's older sons. Intelligent, they eagerly learned the arts of warfare from their foster father, and it was expected that they would join the army when they returned to Qasr-al-Hêr.

The Palmyran celebration was to last six days, with all entertainments free and open to everyone. Food and drink were available to all, courtesy of the royal council. Certain prisoners were released in honor of the king's victory over the Persians. Others would have the opportunity to win their freedom in gladitorial combat in the great Palmyran amphitheater.

The games held in Palmyra were probably the most humane in the entire empire. The Palmyrans did not have the lust for blood that the citizens of Rome did. The gladitorial combat was therefore with blunt weapons, and a man put down by his opponent was subject to the crowd's judgment. A thumb turned upward meant he was allowed to get up and continue; a downward thumb meant the contest was immediately awarded to his opponent. Unlike Rome, Palmyra did not allow man and animal to fight; nor did women battle dwarfs.

Palmyra's open-air theater, which dated from before the Roman occupation, was offering comedies each morning, and its ten thousand seats were always filled. There were no women performers, young boys whose voices were still high played the female parts. Zenobia in particular enjoyed the earthy, ribald humor.

Each night after the celebrations, the rulers of Palmyra held a banquet to which the rich and famous were invited; but on the final day their banquet was limited to their family and close friends. It was not as elaborate a meal as the previous nights, beginning with silver platters of boiled, peeled eggs with a piquant dipping sauce, artichokes in wine vinegar and olive oil, thin slices of onion, and salted fish. The second course offered baby lamb garnished with tiny onions which had been roasted with it and sprinkled with fresh mint, antelope with asparagus and beets, an enormous haunch of beef, chickens roasted with lemon sauce, bowls of beans, peas, and cabbage, platters of cucumbers, lettuce, carrots, and radishes, black and green olives in glass bowls, and round loaves of fine white bread. Mulsum, a drink made of four parts wine and one part honey, was drunk with the first course, and meal wine, a mixture of water and wine was served with the second course because straight wine was considered harmful to the stomach until it had been well filled.

The last course offered fresh fruits: peaches, apricots, green and red grapes, pomegranates, cherries, oranges, figs, and plums. There were honey cakes rolled in poppy or sesame seeds, in chopped almonds or pistachios. There were large dates stuffed with walnuts, and at last the goblets were filled with rich and heady dark red wine. There were entertainments with the final course; a jongleur who delighted the children by being able to handle six oranges at one time; and a clever elderly man from Cathay with a troupe of dancing dogs. The older boys enjoyed the acrobats, the gentlemen the dancing girls from Egypt.

It was a warm and friendly gathering with Cassius Longinus and Marcus Britainus joining Zenobia, Odenathus, and their children; Al-Zena; Antonius Porcius, his Julia, and their children; Rufus Curius, Deliciae, and their children; Linos and Vernus; now elderly Zabaai ben Selim, Tamar, Zenobia's favorite brother Akbar ben Zabaai, and even old Bab. Odenathus stood, raising a fresh goblet of wine to toast them all.

"To Palmyra," he said. "To my beloved wife, Zenobia, and to my sons. To all of you!" He gestured with the goblet, "My family, my friends." Then he spilled a portion of the goblet. "To the gods!" he toasted, and quickly quaffed the wine down.

All stood, and raised their own goblets to him in salute preparatory to drinking; but suddenly a terrible look came over Odenathus's face, and he doubled over, his voice barely a whisper, but clearly heard by them all.

"Don't drink! I have been poisoned!" Then he fell back onto the couch.

Al-Zena screamed in horror, her hand going to her mouth as Zenobia shot her a quelling look.

"Fetch the doctor! Hurry!" the queen cried to the servants.

A servant ran from the room as Julia quickly gathered up the small children, and herded them out along with the king's weeping mother. Fortunately they had seen little, and understood nothing.

"Do not fear, my Hawk," Zenobia whispered, "the doctor is coming."

Odenathus shook his head. "I am a dead man, my flower," and he grimaced as a burning pain tore through his guts. "You must rule Palmyra until Vaba is of age, Zenobia." Painfully he raised himself so they might all see him. "Prince Vaballathus is my choice, my heir, the next King of Palmyra. Zenobia is to rule in his place until he is of age." As he fell back he cried out, "Promise me!"

The men gathered about the king, and said with one voice, "We will protect Prince Vaballathus's rights, Majesty."

"Where is the doctor!" Zenobia's voice was edged with hysteria.

"*Zenobia!*" His voice was weaker now, as if, having settled the succession, little was left for him. "Give me your hand, my flower." She took his slender hand, icy now with approaching death. Her eyes were filled with tears that she could not control. "Ah," he said softly. "How I have loved you!" and then he was dead.

For a moment, silence. Then Zenobia said in a strained voice, "I want to know who did this. *I want to know!*"

The royal physician ran into the room, saw Odenathus, and flung himself on the floor before the queen. "Take my life, Majesty, for what use am I to you by being too late," he cried.

"No, Apollodorus, it is not your fault; but take the other goblets of wine, being careful to mark each one, and tell me if they, too, were poisoned."

The physician stood and, moving to the table, quickly began lifting each goblet and sniffing carefully at it. When he had checked every goblet in the room he looked at Zenobia and said, "It is not necessary for me to make a further study, my Queen. Every goblet but two was poisoned. All in this room but two would have died had they drunk."

Zenobia looked to Odenathus's oldest sons. "Why?" she asked, knowing they were the quiet ones.

It was Linos who answered. "Because I should be the next king. I was the eldest son, not Vaba. Odenathus was going to formally invest Vaba as his heir tomorrow."

"But why everyone, Linos?"

"If you were all dead the people would have to accept me. Besides, the emperor promised that he would support me."

"Gallienus?" Zenobia was shocked.

"He always secretly held my father responsible for Valerian's death at the hands of King Shapur."

"Valerian was responsible for his own death, the fool!" was the sharp reply. Then Zenobia turned to Rufus Curius, and said quietly, "Take your wife from the room, Rufus Curius."

The commander of Qasr-al-Hêr led his numb and sobbing wife out. Whether Deliciae wept for Odenathus or her sons even she did not know.

Zenobia drew her older son forward, and Longinus lifted the

boy up onto the dining table. "The king is dead," Zenobia said in a strangely strong voice. "Long live the king!"

"Long life to King Vaballathus!" the men in the room took up the cry.

"*No!*" Linos shouted, but it was his last word. Akbar ben Zabaai moved quickly behind the young man and slit his throat. Vernus screamed but one word—"*Mama!*"—then the blade silenced him forever.

"Take them out into the desert and leave their bodies for carrion," commanded the high-pitched voice of the new king. "They have killed our father, and do not deserve the honor of a burial." His young voice was strong, but he looked to his mother for corroboration. Her nod was barely perceptible.

"I think that the king and his brother had best be taken to bed now, Majesty," Longinus said. "It is necessary that we call the council together immediately. A check must be made to ascertain if anyone else was involved in the plot against the royal family. The city must be secured against possible uprising or outside attack. The people should be informed, then assured that all is well."

Zenobia nodded. "So be it. See to finding the council, and send my guard to me. Tell Rufus Curius to return immediately." She turned to face the others in the room. "I must ask everyone here to please remain."

As she continued to give detailed instructions to Longinus, Antonius Porcius moved next to Marcus Britainus and said softly, "What do you know of this?"

Marcus's face was grim. "Nothing," he answered. "I have always avoided being involved in imperial politics. I can only suppose that the weak fool, Gallienus, made wild accusations in one of his drunken moods; but how he managed to involve Linos and Vernus, I do not know."

"It is obvious that there is an imperial spy here in Palmyra," was the reply.

Marcus looked at Antonius Porcius in surprise. "I am not an imperial spy," he said.

Al-Zena chose that moment to re-enter the room. She walked slowly over to the fallen body of her son and gently soothed his brow. Odenathus's face was peaceful in death, and although he was but thirty-eight, he looked much younger. Sorrow had etched deep lines in his mother's once proud face, and she who so valued her appearance was oblivious to the fact that her face was dirty with tears. Sadly she shook her head. "I had him such a little time," she said.

Zenobia moved over to her mother-in-law and, in the first gesture of affection that she had ever shown the woman, put her arm about her shoulders. "I do not understand it," she said to Al-Zena, "but surely it is the will of the gods. Why else would this man be taken from us?" Gently she led the grieving woman back to the door, calling to old Bab, who had been in the dining room all along, "Take her to Ala, and stay if you are needed."

Bab nodded and, putting an arm around Al-Zena's waist, led the woman off down the corridor.

Rufus Curius re-entered the room. Turning to him, Zenobia said, "Rufus Curius, I am placing the king and his brother in your charge. See to their safety."

"You can trust me after what happened?" The centurion's eyes misted.

"I do not blame you, Rufus Curius. The damage was done to Linos and Vernus before you became their foster father. I know you did your best, and I thank the gods you have your own children, that Deliciae has something to live for despite this tragedy. Please now, escort my sons to their quarters and arrange that some of the men of my guard watch over them. Then see to your wife, for I know tonight's events have left her devastated."

Rufus Curius saluted his queen, and then bowed to the young king and his brother. "If your Majesty will allow me I will escort you and Prince Demetrius to your apartments."

Demi hurled himself into his mother's arms, weeping, and Zenobia soothed him as best she could, kissing away his tears and chiding him gently that his father would want him to be brave. Firmly she disengaged his hold about her neck, and placed his small hand into the centurion's big one. Young Vaba bowed in a courtly way before his mother, his face grave. "Good night, Mother."

Zenobia reached out and, pulling him to her breast, hugged him tightly. "Good night, my lord," she said, her voice strangely tight. He drew away from her and, nodding to Rufus Curius to go, almost ran from the room.

Watching him go, she sighed. He was so young to have this responsibility thrust upon him; yet a boy. Tonight his childhood had ended—or had it? Was it really necessary for Vaba, only twelve, to be laden with such responsibility? Perhaps she could give him a year or two more before she must teach him how to be king. He would be the better for it, she knew.

The council began arriving, staring at first in shocked fascination at the dead body of their king. Only when they had all come did Zenobia give the order that her husband's body be removed and prepared for its funeral. "Sit down," she commanded, and they quickly obeyed her, seeking seats about the dining table. "I am appointing Antonius Porcius to the Council of Ten to replace the king; and Marcus Britainus will have temporary command of Palmyra's legions. Are there any objections?" Her gaze swept them.

"Antonius Porcius has long been a resident of this city," Marius Gracchus said. "Although he was not born here, he chose to remain upon his retirement. He has married into one of our most distinguished families. I can find no fault with the queen's choice. In the matter of Marcus Britainus, however, I am confused as to why the queen has chosen him over a Palmyran officer."

"The king trusted him," was the reply, "and so do I. He has had several years of military experience with the Praetorian, and it is precisely because he is a Roman that I have chosen him. Rome trusted my husband, and gave him great powers. With his death I do not want them sending someone from Rome to oversee our armies. Rome will not find any fault in my choice, and we shall be left alone."

"Then it only waits for Marcus Britainus to accept your appointment," Marius Gracchus replied. He looked directly at the Roman, his glance searching and not entirely trusting.

Marcus was totally surprised by Zenobia's decision, and he could see the hostility in many on the Council of Ten. He wasn't sure exactly what it was she was asking him to do. Vaba was far too young to take over his father's command, and Rome was eventually going to send someone out. Obviously she wanted a little time to organize the government. He could aid her without being disloyal to Rome; but more important, he would have constant access to her.

"Marcus Britainus." Her voice was soft as she fixed her wonderful gray eyes on him. "Marcus Britainus, will you accept?"

"Of course, Majesty. I am honored at the faith you have in me."

"It is settled, then," she said, and only Longinus, who knew her best, heard the relief in her voice. "Now we must get to the succession. Those who were with us this evening heard my husband name our eldest son, Vaballathus Septimius, his heir, the next king. The Council of Ten must honor Odenathus's dying request."

"What of the king's elder sons?"

Zenobia froze, her eyes darkening with anger, and she looked at a council member named Quintus Urbicus. "Do you refer to the king's two bastards?" Her voice was icy. "They are both dead." The council gasped. "The eldest, Linos," Zenobia continued, "was responsible for his father's death; the younger was guilty also. They killed the king, Quintus Urbicus, and it was a miracle that they did not kill all of us! There were five women, and ten children here this night. Ten children including Palmyra's rightful heir!"

"Prince Vaballathus is only twelve, my Queen."

"It is true that *King* Vaballathus is yet young, but he is of the true line of Palmyra."

"This is a dangerous situation," said Macro Cursor, another council member. "A child king is always vulnerable. He cannot be allowed to rule until he is of age. If the king's older sons are dead, and unavailable to us, then the Council of Ten must take over for our boy king." He looked around the table for support, but only Quintus Urbicus seemed in open agreement with him.

Antonius Porcius cleared his throat. "We cannot have ten people ruling Palmyra. It would lead to chaos; and in the end Rome would send another governor. It only remains for us to choose a regent to rule in the king's place until he is of age. What more natural choice can we make than to appoint the queen regent of Palmyra. The king wanted it so."

"*The queen!?*" The council looked to Zenobia.

"Antonius Porcius is correct." The speaker was Marius Gracchus. "The queen is a perfect choice for regent. Rome will accept her, for she is a known quantity to them, and with a former Praetorian officer in charge of the legion . . ." He allowed them all to absorb the obvious. "When you think on it, my friends," he continued, "the queen is the only logical choice. She has an excellent grasp of government, and has ruled well in our late king's many absences. Does anyone else wish to put forward another candidate for this post?" His gaze swept the table. "Then I can assume there is no need for us to vote on this, and that the matter is settled. Queen Zenobia will rule in her son's stead until he is of age." Marius Gracchus looked again to the queen, and then sat down.

Zenobia stood and faced them all. "I will rule alone for the next two years," she said bluntly. "My son needs more time to grow. He will attend council meetings only once a month, but of course will be present on all state occasions. My husband's body will lay in state tomorrow, and be buried the following day."

"It will be as the queen has said," Marius Gracchus intoned.

"I thank you all for coming," Zenobia said. "The council is now dismissed, Longinus and Marcus Britainus to remain for a moment. Good night."

No sooner had they gone than Zenobia's face crumbled, and she began to cry. Longinus dismissed the guard and, turning back to her, was not surprised to see his queen held firmly in Marcus Britainus's strong arms. For some minutes she sobbed her grief, and Longinus could hear the Roman's voice softly comforting the woman. What a remarkable creature she was, he thought. Never once in the few hours since Odenathus's death had she allowed herself one moment of weakness. She had been firm and resolute, even ruthless, taking charge of the very dangerous situation. She was amazing!

As her pain abated Zenobia was suddenly aware of the fact that warm arms encircled her; beneath her cheek a hard chest cloaked a heart that beat steadily. To her confused and numbed mind it felt right, and she snuggled deeper into the embrace. She was so tired, so suddenly and terribly tired. Her legs gave way, and as they did she felt herself being lifted up. Marcus Britainus looked to Longinus for aid.

"Follow me," was the reply. "There is a guest bedroom nearby. If we go to the queen's apartments old Bab and all the queen's maidens will flutter and fuss."

"I will stay with her," the Roman said. "If she awakens in a strange place it could frighten her."

Longinus almost laughed aloud at this weakness being attributed to Zenobia. Ah, well, let the Roman have his dream, he thought. "Yes, that would be best, Marcus Britainus," he answered, ushering the man and his burden into a pleasant room reserved for state visitors.

"I will leave you," Longinus said. "I want to see to the young king and his brother." He hurried out.

Marcus carefully lay Zenobia on the bed, drew up a chair,

and sat down. For a long time he stared at Zenobia. She was so incredibly beautiful. Her skin! By the gods, it was flawless, perfect! Venus herself could not have had more beautiful skin. Hesitantly, he reached out and touched it, finding it as he had suspected, smooth and soft. Growing bolder, he let his fingers trail down her face, her neck, her shoulder. Reverently, he fondled the rounded shoulder, admiring how marvelously proportioned she was. His hand seemed to move of itself, slipping lower and lower until it moved past the neckline of her violet stola and he cupped a warm, full breast. He almost cried aloud with the pleasurable pain of the act, and then he snatched his hand away as if her skin had been a hot coal.

He looked at the hand with revulsion. What kind of a man was he to take advantage of an unconscious woman? A woman who had just lost the husband she loved. Had his own love rendered him mad? Burying his face in his hands he groaned with shame. Then her voice touched him.

"Marcus Britainus, what is it?"

Slowly he raised his head, and then his deep blue eyes met her gold-flecked gray ones. For the longest time they stared, each transfixed by the other's eyes, and then he lowered his head and his mouth found hers in a deep and burning kiss, a kiss he had waited so long to give her.

Into Zenobia's mind came the single and simple thought: This is how it was meant to be. And as his hungry lips moved over her own, as her own lips returned the fire, it came to her with startling clarity that this was the man she had been waiting for all of her life. How could that be? she thought wonderingly. *How?* The question brushed through her mind briefly, and then she gave herself up to the wonder of his embrace. The kiss deepened, and she could feel him trembling with the depth of his emotion. Putting her arms up, she drew him closer to her, her graceful, strong hands caressing the sensitive back of his neck, her fingers entwining themselves in his thick, chestnut-colored hair. She could sense the natural wave of it as her fingers slipped through its soft silkiness.

She could feel his tongue against her lips, gently encouraging her to allow him that first, most intimate embrace; and without hesitation she acquiesced. Velvet fire filled her mouth, probing, exploring, caressing with infinite tenderness. A first flush of heat poured over her body, and she shuddered with delight. Finished with his exploration, he kissed the corners of

151

her mouth, moving to the soft spot beneath her ear, down her slim neck to the hollow between shoulder and neck. There he buried his face for a moment, inhaling the natural fragrance of her that mixed with the hyacinth scent of her perfume.

Finally he sighed, raised his head from its sanctuary, and looked deeply into her eyes. "I want more," he said simply, leaving the decision to her.

Zenobia said not a word; but she swung her legs over the edge of the sleeping couch and stood up. Her eyes never left his as she loosened her stola and let it slip to the cool marble floor. Her camisa, finely spun white linen that gave a glimpse of the glories to come, followed. Reaching up, she drew the jeweled pins from her midnight hair, and it tumbled free. Her piercing look spoke as clearly as words would have.

He obeyed, standing to disrobe quickly, all the while filling his blue eyes with her golden beauty. If Venus came down to the world of mortals, he thought, she must surely look like this. He was enchanted by her body, which was the most beautiful he could ever remember seeing. She was tall for a woman, yet despite wide shoulders, her bone structure was really quite delicate. And the shoulders served to enhance the large breasts.

Naked now, he reached out to place a hand about her small waist. Because of his height most women were always too tiny against him, but Zenobia was just right, her dark head almost to his shoulder. He drew her nearer, feeling the small round of her belly as it pressed against him. Reaching out, she caressed his cheek. There was neither shame nor shyness between them.

He tipped her face upward so he might look at her. "I love you," he said quietly. "I have always loved you. I have loved you from the beginnings of time, and I shall love you long after our memories have faded from this earth." Then, picking her up in his arms, he returned her to the sleeping couch and lay down next to her.

For some minutes they lay together holding hands, and then her voice, soft with confusion, said, "I do not understand this, Marcus, and yet I desire you. I want you to make love to me. *Why?*"

"You must find your own answers, my beloved, but I shall never force you to anything you do not want. I will rise now, and go if that be your wish."

"*No!*"

At that he drew her into his strong arms again, and kissed

her with such passion that she could not restrain herself from responding. She matched him kiss for kiss, tasting him, scorching him with her own fire until a flame began to leap upward within him; a flame born from the ever-burning embers of his love for her. It burned and twisted within him, and he grew warmer and warmer with his own desire to possess her.

Straddling her, he sat back upon his heels. His big hand reached out to cup and admire her breasts. They overflowed his hands again and again as he attempted to contain their beauty. Her eyes had closed, and as he gazed down upon her purple-shadowed eyelids, he wondered if she was even aware of him. "Zenobia," he said, and her eyes opened and she smiled up at him.

"I am here."

Drawing him down, she brushed her lips over his, and once more they kissed with steadily building passion. Now he allowed his hands the freedom they had so longed for, the freedom to caress her marvelous body. He stroked her back, revealing in its long line, the curve of her buttocks. Turning her over so that she lay face down, he began a worshipful adoration of her body, and kissed slowly and hungrily along the same path that his hand had taken, not stopping at her buttocks, however, but continuing down her legs to her slender feet.

Zenobia sighed luxuriously, for Odenathus had never made love to her like this. Marcus was a tender lover, considerate and passionate, preparing her carefully. Why she did not feel guilt she did not understand. Perhaps it was because she had not sought this wonder, this delight, and to find it now on this night of great tragedy was a miracle, a gift from the gods. She would not question further.

Turning her onto her back again, he pressed feathery kisses up her legs to the soft insides of her thighs, but going no farther for that was a special pleasure to reserve for another time. His tongue teased her navel, and she wriggled with pleasure as once more he found her breasts. This time he sucked her honey-colored nipples until they were tight crests of pure sensation.

Now his large body covered her, their mouths warred together again, and she felt him pressing against her. With a sigh she opened her legs to him, murmuring against his mouth, "Oh, yes, my darling! Yes!" Tenderly and with infinite care, he entered her. Zenobia quickly realized that his lance must be enormous, and she winced slightly. He stopped, giving her

153

body time to stretch for him. Once more he thrust, and to her amazement she began to feel the magic beginning. It was too soon, she thought frantically, but she could not stop it.

With a gasp she cried out, opening her eyes to find his blue eyes blazing down on her. He saw her gray orbs glaze over as the first wave of pleasure washed over her. "No!" she sobbed. "It is too soon!"

But he soothed her. "It is just the beginning, beloved! I will give you more joy than you ever believed possible." He kept his word, bringing her pleasure several times before he finally took his own, his powerful seed overflowing her womb.

They fell asleep, clutching each other, their strong, beautiful bodies intertwined. But afraid for her reputation, he slept lightly, waking fully before dawn. Looking down on her, he was filled with tenderness. He wanted to waken her and make love to her again, but she slept very, very deeply, her body healing itself from the shock of last night's events. So he rose quietly and dressed himself. She would be all right when she awoke, and he had best leave lest some gossip see him.

A faint noise caused him to turn to the door where, to his surprise, Longinus stood, shocked. "How could you take advantage of her?" he whispered furiously. "She trusted you, Marcus!"

"I did not take advantage, Longinus. It happened."

The simplicity of the explanation convinced Cassius Longinus of its truth, although he found that he was still distressed. In his own way he loved Zenobia, too.

"Come with me," he said coolly. "I will take you to my own quarters, for it will be necessary for you to be here this morning."

"I would never hurt her, Longinus."

Cassius Longinus turned to the Roman, a look of sadness in his brown eyes. "I know that," he sighed. "How long is it that you have loved her, Marcus? I understand, but you must be cautious. Her position is so very precarious right now."

"We will be careful, Longinus."

"Love her if you will, Marcus, but be warned that Palmyra must come first. If Zenobia was given the choice between you and this city today, Palmyra would come before you. Never force her to that decision."

The Roman was somewhat taken aback. "Surely you make mock of me, Longinus. Zenobia is a woman who needs to be loved. She cannot live without it."

Cassius Longinus shook his head. "Because she melted into your arms last night in a moment of weakness, do not be fooled. Zenobia is not a weak-willed woman who can be content keeping her husband's house, and wiping the runny noses and wet bottoms of her children. She was born for greatness! The signs were all there at her birth, and she has only just begun to fulfill her promise."

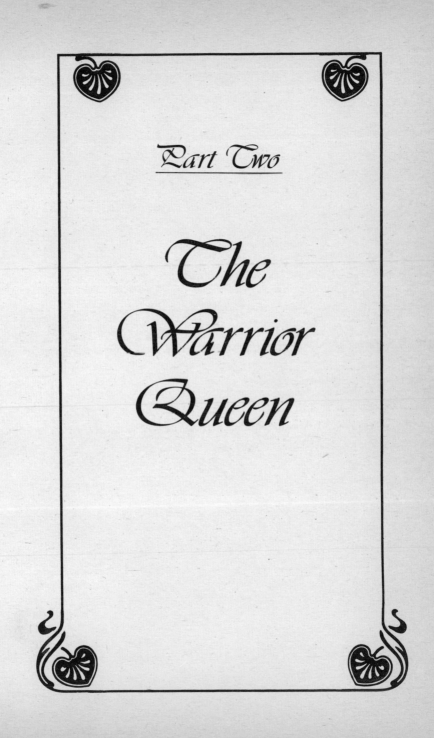

Part Two

The Warrior Queen

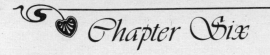

"You behave like a girl having her first child instead of a woman who has already birthed two sons," old Bab snapped to Zenobia.

Zenobia gritted her teeth as another pain rippled across her belly and back. "Vaba and Demi were easy births," she groaned. "This child seems not to want to be born."

"Poor little mite," Bab murmured. "It will never know its father. It is almost as if the gods had gifted you after all these years—to give you this last child of King Odenathus but nine months after his death." She shook her head again. "Poor little mite," she repeated.

"It truly is a miracle," said Julia, leaning over her old friend and wiping the perspiration from her forehead.

"At least the succession is well served," said Zenobia, breathing easier as the pain receded. "Three sons is even better than two."

Julia laughed. "It could be a daughter this time, Zenobia."

"No," came the certain reply. "Odenathus and I spawned only sons—strong sons for our Palmyran dynasty!"

"Well," Julia said, "I, for one, am delighted to have a son and a daughter. Gaius was for Antonius, but Flavia is for me."

"She certainly is," Zenobia chuckled. "Not only is she your image, but even her mannerisms are yours." A spasm crossed her face. "Ah, Mother Juno!" she cried out.

"Push, my baby, push!" Bab commanded.

Zenobia did as her old nurse commanded, but even though she worked hard at birthing this child, it would still be several hours before she gained her goal.

Outside, in the queen's antechamber, Cassius Longinus and Marcus Britainus waited. The two men had become quite good friends over the last months. Indeed, Marcus did not know what he would have done without the wisdom and friendship of Zenobia's trusted councillor. He might have gone mad without it, for fate had dealt him one more blow, the gods having given him a glimpse of paradise had then as quickly snatched it away.

The morning following Odenathus's death he had waited for Zenobia to summon him, but instead he had been summoned to a council meeting to receive his instructions. Her behavior toward him was as it had always been, polite and pleasant. Ah well, hé had thought, she is the queen, and will wait until after the nine days of sorrow and the funeral are over. It is only right.

The king's body had been washed and prepared. He had been dressed in a finely woven *tunica palmata,* which was a purple and gold embroidered ceremonial tunic reaching to the ankle, and worn with a beautifully spun light wool *toga picta* of Tyrian purple embroidered in gold-thread figures representing the gods. Upon his feet were gold sandals, and a victory wreath of beaten gold laurel leaves adorned his dark head.

He was placed on his funeral couch in the atrium of the palace, his feet toward the door, to lie in state until the time came for his funeral. About the couch were masses of flowers, and incense burned in silver braziers. At the head and the foot of the couch were gold lamps burning scented oil. Before the doors of the palace were set branches of pine and cypress, a warning that it was contaminated by death. When all was in readiness the doors of the palace were opened to the public in order that they might enter in and mourn their king. The people came in a steady stream for a full day and night and another morning before Odenathus's body was carried to his tomb outside the city walls, for it was forbidden for a cemetery to be within the gates of a city.

The funeral procession from the palace was followed by every citizen in 'the city who could walk; men, women, and children alike. At the head of the procession was a band of musicians and singers who played and sang mournful dirges in praise of Odenathus Septimius and the greatness of his reign.

Because Odenathus had been a great military leader memorials to his victories, especially those over the Persians, were carried in triumphal procession. Next came the body upon its funeral couch, the face uncovered. The couch was borne by the Council of Ten. The family followed the body, Zenobia garbed in deepest black, which strangely suited her golden skin and only made her look more beautiful; Al-Zena, proudly erect although the grief was etched openly in her face; the young king and his brother, vulnerable, but as their mother and grand-mother, proud and straight.

At the end of the city's main avenue, the procession exited Palmyra, passing beneath the great Triumphal Arch through which Odenathus had so often entered when returning from his many victories. A half-mile beyond was the cemetery, and it was here at Odenathus's family tomb, a great marble construction, that the procession came to a halt. All grew silent as the young king stood before them and eulogized his father.

The priest of Jupiter reconsecrated the tomb, and the marble sarcophagus into which Odenathus's remains would be put. He then sprinkled purified waters three times over all the mourners, and they departed, leaving only the immediate family at the tomb. An animal was sacrificed to make the burial ground sacred, and upon its burial couch Odenathus's body was finally lowered into the sarcophagus. They left Zenobia with him for a minute before the tomb was closed.

Zenobia looked down upon the face of the man who had been her husband and her friend for the last thirteen years. Although he yet seemed familiar, the life spark that had made him the man he was was long gone. There was a finality about the body shell which was all that remained of Odenathus Septimius. Reaching out, she touched his face, but it felt waxlike now, no longer like living skin.

"Oh, my Hawk," she said sadly, "it should not have ended like this. That your life force has been snuffed out by two bitter and useless boys, your own seed, is not to be borne; and yet I must bear it." She paused a moment, considering her words carefully, for a promise to the dead must not be given lightly. Finally she spoke again.

"I will try to raise our sons as you would want them raised; and I will govern Palmyra as you would—with justice and strength." Bending, she placed a kiss upon his icy lips. "Farewell, my husband! May Charon guide you across the Styx to that place where all the great end!" Then, turning, she hurried from the tomb.

Al-Zena withdrew within herself, and even her faithful slave woman, Ala, could not reach her. She blamed her son's death on herself. "If only," she wept to Zenobia, "I had not sought to make mischief by using Linos and Vernus, Odenathus would be alive today. I have caused the death of my own son, and two of my grandsons! The gods have indeed punished me for my wicked meddling!'' Not even Zenobia could reason with her. She mourned deeply, stopped eating, and within the month was dead, too. She was buried with suitable pomp in the same tomb as Odenathus.

Returning once again from the cemetery, Zenobia burst out, "The gods! I am so sick of death!" And then she fainted. Her female weakness was put down to the great pressures she had been under. Within the next few weeks, however, the queen found her appetite not at all as it had always been. She grew queasy at the mere sight of her favorite foods, and developed longings for fruits out of season. Finally old Bab said to her tartly, "Is it not obvious to you what your trouble is?" The queen shook her head in the negative. "You are with child," the old woman said. "The king has given you a final gift."

The second the words were out Zenobia knew them to be true. She was pregnant! Strange, she pondered, I cannot remember being with Odenathus recently; but then she pushed the thought from her mind. Shock could do strange things to a person, and there was no other explanation. She was with child. She liked the idea. Another baby. Ah, how pleased he would have been with her. Three sons, for of course it would be a son. She had always been a mother of sons.

The next week made her certain. Her moon link had been broken for close to three phases now, and it was time to publicly announce her condition. She told Longinus first, and briefly wondered at the strange look that fleetingly passed over his sensitive face. Given his sexual preferences, he probably didn't like pregnant women, she thought.

Cassius Longinus had his suspicions, and so he cornered old Bab one day. "I need information, lady," he said quietly.

"What could I possibly tell the queen's favorite councillor and private secretary, Cassius Longinus."

"You must not misunderstand, lady. I have only the queen's best interests at heart, but I must know when the queen's last show of blood was."

Bab looked scandalized. "What kind of question is that for *you* to ask?!" She had grown plump with age and good living. Her three chins bobbed indignantly, and her ample bosom heaved with righteous outrage beneath the rich fabric of her dark gown. "Well, Cassius Longinus?"

"Lady, I know that you love the queen; have been with her since birth. I also know that what I tell you will remain with you alone." He moved next to the old woman, and lowered his voice. "The queen was with Marcus Britainus the night of Odenathus's murder. I saw them. Yet never since that night has the queen acknowledged Marcus Britainus as more than an old friend. His heart is breaking, for he loves her truly. Now the queen says she is to have a child."

He had expected old Bab to fly at him in a rage, but instead she shook her head back and forth. "Aiiiiieee," she intoned softly "I knew something was wrong. I knew it!" Then she looked frightened. "Does anyone else know?"

"No," he said. "No one else knows, and certainly, given the queen's reputation for chastity, they do not suspect." He looked closely at the woman. "This is not Odenathus's child, is it, lady?"

"No," Bab replied. "It cannot be, and yet I hoped." She took Longinus's arm, and slowly they began to walk through the queen's garden. "When the king came home for the celebrations, she was unclean. Her link with the moon was in force. I am certain he did not go to her. They were quite strict about that. Then he was murdered. And yet when the signs became obvious I still hoped. Oh, Cassius Longinus, will anyone guess? Is she in danger?"

"Does anyone else know her personal habits as you do, lady?"

"No. I alone serve her. Those silly butterflies she calls her maidens do naught but sing and giggle. They have not one intelligent mind between them."

A ghost of a smile flitted over Longinus's lips. "No one will suspect, lady; but I am yet unsatisfied as to why the queen has not acknowledged the Roman."

"My baby has never been devious." Bab said. "She has made no mention of him to me, and if there were something to tell she would share it with me. No, Cassius Longinus, she has said nothing because she remembers nothing. She honestly believes this child to be Odenathus's child."

Longinus nodded. "It is possible," he said. "Yes, it is quite possible. She was in shock that night. While everyone about her mourned, Zenobia was forced to take charge."

"Cassius Longinus, what you would advise in this situation? What shall we do?"

"Nothing," he said. "If the queen remembers what happened the night of Odenathus's murder, then I believe she will come to terms with herself."

"What of the Roman?" Bab demanded. "He moons about her like a lovesick puppy."

"I will explain to him what has happened."

"And will you tell him that the child is his?"

"No. It is unlikely the child in its infancy will bear any great resemblance to him. It is better he not know."

Bab peered closely at Longinus. "Why?" she said.

Longinus sighed. "If he learns the child is his it will only bind them closer."

"Would that not be good for Palmyra?" she demanded.

Again Longinus sighed. "Lady, I do not know, but I cannot take the chance of his turning her from her obligations. Marcus Britainus is an old-fashioned Roman. Women are the home-makers, no more. Until he can be taught differently I cannot allow him to seriously influence the queen in any way."

"I understand your reasoning, Cassius Longinus, but I am not sure you are right. Yet, I will abide by your decision."

They parted then, and Longinus found himself encouraged to have an ally in the queen's old nurse. Now he had but to convince Marcus Britainus that the queen remembered nothing with regard to their brief relationship. He grimaced. The gods had given him an awesome task indeed when it fell to him to convince a virile man that the woman he adored and had made love with did not remember the occasion. He wondered if Marcus Britainus had a sense of humor.

If he had expected outrage he was surprised and relieved to find concern instead.

"Will she be all right, Cassius Longinus?"

"Other than the fact her memory of your liaison is gone, she is in perfect health," he replied.

"Will she ever remember?"

"I am not a physician, Marcus. I do not honestly know. There is one thing, however, that you should know. The queen is to bear Odenathus a posthumous child." He watched to see the Roman's reaction. Would he guess?

"I shall have to begin again with her, and perhaps it is better," Marcus replied absently. "A posthumous child, you say. Poor baby, not to know his father."

And that was all. Cassius Longinus almost cried aloud his relief was so great.

Now, six months later, he and the Roman paced back and forth in the queen's antechamber waiting for the birth of the child. During those intervening months Marcus had taken the opportunity to court the queen, and she was beginning to respond. How many times had he seen them walking in the palace gardens? How many meals had she shared with him? He ate the final meal of the day with Zenobia and her sons, almost every night. The young king and his brother were succumbing to the Roman's charms. Marcus was the most prominent male figure in their lives, he thought, with just a trace of jealousy. They admired him and respected his views, which Longinus was forced to admit were practical and sound. He could not help but wonder what would happen once Zenobia had delivered the child and been purified. Would the passion that had enveloped them on that one night consume them again?

From within the queen's bedchamber came the sounds of groaning, and the Roman paled. "It will be soon," he said.

"How do you know?" Longinus asked.

"I am the eldest of four."

A shriek came from the queen's chamber, followed by a lusty wail. Within the room Zenobia pushed a final time, expelling the afterbirth, and demanded, "Is my son all right? Is he perfect?"

Julia, cleaning the baby with warmed olive oil, looked up a moment from her task, and said, "Your *daughter* is perfect, dear friend. She is an adorable little beauty."

"Daughter? I have birthed a daughter? Surely you are mistaken, Julia. Look again! I cannot have birthed a daughter."

"But you have, Zenobia. It is not the end of the world."

Zenobia lay back, physically exhausted but mentally alert, as Bab, faithful Bab, removed all traces of the birth from her mistress's body. "I shall enjoy having a little girl to take care of again," she chortled. "You have two fine sons, my baby. A daughter will be a comfort to you in your old age."

She helped to support Zenobia as two of her maidens changed the linen on the queen's couch. Zenobia was restless, and demanded of Julia, "Give me the baby. I want to look at it." She could not yet bring herself to say "her."

"But a moment," Bab protested, and she sponged her mistress with perfumed water before placing a fresh linen chamber robe on her and helping her back into bed. The covers were lightly tucked around her, and then Bab stood sternly by as Zenobia was given a nourishing beverage. The queen drank it down, grimacing.

"Why does everything that is good for me have to taste so awful?" she demanded, handing Bab the empty goblet. "*Now, bring me the baby!*"

Julia approached, cradling a swaddled bundle that made soft little mewling noises. "There you are," she said, placing the infant in Zenobia's arms.

Zenobia turned her eyes to the child. It looked nothing like either Vaba or Demi. The baby whimpered, and looked up at her mother. Zenobia stared in shock. She had *blue* eyes! *Her daughter had blue eyes!* and the expression in them was strangely familiar. She clutched the infant to her as her head began to whirl; and in the midst of a roiling reddish darkness she heard a voice:

"*I love you. I have always loved you. I have loved you from the beginnings of time, and I shall love you long after our memories have faded from this earth.*"

Her head cleared as quickly as it had grown dizzy just seconds before. "Take it away!" she almost shrieked, holding out the bundle. "*Take it away!*"

The baby began to wail, either from fright at the sound of her voice or out of some sense of her mother's rejection. Julia quickly took the child and looked strangely at Zenobia.

"What is it, my baby?" Bab hurried to the queen's side. "What is the matter?"

"I don't want her! I don't want her! I birth sons for my Hawk, not daughters."

"This child is the lord Odenathus's last, and surely most precious gift to you, my baby," Bab said sternly. "What do you mean you don't want her? Of course you do! Your travail was long, and it has addled your wits."

"*Leave me!*" Zenobia cried, "and take *it* with you!"

Bab nodded to Julia, and together they hurried from the room, leaving the queen alone. Zenobia lay very still, but her mind was almost boiling with confusion. The voice she had heard had been that of Marcus Britainus! The half-images of memory began to grow whole as she concentrated with all her might, endeavoring to discover the key that would unlock this mystery. The key, however, eluded her, and coupled with the hard birth, she fell into an exhausted sleep.

When she awoke several hours later it was deepest night. The lamps had been trimmed and lowered and now cast flickering shadows on the walls, ceiling, and floor. The early-spring night was yet cool, and she drew her covers about her. She had remembered. She remembered all of that hot, hot July night that Odenathus had died. She remembered how she had willingly given herself to Marcus Britainus; and how he had made tender, passionate, marvelous love to her.

"I love you," he had said. "I have always loved you. I have loved you from the beginnings of time, and I shall love you long after our memories have faded from this earth."

The power in that commitment was in itself overwhelming. The child of course was his. There was no way it could have been Odenathus's daughter. Did he know? More important, who else knew? "Adria!" she called to the slave girl who lay sleeping on the floor at the foot of her bed. "Adria, awake!"

The girl scrambled to her feet, rubbing the sleep from her eyes. "Yes, Majesty? What is your wish?"

"Fetch old Bab," Zenobia commanded, "and then fetch Cassius Longinus. Hurry, girl!"

The slave girl ran from the room.

Zenobia willed her mind blank for the next few minutes. Then the door to her bedchamber opened, and old Bab hurried in, demanding, "Are you all right, my baby? What is it?"

"I have sent for Cassius Longinus," Zenobia replied. "We will talk when he arrives. Be sure no one lingers about my door to hear us. Do you understand?"

Bab nodded.

The door opened again, and Cassius Longinus entered, looking slightly disheveled. "Majesty."

"Adria, I would speak privately. I will not need you again this night. Go to the women's quarters and sleep."

"I obey, Majesty," the girl replied as she backed from the room. Bab held the door to the bedchamber open to be sure the girl departed the anteroom, and did not linger to eavesdrop. The guards at the entry to the apartment would let no one else enter. She turned back to Zenobia.

The queen looked from Cassius Longinus to Bab. "The child is not Odenathus's," she said, watching for their reaction.

"Nevertheless," was Longinus's quick reply, "no one is likely to suspect the child's paternity, Majesty. The little princess is not apt ever to inherit the throne, and so the dynasty remains unsullied."

"You knew from the beginning, both of you," Zenobia said.

"I knew. Bab suspected, although she hoped her suspicions would come to naught. Once we had talked we both understood the truth of the matter."

"Does *he* know?"

"No," Longinus said. "I thought it best he did not."

"*You* thought it best?" Her voice was chilly, but he was not intimidated.

"What happened was the result of your shock over the king's death; and then your mind blocked out the incident. I could not tell you the truth of the matter for fear of endangering your health or that of the child. You are Queen of Palmyra. It is what you were born for, your destiny! I do not know if he can readily accept that if you become lovers."

"It was not your decision to make!" Zenobia said furiously.

"You could not make it!" he countered. "I but sought to protect you and the young king! Would you really give this all up simply to lie beneath your lover? I do not think so, Majesty. You may love him, but first and foremost you are Zenobia, Queen of Palmyra."

"Can I not have both?" Her eyes were fast filling with tears.

"That depends on Marcus Britainus, Majesty. You, I know, can both love and rule. It is he who must love you despite the fact you are the queen. I do not think it will be easy for him, Majesty."

"He must know that Mavia is his daughter," Zenobia said.

"*Mavia?*" they both exclaimed.

"My daughter," was the queen's reply. "I have decided to call her Mavia."

"Is it really necessary to tell him?" Cassius Longinus looked distressed.

"Oh, Longinus, you fret too much," Zenobia said softly. "I cannot keep such a thing from him, and besides, she looks like him. Her hair is reddish, and her eyes quite blue."

"All babies have blue eyes," Longinus said hopefully.

"Not this color blue. Mavia's eyes are the same blue as her father's, even to the same expression."

"He cannot publicly acknowledge her. Even now there are yet those who would discredit you, and remove you from the regency."

"I am sure that Marcus will be as anxious as we all are to protect Mavia, Longinus." She turned to old Bab. "Is Marcus Britainus within the palace tonight?"

"Aye, my baby. He is even now sleeping in his apartments."

"Fetch him secretly, Bab. When he is safely here you must bring my daughter to me."

"I will go," the old woman said, and hurried out.

"What do you plan?" Longinus asked.

"He must acknowledge her as his child before you and Bab. If anything should ever happen to me then Marcus Britainus must see to his daughter in my stead. Surely you approve?"

Longinus nodded. "You are wise, Majesty."

"Longinus, you are my best friend! What should I do without you?"

"You will never have reason to wonder, Majesty," he said fervently. "I will ever serve you!"

The chamber door opened to admit Marcus Britainus. It was obvious that he had come quickly, for he wore only a short tunica interior. His eyes sought hers, and she said quietly, "Leave us, Longinus. Wait outside with Bab. I shall call you when I want you."

Longinus left without even a backward glance, and hearing the door close behind him, Marcus slowly approached the bed where Zenobia lay propped up by several pillows. His eyes never left her face, and his heart leapt with hope when he heard her say in a soft voice, "I remember, Marcus. I remember all."

He didn't know what to say, and so she patted the bed, encouraging him to sit by her. "I remember," she repeated, "and I regret nothing."

"Then my prayers are answered, beloved," he said.

"The child is yours."

"*What?!*" His face was a dual mask of shocked surprise and incredulous delight. "How?"

She bit her lip in amusement. "Don't you know?" she teased him lightly.

"I mean, how can you be sure?"

"I had not been with Odenathus in many months, my darling. Mavia, for that is what I have chosen to call our daughter, was conceived on the night of Odenathus's death. You cannot, of course, publicly claim her, Marcus. My enemies would use such knowledge to destroy my dynasty, and I cannot, nay, I *will* not allow that to happen! Will you, however, in the presence of my faithful Bab and my good Longinus, accept her as a true Roman father would?"

He heard both the queen and the woman in the request. A daughter. He was the father of a daughter! "I will acknowledge her, beloved," he said.

169

"Thank you, Marcus," she answered him. "I know it will not be easy for you, for everyone will believe her to be Odenathus's child."

"May I see her?"

"Only if you will kiss me, Marcus Britainus. You see, I am really a terrible woman, for I will exact a penalty from you for what should be your right."

A slow smile lit his features, crinkling the corners of his deep blue eyes. A large hand cupped her head, while the fingers of his other hand tenderly re-explored her face. She sat very still as he moved over her eyelids, down the bridge of her nose, across her high cheekbones, and gently touched her petal-soft lips. As he did she kissed his fingertips. Then his head descended to cover her mouth with his own. The sweetness that flowed between them brought tears to her eyes. Feeling the wetness on her cheeks, he raised his head and gazed deeply into her eyes.

"Beloved, why do you weep?"

"Oh, Marcus, haven't you ever known a woman to weep from pure joy? I am so happy!"

"Do you love me, Zenobia?"

"Yes," she said simply, and without hesitation. "I love you."

"Let me see our daughter," he said, and she called to old Bab and to Longinus, who re-entered the room. In her arms Bab carried the sleeping infant, whom she laid at Marcus's feet. Immediatey he took the baby up into his arms, and by that simple act acknowledged Mavia as his own. Whatever happened now the baby girl was admitted to all the rights and privileges of membership in a Roman family. No one, however, should ever know this, for Mavia would be believed Odenathus's posthumous daughter, and Princess of Palmyra.

Marcus Britainus looked down at his child, and his face softened. "She is beautiful," he said softly so as not to awaken her. He almost trembled so great was his emotion. This tiny bit of humanity was his daughter; created by the gods as proof of his love for Zenobia. He looked up from the child and at its mother. "Marry me," he said quietly. "Your period of mourning is almost over. We love each other."

"I cannot," she said quietly. "I am Queen of Palmyra, and if we married then we should endanger Vaba's monarchy. If I remained regent there would be those who would claim that you—Rome—influenced me against Palmyran interests. More likely, however, would be my removal by the Council of Ten from the regency. I cannot trust anyone else to guide the city's destiny for my son."

"And when Vaba is a man, Zenobia? Will you then release the reins of power to him and live for yourself?"

"Do not quarrel with me, my love," she said, avoiding his question. "Are you not my husband in all but the formal sense? You love me, I love you, and we have a child."

He looked at her, and she could see the pain, the hurt, the anger, the resentment, and the resignation all swirling about in his eyes. "So, I am to be known as the queen's lover instead of the queen's husband," he said softly.

"It matters not," she answered him as softly, "if I am your legal wife, for even if I were you should still be my lover, Marcus. Is it so terrible a thing?"

Longinus had been right, Marcus thought bitterly. The woman he loved put her duty above all. He could not have her to wife, nor could he have his own child. Still, he loved Zenobia, and if having her meant swallowing his own male pride then swallow it he would. When he thought on it he realized that her attitude to duty was actually no different from his own. "Am I your lover?" he asked.

"You will be," she said with certainty, looking directly at him.

He felt a chill of desire sweep over him. "When?" he demanded, the smile returning to his eyes and once more crinkling the corners.

"You must give me time to recover from Mavia's birth, my darling."

As if recognizing her name, the infant opened her eyes and looked up at the great man who held her. Making small noises, she instantly attracted his attention, and looking down again on his daughter, Marcus was enchanted. Gently he touched her pink cheek, and Mavia turned her head, her small bud of a mouth opening.

"Give her to me," Zenobia said. "She is already hungry. Longinus, go back to bed. We will speak in the morning. Bab, do you mind waiting in the antechamber until Mavia is ready to return to her cradle?" Reaching out for her daughter, Zenobia put her to her plump breast, not even seeing Longinus and Bab leaving. At first the baby was not certain of what to do, but the queen, all mother now, carefully forced her nipple into the baby's mouth, and pressed gently to expel some of the clear fluid already flowing from her breasts. The second the baby tasted the nourishment, instinct took over and she began to suck, tentatively at first, more vigorously as she met with continued success and became surer.

Marcus watched, fascinated. He was enchanted by the sweetly maternal picture Zenobia presented; and yet at the same time he felt a strong tug of hot desire watching the child as she nursed. In the months since the infant's conception he had found himself unable to enjoy the beautiful and skilled whores for which Palmyra was famous, and finally had stopped trying. Now celibate for many months, he watched as his daughter suckled on his beloved's plump golden breasts, and he found himself consumed by a lust that had become highly visible beneath his short interior tunic.

Transferring the baby from one breast to the other, Zenobia saw his state. "Oh, my darling," she sympathized, "I will send a slave girl to your bed."

"*No!*" he almost shouted through gritted teeth, and the baby started, giving a little hiccough before settling back down again to nurse. "I cannot . . . I mean I don't want anyone else but you."

"Are you telling me that there has been no one since *that* night?"

"No one," he said.

"Oh, Marcus!" The baby cradled in one arm, she reached out the other to take his hand in hers, and they stayed thus bound together until Mavia, sated at last, fell asleep against her mother's breast.

"If I were just a woman," Zenobia said quietly, "I should be so proud to be your wife. I could not say that while Longinus was in the room, for he would fret so. You know what he is like, my darling."

"We could wed in secret," he suggested.

"Marcus, there will come a day when I will marry you if you still want me. When that day comes it will be done with much pomp and public show; and you will escort me through the streets of Palmyra to your house, as befits an honest man. I will be your wife for all the world to see, and I shall not be ashamed. Until that time we will be lovers, and I shall not be ashamed of that, either. For now my duty is to the memory of Odenathus Septimius, his son—*my* son—Vaballathus, boy king of this city; and to Palmyra itself. I will not shirk my duties, Marcus. It is not my way."

In an isolated part of the palace she set aside a private apartment where no one but old Bab and himself were permitted to enter, although he rarely saw the queen's old nurse. It was one large, square, bright and airy room that she transformed into a retreat of sensuality where they might play with each other and be safe from prying eyes.

The floor of the room was made of great blocks of pale-gold marble, carefully fitted so that they appeared to be one piece. Near the entrance was a sunken black marble bathing pool filled with tepid scented water sprayed by the distended male organs of four mischievous gold cupids. To the left was a large, beautifully carved standing cabinet for storage, and beyond that a round table—in fact the very one of African cedar that Zenobia had bought from Marcus many years before—with two round backed chairs with carved arms and legs. Bright peacock-blue silk cushions had been placed on each chair.

In the far left corner of the room was a large, square sleeping platform that sat upon a dais set up two steps. An enormous striped mattress made of coral and gold silk, and filled with the finest, purest white lambswool was placed upon the sleeping platform. The dais and the platform has been overlaid with several layers of gold leaf. Upon the mattress were spread peacock- and emerald-colored silk pillows.

On the wall opposite the sleeping platform were seven marble pillars, gold-colored, veined in red, and between them hung sheer silk curtains of palest gold shot through with gold thread, which blew gently in the soft evening breezes. On the coldest days the silk would be replaced by heavy woolen draperies of an earthy gold color.

The walls had been painted with colorful frescoes of the gods and goddesses as they played at love. Diana, chaste goddess of the hunt and the moon, was held in captive embrace by the sun god, Apollo, who boldly fondled her unclad breasts; while about them Diana's equally chaste handmaidens were hunted by a band of rapacious satyrs. A very voluptuous Venus, goddess of love, reclined upon a couch, her pink, white, gold, and blue-eyed beauty totally nude for all to see while two very handsome and extremely well-endowed young mortal males sought to please. Juno, queen of those fortunates who resided upon Mount Olympus, lay upon her back, legs spread wide, her face a mask of ecstasy, while the blacksmith god, Vulcan, labored mightily. Jupiter, King of Olympus, was shown in both his guises: as the swan seducing the beautous Leda, wife to Tyndareus, the King of Sparta; and as the chestnut-colored bull who abducted and seduced the virgin, Europa, daughter of Agenor, the Phoenician King of Tyre. Both ladies seemed quite pleased with the god's attentions, however. Among the gods and goddesses nymphs and centaurs sported in various and some quite interesting attitudes of play.

Carefully studying them during his first visit to the apartment, Marcus noted somewhat wryly, "I am not sure such a thing is possible when one has a body that is half-human, half-equine." He reclined in a chair along one of the walls.

"The ladies seem content," Zenobia noted from the black marble pool where she was swimming. In the crystal waters of the pool her own very voluptuous form was quite visible.

"Still, I wonder . . ." he mused, and then he turned to face her. "Come to me, beloved. It has been more than three hundred nights since you have lain in my arms. The gods know that I have always been a patient man, but now I am no longer patient."

Her gray eyes darkened with the remembered passion of that one night that they had had, and a soft smile curved her lips for a moment. Then she swam over to the steps of the pool and stood up. She slowly ascended the stairs as he watched with intense desire her lush golden body, the water droplets glittering like diamonds as they ran down her. Lazily she dried herself off, picked up an alabaster flask, and walked across the room to him. Handing him the flask, she purred, "Will you rub me with this cream, Marcus," and without waiting for him to answer continued on to the sleeping platform, where she lay down upon her stomach.

Standing, he whipped the wrap of cloth from his loins, and, naked, joined her. The night was warm with early summer as he straddled her, using her bottom as a seat, and poured the fragrant, pale mauve-colored cream into one big palm. Carefully he set the flask upon one of the platform steps and, rubbing his hands together to spread the cream, he began to massage her.

"Ummmmmm," she murmured huskily as his large hands swept up the long length of her back and over her shoulders.

He continued this way for some minutes until all the cream had disappeared into her skin, and then, reversing his position, he crouched over her facing her feet. Taking more of the mauve cream, he began to massage her buttocks with expert fingers.

"Ohhhh!" Zenobia gave a little shriek of pleasure, and he smiled to himself. She had thought to play this teasing game with him, but when he had finished with her it would be she whose fires would rage uncontrolled.

Finished with her buttocks, he began to rub each leg in its turn, and then her arms, with the scented cream. As he did so he was not averse to pressing teasing little kisses upon the back of her neck, having first pushed aside her long black hair, which had come free of its jeweled pins. It gave him great satisfaction to note that her delicious body was unable to remain still.

"*Marcus!*" Her voice was somewhat strained.

"Yes, beloved?" His voice was smooth, devoid of any emotion.

"I think you can stop now." He certainly could stop, she thought frantically. Her skin was absolutely tingling; in fact, she was tingling all over.

"*Now?*" His voice had turned innocent, and he slipped his hands beneath her to grasp her marvelous breasts. Teasingly, he pinched the nipples, very much enjoying her gasp of surprise. Covering her body with his own, his weight crushed her into the mattress as he murmured into her ear, "My beloved goddess, did you think to tease me to madness? You have succeeded!" And he gently bit at the back of her neck.

She shuddered as the flames of desire began to lick at her in earnest. "*Marcus!*"

He heard the plea, and lifted himself off her to turn her over onto her back. Her beautiful breasts rose and fell in quick rhythm. His dark chestnut head lowered to capture a pert nipple, which he then caressed with his tongue, circling round and round it, until she moaned a low, keening sound that was half-pleasure, half-frustration. Lifting his head, he moved over to her other nipple while his hand kneaded the breast he had just left. Her breasts had been extremely sensitive since she had stopped nursing Mavia and given that chore to a wet-nurse.

He was going to drive her mad, Zenobia thought. Reaching down, she grasped his thick hair and pulled him from her breast. "Kiss me!" she demanded furiously, and he laughed softly for a moment before his lips took fierce possession of hers. His tongue filled her mouth, skillfully doing battle with hers, which would not be subdued but fought him with equal cunning, bringing quick liquid fire into his hot loins.

175

Mischievously she bit him, and he swore softly while she laughed and, moving provocatively, murmured, "Now, my darling! Now!"

"*No!*" he told her. By the gods she might be Queen of Palmyra, but while she lay in his arms he would be the master! "Not yet, beloved! You are too eager."

"Yes, now!" She thrust her pelvis upward against him.

"*No!* There are pleasures yet to be savored, my beauty," and before she could stop him he shifted his body downward to push his head between her thighs. His fingers pushed the yielding flesh apart, and his mouth found the bud of her womanhood.

Zenobia struggled frantically for breath. Her husband had *never* done what Marcus now did to her! Such delights he was unleashing within her body! They came quickly one after another in explosions of incredible rapture that left her close to swooning. It was only when he heard the tone of her voice become distraught that he stopped and covered her body again with his own, murmuring soft love words, plunging deep into her burning flesh to soothe and comfort her. Her arms went about him, and she held him tightly against herself, her breasts flattening against the soft fur of his chest.

Together they found the perfect rhythm, and ascended an Olympus of their own, rising higher and higher until finally they gained a paradise far above that of mere gods. Together they clung to each other in that incredible world of instant immortality before descending again to the world of man. Neither remembered the return, awakening much later wrapped within the other's arms; Zenobia, suddenly clearheaded, could hear the strong beat of his heart through his ribs.

"Are you awake?" she whispered softly.

"No," he answered. "I can't possibly be, for if I am then I am in paradise."

"I love you," she answered him.

"No," he said. "I love you!"

Pushing herself up onto one elbow, she gazed down into his strongly chiseled face. "That first night," she said. "I remember thinking that you were the one I had waited for all my life, and I did not understand it. How could I love my Hawk, and yet so quickly love you? I still am not sure I understand."

"Did not your father arrange the marriage?"

"Yes."

"Then you were expected to marry Odenathus, and there was an end to it as far as your family was concerned. Tell me if I am wrong. He was the first man ever to come into your life other than your father and your brothers. He was the first man to make love to you. He was intelligent, and sensitive, and gentle. He adored you above all women, even to putting aside his concubine for you. Is all of this not so?''

"Yes."

"Then how could a woman of sensitivity fail to respond to him? Did you know what love was, beloved? Do you know now?"

"My love for my Hawk was a child's love," she said slowly. "Very much the same as I feel for my father and my brothers. He awakened my body, it is true; but never did I feel for him what I feel for you. Yet that, too, is confusing.

"I remember that all my life until she died my mother always told me of how when she and my father met they fell instantly in love, and knew without reason that they were meant to be together. She did not hesitate to marry him, even though his life as a Bedawi chief was a great deal different from hers as a wealthy Alexandrian.''

Gently she brushed a tousled lock of his chestnut hair back from his forehead. Catching her hand in his, he kissed it, and then pressed it to his heart. "When we met it was hardly love at first sight," she continued. "Oh yes, Marcus, I remember it well, although I have not until now spoken of it! We met on the desert road at dawn, and I was insufferably rude to you; but oh my darling, the pain of my mother's death still lived close to me.'' Tears sprang to her eyes as she remembered that terrible morning so long ago when her beautiful mother was savaged, raped, and murdered by Roman mercenaries.

"Don't, beloved," he urged her, sitting up and gathering her into his embrace.

"I have never really spoken of it to anyone since that day, Marcus. I told my father what had happened, and after that I tried to put it from my mind; but I have never forgotten. They used her body. Then they slit her throat. Perhaps they did her a kindness, for I do not think she could have lived with her shame. Blue-eyed Romans. They were blue-eyed Romans. When I met you the hate still boiled in my heart.''

"Hate, beloved, is the opposite of love. From the very first moment I saw you I was lost." He chuckled. "You were such a little spitfire that I wanted to drag you from your horse and kiss that angry little mouth until it grew pliant and loving. I knew, however, that you were shortly to be married to the

177

prince of the city. I wanted you then, and having possessed you now, I still want you!''

Her beautiful gray eyes, filled with their tiny golden lights, looked deeply into his sapphire-blue ones. ''You have loved me all these years, Marcus, and I never knew it. I have loved you but never did I dare face that love.''

''Yet the night of Odenathus's death you came willingly to me, beloved. It was as if your soul understood what your mind never dared to comprehend.''

''I ought to be ashamed,'' she said quietly, ''and yet I am not. My husband lay dead and I gave myself to another man.''

''You were in shock, beloved; without the least thought or care for yourself you took immediate charge of the situation and thus saved Palmyra from a civil war.''

''I did not even remember! All those months while I carried Mavia I believed her to be Odenathus's child, and when I first saw her and remembered, I rejected her.''

''No, Zenobia, you didn't reject our child. At your first sight of her you were frightened and confused, as your memory had begun to return. What you were rejecting was the possibility of having behaved in a manner contrary to what you had always done.''

She moved so that he held her but lightly and she might gaze into his face. ''I love you, Marcus Alexander Britainus, and for some reason I cannot fathom I am loved by you in return. Stay by my side, my darling. Be my rock; my fortress and refuge in this world. Be my love, and never leave me!''

''I will never leave you, Zenobia,'' he promised. ''You are my wife, my beloved one, and as long as you want me I shall stay by your side.''

''Then you must remain with me for eternity, Marcus. Eternity and beyond!''

''You do not set me a very harsh task, beloved,'' he said and, bending his head, he brushed her lips with his own.

Her arms wound about him, and she murmured against his marvelous mouth, ''Then I shall have to think of something, my darling, and do not fear, I shall!''

''You will not be easy to live with,'' he teased her, ''will you?''

''No,'' she said, and then a smile lit her features, ''but then, I suspect, neither will you, my darling!''

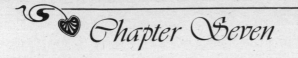

The soldier emperor, Gallienus, considered the letter he had received from Antonius Porcius Blandus, hot upon the heels of the news of Odenathus's murder. He had thought about sending a military governor out to the East, but old Antonius Porcius, a loyal fellow as he remembered, assured him that the young queen, Zenobia, had all in hand; and had already appointed a former Praetorian prefect, one Marcus Alexander Britainus, to be commander of the Eastern legions.

The Alexander family were well known here in Rome, and this was the eldest son. There were those who thought it amusing that the Alexanders kept to the old ways of loyalty, honest industry, and piety toward the gods, but Gallienus thanked Jupiter himself for such rare servants. The Eastern frontier would be safe with Marcus Alexander, and in a rare burst of goodwill even the senate confirmed his appointment.

Feeling confident, Gallienus went off to subdue the Goths, who were once more overrunning Roman territory. Unfortunately his departure encouraged his general, Aureolus, who commanded the cavalry in Milan, to rebellion. Gallienus hurried to lay siege to Milan. Once there, he was murdered by a group of his dissatisfied generals, who then put forth one of their own as the new emperor. Claudius II quickly subdued Aureolus, put him to death, and then went on to conduct a successful campaign against the German tribes. The Eastern Empire was forgotten.

It was some weeks after Gallienus's murder that word of it reached Zenobia in Palmyra. It was obvious that Claudius would pay no attention to their part of the world, and looking at Longinus, Zenobia said, "Odenathus told me that the right moment would come someday. The time is *now!*"

"Just what is it you want, Majesty? Palmyra's freedom from Rome?"

She laughed, and he could hear a triumphant note in the sound. "Once, Longinus, freedom for Palmyra was all I wanted, but I was young and I lacked experience. It is not enough that

Palmyra be free. We need much territory about us to keep our near perimeters safe. I want all of Rome's Eastern Empire for Palmyra, for my son; and I shall have it!''

She had said it, and it was as he had suspected. "You must move very carefully, Majesty," he said slowly. "In the beginning all must be done in the name of the Roman Empire. After all, you will be using the legion they left here in Palmyra.''

"A legion of mercenaries, Longinus; legionnaires from Numidia, Mauretania, and Cyrene! They can be bought.''

"It will take more than money, Majesty.''

"I know, Longinus. It will take victories, for these mercenaries love the taste of victory as well as the sound of gold. First I must win their confidence, and then I will buy them; first with the victories so dear to their hearts, and then with the gold they desire. You are correct. It will be done first for Rome, and only when I have Rome's legion in the palm of my hand will it be done for Palmyra.''

"And Marcus Britainus, Majesty? Will he desert Rome for Palmyra?''

"I don't know," she said honestly.

"And will you give up your own happiness, Majesty, for Palmyra?''

"Why should I have to, Longinus? While Rome's legion and my own army fight together for Rome, there is no conflict. Rome is not competent to rule in the East, for she is too far away to administer the governments properly. Marcus will be on our side. After all, it is not as if he were involved in the government of Rome. Like me, he springs from two peoples— from Britain, and from Rome. He has spent the last fifteen years here in Palmyra, and become more Palmyran each day.''

Longinus shook his head. Where Marcus Britainus was concerned Zenobia was blind in both eyes.

"As always, Longinus, you worry too much," Zenobia teased him. "This is not the time to make a decision, and perhaps there never will come such a time for Marcus. We are friends as well as lovers. When Vaba is eighteen I will marry Marcus and let my son rule alone. I want children for Marcus.''

Again Longinus shook his head. She was a brilliant ruler, but where her lover was concerned she simply did not understand. Love was indeed blind in the case of Palmyra's queen.

"Stop frowning, Longinus! You are beginning to resemble a thundercloud.''

"I think ahead, Majesty.''

180

"And you obviously do not like the conclusions you have reached," she replied. "Do not fear, Longinus. Everything is going to be all right. Tomorrow I begin to ready the army for Syria."

"Will you go with them this time, Majesty?"

"Yes," she answered. "This time I will go with them. You, old friend, will remain behind in Palmyra to guide the king in my absence. This will not be a long campaign, but the Syrians must be brought firmly under my control."

"The Syrians are used to being conquered," Longinus said drily. "They will give you no trouble, Majesty."

It was doubtful that Zenobia even heard him, for she was lost in thought at her map table. Her fingers wandered restlessly across the parchment, touching the main cities of Syria: Damascus, Antioch, Emesa, Beirut. And above Syria lay all of Asia Minor. There was Cilicia, Cappadocia, Bithynia, and Pontus; Galatia, Lycia, and Pamphylia; Lydia and Paphilagonia; Mysia, Phrygia, and Commagene. Her fingers moved downward, brushing across Palestine, Arabia, and finally into Egypt. A small smile played about the corners of her mouth. Yes, Egypt should be the outer boundary of her Palmyran Empire, and the far west of Asia Minor her other boundary. She gazed out the window toward the east. She would need eastern boundaries. Perhaps Armenia and Parthia; but right now her chief enemies lay to the west. Rome. In Persia, King Shapur was old and beaten, holding his hollow court and speaking of past victories; victories before Odenathus; victories before Zenobia.

She could feel the power filling her soul, and she knew that she would be victorious in her endeavors. She did not understand how she knew it, but she knew. Marcus, of course, was not happy at the prospect of her going on campaign.

"You have made me commander of the legions," he said. "Do you not trust me to lead them well?"

"I am not questioning your competence, my darling, but I am the queen. This time I must go with the armies. When Odenathus was alive it was not necessary, for he as their king led them, and I remained here in Palmyra to rule in his name. Now, however, I am the power in Palmyra, and I must go with the legions. Vaba is still too young, and he is important to our people. Until he is married and has a son we cannot take the chance of losing him. Therefore I must go with Palmyra's troops." She moved provocatively into his arms and lightly kissed his lips. "Will it really be so terrible to have me with you on this campaign, my darling?"

"It is indeed a burden for me, beloved," he said honestly. "I cannot lead my armies if I am worried every minute that you may be in danger. There are hardships on a military campaign you cannot possibly know, Zenobia. We simply cannot carry along all the fripperies and slave girls necessary to a woman's comfort."

Cassius Longinus sat back in his chair, a wicked smile lighting up his aesthetic face. *This* was going to be quite enjoyable.

Zenobia sighed a long patient sigh. Walking across the room, she stopped before a cabinet, reached in, and withdrew two broadswords. Turning about, she tossed one to the very startled Marcus. "Prepare to defend yourself, Roman!" she said, loosening her long stola and stepping out of it. Beneath it she wore only a thin white linen camise.

Longinus muffled a deep chuckle. Reaching for his goblet, he quaffed down the sweet red wine, and then, his brown eyes darting between the queen and Marcus, he watched to see what would happen.

"Zenobia! Have you gone mad?"

"No, Marcus, I have not. I was born and bred to be a warrior. It is true that I have yet to taste battle, but I am capable, as any of my guard could tell you had you ever bothered to ask. You, however, doubt my capability. Since you do I must obviously prove myself to you. I am now prepared to do so, so you had best defend yourself, my darling, lest I slice off an ear!" She punctuated her speech by whirling her sword in ever-widening circles over her head.

Marcus Britainus was momentarily surprised, but, realizing that she was serious, quickly stripped off his toga and his long tunic, keeping only his short tunica interior to cover him. He was somewhat annoyed by her actions. She was a woman! Why could she not behave like one, and remain home in Palmyra while he took her armies out and subdued the Eastern Empire? Too late he realized that it was he who had brought about this confrontation. If he had simply agreed to her accompanying them and let it go at that—but no! He had to behave like a great masculine brute. He knew her competence. He could not allow her a false victory, for she would know. Wondering how good she really was with the broadsword, he leapt forward, his blade on the attack.

With a grin Zenobia moved backward but a step, and then, rather than taking an attitude of defense, which was what he had expected, she rushed forward, her sword cutting through the air with a loud whooshing noise, and it was he who was forced to retreat. He parried blow after blow, and quickly discovered that she was not only adept with her sword, but tireless. With a leap he got behind her, but she was equally quick, and instantly turned to defend herself.

Metal clanged as weapon met weapon, and they were both soon dripping wet with their exertions. Longinus sat watching, totally fascinated by the spectacle before him. It did not even cross his mind that they might unwittingly hurt each other. Zenobia's concentration was grim as she parried his blow, staggering somewhat for he had put his entire weight behind it. Still she would not give him the victory for she was angry. How could he love her the way he did, and yet be so unaware of the warrior she was? It infuriated her!

He was surprised at her skill and her stamina. She was one of the finest swordsmen he had ever encountered; but the battle was getting them nowhere. Eventually one of them was going to draw blood, and that thought frightened him. He could not bear to hurt her.

"Zenobia! Give over, my darling. I was wrong, and I freely admit to it."

"What?" She lowered her blade and looked at him. Her wonderful breasts were rising and falling with her exertion.

"I was wrong," he repeated. "You are a warrior, a great warrior, but I am terrified that I might hurt you. Please let us stop this battle. If necessary I will concede you the victory."

"*You will concede me the victory?!*" Her voice was filled with righteous indignation. "I *win* my victories!"

He saw it coming and, heedless of the danger, he leapt swiftly forward and wrenched the broadsword from her hand. "No!" he shouted. "No, you little savage, I won't allow you to hurt either yourself or me!" And he flung both weapons across the room.

Furiously she launched herself at him, nails extended to rake his face, but he caught her wrists and squeezed until he saw the pain leap into her eyes. But she would not cry out. Instead her gray eyes darkened until they were almost black in her anger. He was just as angry. Yanking her into his arms, his mouth fiercely savaged hers, stoking the fires of her body until the nipples of her breasts were as hard and as sharp as her swordpoint had been. The desperate need to retaliate was deep within her, and furiously she bit his lips.

"Bitch!" he murmured against her mouth, and then his kisses grew soft, and filled with such intense passion that she could feel the anger flowing from both their bodies as another, sweeter need rose and took its place. The arms that had been locked tightly about her loosened, and she slipped her own arms up and around his neck, molding her lush soft curves to his hard body. How long they remained standing there kissing, she never knew; but suddenly he was drawing her camise off, his big hands caressing her back, cupping her buttocks, drawing her tightly against him, letting her feel his deep and hungry need.

"Longinus," she managed to whisper, wanting very much to satisfy his need and the equally deep need within her.

"Longinus is gone," was the answer, and quickly looking about the room, she saw that Marcus spoke the truth.

"Not here, not now," she whispered again, somewhat shy that they might be discovered.

"Here and now," he answered, drawing her down onto a couch.

"Please, Marcus . . ." she pleaded.

"I very much please," he answered her, and then she felt his hands beneath her bottom, lifting her slightly, felt the hot tip of his shaft rubbing against her womanhood, felt herself encouraging him onward, and knew that she was lost.

There was no subtlety, for the need between them was too great. Again, again, and yet again he drove himself into her, and it was, he thought, like plunging into boiling honey. The sweetness flowed from her until he thought it could come no more; but yet again it flowed and in the end it was she who weakened him, and filled him with such delight that he cried out.

Her hands reached down and raised his face from her shoulder. She loved gazing into his eyes when they lay locked in passion. Kissing him with gentle little kisses, she said once more the words he never tired of hearing from her lips. "I love you, Marcus! I love you! Never leave me! Never!"

His sapphire-blue eyes bore into her, and told her all that his lips could not say at this tender and yet fiery moment. The deep and desperate loving began again, and she felt him growing and filling her with such pleasure that she believed for a long moment that death was but an instant away. Nothing, she reasoned, could be quite that wonderful, but he certainly was. Again, and yet once more he led her down passion's path until the rapture burst over her in a shower of tiny golden lights. Then she tumbled into a velvet abyss of warm, loving darkness that enfolded her, rocked her, protected her.

When she came to herself once more he was looking at her with a bemused expression. "Did all of this come about simply because I questioned your prowess with a broadsword?" he asked.

Weakened by his loving, she could only manage a soft chuckle. Unable to resist, he bent and tenderly covered her face with kisses. "I adore you, my Queen," he said quietly. "I adore you, beloved!"

"Then I have won this victory myself, Marcus," and her voice held a teasingly triumphant note.

He laughed then. He couldn't help it, for she had so very neatly outmaneuvered him. "You have won the victory fairly, beloved," he admitted.

There came a discreet knocking at the library door, and Marcus rose from the couch, snatching up his long tunic, sliding it over his big frame, reaffixing his toga. He looked to Zenobia who had as quickly redressed in her graceful long, white stola with its wide belt of gold squares studded with turquoise-blue chunks of Persian lapis. She nodded, and he said, "Enter!"

Cassius Longinus returned to the room, saying, "I assume you have reconciled your differences now, my children. It seemed to me when I was forced to hurriedly depart that you were well on your way to doing so."

They both laughed, and Zenobia replied, "We have indeed reconciled our differences, Longinus, and I have easily won the victory."

"Indeed the queen is invincible," the smiling Marcus agreed, and it seemed as if his words were prophetic of the months to come.

Palmyra's legions moved across Syria, subduing all rebellion in the name of the Roman Empire. Asia Minor was firmly cowed, and only then did Zenobia return to her oasis city.

There she found that in her absence her son, the boy king, had grown into a young man. He was fully as tall as she was, and so closely resembled his father, Odenathus, that it almost hurt her to look at him.

"Is it that I have been away so long," she marveled, "or have you really become a man?"

"I have become a man," he answered her. Gone was the squeaky voice of change that had bid her farewell. Now his voice was deep and sure.

"He has your knack for government," Longinus said quietly. "He has begun to rule, and rule well."

"Only under your guidance, and that of Marius Gracchus," the sixteen-year-old king replied graciously.

"Strange," Zenobia mused. "I had thought that you would prefer the military, like your father."

"I have not yet had the chance, Mother. You and Marcus have led the armies these many months."

"You were too young to go," she protested.

"But I am no longer too young. I will take the armies into Egypt when they go this winter. Palmyra's kings have always been good generals."

"No," she said quietly.

"What? Do you love war so, Mother?"

"I can see now that only your body has grown, Vaba. Your mind is yet that of a child."

"I am the king, and I *will* lead the armies!"

"*I am the queen,* and you are not yet of age. Until you are, my word is supreme in Palmyra! There is danger all about you. I will do everything in my power to protect you until you have a son of your own."

"I will choose my wife," he said, and she knew in that instant that he already had. She invoked the gods that the girl be suitable.

"Who is she, my son?"

"You will approve, Mother. It is Flavia, the daughter of your friends, Antonius Porcius and his wife, Julia."

"Flavia Porcius? She is but a child, Vaba."

"She is almost thirteen, Mother. She has already begun her woman's flow."

"I don't want to know how you know that," Zenobia said, shocked, and behind her both Longinus and Marcus smiled. The young king might look like his father, but he was his mother's son in that he was determined to have his way.

"Nonetheless she is my choice for a wife, and I will wager even you could not choose a more suitable girl. She is Palmyran-born, of reputable family, and ready to bear children. More important to me, however, is the fact that she loves me and I love her.''

"Then why do you want to rush off into battle?''

"I must prove myself worthy to rule Palmyra; to myself, to my people, and to Flavia. Until I do I am only your son, and that is simply not enough for me. I must be a man in my own right.''

Zenobia turned away so he might not see her tears. Vaba was indeed becoming a man. Gently he put his arm about his mother. "You have given me the greatest gift any woman could give her child. You gave me time to grow, time to learn, time to play. But now the time has come for me to earn my place. All your life you have been so good, so loyal, so generous. Do you not want a life of your own? Do you not want to marry Marcus? You are yet young enough to have children, and I believe that like any man he wants a son.''

She blushed at his words. He, her firstborn, her baby, was chiding her, but when she turned to give him a sharp reply she saw how earnest he was, and instead she said, "You are right. You shall lead our armies into Egypt this winter while I remain behind to rule this city in your stead.''

It was going to be devastating, she thought. Both Vaba and Marcus, two of the three males she loved best in this world, away from her this winter; for of course Marcus was still commander of the legions, and would go to guide Vaba in military matters. Then suddenly she thought that it was not so terrible after all. Egypt would be easily subdued, and Vaba would have his first taste of battle. He would return to marry Flavia Porcius, then she, Zenobia, would be free to marry Marcus Britainus. Together they would guide the young king and his wife in their rule of the Eastern Empire. Zenobia smiled. When Vaba's first child was born she would declare her son Augustus, supreme ruler of the Eastern Empire. With all the lands from Egypt to Asia Minor under their rule, who would dare to dispute them? Certainly not Rome, weakening Rome with its succession of soldier-emperors, and its northern and western borders constantly challenged by barbarian tribesmen.

Later she sighed within the comfort of Marcus's arms "Soon we shall be able to marry. Make this Egyptian campaign a quick one, my darling!''

"Do I not always do my best to oblige you, beloved?'' he teased her, his hot mouth finding a ready nipple. Slowly he sucked on her sweet flesh, taunting her with his tongue while his fingers moved to torture her in yet another sensitive spot. They loved almost without ceasing in that short period between military campaigns. Zenobia allowed her son and the Council of Ten almost complete freedom while she and Marcus locked themselves within the love chamber she had created for them. They could not be sated in their consuming desire for each other.

Less than a month before Palmyra's legions were due to depart, a trusted household slave of the Alexander family arrived from Rome, bearing tidings from Marcus's mother. The slave had been admitted into the queen's private apartment, and stood staring in amazement at the colorful, rather explicit frescoes that adorned the walls. Watching him, Zenobia thought that the Alexander household in Rome was sure to get quite a report.

"Is everything all right?" she asked Marcus

"No." He paused in his reading. "My father is ill, beloved. He is seriously ill, possibly dying. My mother has sent to Britain for my younger brother, Aulus, to come home." He turned to the slave. "How long ago did you leave Rome, Leo?"

"This is the fiftieth day, Marcus Britainus, since my departure."

"It's thirty-three days to Britain. My brother is halfway to Rome already. Zenobia . . ."

"I will lead the legions, Marcus. You must answer your mother's plea. If the worst is to happen I could not live with myself knowing that I had kept you from your father in the hour of his death. Go back to Rome, and then come home to Palmyra, and to me."

"You will be able to manage?"

She smiled at him, a slightly wry smile. "I can manage, my darling, although I am not sure I should admit to that. Nor would I, but I don't want you to worry. Perhaps it is better that I take my son, the king, and teach him the art of war. Do not fear for us, Marcus. Longinus shall remain here with Demetrius. The succession is safe. Go to Rome."

"Leo and I will start at dawn for Tripoli. There will be a ship sailing for Brindisi."

"Do not take just any vessel, Marcus," she pleaded with him.

His blue eyes drove into her very soul. "I am coming back to you, I promise, beloved."

"I cannot survive without you, Marcus!"

He laughed gently. "Zenobia, Queen of Palmyra, I do not believe that for a moment." He wrapped his arms about her, and felt her trembling against him. Small tears matted her black eyelashes, tears she fought to hold back. Tenderly he tasted of her mouth, kissing at the corners of it, nibbling at her upper lip affectionately. "Oh, queen of my heart, do not make my going any harder. How I wish that Vaba ruled in his own right, and that you were naught but my wife and might go with me!" He sighed, and then said quietly, "I will take Leo to my house. Severus must be informed so that he may assume the responsibilities that are mine while I am gone."

"You will return to me tonight?" She brushed a tear that had dared to slip down her cheek.

"Yes."

When he was gone, taking the slave, Leo, with him, she sat squarely in the middle of the sleeping platform, legs crossed, very much like the child she had once been. It would be the first time that they had been separated. Thank the gods for the winter campaign against Egypt. She needed it to keep herself occupied. Rome was so far away, across a vast sea that she hadn't ever seen. There was a finality about Marcus's trip that frightened her, and set her imagination to playing tricks on her. Would he return to her if his father died? He would then be the head of his family, and it was not a responsibility he could pass on to his younger brother. Aulus, after all, had a life in Britain, and lands that needed his management there.

By the time Marcus returned to the palace that evening Zenobia was a bundle of nerves. He had never seen her that way. For that matter in her entire life she had never behaved that way. She picked at her food, but so did he even though she had ordered that his favorite dishes be prepared.

"I don't like leaving you, beloved," he said. "I wish you could come with me. I am beginning to see disadvantages in loving a queen."

"Then I *shall* come with you! Oh, Marcus, yes! I will come with you! I know it will shock your family, but I do not care if I may be with you!"

"No, it is impossible, Zenobia. You cannot come. If you come then you must send Vaba into Egypt alone. Without your tactical skill he is sure to lose."

"If your father dies you will not be able to return to Palmyra," she said, admitting to what really concerned her.

189

"I will return to Palmyra, beloved. I promise you that, and never have I broken a promise to you."

"If you are head of your family, how can you leave them?"

"I can leave them to return to Palmyra to fetch my wife, for you are my wife, beloved. Zenobia, marry me before I go! Be my wife legally, before the gods."

"We would have to wed secretly, Marcus, and that I will not do as long as I am the reigning queen. You know it! We have spoken it before."

"As always, you put Palmyra before all else," he said, his voice a trifle bitter.

"And you!" she accused him. "Are you not putting your family before our love? You see your duty, and you do it. Why, then, is it so different when I do the same?" Suddenly she stood up from the table with its barely touched meal. "I will not quarrel with you, my darling. Not tonight; this is the last night we will have for so many months! Come!" She held out her hand to him. "Let us bathe, and then let us spend the hours we have left in making love to each other."

"I don't want to leave you," he said low. "You know it, beloved!"

"I know it, Marcus, but we are two people who have been trained to duty and loyalty. Return to Rome, and receive your father's final blessing. I will be waiting when you come home to Palmyra."

Together they walked across the room to remove their garments by the side of the pool. He stood watching as she descended the steps down into the tepid water, and felt himself grow warm with longing at the sight of her golden body moving languorously in the black marble pool. Her dark hair streamed out behind her, a feathery cloak. Turning, she swam back toward him, her gray eyes devouring his tall body. His long legs were to her like the marble columns that lined the portico of the ancient Temple of Baal, and she shivered in anticipation of feeling his hard thighs.

Already his shaft was straight and firm, thrusting from the dark forest of his groin. Their eyes locked, and he moved down into the pool, walking slowly toward her. Zenobia felt herself growing weak with desire as she floated, her limbs losing their will. His hands closed gently about her ankles, and he drew her forward, his sure grasp moving up her legs. She ached for him, a yearning clearly visible in her beautiful face, as he tenderly entered into her body, filling her with the fiery fullness she loved. He stood in the waist-deep water, his throbbing lance buried deep within her as she floated before him, her legs wrapped lightly about his body, her marvelous hair billowing in the soft swell of the waters.

The fingers of both his hands began to rub the nipples of her breasts with delicate little touches. She shivered, and while he smiled a slow smile her eyes closed in rapture and small waves of pleasure began to lap over her. Her entire being was finely tuned to the pleasure of their lovemaking, and she almost screamed aloud her bliss as she felt him throbbing and growing within her. Yet he remained perfectly still but for his fingers, which continued to tease at her velvety nipples.

Finally she could bear no more of such exquisite torture, and her body began to shiver as the honied sweetness flowed from her, crowning the ruby head of his manhood. She heard his soft laughter. "Oh, beloved, you are as ever an impatient and greedy creature." Then he withdrew from her, gathered her up, and carried her from the pool.

"I hate it when you are so superior," she murmured as she stood on trembling legs that threatened to give way beneath her at any minute.

One strong arm locked about her slender waist, and with his other hand he carefully dried her off. "I am not superior, I am only delighted that I can give you such pleasure," he said as he toweled her long hair free of excess water.

"But I want you to be pleasured, too!" she protested.

"I am," he answered, "and even more so when I see the look on your face." He picked her up again, walked across the room, and gently deposited her upon the sleeping platform. Lying down next to her, he said, "In the lonely nights to come, beloved, I shall relive a thousand times each moment we have spent in this room; each night I have lain by your side and loved you. I have never loved anyone else, and I swear to you that I never shall." He took her into his arms then, and they kissed until they were breathless.

Now he was afire to possess her once again, but Zenobia squirmed away from his eager grasp. Turning her body, she moved downward, covering his flat and lightly furred torso with little kisses. Teasingly, she nipped at him with her sharp little teeth, and he groaned as the tip of his shaft tingled with her assault. A warm, soothing tongue followed, and then she took him in her mouth for a few moments while he fought to retain control of himself. Just when he thought he would lose the love battle between them, she moved again, mounting him and plunging downward to envelope him deep within her hot sheath.

Reaching up, he crushed her beautiful breasts within his big hands, aching with incredible pleasure. Through slitted sapphire eyes he watched her as she flung back her head in ecstasy, the delicate veins in her smooth throat standing out as the blood pumped visibly through them. She shuddered again in pure fulfillment, and it was then that he regained control, turning her over so that he now rode her.

Slowly he withdrew from her, chuckling at her soft cry of distress. Taking his shaft in his hand he softly rubbed it over her lower belly, and she moaned, seeking him with hot, eager little hands. "No, beloved," he murmured, bending to caress the inside of her ear with his tongue. "Do not be too eager, for there is time for us." His tongue followed the intricate path of her other ear, tickling it lightly for a moment.

Beneath him she writhed, her desire growing again with each touch, each caress. His hands moved with love over her trembling form as he committed to memory the line of her body; the feel of her satin skin; her wonderful breasts—those honeyed hills of softness that reminded him of the great mother goddess herself; her long, strong legs that could grip a man in passionate embrace as easily as the sides of the great gray stallion she rode; the marble smooth twin moons of her bottom. He adored her completely, worshiping at the shrine of her, his love, his very soul.

"Oh, my love," he murmured into the damp tangle of her hair, "I do not know if I can bear the separation from you!" His voice throbbed with emotion, and Zenobia could feel the unbidden tears begin to straggle down her cheeks.

"Make us one, my darling," she begged him. "I shall die if you do not," and she arched to receive him as he thrust vigorously into her aching body.

Over and over again he drove himself into her willing flesh; and Zenobia wept as much with the joy of his possession as she did from the knowledge that in the morning he would be gone. At last his passion peaked, and his seed rushed into the warm darkness of her womb as he collapsed upon her breasts. She wept silently as he shuddered with his own pleasure. How would she manage to exist without him? He was her very life. Oh, Mama, she thought, if this was how it was for you and my father then at last I can understand the love you bore each other.

For some minutes they lay locked in embrace, not speaking.

He could hear her heart gradually growing quieter beneath his ear, and he knew that his own heartbeat was slowing. She was the most incredible woman, he thought, and he didn't intend spending any more time in Rome than he had to. If his father was truly ill to death—and his mother was not a woman to exaggerate—then he would have to accept his responsibilities as head of his family; but first he would return to Palmyra for Zenobia. Then it occurred to him that there was no reason he should have to remain in Rome. He didn't like Rome, and he never really had. His younger brother, Aulus, was settled in Britain; his two sisters, Lucia and Eusebia, lived with their husbands away from Rome—Lucia in the north outside of Ravenna, and Eusebia in the south at Naples. His mother would probably choose to return to Britain with Aulus. He would be free to live in Palmyra, to make it his home, their home. He shared his thought with her, and he could hear the joy in her voice when she answered him.

"You mean you would really make Palmyra your home? You would desert Rome?"

"I deserted Rome fifteen years ago, beloved. What is there for me? A house? A business? These I can sell. They have no meaning, hold no sentiment for me. My home, beloved, is where you are. My home is here in Palmyra."

Zenobia wept with joy, her hot tears pouring down her cheeks to soak the pillows, running into her ears. "Now," she said, finally gaining control of herself, "now I can bear your going! I will send six of my guard with you, Marcus. The first will return from Tripoli to tell me the ship on which you have sailed. The second and third will bring me letters from your ports of call; the fourth will come directly from Brindisi to tell me that you have reached Italy safely; the fifth will bring me news from Rome; and the last man will stay with you until you are about to return to me. He will bring me the gladdest tidings of all; the news that you are coming home!"

"So be it, my beloved!" he agreed, and then his mouth found hers again, drinking in the sweetness of her, quickly seeking to possess her once more as she joyously opened her arms to him and received him again. They loved almost without stopping that night, with lips, and tongues, and hands, and eyes. They touched, and caressed, and tasted until they thought there were no more pleasures. And then they were astounded to find that that was not so—their bodies turned, and twisted, and molded themselves a hundred different ways, and the rapture never ended, but grew sweeter, sharper, better each time. Finally, but an hour before the dawn, they fell into a restful sleep. When they awoke but a short time later they were both at peace.

Their private good-byes were said within their love chamber, their lips clinging for a moment to each other, their eyes locking in silent understanding. "Nothing will keep me from returning to you, beloved," he said.

"I will be waiting," she answered.

Their public farewell was said in the main courtyard of the palace, surrounded by Longinus, the young king, his brother, and the other members of the Council of Ten.

"Please bring our loyal greetings to the Emperor Aurelian, Marcus," the king said. "We hope his reign will be a long and prosperous one. It is unfortunate that Claudius died of plague."

Marcus smiled. "I shall be happy to convey your Majesty's greetings to the Emperor Aurelian. He is married to a distant cousin of mine, and he is a fine general. I suspect if the senate will cooperate Rome will prosper under him."

The king nodded, then said, "Farewell, Marcus Alexander Britainus. The gods go with you, and keep you safe until you return to us here in Palmyra!"

Marcus bowed to the young king, and then nodded to the others before his eyes found Zenobia again. They gazed lovingly at each other. "Farewell, beloved," he said softly, and he heard her answer, "Farewell, my heart! I will wait!"

He did not look back again, but mounted his white stallion and rode off through the main gates of the palace accompanied by his family's slave, Leo, and six of Zenobia's personal guard. He did not know that she went immediately to a tower in the palace that overlooked the main caravan road west, and watched until he and his party became but specks upon the horizon.

Several days later the first of her guards returned. Marcus Britainus and his party had taken passage from Tripoli upon a first-class merchant vessel, *Neptune's Luck,* which would be stopping only at Cyprus and Crete before it reached Brindisi. The second messenger returned, and shortly thereafter the third. The voyage was progressing smoothly, the seas calm, the winds perfect. He would shortly be in Rome. In two months' time the fourth messenger returned back to Palmyra: the queen's beloved had safely reached Italy. Zenobia stopped fretting. The Appian Way, the empire's most famous road, ran directly from Brindisi to Rome, and was eminently safe.

Now Zenobia turned her eyes toward Egypt. They departed Palmyra on an early winter's morning, the queen and her handsome son both riding within the same magnificent gold chariot drawn by four coal-black horses. The citizens of Palmyra lining the way to the Triumphal Arch screamed themselves hoarse at the sight of their beloved queen and their king.

"How they love you," Vaballathus marveled over the cries of the crowd.

"How they love *you*," she corrected him. "You are the king."

"No," he replied. "I have not yet earned their adulation. It is you for whom they cry, but when we return through this Triumphal Arch they shall cry my name, and *I will deserve it!*"

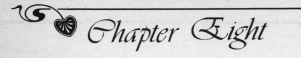

Chapter Eight

Dagian, the wife of Lucius Alexander Britainus, hurried into the atrium of her home, arms outstretched in joyous welcome. "Marcus!" She flung her arms round her eldest son, and then kissed him on both cheeks. "Praise the gods, you have arrived home safely!"

He stood back and studied her. She was nearing sixty, and yet he could see little change in the fifteen years he had been away. Her wonderful, once golden hair was gray, but the blue eyes he had inherited were as clear and sharp as ever. There were few lines in her beautiful face. "Did Aulus arrive safely?" She nodded in the affirmative. "And Father? He is still alive?"

"Yes, but only because he did not choose to depart for the Underworld until he had seen you, Marcus. He is sleeping now, but I will take you to him when he awakens."

"Marcus?" A woman, very like his mother but with red-blond hair, had come into the atrium.

"Lucia?" By the gods, she had been but a slip of a girl when he last saw her!

"I did not think it possible, Marcus, but you have grown even handsomer with age," Lucia said, coming up and kissing him as his mother had done.

"And you, my sister, have also grown lovelier," he answered.

"No, Marcus," she answered him wryly. "I have simply grown," and she laughingly patted her matronly form. "The result of five children, and too good a cook. Wait until you see your nieces and nephews, Marcus. They are young men and women."

"Yes, Marcus," Dagian put in quietly. "Lucia's children are almost all grown, and you, the eldest of my children, are not even married."

He might have put it off, but suddenly he realized it was better to speak the truth now, so they might get used to it, rather than wait until after his father had died and then suddenly spring it on them. "I will not be making my home in Rome, Mother. I will be returning to Palmyra."

"Marcus! Why?"

"I am afraid, Mother, that my fifteen years in the East have made me prefer a dry and warm climate."

"And what else? You cannot fool me, Marcus. Warm weather is simply not a reason for deserting your home."

He laughed. He was not going to escape her curiosity. He had never been able to, even as a child. "There is a lady whom I wish to marry. She has consented, and so I will return to Palmyra."

"Who is she, Marcus?"

"I cannot tell you yet."

"Is she married?"

"She is a widow."

"Young enough to have children?"

"Yes, Mother. She is young enough to have children."

"Is she beautiful, Marcus?" Lucia asked softly.

"Little sister, if the goddess Venus came to earth, she would take my beloved's face and form."

"*You are in love!*" Dagian was amazed.

"I am in love, Mother," he admitted with a smile.

For a moment Dagian stared in surprise at her son. He had always kept his feelings in complete check, never exhibiting undue emotion, even as a little boy. He had grown into a big, elegant, intelligent man who always appeared a bit severe to her. He was not like her younger son, Aulus, always laughing, light of heart, deeply involved in life, unafraid of being hurt. He was not like his sisters, passionate and gentle women whose emotions were always quite visible. No, Marcus had been the reserved one, and now suddenly to see his face alight with love was somewhat startling.

"*Marcus!*" The cry was almost a shriek, and came from a short, plump young woman with her father's dark hair and eyes who ran across the atrium and hurled herself into his arms.

He swung her high above him, and she giggled with glee as he put her down. "Eusebia, my little bird, you have not learned to curb your passion for sweets, I see."

"Calvinus says a skinny woman is no use on a cold night," came the prompt reply. She eyed him frankly. "Jupiter! You have grown positively gorgeous! Perhaps I should move to Palmyra."

"It is love that has softened him, Eusebia," teased her older sister.

"Love? Marcus is in love?" Eusebia's dark brown eyes were round with curiosity. "Tell me! Tell me!" she begged her oldest brother.

"There is nothing to tell. I will marry the lady when I return to Palmyra."

"You aren't going to stay in Rome?" His oldest sister spoke.

"There is nothing here for me, Lucia. You live in Ravenna, Eusebia in Naples; and Aulus in Britain. Father is the first of the Alexanders to make Rome his permanent home. He likes it. I do not. I will return to Palmyra which I have grown to love, Lucia."

"Do you plan to sell the business?" A man almost as tall as Marcus entered the room. "Welcome home, brother."

"Thank you, Aulus." Marcus was amused at his brother's question. "I think we shall wait until the matter need be settled to settle it."

"That's right," replied Aulus. "After all it will all be yours as the elder son, won't it, Marcus?"

Marcus laughed pleasantly. "You haven't changed, Aulus. You are still spoilt."

Aulus shook his head wearily. "The gods, Marcus! How long has it been since we have seen each other; and the second I lay eyes upon you I become the whiny little boy trying to compete. Forgive me, brother. I thought I had outgrown it."

Marcus looked at his younger brother. Aulus was not quite as tall as he, but they looked very much alike with their blue eyes and chestnut-brown hair. He had been almost six when Aulus was born, and he had, he recalled, been totally unimpressed with the baby. Aulus, from the moment of his birth, had competed with his elder sibling, imitated him, followed him; but alas, the gap had been too great between the boys. Aulus had never been able to keep up, and although totally charming with everyone else, he eventually became embittered toward his brother, finding himself only when his maternal grandfather left him his estates in Britain and he could be his own man away from Marcus.

"We will make the decisions necessary together, when the time comes, Aulus," Marcus said quietly, and Dagian was silently proud of her eldest child.

"You have had a long journey, my son," she said. "I will

show you to your room, and then perhaps you will want to bathe the dust of the road away.''

Knowing that his mother wanted to be alone with him for a few moments, he followed her from the atrium, leaving his sisters and his brother behind to gossip. They ascended to the second floor of the house, and she led him into the simple bedchamber of his youth. Gone, however, were all the small things that had made the room his.

Dagian seated herself in the room's one chair and looked piercingly at her son. "Now, Marcus," she said. "I wish to know of this woman you propose to make my daughter-in-law.''

"Her name is Zenobia. She is the Queen of Palmyra.''

"The gods, my son! You aim high! How can you marry this woman if she is the Queen of Palmyra?''

"Her late husband Odenathus left her regent for their son, the young king. Once the king is married, her obligation is over, and Zenobia will be free to marry me.''

"But if her child is old enough to be king in his own right, then this woman is far too old to bear your children," Dagian protested.

"We have a child, Mother. A daughter. Her name is Mavia, and she is the Princess of Palmyra.''

"What?!'' Dagian gripped the arms of the chair and leaned forward, her lovely face very white.

"Hear me, Mother, before you speak again. I had barely arrived in Palmyra when I saw Zenobia and fell in love with her. Regrettably, she was about to marry Odenathus, who was then Prince of Palmyra.''

"She returned your feelings, though?''

"She didn't even know, Mother. She was young, and very innocent, for after her mother's death her father and her brothers all overprotected her. You would like her, Mother. She is very much like you in certain ways.''

Dagian looked like she might cry, but she fought back the emotion that threatened to spill over and asked in a voice that was less than steady, "How is she like me, Marcus?''

"She is stubborn, yet compassionate, intelligent, and kind. She was a good wife to her husband, and is a good mother to her children.''

"Yet she has borne you a child, Marcus. A child that you tell me is known as the Princess of Palmyra. I do not understand.''

"The night that Odenathus was killed, Zenobia collapsed with the shock, and we made love, Mother. In the morning I was gone and she remembered nothing. She believed the child to be her husband's until she saw it, and then she remembered. We both thought it best that Mavia believe she is Odenathus's child. To do otherwise could have compromised the rule of young King Vaballathus, for although the boy is his father's image, there are those who might say *he* was not Odenathus's son.

Dagian nodded, understanding Zenobia's protective maternal instincts toward her children.

Marcus spoke again. "Now I wish to see my father, receive his final blessing, make his passage from this life to the next a happy one, and then return to my beloved in Palmyra. Zenobia is my very reason for living, Mother, and I ache with the separation from her."

Dagian was now unable to control herself, and a flood of tears rushed down her face. "Oh, Marcus, you are my eldest child, and although I would never admit it before even to myself, you are my favorite child. I want you to be happy, but you cannot marry your Zenobia. Your father has arranged a match for you. He so wanted to see you married before he died. You must not be angry with him!"

Marcus was astounded. *"He arranged a match for me?* Has his illness rendered him mad, Mother? I am no boy for him to arrange a wife for me. I am past forty! Could he not have waited until I got home, and consulted with me on this matter?"

"Marcus, try to understand! He is dying and he wants everything in his life in order before he must make that crossing from here to the Underworld. His eldest son, a man these many years, remains unmarried. If you were a lover of boys he would have long since given you up, but you are a real man, and his only immortality."

"Aulus is married, Mother, and he is also father's son. Aulus is the father of several sons."

"You are Lucius Alexander's eldest son, Marcus, and he wanted you settled. He wanted you happy, as he and I have been all these years. He did not seek to harm you. Besides, why did you not write to us of your love for Zenobia. As always, you have been secretive."

"I could not write to you under the circumstances, Mother. Surely you must see that. Zenobia's situation is far too politically sensitive, and if such a message had fallen into the wrong hands it might have brought down her government and endangered the empire's eastern boundaries that she and her late husband protected so well for Rome. No, it is unfortunate, but this betrothal will have to be broken."

"It cannot be," Dagian almost whispered.

"*Cannot?*" His brow darkened with anger. "What do you mean, 'cannot,' Mother?"

"Your father secured a great match for you, Marcus. You are to be married to the emperor's niece, Carissa."

"The match will have to be broken, emperor's niece or no, Mother."

"Marcus, you cannot offend Aurelian!"

"Do not fear, Mother. I will go to Aurelian myself, and explain the situation. Zenobia is vital to the empire's eastern defenses. I know the emperor will approve my match with the queen and find another husband for his niece."

They walked from the room and back downstairs again into the atrium, where Marcus called for a chariot. Within moments the vehicle was at the front door of the house, and with a quick smile to his mother he was gone through the door. She stood listening as the chariot rumbled off down the quiet residential street. An arm went about her shoulders, and Aulus said. "You look as if you have been crying. What has my big brother done now, Mother?"

"He has done nothing, Aulus. Your father made a match between your older brother and the emperor's niece, Carissa. Marcus, however, is in love with a woman in Palmyra. He has gone off to tell the emperor that the betrothal must be canceled."

Aulus had paled at the mention of the emperor's niece's name. "Carissa, Mother? You are sure of the name?"

Dagian nodded, and then asked, "What is wrong, Aulus? You look as if you have seen an evil spirit."

"Oh, Mother, Carissa is the most venal creature alive."

"That sweet-faced child?"

"That is the paradox of Carissa. She looks like a vestal virgin, yet is more corrupt than any woman in the empire."

Marcus drove through the bustling streets of the city to the Palatine Hill, where the emperor lived. He could not help but notice the filth in the streets, unusual, for the Rome he remembered had been clean and bright. Now, however, the great marble buildings were in need of repair, and there was obvious vandalism to public places. There were many shops closed and shuttered.

At the palace a slave ran to take his horses, and he strode into the ancient building to encounter an old friend.

"Marcus Alexander!" came the shout, and he turned.

"Gaius Cicero!"

The two men gripped arms in the traditional Roman greeting, and then stepped back to view each other.

Gaius Cicero was a man of forty, of medium height and stocky build with brown eyes and black hair. "I had heard you were coming home from the eastern frontier," he said with a smile. "I am sorry so sad an event as your father's dying brings you. What do you here?"

"I must see the emperor."

"So cries half of Rome, Marcus Alexander, but Aurelian's time is limited."

"This is an urgent matter, Gaius Cicero. It could have far-reaching effects on the empire. Can you help me?"

"By chance, yes. He's in the baths now, and if you don't mind seeing him there, then I will take you."

"I would see him in Hades if necessary."

The Praetorian officer smiled wryly. "I am sure there are those who would wish Aurelian in the very place you mentioned. Follow me, Marcus Alexander." He made several turns into exquisitely decorated corridors that were lit with multilamped candelabrum. "Ah, here we are," he announced as they moved quickly through large double doors that were opened by two Praetorian guards.

A slave hurried to aid them, and Gaius Cicero said, "Tell the emperor that Gaius Cicero has brought Marcus Alexander Britainus to see him on a matter of urgent business. We ask the emperor's leave to come into the bath."

"At once, Gaius Cicero," the slave replied, and hurried off.

"If he will see you, Marcus, you will not need me. I do not wish to intrude."

"I thank you again for your help, Gaius Cicero," Marcus replied.

"Perhaps we can have dinner together while you are in Rome," the Praetorian said.

"The emperor will see you, Marcus Alexander Britainus," said the returning slave.

"Farewell, Marcus Alexander," Gaius Cicero said. "I will send a message to your parents' home."

The slave quickly had Marcus divested of his clothes. "The

emperor is already in the caldarium. He will speak with you when you reach the unctorium, Marcus Alexander Britainus.''

Marcus nodded, and walked from the dressing room into the tepidarium where he sat down and waited for the perspiration to flow. When his pores were open and he was dripping, a slave began to scrape him free of dirt and sweat as he stood silently. He moved quickly into the caldarium for a hot bath. The emperor was already gone. There were, however, several young, beautiful nude slave girls who bathed him tenderly with scented soap before leading him to the bath, where he soaked a short time. He decided against a plunge in the frigidarium's icy bath, preferring a quick swim in the open courtyard pool, which had been warmed by the sun. Now he might enter into the unctorium. The emperior was waiting.

"Marcus Alexander!" Aurelian rose and came toward him, smiling.

"Hail, Caesar!" Marcus replied, his right arm extended in salute.

"Put your arm down, Marcus," Aurelian said, gesturing impatiently. "The gods, I shall never get used to being greeted 'Hail Caesar!' '' The emperor was a tall man, over six feet, but Marcus still topped him by a good two inches. "Come and have a rubdown, and we'll talk," he invited.

The two men lay upon the massage benches, and Marcus studied the emperor from beneath apparently closed eyes. He had known him briefly years ago, and he remembered Aurelian as fair but determined. He wondered if the years had altered him any; certainly not physically. He was older than Marcus, and yet Marcus noted the emperor's body was yet that of a younger man—firm and hard. His blond hair was just faintly touched with silver, as was his barbered beard; but his light blue eyes were as clear and sharp as ever. He had a nicely-shaped head, his eyes were well spaced, his nose was long and surprisingly aquiline for a man with peasant roots, his lips narrow, almost scornful.

"How is your wife, Ulpia?" he asked.

"Your cousin Ulpia is well, Marcus, but that is not what you came to see me about. What is it you want?"

"Release me from the betrothal my father made with you between myself and your niece, Carissa.''

"No.''

"I will not marry your niece, Caesar. I came home for two

203

reasons; because my father was dying, and to tell my parents
that I was to marry at long last. I am already betrothed. When
I return to Palmyra I shall marry its queen, Zenobia. Her son
will shortly rule in his own right, and I shall then wed his
mother. Is it not of more importance that I wed such a valuable
ally to Rome?"

"Do you love the Queen of Palmyra?"

"I have loved her for many years, Caesar."

"And she loves you?"

"Yes."

"It is unfortunate then that you must wed with my niece.
Take her back with you to Palmyra if you desire to live there,
Marcus. The queen will remain your mistress if she loves you."

Marcus felt the anger welling up within him. Who was this
peasant, chosen emperor, that he might control the life of a
member of one of the empire's oldest patrician families? "I
will not marry this girl you have chosen for me, Caesar,"
Marcus said quietly, attempting to mask his fury.

"But you will, my friend, because if you don't I will destroy
your family. They are all here in Rome now, aren't they? How
would you like to see Aulus executed on the charge that his
loyalty to Britain is greater than his loyalty to Rome? It is, you
know. I would then send word that his foreign wife and half-
breed children be expediently dispatched, and that his wealth,
as well as that of your father, be confiscated by the government.
Your parents would be forced to beg for their very existence. I
wonder how long your beautiful mother would survive, Marcus.
As for your luscious sisters, my friend, a short stay in the
whorehouse of the Praetorian Guard would make them welcome
death. As for you, defy me in this, and you will never see your
beautiful mistress again."

Marcus felt frustrated and helpless. Aulus might run; the
husbands of his sisters use their wealth and influence to protect
them; but who could protect his parents? His father must be
allowed to die in peace in his own home. His mother must be
comfortable in her old age. "Why?" he asked.

"Because I am Caesar, and I command it."

"You can force me to wed with your niece, Caesar, but you
will do her as great a disservice as you are doing me. I will
never touch her, and she will be condemned to a life of total
loneliness. Is this what you want for her?"

Aurelian smiled. "You have not seen Carissa yet, my friend.
She is exquisite."

"There is nothing your niece can offer that I want. I will marry her because you have given me no choice, but I will not honor her or love her." Marcus arose from the massage bench, and strode toward the door to the dressing room.

"The wedding will be in two days," the emperor called to him. "Would you not like to meet Carissa before then?"

"*Why?*" was the acid reply, and Marcus disappeared from Aurelian's view.

"I do not like him, Uncle," said the beautiful nude girl who had been massaging the emperor.

"You do not have to like him," Aurelian replied laughing, "I have most kindly supplied you with the son and heir of one of the most patrician families in the empire for a husband. He is handsome, he is wealthy. What more can you want, Carissa?"

"He will not be manageable, Uncle."

"Nevertheless he is a Roman of the old school, and as his wife you will lack for nothing."

"You speak of his returning to the East. I do not want to go to the East."

"Then don't, my pet. Many a Roman wife has remained behind while her husband served a term in Syria or Palestine. You are most fortunate, Carissa, that Lucius Alexander chose this time to die. Else I had not gotten you such a prize."

"But I don't want him, Uncle. Find me someone else!" the girl pouted.

Aurelian smiled a slow and lazy smile as he turned over on the marble bench. His staff was straight and hard. "You do not have a choice," he said softly, pulling her atop him, and burying himself inside her. "You simply do not have the choice," he repeated, thrusting deeply, sinking his teeth into her smooth shoulder.

"Then make him stay in Rome, Uncle," she murmured, imitating his pelvic movements.

"I will try, my pet," he said. "I will try," and he crushed her in his embrace.

"Try hard, Uncle," she said, and then her mouth took his in a flaming kiss.

Marcus had dressed and left the palace. He was in a high fury, for he could not think of a way to extricate himself from this situation that would not involve his entire family. He did not doubt for one moment that Aurelian would carry out his threats. What was he to tell Zenobia? How could he possibly explain to her in a letter all that had transpired? In two days he must marry the girl. *Two days!* He had not yet seen his father, but when he had obtained his blessing, and the wedding was over, Marcus intended to return to Palmyra alone. There, he would explain to Zenobia what had happened. Then, as soon as his father died, his sisters had left Rome and were safe with their husbands, and his brother had taken their mother to safety in Britain—for whatever Aurelian might think, there were places in Britain that Roman "justice" could not touch—then would he act to divorce this woman he was being forced to take to wife. He would divorce her and marry his beloved.

If he left the day after the wedding he could reach Palmyra before any letter could; before any gossip could. Furiously he whipped his horses and, as he raced through the streets, took savage pleasure seeing the pedestrians scatter and scramble out of the way, hurling curses at him that flowed off his shoulders like rainwater. If they hated, he hated right back.

His father was awake when he arrived home, and he went quickly in to see him. "Do not upset him," Dagian begged her son, and Marcus nodded. He was shocked by his father's withered and shrunken appearance. Marcus had long ago topped his father by several inches, but the tiny, frail man who lay in his bed was almost a stranger until he spoke.

"You are growing older, my son," he said. "Your mother has told me that she informed you of the fine match I have made for you. I would that she had given me that pleasure, but then," and here he gazed affectionately at Dagian, "your mother was never one to keep a happy secret. We must have the wedding soon, Marcus. Charon already waits to ferry me across into the Underworld."

"I have already seen the emperor, Father. He tells me that the wedding will be in two days."

"Good, good!" the old man enthused. "I ask nothing more of the gods but to see you safely married." He fell back upon his pillows and was soon snoring lightly.

"Oh, Marcus," Dagian whispered, "when I think of the strong and virile man he was. And now—now he is so weak." Dagian took her son by the hand, and led him from the room. "Tell me what transpired between you and the emperor."

"Aurelian is adamant that I marry his niece. He has threatened violence and destruction against this family if I do not. However, I shall leave the day after the wedding for Palmyra. I can stay no longer, and Father will die whether I am here or not. This is hardly something that I can tell Zenobia in a letter. Once Father has passed on; once my sisters are safe with their husbands; once you and Aulus are safely returned to Britain; then I shall divorce this Carissa and marry Zenobia.''

Dagian nodded slowly. His plan was sound, and although she could see that he was angry it was a contained anger. She could not understand Aurelian's immovable intent. Why did he so fervently desire Marcus for his niece? Surely there were other young men in Rome who could be brought into line, or even bought. *Why Marcus?*

She wondered again two days later after her eldest son had been married to Carissa. Because of her husband's illness the ceremony had been performed in her husband's bedchamber, and for a brief time Lucius Alexander exuded the power and the charm that had once been his. It was as if he had gathered all his strength for a final performance. He greeted the emperor heartily, and complimented the bride.

The Bride. Dagian gazed upon Aurelian's niece and marveled that any woman could be that perfect. Carissa was a girl of medium height with an oval face and two adorable dimples on either side of her rosebud mouth. Her skin was milk white, her cheeks were touched with rose. Her features were quite delicate for a girl of peasant background. Her small nose was straight, her black eyes round and fringed with thick, long gold eyelashes. Her forehead was not quite as high as one might have wished, but her small, square chin was also blessed with a dimple. The lovely head was crowned with thistledown hair, of the natural gold color that the women of Rome so desperately sought in their wigs.

Carissa had slim hands and feet; a reedlike waist; slender hips; and firm, high young breasts. She moved with complete grace, and her manners appeared excellent, for her voice was soft but clear, and she deferred to her uncle and her Aunt Ulpia. She had chosen white and silver as her wedding colors, and they suited her admirably.

Marcus glanced at the girl, his distaste obvious. The augurs were taken, and declared highly favorable. Dagian hid a smile. The soothsayer could have opened a lamb that was filled with writhing snakes and he would have found it favorable to this match. The ceremony was quickly over.

The emperor and the empress were quite jovial at the feast that followed. They and their friends ate and drank liberally.

The bride was quite animated, chatting with all the guests. But not once did she speak to her husband, nor he to her.

The rest of the wedding customs were forgotten, and Marcus was glad, for this marriage was a mockery of everything he had ever been taught. *Zenobia!* He almost cried her name aloud in his anguish, and Dagian, seeing the spasm cross her son's face, reached out and squeezed his hand.

When it was no longer possible to prolong the festivities, the emperor and his wife stood, and both bride and groom escorted them to the door, bidding them a good night. Ulpia Severina wept matronly tears as she kissed the beautiful girl she had raised. "Be happy, dear child," she murmured, and with a maidenly sigh Carissa assured her aunt that she would be. The emperor looked directly at Marcus, and said in a very public voice, "I know that you will make my niece happy, Marcus Alexander."

Marcus smiled broadly. "You may be certain, Caesar, that I shall see that Carissa has everything she deserves," he replied.

The emperor and the empress departed, and with them all of the other guests. Turning, Marcus looked at the beautiful girl who was now his wife.

"We will sleep in the atrium tonight," he said. "I see that the wedding couch is already there."

"Very well," she replied coldly, and walking over to it kicked off her sandals. "Do you want me naked?"

"I don't want you at all, Carissa. Surely you know that I was forced into this marriage. That I am betrothed to another woman."

"Whether you sleep with me or not, I do not care," was her answer. "The child will come anyway."

"*What?!*" He felt a throbbing begin in his head.

"I am with child," she said. "It will be born in four months." A small smile played about the corners of her mouth. "You surely do not think I wished to marry *you?*" She laughed her tinkling, irritating laugh.

"Whose bastard do you carry? Why did you not marry him, or is he perhaps already married?"

"Yes, he is married. Unfortunately he could not divorce his dull wife to marry me, for it is forbidden that an uncle marry his niece. My child should be the next emperor of Rome after Aurelian, his father, but it cannot be. Therefore it was necessary that I have the most patrician of husbands to give my child a name. Aurelian will eventually name our child his heir, for he has promised me that.''

"A worthless promise," Marcus replied. "Aurelian will be emperor for a few years if we are lucky, but eventually one of our power-mad generals will assassinate him and declare himself Augustus.''

"That is a possibility, of course," she answered coolly, "and that is why this child will be considered an Alexander. He will be safe if his real father should die before he is old enough to take command of the empire. My child will be safe until his time comes.''

"Since I have just arrived home, Carissa, there is no one who will believe the child mine.''

"It makes no difference. You are my husband now, and therefore my child will be legally yours, heir to this fine, old patrician family! You will never have a child of your own, Marcus Alexander, for I will never couple with you! Never! Nothing shall endanger my child's place in life!''

It was then he slapped her, his big hand flashing out to make contact with her smug, beautiful face. The red imprint of his long fingers crossed her smooth, white cheek. Carissa screamed with outrage, her high voice pealing throughout the entire house again and again until finally the room was filled with Dagian, Aulus, Lucia, and Eusebia, and numerous wide-eyed slaves.

Carissa, the shoulder of her tunic suddenly shredded, flung herself into Dagian's startled arms, weeping wildly. "Oh, Mother Dagian, he tried to make me—make m-m-me—it was foul and unnatural! Nothing like what dearest Aunt Ulpia told me was expected of me on my wedding night." Then she sobbed again, hiccoughing a few times for effect.

"Back to your quarters, all of you!" commanded old Castor, the Alexander major-domo, in an attempt to herd the slaves away from what was obviously a family dispute.

"Oh, no!" Marcus said loudly. "Since my *wife* has started this thing publicly we will finish it publicly. You will all stay." He turned to his mother. "Don't bother attempting to comfort her, Mother. She is a consummate liar and a skilled actress as well as an obviously competent whore. My blushing bride has just told me that she is some months pregnant, and was married off to me to supply the child with a good name.''

"Aurelian will kill you for this!" Carissa hissed, suddenly in full control, her beautiful face contorted with fury.

"I would kill *you*," Marcus replied, "but instead I intend leaving Rome tonight. I will divorce you as soon as I reach Palmyra."

"You will never divorce me!" she screamed at him. "Aurelian will not let you divorce me!"

Marcus looked to his two sisters. "Take her out of my sight!" he commanded them. "Lock her in some room far away from the rest of the household where she cannot cause any trouble! I cannot bear the sight of the whore!"

Aided by two strong young slaves, Lucia and Eusebia did as their brother bid them, removing Carissa from the atrium as she screamed threats and curses at them in high fury.

"Now," Marcus said, turning to old Castor, "you may send the slaves to bed."

"You should have let me tell him," Aulus said to Dagian.

"Tell me what?" Marcus asked.

"I knew of Carissa's reputation, for though she and the emperor have been discreet, they have not been that discreet."

"It would have made no difference," Marcus replied. "I went to the emperor, and was told if I did not marry her he would destroy our family."

"I should not have allowed you to sacrifice yourself for us, Marcus. Return to Palmyra this night. We will weather the storm.

He sat down heavily, and his head wearily dropped into his hands. "You are welcome to come to me, Mother, but I somehow feel that you will want to return to Britain with Aulus. Go with him if that be your desire, or live with Lucia or Eusebia, but leave, I beg you, this sewer that has become Rome. When I ride through its gates I shall never return. I swear it! I shall never return!"

"Oh, Marcus," Dagian replied brokenly, "I am so sorry. I am so very sorry!"

"Marcus is correct, Mother," Aulus spoke up. "Rome is no longer a decent place to live. Why do you think I chose to settle in Britain? The immorality and corruption here is worse than ever. Each day the rich become stronger, the powerful more powerful. The simple citizen who would normally be honest and hard-working is being ground into the earth, and the idle are being rewarded for their very laziness. This is not the Roman way, yet mention the old ways of diligence, hard work, honesty, manners, and honoring the gods, and the people mock you. Well, the new ways are not my ways, nor are they better ways, and I will not abide by them.

"Aurelian chose to foist his whore off on Marcus because of the very virtues we believe in, Mother. He knew that Marcus would not, like so many of these *new* Romans, desert his family or his obligations."

"*Mother!*" Lucia hurried into the room. "Mother, it is Father!"

"I will come immediately," Dagian replied, and she hurried from the room.

"Is he dying?" Marcus questioned his sister.

"I think so," was the answer.

"Will you and Aulus come now?"

"In a few minutes, Lucia. Where did you put Carissa?"

"In nurse's old room on the second floor in the far back of the house."

"Go now, Lucia. We will come presently."

"What are you going to do, Marcus?" Aulus cocked his head to one side curiously.

"If he is dying then he will want to see us all, and that most certainly includes his new daughter-in-law. I know I can rely on your aid, younger brother."

"You can, older brother," was the smiling assent.

As they went Marcus said, "There will be time for us to talk before I return to Palmyra, Aulus. I intend selling the business here in Rome, but it will be to someone who will broker for us the goods you send from Britain and those I send from the East."

"Agreed, and I think I may know the man we can trust."

They reached Lucius Alexander's room, and when they looked inside Dagian left her husband's side and hurried toward her sons. "It is the end," she said softly. "He will die before dawn."

The two brothers disappeared down the corridor of the upper floor and, stopping before a heavy wooden door at the corridor's end, lifted the heavy bar that lay across it.

"You bastard!" Carissa was across the floor, her nails extended to rake at him.

With a wolfish grimace he caught her wrists and brutally forced her arms down. "Be silent, you bitch, or I swear I will throttle you, emperor's niece or no!"

She glared at him furiously. "You are hurting me," she said.

He ignored her complaint, continuing to hold onto her wrists.

"My father has chosen this moment to die, Carissa, and he wishes his entire family about him. You are going to come with me now, and you are going to behave like a good Roman wife would behave. Modestly, quietly, and reverently."

"No I'm not! I shall tell your father that I carry Aurelian's son, and that my bastard will bear *his* proud patrician name! Let that be his last thought in the mortal world, and let him know he is powerless, even as you are powerless to do anything about it!" Her beauty was suddenly marred by her hatred, which made her look quite common.

Marcus's voice was low, but Aulus could hear that it held a dangerous note. "No, Carissa. You will behave as I have said. Modestly, quietly, and reverently. If you do not I swear to you that I shall throw you from the roof of this house, and tell the world that you committed suicide when I attempted to claim my conjugal rights." He smiled, but his eyes were pitiless. "I almost hope," he said, "that you give me the chance to kill you."

Looking into that hard and ruthless face, Carissa knew that Marcus meant exactly what he said, and she shivered, suddenly afraid. She didn't want to die, nor did she want her unborn child killed. "I will do what you want," she said.

"And remember," Aulus said, "that I, too, shall be by your side."

Carissa brushed her hair into a smooth coil, and affixed it with silver pins. Then she quickly shed her torn tunic and replaced it with a fresh one. They walked down the hallway to Lucius Alexander's death chamber, where Dagian and her daughters clustered about the old man's bed. "Here are your sons and Carissa to see you, my dearest," Dagian said as they reached the bedside.

Lucius Alexander opened his dark eyes, but for a moment he could not focus clearly. Then as the fog cleared from his eyes he struggled to speak. "You have both been sons to be proud of, and I know you will keep the family and its traditions alive in the hearts of your own children. Kneel, my sons," and both men knelt by Lucius's bedside. The old man struggled to raise his hand to Aulus's head. "My blessing, Aulus. May only good fortune smile upon you and your family throughout your lifetime." Aulus felt the sob rising in his throat, but quickly forced it back. "Marcus, my son, my heir, upon you falls the responsibility for this family. Will you honor this responsibility?"

"Yes, Father, I will." Marcus felt his father's bony hand upon his own head.

"I am pleased with you. Pray that tonight you will plant the seed of life within this sweet child's womb."

"It will be as the gods will, Father."

"Carissa, my newest daughter, I know you will be to Marcus as my faithful Dagian has been to me."

"Yes, Father Lucius," came the demure reply. "I promise to follow her example."

"You are a good child," Lucius whispered. "I was right to pursue this match. Marcus will see I was right." The dying man fell back upon his pillows, his breathing a harsh rasp. Soon he slid into a half-conscious state. As the minutes turned to an hour, and then two, and three, Lucius Alexander seemed to shrink before their very eyes. Each breath he drew was a tortured struggle, and it seemed as if his chest would split with the effort. In the loneliest part of the night, those hours just before the dawn, Lucius Alexander opened his eyes a final time, and stared at the woman who sat patiently by his side. "Farewell, my heart," he said distinctly in the voice of his youth, and then he died.

For Dagian it was as if a spear had pierced her heart. One minute he was there, and then as quickly he was gone. As she sat frozen with shock and grief her eldest son reached over and closed his father's eyes. *"Conclamatum est,"* he said as he closed them.

"It is over, Mother," Marcus said quietly, helping her to rise from her place by the bedside. She looked helplessly at him, unable to speak. "Lucia, Eusebia, take our mother to her room to rest, and stay with her. Aulus, return Carissa to her place of confinement."

"You cannot mean to lock me up again?" Carissa protested.

"Do as you are told else I take a stick to you!" he thundered.

Had Lucius Alexander Britainus died but several days later, his eldest son, Marcus, would have been safely on his way back to Palmyra. As it was, the old man's death and the settling of his estate took longer than Marcus had anticipated.

Lucius was buried the same day he died. In the confusion the two young slaves appointed to carry the lifeless body of their master to the atrium mistakenly placed him upon the wedding couch that had been set up for Marcus and Carissa. Marcus laughed at the irony of it. "The marriage was dead before it was even celebrated," he said bitterly.

213

At the hour appointed for the funeral the public crier gave notice according to ancient custom, going about the city and saying, "The citizen, Lucius Alexander Britainus, has been surrendered to death. For those who find it convenient, it is now time to attend the funeral. He is being brought from his house."

Lucius Alexander's funeral was well attended, for he had been a respected man. He was escorted by many to the Alexander family tomb, which stood along the Appian Way on the road to Tivoli. Afterward the family hosted the funeral dinner, and their nine days of sorrow began. The emperor and his wife had come, of course, and Marcus had seen Carissa deep in conversation with her uncle.

"I can only hope," he warned her later, "that you have done nothing foolish."

The nine days passed slowly. Within the house Dagian and her daughters carefully packed up all of Lucius's belongings until very little trace of the man remained except within their minds and hearts. Carissa, no longer confined to her room, spent most of her time lying about, eating outrageous delicacies that she had ordered the kitchen to prepare for her alone, and having her golden hair brushed, did not bother to help.

Marcus and Aulus spent the time preparing their father's trading house for sale. The younger Alexander son knew a man who would be more than delighted to have the business, and would cooperate with the two brothers in marketing their goods from Britain and from Palmyra. Since they could not leave the house or conduct business during this time, however, they could do nothing concrete. Finally the nine days were over, and Julius Rabirius was contacted. As expected, he wanted the Alexander business interests; offered a generous amount for them; and agreed to deal with Aulus Alexander Britainus exclusively in Britain and Marcus Alexander Britainus in Palmyra.

Eusebia and Lucia, assured that their mother would be well taken care of by her sons, returned to their homes. They had both been gone several months, and their own families needed them. Lucia, the sister nearest to Marcus in age, spoke the thoughts that had occurred to both sisters before they departed.

"Will we ever see you or Aulus again in this life, Marcus?"

"I do not know," he replied honestly. "I have given Aulus permission to form his own family, independent of mine. You and Eusebia belong now to your husband's families. Mother has decided to return to Britain with Aulus, and will be a part of his family. Zenobia and I will found our own family in Palmyra. I think it unlikely that we will meet easily again."

Lucia began to weep softly, and Marcus comforted her. "It is not easy for a family to part, dear sister, but it is the way of the world. Nothing ever remains the same. The seasons change; the years change; often too quickly to suit me, but none of us can hold back time any more than we can hold back a sunset or a dawn. One moment we are carefree children, the next we are grown, and as suddenly we are old. There is nothing for it, my sister, but to enjoy that which we have, and not waste time bemoaning what we do not have. Give thanks to the gods that we are all happy and taken care of, my sister. So many are less fortunate than we of the Alexander family."

"You make it all sound so simple," Lucia sniffed.

"That, my dearest sister, is the secret of life. We spend so much time seeking the solution to it; and what it all boils down to in the end is simplicity."

The sisters departed, Lucia north to Ravenna, Eusebia south to Naples. Now it was time for Aulus and Dagian to leave for Britain. "What of your Zenobia?" asked Dagian. "Have you written to her of your marriage, and what you plan to do?"

"If I were to communicate with my beloved the message would certainly be intercepted by the emperor. I have here with me one of the queen's own personal guard who will go before me when I am ready to return to Palmyra. He will take my message then, but I fear to send him before I am ready to leave myself."

"When will you go?" Aulus aked.

"Not until I receive word that you and mother are safe from imperial retribution."

"It will be over two months before we can get word to you, Marcus. Dare you wait that long? You have already been gone three months from Palmyra."

"I do not have a choice, Aulus. Only when my family is safe can I act."

He escorted them to the western gate of the city, but there they were stopped. "I am sorry, Marcus Alexander Britainus," said the centurion in charge of the gate, "your brother is free to return to his home in Britain, but neither you nor your mother may leave the city without the emperor's permission." Realizing the futility in protest, he turned to Aulus. "Go,

215

brother. I will care for our mother, and see that she eventually returns to the land of her birth. Make ready a place for her, Aulus.''

Dagian nodded her agreement. ''Give my love to Eada and the children,'' she said, and then she hugged him tightly. ''I will come soon, I promise you, Aulus. It is not meant for me to die in this foreign land.''

The two brothers embraced. Both had tears in their eyes as a thousand memories assailed them; memories of happier times when they had been one family. ''We will meet again, Marcus,'' Aulus said softly.

''Perhaps,'' was the quiet reply. ''Now, go, youngster! Never forget you are an Alexander! Never allow your children, or their children, to forget it.''

Then Dagian kissed her younger son tenderly. ''I will come as soon as I can.''

''Take my chariot, Aulus. Without Mother it will help you go quicker,'' Marcus said.

Aulus climbed down from the raeda, which was a large, heavy, covered wagon with four wheels, drawn by four horses, used for family travel. One of Dagian's slaves hurried to remove his scant baggage, and store it in Marcus's elegant chariot. Quickly Aulus climbed aboard the chariot, and with a quick smile at both his mother and his older brother he drove off down the Via Flaminia. Dagian's eyes were wet with unshed tears as she watched him go.

They spoke little as the raeda rumbled back through the streets of the city, and out into their suburb. Startled servants hurried to greet the wagon as it entered the grounds of the Alexander house. Marcus helped his mother down and quickly gave orders that her baggage be returned to her rooms, then together they hurried into Marcus's study. Tenderly he settled his distressed mother, pouring her some wine.

''How did Aurelian know that we were leaving?'' Dagian wondered aloud.

''Carissa,'' was Marcus's flat reply. ''The bitch has an uncanny instinct for survival.''

''Then why let any of us go?''

''You, Mother, are the only hostage he needs, and that is why you were forbidden exit from the city. Aurelian knows that as long as I must worry for your safety, the safety of his whore and his bastard are assured.''

''What of your Zenobia?'' Dagian asked.

216

"I do not know," he said helplessly. "How can I send her a letter explaining *this?*"

"What of her personal messenger, my son?"

"The Palmyran was found strangled in his quarters early this morning, Mother. I did not tell you because I did not think you would need to know. I expected that you would be on your way with Aulus, back home to Britain."

"There is more to this, Marcus, than meets the eye," Dagian said thoughtfully.

"I know that, Mother, but what is it? *What is it that Aurelian really wants?*"

"You would do well to ask me that yourself, Marcus," said the emperor, striding into the room. "Good day to you, Lady Dagian."

"How did you gain entrance to my home?" Marcus demanded angrily.

"I was visiting my dear niece, Marcus. Surely you don't object to a fond uncle visiting his favorite niece. She is quite pettish as her pregnancy advances, I find, and suddenly, my dear Marcus, she grows fat. Carissa should not allow herself to grow fat. It coarsens her. I do hope that after she has delivered the child you will insist she regain her divine form."

"I will leave you," Dagian said, rising.

"No," commanded the emperor, waving her back into her chair. "I wish you to hear what I have to say to your son, Lady Dagian. It will save him the trouble of repeating it." He turned back to Marcus. "You wonder aloud at my purpose, Marcus. It is really quite simple. Of course it was necessary that I supply Carissa with a husband, due to her state; but it might have been any of a number of young patrician fops rather than you. I chose you because you were the betrothed of Palmyra's queen. It serves my purpose well.

"You see, Marcus, I know the history of Zenobia's youth. I know how she has hated Rome for the murder of her mother. I know how, as a child, she watched her mother's murderers as they slowly died. I know how after Odenathus's death your love for each other grew, and her hate subsided; but that hate is still there, Marcus. It exists just below the surface, waiting to be rekindled. I intend to rekindle Zenobia's hatred of Rome. Her cooperation does not serve my purposes.

"I do not want Palmyra ruled by a client king. I want it returned to a Roman governorship, as it was in the great days of the empire. I want to return imperial Rome to her glory, and

217

I have already begun with the resubjugation of Gaul. In the East Zenobia has kindly subdued all, and now I will subdue her!"

"She has shown no disloyalty, Caesar. You have no just cause."

"I will have," Aurelian smiled. "When Palmyra's queen hears that her lover, the man she expected to marry, has married another . . ." he chuckled, and then said, "I expect that her fury will know no bounds. She will want to revenge herself on Rome once more, and believe me, Marcus, she will try. When she does I will do what any Roman emperor would do when faced with a threat to the empire. Your fair Zenobia will walk in golden chains behind my victory chariot, Marcus. A year, two at the most if she is as good as they tell me she is in battle, but she will crown my triumph, and settle me firmly upon the throne sooner or later. The empire will be preserved." He paused, looking at the stunned faces of his audience. "It is but an added bonus that she is beautiful. I always enjoy making love to beautiful women, especially if they are intelligent as well."

"If you touch Zenobia . . ." Marcus suddenly had come to life again.

"My dear Marcus, you're a married man with a pregnant wife. For shame, dear boy!" He chuckled indulgently. "Oh, you may have her back when I am through with her . . . if she wants to go to you. Of course, I imagine she will be quite piqued with you. Quite piqued, indeed." He looked to Dagian. "I can trust you to look after my little Carissa, Lady Dagian? A young woman having her first child needs the comfort of an older woman."

"I assumed that was why you forbade me exit from Rome, Caesar. If you had but told me it would have saved me a great deal of packing and unpacking," Dagian said tartly.

"I will allow you to return to Britain when Carissa is safely delivered and Zenobia of Palmyra is properly beaten. You have my word on it, Lady Dagian. Until then you must content yourself to remain with your eldest son."

"As Caesar wills it," Dagian replied acidly.

Aurelian chuckled again, then spoke once more to Marcus.

"I do not think the city is good for Carissa right now. You have two days in which to pack all you need, and then you will depart for an imperial villa in Tivoli. You will be forbidden Rome once you leave. Only when I have the Eastern provinces firmly under imperial control again will you be allowed to return to the city.''

"My business requires I remain in Rome, Caesar. I will give you my word not to leave the city, but you cannot exile me from it.''

"You have sold your father's trading business to Julius Rabirius, Marcus. I know that he has agreed to broker for both you and your brother. You may communicate with him, of course, but be advised that every message you send will be read by me before it goes on its way. I will allow you no chance to warn your queen of my plans for her—and the Eastern Empire.''

"Are we restricted to your villa, Caesar?''

"I think for the time being, Marcus, that it would be wisest.'' He rose from the chair in which he had been sitting and stopped before Dagian, who remained seated in a gesture of disrespect he did not miss. Aurelian smiled brightly and bowed to her. "Good day to you, Lady Dagian. I hope I shall see you soon again. Come, Marcus, walk out with me.''

The two men left the study, and moved into the atrium. "Make no mistake, Marcus,'' the emperor said quietly. "If you attempt to warn Zenobia of my plans, or plot against me, or embarrass my family, I will act swiftly. Do you understand, Marcus?''

"Yes,'' was the terse reply.

"Good,'' Aurelian said. "Now I have a project for you to do. I want a detailed map of Palmyra, and her border fort, Qasr-al-Hêr.''

"The gods curse you, Aurelian!'' Marcus swore angrily. "It is bad enough that you make it appear to Zenobia that I have betrayed her. Must you also see that I do so in fact as well?''

"I wish to take Palmyra with as little bloodshed as possible. A blackened city with a dead populace is of no use to us. Your lovely queen will fight me to the last man if I let her. It is her reputation to do so. If I can prevent this I would prefer it so.''

"Caesar. I cannot betray Palmyra any more than I could betray Rome.''

"I understand,'' the emperor replied, and then with a quick nod he was gone.

With a deep sigh Marcus returned to his study. Dagian was gone, and he was alone. Wearily he sat down, reached for the wine, and poured himself a full goblet, which he quickly drained and as quickly refilled. He stared into the dark red liquid, which mirrored his own face, severe with sleeplessness and worry. He was trapped. If Dagian had been allowed to leave Rome perhaps he might have made a run for it; but, of course, Aurelian had had no intention of allowing it. He drained the second goblet, and felt its warmth beginning to suffuse his body.

The emperor was correct in all he said. When Zenobia learned of his marriage to Carissa, she would, of course, assume another Roman betrayal. If only Longinus could hold her in check . . . But in his heart he knew that Longinus would not be able to do so. Hurt, she would seek to hurt.

Oh, beloved, he thought sadly, Aurelian will eventually crush you, for never have I known such a determined man. But then, you are a determined woman. Perhaps you will prevail over him if the gods will but allow. May they guard you, and protect you now, my beloved, for I cannot.

Marcus sipped at the wine, sinking deeper into depression until suddenly he realized that to give in even in the face of such incredible odds was totally out of character for him. Never in his life had he allowed self-pity to gain the upper hand. Never in all the years that he had yearned for Zenobia, then another man's wife, had he ever given up hope. He would not give it up now! *Not even now!*

Resolutely he stood up, feeling the wine in his head and swaying.

"You're drunk," came the petulant voice from the door.

"And you are fat, Carissa," came the scathing reply. "Your uncle is correct. It coarsens you." He moved to the door, and with surprisingly firm hands pushed her out of his study. "This room is forbidden you, Carissa. If you are to have the run of the house, there must be one place where I may escape the sight and sound of you."

"Once we get to Tivoli things will change," she snarled at him.

"I don't think so, my dear," was the acerbic reply. "I will still be the head of this household whom you must obey."

"I hate you!" she screamed at him.

"No more than I hate you, Carissa!" he laughingly replied "No more than I hate you."

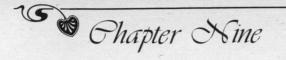

Chapter Nine

Zenobia, Queen of Palmyra, stood looking out upon the Mediterranean sea. She could not get enough of the sight, for she had discovered that it was very much like her desert; a constantly changing pattern of color and movement. It was close to sunset, and the sea was very still at the moment, a smooth and silken surface, wine-colored, reflecting back at her the palace from which she watched it. Above her a flock of pink flamingos whirled, their black underwings in stark contrast to their vividly colored upper bodies. She turned to watch the beautiful birds as they flew over the palace to settle down along the shores of Lake Mareotis, where they nested. All was quiet now, and she stood for some long minutes watching the beacon to the east harbor, the Pharos lighthouse. It was a view seen many times by her ancestress, Cleopatra.

Her gaze moved back to the sea, and she could feel her eyes straining as if by only looking hard enough she might see Rome across the water; see Rome—and her false lover, Marcus Alexander Britainus. There was still pain when she thought of him; but it was not as sharp today as it had been yesterday, nor would it be as sharp tomorrow as it was now. She had always believed she could not live without love, but now she knew that to be untrue. Hate was a magnificent substitute, and she had vowed privately that she would never love a mortal man ever again. Death had taken Odenathus from her, and now an emperor's niece had taken Marcus.

Why? she wondered once more. Why had he married another woman when he had sworn to return to her? She could find no explanation. He had not even written to her.

"Are you all right, Majesty?" Cassius Longinus had come out on the long open portico.

"Yes, Longinus, I am fine," she replied, but he could hear the sadness in her voice.

"There has to be a logical explanation," he burst out, and she turned to look at him with haunted eyes.

"Why do you attempt to find excuses for him, Longinus? You never really approved, I know that. There is no explanation other than the fact that the Roman used me; but I have always learned from my mistakes, and I will never be used by any man again."

He did not argue. But still, Longinus wondered. He believed that he knew the Roman very well, and this sudden marriage to Aurelian's niece and his failure to communicate with Zenobia were totally out of character for Marcus Britainus.

"I intend declaring Vaba Augustus, and myself Queen of the East," she said, and he was quickly jolted from his thoughts.

"You will bring Rome down on you, Majesty."

"Rome is weak," Zenobia said scornfully. "One general after another declares himself emperor, and the path to their empire's throne is littered with the bodies of the assassinated. None can hold power for very long. The barbarian tribes to the west and the north of Italy are constantly encroaching upon the empire's territory. Can Aurelian divert enough soldiers from Europe to make war on me? I do not think so, Longinus. Rome must face the fact that I now control the East, and I will not let it go! This I can do to insure Vaba's future, and that of his sons and grandsons."

"Is it for Vaba you do it, Majesty, or is it to revenge yourself on Marcus Alexander Britainus? Hate is a two-edged sword, Majesty. It can injure those who wield it as well as an enemy."

"You worry too much, Longinus. Did not the augurs at my birth say I should be fortunate at war? And have I not been?"

"The augurs also said you would be fortunate in love, Majesty," was the devastating reply.

"And so I have been!" she argued. "Was my Hawk not the most wonderful of husbands?"

"But he is dead, Majesty, and the man that you truly love with every fiber of your being has appeared to betray you. I do not consider that fortunate." Longinus's logic was a sharp knife cutting away at her confidence.

Zenobia tossed her head angrily and chose to ignore his remark. "I repeat, Longinus, you worry too much."

Longinus bowed his head in acceptance of her will. "Will you make this announcement here in Alexandria, Majesty?"

"Yes," was the reply. "By the time my announcement arrives to ruin Aurelian's digestion, I shall be back in Palmyra." She laughed. "This could very well topple the latest of Rome's military rulers, and who shall be next, and for how long?"

He wondered about her overconfidence, and he worried, yet all had gone well so far. The armies of Palmyra had passed easily and quickly through Syria and Palestine and across the Egyptian desert. They had crossed the Nile River Delta, attracting only curious glances from the peasants, and entered into Alexandria with no resistance. There, Zenobia's uncles Paulus and Argus Simon had been busy spreading her doctrine of an Eastern Empire free of foreigners; free of Rome.

Alexandria, never treated well by the Romans, had responded to that message by welcoming Palmyra's queen, and taking her as their own. After all, was she not the child of a daughter of this city? Was she not a descendant of the last great Ptolemaic queen, Cleopatra? By the gods, they would once again rise to the greatness that had been theirs before the Romans. The Romans! Since the days of Julius Caesar they had been bad luck for Alexandria.

The Ptolemaic pharaohs and their queens had made Alexandria the academic center of the ancient world. The great Alexandrian library and museum were world-famous. So were the many schools of rhetoric, medicine, mathematics, philosophy, art, literature, and poetry. In the beginning of Roman rule nothing had changed; but then it became intolerable and various segments of the population began to chafe. A revolt by the large Jewish population resulted in their annihilation and the destruction of the Jewish quarter, fully a third of the city. And with the Jews went Alexandria's commercial prosperity.

It was now merely a beautiful ancient city whose schools and great library attracted scholars. There was a certain amount of commerce, but nothing to compare with its days of glory. The Alexandrians had little love for the Romans, whom they rightly blamed for their plight. The chance to strike back at them was irresistible, and Queen Zenobia of Palmyra appeared the very person for them to follow.

The pronouncement of King Vaballathus and his mother, Zenobia, was made from the main portico of Alexandria's royal palace. Zenobia had sworn never again to wear Roman garments, and had taken to the opulent clothes that were a mixture of Egyptian, Persian, and Parthian.

Her dress that day was called a kalasiris, a long, sleeveless garment with a simple, round neck that was totally accordion-pleated to the ankle-length hem. Its color was a pale Nile green, and the linen of the garment was so sheer that Zenobia's flawless body could be seen through it. Her firm and full breasts thrust the fabric boldly out beneath the great jeweled collar of gold inlaid with emerald, lapis lazuli, turquoise, and amber. Upon her arms were beautifully carved gold armbands which were easily visible despite the floor-length cape that she wore. The cape was an incredible piece of workmanship, the lining cloth-of-gold, the exterior of male peacock feathers. It was fastened to her shoulders by means of hidden gold clasps attached to her collar. Upon her feet were simple gold sandals; her long black hair was entwined with lotus blossoms, and the beautiful gold fillet she wore was decorated in front by Egypt's royal asp.

In contrast to his mother's barbaric beauty, young Vaba was dressed quite simply. He wore the flowing white robes of his Bedawi heritage, but the hood of the garment was pushed back to reveal his strong, handsome face, the dark head topped with a magnificent gold crown. Standing next to his mother on the top steps of the portico, he listened with impassive face as Cassius Longinus, several steps down from them and dressed in an impresive white tunic, intoned in a loud, clear voice to the great mass of humanity who had crowded into the square before the palace.

"Behold, Egypt! Behold Zenobia, Queen of the East, and her son, Vaballathus, Augustus of the Eastern Empire!"

Three times the queen's favorite councillor called out, each time followed by a great trumpet fanfare. The crowds cheered and shouted their approval of Zenobia and her son. Longinus looked up at the queen, and said so just she might hear, "Rome will not fail to notice this demonstration, Majesty."

"Then let them be warned, Longinus," was the icy reply.

Aurelian was indeed warned, and in far less time than Zenobia had anticipated. On the very day that Zenobia had proclaimed herself Queen of the East, and her son Augustus of the Eastern Empire, a Roman spy in Alexandria let loose a pigeon. The pigeon, a small capsule attached to his leg, flew to the city of Cyrene, where his message was transferred to the leg of another bird, who flew to Lepcis Magna; then to another who flew to Carthage; and yet another who traversed the length of Sicily. The last bird left Sicily, rested overnight at a cote in Naples, and within a week the message from Alexandria had arrived in Rome.

Eagerly the emperor removed the message from the capsule carried by the last bird; and a slow, satisfied smile spread over his face as he read it.

"It is good news, Caesar?"

"Yes, Gaius Cicero, it is very good news. Praise the gods for creating women to be predictable. The Queen of Palmyra has done exactly what I expected her to do, and now we may march against her."

"Zenobia of Palmyra, sir? But I thought she was our ally?" Gaius Cicero looked puzzled. "Has she not kept the peace for us in the eastern provinces since her husband died? Why are we to march against her?"

"Because, my dear Gaius, the Queen of Palmyra has just seven days ago had the temerity to declare herself Queen of the East, and her son Augustus of the Eastern Empire."

Gaius Cicero sought out his old friend, Marcus Alexander, at his new home in Tivoli. "The Queen of Palmyra has revolted against Rome, and the legions will soon march," he announced. "Will Rome prevail, Marcus?"

"Rome must prevail, Gaius, although I now question my own loyalty to a rotting empire."

Gaius Cicero shook his head. "It will take more than a war with Palmyra to turn Rome from the path of decay."

"Will you be going with the emperor?"

"Of course!"

"Then you will have an opportunity that I have not had, Gaius. The Queen of Palmyra was to have been my wife. Tell her that I yet love her, that my marriage is but a sham. I was not able to communicate with Zenobia after my return. Do this for me, Gaius, for the sake of our long friendship, I beg you!"

Gaius Cicero saw the pain that lurked within his friend's eyes. He knew the cost to Marcus's pride to have to ask even as old a friend as he to relay such a personal message. "I will gladly take your message, Marcus," he said. He was very surprised by his old friend's revelation, and for the briefest of moments Gaius Cicero had doubts about the emperor's conduct in this matter. Then he thought of the good Aurelian had accomplished in his short tenure as emperor. What were the problems of two lovers in light of such greatness?

Aurelian marched east, his troops departing from Brindisi, then ferrying across the Adriatic to Apollonia in Macedonia. From there they marched into Thrace, crossing the water once again to Dardanus in Asia Minor. The emperor moved at a steady pace, stopping to reassert imperial authority in major towns, allowing the local officials to tell him that they could not be blamed for assuming that Zenobia, like her late husband, Odenathus, spoke for imperial Rome. Aurelian agreed, nodding wisely, laughing silently to himself at their quick defection from Palmyra's queen, and levying token fines to impress upon them Rome's authority.

Before the walls of Antioch Aurelian met in battle with Zenobia's general, Zabdas. No one was more surprised than the Palmyrans, for they had not expected the Romans for some time, and yet suddenly here they were. The force commanded by General Zabdas was small, the bulk of the army being with the queen in Alexandria. Though they fought well, and bravely against the legions, they were overcome. Zabdas fell back to Emesa, leaving Antioch to the Romans. But securing the city, they quickly followed him and defeated him a second time at Emesa. His small force virtually wiped out, Zabdas fell on his sword, ending his life, but satisfying honor.

Aurelian might then have crossed the hundred miles between Emesa and Palmyra, securing Palmyra in its king and queen's absence and taking its regent, Prince Demetrius, prisoner. That he did not he was to regret. So far he had not lost many men to battle, disease, or fatigue, and he was feeling invincible. Swiftly he moved his army down through Palestine, avoiding as many towns and villages as he could, for surprise was to be his greatest weapon. In Emesa and Antioch his authorities made very sure that no messenger escaped the city to warn Palmyra's queen. They would meet in Alexandria!

The emperor, however, was doomed to disappointment for in a quirk of fate the armies of Rome and those of Palmyra passed within a few miles of each other in the Egyptian desert of Gaza, and neither saw the other. Zenobia, having made her position clear in Alexandria, was hurrying home to await Rome's answer. Aurelian arrived in Egypt's premier city to find his quarry gone, and what was worse, the Alexandrians were not one bit repentant of their support of Palmyra's queen. In retaliation Aurelian set fire to their famous library. By the time the fire was contained, many of its valuable books had been destroyed.

When Zenobia reached her beloved city she found surprising news waiting for her. The enemy was almost at her gates. On the battlefield at Emesa one Palmyran had pretended to be among the casualties, then waited until dark before making good his escape. He had had no supplies or water to aid him; but he was of Bedawi parentage, and tough. It had taken him five days to reach the Qasr-al-Hêr fortress, where he told his story before collapsing. Rufus Curius had immediately sent word to Palmyra.

"But how could Aurelian have heard so quickly?" Zenobia was puzzled.

"The Romans have been known to use pigeons to carry messages," Longinus said. "The message was most likely sent from Alexandria, Majesty."

"And Aurelian has come himself?" she mused. "He will find that Palmyra's legions are not so easily beaten. General Zabdas's defeat will have made the Romans overconfident."

"You don't propose to meet them in open battle, Majesty?"

"No. We will withdraw within Palmyra, and then wait. I am curious to see how long the Romans can survive in our desert, Longinus. Send a message to Rufus Curius. I want all civilians withdrawn from Qasr-al-Hêr immediately, and only a token force left at the fortress. Those who remain are to poison the wells and build upon the highest tower the makings of a bonfire. At the first sign of Aurelian they are to light the fire as a beacon to Palmyra and then retreat. It is easy to fight in the forests of Gaul, where the dew drips from the very branches of the trees, but here in the desert how long will Rome's legions last without water? With luck we will not lose one Palmyran to Aurelian's armies."

The order was sent, and soon the people who had made the Qasr-al-Hêr fortress their home began arriving, crowding the desert road from the west with their carts and livestock. Most had relatives within the city that they might stay with. For those who did not, the queen offered shelter within properties owned by the royal family.

Word was sent along the desert road to the east that Palmyra would soon be under siege, and should be bypassed by those who did not seek to have their goods confiscated by the Romans. Zenobia felt she owed this courtesy to those merchants in Cathay and India who regularly did business with the city.

Confident of their triumph, the people of Palmyra went about their business, the city taking on a festive air for the wedding of the young king and Flavia Porcius. After the festivities, Zenobia and Longinus sat together getting companionably drunk on Cyprian wine. "Marcus has betrayed me," the queen mourned. "Why did he betray me, Longinus? Am I not beautiful? Intelligent? Rich?" A tear slid down her cheek. "What does Aurelian's niece have that I do not have?" Then she giggled. "I shall ask him when I capture him, Longinus! That's what I shall do! I will say to him, Aurelian, what does your niece have that lured Marcus Alexander from my side? Am I not clever, Longinus?" She was happily drunk.

Her answer was a soft snore, for Cassius Longinus had fallen asleep in his chair. His goblet tipped from his hand, drizzling sweet red wine across the marble floor. Zenobia watched the blood-colored trickle of liquid, as it ran slowly across the white floor. She sighed again and, standing uncertainly, she reached for the decanter, picked it up, and wandered slowly down the corridor that led to her private apartments.

She awoke late the next morning, and her head immediately regretted her actions of the previous night. The bright sunlight streamed in across her bedchamber, causing her to wince with genuine pain. Warned by her aching head and roiling stomach, she did not dare to rise else she be sick. She lay very still, finding that the closest thing to comfort.

Old Bab hurried in, her sandals slapping against the floor in a most aggravating manner. "So, you are finally awake."

"Do not shout," Zenobia whispered. "My head pounds."

"I am not surprised. But there is something you must know. The beacon from Qasr-al-Hêr has just a few minutes ago been spotted burning. The Romans are coming."

"The gods!" Zenobia swore irritably. "Today of all days!"

"Aye, they were ever a thoughtless bunch," Bab observed wryly. "Come, I will mix you a potion that will take the ache from your head and the sickness from your belly." Bab bustled out, and Zenobia could hear her giving orders to the slave girls in the outer room. In a few minutes she was back again, carrying a small goblet, which she handed to Zenobia. "Drink it," she commanded in a voice that brooked no nonsense, and the queen obeyed.

Within minutes the symptoms that had made her so uncomfortable were magically gone. "What was in *that?*" she demanded of Bab.

"It is a mixture of honey, fruit juices, and herbs," was the reply. "Let me help you up now, my baby, and it is off to the baths for you."

An hour later Zenobia stood atop the highest tower of Palmyra gazing west toward the Qasr-al-Hêr fortress, where the sentinel beacon blazed brightly even in the midafternoon sun. On the westward road she could see in the distance faint puffs of dust made by the hooves of the approaching camels who carried

Rufus Curius and his small patrol to safety in Palmyra. She stayed watching until she could make out the riders quite plainly, and then she descended the tower and, mounting her chariot, drove through the city amid her cheering people to greet the riders.

They thundered through the gates, which quickly closed behind them, coming to a quick halt before the queen's chariot. The camels knelt, and their riders swiftly dismounted and stood making their obeisance before Zenobia.

"It has been done as you commanded, Majesty," Rufus Curius said.

"The Romans?" she asked.

"At least two legions, Majesty. Possibly three."

Zenobia turned to Cassius Longinus. "Have them sound the alarm, Longinus, so those outside the walls may enter before it is too late."

"What of the Bedawi, Majesty?" he asked.

"They have disappeared into the desert," she said with a small smile.

"The better to watch for us," he murmured with an answering smile, and left to do her bidding.

Zenobia returned her attention to Rufus Curius. "You have done well, old friend, and I thank you for your loyalty, you and your men. Go now and spend the evening with Deliciae and your children. I do not expect the Romans before our gates until tomorrow, when they will attempt to frighten us with a show of force."

He saluted her, and Zenobia, remounting her chariot, drove quickly back to the palace. Throughout the city the echo of the warning trumpets sounded again and again as latecomers and stragglers from the unwalled suburbs hurried to safety within the gates. Arriving at her destination, the queen hurried to the council chamber for a prearranged meeting with the Council of Ten. She found them and both her sons waiting.

Questions were fired at her with great rapidity, and impatiently she held up her hands demanding that they stop so she might speak. "We do not expect the Romans before dawn," she said, "and then they will do one of two things. Morning will possibly show Aurelian in full battle force before our gates. Often the legions sneak up upon a city in the night so that the dawn reveals their battle formation. It can be a formidable sight.

"The other possibility is that dawn will reveal an empty

desert. Suddenly in the distance will come the faint sound of the war drums, which will grow louder and closer as each minute passes. As suddenly, the Romans marching in perfect ranks will begin to pour over the horizon until they are lined up before our gates. Both of these ploys are used to frighten a civilian population, and so our people must be told in order that they not be afraid. Terror is the prime weapon used by the Romans.

"Marius Gracchus, have foodstuffs been laid in as I commanded?"

"We have several months' supply of grain, oil, olives, figs, and dates in government storehouses, Majesty. We have spent the last few weeks buying livestock, which will be slaughtered as needed and distributed when necessary. Practically every family in the city has some sort of poultry in its keeping. Palmyra is well prepared to withstand a siege of several months."

Zenobia nodded. "The Romans will not last that long, Marius Gracchus." She then looked to her younger son, Demetrius. "You have seen to the wells in the suburbs?"

"My men and I personally visited each house, Majesty, and impressed upon the owners the importance of destroying the water supply so that the Romans could not have it," he said. At seventeen, Demetrius was an extremely handsome young man, far better-looking than his older brother, who favored their father. Demetrius was his mother's son, with her dark hair, a pair of languid gray eyes, and a most sensuous mouth. Like his mother, he was impetuous and passionate; but Zenobia suspected that, like his father, Demetrius would not marry until he was considerably older. There were too many delicious treats the prince wanted to taste before settling down.

She inclined her head in response to his reply, and then she turned to Vaba. "Is there anything you wish to add, my son?"

The young king shook his head in the negative. "You seem to have thought of everything, mother," he said quietly.

Zenobia threw him a sharp glance, and then turned back to the entire council. "Does anyone else have anything further to say?" she asked, and the reply being in the negative she dismissed them. "Stay, Vaba," and he heard the command in her voice. When the room was at last empty she turned on him furiously. "Do not ever fence words with me again in open council!" she said. "Why do you choose this time to quarrel with me?"

"You behave as if Palmyra has no king, Mother. Everyone

230

defers to you. The council, the people, even the damned Romans! I am consulted on nothing.''

"Vaba, Vaba," she chided him. "The very life of this city is at stake. Tomorrow morning the Romans will arrive. They seek to destroy us. Do you really believe you are experienced enough to plan the defense of Palmyra? I am sorry that in all the tumult you have not been properly deferred to, but there is no time. I did not expect the Romans for another three months, and suddenly they are on my doorstep.''

"In other words, Mother, they have already outmaneuvered you," he said quietly.

"Yes, Vaba, they have. I am not ashamed to admit it. I am human as are they, and I learn from my errors.''

"If going to war against the Romans is an error, Mother, then all of Palmyra shall learn,'' he answered her.

"Rome has no business here in the East. Your father believed it, and I believe it.''

"This war would not have happened if Marcus had returned to you," he accused. "I wish to the gods that he had, for then you would have married him and I might have ruled in my own right!''

"You ungrateful little whelp!'' she hissed at him. "You rule this city?! What a joke, Vaba, my son! What a fine joke! When your father was murdered *I* secured the city for you. For six years *I* have ruled it for you, and what have you learned from me, my son? You have learned nothing! All you know of kingship is the bowing and scraping of your courtiers!

"The Romans are not to be trusted. Your grandfather was loyal to Rome, and what was the result? His wife, my own sweet mother, raped and murdered by Romans! I loved Marcus Alexander more than I ever loved any man. Aye, I even loved him more than your father; but he betrayed me to marry an emperor's niece. I do not deny that I am bitter, but I have not gone to war with Rome out of that rejection. For many years your father and I planned to consolidate the Eastern Empire, and rule it ourselves. Now I have done just that. I have but one piece of unfinished business, and that is to defeat Rome once and for all. I shall do it, Vaba! On your father's memory I swear I shall do it! When I have, and there is once more stability in the region, you may rule alone and to your heart's content. I will have given you time to learn this business of kingship the way I have always given you time, Vaba. Do not be impatient with me, or with yourself. You will be a good king one day.''

"You loved Marcus more than my father?" His face was a mask of shock, disbelief, and hurt.

She sighed, and wondered if he had heard anything else that she had said to him other than that. "Your father was the only man I knew until his death. Odenathus was chosen to be my husband. He was a good man. I loved him, for he was good to me, and he loved me in return; but with Marcus it was different.''

"I don't know if I will ever understand you," he said softly, rising from the council table and walking to the door. At the entry he turned. "Good night, Mother," and then he was gone.

She sat for a few minutes longer, but she would not allow herself to think. She needed to free her mind.

"Mama?"

Startled, Zenobia looked up and saw her small daughter standing in the doorway to the council chamber. Her heart contracted at the sight, for the little girl was so like her father. Tall for her age of five and a half, Mavia was slender with a heart-shaped face, Marcus's startling blue eyes, and long chestnut curls. Her skin was lighter than Zenobia's, but still it held a golden tone.

"What is it, Mavia?" she answered the child. "Should you not be in your bed?"

"Mama, is it true the Romans eat little children?"

Zenobia felt anger well up within her. Who had been frightening the child? "No, Mavia, Romans do not eat children. Who has told you such silliness?"

"Titus says that the Romans eat little children." The little girl nervously twisted the side of her blue gown.

"Deliciae's son, Titus?"

"Yes." Mavia's eyes were very large and fearful.

"Come here to me, Mavia," her mother commanded, and the child ran across the floor on small, bare feet to climb into her lap. Zenobia cuddled her close against her ample breasts, and felt the little girl trembling. "Titus is a silly little boy, Mavia. Boys his age like to tease younger children, and you have made him very happy by being afraid. If he should attempt to frighten you again with such nonsense then tell him that the Romans particularly love to munch on nine-year-old boys.''

Mavia giggled. "I love you, Mama," she said.

"And I love you, my darling. I love you best of all!" Zenobia rose up, her daughter still in her arms. "I am going to take you to your bed, my chick.'' She left the council room and carried her daughter through the palace corridors back to the child's own rooms. ''You must not be afraid, Mavia,'' she said as she walked. ''The sound of battle is noisy, and can sometimes be frightening; but the Romans cannot enter Palmyra, and they will not hurt you, I promise.''

Mavia nodded, and whispered, ''Yes, Mama.''

Reaching Mavia's rooms, the queen handed her now sleepy child over to her nurse. Kissing Mavia's cheek, she said to the nurse, ''You will remain in the palace until further notice, Charmian. Mavia is only to be allowed to play in the inner gardens.''

''Yes, Majesty,'' the slave woman murmured.

Zenobia hurried to her own apartments, where Bab was waiting. ''I have dismissed your butterflies,'' the old woman announced.

''How well you know me, old friend,'' Zenobia said. ''I do want to be alone this night.''

''What can I bring you to eat, my baby?''

''Anything simple, and something to drink.''

''Wine?'' the old woman inquired mischievously.

''Never again!'' Zenobia said fervently. ''Fruit juice will be quite nice, thank you, Bab.''

Bab exited to return a few minutes later with a heavily laden tray, which she placed on a low ebony table. ''The gods grant you sweet repose and a clear mind, my baby,'' she said as she left the room.

The queen shrugged out of her kalasiris and crossed the room out into her private garden. There, a pool warmed by the late-afternoon sun beckoned invitingly. Diving in, she swam for some minutes until her body grew tired and began to relax. Climbing out, and taking a large linen towel she began to dry herself off. As she did so, Zenobia carefully scrutinized her body and did not find it wanting. Her large breasts were as firm as when she had been a girl, her belly flat despite three children, her bottom rounded and not overly large. There was nothing that should be displeasing to a man. Why then had he left her?

''The gods!'' she swore aloud. How deeply he had hurt her. He had probably returned to his own world, and seeing about him all those proper Roman wives had finally desired one of his own. He had been ready to marry and, unable to publicly claim Mavia, had longed for children of his own.

Sitting by the pool, she wondered once more why he had not written to her, and then she laughed ruefully. How could he possibly have explained his actions to her on dry parchment after all that had passed between them? Still, to find out in the manner in which she had was cruel, and she would not have thought him a cruel man.

Dear Longinus. It was he who had first learned of Marcus's betrayal in a letter from his former pupil, Porphyry, who now studied in Rome with Plotinus. Longinus did not wait for the gossip to reach her, but quickly joined her in Alexandria, leaving Prince Demetrius in the capable hands of Marius Gracchus. Longinus, her dear and good friend, her loyal councillor, had known how devastated she would be. Longinus, who had held her in his arms while she cried away the first hurt. What would she ever do without Longinus? She would never have to wonder, Zenobia realized, for Longinus was the one man other than her father and her brothers upon whom she might rely.

The afternoon became desert twilight, and then, quickly, night. The dark skies sparkled with thousands of bright stars, casting their lights upon Palmyra as they had for all the centuries since time began. She loved them for their beauty, and she loved them because they were constant and never-changing. Should not a relationship between lovers be a constant thing, or was she simply idealizing love?

Standing up, she flung the towel aside and walked back into her chamber where she put on a simple, long, natural-colored soft cotton gown. She then began to examine the tray that Bab had left her. Upon it were very thin slices of chicken breast and baby lamb alternating with equally thin slices of pomegranate. A woven round basket, a hot stone within its bottom, held small, flat loaves of bread. There was a salad of lettuce and tiny fresh peas that had been dressed in olive oil and herbed vinegar; and a footed silver bowl that held a small bunch of plump, green grapes and half a dozen fat apricots. A matching tall silver pitcher was filled with cool juice. Zenobia's appetite had never been a poor one, and she fell upon the meal, devouring it thoroughly.

Afterward she bathed her hands in rose water, and went again out into her private garden, where she once more began to think. The moonless night was unnaturally quiet, and she wondered if the Romans were already before her gates, or if they would choose to come by daylight. She somehow thought the latter, and knew that she would not have long to wait. It was a strangely comforting thought. She would be glad to begin this confrontation—the sooner to get it over with. The queen retired to her empty bed to sleep a dreamless sleep. For one night she was not haunted by his face with its deep blue eyes; nor the sound of his voice promising to return to her.

In the hour just before the dawn old Bab gently shook her mistress awake and offered a goblet of sweet pomegranate juice. Zenobia lay quietly, allowing her spirit to return to her body after its long night of roaming within the shadow realm. Finally she asked, "Are they here yet?"

"Not a sign, my baby."

She sipped at her juice. "Is the city calm?"

"For the most part," the old woman answered. "The people are like a virgin going to her wedding couch, a little frightened, but sure that all will be well."

"It is natural," the queen said. She put the empty goblet down. "Today I must dress like the queen I am, Bab. It will hearten the people, and the Romans will expect it. I will be on the walls awaiting them, and afterward I shall roam the city to assure my people."

Bab nodded. "I expected you would wear your finest feathers, my baby. All is in readiness for you this very minute. I have personally chosen your wardrobe. You have only to pick your jewels."

"Show me."

Bab clapped her hands, and instantly a slave girl appeared carefully holding out for Zenobia's approval a kalasiris made of a cobweb-sheer linen cloth that had been interwoven with very thin strands of finely beaten gold. The sleeveless gown had been skillfully constructed in narrow pleats from its round, high neck to the ankle-length hem. Zenobia nodded her approval, and after bathing her face and hands in a basin held by a slave girl she rose from her bed, holding out her arms. Swiftly Bab removed her simple sleeping gown, and taking the kalasiris from the slave dropped it over the queen's head.

Zenobia walked across her bedchamber to stand before the enormous full-length polished silver mirror. "Adria," she commanded the slave, "bring my jewel caskets." The girl scurried off, and the queen said to Bab, "Your choice is a perfect one, old woman." Bab smiled broadly. Adria returned balancing several jewel caskets in her arms. "Fetch me the soft gold leather belt for this," Zenobia asked Bab as she began opening the jewel boxes. Carefully she studied the contents of each box, removing the upper trays in order to see what lay beneath. Swiftly she closed several lids down, and said to Adria, "Remove these boxes. I do not choose to wear silver today."

"Here is the belt you desire," Bab said, carefully fastening it about Zenobia's slender waist. The wide belt was made of soft kidskin overlaid with twelve layers of gold leaf over which were sewn tiny beads of fine gold and pale-pink rock quartz. The front of the belt rose up to a narrow peak that ended just below her breasts.

The queen now began to choose her jewelry. From one jewel box came two wide gold armbands with raised designs which Bab fastened about each of Zenobia's upper arms. Around her wrists the queen slipped on several gold bangles, some plain, some with blue Persian lapis, some with rose quartz. Into her earlobes she fastened enormous diamonds, pale pink in color, which had come to her from mines located far to the south. They dangled, sparkling, from their thin gold wires.

"Rings?" Bab asked.

"No," was the reply. "They will not be close enough to see them." She thought a moment as Bab made to close the ring casket. "Wait! Perhaps just a ruby on this hand, and the matching pink diamond on the other. If I use my hands to punctuate a point, they will sparkle and add effect."

"Necklaces?" Bab inquired.

"No, but I think one of those marvelous jeweled collars. Adria?"

"Majesty?"

"Do we not have a gold collar inlaid with rubies, and rose quartz, and small diamonds?"

"Yes, Majesty. Shall I fetch it?"

Zenobia nodded, and Adria quickly complied, returning to fasten the exquisite collar about the queen's neck. It lay flat upon her chest, the alternating jewels just above her full breasts. Zenobia smiled with satisfaction. "Brush my hair out, Bab, and then let us place upon my head that elegant small circlet of beaten gold vine leaves that has the long gold ribbons sewn with brilliants."

Bab nodded vigorously, and instructed Adria where the circlet might be found. When Zenobia's long black hair had been brushed silken smooth, Bab placed the wreath of golden vine leaves atop her mistress's head, and carefully arranged the ribbons out behind her. Then she stepped back, and nodded again. "It is perfect, my baby. You are a queen!"

"Come now, old woman, I must hurry. I would be on the walls to greet our visitors."

Giving her old nurse a quick hug, Zenobia hurried from her apartments and through the palace to its main courtyard, where her magnificent gold chariot with its four coal-black horses waited. She could see Vaba and Flavia coming down the path from the tiny palace within the larger palace gardens. She had given them the house that Odenathus had given her as a wedding gift those long years ago. Since his death she had been unable to live in it again, and she believed that the newly married couple would enjoy their privacy as she and Hawk had enjoyed theirs. Flavia, of course, had accepted the gift in the spirit in which Zenobia had intended it; but Vaba had sarcastically asked if she was attempting to keep him from *his* palace. Only sweet Flavia's quick intervention had saved the bridegroom from his furious mother.

"Good morning, Aunt Zenobia," Flavia said, going to the queen and giving her a loving kiss on the cheek.

Zenobia couldn't help but smile. Her new daughter-in-law, the child of her two friends, Antonius Porcius and his Julia, was a dear girl, and she had to admit, the perfect wife for Vaba. "Good morning, my dearest," she answered Flavia. "Good morning, Vaba."

"Good morning, Mother. Have the Romans been sighted yet?"

"If they have I have not been told, Vaba. Come, my son. Let us hurry to the walls, and be prepared to greet our guests, unwelcome though they may be. Flavia, would you come with us?"

"May I?"

"Of course, child. You are Palmyra's queen."

"Oh, no, Aunt Zenobia! You are Palmyra's queen. I am only Vaba's wife, and it is all I seek to be."

Zenobia threw her son an arch look, and then put a loving arm about Flavia. "We are both Palmyra's queens."

"Let us go if we are going," Vaba said impatiently.

"Very well," his mother replied, climbing without any help up into her chariot. "I will drive, Vaba. Your hand is too heavy on my horses' mouths. Besides, I think Flavia would enjoy being held by her husband rather than clinging to the handhold for dear life."

For once Vaba did not disagree with his mother, and Flavia colored becomingly. Zenobia smiled to herself, remembering how it had been to ride with Odenathus's arm tight about her. She looked over at the pair as she started the horses off, and thought how pretty Flavia was. She was a small girl, her delicate build belying her great strength of character. Her eyes were a clear amber in color, her hair a lovely golden brown, her skin tones peachlike. All of her features—a round face with well-spaced eyes, a turned-up nose, and a coral-colored, generous mouth—had combined to form a most pleasing appearance. Her neck was slender and graceful, and she had a way of holding her head that gave her a presence usually associated with taller people. She was intelligent, and had a kind heart, both of which Zenobia thanked the gods for, because had Vaba chosen simply a pretty but vapid girl, the results would have been disastrous.

As it was still early the broad streets of Palmyra were empty, and it was but comfortably mild in temperature. A light wind teased at both Zenobia's gold kalasiris and Flavia's pale-blue tunic dress. As they reached the walls of the city the activity increased, the military in control of the streets leading to the walls. The populace cheered Zenobia and her family as the chariot thundered by them, and a faint proud smile touched the queen's lips.

Reaching the walls of the city, Zenobia brought her vehicle to a halt, and leapt out without waiting for Vaba and Flavia. Striding to the narrow steps built into the thick walls, she began climbing. At the top she was greeted by a captain in her personal guard, and her younger son, Prince Demetrius. "Good morning, Demi, Captain Tigranes," she said. "Any sign?"

"Not yet, Mother."

"Longinus is here?"

"Over there, Mother."

The king had reached the ramparts with his young wife. Zenobia moved down the ramparts to stand with Longinus.

"Here I am again rousing you early in the morning," the queen teased her chief councillor.

"One of the hazards of being in your employ, Majesty," he chuckled.

Together they stood looking out across the desert that surrounded the oasis city of Palmyra. The wind had blown the sands into small wavelike ripples so that the city appeared to be an island amid a vast golden sea. Behind them the sky flung out dawn streamers of scarlet and coral, mauve and pink, burnished copper and narrow bands of dark purple edged in palest green. To the west it was yet dark with one lone and cold star gleaming ominously down upon all. There was no wind. All was very still. Looking about her, Zenobia saw that the ramparts along the walls were now crowded not only with soldiers, but with Palmyra's citizens, who had come to see the arrival of their unwelcome guests.

The sun began to spill over the horizon, and suddenly very faintly from the distance came the sound of drums and marching feet. Zenobia turned to Longinus and her sons. "Did I not tell you?" she said. "They are exactly on time—sunrise—with their booming drums and stamping feet, all calculated to put abject fear into the hearts of the citizenry."

"You cannot blame them for lack of originality," Longinus said wryly. "This has always worked for them, and the Romans are not a people easily persuaded to try something new."

All along the walls the citizens chattered busily, not at all impressed by the distant noise, for had they not been told that this was how it would be? Now they watched curiously to catch the first glimpse of the enemy. It was like some vast show presented in the arena.

The queen strained her eyes. Upon the horizon she could see the sun reflecting off a veritable sea of spear tips. Fascinated, she was unable to tear her eyes away as the spear tips became soldiers, marching soldiers, soldiers dragging great war machines and battering rams across the shifting sands of the western road, thousands of infantry urged on by officers mounted upon a variety of prancing horses.

"How many legions do you think there are?" Longinus asked.

"I cannot tell yet," was the reply.

Closer and closer the Romans came to the city walls, until at last they stopped, and Zenobia breathed softly, "I count four full legions, Longinus. Aurelian wants us very badly, but he shall not have my city." Boldly she stared down upon the army amassed below, and suddenly the ranks opened to allow a war chariot through. In the chariot was a driver and one man. The vehicle stopped before the walls, and in the great silence that followed the man in the chariot began to speak.

"People of Palmyra, I am Aurelian, Emperor of the Romans."

"I believe the archers can get him from this distance, Mother," said Demetrius.

"No," Zenobia said. "Let him speak. I wish to hear what he has to say."

"I come in peace. I have no quarrel with the people of Palmyra. It is the woman who calls herself your queen who has rebelled against the empire. Give her over to me, accept my governor, and we will live in peace as we always have."

From the ramparts of Palmyra came shouts of outrage, and almost at once the spectators began hurling the remains of their morning meal at the Romans. The emperor's chariot was forced to move backward. The queen nodded to her trumpeter, and a clarion call rang in the still air, silencing everyone. Zenobia stepped up on the walls so that she might be visible to the Roman army and its emperor. Behind her the sun blazed, and with the blue sky above her as a background, her golden garments and jewelry sparkled and gleamed impressively. Below, the Roman soldiers murmured superstitiously at the sudden appearance of this golden woman. There were murmurs of "The goddess Athena!" "Venus!" "No, fools, 'tis Juno herself!"

"I am Zenobia of Palmyra, Queen of the East. Aurelian of the Romans, you are unwelcome here. Go while you still have the opportunity, else the desert become your final stop on the road to Hades."

"Woman! You have rebelled against Rome! Give yourself over to me for judgment, and I will spare your city."

The answer to Aurelian's impertinence was a spear that sang swiftly through the air to bury itself in the ground before his chariot. Startled, the horses reared, but were quickly brought under firm control by their driver. No one, even the queen, had seen who threw the spear, but its message was far more eloquent than words.

"You have the answer, Aurelian of the Romans. My people have spoken, and as always I am an obedient servant of my people."

A small smile played upon his lips, and he nodded almost companionably at her. "As am I, Zenobia of Palmyra," he said.

"Then it is war between us," she answered.

"It is war," was the reply.

"We have the advantage, Roman, safe here behind our walls. We are prepared to hold out for months. Are you?"

"We are."

"Without water, Aurelian? You have no water. I would have no innocent lives on my conscience, so I give you fair warning

240

that the wells serving the suburbs surrounding this city have been poisoned.''

"Can you be sure, Zenobia?" was the mocking reply. "Do you really think that those who expect to return shortly to their homes have poisoned their own wells? What would they use for water then upon their return?"

"Unlike Romans, Palmyrans are loyal, Aurelian, and they follow orders."

"Palmyrans are people like any other, Zenobia. Perhaps most of your people have obeyed, but there will be some who have not, and we need only one well to survive."

"Do you really think you can water four legions and all your livestock on one well, Aurelian? Do not be a fool! You will have not enough water, and without water you will die! Go while you still have the opportunity. Were not all the wells at Qasr-al-Hêr destroyed?"

"They were indeed."

"Does that not tell you something?" she demanded.

He smiled up at her, looking a long moment upon her incredible beauty before he spoke again; and then he said quietly, "Remember Masada!"

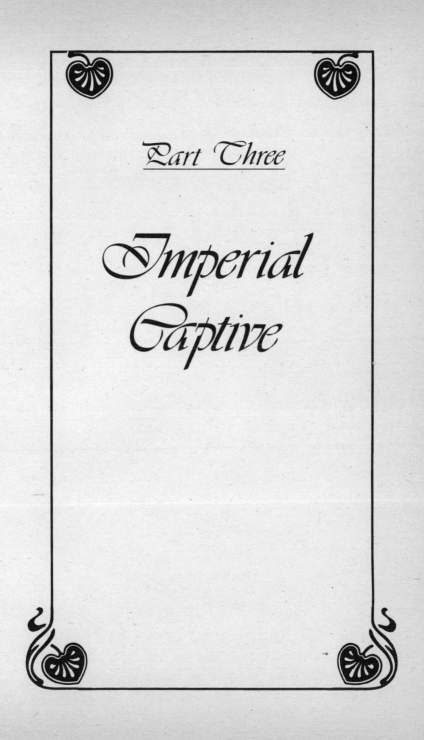

Part Three

Imperial Captive

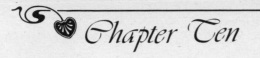

Zenobia looked down the table at Palmyra's Council of Ten, assembled five to a side. At the opposite end sat her son, the king. "It has been four months since the Romans appeared before our gates," she said, "and what I have learned this day has told me that if we do not get aid from another quarter we shall not be able to rid ourselves of them. Before our stores run out, before one Palmyran life is sacrificed, I must get aid!"

"What is it, Majesty?" Marius Gracchus asked. "What have you learned?"

"Aurelian was correct when he said that all the wells within our suburbs would not be destroyed. Less than half of our people obeyed, and of the other half most simply filled their wells with debris that the Roman soldiers have been carefully removing. They have more than enough water, and their lines of communications and supply are totally unfettered. They can hold out forever. We cannot."

"What must we do then, Majesty?" the venerable old councillor asked.

"I must ride for Persia. When my late husband beat Shapur, their king, in battle, it was for Rome. Perhaps Shapur will aid us. If he does, and attacks the Romans from the rear, and we attack them from the front, we can destroy them between us."

"Surely you do not propose to go yourself, Majesty?"

"I must. Our need is great, and I believe that only I can convince Shapur to join us."

"Who will you appoint regent in your absence, Majesty?" he asked.

Zenobia looked directly at her son, who sat unsmiling in his chair. "There is no need for a regent, Marius Gracchus. Palmyra has a king, and it is past time that he ruled in his own right. I have been fearful that perhaps my son was not mature enough to assume his full responsibilities, but his conduct during these months of siege has proved that he is more than ready. Vaballathus has my loyalty, and my full confidence." She smiled at him, and then bowing her head said, "I beg your Majesty's leave to ride to King Shapur of Persia."

"You have my permission, Queen of Palmyra," Vaba said, and then he stood and looked at them all. "I am your king, but she is the queen. Remember it!"

Afterward, when they had all been dismissed, he chided her, "You might have at least warned me what you were going to do, Mother."

"I wanted it to be a surprise," she answered.

"Do you really mean it, or will you take over when you return again?" he asked.

"No, Vaba, Palmyra is yours. But at least listen to my advice, and let us work together until the enemy has been driven from our lands."

"How will you reach Persia?" he demanded.

"The Bedawi," she said.

"Is that how you found out about the wells?"

"Yes. Your uncle Akbar and his sons have been camped just over the dunes, playing the desert nomads for the Romans. They sell them goat's milk, cheese, dates, and women. Indeed, they have become quite friendly with Aurelian himself."

"Where is Grandfather Zabaai?"

"With the main part of the tribe, several days to the east."

"When will you go, Mother?"

"Tonight. There is no moon, and I can safely slip out of the city without being caught. I must not delay, Vaba. We have barely three months' supplies left even with strict rationing."

"Will any of your men go with you?"

"Only Rufus Curius. I would prefer to go alone to meet Akbar, but he insisted that someone come with me, and Rufus Curius asked to accompany me." She shrugged irritably. "They are a pair of old women, both of them. They were afraid if a stray Roman caught me I might be assaulted. I am not so feeble that I cannot put a knife between some Roman's ribs."

He smiled at her. "I have no doubt that you could knife a Roman with ease, and butcher him without a sound, but I agree with them. It is better this way."

She laughed. "A fine opinion you have of your mother, Vaba."

"Have you any suggestions for me while you are gone?"

"Several," she answered mischievously, and then she grew serious. "Rely on Longinus first, and then Marius Gracchus.

They are the best of the council. The others have a tendency to be too cautious, even my good Antonius Porcius. My absence must be kept secret for as long as possible, for once the Romans know they will come after me. I must reach the Euphrates River and cross it before they can catch up with me.''

"We will offer the information that you have a mild fever," Vaba said, "and that you are keeping to your couch for a few days."

"I will need three days."

"You will have them, Mother."

She stepped forward and embraced him. "If I do not return, Vaba . . . remember that I have always loved you. Remember that, and remember the dream that your father and I always had for Palmyra. We wanted her free of Rome."

"I will remember," he said, and kissed her affectionately. "I do love you, Mother."

She laughed. "I know, Vaba, and I also know that it has not always been easy to love me."

He gestured helplessly, and laughing again, she left him.

In the darkest part of the night Zenobia left the city with Rufus Curius. Together they had mounted the walls on the eastern side of the city, and been lowered down in the darkness by two of Zenobia's personal guard. In silence they had skirted the city, carefully avoiding the Roman camp and their pickets, to walk quickly to the encampment of Akbar ben Zabaai. With a skill that amazed Rufus Curius Zenobia managed even to evade the Bedawis who guarded that campsite, and enter her brother's tent unseen.

Akbar ben Zabaai came forward smiling broadly. "You have not lost your touch all those years in the city," he said, chuckling with pride.

"This is Rufus Curius," Zenobia said. "He was commander of Qasr-al-Hêr. He is to accompany me. Are the camels ready?"

"They are, my sister. I am sending five of my men with you also."

"No!"

"Yes, Zenobia, my sister. You must be protected. Do not think you can keep this from the Romans. They have spies everywhere, and will know of your departure quickly."

"I only need three days, Akbar! Three days!"

"You will be lucky to get twelve hours. Then may the gods

247

make your camels swift, for they will be after you! The Bedawi can make up a rear guard. Should the Romans get too close, they can slay your pursuers.''

"Your brother is right, Majesty. I, for one, am grateful for the extra protection,'' Rufus Curius said.

"Very well,'' Zenobia replied. "I agree. Let us go now!''

Without another word Akbar led them out of the tent and to the edge of the encampment where his men and the camels awaited "This is my sister,'' he said, "and her aide, Rufus Curius. Obey her, for she is far wiser in the ways of the desert than any of you. Should you be pursued protect her with your lives. Her mission is to get to Shapur of Persia, and gain his aid. Without it the Romans will again control this region, and we do not want that, my friends.''

Zenobia mounted her camel and, leaning back in her saddle, kicked it into a standing position. "Thank you, Akbar,'' she said.

"The gods go with you, my sister.''

The other men had mounted their beasts, and the little party left the Bedawi camp, traveling east toward the Euphrates River. Once they had crossed it they would be in Persia. Although the Palmyrans had beaten Persia in battle, there had been peace between the two lands for several years now. Zenobia thought that despite their past differences Shapur would aid them, for he hated the Romans. Besides, there were several valuable trade concessions she would give him in return for his aid.

The night began to give way to a gray dawn, and dawn in its turn to a rainbow-colored sunrise and a magnificent day. The sun slowly climbed up into the cloudless blue sky while across the seemingly endless desert the seven camels plodded onward. Finally, at two hours past noon, they stopped in the shelter of some tall dunes. The sun beat mercilessly down upon them as the camels knelt to allow their riders to dismount. It had been a long time since Zenobia had ridden across the desert under a midday sun. She longed to throw off her enveloping cloak, but to do so would be to risk severe sunburn, and dehydration. Instead, she made a small hollow for herself in the sand within the shadow of one of the dunes, and settled down to rest. After a bit she accepted some lukewarm water offered her by Rufus Curius and, digging her hand into a leather pouch hanging from her belt, she drew out some dates and two figs, which she began to slowly eat. Her hunger and thirst both satisfied, the Queen of Palmyra slept for the next several hours.

"It is time to go, my Queen," Rufus Curius's voice penetrated her wild and formless dreams.

Zenobia opened her eyes, suddenly aware of where she was. "I hear you, Rufus. Give me but a moment, and I will be ready." He offered her another drink, which she accepted, and then she rose and mounted the kneeling camel. Irritably the beast stood, swung his head around, and attempted to bite her foot. Quickly she escaped him, administering a smart slap to the camel's nose with her reins at the same time. "They are the most irascible creatures," she muttered to Rufus Curius, who then warily mounted his own camel.

It was late afternoon and still quite hot, but quickly night descended upon the desert, and Zenobia was glad for her long black wool cloak. During the long night they made but one short stop to rest the camels and to relieve themselves. The second day was an imitation of the first, but when they prepared to travel on the third night, one of the Bedawi announced, "We are being followed."

"How do you know?" demanded Rufus Curius, anxiously scanning the horizon and seeing nothing.

"I know," was the reply.

Rufus Curius nodded. "How far behind us?"

"Several hours," was the answer.

"Can we make the river before they catch up to us?" Zenobia spoke.

"With the gods' blessing, Majesty," the Bedawi said.

"Let us go then, Hussein, and pray that the gods are not fickle toward me now at the crucial moment." She clambered up onto her camel.

Throughout the night they rode relentlessly on toward the Euphrates, eventually exiting the desert and riding along through the lush farmland that was the great river's heritage. Ahead of them the skies began to grow gray with light, spreading slowly westward until they found themselves riding in a dove-colored gloom that allowed them to see the green of the land and the black outlines of occasional farmsteads and small villages.

The horizon was soon edged in gold, and slashes of crimson also spread westward as the great round of the blazing sun pulled itself slowly over the edge of the world and began to rise upward into the sky. The camels were tiring, but ahead of them they could just begin to make out the wide, greenish-brown ribbon of the Euphrates as it wound through the great and ancient plain of Sumer and Akkad.

249

Safety, thought Zenobia, heaving a sigh. Once they had crossed the river they were safe, for the Romans would not cross into Persia. Closer and closer they came to the river, and then suddenly Hussein turned and shouted, "Behind us! The Romans!"

Zenobia turned in her saddle, and saw with horror a troop of mounted men gaining on them. She glanced over at Rufus Curius, and heard him say, "Too many for us!"

"Can we reach the river?" she shouted to him.

"Possibly," came the reply.

"Stay with me," she commanded him.

"I will, Majesty!"

Zenobia leaned forward, and kicked her reluctant camel into a gallop. The poor beast was exhausted after the night's travel, and she had intended to rest him on the other side of the river for several long hours. Now the tired beast was forced to expend what little energies he had left. Bred for toughness, however, he responded, and the river came even closer. Behind her the Bedawi warriors dropped back to cover her flight, and soon she could hear the fierce sounds of a short battle. She knew the five tribesmen who had accompanied her would die in that battle. They were pledged to defend her, and there would be neither surrender nor quarter given. The few minutes that they would give her, though, could mean the difference between escape and capture.

Then they were at the river bank, and flinging themselves from their mounts. The Euphrates stretched wide, and in midstream a small boat with a fisherman floated. Rufus Curius called to the boatman. "A gold piece if you will ferry us across! Hurry, man, we are pursued by the Romans!" He held the shiny coin up so the fisherman might see it and know he told the truth. The man began to pole quickly toward the shore. "Wade out as far as you can go, Majesty," Rufus Curius commanded. "We can't waste time."

"You aren't coming with me?"

"I must cover your retreat, Majesty. Now even the moments count. I will come if I can."

She looked searchingly at him. "Rufus Curius, I thank you."

"It has never been hard to serve you, or to serve Palmyra, my Queen."

Zenobia hoisted her cloak up and tied it about her middle before she began to wade out into the river. The water was sun-warmed, the bottom at first sandy, then muddy, squishing through her toes. She looked toward the fisherman, shading her eyes with her hand, and saw that he was getting closer. Suddenly behind her on the bank she heard shouts, and Rufus Curius's voice cried out, "Swim, Majesty! Swim!" Turning, she saw him surrounded by almost a dozen men, and then she saw him no more.

Frantically Zenobia flung herself into the water, and began swimming toward the fishing boat. Behind her she heard splashing, and knew she was being pursued. *Venus! Mars! Jupiter for whom I was named! Help me now! Help me to escape them!* she prayed silently, her arms moving rhythmically as she swam as quickly as she could. Ahead of her she could see the fisherman had stopped poling, and was watching curiously. Then suddenly a hand grasped her ankle. Furiously she struggled to escape, kicking out, but she quickly found herself surrounded by Roman legionnaires, and weighed down by her heavy, wet cloak she was powerless. They hauled her none too gently back toward the shore, and when it was possible to stand again they closed in about her, their hands moving roughly over her body in a "search" for weapons; but their real intent was quite clear. The sodden cloak was pulled away and her short tunic was torn from her; she was weaponless, powerless. One of the men shoved her backward onto the sandy beach, loosening his own clothing. In that terrible and short moment Zenobia remembered her mother. I will not beg, she thought. I will not beg!

"Halt, you men!" The centurion of the unit came hurrying forward, and taking off his long red cloak put it around Zenobia, who had quickly struggled to her feet. "I offer my apologies, Majesty," he said quietly, and then swung around to the men who had captured Zenobia. "This woman is the Queen of Palmyra, and a great warrior. She is entitled to the same respect as any male adversary of equal rank. She is not to be touched by any of you. Those are the emperor's orders. Do you understand?"

Grumbling, the soldiers nodded, and the centurion spoke again to Zenobia. "I am Gaius Cicero, Majesty, personal aide to the Emperor Aurelian. You are now a prisoner of the state."

She wrapped the cloak tightly around her and lifted her head proudly. She would not beg! "Where are my men?" she demanded in a voice that required a reply.

"I regret, Majesty, that it was necessary to kill them. They were all valiant fighters."

"I want to bury them," she said tonelessly. "I will not leave them to be picked clean by the vultures and the jackals. They were brave men, and deserve that courtesy."

"We cannot take the time, Majesty."

"You cannot begin your return immediately, Gaius Cicero. You, too, have been traveling all night, and need to rest your mounts. This place is far more hospitable than the desert, which we must cross again. Ask your men to bring me the bodies of my people and give me a digging tool. I will bury them myself."

"You cannot . . ." he began.

"*I can!*" she replied fiercely, and he saw that she was not a woman to be dissuaded.

She was correct. They needed to rest after the three-day pursuit, and the fertile river bank was most pleasant. "Lucillus," he called to one of his men. "Bring the bodies of the slain tribesmen here for burial; and send several men to that nearby village to buy food."

"Thank you," Zenobia said.

"I will have my men help you," he said.

"No! Those who protected me are my responsibility, Gaius Cicero. It is my duty as Queen of Palmyra to help them to their final resting place. Never have I shirked my duty. I will not do so now."

He understood, and he admired her for such strength of character. Now more than ever he understood Marcus Alexander's great love for this woman. He didn't think that this was a particularly good moment to deliver her a message from him, and so he simply found a spade among their equipment, and gave it to her. Wordlessly Zenobia began digging, heedless of the long cloak that opened with her efforts, displaying her nudity to all. Desperately Gaius Cicero looked for the queen's tunic, but upon finding it saw that it was ripped beyond repair. There had to be an extra one among his hundred legionnaires that would fit her. He set off to find it, posting a guard near the queen, forbidding all others to come near her.

Methodically Zenobia dug one grave after another in the soft earth. She was tired but worked on, despite the blisters now swelling up on her hands. At first the legionnaires watching from a distance had been scornful and even amused by her efforts, but now as she completed the fifth grave their admiration was open.

The last grave was dug, and Zenobia stood over the bodies of her slain companions. Suddenly she looked up, and her gaze was fierce. "Who among you robbed these men?" she demanded furiously. "Come forth now, and return them their property. They will have little enough to take with them into the Underworld."

After a moment the shamefaced culprits came slowly forward and, checking the bodies themselves, returned what they had taken from the dead.

Again Zenobia spoke. "Tell Gaius Cicero I want six coppers. Charon will not ferry them across the Styx without payment."

A legionnaire detached himself from the crowd and ran to find Gaius Cicero. Returning a few moments later, he bowed politely to Zenobia and gave her the coins. Taking them, she placed one between the teeth of each corpse. Suddenly a legionnaire was at her side.

"I would consider it a privilege if you would let me help you to lower the bodies into their graves, and cover them, Majesty," he said.

Their eyes met, and she was touched to see in his honest sympathy, not for her plight but for the sorrow he knew she must be feeling over her fallen comrades. She graciously accepted his help.

At last the task was done and Zenobia stood just a moment, offering her silent prayers to the gods for Rufus Curius, and the Bedawi who had fallen in her defense. Suddenly Gaius Cicero was at her side, gently taking her arm and drawing her away to a secluded spot. Without speaking he handed her a linen tunic, turning his back as she removed his long cloak and put it on.

"I lost my sandals in the river," she said quietly.

"I will see if I can find you a pair," he promised. "Are you hungry?"

She shook her head in the negative. "No, just very tired, Gaius Cicero. I am suddenly very tired."

"We will camp here until nightfall, Majesty. You may sleep in safety. No harm will come to you while you are in my charge."

"Where do you want me?" she asked him tonelessly.

"Here would be satisfactory," he replied, "but before you rest I would speak to you. I bear a message to you from an old friend in Rome."

"I have no friends in Rome." she answered.

"I speak of Marcus Alexander Britainus," Gaius Cicero said.

"*Don't!*" was her sharp reply. "I do not want to hear even the mention of his name, Centurion."

"He did not betray you, Majesty."

Zenobia looked directly at Gaius Cicero. "Romans always betray those who trust them. I am your prisoner, but I do not believe I must listen to the pretty lies you have been told to tell me. I will never forgive Marcus. *Never!* Now speak no more to me of it."

Her voice had been strong and even, but he could hear a ragged edge to it, and he saw in her eyes the most terrible pain. She was close to tears, which she valiantly fought back, and ashamed, he lowered his own gaze. "It will be as you wish, Majesty," he said. Then he left her to rest.

Zenobia pulled the long red cloak about her and lay down upon the ground, curling herself into a ball. Her mind began to sort out all that had happened. She had failed in her attempt to escape the Romans, and gain help from the Persians. She had been so close to succeeding.

Through hooded lids she looked to the river bank, weighing the possibility of escape. The fisherman was long gone, and the river was broad here, but possibly she could swim it. If not, then at least the Romans would not have a hostage to hold over Vaba and the city. To her vast annoyance, however, Gaius Cicero had placed pickets at intervals of three feet for one hundred and fifty feet along the river bank. She smothered a particularly ripe curse and, unable to think of another way, sighed and put her mind to falling asleep.

When she awoke the sky above her was streaked in gold and peach and lavender; the narrow ruffled clouds were pale pink edged in dark purple. She could hear the soft sounds of the river as it lapped against the shore, and for a brief minute she experienced a feeling of incredible peace. Then reality quickly surfaced, and she remembered all that had passed. There was a faint breeze, and upon that breeze wafted the scent of lamb. Her stomach rumbled appreciatively, and with a small smile of amusement at herself she realized that she was hungry. Except for some figs and dates, she had not, after all, eaten in several days.

Slowly standing up, she stretched, spreading her arms wide and tensing her muscles for a moment, then relaxing again. Shaking the sand from the long cloak, she set off down the beach seeking the cook fire. She did not have to go far. She regally accepted a tin plate with two smoking-hot portions of lamb kabob from the legionnaire who was designated cook. The chunks of lamb had been skewered on peeled sticks and interspersed with small onions and pieces of sweet, green pepper.

"Would you like some wine, Majesty?"

"The privileges of rank, Gaius Cicero?"

A small smile lifted the corners of his mouth. "Perhaps," he answered her, holding out a tin cup.

She hesitated for a moment, then took it from him with a nod of thanks.

"Do you wish company?" he pursued her.

"No," she said shortly, not even bothering to turn around as she made her way back down the beach.

He sighed. What a pity, he thought. He would have enjoyed her company. She was a beautiful woman, and her reputation was that of an intelligent and witty woman. He could understand, though. This was hardly a comfortable situation for her. Zenobia of Palmyra had never been beaten before, and defeat was never a pleasant thing. At least her capture would serve one good purpose. The Palmyrans would certainly surrender once they learned that their queen was in the hands of the emperor. A frown crossed Gaius Cicero's face. He did not have to wonder what Aurelian would do with Zenobia. The emperor had been like a young boy from the day of their arrival before the gates of Palmyra. He could not stop talking of her. It was obvious that he had been quite smitten, and Aurelian had never been one to deny himself a woman who took his fancy.

Shortly after sunset they departed the shores of the River Euphrates, retracing their steps of the last three days as they traveled westward back toward Palmyra. Zenobia sat her camel stoically, never complaining at the brisk pace set by Gaius Cicero, who was determined to bring his prisoner before the emperor as quickly as possible. There was always the chance that the Bedawi would learn of her capture and seek to rescue her.

As they moved across the desert, the shock of what had happened finally began to sink into her very soul. Why had the gods deserted her so cruelly in her hour of deepest need? How was she to tell Deliciae and her children of Rufus Curius's death? And what of the families of the Bedawi? How many widows and orphans had been made? Curse the Romans! Curse them all! Yes, even Marcus, who had betrayed her! How she hated them, and the hate was the first thing that she felt as she began to rise, phoenixlike, from the ashes of her first defeat.

255

I will not be beaten again, nor will I beg, she thought fiercely. Even if they take me to Rome, I will escape them somehow and return to Palmyra to rebuild my empire, Odenathus's empire. As the banners of the Roman army came into view and their enormous encampment became visible, as she saw the walls of the city once more, she sat proudly upon her camel, her head held high, looking straight ahead. Finally they stopped before a large tent, set upon a platform deep within the encampment.

Gaius Cicero was quickly at her side, helping her to dismount and then escorting her into the tent. As her eyes grew used to the gloom she saw a tall man with blond hair and a long, elegant bearded face standing in profile by a map stand.

"Hail, Caesar!" was Gaius Cicero's greeting.

The man turned. "Ah, Gaius, you are back." His glance flicked to Zenobia, swiftly taking her in. "I assume this is our rebellious queen?"

"Yes, Caesar!"

"You may leave us, Gaius, but wait outside. I will have further need of your services."

Aurelian now turned back to look at Zenobia again, and their eyes instantly locked in a battle of wills. He felt his heart quicken at the sight of her, for close up he realized that she was the most beautiful woman he had ever seen. She was filthy from her travels, and her dark hair was dusty and matted; but still she was beautiful. She stared boldly at him, making him a little uncomfortable, although he would not show it. Finally he said, "You need a bath, Queen of Palmyra. You stink of camel."

She never even blinked. Instead, her sultry voice replied, "I have always hated blue-eyed Romans, and you do nothing to change my opinion, Emperor of the Romans."

His narrow lips twitched faintly as he suppressed a smile. She was not beaten, and he was glad. He wanted to tame this wild creature himself, and by the gods he would! "You are now my prisoner, Zenobia," he answered.

"You speak the obvious," was her quick retort. "I am your prisoner, but it will do you no good, Aurelian. Palmyra will not surrender!"

"No? Why did you flee to Persia?"

"I wanted Shapur's help," she said irritably, as if he were an idiot child. "I needed an ally to attack you from the rear in a pincer movement. You disturb the economy of this entire region, in fact the entire world, by this stupid attempt at war on us. I want you, and your puny army gone back to where you belong so the trade routes may once more be open."

"You wanted to end this war because you are running low on provisions in Palmyra," was his answer.

"Palmyra is more than well stocked with provisions for a long siege, Aurelian, but I do not choose to play with you any longer. Had I reached Persia I might have ended this madness quickly. Now it is not to be. Very well," and she shrugged, "I bow to the wisdom and the will of the gods."

"Without you your son will collapse. Once he knows that I possess the Queen of Palmyra, he will open the gates of the city and we will march triumphantly in."

"The king will never give in. I am ready to die for Palmyra, Aurelian, and Vaballathus knows it. For me there can be no greater honor than to give my life for my city."

Into his eyes crept an admiring look he could not suppress, and he said quietly, "You are too intelligent and too beautiful to die so needlessly, Zenobia of Palmyra. I will not allow it!"

"*You will not allow it?*" Her mocking laughter startled him. "What I will, Aurelian, you cannot prevent! How can you understand? You are a peasant who has clawed his way up the ladder of the Roman military! I descend from the great Queen Cleopatra."

"Who was beaten by the Romans," he reminded her.

"You will have another Masada on your hands before you take Palmyra from my son," she threatened.

"We won at Masada, too," he said quietly.

"A victory over a fortress of corpses?" she replied scornfully.

"A victory nevertheless, Zenobia. But enough of this! Gaius," he called, and instantly Gaius Cicero re-entered the tent. "Gaius, take the queen to my sleeping tent, and see that she has a bath." His bold look told her what would come later.

Zenobia drew her breath in sharply.

A slow smile lit his features, and his light blue eyes danced with amusement for a moment.

"Come, Majesty." Gaius was at her elbow, leading her away.

She followed him down the line of tents, her mind quickly working. Aurelian lusted after her. She shuddered. He would have her, she knew. But if she must take the emperor as a lover then it would be on her terms, not his. He would expect resistance, she knew, and instinctively she realized that resistance would give him pleasure. Therefore she would not fight him physically, but with her mind. She would yield her body, but nothing more. Aurelian might be a peasant, but he was an uncommonly intelligent one. He would want all of her. He would not get it, and it would drive him mad. This was one Roman who would not betray her because he would not control any part of her mind and heart. Rather, she would control him.

Gaius Cicero stopped before a large tent and ushered her into it. "I will send some men with water and a tub for you," he said, and he flushed with embarrassment.

"Be sure the water is heated," she said calmly. "I dislike cold baths, and I will need warm water and soft soap to clean the desert from my hair and skin. I assume that you have soap in your encampment, Gaius Cicero? Of course you do. The camp followers would bathe, at least occasionally, wouldn't they?"

"I will see what I can find," he muttered, turning his flushed face away from her.

"Thank you," was her polite reply, and he was quickly gone. Zenobia sighed and gazed around the tent. It was divided into two sections. The larger section, in which she stood, was simply furnished with a low round table where, she assumed, the emperor must eat. There were several large seating pillows strewn carelessly about it. There were two chairs set up in another part of the tent and some trunks, but nothing more. The wooden floor was well worn from many campaigns, and spread with several sheepskins. There were a few brass oil lamps, nothing opulent. All in all, it was quite plain. A soldier's tent without a doubt.

Walking across the floor, she pulled aside the woven woolen divider. Behind it was a rather large and comfortable sleeping couch, but other than that the smaller section was empty.

"It certainly lacks the amenities," Zenobia observed softly to herself. She heard the sound of feet coming in and out of the main section of the tent, and turned to see a procession of straining legionnaires lugging large containers of water into the tent and emptying them into a round, wooden tub. "Is there a respectable woman in this camp?" she demanded loudly.

The legionnaires stopped, startled, at the sound of her voice. They stared openmouthed at her for a moment, and then one, braver than the others, replied, "There are several good women, Majesty."

"Have one sent to me then," she said. "I will need help washing my hair."

"Yes, Majesty," the brave legionnaire answered. "I will fetch a woman immediately," and he hurried from the tent.

Zenobia hid a smile as she stood watching her water bearers. The last of them gone, she saw a woman standing in the entry of the tent. Zenobia waved her into the room. "What is your name?" she asked.

"I am called Keleos, Majesty."

'What do you do among the Romans? Your speech is of Palmyra."

"I am Palmyran, Majesty."

"Then why are you not safely within the gates of the city, Keleos?"

"I am a widow, Majesty. I live with my aged father and my son, who is a cripple, just outside the walls. Neither my father nor my child could be moved, and so I was forced to remain in my home despite the Romans."

"Could your neighbors not help you, Keleos?"

"Majesty, they were terrified, and could not get themselves and their valuables into the city quickly enough. They had no time for us. I have a small bake shop. Normally I baked for my neighborhood, but now I am forced to sell my wares to the Romans. I still have my father and son to support. Please forgive me, Majesty," and Keleos fell on her knees, her hands outstretched in supplication.

"You are forgiven, Keleos," Zenobia replied. "You did what was necessary to survive, to insure the survival of your family."

The woman crawled the short distance between herself and the queen, and prostrating herself further kissed Zenobia's feet. "May the gods bless you, my Queen," she sobbed.

"Get up, Keleos!" Zenobia commanded, and when the woman had scrambled to her feet the queen said, "I would like you to help me wash my hair."

"Gladly, Majesty!" Within minutes Keleos had everything prepared, and was washing Zenobia's hair with some of the soap that had been brought for the queen's bath. They used one of the extra wooden buckets filled with warmed water that had been left. Zenobia could feel the sandy grit of the desert as Keleos soaped it free, and with another bucket of water rinsed it away. It took three latherings, but eventually Zenobia's hair was clean. Keleos wrung the queen's long mane of excess

259

water, and then taking a towel rubbed and rubbed. The hair was quickly dry in the hot desert air. Thanking the woman for her aid, Zenobia dismissed her.

Quickly she stripped her filthy clothes off, and kicking them aside sat down in the round, wooden tub, laving warmish water over her shoulders. Taking a bit of soap, she washed herself and then settled back a moment to enjoy a small soak and the solitude. She wondered how soon he would come and demand her surrender. It would take everything strong within her character to give him her body without flinching. She hated the very thought of his touch, for instinctively she knew he would demand far more than she was ever going to give, and the ensuing battle would be exhausting. Finally she stood up, and with a little smile realized that she faced a predicament of sorts. She could not redress in her dirty garments, and there was no large and dry towel with which to dry and wrap herself. The small towel that had been used for her hair now lay in a sodden lump upon the floor.

Stepping from the tub, she reached for the towel and mopped herself damp. The air would quickly dry the rest of her, but there still remained the problem of what to wear. She looked about the room. There was nothing. She made a sound of annoyance, which was answered by a soft laugh. Furious, and quite heedless of her own nudity, she whirled about to face Aurelian.

"How dare you spy on me!"

"It is my tent," he answered.

"You ordered me placed here," she snapped. "I should as soon have had my own tent."

He walked across the floor to where she stood and, catching her face between his two hands, looked down into her angry eyes. "The wishes of a captive are never considered, Zenobia." Then, to her surprise, he released her. Slowly he walked around her, studying her from every angle, but not yet touching her. Finally he said, "You were once described to me as the goddess incarnate, but seeing you now I must say, with apologies to the beauteous Venus, that the gentleman was not generous enough in his praise. If I put you on the block there is not enough gold in the entire world to secure your purchase, Zenobia."

"Then I may assume you will not put me on the block," she answered him coldly.

He laughed. "Only because I cannot gain enough for you," he teased.

"I did not think you were a procurer, Aurelian. Your reputation is that of a warrior."

He laughed again. "You can fight like a guttersnipe, goddess, but it will avail you nothing. I am Aurelian, and I never lose a battle."

"You may have *me*, Roman, for I cannot hope to overcome your physical strength; but Palmyra's gates will still be closed to you!" She stood tall, glaring icily at him, totally unconcerned by her total nudity; and Aurelian was further intrigued and inflamed by Zenobia. *This is a woman,* he thought admiringly.

"You are a brave creature, goddess," he said quietly, "but you are still just a woman as I am just a man. My spies tell me that there has been no man in your life since Marcus Alexander Britainus left you to return to Rome." He was pleased to see her grow pale at the mention of Marcus's name, and he continued. "He was your lover, and I do not doubt that he was a magnificent one. My niece is already with child." Zenobia's eyes closed for a moment, and she clutched at the hanging divider to keep from swaying.

"You are a bastard!" she managed to hiss at him.

He laughed pleasantly. "You are beautiful, and I desire you, goddess." Now he reached out with gentle fingers to caress her creamy shoulder, stroking with a delicate touch, watching while she fought down the urge to shudder, which finally she was unable to suppress. "Are you beginning to understand what it means to be an imperial captive, goddess?" he asked her.

"I am not afraid," she said low.

"I know that," was his answer, "but you have caused me no end of trouble, goddess, and you must be punished for it."

"So you will force me to be your mistress? Yes, Aurelian, that will indeed be punishment," she replied. "I am accustomed to choosing my own lovers."

Again he laughed. "What a defiant goddess you are, Zenobia. You were a virgin when you married Odenathus at fifteen. Marcus Alexander Britainus has been your only lover. You are an appallingly moral woman, goddess. Half, nay, most of the women in Rome have had half a dozen lovers before they marry. You have known two men, and it shall be for me as if you were a virgin."

261

"Take me then!" she cried half angrily, half fearfully. "I will neither yield nor give you anything of myself!"

His light blue eyes glittered with anticipation, the tiny flecks of black and copper within them dancing wildly. His fingers closed about her shoulder, and he drew her to him. She stood perfectly still, neither resisting him nor accepting him, as his arm went tightly about her waist, molding her hard against him. The hand that had been on her shoulder took her face between thumb and forefinger, tipping it upward as his head came slowly down to claim her mouth with his. With frightening expertise he forced her lips apart, invading her mouth with a velvety tongue, exploring, taunting, *demanding!*

I will show no emotion, she thought, but it took every bit of control not to struggle, not to tear herself away from this man whose mouth was so insistent. She wanted to run, to hide from him, for he frightened her although she would never admit it. There was a look about him that said he would not be denied, and in her entire life she had never known that a man could be like this. She had always been loved gently as a woman, first by Odenathus, and then by Marcus. This man did not seek her love, he sought her very soul! She had to stop him, but without his knowing the terrible effect he was having on her. Pulling her mouth away from his, she said coldly, "Enough! If you wish to couple with me then let us get on with it!"

If she had hit him the effect would not have been any more jolting, but then he began to chuckle, and the chuckle grew into a rumble of pleased laughter. "Brava, goddess! *Magnificent!* And it almost worked, but almost is not good enough." He set her back from him and studied her once more.

Zenobia was shocked. She had expected to cool his ardor by her disdain, and she had instead aroused his admiration. The next move was up to him, so she stood silently sneaking a careful look at him from beneath her thick, black lashes while she waited. She had to admit that he was a very handsome man in a virile, rugged sort of way. He was at least an inch over six feet in height, with a powerfully built body. He had a surprisingly elegant head for one of low birth, she thought. It was oval in shape, with high, well-sculpted cheekbones, a straight patrician nose almost classic in its perfection, extremely sensuous lips, a square chin with a deep cleft that was fairly well hidden by his well-cropped, short beard. The beard, like his close-clipped curly hair, had only faint touches of silver to mar its beautiful golden-blond color. The well-spaced, round eyes were sky blue with their odd-colored flecks, and edged in short, sandy lashes. They were eyes that pierced, but never divulged what they thought.

He began to undress. "Help me with this chest armor," he said briskly as he undid the buckles that held his protective plating.

"Call a slave," she said.

"I am at a loss for what to do with you," he said slowly, pulling off the beautifully decorated breastplate and then undoing the belt that held the strips of armor that hung from his waist. Warrior that he was, he carefully placed the armor in a small chest for safekeeping, then turned back to her. His muscular arms pulled the short-sleeved, knee-length red tunic off, and this garment was followed by a natural-colored linen tunica interior. He was nude except for his sandals and leg shields. Sitting down, he held out a foot. "Will you undo my sandals?"

"I am not your servant, Aurelian."

"You highborn wenches aren't good for very much at all. You refuse to help me undress, and you kiss like a child. I wonder if you will be worth all the trouble I am going to have to take with you."

"Then return me to Palmyra!" she spat at him. "Return me, and then fight me like a man, Roman!"

He looked up at her, now free of his sandals and leg shields. "I am going to fight you like a man, goddess, and for probably the first time in your life you are going to have to fight like a woman!" She gasped, outraged by his words, but he continued. "There will be no emperors or queens in this tent tonight, Zenobia, just a man and a woman waging the age-old battle between men and women!" His eyes blazed blue fire at her, and, startled, she stepped backward. It was all the advantage he needed. Stepping swiftly forward, he lifted her and tossed her over his shoulder.

He had made no attempt to be gentle, leaving her helpless to struggle, for she was too busy trying to catch her breath. Walking across the tent into his sleeping chamber, he unceremoniously dumped her upon his bed and then flung himself down atop her, trapping her face between his two hands.

"I have nothing to give you!" she hissed.

"You will before this night is finished," he promised, and then yanked her head back to his. His lips claimed hers again.

This time Zenobia struggled against Aurelian. As his mouth ground down upon her an unreasoning fear welled up within

her, destroying her intent to remain cool, increasing her panic
as her heartbeat accelerated violently.

He quickly felt her terror, and suddenly his lips were gentle,
barely brushing hers as he murmured against them, "No,
goddess, don't be afraid. Shhh. Shhh, I will not hurt you."

She was unable to prevent the shudder that ripped through
her. This was worse, she thought. She didn't want him to be
gentle. She wanted him to assault her with violence so she
might hate him even more. With an angry cry she raised her
hands and clawed at him.

Forcing her arms above her head, he held them there with
one hand while the other sought to gentle her. "No, goddess,"
he chided her, and then, "What are you afraid of, Zenobia?
Give me some of the sweetness of your mouth, beloved. There
cannot be great harm in that."

She almost wept then. *Beloved!* He had called her beloved—
until now only Marcus, Marcus who had betrayed her and left
her to this man, had called her beloved.

Aurelian sensed the weakness, and in that instant he descended
on her agian, his mouth tenderly taking hers in a kiss so
passionate, and yet at the same time so gentle, that she was
unable to resist any longer. Her lips softened beneath the insistent pressure of his. Finding her tongue, he sucked a long
minute upon the tempting morsel, then released her from the
kiss.

Zenobia was stunned by the sense of loss she felt. Why did
she feel this way? She detested this man, and had a weapon
been available she would have used it on him. Opening her
eyes, she found him looking down on her, unsmiling. His free
hand came up to caress her face. "Your skin is like silk," he
said softly, and then his hand began a lengthy exploration of
her body.

Shifting his weight off her, he released her hands and put the
arm that had imprisoned her about her shoulders, pinioning her
as effectively as he had before, but allowing him the freedom
he needed to caress her. A warm hand moved down her throat,
a hand, she thought, that could as easily strangle her as make
love to her. He read the thought in her gray eyes.

He dallied a moment in the soft hollow of her neck, and she
could feel the blood coursing beneath his fingers. His hand
next moved down to stroke the high swell of her breasts, trailing leisurely downward between her cleavage. A single finger
teasingly encircled each nipple, shocking them, despite her

best efforts to resist, to tight and tingling peaks, which he bent his head to kiss.

She could feel the cry welling up in her throat, and with a supreme surge of willpower she forced it back. He must not know—she would not let him know that his hungry mouth now sucking on her breasts was beginning to elicit a tiny response deep inside her. She could not understand it, and it not only puzzled her, it frightened her. She began to tremble, and tried to draw away from that insistent mouth.

Slowly he raised his head. His eyes were glazed with passion, and something else she could not fathom. She turned her head away from him so he might not see her fear. "You will not deny me, goddess," he said softly. "I will possess you."

"No," she managed to whisper, "my body, but nothing else!"

"I will possess all!" he answered her. "You will belong to me alone, goddess, for never have I been beaten in battle, and I will not be beaten in this one."

Scalding, slow tears began to course down her cheeks, but no sound came from her throat. This was what it had been like for her mother those long years ago; pinned beneath a Roman who demanded everything of her and took it without a care for her soul. They had destroyed her mother, but whatever happened between Zenobia and this Roman, she would not allow him to destroy her.

"No, goddess," and his voice was deceptively soft. "Don't weep. I will not hurt you. I will only love you," and he raised himself up so he might kiss the wetness on her face.

It was too much for Zenobia. With a wild cry she fought to escape him, but could not fight her way free, for his strength was too great. Aurelian laughed, her confused and terrified resistance seeming to give him great pleasure. He shifted his body once more, this time to cover hers. She could feel his muscular thighs with their soft blond down pressing down upon hers, and to her horror she felt a great flash of heat suffuse her body. His broad chest crushed her full breasts, his mouth again captured hers in a kiss of such blazing passion that she could feel her strength ebbing away. Against the inside of her thigh she felt his staff lengthening and growing hard with his desire for her.

He caught at her tongue and began to suck upon the velvet of it again, sending shock waves of desire—*dear Venus, it was desire!*—throughout her feverish body. With that admission to herself it was as if a dam had burst within her. Unwillingly her arms went about him, and she felt him seeking entrance to her unwilling, yet willing body. He thrust deep, and she cried out, her breath coming in quick pants, her long golden legs wrapping themselves about him. Again and again he plunged himself into her burning and wet sheath, making her cry with pleasure in spite of herself. And then with a pitiful sob she whimpered low "*I do not understand! I do not understand!*"

He stopped in his rutting, and with a roar of laughter he caught her frightened face in his hands. "It is *lust,* Zenobia! *Sweet, hot lust!* How is it that you have never before experienced lust?" He drove again into her and, bending, murmured against her ear, "I will teach you to enjoy lust, my goddess, to revel in it, to yield to it!" His hands moved beneath her to cup her buttocks, and he squeezed them possessively. "Do you feel it, Zenobia? Do you feel the fire coursing through you? *Lust!* It is lust, and you have no choice but to give in to it; give in to me! The victory will be mine, goddess, as I warned you! The victory will be mine!"

Shocked, Zenobia realized that what he was saying was true. She had no control over her body at that moment. Ripple after ripple of pure, sensuous pleasure was starting to wash over her, and she had not the strength to resist it. A tension was beginning to build deep within her, and the force of it was so great that it threatened either to consume or destroy her. She would either give in to it, or die from it; and as shameful as she found her situation, she did not want to die. The victory would be his whatever way she chose, but she would find a way to revenge herself upon him. This was only the opening battle in the war between them.

With a soft cry her nails dug into the muscled skin of his upper back; and his laughter was triumphant. With slow, deliberate thrusts of his pelvis he began to move upon her again, and this time Zenobia pushed her own body up to meet him. "I hate you!" she snarled at him through gritted teeth.

"But your delicious body wants mine," he murmured.

She caught his head between her two hands, and kissed him fiercely, then finding his left ear she provocatively ran her pointed tongue around it, pushing it into the cavity insinuatingly, blowing softly, laughing low when he groaned. He countered by sliding his hands beneath her rounded buttocks and caressing them. Leaning forward, his mouth began to play with her taut nipples, licking and nipping at them until her breath began to come again in short, quick gasps. She tried to push him away so she might counterattack, but grasping her bottom he drove hard into her, pinioning her once more beneath him, subduing her cruelly. Soon Zenobia writhed, mindless, beneath Aurelian while he brought her to the brink of pleasure once, twice, three times, until at last she cursed him, "Damn you, Roman, give me release!" And he did, climaxing with her with a sound somewhere between laughter and a groan.

Afterward they lay sandwiched together for some minutes before he rolled off her, and shortly she heard him snoring. Only then did Zenobia pull herself into a tight little ball and weep softly into the pillows until at last she fell into a deep, healing sleep. When she awoke she found that she was lying upon her stomach, caught beneath his hard arm. She debated the wisdom of moving, for she feared that if he was awake too he might want her again, and Zenobia was not yet ready to undergo another such battle.

"You are awake." Aurelian's voice decided the matter for her.

"I am awake, Roman." Deliberately she made her voice flat and emotionless.

"Are you all right?" he demanded.

"Why should you care?" she countered, rolling over, then sitting up and dragging the coverlet over her chilled body. "You have had your victory, haven't you? You won the battle between us, Roman. What more do you want?"

"You." He made the word sharp and clear.

"You had me." Her voice trembled slightly, and she silently cursed herself for the weakness.

"I possessed the body, Zenobia, but I did not possess you."

"You never will, Roman! No man ever has, nor ever will!" she lied.

"Not even Marcus Alexander Britainus?" he asked.

"Damn you, Aurelian! Damn you a thousand times over," she said in a tight voice, and she forced back the tears that threatened to begin again. "What do you want of me? Perhaps the truth will silence you once and for all. Very well, then. I loved Marcus as I have loved no other man. When he married your niece I ached not only with the loss of him, but for his betrayal, for I thought I knew him. Yes, I gave myself wholly to him, and I shall not make that mistake again. Each time you desire me you will have to force me, and perhaps you will again make me cry out a surrender of sorts, but you will never really have me. And you will never be able to use Marcus as a weapon in your war with me. You cannot hurt me." She felt drained by the speech, but, incredibly, she also felt strong again.

He had lain on his belly throughout this exchange, and now he rolled over and looked up at her. "How strangely naive you are, goddess." His blue eyes regarded her with a funny mixture of compassion and determination. Then quickly the look was gone, and his glance was once again unreadable. Calmly he arose from the bed and, turning, said to her, "Get up, goddess. I sent a message to your son last night, and this morning I will present you to the city of Palmyra as my prisoner. They will have the space of one day in which to decide their fates."

"They will not surrender," she insisted.

"Then I will destroy the city about their ears," was the reply.

They glared at each other, each immovable in intent, each sure of rightness. Finally Zenobia said sulkily, "I have nothing to wear, Roman. Surely you aren't going to make me stand naked before my own city walls?"

A wicked grin creased his mouth. "A delectable thought, goddess, but no. I rarely share with others what belongs to me. Late last night before I joined you there came into camp a querulous old woman who claims to be your servant. Your son sent her with garments and other things that a woman needs. Poor Gaius Cicero had a terrible time with her. Only when one of the Bedawi women spoke to her could she be calmed. I will send for them now."

Aurelian dressed quickly and left the tent without another word to her. Shortly afterward he returned with two women.

"The gods be praised! You are unharmed!" cried Bab, tears running down her weathered old face as she fell on Zenobia's neck.

The bed's coverlet wrapped around her, Zenobia soothed her nursemaid. "Hush, old woman! As always, you fret too much over me. Am I not the beloved of the gods?" Aurelian, however, noted the concern on the queen's face. So, he thought, her heart is not entirely cold.

"Zenobia."

She looked curiously toward the other woman, who threw back the hood of her robe. "Tamar! Oh, Tamar, is it really you?"

"It is me, child." Tamar eyed Zenobia's garb. "Is all well with you?"

Zenobia nodded quietly. "It is as expected," she answered. "Who are these women?" the emperor demanded.

She looked at him. "My old nursemaid, who has always cared for me. Her name is Bab, and this," she drew Tamar forward, "is Tamar bat Hammid, my father's wife."

"Then you are in good hands, and I may safely leave you," he answered. He turned to the two older women. "Prepare the queen in her finest garments." He raised Zenobia's hand to his lips and, turning it, kissed the inside of her wrist. "Until later, goddess," and he was quickly gone from the tent.

For a moment the three women stood in silence, and then Tamar said quietly, "Bab, show Zenobia what you have brought so we may choose from among her garments for something suitable."

Bab shuffled to the entry of the tent and, bending, dragged a small trunk inside. Opening it, she brought forth a diaphanous dark garment. With a ghost of a smile she held it up, saying, "I have chosen this for you, my baby."

Zenobia's own lips twitched with delight. "Are you becoming a rebel in your old age, Bab?"

The old woman cackled. "I thought it fitting under the circumstances."

"Have you gone mad?" Tamar demanded. "Black is for mourning."

"Should I not be in mourning?" Zenobia shot back. "I mourn for my virtue, torn from me last night, and I mourn for Palmyra, my beloved city. I sense that this battle with Rome will be to the death."

"Can we not win?" Tamar's voice had dropped to a whisper.

"If I were in the city instead of here, yes; but I am not within the city; and Palmyra's king, my son, is not as skilled in the art of ruling as I would wish. I fear that Aurelian will outwit Vaba, for he is a clever man."

"Then why did you turn over the full responsibility for Palmyra to Vaba before you rode for Persia?" Tamar was curious.

"If I were not to return I wanted no misunderstanding among the council as to who the king was. I can only pray that Vaba will be the king his father was; that he will hold firm even though Aurelian holds me prisoner. I shall pray to the gods, if they have not deserted me entirely, that he will be strong."

Outside they heard the trumpets call, and Bab said, "We must dress you, my baby. Soon they will come for you, and you must be ready."

A few moments later Gaius Cicero arrived with a six-man escort that he left outside to await their prisoner.

Zenobia greeted him pleasantly enough, and unable to conceal the admiration he felt, his eyes widened at the sight of her. "Are you ready, Majesty?" he inquired politely.

"I am ready, Gaius Cicero," was her calm reply.

Tamar and Bab stood at the entry to the tent and watched as the Roman centurion and his men marched Zenobia from their sight. They brought her to the edge of the camp that faced the main gates of Palmyra, and there she saw a raised platform with a small tent upon it. They led her up a small flight of steps behind the little tent and then into it, leaving her there. Within the little enclosure Aurelian awaited her. He raised one blond eyebrow at the sight of her and then he chuckled.

"Thought you to irritate me by wearing mourning, goddess? I believe your gown an excellent choice, for it implies defeat. Defeat for Palmyra."

Her heart sank. He was right, but she had not thought of it that way and neither had old Bab. She had indeed sought to annoy him by wearing a plain, black kalasiris and no jewelry other than her royal circlet of golden vine leaves atop her unbound black hair. "Will you allow me nothing, Roman?" she said low.

"It is dangerous to *allow* you anything, goddess. We gave you a city, and you took an empire. You are known to bite the hand that feeds you, Zenobia."

Her hand flashed out, catching him off guard as it slapped his face. Instantly rage suffused his features, and grasping her arm, he brutally forced it behind her. "Were it not necessary for me to present you publicly to your people, and your son in a few moments," he said through gritted teeth, "I should beat you. Never raise your hand to me again, goddess!"

"You are hurting me, Roman," she spat back, not daring to struggle for fear the movement would break her arm.

The anger drained from his face, and he released his hold on her. "I give only one warning, goddess," he said coldly. "Stay here and do not move. You will know when I want you."

He exited the tent, and she was left alone to listen to the sounds whose sources she could not see. She could hear the movement of many feet, the undertone of voices, and then suddenly silence followed by the flourish of trumpets, which was answered by Palmyran trumpets from atop the city walls.

Zenobia's heart quickened. She heard Aurelian's voice in the clear air.

"People of Palmyra, I am Aurelian. Hear me well! I have now in my possession your rebel queen, Zenobia. Surrender to me, and I will spare not only her, but all of you and your city as well. I will not impose fines upon you, for the fault has not been yours but that of your overproud queen. You have until this time tomorrow to make your decision."

Zenobia felt her anger rise. The cheek of the Roman! Overproud, indeed! Then she heard the voice of Cassius Longinus.

"You say you will spare the queen, Emperor of the Romans, but surely you will not leave her here to rule in her city. What say you?"

"Who is that man?" Zenobia heard Aurelian demand of Gaius Cicero.

"His name is Cassius Longinus. He is the queen's chief councillor."

"Not the king's?"

"I do not know. He came to Palmyra from Athens many years ago to serve Zenobia. Possibly he also advises the young king. I can see the boy standing near him. You could answer him without losing your dignity, Caesar."

"Your queen, Cassius Longinus," Aurelian said, "will not be allowed to rule Palmyra ever again. She is now a prisoner of the empire. She will go to Rome to be marched in my triumph. Afterward, I do not know. It will be up to the senate, but if the citizens of Palmyra are once again loyal citizens of Rome the senate could be merciful."

"And who will rule Palmyra, Roman?" Was Longinus's next query. "Will our king be allowed to keep his place if we surrender to you?"

"Possibly," Aurelian replied. "King Vaballathus has never shown disloyalty to Rome, only his mother has."

Liar! Zenobia thought furiously. I know exactly what you mean to do. Oh, Jupiter father, hear my prayer! Do not let my people be swayed by the silken tongue of this Roman! Minerva, great wise one, grant my son the wisdom to see the truth.

"You claim to have our queen, Aurelian," came Longinus's voice once more, "but how do we know that you speak the truth? Show us Zenobia of Palmyra so we may know for certain."

Suddenly the tent top above her was pulled away and the body of the small enclosure fell away to reveal Zenobia to all

271

those who stood upon Palmyra's walls. "Here is your queen!"
Aurelian declared dramatically.

Zenobia knew that she would have but one chance, and so
at the top of her lungs she cried out for all to hear, "Do not
surrender, my son! I die gladly for Palmyra!"

At Aurelian's signal a legionnaire leapt forward to silence
her by placing one arm about her waist while a hand was
clamped firmly over her mouth. Zenobia did not bother to
struggle. She had said what she had to say, and it had had its
effect. Upon the walls of the great oasis city the populace
began to chant her name softly at first, and then louder, and
louder until it became a roar of defiance.

"*Zenobia! Zenobia! Zenobia! Zenobia! Zenobia! Zenobia!*"

"Take her back to my tent," the Roman emperor commanded
angrily.

Zenobia pulled away from the offending hand over her mouth,
and laughed mockingly at Aurelian. "We are even now, Roman.
You won last night's battle by brute force, but I have won this
morning's by better tactics." Then she easily shook off the
legionnaire's grip. "Let go of me, pig! I am capable of returning to my quarters without your aid." To prove her point she
walked swiftly away.

Gaius Cicero looked at the emperor. "Will they surrender, I
wonder?" he said quietly. "You see how she holds the populace
within the palm of her hand."

"The decision isn't theirs, but rather the young king's," the
emperor returned irritably. "He will surrender if for no other
reason than his mother told him not to. My spies tell me that
he resents the queen and very much wants to be his own man.
He will open the gates tomorrow. Wait and see if I am not
right, Gaius."

"The men are restless, Caesar. What will your orders be for
today?"

"I think it best that they drill for several hours beneath this
charming sun. It will take the meanness from them. Afterward
they will return to their quarters, where they will spend the rest
of the day polishing their gear for tomorrow's triumphal entry
into Palmyra. Only when they have completed these tasks may
they have some time to themselves. Encourage them to visit
the whores, for I want no rape tomorrow when we enter Palmyra.
A city of resentful rebels is not to our best interests.

"I want to remove the government and replace it with our

own people; but other than that it will be business as usual in Palmyra."

Gaius Cicero saluted the emperor. "It will be as Caesar commands," he said and, turning, hurried off to give the order.

Aurelian sat down, his legs swinging over the platform's edge. The hot sun felt good on his body, which might be lean and hard but was nonetheless the body of a man in his late-middle years. He chuckled to himself, remembering the old men in his Illyrian village sitting and gossiping together in the winter sunshine. Was he getting to be like them? he wondered. In his lifetime neither generals nor emperors were particularly noted for long lives, and so perhaps he would not have the time to find out.

He chuckled again. What strange thoughts he was having today. It was truly a sign of old age. Here he was on the day before his greatest triumph, and he sat like an old turtle atop a rock in midpond, philosophizing in the sunshine. He looked up at the walls of Palmyra, but the white-marble barriers told him nothing of the beauties that lay hidden behind them. It was said to be the Rome of the East; and there were some who said it was lovelier. Well, tomorrow he would find out.

A wolfish smile lit his features. Zenobia was going to be very angry at the boy. Now the young king of Palmyra would be making his first serious royal decision, and that decision was going to cost him his throne. Yes, Zenobia was going to be very angry, and he could not blame her, for as a ruler himself he understood. She and her late husband had worked hard to rebuild the Eastern Empire, and now he would take it.

Aurelian pushed himself off the platform and walked back into the heart of the encampment, noting as he went that the centurions were already drilling smartly.

It was not to his sleeping tent that he returned. Rather, Aurelian hurried to his main tent, where the business of the empire awaited him. Durantis, his secretary, was already hard at work opening the dispatches and separating them into piles according to their importance.

"Good morning, Durantis. Any emergencies?"

"No, Caesar. Nothing serious."

"Anything personal?"

"A letter from the Empress Ulpia. She writes that although she is well, your niece, Carissa, is not. The late months of the young lady's pregnancy do not seem to agree with her."

"Any mention of my niece's husband, Marcus Alexander?"

"No, Caesar."

"Well, let us get to work then on the correspondence," the emperor said. "I have plans for the afternoon hours." He settled himself in a chair and began to dictate rapidly to the wheezing scribe who sat at a side table, while Durantis murmured small asides and reminders into his ear.

In Aurelian's sleeping tent Zenobia was busily talking to Bab and Tamar. "What was his state of mind when you left him, Bab?" she demanded of her old nursemaid.

"He was very distressed by your capture, Majesty, and quite worried as to what he should do. The lady Flavia never left his side."

"Good for Flavia," Zenobia remarked. "She is stronger than her sweet appearance would tell. He must not surrender."

"He is not you, my dear," Tamar said with an air of finality, "and he is not Odenathus, either. If he does not surrender your life could be forfeit. Palmyrans would follow you anywhere, Zenobia. They would starve themselves to death and murder their children to please you; but you have not the right to ask them, my dear. You cannot repay their loyalty with death and destruction. You have lost this war. Do not drag Palmyra and all its peoples into the war you wage within yourself."

Old Bab drew her breath in sharply. Tamar's words had been a truth that no one else had ever spoken to Zenobia, but the beautiful queen tossed her dark head angrily and replied, "My only war is with Rome. From the day that they killed my mother Rome has been my enemy. If Vaba opens the gates to them he is no son of mine. I will fight the Romans till my death!"

"Is there no reasoning with you, Zenobia? Since you learned of Marcus's marriage this hatred of yours has been a burning spur to drive you onward toward your own destruction. No, do not glower at me. Everyone but you sees it. I am here with Bab because your father asked it of me. He will not live much longer, Zenobia, and his greatest fear is that you will ruin all that Odenathus worked so hard for, and by your own impetuous and stubborn acts steal Vaba's heritage from him. You are his favorite child, my dear, and all Zabaai ever wanted for his daughter was that she be happy."

"*Happiness?*" Zenobia's laugh was harsh. "There is no

such thing, Tamar! There is survival, which goes to the victorious, to the wisest, the wealthy, the clever, the strong! With survival one may gain a measure of peace, but that is all."

"Do not be cynical with me," Tamar snapped, her good nature and patience coming to an end.

"You are a disciplined woman. Use that self-discipline now, if not for your own sake then for the sake of those who love and care for you." She put a loving arm about Zenobia, and for a brief moment it was as it had been so long ago in that other time when everything had been so simple and there was no Marcus Alexander Britainus.

Then Zenobia shook Tamar's arm from her shoulders and said, "I can promise nothing, Tamar. Go back to my father and tell him that I love him. It is the best I can offer."

With a sigh Tamar kissed Zenobia upon the forehead, and with Bab to escort her safely through the encampment back to the tents of her son, Akbar, she left the queen to her solitude.

Furious, Zenobia looked for something to throw, but Aurelian's spare quarters offered nothing, frustrating her further, and she burst into tears. She was horrified at her own actions, but she could not stop the copious flow that poured from her eyes and down her cheeks, streaking them with hot salt. It was as if all the sorrow, the pain, and the disappointment of the last months was finally purging itself.

In the heat of the afternoon Aurelian returned to his own quarters with the idea of pleasuring himself once again with his beautiful captive. He was hardly prepared for the sight that greeted him. Zenobia lay upon her back on the couch; her exquisite golden body gleaming temptingly through the sheer black silk of her kalasiris; one arm flung protectively over her eyes, the other by her side, the hand curled into a fist. One leg was up, the other stretched straight. The evidence of weeping was plain upon her face, and for the briefest moment Aurelian felt pity for the brave queen she had been, but this was a woman as he liked them: pliant and helpless. He sat beside her.

She opened her silvery eyes with their black and gold flecks, and the hatred leapt forth to scald him. "What do you want?" she hissed venomously.

In an instant Aurelian's compassion vanished, and reaching forward to hook his fingers into the neck of her gown, he ripped it in two with a swift motion. "I wouldn't think after last night, goddess, that you would have to ask me that question," he replied mockingly; and when she attempted to rise he held her down, a cruel arm across her throat, effectively pinning her while his other hand began a leisurely exploration of her magnificent breasts.

She lay mutinous, her fury quite evident, while he played with the full silken orbs. Zenobia's nipples had always been sensitive, and now she quivered as he rolled first one and then the other between his thumb and his forefinger. "You will soon bore me if you are so quick to passion, goddess," he mocked her, and then he laughed, for if looks could slay then he knew he should lay this minute cold and lifeless upon the floor of his tent.

"Pig of a peasant," she snarled at him. "Is force the only way you can have a woman?"

"You were quick enough to beg for release last night," he countered, looking down into her angry eyes.

"Did you not teach me that it was lust, Roman?"

He chuckled. "Lust may generate your desire, goddess, but the results are the same as if you loved me. *You yield!*"

With a shriek of outrage she began a struggle against him. Quickly he removed his arm from across her throat, and catching her hands yanked them above her head as he bent to kiss her. She tried to bite him, but he only laughed, and bent again to kiss her passionately, his warm lips pressing hungrily upon hers, and forcing them apart so that he could run his tongue across her clenched teeth and murmur against her mouth soft entreaties all the while seductively fondling her breasts. She fought, desperately trying to avoid the tingle deep within her that now began to fight its way to the surface of her consciousness regardless of her struggle to avoid it. She fought, desperate to avoid this strange emotion that he called *lust,* an emotion that seemed to control her very thoughts.

He was enjoying their battle, for he understood the war that she now fought within herself. He knew that he had simply to persevere, for she was by nature an extremely passionate woman; and she would not give up at the first breach in her defenses. She would fight on until he plunged deep within her warm, wet body; until she climaxed beneath him, a curse upon her lips for him. And strangely, the prospect excited him more than if she had yielded to him without a struggle. He would never really tame her, he knew now; but eventually she would stop resisting him.

Beneath him, Zenobia fought to free one of her hands. If she could just get one arm loose she might use it in her defense. His big, hard body pressed down upon her, forcing the breath from her until, tearing her head from him, she gasped for precious air. He used the opportunity to release her arms and catch her face between his two hands. "Look at me!" he demanded of her in a voice she found she was powerless to resist. Her anger-blackened eyes confronted his sky-blue ones. His knee forced itself none too gently between her thighs, and then he was slowly, deliberately entering her. With a gasp of shock, and a terrible fear she could not explain rising up almost to suffocate her, she attempted to turn away. "*No!*"

His voice whipcracked sharply. "I want you to look into my eyes when I enter into your body."

"*No!*" Her voice had become a desperate whisper.

"*Yes!*" His hands held her head so tightly that she thought he might easily crush her skull. She trembled, mesmerized like a small bird caught before a snake, unable to look away as he slowly pushed himself into her helpless body. With deliberate and provocative movement he took her. His blue eyes bore deep into her soul, and the last thought Zenobia had before she fainted dead away was that he was somehow taking over her entire being and she had not even the strength to protest. Instead, she gave way to the rich, warm darkness that enfolded her and took away all need for thought.

"*Zenobia! Zenobia!*" Through the mists she could hear someone calling her name, and with a small protest she struggled to return to the sweet darkness; but the voice persisted. "*Zenobia! Open your eyes, goddess! Open them!*" Still protesting, she finally opened her eyes, although the effort was a mighty one, for her eyelids felt heavy. Before her foggy gaze Aurelian's face loomed, and to her surprise he appeared worried. Now as she focused and he became clearer, she could see relief etched upon his handsome face, even tenderness.

"I hate you," she managed to say weakly, and he laughed, elated.

"I thought I had killed you," he said, "and a dead queen is of no value to me."

She struck at him futilely, and with a growl of delight he gathered her into his arms and held her close. "Be quiet, goddess. I'm not going to hurt you. Just be quiet now." Because she was too ravaged to do anything more she lay quiet within his embrace; then reluctantly she began to relax. Soon she was dozing against his chest, and a lovely warmth began to penetrate her chilled frame.

When she awoke she knew that several hours had passed, for she could tell through a loose place in the tent that it was night. Carefully she eased herself out of his embrace. Her body ached in every joint. More than anything else in the world she longed for a hot bath, sweet-scented and soothing to ease her tired and sore mucles. With a sigh she knew that it would have to wait.

She looked over at Aurelian. He lay quiet, his breathing soft and even. Zenobia studied the emperor carefully. Her first brief impression of rugged handsomeness still held. He was surprisingly youthful-looking despite the fact that she knew him to be in late midlife. About his eyes and very gently etched into the skin on his upper cheekbones were the telltale signs of aging. Still, she thought, a touch bitterly, he was a damned satyr below the waist. He hadn't bothered to remove his short red military tunic during this last assault upon her, so she could see little of his body, but where the tunic rode high she could see the beginnings of a scar along his left thigh. From the width of it she suspected it was probably a spear wound. There were several other smaller scars upon his legs and arms, enough to show he had done his battle time, but not enough to say he was careless.

Even in sleep the line of his mouth indicated that he was a tough, stubborn man rarely given to softness or compassion. She shuddered remembering their battle of that afternoon. Never had she felt so . . . so possessed, or less in control of her own body and mind. When he had forced her to look at him she had come totally under his control, and she knew that he had reveled in her weakness. Zenobia vowed that she would not let that happen again. The next time he demanded she look into his eyes, she would appear to give her complete concentration, but in reality she would unfocus her eyes.

Quietly she rose from the bed and stretched slowly, easing some of the tension from her battered body. She was unaware that he watched her through slitted eyes, for not once had his breathing altered to warn her that he was awake. She had a fine body, he thought, despite the fact that she was over thirty. He liked her long legs, sleek flanks, barely rounded belly, and particularly her full but firm breasts. He liked women with big breasts, but often with age those fine breasts sagged. Ulpia's certainly had.

As he watched Zenobia raise the lid on her small trunk and pull forth a robe in which to clothe herself, he wondered about Carissa. She would have had her child by now. Was it the male child she had been so sure she carried? He also wondered whose child it actually was. Oh, there was always the possibility that he had finally fathered a child, but he seriously doubted it. People liked to believe that his lack of sons was poor Ulpia's fault, but he knew that it was not.

Before his marriage he had occasionally kept a mistress, and none had ever presented him with a bastard child. Since his marriage he had kept a steady stream of minor courtesans, and certainly none of them had borne him children. Only Carissa had ever claimed that he had fathered her child. He was dubious, but since he had never intended divorcing Ulpia to marry his venal little niece, he did not argue with her. Possibly the child was his. He had to admit that he was curious.

Aurelian opened his blue eyes and watched Zenobia as a cat watches its prey. He certainly felt sorry for Marcus Alexander, but then to the victor belonged the spoils, and he, Aurelian, was the victor.

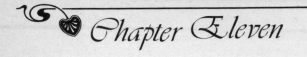

Chapter Eleven

"Please, Carissa, please help yourself and let us be done with this birth." Ulpia Severina, Empress of the Romans, leaned over her niece and tried to encourage the girl.

"It hurts," Carissa whined petulantly.

"I know, dearest, but you must push the babe out."

"How could you know? You are barren, aunt," was the cruel reply. Carissa turned her head away from Ulpia, and groaned.

"Come, Ulpia," said Dagian's soothing voice, and her strong, kindly hands gently pulled the empress away from the bedside. "Come and have some wine with me. The midwife will care for Carissa quite well."

Dumbly Ulpia nodded and allowed herself to be led from Carissa's bedchamber and back into the sunny atrium. Two slaves hurried forward bearing comfortable chairs, which they placed by the pool. A third slave placed a tray with a decanter of wine and two chased silver goblets upon a low round table. Dagian waved her servants away, then poured out the sweet golden wine and handed Ulpia a gobletful.

"Marcus should be with her," the empress murmured. "This is her first child."

"Ulpia, you cannot keep up the pretense any longer. Theirs was not a love match. If you do not know the truth then I will tell it to you now. The emperor forced this marriage upon my son. He was contracted to a lady in Palmyra with whom he is deeply in love. I know that however much you may love Carissa you do not for a moment believe the baby she is about to birth is my son's. They have been married four months, and he has been back in Rome just over that time."

"She thinks her child is Aurelian's," the empress whispered low, and Dagian's eyes widened slightly. "She does not know," Ulpia continued softly, "that my husband is sterile. Never once in all the years we have been married have I conceived; nor have any of his women." Her faded brown eyes grew wet with tears. "I had a baby once, Dagian. He was a beautiful little boy. They took him away from me. That is why I was married to Aurelian. He knew my shame, and threatened to expose it if my father did not allow the marriage.''

She sighed and wiped the tears that had strayed to her cheeks. "You must not think badly of him. He has always been a good husband to me; respectful and kind. He is a weak man where women are concerned, though, and Carissa is ambitious. I doubt even she knows the child's father.''

"Does the emperor know you know all this?'' Dagian asked.

"Of course not. In the tradition of this family, I have all these years been the perfect Roman wife. I have ignored his women as beneath my notice.''

"But your own niece?'' Dagian was somewhat taken aback.

"I am well into my middle years, Dagian. I did not want to lose my husband, and by keeping silent I have kept him all this time.''

Dagian smiled in spite of herself. There were those who thought Ulpia Severina stupid, but she was really quite clever. "But how can you love your niece when you know that she has betrayed you so disgracefully?''

"I cannot stand the little bitch,'' was the reply. "But I will never give Carissa the pleasure of knowing she has hurt me.''

A terrible shriek rent the stillness of the house, and the two women rose and hurried back to Carissa's bedchamber. They were joined by Marcus, who had come from the study where he now spent most of his time. Within the room was a sweet, unpleasant smell, and the two women wrinkled their noses slightly. Marcus strode to the windows and flung open the shutters, allowing in some fresh warm air.

Upon the bed Carissa writhed, moaning and praying for release. "Help me, Mother Juno! Help your daughter to birth an emperor!''

"The pretensions of the vixen,'' Ulpia murmured.

The midwife took the three aside for a moment while her assistant aided the straining women. "There is something wrong, noble master and ladies. The child was not positioned properly, but I turned it. Still, it did not feel right, and the mother will not help herself. The longer the birth takes, the harder on both her and the baby. She has lost too much blood already, and I am truly worried.''

"Can I be of help?'' Marcus asked.

"Sit by your wife, and encourage her.'' The midwife looked apologetic. "She is not an easy patient, sir,'' she explained.

"I don't imagine she is," he answered. "Carissa likes things easy, and instantly. It must have come as quite a shock to her that the child has not leapt fully clothed from her womb."

"Marcus!" Dagian was scandalized, but Ulpia put a gentle hand upon Marcus's arm.

"We have all suffered by Carissa's actions, Marcus," she said.

He looked long at her, and then with a sigh he sat down next to his wife. "You are going to have to push, Carissa," he said quietly. "The longer you delay doing your part the harder it is on your child."

She turned her face to him, but seeing concern in place of his usual mockery, she relaxed. "Will you stay with me?"

"Yes, I will stay until the child is born."

"And you will accept the child as your own?"

"No," he said. "I will not."

"*You must!*"

"No one in Rome believes for an instant that I fathered your child, Clarissa. I will support you both, but that is all!"

"My uncle will punish you," she whined, and then she cried out again with her labor.

"Push!" he commanded her, and she obeyed him, for the child was precious to her. It would guarantee her wealth and power for her lifetime. It was the beginning of a new line of imperial Roman Caesars. Gritting her teeth, she bore down. She would be the mother of a race of kings! Rome would be at her feet, and even this proud patrician who was her husband would eventually desire her; but when he finally did she would scorn him.

Soon! Soon she would hold her baby in her arms. Another pain clawed at her, and she bore down, elated to hear the midwife's cry, "I can see the child's head!" Carissa was greatly encouraged now, and from that moment on she strove to deliver her baby. Through the mists of pain she could hear them all driving her onward to her ultimate victory. The pain was becoming worse as the child pushed itself forth with her help. Finally with a mighty effort she expelled the infant with a shriek, and then she panted eagerly, "Give me my son! Give him to me now!"

They were silent. Why were they so silent? Despite her devastating weakness she struggled into a sitting position. "Give me my baby!" she demanded.

Why wasn't her son crying?

Marcus Alexander sighed, and there was a look of pity upon his handsome face. "The baby is dead, Carissa," he said quietly. "I am sorry."

"No!" They were lying to her. The baby couldn't be dead! "Give me my son!" she screamed.

Marcus nodded to the midwife's assistant, and the woman handed a swaddled bundle to Carissa. Eagerly she unwrapped the white linen stained brown with birthing blood to reveal— her watery blue eyes bugged in horror. "This isn't my baby!" she whispered in a tight, little voice, a voice that quickly rose to an hysterical scream. "What have you done with my child?!"

"You are holding your child," he said tonelessly.

Carissa looked down for several long moments at the thing in her lap. It had a head, a head with a flattish top, and a face with a grotesquely twisted mouth. At the base of the neck the thing's body divided itself into two sets of shoulders, which sprouted between them three arms, three legs, and two sets of fully developed genitals. The umbilical cord was wrapped tightly about the unfortunate infant's neck, and its whole body had a bluish cast. With a horrified shriek Carissa flung the thing from her lap, and screamed at Marcus, "It is your fault! You cursed me! You cursed me!" Then she gasped twice, and suddenly a stream of rich, red blood began to pour from her mouth while at the same time she began to bleed heavily from between her legs.

It was over so quickly that the spectators hardly had time to realize what was happening. Carissa fell back. She was quite obviously dead; and with an oath Marcus rushed from the room. Ulpia Severina stepped forward and closed her niece's eyes before turning to the midwife and her assistant to say, "You must disregard my poor niece's ravings. She was not herself in these last days of her pregnancy. Marcus Alexander was a fine husband to her, and she was fortunate to have him."

The midwife and her assistant nodded. "We have seen it happen before, lady. The sweetest-natured girls become totally deranged when told a child is dead. Poor girl. But, 'twas the will of the gods." She began gathering up her instruments. "We will leave you to prepare her for burial, lady."

The empress smiled graciously. "You will, of course, be paid double your fee for your trouble; and we may rely upon your discretion with regard to the matter of my niece's unfortunate infant."

"Of course, lady," was the smooth reply. The midwife bowed respectfully, and then departed the room with her assistant.

"Lady," Ulpia said quietly, "call your slaves and let us prepare my niece's body as quickly as possible. With your permission I should like to put her in our family's tomb rather than yours."

Dagian nodded gratefully. "It would be better," she said, "and I thank you, Ulpia."

"Call the slaves," the empress repeated, "and then go to Marcus. Now, perhaps, he may marry his true love. Aurelian will soon have Palmyra safely back within the fold. He is totally dedicated to reuniting the empire. Once Palmyra is subdued, your son may travel east and wed with his lady."

"I do not know if that will now be possible," Dagian said. "The woman to whom my son was betrothed is Zenobia, the Queen of Palmyra."

"Oh dear," Ulpia murmured. "That does put a different complexion upon the matter, doesn't it? Aurelian would be very angry with me if under those circumstances I allowed Marcus to leave Italy." She sighed, perplexed, and then her face brightened. "Well, Marcus will simply have to wait for his queen to come to him. I know that Aurelian plans to march her in his triumph when he returns to Rome. The queen will, of course, be an imperial captive, but I shall see that my husband gives her to Marcus. Aurelian is always very generous with me, for I ask little of him and I have always been discreet." She smiled at Dagian. "Go to your son, and tell him that everything will be settled soon. I will help to prepare Carissa for her last journey."

Dagian left Carissa's bedchamber. She wondered if Zenobia would survive her war with Rome. Was she already defeated, or had she surprised imperial Rome once again by defeating them? News took so long to get to Italy from Syria. Marcus's mother said a quick prayer to the gods that they protect Zenobia of Palmyra.

The gods, however, had chosen to be fickle toward the mortal who until recently had always been their favorite. She had spent another night of unrelenting combat in Aurelian's bed, and she wondered why Venus had left him so long upon the earth. The man was insatiable and apparently inexhaustible; but then, Zenobia thought with the barest hint of a smile, even the goddess had to rest. It was a pity she could not. The dawn had barely broken when they were engaged in battle of another kind.

"You will walk behind my chariot," he had announced to her as they rose from the bed.

Shocked, she had taken a moment to comprehend him, and then she had spun about, shouting, *"Never!"*

"Or I can drag you behind my chariot," was the choice offered next.

"Then you will drag me," she declared dramatically. "I will never enter *my* city in defeat! You have not defeated me, Aurelian!"

"Yes, I have," he mocked her, his sky-blue eyes crinkling at the corners with amusement. "What a stubborn goddess you are, Zenobia. I have defeated you honestly, both in the field and in my bed. If you do not play your part today in my triumph then I shall not allow you ever again to set foot within your city. How will you then spin your webs, my adorable spider? More important, how will you guide your son?"

Her teeth bared at him and her fists clenched angrily, she realized how securely she was entrapped. She knew that he would not relent once his decision was made.

"You will come meekly?" he demanded.

"I will come."

He chuckled at the fine disjunction between his question and her answer.

A slave brought them breakfast, and he noted with some amusement that her irritation had not affected her appetite. She neatly peeled and sectioned a small orange, which she then placed in a little bowl and covered with yogurt. A thick slice of freshly baked bread was lavishly spread with honey and set upon the red Arrentine pottery plate with two hard-boiled eggs and a handful of plump, ripe black olives. Totally ignoring him, she proceeded to consume this bounty, washing it down with a goblet of pomegranate juice. Then, without so much as a word to him, she rose up and left the tent. He wanted to laugh, but Zenobia's dignity was already worn thin and the emperor needed her cooperation.

To drag her shrieking into Palmyra would not win the city's sympathy, and even the young king might think differently about cooperating with Rome under those circumstances. He was, after all, her son, for all her usurpation of his office. He wanted her walking under her own power behind him, in a gesture that all of Palmyra would understand. Seeing her acceptance of Rome, the citizenry would then bow their own necks to the imperial yoke. Let her walk off her bad temper and come to terms with herself before his triumph. Had their positions been reversed she would, he knew, have treated him no differently. Let her be aware of that. Having settled it in his own mind, Aurelian proceeded to eat his own breakfast.

When he had finished he called for Gaius Cicero. "You are responsible for the queen," he said quietly. "I do not believe you will have any difficulty with her. We have spoken this morning, and she understands my wishes completely. You will see that she is in her place behind my chariot as I enter into Palmyra."

"Yes, Caesar!" came the dutiful answer.

At the appointed hour the Roman army was drawn up in full formation before the main gates of Palmyra. At their front was Aurelian in his battle chariot, looking eminently powerful and regal. His gold breastplate, with its raised design of Mars, the god of war, in various victories, gleamed in the morning sunlight; his long red military cloak blew gently in the faint breeze; but his elegant helmet could not hide the stern features of his face. He stood tall, erect, quiet. Behind him his waiting legions shuffled nervously.

The emperor turned to see Zenobia, in her place behind his chariot, turning away from his gaze. The gods! he silently cursed. Just to look at her aroused his desire. She wore no mourning this day, but rather was dressed as she had been the first day his army had arrived at Palmyra's gates those months back. In her golden kalasiris she looked no more like a beaten adversary than a bird of paradise. Her collar of rubies, rose quartz, and diamonds glittered brightly, its brilliance echoed by her golden circlet of vine leaves with their ribboned brilliants. She was in truth a golden goddess incarnate, and she had managed by her dress to change the lesson he had intended to teach the people of Palmyra.

A tiny smile twitched his lips, softening for a moment his stern features. She had somehow turned another defeat into a victory for herself. He would remember that. He had once accused her of being overproud, and by the gods she could give lessons in it! He turned back to face the gates of Palmyra, and as if his look were a signal, they began to slowly open.

Aurelian felt tense. He wondered if they would choose to fight at the last minute. Usually the walls of the city were crowded with spectators, but this morning not one person was to be seen upon them. He could plainly hear the creak of protest from the gate's hinges as it yawned wider and wider.

Once open, the entry to Palmyra resembled a gaping mouth void of teeth.

Then from out of the entry came a man in a simple white linen tunic and a red-and-white-striped toga bordered in purple. In his hands he carried the symbolic gold keys to the city. With great dignity the man made his way forward to stand before Aurelian's chariot. "Hail, Caesar!" he said in a loud voice. "I am Cassius Longinus, the king's chief advisor. On His Majesty's instructions I present to you the keys to Palmyra."

"Where is the king?" demanded the emperor.

"His Majesty awaits you at the palace, Caesar. The young queen was ill this day, and as they are recently wed, the king would not leave her side."

Aurelian raised an eyebrow. No wonder Zenobia was loath to let the boy rule. A king who put his woman before his position was certainly doomed. "Walk beside your queen, Cassius Longinus, as I enter the city. I assume your main avenue leads to the royal palace."

"It does, Caesar." Longinus moved behind the chariot to where Zenobia stood. "Majesty," he said low. "Thank the gods you are safe!"

"By rights, Longinus, I should be dead now but that my son has forgotten his duty."

He put a comforting hand upon her. "We will talk later," he said, and then they moved forward.

The Roman legionnaires jogged along nervously, facing straight ahead, their eyes shifting from right to left. The streets were quiet and empty, the shops closed, the people seemingly nonexistent. An unnatural silence hung over the city as Aurelian and his army made their way down the main avenue.

It was a wide avenue, fully able to accommodate four large chariots. The avenue was paved with interlocking blocks of black and white marble, and lined with magnificent white marble pillars that supported the roofs over the walkways in front of the shops and houses. Driving his chariot at a sedate pace, Aurelian was able to take it all in. He was impressed by the city's cleanliness and its graffiti-free statues, quite unlike Rome's.

Behind him Zenobia spoke quietly to Longinus. "Where are the people, Longinus?"

"At the council's suggestion, Majesty, they decided it would be better not to show themselves when the Romans entered the city."

"Not the king's suggestion?"

He hesitated, and that hesitation told her all she need know. "The king fears for the city's safety," Longinus attempted to excuse Vaballathus.

"Please thank the council for me, Longinus. I must assume that I will be kept from them."

"Has he said what he means to do about the government, Majesty?"

"Government has not been the main focus of our discussions," Zenobia said somewhat wryly.

Cassius Longinus flushed. "Majesty . . . " he gestured helplessly.

"I know, Longinus. It is the way of war, and for all my rank I am nought but a woman in the eyes of the victorious general from Rome."

"He has not hurt you?" Longinus looked concerned.

"Only my pride, old friend, and that, as you are well aware, is great. I expect I can spare a small piece for Aurelian to play with." She chuckled. "Despite my status as the defeated queen I seem to continue winning small battles." She gestured gracefully, and he smiled back at her.

"The city would have died for you, Majesty!"

"I know that, Longinus. Perhaps, however, I have been wrong. I have been told that I have not the right to ask that of my people. In the end what is important? That Palmyra survive! I took my chance with Rome, and I lost." She sighed sadly, and had he not known her better, he would have sworn that he saw a tear in her eye.

"They will probably exile you, Majesty."

"I know, Longinus, but if Vaba can remain here to rule, then Odenathus's dynasty continues. There will come another time, another age, another Palmyran king, and we will finally be free!"

"Do you really think that the emperor will leave Vaba here?"

"Vaba is hardly a threat to Rome. His ploy of not coming to give Aurelian the keys to the city because of the young queen's indisposition was a brilliant stroke. He has made himself look like a lovesick young fool who puts a woman above duty. That should give Rome a solid feeling of security."

Ahead of them Aurelian suddenly stopped his chariot and, turning about, called to Zenobia, "Come, goddess, and ride with me. We both know it does no good for you to walk behind me in defeat if no one is looking to see your defeat. You, too, Cassius Longinus. Perhaps you can enlighten me as to why

Palmyra appears so deserted." He reached down to her and, taking her outstretched arm, pulled her up, sliding an arm about her waist as she reached the chariot floor. Longinus was left to draw himself up by means of the handhold.

Once they were all safely within the chariot, Aurelian let the reins loosen a bit, and his cloud-white horses pranced forward again. The emperor turned his blue eyes upon Cassius Longinus. "Well?" He said. "Why is the city in hiding?"

"Palmyra loves its queen, Caesar. We will not be party to her shame."

Aurelian smiled coldly. "Palmyra has no queen," he said, and felt Zenobia shiver in his tight grasp. But when he looked over at her, she was staring straight ahead, seemingly unperturbed. Leaning over, he murmured against her ear, and the heady hyacinth fragrance she always wore battered his senses. "What sorcery is this, goddess, that you can arouse me without even seeming to try to arouse me?"

"You imagine it, Roman," was her cold reply.

He laughed low, and his laugh was intimate and insinuating, implying things she didn't even want to think about or consider. "You are the most intriguing captive I have ever taken," he said. "Fight me all you wish, goddess. I know how to defeat you."

Zenobia laughed scornfully. "You know how to overcome me physically, Roman, which is not surprising considering your height and girth."

Aurelian pressed his lips together, making his face appear even more severe. She had stung him successfully.

The royal residence came into view, and Aurelian had to admit to himself that the beautiful marble buildings easily rivaled his own official palace on the Palatine Hill in Rome. The entry stood open, and the emperor's chariot swept through into the courtyard, the men of his own legion positioning themselves about the palace in prearranged order. Not all of the army had entered the city, although part of each of the four legions had come; and as they had marched through the city toward the palace, *centurias, maniples,* and even full cohorts had dropped from each legion, taking control of government buildings, the great merchant houses, the university. Rome was quickly in control.

In the courtyard of the palace the first signs of life were visible as slaves rushed forward to catch the heads of the emperor's horses. Then upon the portico of the palace the

Council of Ten appeared, surrounding the young king almost protectively. Cassius Longinus leapt from the rear of the chariot as soon as it had stopped, and reached up to lift Zenobia down. Without so much as a backward glance at Aurelian she walked swiftly toward her son.

The Council of Ten, the attending soldiers, and the slaves all bowed before the queen, parting to allow her a path to the king. Mother and son looked at each other, and then Vaba said with honest emotion, "Praise be to the gods that you are safe, Mother!"

For a moment Zenobia closed her eyes, and then a deep sigh rent her slender frame. "I would have given my life for the city, Vaba," she said quietly.

"It would have been a needless sacrifice, Mother. We both know that, don't we?"

How can I be angry with him? she wondered quickly. He has done his duty toward Palmyra as he has seen it, and I was the one who gave him the king's power. It is not my way, but he is as steadfast as I am.

Zenobia held out her arms to her son, and he quickly stepped into her embrace. "I know that you are angry with me," he whispered, "but they would have had the city no matter the cost. I could not let you die, Mother. I could not!"

Without warning the tears appeared and spilled down her cheeks, "Perhaps they will let you rule still," she whispered back, hugging him tightly. "I shall take all the blame, Vaba. I will not allow you to be punished for me, and I will have no more gallantry from you!" She stepped back from him, her beautiful face serious in her intent.

Gently Vaballathus brushed the stray tears from his mother's cheeks. "For my father's sake?" he gently teased her.

"Yes," she smiled at him, and then suspiciously, "Why are you suddenly so amenable. Flavia has indeed wrought a miracle if she has matured you in six short months of marriage."

"I am beginning to realize what it is not only to be a king, but a parent as well, Mother," was the quiet answer. "Flavia is with child."

"Then she really was indisposed?" Zenobia was pleased, but at the same time a tiny voice said that she was too young, too beautiful, too sensual to be a grandmother. She was but thirty-four!

Then a sharp voice destroyed her reverie. "If this is your

son, goddess, I should like to be presented." Aurelian was at her side.

Zenobia looked up, faintly annoyed. "Vaballathus, my son, here is the mighty Roman conquerer, Aurelian." Her gaze flicked insolently to the emperor. "My son, the King of Palmyra," she said.

The two men stared coldly at each other, and then Aurelian said mockingly, "Will you not bid me welcome to Palmyra, Vaballathus?"

"I did not think it necessary," was the quick reply. "You Romans seem not to mind if a city welcomes you or not."

Aurelian looked carefully at the young man. "There is a lot of your mother in you, *boy,*" he replied.

"Thank you, sir." Vaba was totally unruffled, and Zenobia was quite proud of him.

"We will talk inside," the emperor snapped. "All of you," he continued, including the nervously waiting Council of Ten with a wave of his hand. "Cassius Longinus, lead the way. Gaius Cicero, attend me!"

At the door of the main council chamber, Aurelian stopped and said to Zenobia. "Not you, goddess. This is men's work."

Longinus saw the furious retort rising to her lips, but before he might intervene the king spoke. "The queen is a member of the council, Caesar. Without her we cannot legally meet."

"And we will not," put in the white-haired, elderly Marius Gracchus.

"If you would treat with us," Antonius Porcius contributed, "then the queen must be with us, Caesar. We mean you no disrespect, but these are *our* ways. We know that, understanding them, you will be fair."

Aurelian looked at the council and, seeing that they were adamant, relented. He had hoped to humiliate her with the government, but, by the gods!, she certainly commanded loyalty. He felt almost envious of such devotion.

"If it is your custom," he said casually, "then the queen may partake of this meeting." He entered into the council chamber and seated himself at one end of the long table.

"You sit at the other end, Mother," Vaba said softly, and Zenobia knew that her son was giving his permission for her to take a leading role in the negotiations to come.

Regally she settled herself, nodding as she did so to Vaba and the council to sit down.

Aurelian noted all of this. It seemed almost a shame to break her, but as much as he admired her, she was a dangerous enemy; an enemy Rome could not afford. She wanted the entire Eastern Empire, and she had taken it. Left in Palmyra, she would rise again. He looked down the table at the faces turned to his, and said, "Palmyra is no longer a client kingdom. It will return to province status effective immediately."

Then the emperor sat back, expecting the uproar that followed. The Council of Ten was speaking all at once, their voices raised in strong protest against what seemed to them an arbitrary decision. They had expected negotiations, the removal of Zenobia, even trade sanctions and heavy fines; but not *this*. They had opened their gates allowing the Roman emperor inside their city and this is the way he responded.

"Be silent!" Zenobia's voice stilled the cacophony. She looked down the table at the emperor. "You are overly harsh, Caesar." He noted with amusement that it was the first time she had used his proper title, and without sarcasm. "It is I who am at fault, not Palmyra. Do not punish the city, nor my son; rather, punish me. Vaballathus will serve you well. He is his father's son before he is mine, and my husband was always loyal to Rome. It was he who kept the eastern boundaries secure for the empire against the Persians. Surely you will bear this in mind before you make a final decision."

It was as close to begging as she was going to come, and Aurelian knew it. "Why should I heed your words, *Queen* of Palmyra? Your son has not proven himself, as did his father, and he is young besides. Give me one good reason why I should listen to you?"

Zenobia stood up and gave the emperor a long, slow look. "Because *I am Palmyra*," she said quietly.

He was frankly astounded by her words, but a quick look at the others confirmed that she had spoken from truth not vanity. "I will think on it," he said. This was a far more dangerous woman than he had realized. Better he spend a little time assessing the situation before making a final decision. "The council is dismissed," Aurelian concluded. Then he rose and walked from the room.

"Go with him, Antonius Porcius," Zenobia begged. "You were the last imperial governor before we were freed of Roman control. Plead for my son! For your daughter, the young queen, for our unborn grandchild who will be Palmyra's rightful heir!"

Antonius Porcius arose dutifully and followed after the

emperor. He had not changed a great deal over the years, but Zenobia noticed that he moved more slowly than she remembered and that silver was beginning to streak his remaining hair.

"What are we to do, Majesty?" Marius Gracchus asked.

"Wait," was the reply. "He is not an easy man. I suspect that he truly wants Palmyra to return to province status, but we must prevent that at all costs. Vaba must be allowed to remain king. Perhaps not in his lifetime, but one day we will again rise, and the inheritors of Odenathus's dynasty must be ruling the city when the time comes! To this end I expect you to all work, and if the people really love me then they will work toward this goal, too."

"But what will happen to you, Majesty?"

"I shall go to Rome, Marius Gracchus. Aurelian has already told me that much. He will not, I fear, trust me out of his sight, and he is wise not to." She smiled at the elderly councillor. "Given the chance, I should do it again, old friend."

Marius Gracchus chuckled. "With you will go our greatness," he replied.

"Do not say that," was her quick answer. "Vaballathus is a young man now. Who knows what miracles he will accomplish in his time. And what of those who come after him? This city has stood since the days of the Hebrew king, Solomon, its founder, and it has seen its share of greatness. It will again." She stood up. "I am tired," she announced. "I have not slept well these last months, but now I think I might." She looked over her council. "I do not know if we will be allowed to meet again," she said. "I thank you for your loyalty to Palmyra, to me, and to my late husband. I know you will give that same loyalty to my son, the king. Long live Palmyra!" Then she was swiftly gone from the council chamber.

There was not one member of the Council of Ten who did not unashamedly wipe the tears from his eyes; and then slowly each one of them moved forward, kneeling before Vaballathus to pledge fealty to him as they had done upon his father's death those long years ago. Then each departed to his own section of the city to do the queen's bidding. It was not an easy task, for the Romans were everywhere and public gatherings had already been forbidden; but slowly the council members moved, in some cases from house to house, spreading Zenobia's words. The city must rise behind their young king in order to preserve the dynasty. The queen's day was done, but the Roman emperor must feel the weight of public opinion behind the House of Odenathus.

Zenobia had retired to her own apartments, where she had a long, leisurely soak in a hot bath scented with oil of hyacinth. The queen's long hair was washed and brushed dry so that it floated about her like a veil. A soft Egyptian cotton robe was slipped over her head, and then she lay down upon her couch to sleep.

Sleep came quickly. The last thing she remembered was the bright sunlight of midday streaming in a blazing shaft across the marble floor of her room. When she awoke a single lamp burned in the darkness of the room and in the gardens outside she could hear the crickets singing their evening song. Slowly she stretched herself, one leg, one arm, then her entire body, feeling the tension entirely gone. She sighed deeply, and then started at the sound of Aurelian's voice.

"You have slept long, goddess. Are you feeling better?"

"What are you doing here, Roman?" but her voice lacked any anger.

"Watching you," he replied. "I like watching you in sleep. It is one of the few times you are not spitting and snarling at me like a wild thing."

"We cannot be friends, Roman," she said quietly.

"Perhaps not right now, goddess, but I enjoy looking at you. You are extravagantly beautiful."

"Like the ladies of Rome?"

"Great Jupiter, no! You are exotic; they are . . ." he thought a moment, and then he said, "they are not exotic, goddess, as you are. You are as fair as a dawn, and as elusive as a soft desert wind."

"Why, Roman, you are quite poetic."

Aurelian arose, came across the room, and seated himself on the edge of Zenobia's sleeping couch. She tensed, and he said, "You are not afraid of me, and yet—" He looked piercingly at her. "What is it, goddess? Why do you grow stiff when I but sit by your side?"

"Because I know what your sitting by me portends, Roman. You will force yourself upon me once again, to impress once more the imperial victory upon my body and soul." Her voice was bitter, almost raw in its tone.

"You still love Marcus Alexander, don't you, goddess?" She said nothing, and so he continued. "He is my niece's husband,

and already they are parents. It is a futile love you hug to your heart, goddess. Let me love you.''

Her eyes widened in surprise. ''*You?*'' The scorn in her voice was fierce. ''I shall never give myself into the keeping of any man ever again, Roman; but *you? You* love me? What madness is this? What of your poor wife who waits for your return? I am a queen! No matter I am a defeated queen, I am still a queen. I am not some poor innocent to be honored by the position of mistress! You insult me!''

''Your illustrious ancestress, Cleopatra, was honored to be the mistress of two Romans,'' he said.

''It cost her her life,'' was the cold reply. ''She put herself into the keeping of Romans, and in the end it destroyed her! I will not be destroyed by you—or any other Roman!''

''I cannot destroy you, Zenobia—only your own bitterness can do that,'' was his reply. ''You will be my mistress because I make that decision, and not you.'' He reached out for her, but Zenobia drew back.

''And now,'' she said angrily, ''now you will once again rape me to prove the truth of your words.''

''I have not once raped you, goddess. Each time I have made love to you, you have wanted me to do so. The only one you have been fighting is yourself!''

''I despise you,'' she whispered half fearfully. ''I hate you! How can I want your lovemaking when I detest you so?''

''Lust, Zenobia. Did I not tell you that first night? You may not want me, but your beautiful body does. You are a woman; you have known a man's love and you have known a man's passion. Neither of these things have frightened you. Why then should a man's honest lust cause such a turmoil within you, goddess?''

''It is wrong,'' she said firmly. ''Lovemaking without affection or caring is wrong.''

''Who has told you these things, goddess? You are young yet, and certainly your small experience with but two men cannot qualify you to make such a judgment.''

He reached out for her again, and this time his arm slid about her waist and drew her resisting body close to his. ''I have never experienced *love,* and yet I enjoy lying with a beautiful and passionate woman. None have ever complained to me before, goddess. This foolishness is but in your mind. If you would simply enjoy the feelings I can engender within your body, you would see that I am right."

"You are a wicked man," she said softly. "I will not allow you to destroy me."

"I will not destroy you, goddess," he murmured, and his breath was warm against her ear, the little puffs of his words causing her to shiver slightly. "Let me love you, Zenobia. Don't fight me." A hand began a slow, gentle caressing of her breasts. "Ah, goddess, my beautiful goddess," Aurelian whispered, his lips moving against her soft, fragrant hair.

Zenobia felt his hands and his lips tenderly questing. She heard the restrained passion in his voice, and her soul seemed to draw back deep within her where she might watch him in safety. She was, despite her long nap, still so very weary, and she had no strength left to fight him. Opening the delicate silver filigree fastenings of her sleeping robe, he pushed it back and off her shoulders. He was being very careful, very gentle. For several long moments he simply sat and stared at her firm golden breasts as they rose and fell with her breathing.

Then he tenderly pressed her back among her pillows, and began to place delicate kisses upon her chest and breasts. His lips touched lightly, quickly, moving here and there, never lingering very long in one place. "I am a soldier, goddess," he said low. "A rough soldier, and I have never had the time to make proper love to a beautiful woman; but here in your perfumed palace I shall linger, and adore you until it is time for us to depart for Rome." Then his lips returned to her flesh, this time moving slowly and sensuously, coaxing alive within her tiny flames of pure desire.

She did not fight him—whether from simple exhaustion or because she was admitting her surrender to Rome even Zenobia did not know. What she did know was that his lips, his hands, his seductive words all combined to vanquish her. She had lost Palmyra to him, and whatever she said, or did, he would take her body, for, as he had said, he was the victor. Perhaps by yielding she might regain some measure of control over the situation. Briefly she thought of Deliciae. Was this what it had been like for her in the days before Odenathus had given her in marriage to Rufus Curius? Forced to barter her body in order to survive. How scornful Zenobia had been; but then she had not known. Still, she had sworn to herself that she would survive; and if to survive she must use her body, then by the gods she would do so!

Zenobia focused her silvery eyes upon Aurelian, and said simply, "Love me."

Startled, he looked up at her, and when she repeated those two words he groaned like a starving man being offered a fine feast. She would have sworn that his hands trembled as he bared her completely. Gazing at her passionately, he ran his hands over her silken skin, moving upward to cup her large breasts, then sliding down across her thighs; his fingers hesitant at first, then surer, probing tenderly between the plump lips of her Venus mount. She wasn't really quite prepared when his blond head dipped quickly and his tongue touched the tiny secret, sensitive flower of her womanhood. She gasped, but then his fingers were gently spreading her nether lips, and his tongue was caressing her expertly, forcing the liquid fire to flow, and she realized she didn't care. There would be no escape from this man, and so, uncaring, Zenobia allowed herself to be swept up in the whirlwind of pleasurable sensations that Aurelian aroused within her body.

He was a lover of incredible stamina, and having suffered these last nights from his brutality, she was quite surprised that he was capable of such sensitivity and gentleness. His hungry mouth was beginning to wreak havoc with her senses as he sucked sensuously upon that tiny morsel of tender flesh, yet she was unready when the first starburst exploded within her, and she cried out still fearful of the feelings that this man could arouse within her.

Aurelian understood, and pulling himself back level with her, he smoothed the tangled hair from her forehead and placed a kiss upon it. "You are so beautiful in your passion," he said softly.

"Hold me," she whispered in a shaking voice and, turning, clung to him, her whole frame trembling.

He was instantly protective of her, enfolding her within his strong arms. "Here," he said quietly, "within the privacy of your chamber, I am with you as I have never been with any woman. I know that I stir your senses, goddess, but do you know how much you stir mine? It is with me as it has never been before. I do not think that I shall ever get enough of you!" His voice was thick with his emotion, and she felt his staff, hard and eager against her thigh, yet he made no move to force her this time.

Suddenly Zenobia realized that if Cleopatra's Roman lovers had destroyed her, it was surely because her ancestress had loved and trusted them. I will never love or trust this man, she thought, but if I can please him, and obviously I can, then perhaps I shall yet save my son's inheritance. She shifted her body so she might see his stern face, and freeing her hands from her sides, she reached up, drew his head down, and kissed him sweetly, her soft lips moving against his almost shyly. "You are right, Roman," she said low. "Lust is a powerful thing, and not altogether unpleasant. Would you be very much shocked if I said I wanted you?"

Looking down upon her, his blue eyes searched her face for signs of mockery, but finding none he said, "No, I should not be shocked, goddess."

"Love me," she answered him, her lush body beginning to move provocatively beneath his.

Aurelian needed no further encouragement, for his manhood felt close to bursting with his desire. Feeling her long legs parting to encourage him, he pushed his aching weapon deep within her warm, wonderfully willing body, a groan of pleasure escaping his tightly clamped lips. The long and lovely legs wrapped themselves about him, and he had the fleeting thought that she was really the goddess Venus herself, come to earth to give sweet pleasure to him. Her hands ran smoothly down his back, then caressed his taut buttocks; her touch was more exciting than anything he had ever known. She was making love to him!

Zenobia quickly realized the effect that her boldness was having upon Aurelian. It roused him more than anything she could have done, and his excitement communicated itself to her. Together they fanned the flames of their desire, their bodies writhing passionately, both seemingly inexhaustible as he drove again, and again, and again into the lush and lovely woman panting beneath him. Her movements encouraged him onward. Never had he felt so strong, so manly, so immortal as within the throbbing sheath of this magnificent creature.

Then suddenly Zenobia cried out, "Ah, sweet Venus, I die!" and Aurelian, with a low growl of triumph, waited but a moment to assure himself that she had attained Olympus before releasing his own boiling offering to the goddess of love. He was shaken to the core of his being, and he could see that Palmyra's queen lay in a deep swoon, her beautiful body covered in a faint silvery sheen of dampness that highlighted the pale-golden color of her skin. He would have believed her dead but for the pulse that fluttered in a tiny, provocative hollow at the base of her throat.

She soared upward, floating free and happy, seeing below her the mountainous home of the gods; and then as suddenly she plunged downward into a whirling, light-filled abyss that battered both her body and her soul. Something was wrong, but she could not understand what it was. With a low moan she tried to escape the sinking feeling. Slowly, almost painfully, she fought her way back to consciousness, her first realization of returning feeling being the firm kisses being placed upon her lips. Zenobia opened her eyes, and Aurelian smiled down at her before his lips took charge of hers once again.

His mouth demanded and she aquiesced, kissing him back with equal fervor, opening her mouth to receive his questing tongue. The tongue touched the sensitive roof of her mouth, and she shivered. It rubbed against her tongue in a sensual gesture, then sucked, attempting to draw her very spirit from between her lips. She eluded him, and attempted to imitate his actions. She was pleased when he shuddered against her, and then he drew away from her. "Goddess, you will destroy me yet," he murmured against her ear, and for the first time in months Zenobia felt genuine amusement bubbling up within her. Her laughter sounded warm and mischievous in his ear, and he was forced to chuckle himself.

They lay together for some time, and then she realized that he had fallen asleep, and so Zenobia slept, too. In the morning he made no attempt to hide from her servants the fact that he had slept with her, and Zenobia wisely refrained from comment. She desperately wanted to ask him what, if anything, he had decided for Palmyra; but she believed to ask such a sensitive question after their extraordinary night together would make it appear as if she had deliberately set out to use her body to influence him. She had, of course, but although she was willing to be totally honest with herself, she would not, could not be with Rome's emperor. He would ever be her enemy, though she be his mistress. He would tell her when he was ready to tell her, and then, if necessary, she would try to soften his terms and see that Vaba remained Palmyra's ruling king.

She helped to bathe him, and then bathed herself. When young Adria, Bab's assistant, attempted to brush Zenobia's long hair, Aurelian took the brush from her hand and did it himself, reveling in the silken swath that fell to the middle of her back. His big hand smoothed it after each passage of the brush, and when Bab, scandalized, clucked her disapproval he mildly ordered her to be silent. Then, on reflection, he said, "Bring your mistress a kalasiris the color of flame. I want to see her gowned in the bridal color." Then he bent and whispered in Zenobia's ear, "For you are my bride, goddess. You are the only woman who has ever made me feel. I believe that I am falling in love with you."

"Is this how you treat all your captives?" she half-teased him.

"Do not jest with me, goddess. I mean what I say."

Zenobia sighed. "Do not fall in love with me, Roman. I have warned you that I shall never again give myself into any man's keeping. You are my enemy, yet in this I cannot hurt you. I am being honest with you."

"You have been hurt," he answered her. "In time you will come to trust me, goddess."

"Will you call the Council of Ten into session today?" she asked him, attempting to change the subject.

"The meeting is already arranged for the midday hour, goddess. While you slept yesterday afternoon I gave orders that Gaius Cicero see to it."

She turned her head to look at him, and could not resist asking, "What have you decided, Caesar?"

"As you come to know me, Zenobia," he said slowly, "you will learn that the secret of my success is always to keep my private life and my public duty separate. We will never discuss the business of the empire within the walls of our bedchamber." He then bent and kissed her mouth lightly. "I am ravenous, goddess. Do you think we can persuade that disapproving old crone who serves you into bringing us something to break our fast?"

The reproof had been a gentle one, but nonetheless Zenobia felt a chill of premonition. Forcing it down, she called to Bab, "The emperor is hungry. Why have we not been fed?"

"Can I do several things at once?" Bab snapped. "First there was the bath, then the overseeing of this useless wench that you insist aid me, though the gods know she is more trouble than help, then *he* commands that I fetch a flame-colored gown for you! When am I supposed to have the time to get your breakfast?!" With a snort she turned upon the hapless Adria. "You, girl! Go and fetch breakfast for the queen—and *him!* I must remain and see to flame-colored garments. Humph!"

Still grumbling under her breath, Bab waddled off into the queen's wardrobe while the flushed Adria hurried off to see to the food.

"How can you put up with that sour old woman?" the emperor asked.

"She raised both my mother and me," Zenobia said. "She is very dear to me even if in her old age she becomes impatient and frequently oversteps her place. I love her, Roman, and she loves me."

He smiled. "I had an old grandmother like that. She was fierce and gruff, but somehow she always had a sweetmeat for you." He reached out and pulled her into his arms. For a long moment they stood together, their nude bodies touching, his warmth and male scent suddenly familiar and almost comforting in her nostrils. They broke guiltily apart as Bab bustled back into the room, still grumbling beneath her breath about flame-colored draperies.

"Here!" She almost flung the natural-colored chamber robes at them. "That foolish girl, Adria, is deeply shocked by your immodesty, and for once I am in total agreement with her. Are you athletes to run about in public as naked as the day your mothers birthed you? Put these on at once! Your meal will be here shortly, and unless you wish to display each other's charms to the slaves you will clothe yourselves immediately."

Meekly they obeyed her, but Zenobia's lips twitched her suppressed amusement, especially as she could see that Rome's mighty emperor was completely chagrined by the severe tongue-lashing he had just received.

"Is she a slave?" he demanded.

"No," Zenobia whispered. "She was a freedwoman of Alexandria when my grandfather employed her to nurse my orphaned mother. She has always been a part of my life. She always will be."

"She is elderly, goddess. I wonder if she can make the trip to Rome. It is a long way."

"I cannot leave her behind, Roman."

The arrival of their morning meal forestalled further conversation. Adria had brought a tray containing a pitcher of freshly squeezed juice, a mixture of oranges, lemons, and limes, a round red Arrantine bowl with hard-boiled eggs, freshly baked bread, a honeycomb, and another bowl filled with ripe apricots.

They sat facing each other across a round table, eating together as if it had been a habit of long standing between them. Zenobia reached for an apricot and, pulling it apart, removed the pit and popped half of it into her mouth. Chewing it, she changed the subject, asking, "What will you do until it is time for the council to meet?"

"I will have to ride through the city checking upon my men, goddess. I want no friction between your people and mine. We want a return to business as usual here in Palmyra."

She stifled the angry retort that sprang to her lips. It would do no good, and if she were to convince him to allow Vaba to remain as Palmyra's king, she must remain pleasant. They finished their meal with a modicum of small talk, then Aurelian quickly dressed and made to leave her, stopping as he went to place a passionate kiss upon her mouth.

"I should rather remain with you, goddess, than attend to this dull business." He smiled down at her and then he was gone.

Alone! At last she was alone again, if only for a few minutes. She would go out in her garden and walk among the calming flowers and fountains. It was not yet too hot to do so.

She did not know how long she wandered amid the fragrant blooms; but suddenly Bab was there, fussing at her about changing from her chamber robe into what she scornfully called "those flame-colored draperies that *he* wants." Zenobia's amusement eased some of her apprehension, and she dutifully followed her elderly servant back into her bedchamber. Standing quietly, she allowed Bab and Adria to dress her in the crimson gown, but seeing her reflection in her large oval silver mirror, Zenobia suddenly tore the garment off with an oath.

"No! I will not wear this! Rome's emperor will not dictate to me in even so small a matter as my clothing. Today, I expect, will be the last time my council meets—at least with me. I shall therefore be their queen this last time, and I shall dress like a queen—not like the emperor's favorite whore!"

"Ha!" A smile split old Bab's face. "Now you speak like Palmyra's queen! All this morning you have sounded like the Roman's pet bird, all soft and cooing. What shall I bring you, my baby?"

"I will wear Tyrian purple, the royal color. Adria, fetch me the proper kalasiris, sleeveless please, and a matching cape; and Bab, get the jewel cases. It is Zenobia, Queen of Palmyra, who will head this Council of Ten meeting, not Aurelian's mistress."

For a few minutes Zenobia stood amid the shredded wreckage of her torn gown while her two servants hurried back and forth doing her bidding. When the jewel cases were brought, the queen opened them all, staring down at their contents. Already upon her bed lay a gossamer spun kalasiris of Tyrian purple, its embroidered and fitted bodice replete with golden stars that tumbled down amid the narrow pleats of the skirt, glittering and twinkling like the very stars in the night sky.

Carefully, she considered her jewelry. A jeweled collar would have been a simple choice, but she closed the cases containing these pieces and waved them away. The collars were neat, and she wanted to be opulently magnificent. Finally her eye lit upon a necklace of irregularly shaped amethysts, some set within yellow-gold settings, others hanging from their settings by web-thin yellow-gold wires. Smiling, Zenobia lifted it out of its case and handed it to Bab. "This one," was all she said, and then she pulled a rather barbaric pair of matching earrings from the jewel case. "And these." The box was closed, and Adria proffered another leather case, this one filled with bracelets. Zenobia selected two armbands, fashioned like snakes, each golden scale perfect, their flashing eyes of small but choice purple sapphires. The last box offered contained rings, rings of every size and shape, with gemstones of every sort known to the world. Zenobia chose but one: a huge purple scarab beetle into whose back was carved the seal of Palmyra.

The door to Zenobia's apartments opened, and Vaba and Flavia entered. The queen turned to her son and his wife, holding her arms out to Flavia. "Dear child, I should indeed scold you. I am far too young to become a grandmother." She hugged Vaba's wife, and then inquired anxiously, "You are well now?"

"I tend to be sick in the early afternoons, and sometimes in the mornings," Flavia smiled with a little shrug. "Both quite normal, my mother assures me." Then the girl's face grew worried. "What is to happen to us with the Romans in the city, Aunt Zenobia? Will they kill us? Will my child be safe?"

"So many questions, Flavia! Dear child, I do not know what will happen, but I am certain that Aurelian means this family no harm. I believe what he wants is to restore Roman rule to this city again, but that we shall try to prevent for Vaba's sake."

Flavia's face became less fearful. "You have always been a favorite of the gods, my lady."

"Of late," murmured Zenobia wryly, "I have begun to

wonder." She motioned to a chair. "Sit down, Flavia. You must not tax yourself." Then she sat down herself.

Vaba, however, remained standing. "What is happening in the city?" he demanded.

"We do not know," Zenobia replied. "Each district in the city has been cut off from all the others so the people may not mix freely. It is impossible to get from one area to another without a pass, and precious few are being issued."

"Then we must wait for the council meeting," Vaba said quietly.

"Yes," his mother answered, and then, "Where is Demi? I have not seen him since the Romans entered the city."

Vaba frowned. "My brother disagreed quite violently with my decision to surrender to the Romans. He left the palace two nights ago, and I have no idea where he is. I do know, however, that he has banded together a group of young patrician hotheads like himself, and they are considering a guerrilla-type warfare upon the Romans."

"No!" Zenobia's voice was sharp. "We must find him, Vaba. Such behavior could endanger your position. I will not allow him to do that!"

"I have people out looking, but if the city is as tightly closed as you say, then it will be more difficult for them."

"The gods take the young fool!" Zenobia muttered.

"He is your son, Mother," Vaba could not resist saying.

"If you mean he is impetuous," was the calm reply, "then you are right."

"It was not just the surrender," put in Flavia. "We had only just told him about the baby."

"He was jealous," Vaba said.

"No, Vaba," Flavia defended her brother-in-law. "It is not easy for Demi to be the younger son. It is never easy for a younger son. Now Demi is to be upstaged by our child, and he had not the time to adjust. He will come around."

"What Flavia said is true, Vaba," Zenobia spoke. "I know that for some time Demi has chafed from having little to do. He is a natural soldier like your father, and a good leader. I had planned to send him to Alexandria to act as our governor. His thirst for power is not overly great, and that would have satisfied him well."

"I am not angry at him, Mother," Vaba replied. "Believe it or not, I understood how he felt. But now he endangers not only me but Flavia and our unborn child as well."

"He endangers Palmyra," Zenobia said. "He *must* be found!"

"We are doing our best. Can you not speak to Aurelian?"

"What? Are you mad? What should I say? Should I tell Aurelian that I cannot control my family? Please, will the Romans help to find my bad boy? They would execute him on the spot as a troublemaker! Do you want Demi's death on your hands, Vaballathus?"

"There have been no executions, Mother."

"That is no guarantee that there won't be," Zenobia said ominously.

"Oh!" They both turned to see Flavia white and swaying in her chair.

"Darling! What is it?" Vaba was kneeling at his wife's side.

"What if they kill you, Vaba?" Flavia began to sob piteously.

Zenobia could have bitten her tongue. "Do not fret, Flavia. The Romans will not kill this family, I am sure. They will execute a few unimportant people in order to impress their rule upon the masses. There will be messy affairs in the public squares, but we will not be involved. They will go after potential troublemakers, accusing them of things like hoarding and profiteering. Do not fear. Vaba will not be harmed."

"You are sure?"

"Quite sure," Zenobia said with far more certainty than she was feeling. Then she said, "Vaba, take Flavia to your apartments and stay with her until the council meeting. If I get any word before then I shall send to you."

The king stood up, nodding in agreement with his mother, and then he escorted his trembling young wife from the room.

"Now," Zenobia said, "I am ready to dress." Bab and Adria quickly aided the queen, pulling the exquisite kalasiris over her head, fastening her jewelry about her neck and in her ears and about her upper arms. Zenobia slipped the ring upon her fingers while Adria helped her into delicate golden sandals.

The queen then sat at her dressing table, and Adria brushed her dark hair until it shone. Then, taking a section of hair from each side of Zenobia's head, Adria braided it and drew the thin braids back to fasten them high on the back of the queen's head with a jeweled enamel pin. The rest of Zenobia's black hair flowed free down her back, and Bab dusted it with gold powder before placing the vine-leaf crown upon her mistress's head. The queen stood and walked to her polished silver mirror, smiling in satisfaction at what she saw.

"Bab, find me Cassius Longinus!"

Longinus came quickly, sprawling into the chair lately vacated by Rome's emperor. Helping himself to an egg, he dipped it into the salt and took a healthy bite. "Your secret garden gate is unguarded, Majesty. The council advises you and your family escape while there is yet time."

"To what purpose, Longinus?"

"You would be a rallying point for our people."

"There is no point in it, Longinus. Rome is already in full possession of the city. The army is as trapped as I am. There is no help for us. The king made the decision to open Palmyra's gates to Rome that the city and her people might be saved. He was right, and I can only hope Aurelian will let my son remain this city's ruler. To that end alone I will work, Longinus."

Longinus bowed his head in acceptance of her judgment, then standing, he said, "I will go with you to Rome, Majesty."

"It is time," Bab said. "It is midday."

"You have seen to my guard?"

"Need you ask, my baby? They await you outside the door."

Without another word Zenobia walked through her bedroom, through her antechamber, and out into the hallway through doors opened swiftly by her slaves. Instantly the one hundred men in her guard came to attention, and cried out, "Hail Zenobia! Hail, Queen of Palmyra!"

A small smile touched Zenobia's lips as she said, "Good afternoon, Captain Urbicinus."

"Majesty!" The captain saluted smartly.

The queen seated herself in her waiting litter, an opulent affair of solid silver, its raised designs all of a botanical nature. The cushions of the litter were of purple velvet. Immediately the four coal-black slaves in their cloth-of-silver breechcloths lifted the litter, and began moving down the corridor. Before them, behind them, and on either side of them marched the queen's guard.

It was not a long trip to the council chamber, and with much ceremony—the wide double doors to the chamber were flung wide, the waiting trumpeteers played a flourish—the queen's guard marched into the room with the litter. The litter was carried to the head of the table, where the emperor and the young king were already waiting, as was the entire council. Dismounting the litter with Captain Urbicinus's aid, Zenobia caught Longinus's eye and saw secret amusement in it. As she seated herself opposite Rome's emperor the royal guard once more shouted, "Hail, Zenobia! Hail, Queen of Palmyra!" Then they positioned themselves along two of the walls of the room, facing some of the men of Aurelian's own legion, who lined the other two walls.

"The council is called to order," Zenobia said. She looked to the emperor.

By the gods, Aurelian thought admiringly, she yet has the courage to defy me, even now in the hour of her defeat. He almost regretted the decisions he had made regarding the city. Almost. The emperor stood and looked around the table at all the upturned and expectant faces before facing Zenobia. Then he said, "You are banished, Queen of Palmyra, from this city-state that you led to rebellion against your masters, the imperial Romans."

The room was deathly silent. No one's face showed any emotion, for it was as they expected, as Zenobia had led them to expect. What they waited for was his decision concerning Odenathus's dynasty.

"Vaballathus, King of Palmyra, Roman law demands the death of a client king who rebels against Rome; but you were a child when you came into your inheritance. Your mother has ruled for you, and so in fairness—and contrary to what you have been raised to believe, we Romans are fair—I cannot hold you responsible for this rebellion. I therefore grant you your life, but you and your wife and whatever family you have are banished to the city of Cyrene."

"*No!*" Zenobia's voice was ragged.

"For how long?" asked Vaba.

"For life," was the reply.

"*No!*" A low and desperate cry.

"Be quiet," Aurelian said almost gently. "I have not finished." She was amazing, he thought. She cared only for her husband's line. If she might transfer that loyalty to him!

"Roman law will be served in the case of Palmyra's rebellion," continued the emperor. "Your king was scarcely a child, your regent a woman, a woman who was advised in all her plans by you, the Council of Ten. I have spared both your boy king and your queen regent. I will not, however, spare you. I must hold this council responsible for Zenobia of Palmyra's acts. You are men. You could have prevented all that has happened between Rome and Palmyra, but you did not. You allowed a woman total control, and her emotional and unbridled ways, her fierce pride, her ambition, have led you to your own destruction.

307

"Accordingly, I must mete out punishment to all. You are sentenced to death in the name of the Senate of Rome and the peoples it represents. The Council of Ten will not be allowed to re-form. Rome will rule Palmyra henceforth by means of a military governor. You have six hours in which to put your affairs in order. You will be executed just before sunset. Rest assured that your families will not be harmed, nor will your possessions be confiscated."

There was not a sound in the room. The members of the Council of Ten could not believe what they had heard. Zenobia sat wide-eyed. Clutching at the table's edge, she pulled herself up to a standing position.

"Mercy, Caesar," she rasped, for her throat was tight. "Kill *me*! Make *me* your example, but in the name of all the gods, spare these good men!" Her voice grew stronger. "My day is over. I will die willingly for Palmyra. It is not fair that the council be killed. They are not responsible for my actions! I alone am responsible! I willingly, nay gladly, accept my responsibilities."

"A woman could not have accomplished what you have accomplished, Zenobia, without the cooperation of her council. The boy was too young to rule, I grant you; but had this council not gone along with your precipitous behavior, you could not have come so close to succeeding in your foolish rebellion. My sentence is just."

"I will kill you," she said clearly, and the men of the emperor's legion put their hands to their swords. "Someday I will find a way to repay you for this terrible Roman injustice. You have placed the burden of guilt for the murder of ten good men upon my conscience, and I shall never forgive you for it."

"This council is disbanded," Aurelian said coldly, and quickly the men of his legion surrounded the unfortunate members of the Council of Ten. "Each of you," the emperor said, "may return under guard to your homes. You will be escorted back to the palace before sunset." Then he turned on his heel to leave the room.

"*Wait!*" Zenobia's voice resounded throughout the council chamber. Aurelian turned. "Give me leave, Caesar, to bid these faithful friends farewell." She spoke carefully, in a toneless voice. He nodded curtly. "Without their guards?" she pleaded. Again he nodded. "Thank you," she said simply.

When the room had emptied, and only Zenobia, Vaballathus,

and the Council of Ten remained, she spoke. "I will try when I am alone with him to get him to reconsider; but he is a harsh man. I know not with what I may bargain now. I have nothing left."

Marius Gracchus spoke. "He means to separate Palmyra entirely from her past, Majesty. He believes that once this is done the people will be easy to manage, and in truth they will be. Whatever their loyalties to the House of Odenathus, Rome has not penalized them for this war. Nor, I suspect, will Rome penalize them. The royal family will be gone, the council will be gone, and there will be but one authority: Rome. The people's loyalty will not be torn, and the city will remain as Rome wants. Productive and calm. I admire this emperor for all he has condemned me to my death, because he is clever and ruthless. Do not grieve, Majesty. We of the Council of Ten are mostly old, and the gods know that we have lived good lives. We are proud to die for Palmyra!"

There were murmurs of assent from the others, and Zenobia knew that there was nothing left to say. They were all powerless, and they had all bravely faced that fact. "I will try," she said. "I must try! We all know that you could not have stopped me even if you had desired to do so. Aurelian knows it, too! It is not fair!"

Cassius Longinus chuckled. "You are correct, Majesty," he said with a twinkle. "Although it embarrasses us to admit it even now, we could not have stopped you at any time. Nonetheless the emperor needs a blood sacrifice. We are that sacrifice. Let it be. Do not humble yourself before Aurelian again. You may not realize it now, but your lot is far harder than ours. He can kill us only once, but you, Majesty, must live on to take part in the emperor's triumph, and then afterward—who knows. *You are Palmyra!* You will show the alien Roman world Palmyran courage and loyalty; and by doing that, all we have done in our battle for liberty will live on, and we shall never really be dead."

Zenobia felt the tears well up, and then unshamedly she let them roll down her face. There were no arguments left. "I will bid you farewell now," she said quietly, attempting to gather her dignity about her. Each of the council came forward, placing his hands first in hers and then moving on to their young king to bid him farewell. Zenobia said only their names, for there were no words with which she might thank them now for this ultimate sacrifice.

"Antonius Porcius. I fear for Flavia when she learns of your fate."

"My daughter is stronger than she appears, my Queen. My main concerns are for Julia and our son, Gaius."

"I will do everything I can, old friend. Perhaps they will want to go to Cyrene with Vaba and Flavia. My future is so uncertain."

"Cyrene!" Antonius Porcius made a face. "The armpit of the empire," he said scornfully. "A decaying city on the sea with the desert on the other three sides and nothing else for hundreds of miles. Aurelian chose Vaba's place of exile well. The gods help them. They will be bored to death within a year."

Zenobia was forced to laugh, even in the midst of such tragedy, and the sound of her laughter heartened everyone in the room. She and Antonius Porcius, Rome's former governor and Palmyra's loyal servant these many years, embraced, and then he was moving on and speaking in low, urgent tones to Vaba.

Cassius Longinus stood before her, and for a very long moment they looked at each other. "You," Zenobia said, "you I will miss more than the others, even my children. You are my friend." Quick tears sprang to her silvery eyes, and she amended, "My best friend."

Longinus smiled a strangely sweet smile at her, and took her hand in his. "You think that your life is over," he said quietly, "but dearest Majesty, it has barely begun. Palmyra is just your beginning. I am sixty years old, Majesty, and if I have any regrets it is that I was not with you from the very beginning. It is the will of the gods that your life be spared, as it is their will that we ten die. Remember us, Majesty, but do not grieve." He drew her close to him, and gently kissed her forehead. "You are my best friend also," he said, and then he moved away from her to speak with Vaba.

Zenobia stood quietly, tears streaming down her beautiful face. Finally the room was empty, and Vaba came over to put a comforting arm about his mother. "I do not think I can bear it," Zenobia said. "I cannot believe that Aurelian means to go through with this slaughter. It is so unfair!"

"When were the Romans ever fair?" he replied bitterly. "It is as Longinus said. Their honor can only be satisfied by a blood sacrifice."

"Oh, Vaba," she half-whispered, "I am responsible for this. It is my fault that the Council of Ten is to die. If I had not declared you Augustus, and myself Queen of the East, Aurelian would not have descended upon us."

"In the short time I have known this emperor, Mother, I have reached the conclusion that he never does anything precipitously. Each move he makes is well thought out in advance. I believe that in his quest to reunite his Roman Empire he sought to regain full control of Palmyra again. He did not want Palmyra to be ruled by its own king. He would have found some excuse, however flimsy, to conquer us. You cannot—must not—hold yourself responsible for the fate of the council."

His words were comforting, but Zenobia was not sure that she entirely believed them. After all, had not she—had not they all said that she *was* Palmyra? As queen, a queen who ruled for her son, they had all been her sole responsibility. She had failed in that trust.

Vaba escorted her litter back to her apartments and left her. Slowly Zenobia entered her rooms, her mind deep in thought. She suddenly felt very tired, and decided that she would rest until sunset. It would be necessary for her to attend the execution of her council members. They had always supported her, and she owed them this final courtesy no matter how painful it would be for her.

"Why did you not wear the flame colored gown I wanted?" Aurelian's voice cut into her concentration.

"Red is the color of joy," she said dully. "I did not expect I should be joyful this day, and so I chose to be who I am, the Queen of Palmyra. Tyrian purple is a royal color."

"You are no longer Queen of Palmyra, goddess."

She turned to look directly at him, and then she said in a quiet voice, "I will always be the Queen of Palmyra, Aurelian. Your words, the edicts of your senate, they cannot alter who I am. Perhaps I shall never see my homeland again, *but I will always be the Queen of Palmyra.*"

Seeing her standing there, he understood for the first time in his life the word "regal." He knew that he should never possess such presence, such dignity. She almost made him feel ashamed, and it angered him. Why should this beautiful rebel make him feel guilty for doing his duty?

"May I go with Vaba and Flavia?" she asked. "May I take my other children with me?"

311

"You will come to Rome with me," he said in a voice that suggested she not argue. "You have two sons, but I have only seen one. Where is the other?"

"I do not know where my son, Demetrius, is, Caesar. Perhaps he is with his grandfather."

"And perhaps he is sneaking about the city like a jackal with a group of his angry young patrician friends causing trouble," the emperor said, his eyes narrowing.

"What have you heard?" She tried to keep the fright from her voice.

"It is reliably reported that they have been inciting the people to riot and other such seditious acts. I would suggest that you find him, and warn him that any further such nonsense could incur my displeasure."

She nodded, too tired to argue with him now. He looked at her and felt a surge of pure desire. Suppressing it, he realized she was not beaten, simply in shock over his harsh judgments. "Go and rest, goddess," he said in a kinder tone of voice. "It will not be necessary for you to be at this evening's sad event."

"I will be there, Caesar," she replied in a fierce voice. "Cassius Longinus said that you must have your blood sacrifice, but I shall never forgive you for the guilt you have placed upon me."

"Never," he replied, "is a long time, goddess. When you are in Rome with me you will forget."

"I will never forget."

"Go and rest," he repeated.

Zenobia brushed past him and entered her bedchamber. There, Bab and Adria sat awaiting her return. They quickly rose to their feet at her entry and, hurrying toward her, wordlessly began to remove her jewelry and clothes.

Although she did not believe that she could sleep, she did. Shock had taken its toll, and she could have easily slept for hours, but Bab gently shook her awake in the hour before sunset and helped her to dress, again in royal purple. Her numbed mind began to function again.

She was alive. Her children were alive, and they would remain so unless Demi did something foolish. As long as they lived there was hope; hope of returning one day to Palmyra. How long would Aurelian last? Emperors came and went in these days with remarkable rapidity. In a few years what had transpired between Rome and Palmyra would be forgotten; and if she was in favor with a future emperor in Rome, she could possibly regain Vaba's inheritance.

"You are ready," said Bab, who recognized her mistress's mood and had been silent all during the dressing.

"Come with me, old woman," Zenobia said.

"Did you think I would not?" came the quick reply. "You are strong, my baby, but no one is strong enough to bear alone what you must now face. I will always be with you; as long as these tired old legs can move."

"I would come too, Majesty," quiet Adria said, and Zenobia turned in surprise to see the firm, resolute look in the slave girl's brown eyes.

"Yes, Adria," she answered her. "You may come."

Together, the three women left the queen's rooms, and walked slowly along the corridor leading to the main courtyard of the palace. Zenobia silently noted that her own personal guard had been replaced by Roman legionnaires. Though she felt sure that her men had not been harmed, she resolved to inquire of Aurelian what had happened to them.

The Roman legionnaires guarding the entry to the central courtyard snapped smartly to attention as Zenobia passed through with her women. The sight greeting her outside almost made her falter, but old Bab hissed softly, "Courage, Queen of Palmyra!" Zenobia moved regally forward to mount with her women the raised platform that had been erected at one end of the courtyard. Aurelian already sat sprawled in a chair.

"I told you that you did not have to come," he said.

"I told you," she replied half angrily, "that these men you slaughter have served me faithfully, and I would come!"

Aurelian signaled to one of his men. "Bring a chair for the queen," he said.

"I will stand in respect," she quickly replied.

He ignored her. "Whether you stand or sit, goddess, is your choice, but the chair is there should you need it."

Zenobia looked out over the courtyard. The day had been a hot one, but now with sunset fast approaching the courtyard was in shadow.

Zenobia turned to Rome's emperor. "Will it be quick?"

"Yes," was the short reply.

She wanted to cry, but she forced the tears back and swallowed down the lump in her throat. There were ten baskets lined neatly up in a long row at the center of the open courtyard. Realizing their significance, she shuddered with revulsion, then froze as the condemned men came from a side door of the palace. Each was flanked by two Roman guards, one of whom would act as headsman in the execution. The council members had chosen to wear pure white tunics that came to their ankles and somber black togae pullae, mourning garments. They walked proudly, their heads held high. As they turned to face the raised dais where Zenobia stood rooted, they raised their right arms in salute and cried out loudly, "Hail, Zenobia! Hail, Queen of Palmyra!"

She drew herself up proudly then, and said in a voice for all to hear, "The gods speed your journey, my friends, for you are surely Palmyra's greatest patriots! All hail to you, Council of Ten!"

"Enough," Aurelian snapped, and he signaled with his hand.

Each member of the council was forced to kneel before a hateful reed basket, his bare neck bowed, easily accessible to his executioner. Each headsman raised his sword, and as they did Zenobia called out, "Longinus, farewell, my friend."

"Farewell, Majesty," came his dear voice, and then the executioners struck with well-drilled precision, and the ten severed heads fell with a distinct *thump* into their waiting containers.

She swayed, and Aurelian stood up and reached out to put a strong arm about her. "I do not need your help, Roman!" she snarled at him.

"Death to the Roman tyrants!" The cry suddenly echoed about the courtyard, and in a hail of arrows the legionnaires in the open courtyard fell, some dead instantly, some mortally wounded by the poison-tipped arrows unleashed at them by the kneeling archers upon the palace roof.

A tall young man stood up and looked scornfully down upon the stunned dignitaries on the platform. "Hail, Caesar," he said mockingly, "and welcome to Palmyra! Were the queen not in your grasp at this moment, you and the other Roman dogs with you would now be as dead as your execution squad. The people of Palmyra do not like what you have done. It was our craven king who opened the city's gates to you, not the people. Nevertheless we prefer King Vaballathus to a Roman governor. Reinstate him, or this will be just the beginning of our war with you!" Then without waiting for an answer, he and his archers disappeared from the rooftops.

Gaius Cicero leapt from the platform, but Aurelian's voice

was knife-sharp. "Don't bother, Gaius! They are long gone back into their rodent holes, and we will never find them." He turned to Zenobia. "The youth who spoke was your younger son, I presume?"

She pushed his offending arm from her waist then, giving him a long look, smiled. With her women trailing behind her, she walked from the platform and disappeared into the palace. Once safe within her rooms, she said furiously, "Find Demi, Bab! There must be someone who knows where he is hiding."

The doors to her bedchamber opened, and Vaba rushed in, his face dark with anger. "He is your son, Mother! *Your son!*"

"He is also your brother," she snapped back at him. "I have ordered Bab to seek Demi out, for I do not agree with his methods any more than you do, Vaba. You might know where he is. Who are his special friends now? We *must* find him!"

"Why?" countered Vaba. "So you may save his miserable life? I hope to the gods that the Romans catch him and kill him!"

Zenobia's hand shot out and made firm contact with the cheek of her older son. "Don't ever say such a thing again. I want Demi found because I do not want him to throw away his life needlessly. I want Demi found so that he does not ruin your future, and that of your children."

"What future?" he demanded scornfully. "There is no future for me in Cyrene. There is no future for my descendants. Best Flavia miscarry of the unfortunate babe she now carries. Better we never have any children at all!"

"You fool!" Zenobia almost shouted. "You only see what is in front of you! Why can you never see ahead?" Almost absently she reached out, and rubbed at the red imprint of her hand on his cheek. "Vaba, listen to me. Aurelian will fall like all of Rome's emperors in these past years; and the emperor to follow him will fall. I will be in Rome making friends, building my connections, always supporting the right faction. In five years, ten at the most, you will return to Palmyra as its rightful king. I promise you this, my son! I swear it! Have I ever broken a promise to you, Vaba?"

He looked at her wonderingly, and shook his head. Then he said, "Do you never stop scheming, Mother?"

"Will you trust me, Vaba?"

"I have always trusted you, Mother."

"Good! Now, think! Where can Demi be hiding?"

"It has to be at Cassius Longinus's house in the city. Longinus's little friend, Oppian, has been giving Demi and his friends occasional shelter, although I doubt that Longinus was aware of it. He left the boy alone as he did not want him here at the palace, and Oppian was lonely for the company of other young men. I am sure that Longinus willed the house to him, and equally sure you will find Demi there. Or at least Oppian will know where he is."

Zenobia turned to speak to Bab, but the old woman forestalled her, raising up her hand, and said, "I am already gone. I shall bring him back when I find him."

Zenobia sent a message to Aurelian asking that she be allowed the traditional mourning period. To her surprise, he sent back an immediate reply by his personal secretary, Durantis, agreeing to her request, but stipulating that she keep to her own apartments and own garden. She assented. She knew that he acquiesced because it suited *him,* not her. He probably needed the time to consolidate his victory. With Vaballathus deposed, the Council of Ten dead, and the queen out of sight, Palmyra would naturally turn to Roman authority.

It was late that night when old Bab returned, and she was alone. "He is there," she said, "but he will not come to the palace. He fears a trap."

"He said *that?*" Zenobia was furious.

"He does not distrust you," Bab quickly assured her, "but he fears a Roman trap. There is no one left you may rely upon, he says, now that the council is dead."

"Did you use the secret gate in the garden?" Zenobia asked Bab.

"I did, and I was seen by no one. I am not so old that my eyes and ears cannot see or hear properly."

"Then if you can get out, so can I," Zenobia said.

"That is just what Prince Demetrius said!" Bab replied. "He said that you must come tonight, however, for after tonight the Roman is sure to put a watch on you. Tonight he will assume you too devastated to take any kind of action. We will have to walk, my baby, but at this very minute two of Prince Demi's men are waiting for us outside the palace to escort us in safety."

"Adria!" Zenobia called, and the young slave girl came instantly.

"Majesty?"

"You heard?"

"Yes, Majesty."

316

"I want you and Bab to remain here. You will sit outside my bedchamber door as if keeping watch. Bab will sit inside my chamber by my bed; a bed that will appear to have a sleeping woman in it. Should the emperor come you will do your best to prevent his entering my room, but should he ignore you, then Bab will handle it. Do you understand?"

"Yes, Majesty." Adria smiled. "It will be a pleasure to deceive the Roman dogs!"

Zenobia looked with new eyes upon her young servant. Until recently she had not given the girl a great deal of attention, but of late Adria had shown intelligence and loyalty more worthy of a freed woman than a slave. "From this moment on, Adria, you are no longer a slave," Zenobia said quietly. "Tomorrow I shall have the papers drawn up freeing you."

"Majesty!" Adria's usually plain, round face was suddenly pretty with her joy, and her brown eyes were filled with tears of happiness. Dropping to her knees, she caught at the hem of Zenobia's gown. Raising it to her lips, she kissed it fervently and said, "I will *never* leave you, Majesty! I would not want to leave you, for you are goodness itself! Thank you! Thank you!"

Zenobia gently touched the girl's strangely beautiful brown-gold hair, and said, "Get up, Adria. I must go."

"I do not like you going alone," Bab fretted.

Zenobia did not argue with her. She simply said, "I can move far quicker without you," and Bab was forced to agree. Without another word she swaddled Zenobia in a long, totally enveloping, hooded black cape, and watched with worried old eyes as her mistress went swiftly through the bedchamber door, out into the darkness.

Zenobia picked her way through the blackness of her garden, for there was no moon this night. She could not be quite sure where the little hidden door lay, and so she carefully felt her way along the vined wall until her hands made contact with the smooth, ancient wood. Reaching up, she found the key upon its hook. She unlocked the door, slipped through, and relocked it from the other side before returning the key to her robes. Turning, she stood very still and listened, her sharp ears attuned to the desert night. To her right she could hear faint breathing. Turning, she followed the small sound.

"Majesty?" came the voice in the darkness.

"Lead on," she commanded softly, and then followed the two retreating shadows down the street. Together, the three

317

moved swiftly through the back streets of the city, carefully avoiding the watchful Roman patrols. They did not speak until at last they stood before a garden wall. "We will have to scale it, Majesty," one of the shadows whispered.

"Very well," she agreed, and the first young man leapt upon the shoulders of the second, and reaching down slightly pulled Zenobia upward until she was even with him. Then he carefully placed her on the top of the wall, joined her, and leaning down again pulled the second man up. "I can get down myself," the queen said, and leapt down into the garden of Cassius Longinus's house, landing in, from the smell of it, a bed of tangy herbs. The two shadows upon the wall joined her quickly, then led her through the garden and into the darkened house.

Once inside the house, she was taken down a flight of stone steps into the catacombs beneath it. There, in a torchlit underground room, she found herself among a large group of young men, many of whom she recognized as coming from the city's greatest patrician and commercial families. Seeing her, they instantly came to attention, their right arms raised in salute as they cried out, "Hail Zenobia! Hail, Queen of Palmyra!"

She graciously acknowledged them, and then the group parted, and Demetrius came forward to embrace his mother. She was amazed in the difference in his appearance from when she had left Palmyra several weeks back. His face was suddenly more mature, his stature positively regal. "Welcome, my Mother. Welcome to the Brotherhood of the Palm."

Zenobia did not choose to mince words: "If you think to please me or the King by your futile rebellion, you do not."

"What?" Demi demanded imperiously. "Have you become the Roman's champion as well as his lover, my Queen?"

A hundred pairs of young eyes swung to look upon Zenobia.

"You are as impetuous as your brother, Demi," Zenobia said in an amused tone, though she was feeling far from amused. She turned to allow her gaze to encompass them all. "Surely you do not really believe you can force the Romans from Palmyra? What is it you hope to accomplish?"

"We want Vaba reinstated," Demi said in a loud voice. "He may not be the best of kings, but he is a Palmyran king. We want no Roman governor, Mother."

The young men in the room nodded, and murmured their agreement.

"I want Vaba reinstated, too, Demi, but the Romans cannot be forced from Palmyra, and the city is going to have to endure

318

a military governor for the next several years. In time I will return Vaba to Palmyra as its king. It cannot be done overnight, but I will get it done! Trust me, all of you!'' The queen held out her hands in appeal, and the young men in the torchlit room looked as if they might waver.

Then Demi's voice sounded, fierce and angry. "No! I will not have you prostitute yourself to the Romans, Mother! Vaba must be reinstated now. If he leaves Palmyra they will never let him back, and this city will not endure foreign rule!''

"What do you know of foreign rule?'' Zenobia demanded furiously. "Since before your birth the city has been free, but before you and Vaba the Romans ruled here for over a hundred years and Palmyra survived; as did our family. Do you think this city suffered under Antonius Porcius, Demi? We will bide our time again, and in the end we will win again; but you cannot drive the Romans away!''

"*They will go!* We will fight them in the streets unto the last man, but we shall not let them have the city!''

"Your actions will destroy Vaba's chances, but perhaps that is your real motive. Perhaps you believe that if you cannot have the city then your brother will not, either. Is this how I have raised you? To be a betrayer of your family, of Palmyra?'' The room was deathly silent now, and Zenobia looked upon the eager faces before her. "I appeal to you, my sons!'' she said, her look sweeping them all. "Have patience, and Palmyra will be ours again.''

"They slaughtered the Council of Ten,'' a voice said, and the crowd parted to reveal young Gaius Porcius. "My father lies dead this night, my Queen. My mother might as well be, for she has not spoken a word since sunset. She stares into space and there is no feeling or expression in her eyes. How can we simply sit back and accept this injustice?''

"Your father would have agreed with me, Gaius Porcius,'' was Zenobia's reply. "Though he was born a Roman, he was a loyal Palmyran. He would want what is best for Palmyra, and he trusted me to make that decision. There is a time for quick action, and there is a time for patience. Now is the time for patience. Sending Vaba into exile, taking me to Rome, destroying our council—these were all planned by the emperor as object lessons to our people. He will do no more. There are to be no fines, no new taxes, nothing. It will be business as usual in Palmyra under a Roman governor. But in the end we will win!''

319

"How can you be so sure?" Demi persisted. "Has your Roman lover assured you of it?"

"You are a fool!" Zenobia snapped at her son. "I thought that you had more sense than Vaba, but you are just as bad. Aurelian forced me, but I realized quickly I might turn that experience into an advantage for Palmyra. You may scorn me for it if you choose, but what I do I do for Palmyra! When Vaba is restored how many of you will be here to help him? You will all be dead of your own foolishness! Do not rebel any further, I beg you! Palmyra needs her strong and intelligent young men!"

"Go back to your Roman lover, my Queen," Demetrius said coldly to his mother. "If you are suddenly weary of defending our homeland, we are not. Palmyra will rise up against these tyrants!"

"Will you not be satisfied until you have destroyed the city, my son?" Zenobia demanded.

"Take her back," Demi commanded the two young men who had accompanied Zenobia to the meeting, and before she might speak further they hustled her quickly up the stairs, through the quiet house, and back into the garden. Zenobia sighed sadly. Demetrius had become a fanatic. She silently prayed that Demi's followers would fall away, and that he would come to his senses. She could only hope that he was not caught, for Aurelian would not be kind. He would want to make an example of Demi, and that would mean his death. She sighed again before she once more scaled the garden wall and dropped into the street below. There were times in her life when she felt terribly alone.

Slowly the tears began to slide down her face and Zenobia was glad for the darkness that allowed her her privacy. She was not one for weeping in public.

Then they were back at the royal palace, and Zenobia turned to thank her escorts, but they had quickly melted into the night. Slowly she opened her secret door and stepped back through into her private enclave. She blessed whomever it was that kept the hinges of the little door well oiled, for it made not a sound as it swung wide. Relocking it, she hurried through the garden and back into her bedchamber. Old Bab nodded by a bed in which it appeared a sleeping woman lay. Zenobia tiptoed across the floor and gently shook the elderly servant awake.

"Wh-what?" Bab opened her eyes, and Zenobia saw the

relief in them. "Praise the gods, you are back safe!" She slowly rose to her feet. "Will the prince cease his rebellion?"

"No," Zenobia said. "He prefers to think of himself as a great patriot, and he has enough of a following to cause trouble. I do not doubt that when they do they will obtain additional followers. Perhaps, however, I have swayed some of those fiercely loyal young Palmyrans this night. If I have and they desert Demi with his ideas of violence, then maybe he will come to his senses."

"This Roman emperor will kill him without a thought if he continues," Bab noted.

Zenobia nodded her agreement, and then said, "We had best get some rest, Bab. Help me to undress, and then you and Adria go to bed."

Bab quickly helped Zenobia undress, then offered her a melon-colored sheer cotton chamber robe.

Slowly Zenobia put the garment on, and then, walking to a table, she poured herself a goblet of pale rose-colored wine and sat down in a carved wooden chair. "Go along, old woman. It has been a long night." She heard the door close behind her, and knew that she was alone again. She was worried. Why could Demi not see reason? Then she laughed softly at herself. He was exactly like she had been at his age, but she had had Odenathus's loving and kindly influence to temper her rashness. The difference was that she had listened to her husband. Why would their son not listen to her? Because you are a woman, said the little voice in her head. It matters not that you are the greatest queen upon the earth in many centuries, you are still a woman, and your son, barely a man, thinks that his sex gives him greater knowledge of what is right and what is wrong.

I am failing you, Hawk, she thought sadly. I have failed both our sons. I simply could not do it all alone. I needed you. I needed Marcus. Ah, if only Marcus and I had been married, things would have been different. The wine was beginning to make her maudlin. Why did I not marry him when he first asked me instead of insisting we wait?

She drained her goblet, but did not refill it. Instead, she rose up, walked over to her bed, and lay down. Getting drunk was not going to help her, and she did not need a headache. She was needed. Her sons needed her even if they might not admit it. Flavia would need her, for she would be terribly grieved by

321

her father's death. With Antonius gone, and young Gaius behaving like a fool, Julia—Flavia's mother and Zenobia's oldest friend—would need her doubly.

She was awakened at midmorning by Adria, who brought her a large goblet of fresh fruit juice. Between sips Zenobia gave her orders. "I am supposed to be in mourning, but I want you to fetch the lady Julia and her son, Gaius Porcius, here to me as soon as they can come. Also, I will need a scribe so that your papers may be drawn up. Go to the emperor's secretary, Durantis, and say that I have need of his services."

"At once, Majesty," Adria said.

"Where is Bab?"

"With the lady Flavia. She is most distraught, and begged that Bab come to her."

Zenobia nodded. "Run along, Adria."

"But who will dress you, Majesty?"

"It should not detract from my dignity as Queen of Palmyra if I dress myself," Zenobia said with a smile.

A small smile turned Adria's lips up, and bowing to the queen she hurried off on her errands. Zenobia sat in bed sipping at the juice for a few moments; then rose to bathe and dress. She did not dally in the bath, for she had much to do, but the steam, the scraping, the perfumed water and soap, and lastly the massage with the fragrant oil made her feel a new woman. Re-entering her bedroom, she was somewhat surprised to find Aurelian awaiting her.

His eyes widened with appreciation at her nudity, but, choosing to ignore it, Zenobia asked, "What do you here, Roman? You granted me the nine days of mourning. Surely you do not mean to break your word?"

"Why do you want the use of my secretary?" he asked, ignoring her questions.

"Because I am setting my slave girl, Adria, free. My own scribe will draw up the papers of manumission, but I wish your good Durantis to read them, and be certain that everything is correct according to Roman law."

"Why are you freeing a valuable slave?" he persisted.

"Because she is loyal to me; because she is far too intelligent to be a slave; and because she deserves it. Fear not, Roman, I do not plan to do away with myself. I am not setting my house in order prior to my death. There are too many people who need me. My ancestress, Cleopatra, took a coward's way out. I shall not. I will outlive you, I suspect," she finished mockingly, and her eyes caught his and held them. He wanted her! She almost laughed aloud. There was simply no subtlety in the man.

He took a step toward her, and her look challenged him. "I am in mourning, Roman," she said softly. "You promised."

Aurelian visibly gritted his teeth, and said in a tight voice, "You may have the use of Durantis."

"Caesar is gracious," was the reply.

He flushed a dull red and, turning, almost ran from the room. He had recognized the scorn in her voice, and somehow he felt powerless in light of his desire for her to reciprocate in kind. He was falling in love with her, the gods forbid. Better his old friend, pure lust!

Zenobia felt the thrill of triumph run through her as she watched him go. For the first time since she had set eyes upon the Roman she felt good! Suddenly she realized it was because she had the upper hand!

That might not be entirely to her advantage, she thought as she opened a trunk and began to take out a garment to wear. She chose a deep-blue kalasiris of silk that had been woven here in Palmyra. The dress had a wide belt of silvered kid that fastened about her waist with a silver buckle that had a large blue topaz set within it. Zenobia slipped her feet into matching sandals, and sitting down at her dressing table set about brushing her long blue-black hair. When she had freed it of its tangles she carefully twisted it into a single, thick braid that hung down her back.

A knock on her door roused her, and she called, "Come in."

The emperor's secretary entered. "Good morning, my lady," he said.

"You will address me as *Majesty*, Durantis," Zenobia said quietly.

He nodded politely. "I stand corrected, Majesty. How may I serve you?"

"I will have my scribe draw up papers of manumission for my slave girl Adria today. I want you to see that these papers are correct acccording to Roman law so that there will never be any doubt about Adria's status."

"I will be glad to serve you thus, Majesty," Durantis said.

"Thank you. You may go now."

He bowed politely, and then backed correctly from the room. Zenobia stood up, walked out into her antechamber, and instructed the waiting scribe as to her desires. Then she began to pace slowly about the room as she waited for Adria to return with Julia and Gaius. As she walked, her mind went back to the thread of thought she had been spinning when Durantis had interrupted her. To enjoy an open triumph over Aurelian could anger him, embarrass him, even turn him from her. To pretend great passion for him was an equal danger, for he might grow tired of her if she appeared suddenly docile. She would have to tread a very fine line. She would gradually begin to pretend affection for him while resisting him still. That should keep him interested, for she knew that he desperately wanted to conquer her completely, body and soul. If she could make him believe long enough that victory over her might yet be possible, then she would win.

The door to the antechamber opened and Adria entered, leading Julia Tullio, the wife of the late Antonius Porcius. Young Gaius, looking rebellious, yet a little frightened, followed his mother. Zenobia was shocked by Julia's appearance. Her hair was snow-white, her crying-reddened eyes were blank of expression, her slender shoulders were stooped as if from pain.

"Julia!" Zenobia held out her arms, and the woman walked into them. But the queen realized that her friend did not know her. Anyone might have offered the distraught woman sympathy and she would have accepted it. Zenobia's arms closed around her friend and held her close. Over Julia's shoulder she looked incredulously at Julia's hair, and then questioningly at Gaius.

"It had turned white when I went into her this morning," he said quietly. "She has still not spoken."

The queen loosened her embrace then led her friend into the bedchamber and sat her down in a chair. "Julia," she said, raising up the woman's face and looking down into it. "Julia, I know that you hear me. Antonius is dead, and you grieve. When Odenathus died, I grieved too, but I had my children to live for, and you have yours."

Suddenly Julia's eyes focused. "My children are grown," she said. "They do not need me."

"Flavia needs you!" Zenobia persisted. "Did you not need your mother when you were first with child? Gaius needs you. He is involved in a group led by my younger son, Demi, who would continue to fight the Romans. Would Antonius Porcius approve of this? You know he would not! The father is dead, but the children need their mother, Julia. You cannot desert them. Flavia could miscarry of Palmyra's future heir should you destroy yourself. Gaius will most certainly be killed if he persists in following my son. Then Antonius Porcius's family will be gone from this earth, and it will be your fault for not accepting the responsibilities your husband left you. Antonius Porcius never shirked his duty in his entire life. He understood duty, and so do you, Julia.''

"You are a hard woman, Zenobia," Julia said, her voice quavering. She began to weep bitter tears. "Never in his life did he harm anyone or anything intentionally. Why did the emperor order him executed? *Why?* It is not right!'' Julia cried angrily, and Zenobia was glad to see color coming back into her friend's pale face.

"No, Julia, it is not right, but it is a fact! Do not let the Romans have a further victory, my friend. You and your children must live, for in living you keep alive a great man's memory, you keep alive his line.''

Julia brushed the tears from her face. "You are right, Zenobia; the gods damn you for it, but you are right! It would be so easy to give up, but I will not give up! *I will not!*'' She drew a deep breath, then turned her face to her son's. "I forbid you to have anything further to do with Prince Demetrius and his band of rebels! Do you understand me, Gaius? I have lost your father, and almost died from the pain of that loss. Your death will surely kill me! There will be another way to avenge your father, and together we will find it, but do not carelessly throw your life away. I will not allow it!''

The boy flushed, and protested, "But what other way is there? I am the man in this family now, and the decision should be mine." It was, however, a feeble protest.

Gaius needed to save face, and so Julia said quietly, "You are only fifteen, my son. Under Palmyran law you are not yet of age, and if you go against my wishes I will be forced to act in a way you will not like.'' She held out a hand to him, and when he took it she drew him near. "There is no shame in youth, Gaius, but your judgment is not yet fully developed, and you must yet rely upon your only parent.''

Zenobia came and stood next to the boy. "Even my own Demi," she said, "lacks judgment, Gaius, and he is eighteen this year. What you all did following the execution of the council was magnificent, and a great victory for you all. Your group killed twenty-seven legionnaires! Not only that, but you took the Romans completely off guard!"

"*We did?*" Gaius was quite surprised and, Zenobia could see, rather pleased.

"You did," the queen returned with a smile. "Be satisfied for now, Gaius, and do as your mother asks. You have been so wrapped up in your own loss that you have given no thought to your mother or your sister. If you would be a man then you must be strong, and let them lean on you. How can they if you are running about with Demi and his foolish friends?"

She had made it appear as if the choice were actually his, and that was a wise tactic. Gaius responded as she had expected. "You are right, Aunt Zenobia," he said. "I have great responsibilities now as the eldest male in the Porcius family. I cannot afford to jeopardize my inheritance, and I promise you and my mother that I shall no longer involve myself with Demi and his Brotherhood of the Palm."

Julia heaved an audible sigh of relief, and said, "Thank the gods that underneath your youthful exuberance you have your father's common sense!"

The bedchamber door opened without warning, and Aurelian strode into the room. "You say you are in mourning, goddess, and yet here I find you merrily entertaining your friends," he accused.

Zenobia's first urge was to hit him, but she quickly controlled herself and said sweetly, "I do mourn, Caesar. I mourn the murder of my good friend and loyal councillor, Antonius Porcius. I mourn with his wife, Julia, who is my oldest friend. I mourn with his only son, young Gaius. Julia is my daughter-in-law's mother. We fear for the young queen's health. We are but two grieving mothers, Caesar."

"I think you plot at mischief, goddess."

"No, Caesar, I prevent it. Though you say I am no longer Palmyra's queen, I am, and I fear for my people."

"The city is quiet," he said.

"For now," she warned, then added, "I did not give you permission to enter my chambers at will, Caesar."

"Again I remind you, goddess, that you are a captive. I do not need your permission."

Julia looked between the two, amazed. The emperor was obviously not only taken with Zenobia, but in love with her, and jealous of anyone else in her life. Zenobia, however, was

326

playing with him as a cat with a mouse. I would be afraid of him, Julia thought, shaken. She reached out and pulled her son closer.

"Go to Flavia, Julia. You also, Gaius. Your sister will be much reassured by your visit," Zenobia commanded regally. The two rose without a word to the emperor, and quickly left the room.

"Has that youngster been involved with your younger son?" Aurelian demanded.

"I do not know what you mean," Zenobia countered. "I have no idea if my son Demetrius is with those young men who rebel against your rule."

"I don't know why you bother to protect the boy," the emperor said. "He is making no secret of his identity." Aurelian reached into his tunic and drew forth a small parchment, which he handed to her. "These are appearing all over the city today," he said drily.

Zenobia took the proffered parchment, and began to read:

People of Palmyra! The battle with the Roman tyrant is not over! They have deposed our queen, exiled our king, and slaughtered the Council of Ten; yet we will fight on! Join us in our resistance to these tyrants!

Prince Demetrius and
The Brotherhood of the Palm

"Anyone might use his name in order to gain followers," she said with more conviction than she was feeling.

"Then where is he, goddess? It is no secret that your elder son and your younger son quarreled violently the night before I entered this city. Prince Demetrius left the palace in a rage. He has not been seen in public since that night." Aurelian took her by the shoulders and looked down into her face. "Zenobia, I cannot protect the boy if he persists in his behavior. Yesterday I will forgive. What your son and his friends did is understandable to me, but now they must cease this very futile rebellion. Find the boy and reason with him."

"He will not listen," she said.

"You have seen him?"

She nodded. "Last night. He chooses to be a martyr. He thinks it is what his father would want of him."

327

Aurelian smiled a rueful smile. "Your sons have a great deal of their mother in them," he said. "They are both as stubborn as you are, although in different ways. Try again, goddess. Try to reach him before he steps over the line between the acccept-able and the unacceptable. You understand me, don't you?"

She nodded dumbly. He was being unbelievably kind, and she wondered why. Obviously he was trying to win her over, but when he bent to brush her lips with his she turned her head away, refusing for a moment to give any quarter. He could have easily forced her, but instead he laughed softly and released her, then turned and left the room without another word.

In her confinement Zenobia ate, slept, and lived without worry for nine days and nights. At the end of that time she felt renewed, more certain of herself than she had in many years. The city remained quiet. She had not sought to see her younger son again, for she had said what she had to say to him. He would either come to his senses or he wouldn't. She prayed daily that he would, and should he not, she prayed he might escape Aurelian. One thing she did know. He could not possi-bly succeed. The important thing now was Vaba, his wife, and the expected child; their exile and their eventual return to Palmyra. She was almost anxious for the trip to Rome to begin.

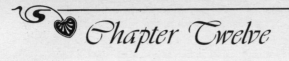

Chapter Twelve

On the morning of the tenth day after the council's death Zenobia found Aurelian waiting for her when she came from her bath. The sight of her after his voluntary absence made his heart quicken. Her golden skin was rosy and dewy, and she seemed to be enfolded in a cloud of hyacinth. Her kalasiris was a delicious bright crimson, her first gay color in many days. "How fair you are," he said almost without thinking, and she smiled.

"Good morning, Roman. Have you given orders to free me now?"

"You are free to roam the palace, and have guests," he answered, "but you may not leave the grounds."

"Why not?"

"Because I want to keep the peace. I need no demonstrations, goddess."

"When do we leave for Rome?" she asked him.

"Are you anxious to go?"

"Yes."

"Why?"

"I want to get on with my life, Roman, and you tell me that my life is no longer here."

"How coolly logical you are, goddess," he smiled, amused. "Well, you should be happy to learn that we leave here in just a few more days. First your eldest son must leave with his wife for Cyrene. I am sending an entire legion with him as escort. His young brother-in-law and mother-in-law will go with them. It is their choice—at least until little Flavia delivers her child."

"Is it safe for Flavia to travel now?" Zenobia asked. "Please do not endanger her or my grandchild."

"Her own physician has examined her, goddess, and has pronounced her most healthy and fit to travel."

"And how is my son to live in Cyrene, Caesar?"

"He will be given a most generous allowance, Zenobia."

"And after they are gone, we shall go?"

"Yes. You, and your younger son if we can find him, and your little daughter. She is a most charming child, goddess. I like her, but she certainly does not resemble either you or your sons."

"She resembles my mother's people," Zenobia said quickly. "Mama was quite blond and fair; but tell me, Roman, you have been seeing my child?"

"She was quite worried about you, goddess, and needed reassurance. I was able to offer that reassurance. I am very good with little girls. You must remember that I raised my niece, Carissa."

"You might have allowed Mavia to be with me," Zenobia said sharply.

"No, goddess. I felt you needed the nine days of mourning to reflect upon your situation. The child would have distracted you." He was telling her once more that it was he who controlled her life.

"As always, Caesar, you are most kind and thoughtful," Zenobia murmured.

Aurelian laughed. "Why is it that even when you are thanking me, goddess, I get the feeling that you are slinging missiles at me?"

Zenobia looked at him, eyes wide, her whole expression one of innocence. "I do not understand," she said. "I thought I was being most polite to you, Caesar."

"The hell you did," he muttered thickly, reaching out and pulling her against him. "You continue to fascinate me and defy me at every opportunity goddess!" A hard arm was tight about her slender waist, and now his free hand cradled her head as his mouth came down on hers in a brief but burning kiss. "I am tired of sleeping alone," he said. "Your mourning is over, Zenobia, and tonight I intend returning to your bed. Have you missed me, goddess?"

"No," she said, smiling up at him, her gray eyes looking directly into his blue ones.

He laughed, but she could see the anger hidden deep in his eyes. "One day you will regret your defiance, goddess. One day I will grow bored with it, and find a more conformable mistress."

"I did not choose to be your mistress, Caesar."

"It is not up to you to choose," he said cruelly. "Remember that when I grow tired of you I may pass you on to anyone it pleases me to, goddess. Perhaps I shall give you to some Gaulish or Germanic chieftain. I wonder how long you would last in the wet, cold, dark forests of the North?'' He bent once more and plundered her lips savagely, bruising them this time, forcing his tongue into her mouth where it darted about, first stroking the sensitive roof of her mouth then sensuously caressing the sides of her tongue.

How I hate him! Zenobia thought. But by Venus and Cupid he can rouse my senses! She shivered as she felt a large, warm hand upon her breast, and struggled to get away from him, but Aurelian lifted his head, saying, ''I desire you now, goddess, and I shall have you!'' Then he swiftly kicked her legs out from beneath her, and together they fell to the thick rugs strewn upon the floor. She gasped for breath as his greater weight knocked the wind from her.

Maddened by his own passion now, Aurelian hurriedly pushed her gown up and yanked it over her head, flinging it across the room. His hands caressed her possessively, slipping over her smooth, cool body, setting her to quivering as the strings of a lyre might vibrate with a sensitive touch. Closing her eyes for a moment, she allowed the sensations to sweep over her. *She hated him!* She absolutely hated him, but the gods! He knew how to pleasure a woman!

Seated upon her hips, Aurelian watched the passion creep slowly into Zenobia's expression. A cynical look swept into his eyes and etched smile lines at the corners of his mouth. She was using him, and he was tempted to get up and walk away. Unfortunately he desired her far too much at this moment to salvage his pride. Why could he not make her love him? He was kind and thoughtful of her and her family and close friends. He was even willing to forgive her rebellious younger son, yet she still scorned him. His one satisfaction was that she did not scorn his body as much as she might want to.

Angry now, he pulled her thighs none too gently apart; then drove immediately into her body, which was already honeyed and awaiting him. She gasped and her eyes flew open with surprise, for of late he had been gentle with her. In and out, in and out, in and out, he moved with increasing rapidity; and Zenobia cried a soft protest. ''I only use you as you use me, goddess,'' he said, mocking her.

''I can't love you,'' she whispered brokenly.

''Then at least give me some kindness, Zenobia,'' he said softly, his anger draining away at the tone in her voice. ''I have tried to be kind to you. At least give me that.'' Bending now, he began to murmur softly into her ear, "You are like a wild rose, my sweet and vulnerable goddess. You are the first star of evening, glittering and alone in the night sky. You are as elusive as the south wind, as beautiful as Palmyra itself, and I am forced to admit that I adore you totally; *but,* I will not be ruled by you, Zenobia." Gently he began to move within her again, and she moaned softly with open pleasure. "Tell me," he whispered to her. "Tell me what you feel, beloved."

She shook her head in the negative, but he persisted, and at last she was forced to speak. "I feel possessed, and I do not like it. I feel consumed, and it frightens me. Why can you not satisfy yourself with a woman who wants you?"

"You have never given yourself totally to any man, goddess, and if you are afraid it is because you are closer than you have ever been in your entire life to complete and sweet surrender. Give me that surrender, goddess! *Give it to me!*"

"*No!*"

Unable to wait any longer, the emperor poured his loving libation into her resisting womb, and Zenobia shuddered beneath him, suddenly lost in her own passion. They lay together upon the rugs for several long minutes, neither willing to be first to break the silence. Then Zenobia said in a shaky voice, "Someone may come," and struggled to her feet. Picking up her kalasiris from where it lay, she put it back on, careful to keep her head averted from his gaze.

"Perhaps you will never love me, goddess," he said quietly, "but I do desire you. You, too, desire me, although you will not admit to it. Let us at least be kind to each other. I am not ready to let you go, and perhaps I never shall be." He rose and pulled down his tunic, then moved across to where she stood and put gentle hands on her shoulders. "Be kind to me, goddess, and let me be kind to you."

"I will try," she promised, "but it is all I can do. Try."

He sighed, knowing that for the moment it was the best he might expect from her. "We will eat together from now on, Zenobia. I dislike eating alone almost as much as I dislike sleeping alone."

"Is there anything that you particularly like?" she asked him in an effort to be amenable.

"I will leave the choices to you," he said, and then he turned and left the room.

She sat down and, staring at the shadows in the rug where they had but recently lain, shivered. There was something unwholesome about making love without love; and yet though it repelled her, it also fascinated her. Aurelian, she thought, was a strange man. He had a peasant's shrewdness and he was harsh, but he could also be kind.

She suspected that he fancied himself a latter-day Julius Caesar, and she was to be his Cleopatra. Well, Zenobia considered somewhat wryly, Cleopatra had survived her Caesar, and she supposed that she might survive Aurelian. He wanted her to be kind to him. Interesting, she mused. Would a pleasant and even relationship keep him content? Perhaps it would. He was a man who liked his personal life smooth and calm, in contrast to his turbulent military and political careers. It was possible he would not be bored with her if she became more domesticated a creature. After all, even if Demi would not come to his senses she had her little Mavia to consider.

Mavia. Mavia, her daughter who was half-Roman, and now, it appeared, was to be raised in Rome. Would they see Marcus? Could she bear it if they did? Marcus had recognized his child at her birth, and even if it had been done in secret she and Bab lived to testify to it. Would he still accept Mavia as his own? Will he provide for her should anything happen to me? Zenobia wondered. *Mavia!* The little girl's name rang again and again in her head. She must see that Mavia was safe whatever happened!

On reflection, she decided that the child would not go to her father. In fact, no one should ever know that Mavia was not the posthumous daughter of Odenathus Septimius. Zenobia decided to make her will and testament before she left Palmyra, and she would ask Durantis to write it for her. She would leave her daughter, Princess Mavia of Palmyra, in the keeping of her elder brother should anything happen to her. Her personal wealth would all belong to Mavia, thereby assuring her of a respectable marriage. It was the best that the queen could do. Why should Marcus have her? Had he not deserted them? He did not deserve Mavia.

Preparations for the departure of Palmyra's king and young queen moved quickly forward. Aurelian was determined to stop Prince Demetrius and his Brotherhood of the Palm by removing Vaballathus and Flavia as swiftly as possible. As long as the young monarch and his wife remained in the city there lived the possibility of rebellion. Gone, they offered no hope. The people of Palmyra were not going to rise up and retrieve their ruler from distant Cyrene.

Zenobia knew that the journey for her eldest son and his family would begin at night, for Aurelian wanted no one to see their departure lest someone try to take them from Roman custody. He dreaded that a popular demonstration would be started by the sight of the young couple, the lovely girlish queen pregnant with Palmyra's heir. At dawn their departure would be a cold, hard fact.

The queen sent Adria for Demetrius. The servant girl slipped through the secret gate in the wall and hurried through the busy streets to the house of the late Cassius Longinus. The haughty servant who opened the door sought to shoo her away, hardly giving her time to state her business.

"Fool!" Adria hissed. "I am the queen's messenger."

"You?" The man looked down his long nose, then again attempted to shut the door in her face.

"Very well," Adria said. "I shall return to Queen Zenobia and tell her that I was sent from the house of Oppian Longinus without even being allowed to state my business to the master. My mistress does not suffer fools at all, and you are a fool!"

"Oh come in, come in!" the major-domo sniffed, "but if I find you've lied to gain entry to this noble house, I shall beat you through the streets myself."

"What is all this noise? How can I compose my poetry when a constant cacophony reigns within my own house." Oppian Longinus came forth from his garden, his long pale-peach silk robes swaying.

"Greetings, Oppian, adopted son of Cassius Longinus," Adria said politely. "I am Adria, second waiting woman to Queen Zenobia. I have a message for Prince Demetrius."

Instantly a wary look came into Oppian's eyes. "I cannot imagine why you have come here then," he said nervously. "I have no idea where Prince Demetrius is. I am sorry." He turned to go, but Adria's voice stopped him.

"No one accuses you of anything, Oppian Longinus. The queen, having met here with her younger son several weeks ago, believes that you might be able to pass along a message. It is very urgent."

"Well," Oppian Longinus reconsidered, "there is a faint possibility that I might see the prince tonight. Give me the message."

Adria smiled. "The queen wishes Prince Demetrius to know that his brother Vaballathus and his wife will shortly be leaving for Cyrene. If Prince Demetrius wishes to bid the king and the young queen farewell he is to come to the secret gate in the queen's garden at midnight tonight. They and the queen will be waiting for him. He must not be late, for the emperor will be returning from a dinner shortly after midnight, and expects Queen Zenobia's company when he does. Please tell the prince, Oppian Longinus.''

"I will tell him," Oppian Longinus said, and then with a rather incautious curiosity he asked, "Is it true that the queen sleeps with Rome's emperor?"

Adria laughed scornfully. "For a man with the instinct for survival that you possess, Oppian Longinus, you are bold to question the queen's actions. I shall tell my mistress that you will pass her message on to the prince," and with a swish of her skirts Adria left the house of Oppian Longinus.

They could not be sure that he would come, but a few minutes before midnight Zenobia, Vaba, and Flavia all waited in the darkness by the queen's secret gate. It was Flavia who first heard the soft scratching, and unlocked the little door to admit Prince Demetrius.

"Brother," she said softly, kissing him on the cheek.

"Flavia, you bloom," was his answer.

In the faint light from the garden torches they looked at each other, and then Demi said, "Mother, Vaba. How are you both?"

"We are all well, my brother, but we fear for your safety. I feel fortunate that we are all still alive."

"I wonder if you will feel glad to be alive after a year in Cyrene," Demi said.

"As long as I am alive, as long as Flavia lives, and our children beginning with this baby, there is hope, Demi. Mother is right. Why can you not be patient, my brother? Go with Mother and Mavia to Rome. I need you there to look after them."

"Look after Mother?" His voice was bitter. "Mother does not need looking after. She does quite well by herself, and as long as she does Mavia is safe."

"I will need someone in Rome who can travel back and forth between Mother and me," Vaballathus entreated. "Who better can I trust but you, Demi?"

"I remain in Palmyra. At least there will be one of King Odenathus's sons here."

"If the Romans capture you, Demi, you will be killed," Zenobia said. "Aurelian will allow you your life if you come with us."

335

"There is no one in Palmyra who will betray me," was the proud reply.

"There is always someone who will betray you, you young fool!" said Zenobia impatiently. "If it is not for gold, then it will be for Roman favor; but mark my words, Demi, someone will betray you, and it will be he whom you least expect."

There was a rustle among the bushes, and Adria appeared. "The emperor is just returning, Majesty. He is already in the outer courtyard."

"Demetrius!" Zenobia's voice was impassioned and pleading. "I beg of you, please, my son, come with us!" She pulled him so that he faced her in the dim light.

For a brief moment Demi softened. "Mother, I must stay," he said quietly. "As long as I remain in Palmyra our people have hope. They will know we have not deserted them. If I am your son then I am my father's son, too. Please try to understand."

"You will throw your life away needlessly," she said brokenly. Where was her power now? This was but one more thing she had to thank the Romans for! She huddled in her son's arms for a long minute, alternating between anger and despair; and then she stood straight. "Demetrius, Prince of Palmyra, may the gods go with you, my son, and keep you safe until we meet again." Pulling his head down, she kissed him on the forehead. "Farewell, my son."

"Farewell, my Mother," he answered her.

She looked at him a long minute, committing his face to memory, then she turned and hurried back to the palace.

"You have hurt her terribly," Vaba said quietly.

"She will survive, my brother."

Vaba realized that there was to be no reasoning with his younger brother. The king knew that every minute they now remained in Zenobia's garden brought them closer to discovery, and so he said, "We must go, Demi. You have Mother's blessing, and I give you mine also. I think that you are wrong, but your sacrifice is a great one. The gods go with you, brother." He embraced his sibling a final time.

Flavia hugged him also, saying in her gentle voice, "Mars protect you, dearest brother; and Athena give you wisdom."

"The gods go with you both also," Demi said softly. He kissed her tenderly upon her lips, then saluting his older brother a final time slipped through the little wall door and into the darkness of the sleeping city.

Slowly they closed the door, locked it, and carefully replaced the key. Then together Vaba and Flavia returned to the palace.

In Zenobia's bedchamber the emperor lay back looking up at her. "You are sad tonight, goddess. Have you seen your younger son?"

"Yes," she said.

"He persists in his foolishness?"

She nodded. "You will have to kill him," Zenobia said low, and a single bright tear rolled down her cheek.

Gently he brushed it away with one finger, and reaching up gathered her into his arms. "Perhaps we shall catch him before he does something too unforgivable, goddess. I will give orders, I promise you."

"How can you be so kind on one hand, so cruel on the other?" she asked.

"I don't want to make you any sadder than you are already, beloved, and I know the wrench it is for you to leave Palmyra, be parted from your family. I understand these things, and I can afford to be generous under the circumstances."

She almost wept then and there, but instead she pulled away and looked him in the eye, saying, "I thank you, Roman, for your kindness."

"What a little fraud you are, goddess," he chuckled. "All right, don't weep upon my neck as you really want to do at this moment. I understand pride." He pulled her back into his arms and covered her lips with his in an almost tender kiss, pressing gently, nibbling teasingly. "You silver-eyed sorceress," he murmured against her mouth. "One day you will yield fully to me!" Wisely the queen refrained from an angry retort, closing her eyes in seeming surrender.

The following evening after a busy day of packing—for the royal Palmyran couple were to be allowed to take all their furniture and personal possessions with them to Cyrene—Zenobia found herself bidding most of her family farewell. In the main courtyard of the palace, where only a short few weeks ago the council had been executed, a fair-sized caravan prepared to leave. There were over two hundred laden camels, each with one of the king's slaves walking by its side. All the royal slaves and free servants would walk with the caravan, as would the legionnaires of Rome. Only the young king, Gaius Porcius, and the military officers would be mounted. Julia and young

Queen Flavia would ride in their own litters, each big enough for sleeping.

"We will write you, Mother, as often as possible," promised Vaba.

"Wait until you have reached Cyrene to send me your message," Zenobia replied. "The emperor is leaving to return to Rome in another day or two, Vaba. There will be no place you can send the message to me until I reach their capital."

"Will you too be hastened from the city under cover of darkness, I wonder, Mother?"

"No. Aurelian sends you from Palmyra this way in order to keep his Roman peace. He will march me from the city in plain view of all our people, a captive queen, a lesson to any foolish enough to reconsider rebellion."

"Mother . . ." The worry showed plain upon his face, and she was touched by his caring.

"Vaba, my son," and she put a hand on his shoulder, "do not be afraid for me. Save your caring for Flavia and your unborn child. Aurelian is nothing more to me than a lustful man with whom I can contend quite successfully." She laughed softly at the shock in his eyes. He knew of her relationship with the emperor, of course, but he did not like to admit to a truth that embarrassed him. "It is never easy to be a woman, Vaba," Zenobia said soothingly, "even a woman who is a reigning queen as I have been. What the gods give with one hand, they take back with the other. Remember that always, my son."

"I am a king, and yet I was unable to aid you, Mother. I will never forget that, and it will haunt me always," Vaba declared.

"No, no, dear one!" Zenobia protested. "The Roman had more power, that is all, and that is what I tried to gain for you, my son—power. That and wealth will always protect you."

"When will I see you again?" he demanded.

"When the emperor tires of me, enough to allow me to travel to Cyrene from Rome. Not until then, my son." She took his face in her hands and kissed him on both cheeks, then quickly upon the lips. "Farewell, my son. Farewell, son of Odenathus. Farewell, rightful King of Palmyra. Until we meet again may the gods watch over you and care for your safety."

Quick tears sprang into his eyes, but he forced them away. "Farewell, my Mother," he said in a tremulous voice. Then his voice grew stronger. "No man has ever had a mother as wonderful as you, Zenobia of Palmyra. May the gods watch over you until we meet again! I love you, Mother!'' He quickly returned her kiss and then as quickly turned away, leaving her to say her good-byes to Flavia and Julia.

"I will look after him as if he were my own,''Julia quickly said, seeing her old friend's face begin to quiver. She lowered her voice, "For goodness' sake, Zenobia, do not give way to tears now! The children have all they can do not to cry themselves.''

Zenobia breathed deeply, and replied, "I'm all right now, Julia, it's just that I cannot remember the last time that Vaba told me that he loved me.''

Julia laughed. "You are a sentimental woman for all you deny it, Zenobia. I will write to you, and I shall tell you all.''

Zenobia nodded. "Thank you, Julia. I know I may rely upon you. You are so fortunate. You shall see the baby long before I do. Be sure that he knows of his great heritage, and of me.''

"I will, Zenobia! I most assuredly will.'' Julia hugged her friend and then gave way to her daughter.

"Oh, Majesty,'' Flavia said, openly teary, and clung to the queen.

"Flavia,'' Zenobia admonished her daughter-in-law gently, "I am relying upon you to watch over Vaba and see that he does nothing foolish. Dear girl, what a joy you are to my son, and I am so grateful to you for that! Take good care of yourself, and of the child.'' Zenobia kissed the girl then stepped away from her. "The gods protect you, and my grandchild.'' The queen turned and walked from the courtyard and back into the palace. She would not stand there painfully watching until the vast caravan was out of sight. Instead, she returned to her gardens and walked amid the torchlit paths. Beyond the high garden walls she could hear the soft plod of the camels' hooves, and the tinkle of their harness bells as they wended their way down the back streets toward the gate to the western road.

The sound beat itself into her consciousness until suddenly she was aware that it was gone, and the night was silent. Only then did Zenobia sit down on a little marble bench in the most secluded part of the garden and weep bitterly, unaware that Aurelian, hidden in the shadows, observed her. When she returned to her apartments he awaited her, greeting her as if nothing unusual had happened, making passionate love to her in the deepest part of the night, holding her until she slept, exhausted with the emotion of her son's departure.

The next day was a busy one, for Bab and Adria had begun to pack all the queen's belongings for the trip to Rome. Zenobia was anxious to leave now. Palmyra was no longer hers, and the pain of that knowledge was too great.

She was granted permission by Aurelian to leave the palace and visit her father. She was carried through the streets in a closed litter so that the people might not see her. Aurelian had no fear that she would try to escape. Where would she go? Besides, he had Zenobia's daughter with him at the palace.

Zenobia was conducted to her father's bedchamber by Tamar. Zabaai ben Selim was close to eighty now, and seeing him propped up in his bed, Zenobia realized that her father did not have much more time to live. Yet he was sharp and fierce in mind even if his body now failed him. In his time he had fathered forty sons and a daughter. He had one hundred fifty-two grandsons, and forty-three granddaughters, over three hundred great-grandchildren, and ten great-great grandchildren. His own people often likened him to the Hebrew patriach, Father Abraham.

"It is Zenobia, Zabaai," his elderly wife said. Tamar was seventy-five.

"I can see her!" the old man snapped. "Come closer, my daughter. Come closer so I may feast my tired eyes upon your fresh beauty."

Zenobia bent to kiss her father. "As always, you spoil me with flattery, Father."

"I hear stories about the Roman, about you. Are they true?"

"Would you have me plunge a dagger into my breast in remorse, Father?"

The old man cackled. "By the gods, my daughter, you are a survivor! Good for you! Follow your own instincts, and do not be led by the opinions of others. Do you love him?"

"I detest him, but if I can outlast him then perhaps I may get Vaba restored to his rightful place, Father."

"Hmm," the old man said. "You are wise, Zenobia. When do you leave for Rome?"

"Tomorrow, Father. Mavia goes with me, but Demetrius will not come. Instead, he skulks through the alleys of the city with a group of young men who call themselves the Brotherhood of the Palm. They claim to work for Vaba's restoration, and the total annihilation of the Romans."

"He is a foolish boy," Zabaai remarked, "but then at his age you were as stubborn. If Odenathus had not been your husband, who knows what mischief you would have gotten into, my daughter. Well, do not fear. The Bedawi will keep an eye upon the boy. We will try to save him from himself.''

"Thank you, Father."

The old man looked closely at his only daughter. "I am near death," he said bluntly.

"I know," she answered.

He nodded. "Soon I shall be reunited with my beloved Iris. Do you think she will have forgiven me for the manner of her death, Zenobia?''

The memories rushed back in as they had not in so many years. They rose up to batter and assail her, and she felt the tears starting. Reaching out, she put a reassuring hand on his gnarled old one. "You were never responsible, Father. If anyone was, it was I." Her voice shook with remembrance. "When you again meet with my mother, tell her it is I who need her forgiveness. I have never forgotten, and I do not believe that I ever will.''

"I grow tired," the old man said. "Kneel, my daughter. Kneel, and let me give you my blessing.''

She knelt, and felt his hand, heavy upon her head, as he intoned the ancient words of blessing of their tribe. When he had finished Zenobia rose and, bending, kissed her father a final time. He smiled up at her reassuringly. "Another door closing, my daughter," he said with complete understanding, "but another door will open. Go through it! Do not be afraid! Always go forward and never look back! Those words are your heritage from me! Farewell, child of my heart.''

Zenobia looked the old man full in the face, and said, "I love you, Father. Farewell!'' Then she turned and, never looking back, went from the room.

Zabaai ben Selim died late that afternoon as the blazing sun slid below the horizon. Zenobia's oldest brother, Akbar, was formally and quickly proclaimed patriarch of the tribe, and all came to pay him tribute even as old Zabaai ben Selim was placed upon his funeral pyre, a pyre that burned all night while his children held vigil around the flames. At dawn's first light the old man's ashes were carefully gathered and formally placed in the family's tomb along the eastern caravan road. For the Bedawi a new era had begun.

Zenobia bid her brothers farewell, then entered her litter to be carried back to her palace for a final time.

Aurelian awaited her, a little angry. "You have delayed our departure," he said.

"But give me time to bathe a last time, and I will be ready," she promised.

"No," he said. "You are exhausted. You have been up all night. You need rest as well as a bath. We will leave tomorrow." Before she might protest further he picked her up and carried her into her bath where he personally undressed her and helped to bathe her. Then he carried her back into her bedchamber and tucked her into her bed. "I am glad you have had the good sense not to argue with me," he noted as he bent and kissed her goodnight.

"I am somewhat stunned by your behavior," Zenobia said weakly.

"I just want you full of fight when I parade you through the streets tomorrow as we leave Palmyra," he said, a slightly wicked grin on his face.

She threw the thing nearest to hand at him, a small statue of the little love god, Cupid. With a harsh laugh Aurelian turned and left the room. Feeling somewhat satisfied even if she had missed him, Zenobia lay back upon the soft pillows and fell asleep. She slept almost around the clock, awakening in the gray light of early dawn the following day. Slowly she stretched out, feeling a delicious sense of contentment. Beside her, the emperor appeared to slumber still. He had obviously joined her in the night. He was, she considered, becoming positively doting.

Then Aurelian destroyed her fantasy, reaching out and pulling her close, running his hands across her breasts. To her fury, she felt her body respond, her breasts tightening, the nipples rising up to push against the soft cotton of her chamber robe. "Good morning, goddess," he breathed against her ear, running his tongue around the curve of it.

She kept very still, and said in a detached voice, "Should we not be rising, Roman, and preparing to leave? Surely we do not have much time."

He chuckled indulgently. "There is time, and besides, I have an unquenchable yen for you this morning. When I came to bed last night you were sleeping as peacefully as a babe, your pretty bottom a most tempting sight. I want you, goddess, and I don't have to beg. What I want, I take!" Then he buried his face between her breasts, and breathed deeply of her. The faint scent of hyacinth still clung to her warm body, making her all the more enticing to him. Impatiently, he ripped her sleeping garment away and, dipping his head, took a nipple in his eager mouth.

"That is the second piece of my clothing you have torn," she protested, trying not to admit to the excitement he was stirring up in her body. Damn the man! She could feel the heat beginning, knew that her heartbeat was quickening.

"Then stop wearing these silly gowns to bed," he said, lifting his head but a moment from the sweet fruit.

"Oh, the gods, how I hate you!" she protested, feeling her control beginning to go.

"But you want me," he countered.

"Yes," she whispered. "I want you!"

"Take me in your hand, goddess," he ordered her. "See how much I want you! How ready I am for you!"

She never even hesitated, reaching out to grasp his mighty weapon in her hand. He was warm and throbbing, and so very eager for her.

"It is yours, goddess," he said softly. "When you are ready for it, it is yours!" Then he began a sweet assault, kissing her lips, her breasts, her belly, all the while aching with his want for her as she caressed him.

Finally Zenobia could no longer bear the passion that was building within her. She actually hurt with her desire. "Please, Roman, please now!" And she took his bigness in her two hands again, and guided him home. The pleasure, the relief, was incredible! Her body exploded with starburst after starburst of passion as he thrust again and again and again into her eager body. Finally the release came, and with a sigh she clung to him.

"You are magnificent," he breathed with pleasure.

"Don't you care?" she said. "Don't you care that I don't love you?"

He hesitated long enough to tell her he was lying when he said, "No, I don't care, goddess. I enjoy your lovely body. It is enough."

She squirmed from his embrace and rose. "I must have another bath, Roman. It will be a long time before we reach Rome, and I have traveled enough with the army to know there will be few amenities."

"No mourning today, Zenobia. I want you to wear the golden garments."

"I will not wear mourning, Roman, but I prefer to choose my own clothing. I shall not disappoint you. Remember, it is

343

the last time my people shall see me, and I would have them remember Zenobia the Queen with pride.''

"I will trust you, goddess," he answered.

At the hour appointed for their departure Zenobia walked slowly through her apartments a final time. Although the military governor was to live in the palace, he was a bachelor, and there would be few rooms open. In fact, she suspected that he would take up actual residence in the small house that Odenathus had built for her rather than in the main buildings. The closed rooms would lie in lonely waiting for the return of Odenathus's dynasty.

Aurelian found her in the garden, just leaving a room whose entry was overgrown with a flowering vine. "What is this room?" he asked her, pushing past her to look inside it. His blue eyes widened at the magnificent, but very graphic paintings he saw upon the walls.

"Why have I never seen this room, goddess?" he demanded.
"It is a room for lovemaking."

"I had it walled up last year," she replied in a stony voice. "In the palace corridor its door lies beneath the fine fresco of fruits upon the wall. I do not know why I did not have this entry walled over, too."

"Perhaps you wanted to remember after all, goddess," he said with unusual insight.

Zenobia stepped out into the sunlight of the garden once more. "Do you approve of my costume, Roman?" she demanded, quite obviously changing the subject.

Following her, he eyed her approvingly. "You are every inch the queen, goddess."

"You do not mind that I wear the Palmyran crown?"

"I do not mind," was his answer.

"Then let us go, Roman," she said impatiently. "I no longer belong in Palmyra, and I certainly do not belong in your Rome. I am anxious to find out where I do belong."

"You belong with me, goddess," he said, and taking her arm he led her off to the main courtyard where the procession was forming.

She was to walk behind Aurelian's chariot, and this time the streets of Palmyra would be full to overflowing with its citizens bidding their beloved queen farewell. She had been dressed in a cloth of silver kalasiris with its round neck and very short sleeves. The kalasiris was smooth and molded her body, making it appear as if she had been dipped in silver. She wore a magnificent necklace of deep-purple topazes with equally gorgeous earrings, both set in bright yellow gold. A cape, lined in cloth of gold, its outer layer done in alternating strips of gold and silver, was fastened to each shoulder of her gown by a carved purple scarab beetle set in gold. Her sandals were a mix of silver and gold.

With a polite apology Gaius Cicero fastened a pair of gold manacles about her delicate wrists. The manacles were fastened together by a length of gold chain between them, and in the chain's center another length of chain stretched forth a final link attached to a special ring on the emperor's own belt. "The emperor has promised to release you when we are clear of the city," Gaius Cicero said.

"Caesar is too kind," Zenobia said sarcastically. "Where is my daughter?"

"She is already outside the city with your servants, awaiting us. The emperor did not want her involved in this procession."

Zenobia nodded but remarked bitterly, "He also did not want my daughter's people to see her a final time. The king, he sent from the city like a thief in the night, and now my little girl."

"You have another son," Gaius Cicero reminded, "and he, it appears, will remain behind to remind Palmyra of Odenathus's dynasty."

"Demetrius is impetuous."

"His impetuosity will cost the boy his life."

"You have not caught him yet, Gaius Cicero."

Zenobia turned her head away from the emperor's aide, and said nothing further. The procession began, and there was no more time to think. If she did not keep up with the pace of Aurelian's horses she was in danger of being injured.

She looked back at her palace only once as they passed through its main gates, and she remembered the first time she had entered into its courtyard. It had been almost twenty years ago, and she was barely more than a child. She remembered Al-Zena's frosty welcome, and the lovely Deliciae of whom she had been so fearful and jealous. Poor Deliciae, now widowed with her six children to care for, although between Odenathus and Rufus Curius, she would certainly have no financial problems.

The queen stumbled, then quickly brought herself back to where she was and what she was doing. They were just entering Palmyra's great main avenue, and the colonnaded streets were a sea of spectators. The emperor's own Illyrian legion led the procession, its mounted officers coming first, followed by a vast sea of legionnaires, all marching smartly, their short red military capes flowing in the gentle breeze, the sun gleaming off their polished breastplates. Behind them came Aurelian in his chariot, followed by Zenobia, the captive Queen of Palmyra, and, behind her, representatives of the other three legions. There were no slaves, nor booty carts, for Rome's emperor had been merciful to the people of Palmyra. Only their government had suffered his wrath.

At the sight of their beautiful queen, manacled and chained to the Roman emperor, the people of Palmyra began to sing patriotic songs of freedom and hymns to Palmyra's past triumphs. They flung white flowers before and upon their queen, some of the delicate blossoms catching in her long, flowing black hair, and in the delicate golden wreath of vine leaves that crowned her. Finally the populace began to chant their beloved queen's name; and the emperor's horses danced nervously as the rhythmic sound rose in volume until the entire city echoed with one word: *Zenobia!*

The queen felt her heart swell with pride at her people's tribute, and unbidden tears slid down her face. Proudly she walked behind Aurelian's chariot, her beautiful head held high. She had given most of her life to this city, this great and wonderful city, and she regretted nothing but the fact she had lost the final battle with Rome. *Someday,* she thought to herself, someday as the great gods Mars and Venus are witness, *I will right this wrong!*

Finally the Triumphal Arch of Odenathus loomed before her. Zenobia passed beneath it, and out of the city of Palmyra onto the western road. After they had gone a mile or so along the highway, and the people were no more, Aurelian stopped his chariot, stepped down from it, and came over to his captive queen, freeing her wrists. Wordlessly he rubbed them, for the manacles had chafed her skin. "I apologize, goddess. I will have these manacles lined in lamb's wool before my Roman triumph. I did not mean that you should be injured."

"I never even noticed," she said wonderingly.

He nodded. "Your people's farewell was indeed impressive. I wish that I were capable of commanding such loyalty and love. I do not understand why, with so much, you risked all to rebel against us. Had you not, I might never have deposed you."

"It is quite simple, Roman," she answered him. "We were

346

tired of answering to foreigners across a sea who knew nothing of us but our wealth. We believed that we could rule the Eastern Empire, a place that we knew far better than you Romans could. We could have too, but alas, you were stronger.''

"We will always be stronger, goddess," he answered her, and then he lifted her up to his chariot and, climbing up beside her, drove off once more.

In three weeks they had reached Antioch, and here Aurelian decided to pause for a few days to enjoy the pleasures of the city before moving onward. Antioch would be the last truly great city they saw before reaching Rome several months hence. Strangely Zenobia was more relaxed now with Aurelian than she had ever been. Away from her city with all its familiar sights and memories, and plunged into this new and fascinating environment, her natural curiosity reared its head, and to his amusement she kept Rome's emperor quite busy sightseeing.

The night before their departure, however, all that changed. At dinner with the city's Roman governor they were suddenly interrupted by the arrival of a messenger from Palmyra. The legionnaire, dried blood still evident upon his body even after several days, exhausted and bleary-eyed, stumbled into the room, and croaked. "Hail, Caesar!" Zenobia felt a frightening chill of premonition.

"Speak!" Aurelian commanded.

"Palmyra has revolted," the legionnaire said. "The governor and the entire garrison massacred."

"When?" Aurelian's voice was a whipcrack.

"Nine days ago, Caesar. The governor saw at once we were outnumbered. Toward the end my tribune chose me from among the survivors, and I made my way from the city, stole a horse, and followed you."

"*Nooo!*" Zenobia's voice was anguished.

"Who led the revolt?" the emperor asked, but they both knew the answer.

"Prince Demetrius."

Aurelian turned to Zenobia, and his eyes were icy with his anger. "Better the boy had died in your womb," he said. He rose from the table and left the room.

Zenobia quickly followed him. "I am coming with you, she said.

"I have no time for women and their fripperies."

"Do not speak to me as if I am only some sort of decoration

347

for your pleasure, Roman!'' she snapped at him. "I am Zenobia, the Queen of Palmyra! I have led my armies into battle enough times to be worthy of your respect. Remember, you captured me as I sought help for my beleaguered city. *You never defeated me! Never!*''

He swung around to face her, and his stern face was terrible to behold. "Hear me, goddess. Whether you come with me or not will be your decision, but be warned. I show no further mercy to Palmyra.''

"What will you do?'' Her face was pale with anguish.

"I will destroy the city, and all in it, Zenobia. Your foolish son has left me no choice. I forgave Palmyra its sins once because of you. I will not forgive it now.''

"Please!'' She held out her hands to him in a gesture of supplication.

"No! I cannot overlook this. If I allow Palmyra to escape imperial wrath this time, how many other cities will rebel and slaughter their Roman masters? I swore to rebuild the empire, and by the gods I will keep that vow!''

"I would still go with you,'' she whispered.

"We leave in half an hour, and you will have to fend for yourself. There will be no servants.''

She nodded her understanding and hurried to change her clothes.

During the next few days Zenobia understood why the Roman Army had gained its fame. The disciplined soliders moved out of Antioch and quickly back across the desert in less than a third of the time it had taken them to reach the city. Once more, Rome's mighty military forces stood before Palmyra's closed gates, but this time there were no negotiations.

When they had rested on their journey the emperor had never once come near Zenobia. Only now, when they were outside of the city's walls and preparing to give siege, did she attempt to reason with him, imploring him to offer her people mercy, to spare the great and ancient city.

"No,'' he said coldly, "and you know my reasoning is sound. I will discuss it with you no further.''

"I will give you whatever you want of me,'' she pleaded.

Aurelian grasped her cruelly by the arms, and almost snarled through clenched teeth, "Listen to me, you silver-eyed sorceress, there is only one thing I want from you, but I shall never have it. I want your love, Zenobia!''

348

"I will give it to you!" she promised rashly.

"You cannot," he answered bitterly. "You have already given your heart, goddess. You have given it to Marcus Alexander Britainus, and whatever happens you will never stop loving him though you will not admit it to yourself!"

"No! I will love you, Roman, if you will but let me! Just spare my Palmyra! Spare my people!"

"Oh, goddess," he said in a more gentle tone, "if for one minute I believed you could give me your heart I should relent. I would, for I love you deeply. I would overlook my duty to Rome for your honest love. But you cannot give it. Your body I can take. Your wit and intellect I can enjoy, but you have already given your heart to another man. I am sorry, goddess. You have not doomed Palmyra. Palmyra has doomed itself."

The siege of Palmyra began with enormous battering rams, their heads carved like huge bulls, pounding against every gate of the city until one by one the gates began to crack and give, at last falling open to the tremendous onslaught. Rome's legions poured in. Before long black smoke began to rise from the city as it was cruelly torched. Palmyra's armies were terribly outnumbered, although they fought valiantly. Soon, however, they fell to the vast numbers of the enemy, and then the Romans began their terrible slaughter of the population.

There were to be no prisoners, no quarter was to be given. Children torn from their screaming mother's arms were tossed upon swords and spears; women and girls as young as five were brutally and multiply raped before being murdered; the men and boys of Palmyra were tortured and killed. The priests protesting violation of their temples' sanctuary were callously disemboweled on their pristine marble floors, and left to die in agony amid their own smoking entrails.

The horror went on for three long days and nights as the Romans satisfied their fierce blood lust and avenged their slain comrades. The sweetish smell of death hung over the city as the carrion birds formed black clouds in the hazy, yellowed skies above once-proud Palmyra.

When not a single living thing remained within the city the armies of Rome began the final destruction. Systematically they worked at leveling every building that still stood, every statue and monument, until Palmyra lay broken and battered, a testimony to Rome's efficiency at devastation. Had they been able to haul away the ruins and rake the ground clean and smooth, the emperor would have ordered it. Instead, the demolished city lay as a warning to all those who would even consider rebellion against the mighty Roman Empire.

Throughout it all, Zenobia had stood before the Roman encampment watching with eyes that grew gradually duller as she saw the results of Demetrius's folly. She wondered absently if her younger son were dead, or if he had somehow escaped the destruction. There was no evidence of the Bedawi anywhere, and she suspected that her wise half-brother Akbar had removed the tribe when he saw what Demetrius was doing. No, her second son was dead, as were Deliciae and all her family; as were all of her people. Zenobia suddenly felt hollow and sick.

Still she stood outside in the burning sun watching as the legionnaires carefully wrecked Palmyra. When it was over at last, and Aurelian gave the orders to depart, she crept unnoticed from the encampment and into the ruins to pick up a small piece of marble from the great temple of Jupiter. It was the last thing she remembered for many days.

Missing her, Aurelian took several men and sought Zenobia. He found her wandering aimlessly amid the destruction, a piece of white marble that she would not be parted from clenched in her fist. Her eyes were sightless, she did not speak, although she did appear to hear him. Obedient to his voice, she followed him back to his tent, and then she collapsed into a stupor so deep that the army physicians feared not only for her sanity, but for her life as well.

The slow trek back to Antioch began, the booty carts rumbling along with the army, for this time Palmyra's treasures had been looted. Zenobia lay unconscious in one vehicle, never moving from one hour to the next. Aurelian, visibly worried, rode by her side, tending her when his other duties permitted. His soldiers had never seen him this way, and were amazed. When they finally reached Antioch, Zenobia was carried into the governor's palace. Old Bab and Adria came running to tend their ill mistress, and the queen opened her eyes for the first time in days.

"Am I dead?" she asked weakly.

"No, goddess," Aurelian said, openly relieved.

She sighed sadly. "Once again the gods have chosen to ignore my prayers," Zenobia whispered, and then she fell into a deep and natural sleep.

"She will recover," the head military physician pronounced.

"I wonder if she really will," Rome's emperor mused, and

old Bab looked sharply at him, suddenly aware of Aurelian's deep feeling for her mistress. She might have even felt sorry for him had she not known what he had done. All of Antioch already buzzed with the story of Palmyra's destruction. The news had seemingly preceded the army upon the hot desert winds.

"My baby has always been strong," she told the emperor.

"She should not have come," he said.

"You allowed it," old Bab accused. "Like all the men who have loved her, you allowed her too much freedom, and perhaps this time it destroyed her. Perhaps, but then again, perhaps not."

"Will she live now?" he asked anxiously.

"Give me a week, Caesar, and then ask me again," came the reply.

Aurelian nodded. "You may have your week, old woman, but do your job well."

"I will do it as well as you did yours, Caesar," Bab snapped, and Aurelian laughed for the first time in many weeks, appreciating the jest at his expense.

"See that you do, old woman. See that you do!"

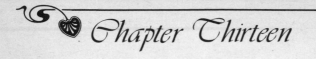

Chapter Thirteen

Marcus Alexander did not publicly mourn Carissa as his wife, for she had never been a wife to him. He did mourn for Carissa herself, however, realizing that she was as much a victim of Aurelian's ambition as he had been.

Upon learning of Marcus's connection with Zenobia, the empress had not permitted him to leave the Tivoli-Rome region. She was not sure what he might do if she let him go. Yes, it was best that he be kept confined, where he could cause Aurelian no difficulty. She felt somewhat guilty about her decision, though. Marcus was such a decent man, her own kin, a Roman of the old school, and the gods knew that there were precious few of those available today. She sighed, and to salve her conscience saw that her distant cousin received all the latest war communiqués before even the senate got them.

Thus Marcus Alexander Britainus knew when Aurelian had reached Palmyra. He knew when Zenobia was captured. He knew when Vaballathus opened the city's gates to the emperor; and he knew when his many friends on the Council of Ten were executed. He knew of the young king's exile to Cyrene, and he knew of Palmyra's revolt and total destruction.

He lived in helpless agony as each communiqué was given him. The word *if* grew larger in his mind with each message. If only he had not left her. It had never occurred to him that such tragedy would happen in his absence. He shook his head at the reckless bravery that had caused Zenobia to try and reach Persia. How like her. She would not have sent her younger son, or a ranking officer in her army. No, she would go because she felt it her duty. Her duty to Palmyra, as he had obeyed his duty to his family.

He had no illusions as to her fate at Aurelian's hands. How could the emperor not desire her? She was the most beautiful, the most seductive, the most intelligent and interesting of women. He wondered if Zenobia had resisted Aurelian; or if she now enjoyed the emperor as a bed partner. The pictures that this thought raised in his mind provoked such pure fury that he could have killed; but he could not decide whether it would be Aurelian or Zenobia, or both, who would fall victim to his righteous wrath!

Dagian might have returned to Britain, but she now chose not to do so. Marcus, she believed, needed her far more than Aulus and his family. There would be time to go back, but now was not the time. With Palmyra destroyed and gone, his Eastern mercantile base was gone too, although Marcus was not impoverished. His faithful Severus had seen the handwriting on the wall, and taken it upon himself to sell everything Marcus possessed in Palmyra to another Palmyran house of commerce. He had left the city for Rome, Marcus's fortune transferred safely to Rome, shortly before Palmyra's demise.

Marcus had greeted him with pleasure when he arrived at the Tivoli villa. He was extremely relieved that the faithful Severus had escaped Palmyra's fate.

"I have saved your fortune, Marcus Alexander," the now elderly Severus said proudly. "Oh, I might have gotten more for you had I stayed longer, and haggled, but I could see we were in for serious trouble. Prince Demetrius would not cease his rebellion."

Marcus nodded his head. "Thank the gods for your instincts, Severus, or I should have been ruined. Palmyra was totally destroyed."

"Yes," came the reply, "I heard that news." A sad look came into his eyes. "It is so terribly tragic, Marcus Alexander. I shall miss that beautiful city."

"The queen, Severus. What of the queen?"

"She was well the last I heard," came the evasive reply.

"You know what I am asking of you, old friend," Marcus said low.

"Marcus Alexander, you know the grist from which rumors are ground. I put no faith in rumors, but if you would hear the chief rumor of Palmyra, when I left, regarding the queen, it was that Aurelian had taken her for his woman. Why do you ask me? You expected no less."

Marcus had sighed and left the room.

"We are relieved that you escaped Palmyra and have come home to us safely, Severus," Dagian said. "You must forgive my son. He is a very unhappy man."

"I can understand that, my lady," came Severus's understanding reply.

Aurelian and his army drew closer and closer to Rome with every passing day; and with each day Marcus grew more grim. Finally, when the emperor was expected momentarily, he told his mother, "I want my daughter. I don't give a damn what that Palmyran whore does, but I want my daughter. I recognized her as mine when she was born, and now I shall claim her. I will not have her raised in any house where Aurelian either lives or is a frequent visitor. Look what he did to Carissa! I won't allow him to do that to my child! Mavia is all that I have."

"You cannot take the child from her mother, Marcus," Dagian protested.

"She is your grandchild, Mother. Knowing Aurelian's influence on Carissa, do you want Mavia to suffer the same fate?"

"Mavia has a mother, Marcus. A very strong and wise mother. Aurelian will never harm the child as long as Zenobia lives. Besides, do you really believe that the queen will hand over her child to you? I somehow suspect that you are not in her good graces."

"She has no right to judge me," he said pompously.

"And you have no right to judge her, my son. It was you who left her, and then did not even bother to send an explanation of your marriage."

"How could I communicate with her, Mother? You know that the emperor had me watched, and every letter going from this house was intercepted and read."

"Marcus, you should have sent her a message as soon as you saw the emperor was adamant in his desire that you wed Carissa; but you did not. I am not blaming you, for you were distraught not only with your fate and your sudden inability to control it, but with your father's impending death. Zenobia, however, does not know these things. Think of how she must have felt if she loved you as you say she did."

"She should have known better than to believe that I would betray that love," Marcus muttered.

Dagian laughed. "I am willing to admit that your Zenobia is a paragon, my son, but even a paragon could not be expected to keep faith with a betrothed who marries another woman. Be reasonable, Marcus."

"I want my daughter."

"Would you place the strain of bastardy upon Mavia? If you claim to be her father and insist on having the child, that is what you will do. You will mark her as surely as if you placed

a burning brand upon her forehead. Even if you adopt her
formally into this family, she will still be remembered as the
illegitimate daughter of Palmyra's queen and one of her Roman
lovers. What kind of a marriage can we make for this child
with that stain upon her innocent reputation? Have you become
so callous in your own misery that you would mark your daughter in order to satisfy your own wishes?"

He looked terribly unhappy, and Dagian pitied him greatly,
but she knew that she was right.

"What am I to do, Mother?" he asked.

"Let us just watch the situation with Zenobia, Marcus. Perhaps
by the time they reach Rome Aurelian will have grown tired of
her. We don't even know what the senate plans to do with her."

He grew pale. "You do not think that they would condemn
her to death, do you?"

"Who can predict the capricious whims of politicians?"
Dagian demanded. "Once they have won their place in the
senate, they behave as if the gods themselves had placed them
there. Only if the public outcry is dangerously great do they
heed the people. They serve only their own interests. However,
if Aurelian has any personal interest in the lady she may be
saved serious consequences."

"You are telling me, Mother, that if Zenobia survives imperial judgment I must regain my lost ground with her and only
then can I hope to have any part in my daughter's life."

"Yes, Marcus, I am. You will gain nothing, I suspect, by
anger."

"What if she no longer cares for me?"

"You will have to begin at the beginning with Zenobia,"
Dagian said quietly.

"You sound as if you are on her side," he complained,
somewhat irritably.

Dagian smiled, her mouth quirking upward with her genuine
amusement, her lovely blue eyes twinkling. "Let us say, Marcus,
that even having never met the lady, I like the sound of her. I
believe she is going to make me a fine daughter-in-law."

Stunned, he gaped at her. "What makes you think that I will
marry her now? After she has been the emperor's mistress?"

Dagian chuckled. "You men are so vain when it comes to
your prowess. Are you afraid to be compared to Aurelian, my
son? Since you conceived a daughter by Zenobia, I am sure the
comparison is already made. Perhaps, though, you do not wish
to know the results."

"*Mother!*" He was visibly embarrassed by her frankness.

"I am sure, Marcus, that if you forgive Zenobia for being Aurelian's captive, she will forgive you Aurelian's niece."

"I never touched Carissa!" he protested.

"In Zenobia's mind it will not matter if you did or not. You married her. That is far worse."

Marcus sighed with exasperation, and Dagian quietly left him to his thoughts. He was a good man, her son, and she knew that he was intelligent in many matters. In the matter of man and woman, however, Dagian decided that Marcus was a dunce. He would learn, though, and providing that the senate did not condemn Palmyra's queen to an unfair death, Dagian decided that she wouldn't miss what was going to transpire between Zenobia and Marcus for all the world.

Two days later, Aurelian and his army arrived outside of Rome's walls. The emperor went immediately to the senate, and was hailed a returning hero. A triumph, complete with a holiday, was ordered to celebrate his victory over Palmyra. One rather pompous senator, Valerian Hostilius, suggested that the highlight of the day might be the public execution of the Queen of Palmyra in the Colosseum.

"Her reputation is that of a warrior," he cried in his rather flutelike voice. "Let us dress this barbarian queen in lionskins, give her a golden spear, and have her fight to the death a pack of wild beasts! What a spectacle it will make for the people, Caesar!"

Aurelian yawned, then looked about the senate. What a perfumed bunch, he thought. "A fascinating suggestion, Valerian Hostilius," he said, "but the Queen of Palmyra has already suffered for her rashness in rebelling against us, and once she realized her mistake she strove to give us aid once more."

"Yet you were forced to destroy the city, Caesar. Why was that?" This time the speaker was Marcus Claudius Tacitus, an elderly but extremely competent senator. Tacitus's opinion would carry much weight in the senate's decision.

"I had already sent Palmyra's young King Vaballathus into exile in the city of Cyrene. The queen and I had left Palmyra for Antioch en route back to Rome. Unfortunately, the queen's younger son, Prince Demetrius, could not accept defeat, and with some young friends inspired a second rebellion. The queen was not responsible. She returned with me to Palmyra, and we took our revenge. She tried very hard before we originally left the city to stop her younger son's foolishness."

"You do not think she deserves to die?" Tacitus questioned.

"No, I do not. She is a woman," Aurelian said scornfully. "It was up to her council to control her as her son, the king, was just a boy. I executed the council for not doing their duty, but Palmyra's queen does not deserve death."

Tacitus turned and looked on his fellow senators. "The noble Senator Hostilius has suggested we make a death spectacle of Palmyra's queen. I disagree with him, and I agree with the emperor. This woman has been a noble enemy to Rome, but she is now beaten, her homeland destroyed, her younger son dead. She has paid the price of her folly. Now let us show the world Rome's beneficence. After the emperor's triumph is completed, let us retire her to one of the state's villas at Tivoli. She will live out her days there a forgotten woman, and what greater punishment can there be for one who was once so powerful?"

"But the people love a good spectacle," Hostilius protested.

Tacitus raised a bushy white eyebrow. *"The people?"* he said.

A rumble of laughter echoed around the chamber. For once all the senate was in agreement. Hostilius sank back onto the bench feeling foolish, and wishing that he'd never opened his mouth.

"It is decided then," Aurelian said. "Palmyra's queen will be pensioned, and retired to Tivoli."

"It is agreed," the senate said with one voice, and a smiling Aurelian left them.

The emperor hurried to his home upon the Palatine Hill. He was anxious to see Ulpia and to hear about Carissa's baby. His wife, however, was not at the door to greet him. She was, it seemed, ill and in her bed. Aurelian entered Ulpia's bedchamber, and was shocked by her appearance. She who had always been of such robust constitution was thin and wan.

"My dear," he said, his voice full of concern. "How are you?"

Ulpia smiled joyfully at his entrance, and held out her arms to him. "I have not been well, husband, but now that you are here I will feel better. I know it!"

"Has Carissa been to see you? How is she? Is the child a boy or a girl?"

A shadow passed over Ulpia Severina's pale face. "Carissa is dead," she said bluntly. "She died in childbirth despite the fact that everything was done that could be done for her. She had the best of care.''

"The child?''

"The child was born dead, and thank the gods it was. It was a monster of incredible ugliness, my lord.''

"Poor Carissa,'' Aurelian mused, but it was Marcus Alexander Britainus that he was thinking about. *Marcus and Zenobia.* By the gods, Marcus would not have her! She was his, and he had no intention of letting her go! He was in love. He was in love for the first and only time in his entire life, and the feeling was one of both Heaven and Hades. Suddenly he realized that Ulpia was staring at him. "And you, my dear,'' he said solicitously, "you have obviously not been well. Have you seen a physician?''

She nodded, and then tears came to her eyes. "I have seen three. They all say the same thing. I have a canker in my breast, and I shall die from it.''

"How long have you been ill?'' he demanded. "Why did you not write to me?''

"I grew ill shortly after Carissa's death. I did not write you about it for the same reason I did not write you about Carissa. Carissa was dead, and there was nothing that you or anyone else could have done to prevent her death. I am to die, and there is nothing that can prevent *my* death. The physicians did, however, assure me that I should live until you returned home, and so I saw no need to worry you.''

"By the gods, Ulpia, you are a perfect wife. You have always been. I have been most fortunate in you.''

Ulpia beamed with pleasure. He could not have said anything more calculated to delight her. She always had tried to please him, and now with death staring her in the face, the knowledge that she had, sent a joyful wave of warmth coursing through her ravaged frame.

Aurelian bent and placed a fond kiss upon Ulpia's brow. "I will leave you to rest, my dear,'' he said. "My triumph is just two days hence. There is much to do.''

"How I wish I might see it,'' Ulpia said sadly.

"I wish you could too, but alas, our house is not near the route of march; and I do not think you strong enough to go.''

Ulpia sank back amid her pillows. Now she was truly curious as to what the Queen of Palmyra looked like. Aurelian did not seem particularly anxious for her to see his triumph, and it could only be because he did not want her to see Zenobia.

Nonetheless Ulpia vowed that she would. She would find out who among Rome's patrician families had a home along the line of march, and she would use her imperial prerogative, and invite herself there.

She called for her secretary, and told him what she wanted. After that it was simple. Fabius Buteo, she was told, had a fine home where she might watch her husband's triumph, and he was overwhelmed at the honor being done him by the empress's presence.

On the day of Aurelian's triumph she was settled quite comfortably on a second-floor balcony with the pleasant women and girls of the Buteo family, who chatted quite companionably with her. She was offered the finest wines to keep her strength up, and the choicest of delicacies. The warm sun beat down, there was a faint flowery breeze, and, in general, Ulpia Severina felt quite well. After all, Aurelian had not forbidden her to watch his triumph. He had merely lamented that she was not strong enough to do so. But she was strong enough!

Below them, the streets were crowded on both sides by the citizenry jostling with one another for a good place. The vendors were busy hawking cheap wines, sausages, and sweetmeats to the excited population. Then in the distance came the sound of marching feet, the rhythm of the drums that beat out the measure of the military step.

Leading the triumph was the Ninth Illyrian Legion, Aurelian's own. The Ninth consisted of ten cohorts of six hundred men each, and was led by six tribunes, each riding before his own unit of cavalry. The legionnaires marched with perfect precision, the sun gleaming off their spotless weapons and helmets. Following them came the plundered wealth of Palmyra in flower-bedecked carts; the gold and silver booty sparkling in the clear Roman light. The crowds ohhed and ahhed.

Following this came the Third African Legion, its tribunes and centurions wearing leopardskins and a toothed leopard's head to cover their own, almost appearing as if they were being devoured by the beast itself. Their men wore the simple skin of the leopard thrown across their left shoulders, without its fierce head. Following the Third African came enormously tall black warriors, their heads capped by wavy grass headpieces that swung with the rhythm of their dancing. The blacks were oiled so that the sunlight made them appear even darker, and about their loins they wore a covering made from the black-and-white-striped skin of some exotic animal. They brandished their carved spears in mock ferocity, much to the delight of the watching children along the route.

Now came what all of the citizenry had awaited so eagerly: the emperor who had given Rome such a great victory. Aurelian himself drove the magnificent triumphal chariot; an incredible piece of workmanship. The vehicle was all overlaid in gold leaf over the raised figures of Mars, the god of war, in a scene of an Olympian triumph. The chariot was drawn by four magnificent white stallions, each more vicious than the next, but kept well in hand by the emperor, who was acknowledged to be one of the empire's finest drivers.

Aurelian was dressed as befitted a triumphant soldier-emperor. He wore a purple-and-gold-embroidered *tunica palmata* that reached to his ankles, and over that the official robe of the emperor, a *toga picta*, also of Tyrian purple and embroidered with gold. Both garments were of the finest silk. Upon his feet the emperor wore a high-soled strapped shoe of gilt leather laced with hooks and decorated with a bejeweled crescent-shaped buckle.

Behind him stood his personal body slave of many years, dressed simply in a natural-colored tunic and holding the laurel wreath of victory over the emperor's blond head. *"Remember,"* the slave intoned with regularity, *"thou art but a man. Remember, thou art but a man."* This ancient custom of the triumph was supposed to keep the victorious general humble with the constant reminder of his mortality.

Ulpia looked with pride upon her husband as he came into view. Then she, along with the other ladies of the Buteo family, let out a collective gasp of shock. Behind Aurelian's magnificent chariot came the Queen of Palmyra—stark naked! Ulpia felt sick with shame that her husband would do such a thing to any woman, let alone the gallant captive Queen of Palmyra. How could he have been so cruel!? So brutal!

"Look at the hussy!" the wife of Fabius Buteo snipped. "She does not even lower her eyes in shame, but stares straight ahead, her arrogant head held high."

"She is incredibly beautiful, Mother," said the eldest Buteo daughter, a gentle matron. "How awful for her!" Then she turned apologetically to the empress. "I mean no disrespect, my lady, I only . . ." her soft voice died away.

"I agree with you, my dear," the empress said quietly. "How awful for her."

Still, the women watching Zenobia were envious of her. They could not help it. Here was a woman who had borne her late husband three children, and yet her body was that of a young girl. Her breasts, firm globes of perfection, thrust boldly forth. Her well-shaped arms and legs were in perfect proportion to her tall height. She had only a faintly rounded belly, and her buttocks were round and firm. Around her slender neck she wore a magnificent necklace of pigeon's blood rubies that set off her pale-golden skin and her flowing blue-black hair. Her high-arched feet were shod in the faintest wisps of red leather sandals. She held her arms before her as her slender wrists were imprisoned by the golden manacles she had worn when she left Palmyra. True to his word, Aurelian had had them lined in soft lamb's wool so they would not chafe her tender skin.

Aurelian! She wanted to kill him as she walked so bravely along, neither looking to the right or the left, hearing none of the lewd comments sent her way by the populace of Rome. That they hadn't rushed out to fondle her was only due to the fact that she was well guarded by a maniple of sixty men. Aurelian didn't mind showing off his new possession to all of Rome, but they might not touch that which was the emperor's toy. She had almost begun to like him, but thank the gods he had reverted to type so she might hate him again, and plot his downfall with a clear conscience no matter how kind he had been before this damnable triumph. No matter how kind he would be afterward, for he would be kind again.

They had quarreled that morning because he had wanted her small daughter, Mavia, to walk with her behind his chariot. She had screamed and railed at him for the suggestion, forbidding him to even come near the child; threatening mayhem if he so much as touched her little daughter. What kind of a monster was he, she had demanded, to attempt such brutality upon an innocent baby? The trauma could destroy Mavia, who had lived through the first siege of Palmyra, and still had bad dreams.

In the end the emperor had relented, and Mavia was taken on ahead to the villa in Tivoli that would be her new home. Aurelian, however, was furious, for Zenobia's anger had come not in private, but before his officers. When she had appeared for his triumph dressed in her gold and silver garments, he had furiously torn them from her beautiful body in front of all of his officers, stating that it was his wish she walk in his triumph nude, wearing only her ruby necklace and her sandals. She had been shocked by his actions, but had looked him straight in the eye, and said in her mocking voice, *"As Caesar commands."*

He had looked as if he wanted to hit her then and there, but instead he had replied as mockingly, *"Yes, goddess, as Caesar commands. For you it will always be as Caesar commands, and should Caesar order you to couple with his entire Ninth Illyrian you would have to do so because Caesar would command. Remember that!"*

His triumph was the hardest thing she had ever done in her entire life; but he would never know it, for her face and carriage were proud and defiant. Gaius Cicero had been visibly embarrassed as he had fastened the golden manacles around her wrists. She had come close to giggling hysterically at him because he was in such a quandary as to where to look next, and his eyes kept coming, fascinated, back to her marvelous breasts with their dark, honey-colored nipples. When he had led her from the emperor's tent, however, all mirth left her. Four entire legions had gaped at her beauty, and she saw many glances of lustful envy.

"It's a wonder one of his men doesn't assassinate him just to possess that woman," one tribune muttered softly to another, but she heard.

For a moment she thought she might be sick, for her stomach churned violently, bile rising up to the base of her throat before she was able to gain control of herself and swallow it back down again. Despite the warm day, she was cold, a coldness only intensified by the gentle breeze that brushed against her body, faintly damp with a sheen of perspiration. Briefly her legs were weak and she was unable to move for the shame, and then she slowly lifted her head and saw him staring at her, his lips curled in a faint smile of triumph.

Zenobia took a deep breath. As the sweet air filled her lungs, strength filled her soul and her silvery eyes mocked him back. The queen closed her ears to everything about her and, looking straight ahead, took her place behind the emperor's chariot. That was the trick, she realized with sudden clarity, to notice nothing, to hear nothing.

As she walked she sang songs in her head, and focused her eyes upon the chariot ahead of her, never looking either to the right or the left. She did not see the mob with its envious, lustful, pitying, vengeful, and cruel glances. She did not hear the ribald, even filthy comments hurled her way. She was Zenobia, the Queen of Palmyra, and could not be humbled by mere Romans.

Marcus Alexander stood amid the front rank of the crowd near the senate, and when he saw her his heart leapt within his chest. Then, realizing that she had been forced to walk naked before plebes and patricians alike, his anger toward the emperor burned hot, almost consuming him where he stood.

Zenobia! Beloved! Aching with her shame he called to her with his heart. There was much he owed Aurelian for what the emperor had done to their lives; and he intended to repay him in full, measure for measure. Marcus Alexander Britainus could no longer fool himself. He loved Zenobia. He would love her always. Once he had told her that he had loved her from the beginnings of time, and that he should love her until long after their memories had faded from the earth. In his disappointment and his anger he had believed that that had changed. But nothing had changed. He loved her. He wanted her for his wife still, and by the gods he would have her if he had to strangle Aurelian with his bare hands.

Turning, he pushed his way through the crowds and walked back to his chariot. Grimly he drove back along the Via Flaminia to Tivoli, and to his waiting mother.

"Did you see her?" were Dagian's first words as he entered the villa garden.

"All of Rome saw her," Marcus said furiously. "Aurelian made her walk nude, the bastard!"

Dagian's usually pale skin lightened even more. "The poor thing," she said.

"*Poor?*" he laughed harshly. "Praise the gods that Zenobia is prouder than Venus herself! She walked like the queen she is, her head held high, her eyes straight ahead. If Aurelian meant to humble her he only forced her to build her defenses higher. She won't forgive him the insult, Mother."

"And you, Marcus? Do you *forgive* her?"

He had to laugh. "Yes, Mother, but I beg you in the name of all the gods I know, and those that I don't, never to tell her that. You were right. There is nothing to forgive, and I've been a fool. Whatever Aurelian thinks, Zenobia is not his."

"She is not yours either, my son."

"I know that, Mother. I am the one who must ask the forgiveness of Zenobia."

Dagian smiled. "At last you grow wise, Marcus!" she said.

"Do you think I have a chance to regain her, Mother?"

"Who can predict a woman's heart, Marcus," Dagian said wisely. "We must remember all the suffering that she has undergone at Rome's hands. I sense that Zenobia will not forgive that easily."

Had Dagian, however, seen Zenobia at the very moment she spoke she would have been astonished. Having reached the senate buildings, and the end of Aurelian's formal triumph, Palmyra's queen was wrapped in a cloak by the emperor himself, and led inside to hear the senate's judgment on her. The senate, recognizing their captive's bravery, applauded her wildly as she entered their chamber, and with a soft smile upon her lips Zenobia accepted their tribute with all the graciousness she possessed. It had been a far better show than if they had pitted her in the arena against the beasts, and they were all now quite pleased with their decision to grant her life and pension her off. She would be an interesting addition to their jaded social life. Now after she thanked them for their mercy, a faint smile of amusement upon her lips, the emperor bundled her off, then returned to escort the senate to the public games that he was sponsoring this day to honor his triumph in the East.

Taking Senator Tacitus by the arm, the emperor led them forth from the senate. Since the distance between the Forum and the Colosseum was not great, they walked, and the populace gave way to them as they came forward, cheering Aurelian, who had given them this day off, and free food and entertainment.

Zenobia awaited Aurelian at the Colosseum, and together they entered the imperial box. Seeing them, all Rome rose to its feet and cheered the handsome emperor in his purple and gold robes; his beautiful captive queen, an exquisite vision now in a simple white silk kalasiris, a jeweled collar of silver set with rich turquoise-blue Persian lapis resting upon her chest. She had dressed to please the Roman crowds, with carved silver snake bracelets on her arms and chunks of Persian lapis hanging from her ears. They would never forget her nude beauty of this morning, but her magnificent attire equally pleased them. Her fantastic cloth-of-silver cape blew in the afternoon breeze, and once she and Aurelian had finished acknowledging the crowds, she removed it.

Suddenly at the back of the box a small commotion arose, and Zenobia turned to see a woman being helped into the box by Senator Tacitus. She was of medium height, and had a faded prettiness about her. "Who is that woman?" she asked the emperor.

He turned, and swore softly beneath his breath. Then he rose and assisted the woman forward to seat her at the front of the box.

"Majesty," he said to Zenobia, "may I present my wife, the Empress Ulpia Severina."

Before Zenobia could speak Ulpia said, "Welcome to Rome, Queen of Palmyra."

"Thank you," Zenobia replied.

"You should not have come, my dear," Aurelian scolded gently. "She has not been well," he said then to Zenobia.

"I saw your triumph," Ulpia said, ignoring Aurelian's concern. "I requested that the Buteo family, who have a large home along the triumphal way, allow me access to see the procession. I was shocked, my lord, at the way in which you displayed this captive queen. All decent people were. Had not Queen Zenobia the dignity she has it would have been far worse."

Zenobia instantly felt a liking for the empress and, reaching out, she put a hand upon the woman's arm. "It is over now, Ulpia Severina, and I would not have you distressed on my account."

Ulpia's sad brown eyes met those of Zenobia, and instantly the two women understood one another. Poor soul, Zenobia thought. She loves Aurelian, and although he may respect her, and be kind to her, he does not care for her one way or the other. How hard it is to live without love!

Zenobia found the games boring, and the blood lust of the Roman population quite disgusting. She had never been afraid in battle, but watching the Colosseum audience leaning forward in their seats so as not to miss any of the gore was revolting. There they were, for the most part a useless, lazy bunch living off the dole, almost salivating with delight as they condemned the losers in the games to death. Turning from the games, she spoke for some time with the elderly Tacitus, until finally she demanded of Aurelian:

"Must I remain through this whole thing?"

"You are part of the spectacle, goddess," he said, forgetting about Ulpia, who sat listening.

"I would have thought that I had provided enough of a spectacle for your Romans today," she snapped at him. "I find your games tedious and appalling, Roman. Let me go to wherever it is you are sending me. I far prefer the quiet of the country to this pesthole of a city."

Aurelian looked annoyed, but he realized that Zenobia had taken as much as she was going to this day. To further impress his will upon her was going to result in a scene, and when Zenobia chose to make a scene he invariably ended up looking the fool. This morning burned yet in his memory. He turned to the empress. "You prepared a pleasant villa in Tivoli for the queen, my dear?"

"I have seen to it, my lord," Ulpia replied smoothly. "Although I could not oversee the preparation personally." She turned to Zenobia. "I trust you will be happy there, Majesty."

"It is not Palmyra," Zenobia said softly, "but I shall never go home, so I suppose that I will be happy in your Tivoli. I thank you for all your kindness, Ulpia Severina."

Ulpia smiled at Zenobia, and the queen rose, discreetly saying to the emperor, "There is no need for you to leave your games, Roman. Gaius Cicero can easily escort me, can you not, Gaius?"

"With pleasure, Majesty," the emperor's aide said.

"I bid you good day, Marcus Claudius Tacitus. I have enjoyed your company greatly, and if I am permitted visitors I hope that you will visit me often at my villa in Tivoli."

The elderly senator rose and bowed in a courtly fashion to Zenobia. "My time with you has been far too short today, Majesty. I will come and visit you whether you are allowed visitors or not. I have a villa in Tivoli myself, and the heat in Rome will soon be too much to bear. I will see you soon, I promise you."

When Zenobia had left the emperor's box the senator turned to Aurelian, and said, "You are right, Caesar. She is too lovely and too intelligent to die. What a waste had we followed Valerian Hostilius's obscene suggestion."

Ulpia turned to Tacitus. "And just what did Senator Hostilius suggest?" she asked.

"His suggestion was that we dress Queen Zenobia in animal skins, give her a spear, and have her fight a pack of wild beasts in the arena."

"Hostilius was ever a fool!" the empress snapped in a rare show of irritation.

"Then you are glad that the senate spared the queen's life, my dear?" Aurelian asked.

Ulpia looked directly at her husband, and said, "Yes, my

lord. I am glad that they spared her life." Her level gaze told the emperor what he wanted to know; that she was giving him permission to amuse himself with Zenobia. Dearest Ulpia! Aurelian mused in a generous burst of fondness. She was so thoughtful! So discreet! He regretted that she was dying, but then perhaps he would take Zenobia for his second wife. He was certainly not going to let anyone else have her. He saw the envy in the eyes of the men who looked upon her. He knew that they hoped he would toss her aside, as he had done with so many others; and when he did, then they would vie for her until she chose another protector. It would not happen, though. He *would* marry Zenobia when Ulpia died. There was no need to divorce his wife, for she would be dead soon enough and Zenobia was going nowhere. She was his imperial captive, and would be safe in Tivoli.

The imperial captive could hardly wait to leave the city. She found Rome overwhelmingly dirty and noisy. She would be happy to live in a quieter setting, one much better suited to raising Mavia.

"How long will it take us to reach Tivoli?" she asked Gaius Cicero.

"It will take several hours, Majesty," he answered her. "It is almost twenty miles from the city, and the litter bearers can only go so quickly."

"What about a chariot, Gaius Cicero?"

"A chariot, Majesty?"

"Yes, a chariot. I drove my own war chariot in Palmyra, and if I might have a chariot now we could get there in half the time or less, couldn't we?"

He thought a moment, and then said, "Indeed we could, Majesty. The emperor only ordered that I escort you. He did not say what sort of vehicle we should use."

Gaius Cicero drove as they left the city, but once they were safely on the Via Flaminia, he let Zenobia have the reins. The horses, however, almost drove themselves, as the road was straight and well paved.

Zenobia was fascinated by the landscape around her. It was so very, very different from what she had known all her life. The desert was endless; but here the land was broken up by hills and rivers. The desert landscape was golden and blue; but here the land was lushly green with summer as well as gold and blue. Here and there were patches of bright-red roof tiles, or black earth in newly tilled fields where second crops were already being planted. Even the air was different. The desert air was dry, but this had a soft moistness to it that felt good on her skin.

They drove in silence for what seemed a very short time, and then Gaius Cicero was taking the reins from her. "We will soon be entering Tivoli," he said loudly over the wind that rushed past their ears with the speed they were making.

She nodded. The road now wound up into the mountains, the Sabines, he told her, and below them stretched the Campagna di Roma: a vast and undulating plain filled with many jewel-like little lakes, most within the craters of extinct volcanoes. Zenobia caught her breath at the beauty of it all. Then they were entering the town of Tivoli, perched on a slope of the Sabines with a magnificent view of the Campagna and, beyond it, Rome itself.

Zenobia was delighted, for Tivoli was exquisite, a white-marble town surrounded by olive groves. Tivoli, Gaius Cicero told her, was famous for its vast deposits of Travertine marble. The quarries were located in the mountains just behind the town, and although the marble was exported to the rest of Italy, the entire town had been built of it. Zenobia was pleased to see that it was a busy place with several attractive open-air markets, an arena, and a theater located along the River Anio, which edged one side of the town.

"Your villa is located just outside the town, Majesty," Gaius Cicero told her. "It is on the river itself. All the imperial villas are."

They were shortly there. As Zenobia was dismounting the chariot, Bab and Adria appeared, and Mavia, who came running with her arms outstretched to her mother. "Oh, Mama, it is so beautiful here!" the little girl exclaimed. Mavia was now six. "It is not at all like Palmyra."

"Can you be happy here, my pigeon?" Zenobia asked, hugging her daughter.

"Oh, yes, Mama!"

"Then we will have to stay," Zenobia teased, taking the child's hand and entering into the house. "Gaius Cicero, you will take some refreshment with us, and if I may I will offer you hospitality for the night."

"The wine I will accept, Majesty," Gaius Cicero said, "but your hospitality I must decline. The emperor said I might go home after I did my duty by you. I have not seen my wife and children in over a year, Majesty."

"I understand, Gaius Cicero," Zenobia said politely, and then she nodded to Bab to see that the emperor's aide had refreshment. He quaffed it down with almost indecent haste, and quickly took his leave. Zenobia chuckled. She did not doubt that he wished to be with his wife tonight. Gaius Cicero was one of the few imperial officers who did not indulge himself with the camp whores. Neither had he kept a mistress. Then, too, she could imagine his position if he should spend the night under the same roof as her and Aurelian found out. His military career would be destroyed, not to mention the danger to his personal safety.

"Well," she said to her servants, little Mavia having been taken off by her nurse, Charmian, "is it livable?"

"It is not the palace in Palmyra," Bab said, "but we are lucky not to be in prison or in our funeral urns."

"Is it habitable?" Zenobia said, looking about, for it certainly appeared a pleasant place.

"It is somewhat smaller than we are used to, Majesty," Adria said. "There are two stories to the house," she continued. "On this level is the atrium, where we stand, and there is a nice interior garden beyond. It should be a pleasant place on winter days. There is also a fine large garden out back that goes down to the river. There is a kitchen, a dining room, and a small library. On the second level there is a bath and two bedchambers."

"What of the servants' quarters?" Zenobia asked.

"They are separate from the house, Majesty."

"It will not do," Zenobia said. "You and Bab cannot live in slave quarters."

"There is a nice room off the kitchen, Majesty, but the cook tells me that the slaves use that room to eat and rest when they are not going about their chores."

"More than likely they use that room to hide from their duties," Zenobia noted.

"Just what I thought," old Bab said. "They're a lazy lot from what I've observed so far, my baby."

"Then we shall have the emperor replace them," Zenobia said with a laugh. "That room off the kitchen sounds just perfect for you and Adria. I hope you will not mind sharing a room, but we are obviously cramped, and I want you both here with me."

"Shall I give orders to have the room cleared, and beds brought for Adria and me?" Bab asked.

"Send the majordomo to me," the queen said, and a few minutes later when the man stood before her Zenobia gave the orders to remove whatever furniture was in the room by the kitchen, and bring sleeping couches for her two serving women.

"Why can your women not sleep in the slave quarters like everyone else?" the majordomo demanded.

"Because," Zenobia said, "they are not slaves, and I want them here in the house with me. Hear me well, Crispus. If you should ever question my orders again I will punish you. My orders will be obeyed without question! Go now and do my bidding!"

"Will the emperor be coming tonight?" Bab asked.

"I do not know, old woman, but if he does not I shall send him a message tomorrow demanding that all the slaves in this villa be replaced. I will not suffer rudeness from a slave."

"Come out into the garden, Majesty," Adria said, "and see how fair it is. It will cool your anger."

Zenobia smiled at the girl. "Let us go, Adria, and see this garden that so delights you."

The three women walked through the villa's interior garden and out into the rear of the building. Zenobia gasped with delight. At the foot of the garden the blue river flowed merrily by, and across it the mountains rose green and fair. Upstream a magnificent waterfall ran white and frothing over the high rocks, and plunged in a wide crystal ribbon into the river below.

The garden itself was neatly laid out in colorful flower beds, all accessible by the crushed white marble paths. Zenobia saw roses and lilies in profusion, along with sweet herbs and small fruit trees. There were violets, both purple and white, and sweet pink stock and brightly colored wall flowers within the beautiful garden. It would be a lovely place for Mavia to play. There were several large shade trees nearer the river, and some marble benches for sitting.

"You are right, Adria. It is lovely."

"You will see, Majesty, that we are separated from the neighboring villas by a low wall, and although we can see our neighbors, no one may intrude unless we invite them."

"Good day to you," came the voice from across the wall, and the three women turned, startled. There stood a tall and very beautiful woman. "I am Dagian, the empress's friend. It was my pleasure to prepare the villa for you, Queen Zenobia. I hope it is satisfactory." She walked over to the waist-high wall.

Zenobia moved over to the wall, and smiled at the woman. "I thank you, Lady Dagian. The villa is a bit small, but it will be most comfortable, I am sure. I do, however, wish to remove the slaves there, and replace them with my own people."

"I am sure," Dagian said, "that all you need do is inform the emperor of your wishes, and he will give his permission."

Zenobia looked closely at the woman to see if her remark was merely a statement, or a sly innuendo; but Dagian's face was as smooth as a mill pond. "Will you join us, Lady Dagian, in a cup of wine?" the queen asked politely.

"I should like that," the older woman replied, and walking to a small gate that was set within the wall, she opened it and came through.

"Bab, Adria. See to the wine, and have a table brought. I have an urge to sit in the garden."

The two servants hurried off to do their mistress's bidding. Zenobia indicated with her hand a nearby marble bench, and invited Dagian to sit. "Are you also an imperial captive?" she asked.

"Of sorts," was the reply. "I come from a land to the west, and for many years I was married quite happily to a wealthy Roman. When my husband died almost two years ago, the emperor forced me to remain here in Rome in order to blackmail my eldest son into doing something he did not want to do."

"That's Aurelian," Zenobia replied bitterly.

"You do not like the emperor?"

"I despise him," she said. "Oh, I know, Lady Dagian. You have heard that I am the emperor's mistress, and it is true; but like you, I have been blackmailed. My eldest son and his family live now in Cyrene under imperial *protection,* my little daughter and I have been brought here under the emperor's personal care. Like you, I have no choice. Mothers are vulnerable creatures."

Dagian nodded, fully understanding Zenobia's position, but wondering how well Marcus would for all his assurances to her. Obviously Palmyra's lovely queen did not realize that she was the mother of Marcus Alexander Britainus, and Dagian thought that perhaps that fact was better left unknown for the present. Then she caught her breath as a small child emerged from the villa, followed by a nursemaid. The little girl ran across the garden and up to Zenobia.

With a smile the queen caught the child to her and kissed

her, and the affection between the two caught at Dagian's heart. It was as she had suspected. Zenobia was a good and loving mother. If Marcus wanted his daughter back he would have to win her mother over first. Zenobia looked up, and said, "This is my daughter, the Princess Mavia. Mavia, this is the Lady Dagian."

The little girl looked up, and Dagian felt her heart contract. The look was Marcus's! Could not Zenobia see that look was that of her new acquaintance also? "How do you do, Princess Mavia," Dagian said softly.

"Lady Dagian," the little girl replied. "I am pleased to meet you. You have blue eyes, as I do. I have met few people with eyes the color of mine. Marcus had blue eyes like mine, but he went away."

"Mavia!" Zenobia sharply reproved her daughter. "It is not polite to mention people's personal appearances."

Dagian longed to take the precious child upon her lap and kiss her. Not only did she have Marcus's deep-blue eyes, but she had his chestnut-colored hair as well. It was a wonder that Aurelian hadn't made the connection, but perhaps he had. She shivered.

The slaves arrived with a small table, which they placed in front of the marble bench, and Bab came carrying the wine and Adria, behind her, the goblets. The old woman's mouth was set in disapproval as she set down the wine.

"In Palmyra," she said, "we would not have given our slaves wine like this."

"I do not understand," Dagian said, distressed. "I gave orders that the finest Falernian be bought for you. I ordered it myself in the town at the wine merchant's shop."

Bab held out a goblet into which she had already poured some of the beverage. "Taste, my Lady Dagian. Is this what you purchased?"

Dagian sipped the wine, and her face was a study in quick anger. Her mouth made a little moue, and she spat the wine she had taken onto the grass. "This is awful!" she said furiously. "Either the wine merchant tried to cheat me, or the slaves have stolen what I bought and replaced it with inferior wine, hoping you would not notice."

Across the garden hurried the majordomo, full of importance, as puffed up as a frog. "The emperor comes!" he announced.

"Crispus," Dagian said severely, "this is not the wine that

I bought from the shop of Veritus Pomponio. I suspect that you and your cohorts have stolen that wine! Now the emperor comes, and how can the queen serve him such swill?''

The majordomo blanched and fell to his knees. ''Help us, Lady Dagian! We can return the wine you bought, but not now!''

''You deserve to be flayed alive, but the queen must not be embarrassed.'' She rose and, smiling at Zenobia, murmured, ''I shall send one of my slaves over with some good vintage for Aurelian, and I will see you tomorrow if it pleases you.''

''Yes,'' Zenobia said, ''it will please me if you come—and thank you.'' She, too, rose, and escorted her new friend to the garden gate that separated their villas.

''Good-bye, Lady Dagian,'' little Mavia piped up.

Dagian turned and, bending, kissed the child on the top of her head. ''Good-bye, little Princess,'' she said before hurrying through the gate into her own garden.

When she turned back, Zenobia and Mavia were already hurrying hand in hand across the garden toward the villa. Dagian paused beneath a tall shade tree and breathed deeply. She had not dreamed that she should see her granddaughter so soon. She remembered Marcus! That was good. Perhaps the child would be the bridge that joined her two proud and stubborn parents.

How beautiful Palmyra's queen was, Dagian thought. She was quite different from both Roman and British women, yet the golden skin, the blue-black hair, and the storm-gray eyes combined with her marvelously aristocratic features to make her fairer than any female Dagian could ever remember seeing. She was intelligent, Dagian realized, and that would have attracted Marcus as well.

Zenobia, before re-entering her own villa, had looked back across the gardens. Dagian seemed a pleasant woman, the queen mused, but was she someone whom she might trust? I need a friend, Zenobia said to herself. She was so alone here.

''Hail, Caesar!'' Mavia lisped, and Zenobia turned to see Aurelian standing within the entry of the house.

''Go to Charmian, child,'' Zenobia ordered.

''Yes, Mama,'' was the obedient reply, and Mavia was gone.

''You never give me a chance to really know her, goddess. Are you afraid I will corrupt her?''

''I never know what you will do, Roman,'' Zenobia said coldly.

"You are angry about the triumph," he said.

"I was paraded the length of Rome, naked for all to see!"

"Yet I have not humbled you, have I, proud bitch?" He reached out for her, but Zenobia skillfully evaded him and, brushing past him, gained the inner garden.

"Do not touch me, Roman! Not now! Not ever!" Jupiter, she wanted to get away from him, but she didn't know where to go! It was an infuriating situation.

"Oh, goddess, are we to fight again? I thought we had done with fighting." His voice was very patient.

"Hear me, Roman! I will be your whore because there is no other choice for me; but I will never forget your actions toward me today."

"So you will be my whore," he said softly, but his narrowed glittering eyes belied the gentleness of his voice. "You will be my whore because you have no other choice? If it is choice you desire, my beautiful goddess, let me assure you that every patrician with a pair of balls between his legs would like me to pass you on to him when I am tired of you. I am not tired of you, but if it would please you, I can do as the Emperor Caligula once did, and indeed make a whore of you. How would you like to spend your nights servicing every rich and randy cock in Rome?"

She looked into his eyes, and was suddenly afraid because she saw in them a terrible determination. He *would* make her whore with every man in Rome if in the end she returned to him pliant and obedient; his woman, and his woman alone. "No," she said low. "No, I should not like it, Roman." Oh, how she hated him for making her feel so helpless; she who had ruled an empire. He delighted in it, the bastard!

"Where is your room?" he demanded.

Zenobia looked at him, and then began to laugh. "I do not know," she said, the tears rolling down her cheeks at the absurdity of the situation. He was ready to assert his rights, in reality to rape her, and she had absolutely no idea of where her bed was.

"Haven't you inspected the house yet?" He was looking outraged.

"There was no time," she said. "I arrived, and there was difficulty with the slaves. I want to replace them tomorrow, Roman. Then I went to see the gardens, and the woman in the next villa, a friend of the empress's, came from next door."

Zenobia shrugged helplessly. "I have not seen the house at all. I did not realize that you would arrive so quickly."

"I left the games shortly after you did, goddess. Without you they were boring. I had to see the empress safely to the Palatine palace."

"You should have stayed with her, Roman. She is ill. Even I can see she does not have a great deal of time left to live; and she loves you. How can you leave her?"

"Ulpia is a soldier's wife. She is used to being without me."

"Because she is a soldier's wife makes it no easier to be without the man she loves. She has accepted her lot, but how it must hurt her, Roman. How cruel you are!"

He moved close to her, and his hands gripped her upper arms. "I would not be cruel to you, goddess. All I want to do is love you. Why will you not love me, beloved?"

Beloved! She turned her head to hide the quick tears that damped her eyes. "I have told you before, Roman, that I shall never put myself into the keeping of any man again. Be satisfied that you have my body. It is all I can ever give you."

"But you never give, Zenobia," Aurelian said. "I must always take. Even now you steel yourself for the assault you assume is about to come." He pulled her chin about so that she was forced to look at him. "Just once, goddess, I would like your kiss to be a willing one, not sparked by lust, but rather, caring."

"Never." It was said quietly.

"Then I must take what I can get from you, goddess," he said, and his mouth covered hers in a fierce, possessive kiss.

She shuddered wildly, and then, to the amazement of them both, Zenobia began to cry great wracking sobs of pure anguish. Every agony of the last months shook her slender frame. The terrible destruction of Palmyra, her separation from Vaba and Flavia, Longinus's death, the loss of Demetrius; all of it welled up within her and poured forth, and she was unable to stop it. She was tired of fighting, tired of responsibility, plain bone tired. For the first time in Zenobia's life she wanted to be free of it all; she wanted to be taken care of.

He saw it in her face, in her eyes, and knew that now if he were clever he might have her as he had always wanted her. She was more vulnerable than he had ever seen her, than she had ever been in her entire life, he suspected. Aurelian held her gently, and stroked her shining, dark hair. "There, beloved," he soothed her, "there, my beautiful goddess. Do not weep, my love; do not weep." He caught her face between his hands and, bending, kissed her mouth again, but with tenderness this time. He kissed her shut eyelids, her cheeks, her nose, and her chin, before returning to her mouth once more; but this time his lips were more demanding, and, to his pleasure, she returned his kiss not from lust, but from need.

He gathered her up into his arms, and she nestled against his shoulder, still sobbing. With firm steps he walked through the interior garden and into the atrium of the house. Seeing them, Bab threw up her hands in distress, but the emperor's stern look warned her to be silent as he made his way up the stairs to the second floor and into her bedroom at the end of the hall.

Gently he lay her upon the bed, then sat down next to her. "I cannot bear to see you weep," he said low. "Tell me what you want of me, Zenobia. I will do anything to make you happy." But she only wept on, softer now, yet still she wept. Reaching out, he ran his hand down her trembling body, and she murmured with an almost shy pleasure that intrigued him. He carefully removed her jeweled collar, the snake bracelets, and her earrings. Next he slowly undid and drew off her sandals, massaging her feet until she almost purred. With a smooth, almost lingering movement he pushed the white silk kalasiris upward, revealing long golden legs, smooth thighs, sweetly rounded belly, tempting breasts. The kalasiris slipped easily over Zenobia's head and arms, and the emperor then dropped it carelessly by the bedside.

He bent and kissed each breast, causing her nipples to stand tall. As he raised his head he found that she was looking at him, her eyes wide and wet, the lashes stuck together. Her mouth quivered, and then she said so low that he had to bend to hear her, "Love me, Roman. Please love me, and make it all better. I can no longer bear the pain."

"And will you love me, goddess, or will you simply take from me?" he demanded softly of her.

"I will give," she replied. "Only take the pain away."

He stood and slowly removed his own clothing, his passionate eyes never leaving hers. He might have fallen on her like a beast upon a helpless lamb, for his own desire was great and he feared that she might suddenly come to her senses. Instead, he exerted his great willpower, and moved slowly and quietly. Returning to the bed, he lay next to her and held her hand. "I have adored you from the moment I first saw you, Zenobia. I love you, my fair goddess, and never have I made that statement to any woman. When Ulpia has left this world for the next you will marry me, and I shall make you Queen of the mighty Roman Empire; not just a small piece of it, but all of it, stretching from Persia to the farthest outposts of wild Britain. You are a rare and perfect jewel, my beloved, and now you are mine alone! I will make you happy, Zenobia, I swear by all the gods. If you will but let me, I shall make you the happiest woman alive!''

He raised himself up on one elbow and looked down upon her. Her eyes were shut, but he knew that she heard him. ''I want you to make love to me, goddess,'' he said quietly, and then he lay back waiting.

For a few very long minutes they lay side by side, then she raised herself up and bent to touch his mouth with a sweet kiss. He reached out and lifted her up so that she found herself sitting upon his loins. Zenobia blushed, the blood rushing up to stain her pale-gold cheeks a soft apricot pink. She was long past girlhood, and yet she felt untutored and shy. She wasn't quite sure what he expected of her.

Aurelian chuckled with amusement at her obvious chagrin. ''What, goddess? You never made love to your husband or your lover? Touch me, Zenobia. Don't you like it when I touch you?''

Hesitantly she reached out and put her hand upon his chest. He held his breath. Slowly she explored the muscles beneath her fingertips, the softness of his skin. She sighed.

Her touch inflamed him wildly, yet he held himself in check, watching her through slitted eyes. She was not yet roused herself, but she was curious, and perhaps a little frightened. Reaching out, he caressed one of her marvelous breasts, taking a finger and running it sensuously around the nipple to encourage her. ''You are so beautiful,'' he crooned. ''So very, very beautiful, Zenobia.''

He felt her relax a bit more, and she shifted her weight, leaning forward to brush her breasts against his chest, matching her hardening nipples with his and rubbing against him in a provocative movement. Stretching his arms out, he gently seized the cheeks of her bottom and drew her closer, fondling her, caressing her, beginning to stir the embers of her desire. ''Oh yes, goddess,'' he murmured against her ear, and she shivered as his warm breath touched her.

He was being so gentle, she thought, so kind. All he wanted was to love her, for her to love him in return. It didn't mean

377

that she had to trust him. She could never really trust any man again; but he was willing to take the pain away in exchange for her devotion. She didn't really love him, but she could pretend. All she had to do was stop fighting him, to relax and enjoy making love to him, to make him believe that she cared. Her stubborn pride had brought her to this, she mused, and she was tired of hurting.

She felt his staff, hard and pushing against her, as if it had a separate life of its own. Zenobia moved back and, raising herself carefully, caught him in her hand and guided him into her softness. Surprised by her sudden action, he could only gasp with delight as she gently rode him. Then he put his arms about her, rolled her over, and rode her. Slowly he pushed himself into her sheath, slowly he withdrew himself; repeating the movement until her relaxed body began to shudder with the splendor of her orgasm. Each movement of his weapon seemed to drive deeper, and she moaned with undiluted pleasure, straining to reach greater heights, finally falling away in a shower of stars while his body joined hers in fulfillment.

The terrible tension and ache gone from her frame, Zenobia fell into a peaceful sleep. At her side, the emperor considered the events of the last few minutes. She had been so sweet! So totally and incredibly sweet in her surrender. This was how he had always dreamed she would be with him, and at last the gods had answered his prayers. She was not broken, he knew, but he believed that she was at last his. He need have no fear of any man, even Marcus Alexander Britainus. Aurelian slept, secure for the first time since he had taken Zenobia for his own.

They slept for several long hours, and Zenobia awoke first. She lay quietly, remembering her mood of several hours ago, remembering what had passed between herself and Aurelian. She had not really promised him anything, and yet she had. But *could* she love him? *No*. The word slammed into her brain. She could not. He had taken from her almost everything that she held dear and sacred. Still she must survive to be revenged, and Mavia must be protected. If she suddenly scorned Rome's emperor after he opened himself to her he would surely kill her.

"What are you thinking of, Zenobia?" he asked her, his voice tearing at the silence.

"Of how kind you were to me last night," she replied.

"I love you," he said simply.

"I know," she replied, and he did not push her further than that.

The dawn was not even beginning to stain the east, yet he said, "Let us bathe."

"The slaves are not yet up," she protested.

"We will wake them," he returned.

"No," she said. "We will bathe each other, Roman." And she arose naked from the bed. Turning slightly, she glanced over her shoulder at him, her look provocative, and she held out her hand to him. "Well? Are you coming?"

He could feel his need for her stirring already, but he fought his urges back down and, taking her hand, stood up and followed her. The bath, which was located next door to Zenobia's chamber, was eerily silent, its oil lamps flickering and casting shadows upon the frescoed walls depicting scenes of nymphs being pursued by the usual satyrs and centaurs. She chuckled, and pleased by the warmth of the sound, Aurelian asked, "What amuses you, my love?"

"The walls, Roman. They are so typical."

"One may not expect originality in a state-owned villa," he teased her.

"Must I remain in this villa?"

"Perhaps at a later date we can discuss a larger home for you, goddess; but for now you will stay here."

"As you will," she answered him, and then reaching for the porcelain jar of soft soap, she scooped some out with three fingers and began to spread it over him. She worked slowly, her hands smoothing the soap into a rich cream as they moved in ever-widening circles over his hard body. He began to feel a delicious contentment at her touch, and almost fell back asleep standing in the bath. She roused him from his reverie, rinsing him off with several jars of warmed water and the command, "Go and soak in the hot tub now, Roman."

"Do I not get to wash you, goddess?" he asked.

"You will catch a chill standing here," she protested.

"I will wash you," he said, ending the matter, and then he took the soap from the jar and began to imitate her motions of a few moments earlier. Turning her so that her back was to him, he rubbed soap over her belly and upward to her breasts, cupping those sweet fruits in his palms, his thumbs gently rubbing around her erect nipples. She stood very still, barely

379

breathing, as his hands moved with familiarity over her graceful form. Finally he rinsed her, and together they entered the
hot tub.

"What will you do here in Rome?" he asked.

"Perhaps you should have thought of that before you brought
me here," she smiled. "I imagine, however, that I shall do
what all new residents of the city do. I shall sight-see, and I
shall try to make friends."

"There will be many only too eager to make friends with
you, Zenobia," he answered. "Beware of becoming involved
in any political factions, goddess. There will be those who will
seek to use you, for Rome is a sewer of intrigue."

She looked at him, somewhat amused. "I did not rule Palmyra
all those years by not being aware of what went on around me.
Rome has ever been a hotbed of conspiracy. You change emperors
with the regularity of a popular courtesan changing lovers."

"Until now," he said. "I am the new Rome, Zenobia. I am
leading my people back to the old ways, the right ways. Thanks
to me, the empire is strong again, and it will grow stronger
with each passing day. My heirs will be the new Caesars."

"Your heirs? You have no children, Roman. Of course there
is your niece's child, isn't there?" Suddenly Zenobia wondered
if it had been ambition that had caused Marcus to betray her.

"My niece's child?" For a brief moment he was puzzled,
and then he realized that she had meant Carissa. By the gods
she must not know that both Carissa and her infant had perished,
and that Marcus Alexander Britainus was a free man! Suddenly
Aurelian's old insecurities rose up to haunt him, and he quickly
said, "Yes, there is that child, but perhaps, goddess, *we* might
have a child. Because Ulpia has been barren all these years
does not mean I might not have a son by you." He leaned over
and placed a kiss upon her wet shoulder.

Cleopatra had had children by her Roman lovers, Zenobia
thought, and those children had all met unfortunate ends at the
hands of the empire, for they stood in the way of those who
wanted power.

Aurelian sank his strong white teeth into her golden shoulder, and muttered, "Think of it, goddess! What a child I could
get from your loins! He would rule the world!" He was actually
beginning to believe he might sire a child on this woman.

Suddenly irritated, Zenobia shook him off and climbed from
the heated tub. "I do not know if I want any more children,"
she said.

"It is not your decision to make, goddess," he said, almost smugly. "When Ulpia dies I shall make you my empress. Until then I will continue to pump my seed into your belly, and I will make offerings to the gods praying for a son to come forth from your womb."

Zenobia laughed, the sound a bitterly amused one that echoed about the tiled and frescoed walls of the bath. "The gods have deserted me and mine, Roman. Your prayers will be in vain." Then she walked from the caldarium of the bath, and he heard her splashing in the frigidarium next door.

Aurelian now stood up and came from the hot tub himself. Looking down, he saw that his lance was hard, straight, and very ready. He longed to move quickly into the next room and take her then and there upon the cold tiles of the bath floor; but instead, he stood quietly, breathing deeply, willing his desire away. He wanted her as he had had her last night: warm, and willing, and pleading with him. He was tired of the virago she could be, and he preferred her sweetness. She was gone from the frigidarium when he entered it, and so he quickly plunged into the cool waters of the pool and refreshed himself.

Returning to their bedchamber, he found her still nude, but dry, creaming herself with a marvelously rich lotion that was scented with hyacinths. Wordlessly he took the pale-green glass bottle from her hand, poured some of the liquid into his own hands and rubbed them together, then began to massage her slowly. She was still stiff with her anger, and he said softly, persuasively, "Would it be such a terrible thing to give me a child, goddess? I love you so very much."

"But I do not love you, Roman. I am trying to please you, but I cannot will my emotions, and I will not lie to you."

"The child will bring us closer together," he said as if it was already a certainty. "When you hold our son in your arms; when you put him to your milk-filled breasts as did proper Roman matrons of old; then, Zenobia, will your heart be filled with love for me. I know it!" He turned her about and kissed her passionately, willing her to respond. And suddenly Zenobia was filled with compassion for him.

Pulling her head away, she looked up into his blue eyes, and said, "Oh, Aurelian! Even you have a weakness. I had not believed it until now."

"Yes, Zenobia, I have a weakness. I crave immortality, and only through my descendants may I have that immortality. Give me a son, goddess! *Give me a son!*" He swept her up then, and lay her upon their bed, sprawling near her, pushing his way between her legs to moisten with his tongue that soft and most secret of places to prepare her for his entry.

When he entered her she enfolded him within her arms, and was tender. She was tired of hurting, of being hurt, and afterward he fell asleep upon her breasts for another few hours. Zenobia, however, lay awake. Emperor of the Romans, she thought, you have made me feel sorry for you, but I will still be revenged. Revenged for Palmyra, for my sons, for myself. You have taken almost everything that is dear from me, but I will have mine again! Her eyes strayed to the small piece of white marble set so carefully upon a nearby table. It was the piece she had taken from amid the ruins of the great Palmyran Temple of Jupiter. It was all she had left of her city, except for her memories, which would never die. She felt the tears sliding down her face, but there was no sound. "I *will* be revenged," she whispered softly, and he stirred restlessly upon her breasts. She murmured soothingly as she might have to an infant, and he quieted.

In the weeks that followed Zenobia visited the city of Rome many times, for there were enough wealthy patricians anxious to entertain her that she need never worry about returning the miles to Tivoli come night. Never, however, would she stay at the emperor's residence on the Palatine Hill.

"I will not flaunt our relationship before your unfortunate, dying wife," she told Aurelian.

The Queen of Palmyra was impressed with Rome, but her discerning eye saw the difference between what it had been and what it was now. She saw the great marble public buildings and temples free of graffiti, and the parks cleared of garbage. She was shocked, however, by the thousands of healthy people who loitered and lingered about the streets, unemployed though able to work, for they were provided with food and entertainment. In fact Zenobia suspected that Rome's famous bread and circuses would be the eventual death of the empire. Whatever Aurelian said, the people, used to their slothful ways for several generations now, would not tolerate being returned to the old ways of hard work and honest industry.

Patricians, she found, were a great bore on the whole. There was one exception, however, and that was the elderly Senator Tacitus whom she had met at Aurelian's games following the triumph. He was a witty old gentleman, and for some reason

she felt comfortable with him. There was also her next-door
neighbor, the lady Dagian. Here, too, was someone with whom
she felt at ease, and daily she walked with her in the garden,
Mavia running ahead of them, around them, lingering behind
to watch a butterfly.

Zenobia was touched by the way the lady Dagian had taken
to her small daughter; and Mavia now adored Dagian with a
singular devotion. It was Dagian who now sewed little tunic
dresses for Mavia, and sat in the grass with her weaving daisy
chains and listening to her many confidences.

As they sat thus one late summer's afternoon with the sunlight
upon their bowed heads, Zenobia suddenly looked at Dagian
and her daughter, and a cry escaped her lips. The older woman
looked up and, seeing Zenobia's obvious distress, rose quickly
and hurried over to her.

"Zenobia, my dear, what is it?" she asked.

Zenobia looked into unexpectedly familiar blue eyes, deep-
blue eyes, and cried, *"Who are you?"*

"I am Dagian," was the gentle answer. "I am your friend."

"Dagian who?"

It was then that Dagian understood what had happened, and
closing her eyes a moment, she sighed softly before saying, "I
am Dagian, wife to the late Lucius Alexander."

"You are the mother of Marcus Alexander Britainus?"
Zenobia's voice was accusing.

"I am," came the quiet reply.

"How could you practice such a deception on me?" Zenobia
demanded, and then, turning to her daughter, said, "Mavia,
my darling, run and find Charmian." The child looked up to
protest, but, seeing the angry look upon her mother's face, she
rose and ran off. The Queen of Palmyra turned back to the
older woman. "Is not your son's child enough for you? Must
you steal my daughter away too?"

"Marcus has had no children here in Rome," Dagian replied.

"No children? The emperor says differently! Tell me, Dagian,
did your traitorous offspring spawn a son or a daughter upon
Aurelian's niece?"

"Carissa died in childbirth, and her infant with her."

"Surely the emperor has other nieces," Zenobia said
sarcastically.

"If I did not know how badly my fool of a son had hurt you,
Zenobia, I should slap you!" Dagian said vehemently. "Sit
down now, and I will tell you the truth of the matter—unless,

383

of course, you prefer to clutch your outrage to your bosom for the rest of your life!'' Dagian gestured impatiently toward a marble bench in a small, secluded grotto in the garden and, suddenly wordless, Zenobia sat. Her companion settled herself next to her.

"When Marcus arrived home his father was dying. Not knowing that Marcus had already betrothed himself to you, Lucius had arranged with the emperor that our eldest son marry Carissa. My husband very much wanted to see his heir safely married before he died.

"Marcus, of course, told me that he could not marry the emperor's niece; that he was betrothed to you, that he loved you. He went immediately to Aurelian; but Aurelian refused to allow Marcus to break the contract made by my husband. He insisted that my son marry his niece. He threatened terrible things against our family if Marcus refused to marry Carissa. Marcus had no choice at that point. He had to wed Carissa.

"Immediately after they were married she told him she was pregnant with the emperor's child. She mocked him with the knowledge. Carissa was a terrible creature, Zenobia! My son despised her, for she was evil incarnate."

Zenobia was stone-faced. "Could he not have written to me, Dagian? When he left Palmyra I sent with him an escort of my personal guard, who were to bring back messages from Marcus at each port. The last of those messengers never returned."

"Because he was murdered, Zenobia! After the wedding my husband died. Marcus had planned that I should go back to Britain with my younger son, Aulus, and then he planned to leave Carissa and return to you in Palmyra. The emperor, however, knew every move we tried to make, and stopped us at the gates of Rome. Aurelian wanted a hostage to insure Marcus's good behavior, and what better hostage than a man's mother? As a last resort Marcus decided to send the final messenger back to Palmyra. He should have done it earlier, I agree, but he was afraid of compromising the family. When he sent for your man, our majordomo found him dead in his quarters, his throat slit while he slept. My son was trapped, unable to communicate with you."

A sob escaped Dagian's lips, and she brushed away the tears of remembrance that were beginning to fall. Instinctively Zenobia reached out and patted Dagian's arm. Dagian caught the younger woman's hand and clutched it. "My son was so terribly unhappy," she continued. "Then before Aurelian left for the East he told Marcus that he might have had Carissa marry any one of a number of eligible patrician men; but that he had chosen Marcus deliberately because he was your betrothed. He knew of your hatred for Rome because of your mother's murder years back, and he sought to rekindle that hatred so that you would rebel. The emperor wanted Palmyra back, not as a client kingdom, but as a province."

As the enormity of the betrayal slammed into her, Zenobia asked in a low, tight voice, "Are you telling me that Aurelian deliberately separated me from Marcus in order to take Palmyra from me?"

Dagian nodded.

"Then he is a bigger fool than I anticipated," Zenobia said coldly. "I fully intended declaring my son Augustus of the East long before Marcus left me. I did not, however, plan to do it until after Marcus and I were married. The news of your son's marriage to the emperor's niece left me with no reason for delay, and so I made my declaration in Alexandria." She laughed bitterly. "No, Dagian, I must accept full responsibility for my actions; but I will have my revenge upon Aurelian. Already because I am his mistress he grows to trust me. He will find in the end that that was a mistake."

"Marcus has never stopped loving you, Zenobia," Dagian said quietly.

"I am no longer the woman that Marcus loved," Zenobia said somewhat sadly. "Marcus loved a queen, a woman with pride and spirit. I am no longer a queen, and I have eaten the ashes of my pride in order to survive, in order to save my children. I can never forget that, nor can I forget the things that I must do in order to continue to survive. As long as Aurelian lives there is no hope for Marcus and me. I have not yet the friends nor the power to destroy him, but eventually I will."

Dagian looked upon Zenobia with wondering eyes. "My child, you will destroy yourself," she said.

"If I can destroy Aurelian in the process then it will be worth it," Zenobia replied.

"What of Mavia?"

"She has you," Zenobia said, "and she has her brother in Cyrene."

"She has her father too," was Dagian's answer, "but she needs *both* her mother and her father, my dear."

"It is impossible," was the adamant reply.

"No, it is not!" Dagian declared. "See Marcus! See my son!"

"Are you mad, Dagian? Where? Where will we not be seen and spied upon? Aurelian lives in terror that Marcus will reclaim me. When I first came to the villa he even lied to me about his niece's child, pretending that it was alive and well. He is beginning to trust me. He has even offered me marriage upon poor Ulpia Severina's death."

"You would not marry him?" Dagian was shocked.

"I will do what I must to be revenged!" Zenobia cried passionately, and Dagian closed her eyes in agony.

"Once," she said, "my son's failure to act quickly caused a separation that has brought you both great pain. You have been given a second chance, Zenobia. Do not let your lust for revenge wantonly destroy what the gods have so generously given you both!"

"The gods!" Zenobia laughed harshly. "Do you know what I was called by my people, Dagian? I was called the beloved of the gods; beloved of my people, and of the two men who loved me." She laughed again, and the bitterness in the sound scalded the older woman. "I honored the gods all my life, but they deserted me! If it appears that they have given me a second chance it is only so they may take it away!"

The tears sprang again to Dagian's eyes. In Zenobia's fierce and defiant words she could hear all the pain and hurt that the beautiful queen had suffered. Dagian wanted to reach out and clasp the younger woman to her bosom. She wanted to soothe her, and be a mother to her, and reassure her that everything would be all right; but she could not, for Dagian was not sure herself that everything was going to be all right.

Suddenly the silence of the grotto was broken by a man's voice. "Mother? Ah, there you are. I wondered where you had gotten to." Marcus Alexander Britainus stood within the entry of the little green hideaway.

Both women leapt from the marble bench, Dagian's hands flying to her heart, Zenobia turning pale at the sound of *his* voice. There was no escape! She tried to turn away, but Marcus's eyes were now used to the dimness and filling themselves with her.

"No!" His voice was hoarse with shock, and his hand reached out to turn her about. "No, beloved, don't turn away from

me." Slowly he entered into the grotto, brushing past his mother as if she were not there. Stunned, Dagian could but watch them as they devoured each other with their eyes. Marcus gently grasped Zenobia by her upper arms, and, looking down into her face, now tear-streaked, spoke in a low but audible voice. "I love you," he said. "I have always loved you. I have loved you from the beginnings of time, and I shall love you long after our memories have faded from this earth."

"I have never stopped loving you," she said, "but our time is past. It would have been better if you had not seen me this day."

"Do not say it!" he almost cried.

"I belong to Aurelian, Marcus. Do you understand? I am Aurelian's imperial captive."

"You cannot give yourself to him willingly, beloved. I understand! I truly do!"

"But I do give myself willingly. I must for the sake of my children, and Aurelian is not a fool. In the beginning I fought him, but I am weary of fighting a battle I cannot win, and I have Vaba and Mavia to think of, Marcus." She sighed sadly. "I am no longer Zenobia, the Queen of Palmyra. Palmyra, like my spirit, lies shattered into a million pieces beneath the desert sun. The woman you knew died with her people." Then, pushing past him, she fled through the gardens back to her villa.

He made to follow her, but Dagian blocked his way, hissing at him in a voice so fierce he hardly believed it was his mother, "Do not follow her, Marcus, lest you compromise us all! Aurelian is frantically jealous of her, and fears you."

"He is wise to fear me, for I intend taking her back," Marcus vowed.

"No, my son. He plans to make her his wife when Ulpia Severina dies."

Marcus's face darkened with anger. *"Never!"* he spat. "I will see him in Hades first!"

Dagian shook her head sadly. "Why are you both so destructive, my son? You would fight the emperor openly over Zenobia, and she plots to destroy him even at the cost of her own life. Be patient, Marcus. Aurelian cannot last much longer. His time will come, as surely as it did to those soldier emperors before him. You have but to wait, my son!"

His face contorted with pain. "How can I wait any longer having seen her now, Mother? It has been two years since

Aurelian separated us, and I have ached every day I have been away from her. Who planned that Zenobia live in the villa next to ours? Surely not the emperor?''

"No," Dagian said. "It was Ulpia Severina who arranged it."

"Because she wanted Zenobia and me to be reunited!" he said excitedly.

"Yes," Dagian admitted, "but I do not believe that she knew the depth of her husband's involvement with Zenobia, Marcus. Now she is dying, she will do everything in her limited power to see Aurelian is happy after she is gone; and if Aurelian wants your queen for his second wife then Ulpia will try to see he has what he wants."

"We could flee Italy, Mother. You, and Zenobia, Mavia, and I could flee to Britain!"

"And what of Zenobia's eldest son and his family in Cyrene, Marcus? What fate would await them in Aurelian's anger? Besides, the emperor's passion for her is all-consuming. He would come after her with every legion at his command, and when he caught us he would destroy you, my son. Zenobia loves you, Marcus. I was not sure of it until this afternoon, but when she saw you, spoke with you, left you, every fiber of her being proclaimed her love for you. You can do no less. You must not put her or her family in jeopardy. Trust me—and wait."

He sank down on the marble bench, and with a sob put his head in his hands. *Zenobia!* Her name burned like a brand within his brain. It was almost like a dream now, their brief encounter. Had he really held her in his arms again? Why had he not kissed her? The gods only knew he had wanted to. Another groan escaped his lips.

Heart pounding, Zenobia had fled across the gardens to her own villa. *Marcus!* She wanted to scream his name aloud! "Marcus! Marcus! Marcus!" she whispered softly. "Oh, Marcus, I love you, and I shall die if I cannot be with you again!" She stopped upon the villa's portico, suddenly taken by a terrible fit of trembling. Reaching out, she put her hand against a marble pillar to steady herself. She closed her eyes, but the tears could not be stopped. They rolled unchecked down her face in such profusion that her eyes were soon burning and swollen with the salty stream. Praise Jupiter that Aurelian was in the city this day and could not see her.

She let the pain sweep over her, and for several minutes she wept wildly, unashamedly. Then, taking several deep breaths, she attempted to pull herself back together. Her instinct told her to run back to him; to fling herself into his arms; to flee Aurelian with the man she truly loved! Her conscience sternly reminded her of her duty to those for whom she was responsible: Mavia and old Bab; Adria, Vaba, Flavia, Julia, and young Gaius Porcius. So many people depended on her, and even now in the bleakest and darkest hour of her defeat, she could not think only of herself.

Slowly she wiped the tears from her face and walked into the villa. Luck was with her, and she saw no one in her hurried flight to her bedroom. With a sigh she flung herself upon her bed and fell into a restless sleep; a sleep haunted by his voice, a faceless voice that declared his love for her over and over and over until she awoke to discover that she was weeping again. She decided that this could not go on. If she could not get herself in hand then Aurelian was sure to discover that his dreaded rival, Marcus Alexander Britainus, was separated from her by just a few feet of garden. If the emperor suspected for one minute that they were in contact, she knew that he would kill Marcus without the slightest hesitation. Zenobia shivered. That thought alone was enough to bring her to her senses. I can face no more deaths, she thought.

In the weeks that followed, Ulpia Severina grew weaker. Aurelian's passion for Zenobia, however, grew greater as each day passed, and he could scarcely bear to be out of her sight. He was jealous of any man who spoke gently to the queen, suspecting all of ulterior motives, even the kindly Claudius Tacitus, Rome's elderly and revered senator.

Aurelian was frantic over the fact that he could not stay in Rome for very long after his triumph. His army was quickly ready to march again, its destination Gaul. Zenobia refused to come with him, and Aurelian knew that if he pressed her she would complain to her friend Senator Tacitus. As an imperial captive, she was forbidden to leave the Rome-Tivoli area.

"What do you think will happen to me in your absence?" she mocked him on the evening of his departure.

"The city is full of men who want you," he declared.

"Indeed? Is Rome so barren of women that its men will pant after a woman past thirty? Be sensible, Roman! Why would I accept another man when I can have the emperor of the Romans?"

Strangely, her mockery soothed him. He felt momentarily foolish, for she had never given him any cause to doubt her.

Aurelian departed for Gaul, the last broken link in the Roman Empire's chain to be reforged, leaving his captive mistress to her solitude. For the first time in weeks Zenobia dared to renew her friendship with Dagian, although she had allowed Mavia to visit regularly with her grandmother.

Early one autumn evening the two women sat companionably together, Mavia having departed with her nursemaid Charmian for her cot.

"The news from Gaul is good for the empire," Zenobia said. "Tetricus, the leader of the Gallic rebels, has surrendered, and Aurelian has spared both him and his son. Gaul is once more a loyal subject of Rome."

"Praise the gods!" Dagian said fervently. "Now there will be fewer Roman mothers to weep over their dead sons. How I hate war!"

"Sometimes there is no other choice," Zenobia replied.

"You can say that, having lost your younger son to a war?"

"I would rather Demi lived, but the choice was his. Like his father, he valued his freedom over all else. I see that now, although there was a time when I thought he did what he did merely to spite Vaba. Odenathus would have been proud of him."

"Yes," Marcus Alexander Britainus said, "he would have."

Zenobia looked up, and when their eyes locked hers quickly filled with tears. *"Go away!"* she said in a low, fierce voice. "Would you endanger us all?"

"No one can see us from either villa, beloved," he said, and then he turned to Dagian. "Mother, I want to walk down by the river with Zenobia. Will you keep watch?"

"You are mad!" Zenobia cried softly.

"I will watch," Dagian said. "Go with him, Zenobia. He will persist until you do. Even as a child, he would not give up until he had what he wanted. The servants are abed, and with the emperor away you will be safe."

Marcus took Zenobia's hand and led her to the cliff's edge where, to her surprise, she saw a flight of steps cut into the face of the incline. Slowly they descended, he carefully leading the way, her warm hand tucked into his big one. At the bottom of the steps was a narrow strip of pebbled beach, and in the dim twilight he led her a ways down it, finally stopping before a thick group of greenery. Pushing aside the brush, he drew her into a small cave with a sandy floor. Upon a small ledge was a lamp already burning with a cheery golden glow that cast dark, flickering shadows upon the walls of the cave.

"I have been seeking a place where we might meet in safety," he said by way of explanation, and then he swept her into his arms and kissed her.

Her arms moved swiftly around him, and their hearts pounded wildly with excitement. She molded herself against him, the desire for his love paramount. His mouth worked against hers, seeking, coaxing, drawing from her the kind of response she had never dreamed she would feel again. She was afire with her passion for him, taking his tongue into her mouth to play with, sucking upon it, nipping teasingly at it.

She was wantonly aggressive with him, murmuring against his ear when their lips had finally parted, "I had forgotten how tall you are, my darling. Ah, Marcus, I have missed you so!"

She made no protest when he loosened her long tunic dress and slipped it off her shoulders, allowing it to fall to her ankles. She stood, shivering slightly in her thin cotton camisa, as he stepped back, removed his long cape, and spread it over the sandy floor of the cave. Wordlessly he took off his tunic, toga, and undergarments. A soft smile touched her mouth as his dear and familiar body was revealed to her once more. She reached out and caressed his muscled shoulder. Their eyes met and then he smiled, too.

"Do you not want to tell me how foolish this all is, beloved?" he gently teased her.

In return she reached down and pulled her camisa up and off, flinging it into a corner of the tiny cave.

He caught his breath, seeing her once more as he had seen her so many times before their separation. His deep-blue eyes moved slowly over her lush form, a warm and loving glance; and she glowed in the light of his open and deep love for her. Reaching out, he drew her slowly to him and enfolded her in his arms. He stood holding her, feeling her warmth against him, enjoying the simple sensation of her. She made no move, standing quietly within the circle of his embrace as he reached up and carefully drew the jeweled pins from her hair, letting it fall loose in a dark swirl about her body. Gently he stroked her long hair, and the touch of his hand sent small, delighted shivers through her.

All her lovely memories of him came tumbling back, and she forgot her months of hurt and anger. This great, tall man, this half-Roman half-Briton was her mate; and she wanted no other. Zenobia shifted in order to free her hands and slowly slid them up his broad chest. When her palms rested flat upon him she let her slender fingers entwine and twirl themselves in a circular motion through the soft chestnut hair that covered the center of his chest. It was a lovely teasing motion that he bore patiently until she finally tired of her play and slid her arms up and about his neck, raising her head to look him fully in the face.

They were now practically welded together, her full breasts pressed against his chest; their thighs and bellies matching. Fierce passion blazed between them, and with a low growl he bent his head to take her lips again. With a sweet sigh she surrendered herself to him, her mouth softening beneath his as together they slid to their knees, still embracing. They kissed and they kissed until finally she pulled her bruised lips from his, laughing breathlessly, and with a rueful grin he admitted, "I can't get enough of you, beloved. I have touched no woman in all the time we have been apart."

"I remember," she said softly, "that after Mavia was born, and I remembered her conception, you told me you had touched no woman since me, for you wanted no other. Now you tell me the same thing again, and I am ashamed."

"Because of Aurelian? I understand why you have taken him as a lover, Zenobia. As an imperial captive you had no choice in the matter short of death. You are not a woman to take the easy way, my darling."

For a brief moment she thought of all that had passed between herself and the emperor. No, she would not have willingly accepted him as a lover, lust or no, had he not forced her.

A brief shadow of worry crossed her beautiful face, and he instantly asked, "What is it, beloved?"

"There is now," she said, "but what of tomorrow?"

"I do not know," he answered her honestly.

"So I must remain a choice bone to be fought over by the two of you," she said softly.

He sighed. "My love for you cannot put you in such a terrible position, beloved." Then he groaned. "Zenobia, is there nothing for us? I cannot go on like this. I dare not be seen with you publicly. I cannot even see my daughter except across a garden wall. I must not speak to the child lest she make some innocent remark to the emperor and compromise us both. It is not to be borne!"

Compassionately she put her arms around him, holding him close. He offered her the chance to walk away from this encounter. To remain meant that once more they would become lovers, and then when Aurelian returned and she welcomed him to her bed, she would truly become a whore. It isn't fair, she thought angrily. None of this is of my making, yet I am a pawn. Suddenly his voice cut into her thoughts.

"Zenobia, once I asked you to marry me secretly, but you refused for the sake of your son, and your position. Now will I ask you again. There are many forms of Roman marriage, but legally all that is necessary is that we consent to live together as man and wife. If we make this consent before several witnesses—my mother, old Bab, and your younger servant, Adria—then our union is legal. Will you marry me, beloved? Now? Tonight?"

"But what of Aurelian? He is already on his way back from Gaul. How can I be your wife and his mistress? I do not think that I can do it, Marcus. Not even for you, my love."

"You won't have to, beloved. I promised Gaius Cicero that I should look in on his wife while he was away; and when I visited with Clodia today she read me his latest message to her. Aurelian plans to stay in Rome but a very short time when he returns from Gaul. His next campaign must begin almost immediately. He goes east again toward Byzantium. There are rumblings there of extreme discomfort, and unless he can quell them he will have a great deal of trouble on his hands."

"A winter campaign? Your rumblings must be serious."

"He will be in Rome less than a month. You can hold him off by claiming to be pregnant. Not only will it keep him off you, but it will prevent him from taking you with him on campaign."

"Yes," she said slowly, "I could do that. The emperor desperately wants a child; but Marcus, when he returns from this war with Byzantium? What will we do then?"

"We will not be here then, Zenobia. None of us are kept under guard any longer, a mistake on Aurelian's part. While he marches his army across Macedonia, we will be making our way to Britain. Winter travel is dangerous, but we will survive. No one will come after us, I swear, for who will know we are gone? You do not entertain, nor do you socialize with fashionable Rome. It could be that you will not be missed until Aurelian returns, and our trail will long be cold by then."

"He will know we have gone to Britain," she said, "especially if you and your mother are missing, too."

"We will be where he cannot find us, beloved, I promise you that. We will not go to my mother's people, but rather to a group of small islands at the very tip of Britain. I visited them once when I was a boy. My grandfather owned one of those little islands—it was a dowry from one of his wives. It belongs to Aulus now, but I know that he will give it to us. It is very tiny, but it is warm almost all the year long, and there are palm trees there. Not our beautiful Palmyran palms, but palm trees nonetheless. The Romans have never been seen upon those islands, Zenobia. Aurelian will not find us there."

"My son is in Cyrene," she said. "What will Aurelian do to him, Marcus?"

He smiled. There were so many barriers to their being together, but he would dismantle them one by one until she was content. "If I swear to you that I will arrange to see to your entire family's escape, will you marry me tonight?"

"Yes!"

"Then I promise you, beloved. Everything shall be as you want."

Suddenly Zenobia began to giggle, and when he looked somewhat puzzled she stopped and explained. "How can I ever explain to our children that their father proposed marriage to me while we both knelt naked in a cave?"

A dark eyebrow waggled dangerously at her. "You plan to give me children, my beauty?" he queried.

"Of course!" she exclaimed indignantly. "I may be past thirty, but I can yet give you children!"

"Then let us start now, beloved," he said, and pulled her down upon his cloak with him. "I have hungered for you, Zenobia, for two years. I am no longer interested in talk."

"Then be silent, Marcus Britainus," she commanded him, and drawing his head to hers she kissed him a long and sweet kiss.

Although his head was spinning, he still managed to place an arm about her shoulders and cradle her against him. His big hand caressed her full breasts, and Zenobia felt a thrill run through her. She had never again thought to be loved by him, and now as his passion grew her own rose to match his. He bent his dark chestnut head to nuzzle at her breasts, and shifting so that she lay upon her back, she drew him as close to her as she could, murmuring softly as his tongue encircled her taut nipples. She threaded her fingers through his thick hair, and with one hand rubbed the sensitive back of his neck.

"Oh, Marcus," she murmured, "you will think me wanton, but I am so filled with desire for you, my darling. Do not play long with me, I beg you."

With a low rumble of deep laughter, he lifted his head from her ripe breasts and, shifting his position slightly, gently entered her. Simultaneously they sighed, and then as he began to move in a slow and sensuous rhythm against her, she nipped him lightly upon his shoulder. "Little wildcat," he whispered, "I love you."

"I love you," she whispered back, and then Zenobia gave herself over to the storm of passion that built quickly within her, sending her moaning and thrashing against him as her desire peaked over and over again. Still he would not give her release, and when she roundly cursed him in her childhood Bedawi dialect he laughed aloud, but continued the pleasure-pain until he knew from her mewlings and whimperings that she would bear no more. Only then did he tumble with her into that dark abyss of passion, already longing to possess her again.

With the saucer lamp flickering low, and the chill of the little, damp cave licking at their naked flesh, the lovers did not stay long that night. They now desired only one thing: to pledge themselves quickly in matrimony before witnesses. Neither would feel safe until that sacred promise had been made to the other. Alone each was helpless, together they were invincible.

Silently, hurriedly, they dressed and left the cave, walking swiftly back down the pebbled beach and up the cliff staircase. Although they had been gone less than an hour, night had fallen, and had it not been for the quarter moon they would have had a hard time finding their way. Dagian dozed, her head nodding against her chest as she sat waiting on the marble bench. Gently Marcus kissed her, and she awoke with a small start.

Before she could speak he said, "Zenobia and I intend to marry tonight, Mother. Will you go to her house, and bring old Bab and Adria here to us? We will pledge ourselves here beneath the night sky for all the gods to see. Let Diana, the goddess of the moon, and the hunt, be our chief witness."

"If Aurelian learns of this . . ." Dagian said quietly, but Zenobia cut her short.

"Tonight we have learned that there is no life for us apart. We should rather face the emperor's wrath than ever be separated again, Dagian."

"Besides, Mother, he is not going to know. Trust me, for this time I have a foolproof plan."

Dagian could see that there was no reasoning with either of them. The light of their shared love shone in both their eyes, and she realized that further argument would be useless. Obedient to her son's wishes, she rose from her marble bench and hurried off to Zenobia's villa to fetch the queen's two faithful servants. When she was well out of earshot Zenobia turned to her beloved, and said softly, "I cannot tell Aurelian that I am with child, Marcus. Not when he first returns, at least. He is no fool for all his passion for me. If I say I am to bear his child, he will call in a physician to examine me. He will want to be assured that both the child and I are in good health; he will want to know the birthdate; he will want reassurance. Whether I am your wife, or not, I will have to play his whore a little time longer. If you love me, and value our safety, then you must live with that knowledge. Can you? Perhaps you would prefer that we wait until we can escape to Britain." Her gray eyes looked searchingly at him. "Tell me true, my darling."

For a moment Marcus looked unhappy. The mere thought of Aurelian touching Zenobia infuriated him, yet he knew she was right. If she claimed to be with child, an excited and happy emperor would demand not only proof of her condition, but more dangerous knowledge as well. Still, he did not want to wait. Even knowing that she must bed again with the emperor, Marcus wanted Zenobia for his wife—now, tonight. What she did with Aurelian would mean nothing to her, and in the years to come the memory would fade from both their minds. What she did she did for love of him, for their future together, for their descendants. "I love you," he said quietly. "I do not choose to wait." Then he took her into his arms and kissed her tenderly. "You have always been my wife, beloved."

She brushed the sudden tears from her cheeks. "I think that perhaps the gods have not deserted me after all. Mayhap they were merely testing me, for this night I have found the kind of happiness that is rarely granted to any mortal."

"Are you not Zenobia, the Queen of Palmyra?" he said. "Are you not beloved of the gods, of your people, and of me?"

"Oh yes," she whispered breathily at him. "Yes, my darling, darling Marcus!" And she clung hungrily to him, looking up

396

at him with the shining light of her love, transforming her whole being until she seemed almost luminous.

He stared down at her transfixed, totally unaware that his own love shone as brightly, infusing her with such warmth and well-being that for the first time in months she felt safe, no longer afraid. She had lived with fear these many months, although never once had she dared admit it, even to herself. Now, like a ship escaped from a terrible tempest, she was in a safe harbor.

At a noise on the path they broke apart. Into view came Dagian, Bab, and Adria.

Zenobia's elderly servant looked at Marcus with a sharp eye. "So, Marcus Alexander Britainus, you are finally come back to us."

"Yes, Bab, and tonight I shall claim my own."

"It is good," the old woman nodded.

"The slaves?" Zenobia queried her servants.

"All in their quarters, and sleeping," Adria assured her mistress.

"Very well, then," the queen said, and she turned to Marcus. "Shall we begin, my darling?"

"Yes, beloved."

So in the green, sweet-smelling garden, its flowers lightly touched by the silver glow of the quarter moon, Zenobia, the Queen of Palmyra, turned to her lover, Marcus Alexander Britainus, and said in a low but clear voice, *"When and where you are Gaius, I then and there am Gaia."* It was that simple. They were now man and wife, and he took her once more into his arms to kiss her as Dagian and Adria wiped the tears from their faces and old Bab gave a little hiccough of a sob, and then said, "It has taken you two long enough. I thought never to live long enough to see you both wed. Now may I die in peace."

"You are not going to die yet," Marcus chuckled.

"No, I am not," the old lady cackled, "else who will teach your son manners!"

"And keep me in my place?" he teased her.

"My children," Dagian said, "we must separate now. None of us must allow the least suspicion to fall on Zenobia and Marcus."

Adria and Bab nodded, and began to make their way back to the villa, while Dagian walked in the opposite direction toward her own house. The newly married pair stood hand in hand for a few minutes, talking quietly to reassure each other that they were indeed man and wife.

"Once you said you would not marry me except that it be in the bright light of day, before all; and that I should escort you with much pomp to our new home. Alas, at the moment I have no new home to escort you to, beloved."

"How foolish I was," she answered him.

"I should have insisted, especially when I knew I had to return to Rome. I should not have left you so unprotected, Zenobia. I will never again leave you, my darling! Go now and dream of me, beloved." He kissed her gently once more, and then stood watching as she obediently turned and hurried back to her own villa. She would not always, he thought somewhat amused, be that obedient.

Walking back through the garden, Zenobia's heart soared with happiness. She was *his* wife now, and nothing would ever part them again. She had once warned Aurelian that in the end she would win the battle between them, and now she almost had. It mattered not to her that he would not know, at least not yet. What mattered most was that she and Marcus were finally united, united now and forever; and nothing, not even death, would ever divide them again!

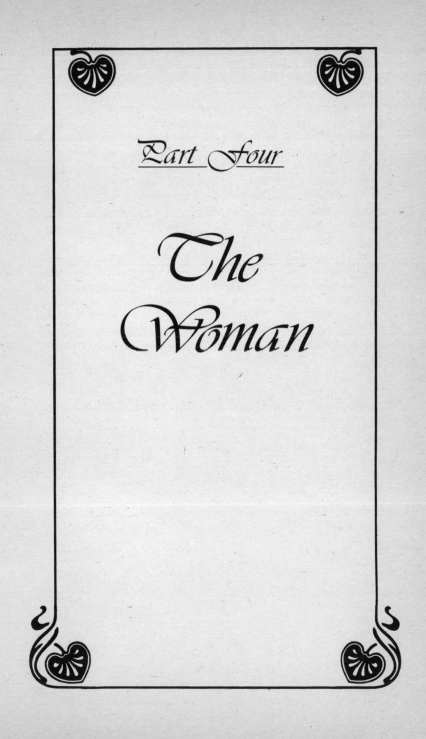

Part Four

The Woman

Chapter Fourteen

Aurelian arrived home victorious from Gaul, and a small triumph was held, this time with the unfortunate Tetricus walking behind the emperor's chariot. In that chariot, Zenobia the captive Queen of Palmyra rode, again with her golden chains fastened to Aurelian's massive iron belt. This time, however, she was garbed in royal purple and gold garments, the Palmyran crown upon her head. Rome's emperor was making a strong point with the people; a point that they did not for all their grumbling miss. *He was Caesar!* His generals were not as easily impressed, for Aurelian had become more imperious as each day passed, and was beginning to believe his own legend.

The queen had been summoned from Tivoli to take part in this latest triumph, and afterward she was escorted to Aurelian's residence on the Palatine Hill. There had been little opportunity for them to speak even though they had shared the same chariot in the procession. She had faintly protested being sent to his palace, but he had quickly overruled her with a wave of his hand. "You will obey me, goddess! Must I again teach you the folly of disobedience?"

"As you will, Roman," she said scornfully, and he laughed.

"I see you have lost none of your spice, goddess. Good! I shall look forward to a long night of playful bedsport with you!"

Zenobia quickly turned away lest he see her repulsion. The moment of truth had finally come for her. She would have to enter into his games with gusto, for when he had left to go to Gaul she had been his willing mistress; now he would expect her to eagerly welcome his advances, having been bereft of him these last months. If she suffered she knew that Marcus suffered too, and whatever happened she would for his sake play the role of the emperor's whore. Just a little while longer, she reassured herself, and I will be free. I will have won!

She was escorted to the royal residence by some half-dozen Praetorian guards, and upon entering it she demanded of the haughty majordomo to be taken to the empress. Ulpia Severina yet lived, and for that small blessing Zenobia thanked the gods. Aurelian would never divorce his wife, and so as long as she lived Palmyra's queen was safe.

The empress lay upon her couch obviously quite ill, but when she saw Zenobia she attempted to rouse herself, smiling a sweet smile. "My dear," her weak voice was warm with welcome, "how kind of you to come visit me. I understand that you keep to your villa at Tivoli."

"I do, Majesty. Rome is too busy to suit me. Nevertheless I must beg your hospitality this night."

"But of course you may stay here," Ulpia Severina said, and Zenobia gratefully acknowledged the empress's consent.

Zenobia was then taken to a suite of rooms where a group of busy slaves awaited her. The chief of these women immediately pressed upon her a goblet of dark red wine, insisting that she drink it down. "It will give you strength, Majesty," the woman wheedled, "and it is the emperor's orders."

Zenobia took the goblet, ready to protest; but the wine, though heavy in appearance, was strangely light and fruity; and the queen was thirsty after the triumph. She quickly drained the goblet, and the slave woman smiled broadly with approval. "Now, Majesty, the bath awaits you," she said, and hurried Zenobia through tall double doors into the baths. There she was scraped, steamed, soaped, rinsed, and scraped again. A final rinse, and she was led to the massage table and made comfortable. A second goblet of wine was offered her. She was hot from the bath, and suddenly thirsty again, and so she again drained the container, the cool liquid slipping easily down her throat.

She stretched out upon the cool marble slab, and at once the slaves about her began to massage her body with a faintly scented pale-green lotion. They worked gently for some minutes as Zenobia grew sleepy with the wine and their ministrations. Then they were turning her over onto her back, massaging her breasts and her belly. She protested faintly, but suddenly all strength was gone from her limbs. She slipped into a half-conscious state, dimly realizing that she had been drugged and wondering why.

Everything became shadowy even though she was quite sure her eyes were open. She was being carried, and yet her body felt weightless, as if she were floating. The dimness began to ease, and once more she could see quite clearly. Zenobia was shocked to find she was in some sort of a temple, and bound by delicate golden chains to a marble altar atop a flight of steps. At each corner of the altar was set a huge standing lamp in the shape of a gold phallus, burning a heavily musk-scented oil, the red-gold flames leaping gently in the coolish night air, swirling about in their carved golden pans. From some hidden place the music of drum and reeds echoed forth.

Zenobia turned her head slightly, and was horrified to see that the altar was set in the very center of a small circular arena, and upon the steps of that arena were men and women, all nude. They were chatting amiably, quite oblivious to their nudity, not the least bit concerned, at least for the moment, with Zenobia. Their lack of interest gave her a chance to inspect her surroundings further. The temple was very simple in design, and obviously within the palace. The only decoration of any kind was a huge sun of pure beaten gold, its giant rays streaked with diamonds and rubies, that hung suspended over the altar.

Aurelian! His name rocketed through her brain with the memory of something he had once said to her. This had to be his doing, and his temple. A temple to the Unconquerable Sun! She was in a temple dedicated to the Unconquerable Sun, Aurelian's pet cult. He had on several occasions spoken to her of his cult, but she had ignored it, not being particularly interested. She still did not understand what it was he was up to, but she imagined she would soon know.

A short but clear trumpet note cut the air, and a deep, stentorian voice called, "Children of the Sun! The time draws near when the incarnation of the great and Unconquerable Sun god upon the earth will come among you to mate with she who is love. Harken, for the sacrifices are about to begin!"

At the instant the voice ceased, powerful and sultry drums began to beat with a sensuous rhythm and a dozen dancers, six males and six females, ran out upon the floor below the altar. The blond women—they were all really girls no more than thirteen or fourteen, Zenobia guessed—were exquisitely and perfectly formed. The men—probably about eighteen—were equally beautiful, also fair-haired, and light-eyed. They were all—both male and female—gilded with beaten gold except for a single stripe of bare skin running up their spines; and they danced the most sensual and wanton dance Zenobia had ever seen; pantomiming the sex act in graphic abandon.

Suddenly one of the maidens broke from the others and fled partway up the steps. At once a young man, his sex rampant, leapt after her. For a moment they sparred upon the marble stairs, and then the man threw the girl down, flung himself atop her, and drove himself into her. There was a pitiful shriek, and the crowd moaned as one as the man withdrew from his victim, turning to face them, his penis bloody with the girl's virginity. "Ahh!" the spectators murmured, leaning forward, eyes glazed with their own lust, mouths open with pleasure, tongues quickly licking lips in undisguised pleasure. The male dancer turned back to the helpless girl, and pushing back into her continued to take his own pleasure as one by one the other gilded men caught and attacked the lovely gilded girls. Cries rent the air as each maiden parted publicly with her innocence to the frantic beat of the drums, while slightly above them the worshipers of the Unconquerable Sun avidly watched, the men now beginning to fondle themselves, nearby women, and in some cases even other men.

Zenobia was horrified by it all, terrified by the thought of whatever might be planned for her, and yet strangely inflamed within her own body. It was madness of the worst sort. Then as suddenly as the dancers had appeared they were gone, the men carrying the weeping women all in their arms. The stentorian voice again spoke.

"What greater sacrifice can a woman make than to offer herself and her innocence to the god? Now he who is the Sun incarnate on earth will mate with she who is love incarnate on earth. This night it is foretold that together they will create a son, a son who will rule the world in the name of the Unconquerable Sun!"

She was to be taken publicly! Zenobia struggled against the seemingly delicate golden chains, but they held firm. Then into her view came Aurelian. She recognized him by a scar upon his thigh, for he wore a carved golden mask. He stood tall, acknowledging the cries of homage that came from the frenzied worshipers. Several women broke from among the spectators and, running down the seat-steps, flung themselves at his feet. They unbound their hair and, writhing about Aurelian, began to rise up, some standing to caress and kiss him, one kneeling and taking his sex into her mouth to stimulate him, others remaining at his feet, licking and stroking at his legs. It was the worst kind of hysteria, Zenobia thought, and yet, to her own disgust she was aroused by it all. While the women worshiped him, Aurelian remained perfectly still until finally their attentions had the desired effect. Gently kicking them aside and pushing them away, he stood before Zenobia. With a swift motion he removed the golden mask, and she finally saw his face, mocking, the eyes glazed with lust and drugs.

The altar upon which she was bound was shaped like an M, and her body had been placed so that her long legs were fastened on either side of the altar's top, a space between them. Now Aurelian stepped into that space and, kneeling, leaned forward to touch her with his tongue. Dear Venus! He couldn't do *that* to her here! Not in front of all of those leering people!

"See!" the disembodied voice cried. "See how he worships at the very shrine of love!"

The emperor's tongue stroked her flesh, sending small shivers of fire through her. *No!* she shrieked silently, for she could not seem to say it aloud. All she was able to do was moan with helpless desire as he probed her delicately, moving slowly, never hurrying her up the path of pleasure but prolonging the torture until finally a long wail escaped her straining throat, and the crowd began to chant: "Fuck! Fuck! Fuck! Fuck!"

Aurelian lifted his head from between her legs and, looking at her, smiled a triumphant smile. Without a word he mounted her, and slowly, very slowly, pushed himself into her; withdrawing as slowly; entering again, withdrawing again, in an unbearable rhythm that would shortly drive her to madness if he didn't satisfy her. "Please!" she managed to moan through now dry lips, hating herself even as she whimpered the word.

"Please what, goddess?"

"Please!" Her eyes pleaded with him.

"Say the word, goddess. Say it, and I will make it good!"

"No!"

He laughed at her defiance, withdrew his lance from her and laid it, wet and throbbing, upon the sweet mound of her belly. "I am filled with special drugs and aphrodisiacs, goddess. When I have finished with you I will take a dozen women before I am satisfied this night. I can wait. Can you?" He punctuated his question by rubbing his organ against her in a provocative manner.

All around her, to the right, to the left, and above, the other worshipers chanted as Aurelian leaned forward to lick at her breasts, which strained to be touched by his talented tongue. "Please!" she whispered again. *"Please!"*

"Tell me what you want me to do to you, goddess. Tell me, and I will do it!"

"No!" She struggled to defy him.

405

The worshipers began to grow restless above them, and their chanting took on a harsh sound. He would lose them if he could not force her, and so, leaning forward, Aurelian took one of her nipples in his mouth and brutally bit it. She screamed with the pain, and the crowd's attention was once more engaged, they groaned together. "Say it, goddess!" he commanded her through gritted teeth.

For a moment incredible hatred blazed from her drugged eyes, and then she whimpered at him, "Fuck me, Roman! Fuck me before I die!"

He rammed himself deep into her, making her cry out again, moving in and out of her with incredible swiftness as around them the other worshipers fell upon each other, men with women, women with women, men with men, in a frenzied orgy of sensual abandon. Mercifully Zenobia fainted, blotting the rest of the horror from her consciousness.

When she once more came to her senses she was surprised to find herself in her bedroom back in Tivoli. Next to her old Bab nodded, and Zenobia struggled to call to her through cracked lips, *"Bab!"* Instantly the faithful servant was awake.

"My baby!" she cried. "You are awake at last!"

"How long has it been?" Zenobia demanded. Her head was pounding.

"The emperor brought you back four days ago. He said you grew ill in Rome, but you have had no fever or other signs of illness. You have been unconscious all that time, and we could not rouse you. What happened?"

"I cannot discuss it, Bab. Do not ask! Where is the emperor?"

"I will fetch him. He asked to be called when you awoke." She hurried off, to return a few minutes later with Aurelian, who looked as cool, elegant, and calm as always.

"Leave us, Bab!"

Bab departed swiftly, closing the door behind her with a resounding bang.

"What happened to me?" Her voice was icy with anger.

"Do you not remember, goddess?" His eyes mocked her.

"I did not dream *it?*"

"I hope not, goddess. We were both incredible, so incredible that donations to the temple the other night reached an unprecedented high."

"You are loathsome!"

"When I had finished with you," he went on, "I took fifteen more women. The gods! How they fought and pleaded to be taken by me. They did everything, *anything* I desired. I was invincible!''

"You are disgusting, Roman! You defile the gods by your obscene worship of this Unconquerable Sun of yours!''

"You are now pregnant with my child,'' he said, ignoring her anger.

She started at him in shock, then said, "You have never in all your years with your wife or your other women fathered a child. What in the name of all the gods makes you think you have fathered one on me now?''

"Because it is foretold in the writings of the Unconquerable Sun that he who is the god upon the earth will father a son upon she who is the goddess upon the earth. From the moment I saw you I knew that you were she who is the goddess upon the earth. Why do you think I have spared you, Zenobia? Why have I always called you *goddess?* You are Venus reborn, my fair one, and from your womb will spring forth a mighty ruler! Were it not so then the other night when I finished with you, you would have offered yourself to the others as I offered myself. You, however, are the goddess, and my seed could not be defiled. So sure am I that you have conceived that in the few weeks I remain in Rome before my next campaign I will not come to you. I will not touch you lest I injure the babe.''

"I am to remain in Tivoli again while you are away?'' she queried.

"Of course! I do not want either you or the child endangered, goddess. You will stay here in Tivoli. Surely Ulpia cannot last much longer, and when I return I will wed with you. If the child is already born, I will legitimize him.''

She could scarcely believe her good fortune. She had looked forward with dread to a month of his insatiable passion, and now he was telling her she was free. Zenobia was careful not to let her joy show. Composing her face, she raised her eyes to him. "I did not like what you did to me the other night, Roman, but I have been without you for several months. Now you say we are not to be together while you are here in Rome.'' Her lips arranged themselves in a pretty pout.

He smiled at her. "I am pleased that you shall miss my loving attentions, goddess; but I will take no chances with you.''

"You are not bored with me? This is not simply an excuse because you have found another?'' Her voice sounded delightfully suspicious in his ear.

"How could there be anyone after you, goddess?" he demanded. "No, I adore you as always! There is no other!" No others that mattered, he thought, pleased.

"You cannot be sure that I am with child, Roman. It is much too soon to know."

"Nevertheless, I will take no risks, Zenobia. I am returning to Rome today, and I will not be back again until just before we march. I have a great deal to do, goddess, and a very short time in which to do it. You must accept my decision. It is for the best."

"Very well, Roman, it will be as you say. I see that you cannot be moved."

Aurelian leaned forward and cupped her chin in his hand while his mouth found hers. His kiss was a possessive one, a demanding one, and remembering the other night, she shuddered. He was a ruthless man. Releasing her from the kiss, he said softly, "I understand that your neighbor is Dagian, the wife of the late Lucius Alexander."

"Yes," Zenobia replied, choosing her words carefully. "She is a pleasant and amusing woman, and she enjoys Mavia greatly."

"And have you seen her son, goddess?" She could hear the dangerous undertone in his voice.

"Yes, Roman. I have seen him several times in his mother's gardens." She must be careful not to lie lest he suspect her.

"You have spoken to him?"

"On at least two occasions," she said, certain now that someone, an imperial spy undoubtedly, had seen them, and reported it to Aurelian.

"And?"

"And what, Roman?" She laughed lightly. "You aren't jealous, are you, Caesar?" Leaning over, she kissed him teasingly. "I do not know now what I ever saw in Marcus Alexander. He is really a very dull, pompous man."

"Then you love me alone?"

"I told you, Roman, that it was doubtful that I should ever love again; but what could Marcus Alexander offer me, pray? You offer me an empire, and I should be a fool to refuse you. Especially since I am to bear your child."

He looked long and searchingly into her face and then, certain that she spoke the truth, admitted ruefully, "I knew that eventually you would see Marcus Alexander again, and I was jealous. I love you, goddess! You are my very life now!"

"I have never given you reason to doubt me, Roman," she

answered him, thinking, somewhat amused: But only because I have been careful, and not been caught!

He rose from the bedside. "I must leave you now, goddess, but I will return before we march."

She smiled up at him, and watched through narrowed eyes as he left her bedchamber. I shall only have to see you one more time, Roman, she thought; and at least I am free now of your eternal pawing.

A few minutes later both Bab and Adria entered her bedchamber, and Zenobia demanded, "Is he gone?"

"He is on the road to Rome as we speak, Majesty," Adria said.

Zenobia turned to Bab. "Go to Marcus, and tell him that I am all right. Then tell him that there is an imperial spy in one of our houses. He is not to come to me until after the emperor has left Rome. If he protests, Bab, then you must tell him that Aurelian asked me if I had spoken to him, and I said yes, for I was certain he knew I had. We are watched, and must take no chances. Dagian will carry messages for us, but I will not endanger either of us when we are so close to escape. Tell him, Bab, that I love him."

"Do not fear, my baby," Bab soothed. "Marcus Alexander Britainus values you above all things. He will understand."

Zenobia prayed it was so.

As the days went by Dagian spoke of her son only once, and that was to tell Zenobia that Marcus was seeing to their departure. The Palmyran queen began to grow curious, and she plied Dagian with many questions.

"What is it like, this Britain of yours?" was her first.

"Ah," Dagian said, a smile lighting her face, "it is very different from your Palmyra, and from Italy. It is an island nation, a land of many contrasts. One day may be sunny, the skies bright blue and cloudless; the next day may be misty, cloudy, filled with rain. The winters can be harsh, with much snow, but the springs make up for all the gray, cold days. There are no deserts as in your land, Zenobia. The only sandy places are by the sea. Britain is a land of hills and valleys, of mountains and fields. The Romans do not control as much of it as they like to think, for the tribes are very fierce and some bloodthirsty."

Zenobia looked troubled. "You make it sound quite savage, Dagian. Is this place that Marcus would take me safe for my children, my children's children? I have only just received word that Flavia was delivered of a little girl in Cyrene. Will your Britain be a safe place for such a tender baby?''

"Dearest girl, is any place in this world safe for children? Somehow they survive. The place that Marcus intends that you settle in is an island, one of several, off the very tip of Britain in the south. You need have no fear, Zenobia. Long ago, so far back that there is no written date, a small Celtic tribe lived upon the island, but today it is uninhabited. The island is a lovely place, as I remember it, its climate mild even in the winter months. Flowers and fruits and vegetables grow year round upon it; and you will be able to raise sheep and cattle. The seas are full of fish, and everything should thrive including your family.''

"Will you come with us, Dagian?''

"No, my dear. I have long planned on living with Aulus and his family in the region of my birth and girlhood. I will come to visit you, though, as long as the gods give me good health.''

Zenobia felt reassured, but now she worried about Vaba and his family. Marcus had promised her that he would take care of them, but how could he, prisoner here in Tivoli that he was? Again Dagian was able to reassure her. "Marcus has been freed of all travel restrictions, as have I,'' the older woman said one day. "We are to return to our own house in Rome within the week.''

"I cannot bear to be without you,'' Zenobia cried. "Curse Aurelian! He says he is no longer fearful of Marcus, but he is. You are the only friend I have, and I need you!''

"Courage, Zenobia!'' Dagian chided gently. "Our return to Rome reassures Aurelian that you truly no longer want Marcus. If you complain to him he will be suspicious. In another week or two the army marches, and with it goes the emperor. You will be free then, my daughter.'' She put her arms around Zenobia, cradling her against her ample bosom.

"I am so afraid,'' Zenobia admitted, suddenly weeping. "I fear that Aurelian will find us out, and prevent Marcus and me from being together. We have waited so long, Dagian, so very long!''

"You were meant to be together,'' Dagian soothed. "Do not fear, my daughter. Prudence will prevent the emperor from knowing our plans. The gods will see to it.''

"The gods are capricious,'' Zenobia whispered.

"Hush, my daughter!'' Dagian looked fearfully about her as if she might see an angry god.

Then as suddenly as she had been fearful, Zenobia became calm again. "You are right, Dagian, and I am behaving like a child. We are so close to victory."

The two women embraced a final time, and then each went her separate way. A few days later the Alexanders, mother and son, left the imperial villa in Tivoli to return to their own home in Rome. Although Marcus Alexander had sold the great trading house that had been his father's, he still had many contacts among the important commercial families. Among them was the son of one of the wealthy Palmyran families slain in the destruction of that city. With Palmyra's fall, the young man had found himself alone and without a market for his goods. He might have gone bankrupt had not Marcus Alexander stepped in and come to his aid. Marcus called in the debt owed, and the young Palmyran was eager to help. Ogga ben Yorkhai was his name, and he had friends in Cyrene with whom he was in constant contact. Now he dispatched his pigeon messengers to that city, and within ten days came word that Vaballathus preferred to remain in imperial captivity than to brave the dangers of escape with his wife and infant daughter.

Marcus knew how disappointed Zenobia would be, but in truth he was relieved. The young man would always remember what he had lost, always unconsciously blame his mother, and between them there would never be any real peace.

A happier note, however, was word that Vaba's brother had been found alive in the ruins of Palmyra by the Bedawi. There had been some half-dozen survivors of the massacre, a woman, four children, and Demi, all of whom had been left for dead. The tribesmen had taken them back to their encampment, and although one of the children had died several days later, the rest had survived. Demi knew that his brother now resided in Cyrene, and that his mother was in Rome. He preferred, he wrote to Vaba, to remain with their uncle Akbar and the Bedawi. If he could not live in Palmyra, now destroyed, he preferred to roam the desert as his ancestors had done. He already had his eye on a strong young girl of fourteen to take to wife once he could earn her bridesprice.

So, Marcus thought as he read the letter from Cyrene, we will start anew, just Zenobia and our daughter and me. We will shed our old lives as the lizard sheds its old skin.

The army's departure was scheduled for the following day. Marcus Alexander Britainus wondered if Aurelian would change his mind at the last moment, and attempt to take Zenobia with him. They had not seen or spoken to one another in over a month. Although his mother had assured him before they left Tivoli that all was well, even Dagian had not seen or communicated with Zenobia in the last few weeks. That afternoon Gaius Cicero came to see him, and Marcus welcomed his old friend warmly.

"Once more," Gaius smiled, "I must ask that you watch over my Clodia and our children while I am away. Clodia is increasing again. Another child I shall not see born," he said ruefully.

"Why do you not resign the army, Gaius? Your family is wealthy, and although your older brother is the heir there is time for you to make a name for yourself in politics. Surely you do not really believe that Aurelian has a long future as Rome's emperor?"

"This is my last campaign," Gaius admitted. "I must think of my family now. As to the emperor, I'll admit I do not know how much longer he can hold on. He is a fine general, a good administrator; but he lacks subtlety. He makes enemies too easily. Take this temple of the Unconquerable Sun of his. He has foresworn the old gods for this strange new religion, and the truth of the matter is it is a scandal.

"After this last triumph he held a fertility rite in his temple. He mated upon the high altar with Palmyra's queen, and then took fifteen more women before he was sated. I know several of the men who attend these rites. They do so for purely licentious reasons. They were extremely annoyed that they could not take the captive queen. Usually Aurelian, who calls himself the god on earth, allows his fellow worshipers to have a go at his woman when he has finished. This night, however, he would not. He claims that Zenobia is the goddess upon earth, and it was foretold that he should get a child upon her that night. He said he did not want his seed defiled by others.

"Just as well, if you ask me. They say that Zenobia fainted and could not be roused for several days from her stupor. Poor woman. She had taken a great deal from Aurelian, and this surely was the worst. The rumor is that he intends to make Palmyra's queen his empress when Ulpia Severina has died."

"Yes," Marcus said in a strangely calm voice. "I have heard that rumor." Keep calm, his inner self warned him. Gaius is your friend, but first he is loyal to Aurelian. Although there were many questions he wanted to ask, he instead changed the

412

subject, pretending lack of interest in Zenobia and Aurelian. He could not be sure that Gaius did not spy for the emperor. "I shall most happily keep Clodia company, Gaius. She is a fine wife and mother in the old tradition, and you are fortunate to have her."

"Why don't you marry?" Gaius asked suddenly.

Marcus laughed. "Because there is no one I love, and I cannot settle for less. My brother will perpetuate our family name, and so there is no need for me to marry. Besides, I prefer my freedom."

"Yes, I have known a few men like you, Marcus," Gaius said. "Some men are like that." He rose. "I shall be on my way now. I thank you for your kindness to my wife and my children. My brother simply doesn't have time to bother with Clodia, and she does get lonely." The two men clasped hands in the traditional Roman salute, and then Gaius was gone, his quick, "Farewell," echoing and then dying.

Marcus sat down heavily once Gaius Cicero was gone, and his mind raced back to his friend's discussion of Aurelian's cult. The emperor had publicly taken Zenobia! Marcus shuddered with the horror of it. He wanted to strangle Aurelian, feel his thick neck beneath his fingers, watch as his face grew purple, as he gasped his last few breaths, as he died!

Feeling the violence welling up within him, he rose quickly and shut the library door. Then turning back into the room, he began systematically to destroy everything in it. Furiously he flung the furniture against the beautiful frescoed walls! Every piece of pottery was smashed, and only the book scrolls escaped destruction due to Dagian's timely entry into the library.

"Marcus!" She looked about her, horrified at the terrible disaster the room had become. "Marcus, what is it?"

Somehow through the red mists of his fury he heard her, and slowly his glazed eyes cleared. "It was either this or I would have killed *him!*" he said.

Dagian did not need to ask who. She simply inquired, "Why?"

He told her, and Dagian's eyes quickly filled with tears. "Poor Zenobia," she said softly, and then, "Marcus, you are not angry at Zenobia?"

"No, Mother, I am angry for her. Rome is truly a sewer, and none of us belongs here any longer. The gods only know how badly I want to take Zenobia from this place."

"You will have to wait until Aurelian has embarked from

413

Brindisi, Marcus, and then it will be another week after he has left. We cannot at this late date take the chance of anyone discovering our plans. You must remain calm, my son."

"I know, Mother, but when I heard what he had done to my wife . . . The gods curse him! I hope he never returns to Rome. I hope they kill him!"

Aurelian, however, at that moment was far from dead. At Zenobia's villa in Tivoli, he held his beautiful captive within the circle of his arms and kissed her passionately. She forced herself to eagerly return his kisses, nibbling teasingly at his lips to further arouse his desires. His hands fondled her full breasts, taunting the nipples to hard peaks. "You are so beautiful," he murmured against her ear, and she purred against him in apparent satisfaction. "Do you know yet, goddess?" he asked her. "Can you be sure yet whether you carry my child?"

"It is much too soon, Caesar," she said, and then she lowered her eyes coyly. "I promise to send a message to you the moment I can be certain. These things cannot be rushed, Roman."

"I do not like leaving you, goddess, but I do not want you exposed to the rigors of travel in your condition."

"I understand, Caesar," she replied, "and I agree with you. I am not a maiden in the first flush of her womanhood. It is better this way."

"If only I could be sure!" He was so anxious, and for a brief moment Zenobia almost felt sorry for him. Then she remembered the rites, those unholy rites he had held within his Temple of the Unconquerable Sun, publicly shaming her.

"You were so virile and potent that night, Roman," she murmured wickedly. "Surely if it is written you cannot doubt the outcome?"

"No, no!" he answered, visibly upset lest his lack of faith cause the gods to turn upon him. "No, you are with child, I am certain!"

"Then kiss me again, Aurelian, and be on your way, for the sooner you leave me the sooner you will return to me—and to our child." She looked him straight in the face now, her silvery-gray eyes dancing with their haunting golden lights. Never had he seen her so beautiful, he thought. Swiftly his mouth descended on her, possessing her lips fiercely, but she would not be subdued, and kissed him as fiercely in return. He was strangely breathless when they parted.

"The gods go with you, Roman," she said.

He could do nothing but leave her now, but he did so feeling strangely dissatisfied. Climbing into his chariot, he turned to look at her once more, and the sight of Zenobia in her flaming red kalasiris, her long black hair blowing free in the afternoon breeze, her proud head held high, was a vision that remained with him. He raised his hand in a gesture of farewell, then slapped the reins upon his horses' rumps, and departed, his chariot wheels rumbling up the drive and onto the Via Flaminia.

She also raised her hand in farewell, wondering if he could hear her laughter following him. "I will never see you again, Roman, and may my memory haunt you through all eternity!" she cried softly, and then she whirled around and re-entered her house.

The time went slowly, the days long and dull, the nights longer and lonely. The only relief for Zenobia during this period was her monthly show of blood. She had never truly believed that the emperor could father a child upon her when he had never before sired one; but the insanity of the Temple of the Unconquerable Sun had left her shaken.

The Praetorian guards about her villa were removed at her request to the senate through Claudius Tacitus.

"I have no wish to cause the government undue expense on my behalf when it is not really necessary," she told him. "It is enough that Rome houses me."

"Perhaps," Tacitus said, "it may soon be possible for you to have your complete freedom, my dear. The senate, however, needs certain assurances." His kindly old face was bland with detachment.

"What assurances?" she demanded.

"The emperor made some rather interesting statements concerning your condition prior to his departure; and there was some gossip about fertility rites in his Temple of the Unconquerable Sun several weeks back."

"If you are referring, Tacitus, to the night in which I was drugged and then raped by the emperor upon the high altar of his temple, then allow me to assure you that nothing came of that night other than my acute sense of shame. Aurelian chose to believe that I was carrying his child before he departed. I chose to allow him to believe it so I might be spared the boredom of accompanying him to Byzantium. If the senate does not believe me then let them question my women, or call a physician in to examine me. I am not with child."

415

"Do you love Aurelian?" Tacitus asked bluntly.

"No," she replied in kind. "I am his captive, and that is all I have ever been."

"He believes that you love him."

"He also believes that I am the goddess Venus incarnate, but I am not, Tacitus." She looked shrewdly at him. "You have all but said aloud that there is a plot against Aurelian. I care not! Why should I? Aurelian has taken everything that I ever held dear from me. My sons are gone from me, my people, my city! All I have left is my daughter, and all I want is to be left alone in peace to raise her. You may tell the senate that, Tacitus! I simply wish to be left to myself!"

"Your reputation was not a lie, Zenobia of Palmyra. You are indeed a wise woman," Tacitus replied, and then he bid her farewell and withdrew from her.

When he had gone Zenobia called for parchment and her writing materials, and quickly wrote a note to Dagian. The note was then taken immediately to Rome by a Tiro, a young slave of Zenobia's. He was a skilled chariot driver, who had been injured in the arena. No longer any good for competition, he had been sold by his master, but he could still drive skillfully enough for the road. She had purchased him, given him a lovely slave girl as a wife, and now Tiro would have died for his mistress.

When Tiro returned after dark that night Marcus Alexander Britainus was with him, muffled in a dark cloak as he slipped into the villa and made his way to Zenobia's bedchamber. Adria gave a small shriek as the large, black figure entered the room without warning; but Marcus flung the long cape off, and Adria sighed, "Oh, master, you gave me such a fright!"

Marcus chuckled deeply. "Did you think I was Aurelian returned?"

Adria made a face that caused Marcus to laugh aloud. "*That one,*" Adria sniffed. "Praise the gods we shall not have to put up with him again, master."

"You sound more like old Bab every day," he teased her.

"Then the girl is finally getting some sense, which is more than I can say for you, Marcus Alexander Britainus! Are you mad to come calling, and the emperor not gone from the country yet?" Bab stood glaring at him, hands upon her plump hips.

"Aurelian sailed two days ago, old woman; and besides, it

was your beautiful mistress who summoned me here. Where is she?"

"Here, my love!" Zenobia stood in the doorway of her bedchamber. "I was in the gardens walking—and dreaming. Find your beds, Bab, Adria."

The two servants scurried out, and waiting until they were just gone, Zenobia threw herself into her husband's arms, raising her face up for a kiss. He stared down at her for a moment, his fingers gently caressing her cheekbones, and then his mouth descended to meet her eager lips. Her heart leapt wildly within her chest, threatening, she was certain, to burst through her skin. He kissed her softly at first, and then as his mouth grew more certain of possession, he demanded surrender, total surrender of her. She joyously gave him that surrender, wrapping her smooth arms about his neck, pressing herself as close to him as she could.

"You are mine now!" and she could hear the triumph in his voice.

"I am yours now and forever!" she answered him, her eyes shining up into his with so much love that he felt humble.

Unable to resist her, he kissed her gently once more, and then he led her to their bed where they sat down so they might speak.

"Aurelian is gone, Zenobia. Two days ago from Brindisi, according to reports received this morning in Rome. The news came by pigeon, and was welcomed by the senate."

"Tacitus came to visit me this morning," Zenobia said excitedly. "I had requested the senate to withdraw the Praetorian guards from the villa."

"On what excuse?" he asked.

"I said I wished to live quietly, and not cause the government unnecessary expense."

Marcus laughed loudly. "Indeed, my love, you certainly must have caught their attention with that excuse."

"He practically admitted a plot against Aurelian. This emperor will not, I wager, return from Byzantium alive."

"How can you be sure, beloved? Tell me exactly what Tacitus said to you."

"I do not doubt that you have heard the rumors, Marcus, of what happened to me in Aurelian's temple," she said slowly.

"I have heard," he said tersely, his face suddenly dark and grim with anger.

"It was not my fault," she whispered, afraid.

He drew a deep breath, and then took her onto his lap to comfort her. "I know that, Zenobia, but I cannot help but be angry about it. I am not angry with you, but at the situation. I am not one of these new Christians who can turn the other cheek. My wife, the woman whom I prize above all others, was taken publicly in a fertility rite! The mere thought maddens me!"

"It was the most horrifying experience of my life, Marcus, and I have lived through much. I was drugged just enough to make me helpless, but not enough to render me unconscious. I was bound upon their high altar for all to see, and all about me those unholy people chanted for Aurelian to take me."

She sighed deeply, sadly, then said, "At least one good thing came of it. Aurelian was so certain that he had impregnated me that he never came near me after that."

He groaned, pained. "How many times have you been helpless, and I not able to defend you, beloved? Never again! I swear by all the gods it shall never happen again! Now you are in my keeping, Zenobia, and I will protect you always."

"And I will protect you, my love. Alone we seem but half a person; only together are we whole."

He was comforted by her words, for he seemed to need the comfort more than she. She smiled with the thought that where she was weak he was strong, but where he was weak she was strong. After a long moment Marcus spoke again, saying, "Tell me what else Tacitus said."

"He said that the senate needed *reassurances,* which, I realized, meant that they wished to know if I was indeed pregnant as Aurelian kept insisting. He said that, given those assurances, I might be granted my freedom entirely. I, of course, told him I am not pregnant. I offered my women to the senate for questioning, and myself for examination by a physician of the senate's choice.

"Why would they want such knowledge if they were not planning to assassinate Aurelian? They would kill me as quickly as Aurelian if they thought there was any chance I was bearing his child. Since he has no other heirs, and poor Ulpia will shortly be dead herself, they seek to tie up all the loose ends. I wonder who will be the next emperor? Are there any generals who stand out in your mind?"

"None," he answered her.

"Then why kill Aurelian? Why—without someone else to take his place—destabilize the government?"

"Aurelian has offended enough men," Marcus explained, "that it matters not to them what happens to the government as long as their own interests are protected. And rest assured, my love, the interests of the conspirators will be safe. The powerful will find a new emperor. And when *he* offends them . . ." Marcus made a slicing motion across his throat with his finger.

"Then surely the time is right for us to flee, my love! Now, while they are involved with their plots."

"Yes, beloved, it is time for us to flee. I have spent these last days planning our escape. I have bought a ship, Zenobia, a Roman merchantman, only two years old. If we are to live on an island we shall need transportation between our new home and the mainland."

"A merchantman? Then you mean to trade?"

"I am not a farmer or a herdsman, beloved."

"Will you leave me then in this strange land that you are taking me to, Marcus. Leave me to pursue your business?"

"No, beloved, I will never leave you again, but my ship will trade for me, and I will have an interest."

She squirmed about in his lap, and looked up at him. "What will I do?" she wondered aloud. "I am a queen without a kingdom, a general without an army. What on earth am I to do, Marcus?"

"You will be a good Roman wife, beloved," he answered, and Zenobia laughed.

"No, Marcus, I should be bored to death. For me there must be something else. Perhaps I shall make this island of ours the new kingdom over which I reign. I must think on it."

"You think too much," he chuckled, falling back upon the bed, still clutching her within his arms. "Come, and be my good Roman wife," he teased, repositioning her to lie in the curve of his arm beneath him as if she were a child's toy. "I think that you should begin by kissing me, *wife*," and he lowered his head to brush her lips with his own. "My wife," he murmured against her mouth. "My beautiful wife, my sweet wife, my adorable wife."

Her smile was deceptively sweet. "I have only been upon the sea once, when Aurelian brought me from Macedonia to Brindisi. I liked it, and I believe that I shall learn to navigate this ship of yours. One may use the stars in the heavens upon the sea as easily as upon the desert.''

He grinned down at her. "Had I wanted to marry a sailor . . .'' He waggled his eyebrows wickedly at her so that she giggled. "I wanted a woman, beloved, and I married woman incarnate.'' His hand drew her robe open to bare her beautiful breasts to him, and he leaned forward to brush them with his rough cheek. Her scent arose from the warmth of her lovely body to taunt and assail him. "Oh, Zenobia,'' he said softly, and she reached out to draw him against her breasts.

They lay together in tender embrace, enjoying the simple pleasure of being together without fear of discovery. She threaded her fingers through his thick chestnut-colored hair, noticing a silver strand here and there. Suddenly she realized that he had fallen asleep upon her breasts, and again she chuckled as she shifted to cradle him more comfortably. There had never before been a time when he hadn't made love to her. Their separation had taken its toll on him, for he was obviously exhausted.

When morning came and he awoke, Marcus was much chagrined. "You were so tired, my darling,'' an amused Zenobia comforted him.

"But I wanted you!'' he protested.

Zenobia laughed. "And I wanted you,'' she said, "but you were tired and you fell asleep.'' Then she roused him up, for it was necessary that he return to the city that morning. "When are we to leave?'' she asked as she helped him to dress in his freshened clothes.

"We will sail from Ostia in three days' time,'' he answered.

"Are we to sail the entire way, my darling?'' She looked a little nervous.

"I would like to, Zenobia, as there is less chance of our being caught; but the sea is so dangerous. We will follow the coast closely as far as Massilia. From Massilia we will take the tin route up across Gaul to the coast facing Britain. It is a very small piece of water, beloved. The ship will meet us there, having gone through the Pillars of Hercules out into the great sea, and around the coast of Gaul. Our ship will then take us across to Britain.''

"Not to our own home?''

"No. First we must take my mother to Aulus and his family. Only then can we seek our own place, Zenobia. Besides, I think it is only polite that I ask Aulus for his island before we take it over.'' His deep-blue eyes were twinkling at her.

She laughed. "How the times have changed, my darling. I pray your brother will be generous."

"He is a good man, Zenobia."

"You must take some of the slaves with you today," she said. "I cannot leave Tivoli discreetly with a large train."

"How many people do you have?"

"You need not worry about the women," Zenobia said. "They can come with me when I go to Rome to meet you, but you must take Tiro, my charioteer, and Otho the gardener. They are the only men with me, and I prefer they go with you today."

"Very well," he answered. "How many women do you have besides old Bab, Adria, and Charmian?"

"Just two slave girls for cleaning, and Lenis, the cook, who is Tiro's wife."

"You'll attract no attention with so small a retinue," he said. "Have your women pack most of your goods and send them with Tiro and Otho to my house in Rome. Then you may travel easily and in comfort."

He left her to return to Rome, and Zenobia spent the rest of her day overseeing the packing. By nightfall all was in readiness. She had instructed both Tiro and Otho that they were to leave before morning in order to be through the town before everyone was up.

In the hour before the dawn she awakened and heard the carts lumbering from the villa courtyard. With a sigh of relief Zenobia turned over and went back to sleep. She was awakened some time later by old Bab, who shook her frantically.

"Wake up, my baby! Wake up!"

"What is it, Bab?" It was a monumental effort to keep her eyes open.

"Gaius Cicero is here, and he is demanding to see you. You must get up and receive him!"

Instantly Zenobia was awake, her mind racing with curiosity. Gaius Cicero was Aurelian's personal aide as well as the emperor's favorite. He had gone with his master to Byzantium. What was he doing back in Tivoli? Was Aurelian in Rome? Had he learned of the plot against him? She rose from her bed, her body gleaming through her sleeping robe. "Get me a tunic, old woman. Where is Gaius Cicero now?"

"He waits in the atrium, my baby," Bab replied, pulling a light white wool tunica over Zenobia and belting it with a length of red leather. "Adria! The sandals, quickly!"

Zenobia slid her feet into her sandals, and hurried from her bedchamber, down the stairs of the house, and into the atrium. There, she saw Gaius Cicero pacing. "Greetings, Gaius Cicero," she called to him, "I thought you with the emperor."

"I was, Majesty. He has sent me back for you."

"What?" she was astounded.

"I am to bring you to the emperor, Majesty. He says . . ." the soldier in Gaius Cicero flushed, "he says he cannot bear to be without you, and I am to bring you to him."

"Have you come alone, Gaius Cicero?" she asked him.

"Yes, it was thought I might travel more quickly. We can pick up an escort in Rome."

"Very well, Gaius Cicero, if the emperor insists then who am I to argue? It will take several days, however, for my things to be packed. I was planning on going into Rome today, and so I shall ask you to accompany me; but first I will give my servants orders to pack." With a smile she turned and retraced her steps back to her bedchamber, where she explained Gaius Cicero's presence to both Bab and Adria.

"What will you do, my baby?"

"I will go into Rome now with Gaius Cicero, and I shall let Marcus handle this. He and Gaius Cicero are friends. Perhaps we should warn him of the possible plot against Aurelian. If he does not return to the emperor then he may be saved. I do not know his wife, but I have heard it said that Clodia Cicero is a good woman, and they have several children. If he returns to the emperor he will surely suffer Aurelian's fate. That, however, must be up to my husband. I will not return here, Bab, and so tomorrow you must bring Mavia and the rest of the servants to me in Rome."

"It will be as you command, my baby," Bab said. "Be careful, Majesty, lest Gaius Cicero suspect anything before you reach Marcus Alexander." She then helped Zenobia to dress for her journey into Rome.

She left the Tivoli villa without looking back. The day was fair with early spring, and the Via Flaminia mildly busy with traffic moving toward the city. Zenobia noted many farm carts filled with the first produce, asparagus, tiny onions, new lettuce, and brightly colored flowers. There were some families, undoubtedly going to visit relatives in Rome; and peddlars come to sell their wares in the streets.

There was little traffic from Rome until a troupe of horsemen came galloping down the road, causing those on foot and in smaller vehicles to scatter to the side of the Via Flaminia. As they were about to pass the chariot in which Zenobia and Gaius Cicero were riding their leader called a halt to his troupe.

"Hail, Gaius Cicero! I thought you were with the emperor."

"Hail, Fabius Marcellus! I was, but I was sent back on an errand."

Fabius Marcellus looked at Zenobia, and then said, "Is this not the Queen of Palmyra, Gaius Cicero?"

"I am Zenobia of Palmyra," she replied before he might speak.

"I have an order for your arrest, Zenobia of Palmyra," came the frightening words.

Gaius Cicero was shocked, and not a little surprised. "On whose order?" he demanded of Fabius Marcellus. "This woman is under the emperor's personal protection."

"On the orders of the senate," came the reply.

"There must be some mistake, Majesty," Gaius Cicero said. "Nonetheless I must let you go with Fabius Marcellus. I will seek to find an answer to this puzzle, and see to your release as quickly as possible."

Zenobia was speechless with fear—not for herself, but for Marcus, for Mavia, for Dagian, for her servants. Why was she being arrested? Had they somehow found out about her marriage to Marcus? A thousand questions flew through her numbed brain, and then to her further terror she heard Fabius Marcellus say to Gaius Cicero:

"I cannot let you go your way, Gaius Cicero. You are not where you should be, and you are in the company of this woman. I must ask that you accompany us until the senate knows of your presence and decides what to do with you."

Gaius Cicero's hand went to his broadsword and then, upon reflection, fell away. He was badly outnumbered. This was either a ridiculous mistake, or else it was a plot against Aurelian. If it were an error he would shortly be free; if it were a plot then his fate was in the hands of the gods. "I will go with you," he said quietly, and Fabius Marcellus sighed, relieved. He had known Gaius Cicero for a long time, and he liked him. He had no wish to kill a good officer.

Zenobia roused herself. "Where are you taking me," she demanded, drawing herself up, her voice impersonal and imperious.

"There is a small prison near the senate, Majesty. I have been ordered to escort you there," replied Fabius Marcellus, now slightly discomfited by the tone of Zenobia's voice.

Gaius Cicero smiled to himself. The queen, he thought, could certainly rise to the occasion.

"*A small prison?*" The outrage in Zenobia's voice was evident for all to hear.

Fabius Marcellus suddenly realized that she was taller than he. He flushed uncomfortably, and then mumbled, "I am not to be held responsible for *their* decisions, Majesty. I only do my duty." He waved his hand in signal, and suddenly the chariot was surrounded by Praetorian guards. With a nod, and feeling that he had now regained charge of the situation Fabius Marcellus moved to the head of the group, and they began to move off toward Rome.

"What do you know of this?" Gaius Cicero asked in a low voice.

"Nothing, really," she answered, "but several days ago Senator Tacitus called upon me and questioned me closely."

"About what?" Gaius Cicero was curious.

"About whether I carried the emperor's child," was her reply.

"*Do you?*" He looked closely at her.

"No," Zenobia replied, "I do not. Oh, I know that the emperor thinks I do, but that is Aurelian's own desperation. You are not a fool, Gaius Cicero. You cannot believe that I care for Aurelian! I am an imperial captive. I have done what I had to to survive, to insure my children's survival. I have loved but two men in my life—my late husband and Marcus Alexander Britainus."

"But I thought you hated Marcus for marrying Carissa." Gaius Cicero shook his head. "Give me a simple woman like my Clodia."

"You must go to Marcus when you are released, Gaius Cicero. You must go to him, and tell him that I have been arrested. He will know what to do. And Gaius, remember your first loyalty is to your wife and family. I have warned you."

"Do not fear, Majesty," was his reply. "It is simply a misunderstanding."

"I know nothing for *certain*, Gaius Cicero, yet I do know that if I have been ordered arrested it is because the senate would be certain that I am not with child—Aurelian's child, his heir. When they are sure of that then I am certain to be released. Still I would have Marcus know where I am, Gaius Cicero. Will you promise to tell him for me?''

''Very well, Majesty, I promise you.'' He paused, and then he said, ''I wonder if they will kill me because I am the emperor's aide.''

''I do not think so, Gaius Cicero. Simply pledge your fealty to Rome, to the new emperor. Seek out Senator Tacitus, and explain to him that you are naught but a simple soldier, not a politician. He is a fair man, and he will protect you. So will your family. Yours is an old and honorable name, Cicero.''

Gaius Cicero looked heartened by her words. ''You are probably right. Had I been with the emperor I surely would have been struck down, but the gods seemed to have arranged differently.''

Too quickly they were in Rome, and Zenobia found herself being escorted into a building of deceptively innocent white marble. Fabius Marcellus took her by the arm and presented her to the jailer.

''I have the prisoner, Zenobia of Palmyra, on the senate's orders. She is to be held for interrogation.''

Fabius Marcellus loosened his grip on her arm, and Zenobia turned to Gaius Cicero. ''Do not forget your promise, Gaius Cicero,'' she said before following after the jailor.

They went through a door, and the stink that suddenly assailed her was worse than anything she had ever smelled. She gasped, and coughed, sudden tears coming to her eyes. ''You'll get used to it,'' the jailor said matter-of-factly.

''Never!'' she said. ''What on earth is it?''

''The stink of human misery,'' he answered her.

Glancing around her as she followed after the jailor, Zenobia shuddered with distaste. They were moving down a flight of stairs and she could see that both the steps and the walls were slippery with slime. Pitch torches stuck in crude iron holders lit the way, flickering smokily and eerily. Reaching the bottom of the steps, he led her along a corridor lined with small wooden doors; there was no sound but the occasional rustle of rodents in the straw that lined the way. At the very end of the corridor he stopped, removed his key ring from his belt, and unlocked a door.

''In there, my fine lady,'' he said, pointing through the open door.

Zenobia ducked her head as she moved through the entry and into the cell. Behind her the door slammed, and she heard the lock scraping as the jailor turned the key in it. A quick look around the room convinced her that she was alone, and she breathed easier. Free now to explore her surroundings, she noted that the cell was small and obviously below ground level, for there was no window. A small pitch torch lit it, and for that she was grateful. If she had been thrown into darkness it would have been utterly terrifying, like being buried alive in one's tomb. There was straw on the floor, and in an alcove in the wall a cracked pitcher of tepid water had been set. There was nothing else to see, and so she sat down on the floor to wait. After a while she dozed.

She was startled awake by the sound of the key in the lock again, and quickly scrambled to her feet with pounding heart to face two men who came into the cell.

"You may close the door," one of the men said to the jailor, who instantly complied.

The other turned to Zenobia and bowed politely. "Majesty, I am Celsus, the physician. I have been appointed by the senate to examine you to determine whether or not you are with child."

"I understand," Zenobia replied. "What would you have me do, Celsus?"

The physician looked to the other man. "This is an impossible place in which to examine a patient, Senator."

"Nevertheless the senate commands it," was the reply.

"Does the senate think I might have a *clean* basin with some warm water, and additional light, Senator?"

The senator flushed. "Of course. You may see to it while I entertain Queen Zenobia. Hurry! This place is disgusting, and I wish to leave as quickly as possible."

The physician bowed sarcastically, called to the jailer, and left with him to obtain what he needed. The other man looked long at Zenobia, finally saying, "I am Senator Valerian Hostilius, Majesty. I have been appointed by the senate to oversee this examination."

"I remember you, Senator. I believe you wished to feed me to the lions the last time we met," Zenobia said scornfully.

"It would have been better if the senate had listened to me," Hostilius said. "We can have no heirs of Aurelian!"

"I am not with child, Senator," Zenobia said calmly.

"So you say! So you say! I, however, was in the Temple of the Unconquerable Sun the night of the rites. The emperor was like a stallion that night! *He was the god! He was!* And you are the goddess! Even I can see it." Hostilius licked his lips excitedly. "Every one of the women he took that night has conceived a child, and you tell me you are *not* with child. I will not believe it unless the physician says it is so!"

"Those women coupled with every man at that obscene orgy, not just the emperor," Zenobia snapped at him. "Aurelian is not capable of siring a child! His own wife says it." Then a horrifying thought crossed her mind. "What has happened to those women that Aurelian took that night?" she asked.

"Dead!" was his answer. "All dead. We could have no spawn of Aurelian coming back to haunt us."

"By the gods," she whispered, "you are all mad!"

At that moment the physician returned with the jailer, and the required items. While the jailer set more light about the cell, the physician placed his basin of warm water upon the alcove shelf and washed his hands.

"You will have to disrobe, Majesty," he said somewhat apologetically, and then snapped at the open mouthed jailer, "Out! Out, you vermin! There is nothing for you to see here." The jailer scuttled away slamming the door as he went.

"Must *he* be here?" Zenobia demanded, looking at Hostilius.

"I remain on the senate's orders lest you coerce this man into lying."

"*What?*" Celsus looked outraged. "My reputation is one of honesty, Valerian Hostilius!"

"Nonetheless I remain on the senate's orders," was the pompous reply.

Celsus looked to Zenobia. "I am sorry, Majesty. I have never before examined a patient under such circumstances, and I do apologize."

She nodded sympathetically at him, and then said, "What must I do?"

"When you have disrobed, you will please to lie upon the straw here."

Ignoring Hostilius, Zenobia removed her clothing and lay down upon the straw. She could feel the chill of the cell now, and involuntarily she shuddered. His look offered commiseration.

The physician palpated her stomach and examined her breasts. Then taking infinite care not to hurt her, he gently examined her internally. Finally satisfied, Celsus arose from his position on the floor and, washing his hands again, said, "Queen Zenobia is *not* with child, Senator. I will tender my report in writing to the senate, but you may tell them that she is absolutely, positively not with child."

427

Zenobia sat up, somewhat lightheaded. "Then I can be released?"

"Unless the senate has other reasons for retaining you in custody, Majesty, I can see no reason why you can't be released now." He looked to Hostilius. "Senator?"

"You are not empowered to make official decisions, physician. You have done your duty, now get you gone!"

Zenobia struggled to her feet, her instincts warning her of impending danger.

Celsus took a quick look at Hostilius, and then said, "I will wait for you, Senator. We came together, we shall leave together."

Hostilius threw him a furious look, swallowed visibly, and then muttered, "Very well, I am ready."

Celsus bowed to Zenobia. "Again, Majesty, I apologize for the inconvenience."

Her eyes spoke her thanks to him before he turned and left the cell with the senator. Slowly Zenobia redressed, then sat back down to await her release. The extra lamps that the jailer had brought helped to cast a more cheerful light about the grim cell, and they even released a bit of warmth into the chill air. The time crawled by. In an effort to make it go faster she began to sing softly to herself.

Suddenly the door to the cell creaked open, and it occurred to Zenobia that she hadn't heard the key in the lock. She rose to face Hostilius. He smiled nastily at her.

"You thought that you were rid of me, didn't you?" he leered.

The door closed behind him. Now she heard the key turning in the lock. "What do you want, Senator?" she said, keeping her voice steady.

"You haunt me," Hostilius said. "Ever since *that* night in the Temple of the Unconquerable Sun, when I saw how beautiful you are, and how passionate, I have wanted you! Soon Aurelian will be dead. The plot is made, the conspirators chosen. It is only a matter of time, and he will be dead! You will need a new protector, Zenobia. You will need someone powerful to take care of you. The empire can be harsh with its captives, but if you will accept my protection, I will shower you with riches!"

Zenobia stared at the senator in genuine surprise, and then she began to laugh. Her laughter shattered the heavy silence of the prison cell, and echoed from wall to wall with open mockery. Hostilius started with surprise, then grew red with anger;

428

but before he could speak she regained control of herself, and said, "You have to be jesting, Valerian Hostilius! I am Zenobia, the Queen of Palmyra, not some expensive courtesan for hire."

"You are an imperial captive, and Aurelian's whore!" he reminded her.

"I am indeed an imperial captive," she snapped back at him, "but if the emperor is to be deposed, then I will no longer have to be *his whore*, Senator, and I will most certainly not be *yours!*"

"*I want you!*" He moved toward her, the violence of his lust clear in his eyes, in his movements.

Her eyes swept the tiny cell for something to defend herself with, but there was nothing. Now it was Hostilius, seeing her predicament, who laughed. "If you harm me I will complain to the senate," she threatened him. "The jailer will identify you, Hostilius, and the physician saw your intent."

"The jailer has been well paid to keep his mouth shut, and Celsus did not see me return." He reached out for her, and she shrank back against the wall. He chuckled, delighted by her reticence. "Come now," he wheedled. "I won't hurt you. I am said to be a good lover, and you are no maid to be coy with me."

She looked at him, horrified. He was a nasty little man, she thought, at least two inches shorter than she, with a balding head of sparse black hair; a fat slug of a man with pudgy, plump hands. He was so white that he seemed almost bloodless.

"You will take off your clothes for me," he said in a soft, dangerous-sounding voice.

"I will not!"

From among the folds of his tunic and toga he suddenly withdrew a small dog whip. "I am very proficient with this," he said, flicking it perilously near her face. "I could put out your eye should I choose to do so." She stood as still as a flushed rabbit as he rubbed the whip against her cheek. "Take off your clothes, Zenobia," he repeated.

"You pig!" she hissed at him.

"Take off your clothes," he smiled, knowing that he had won.

As she slowly removed her tunic dress she debated the wisdom of physically attacking him. She was taller than the senator, but he outweighed her considerably. What would she do with him if she overpowered him? The jailer certainly wasn't going to come to her aid. It was an impossible situation, and Hostilius decided the matter by grabbing one of her arms as she freed herself of her clothing, yanking it up, and imprisoning it within a wall manacle. She gasped as the cold iron bracelet snapped shut about her wrist.

"What are you doing?" she cried, frightened now.

"Don't worry," he soothed her as he fastened her other wrist within the restraint. "I have the key to unlock you afterward."

She hung now from the wall, her toes just barely grazing the straw on the floor. The wall behind her was cold and wet, causing her to arch her body outward. With trembling fingers Hostilius slowly slid her garments over her hips and down her legs to the floor. Then he stood back and stared at her. His eyes were glazed with desire, his mouth hung slack with his lechery.

Finally he spoke, his voice hoarse with hunger. "You are even more beautiful than I remember." As he groaned she saw a wet stain begin to spread on his toga, and she realized with disgust that he had been unable to contain himself.

She hoped that having spilled his seed upon the straw he would be unable to continue, but Hostilius did not even appear to notice what had happened, and reached out to touch her breasts. Zenobia shrank from him, her back making contact with the wet, cold stones of the cell wall. His fleshy fingers began to brush the warmth of her skin, slowly at first, and then as his lust caught up with him, he grasped her breasts in his two hands and squeezed fiercely, making her wince with pain, leaving marks upon her pale golden flesh. With a moan he pressed up close against her, his head swiveling swiftly to find a nipple and then suck it deep within his mouth.

He drew insistently upon her breast, like a hungry child, his mouth ferocious and demanding. She was totally repelled by him, and struggled to twist her body away from him, but he merely grasped her hips to hold her still while he continued his obscene parody. Having wrung all he could from one breast, his balding head moved to the other.

"You are disgusting!" she said. "You are totally repellent to me! Can you not function normally with a woman? Must you force them in order to obtain satisfaction?"

In answer he bit down upon her breast, and she cried out in pain, her arms jerking instinctively to strike him. His hands moved around behind her, crushing her buttocks in a brutal grip. She tried to retaliate, drawing her knees up, and then kicking out at him. Her numbed feet made contact with his soft middle, and Hostilius staggered back from Zenobia with an "offff!" sound. Regaining his balance, he came at her, the little dog whip flying, cutting into her tender thighs and belly, making her cry out in pain again. Still she taunted him, "Monster! Slithering reptile! Free me, and then attempt your rape! You are not man enough!"

"You will see how masculine I am, bitch," he snarled at her, "when I fuck you! You will beg me to continue! To never stop!" The little whip slashed at her again and again, and she was bleeding from several small cuts on her legs and stomach.

Zenobia was more angry than frightened now, and she continued to mock him. "You are a pig, Hostilius! You have already spilled your seed in your lust, and I do not believe that you can replenish it! It is probably the first time in months that you were able to rise to the occasion!"

"I think," he said menacingly, "that I shall share you with the jailer."

She laughed scornfully. "Must you see another man rape me before you are able to function, Hostilius!?"

Valerian Hostilius grew beet red, and then a very evil look came into his eyes. He smiled nastily at her, and said, "I know just how to still your vicious tongue." The dog whip flicked out at her nipple, and she winced, suddenly unnerved by his manner. He walked to the door and pounded upon it. Almost instantly the entry creaked open and the jailer entered, his eyes darting to Zenobia, his own craving evident. Hostilius smiled again. "I need help with this recalcitrant bitch, jailer. Aid me, and she is yours when I have finished. When I am through with her she will be all cozy and obedient, I promise you."

The jailer licked his lips, and whined, "What if she tells, noble Senator? I have not your rank to protect me."

Hostilius laughed. "Do you think this proud bitch will admit to having been humped by a piece of vermin like you? Don't be ridiculous! Help me, now!"

"What do you want me to do, noble Senator?"

"I'm taking her down, and I want you to restrain her across your knees. I have a fancy to beat her bottom for a bit." Hostilius unlocked the iron manacles from Zenobia's wrists, and once again her feet made contact with the floor. "Don't help him, good jailer!" she cried out. "I will say he sneaked into the cell when you weren't looking, and that unknowingly

you locked him in here with me. I will claim you found him
when my cries alerted you! Good jailer, I am a most important
imperial captive!''

Hostilius dealt Zenobia a staggering blow to the side of her
head. ''Pay no attention to the bitch! She is no one!'' The whip
descended upon her tender flesh, forcing a cry through her
clenched teeth.

''Have you ever taken a woman like one takes a boy,'' Hostilius demanded of the jailer, and then he laughed. ''Yes, yes, I
can see you have! Well, I am going to take her like that now!
Lie her flat, jailer! I imagine that she is quite ready for me
now—aren't you, Zenobia?''

The jailer lay her face down in the straw, and then she felt
Hostilius climbing upon her buttocks. The jailer held her arms
down stretched above her head so she might not struggle. The
gods! she thought. Dogs mate this way, but people don't! She
felt his fingers beginning to separate the halves of her bottom,
felt something slimy trying to push at her, and suddenly she
screamed as loud as she could. ''Nooo! Nooooooo!''

There was a roar of outrage from the doorway of the cell,
her arms were suddenly loosened, and she felt Hostilius's weight
yanked off of her. The jailer was already babbling hysterically,
''I only did what he told me! I am a poor man, sir! Don't kill
me!''

''Let him go, Marcus,'' she heard Gaius Cicero say, and
then Marcus's voice replied, ''Run for your miserable life,
man, before I regret my merciful intent.''

She ached all over, but she was too weak to rise. She could
only lie there, face down in the straw, listening as her husband
said coldly, ''You're a dead man, Valerian Hostilius!'' And
then there was a strange sound, a wheezing sigh, and the thump
of a body hitting the floor. She didn't need to be told that the
senator was dead.

She fainted with relief.

Returning to consciousness, she was totally confused as to
where she was. As her eyes slowly focused she became aware
of movement, of the fact that she ached terribly, the very fabric
of her tunic scratching irritatingly against her skin. She was
dressed! She was in a litter! She was in Marcus's arms! She
was safe!

''Marcus!'' she whispered eagerly through cracked lips.

''Beloved!'' His face swam into view, growing clearer with
each moment.

"Praise the gods you came in time," she said softly. "He was going to—"

"I know what the swine was going to do," he said grimly.

"Gaius went to you?"

"Yes. They only held him long enough to be certain there was no counterplot. He has already sworn his fealty to the senate, and will be safe from harm no matter what happens to Aurelian."

"I am free?"

"Yes. The physician Celsus wasted no time in reporting to Senator Tacitus that you were not carrying Aurelian's child; and the order had already been given that you be released. Hostilius knew that it would be."

"Is he dead, Marcus?"

"Yes. I slit his fat throat!"

"We will go tomorrow?"

"Yes. I have requested permission in my mother's name to take you to the seaside to recuperate. Tacitus signed the order himself. I think he suspects that it is not my mother who wants to take you to the seaside. We could not get through the city gates to the port, however, without a pass from the senate. You are still an imperial captive."

"Are you taking me home?"

"Yes, my beloved. I am taking you home."

Her eyes closed again, and when she next awoke she was tucked into a comfortable bed within a house. She was stripped of her garments, but her wounds had been washed and dressed with a sweet-smelling unguent. The coverlet of the bed had been raised somehow, and although it sheltered her, it did not touch her sensitive skin. She sighed with relief, and instantly Dagian was at her side.

"My dearest daughter, praise Mother Juno that you are safe!" Her blue eyes were wet with tears.

"What time is it?"

"Almost dawn," came the reply.

"Have you watched by my bedside all night, Dagian?"

"Only the last hour, my dear. Marcus has been with you all night."

"I am all right," Zenobia reassured Dagian, "just somewhat sore. Marcus should not have sat up all night, especially when we must leave this day."

"We will not leave until the afternoon, Zenobia, and Marcus has changed our plans slightly. When he returned with you late

433

yesterday he sent word to his captain to take his ship from the old harbor at Ostia and move it to the new harbor at Portus. Rather than ride to the coast we are going to go by barge down the Tiber, and through the Claudian canal directly into the Portus harbor. It will be far more comfortable for you, my dear. Our household goods left here yesterday at dawn, and will be awaiting us tomorrow aboard the ship. A rider went after them late yesterday to tell them of the change in plans.''

"Then we sail tomorrow?"

"On the first tide after we arrive, my dear."

"I shall not be sorry to say good-bye to Italy, Dagian, as much as I fear your Britain."

"Fear Britain? Why should you fear my homeland?" Dagian was astounded.

"From what Marcus has told me over the years, Dagian, your land is a wild and fierce one."

"From what Marcus has told me, Zenobia, your homeland is a wild and fierce one," Dagian replied with a smile. "I think, my dear daughter, that it is merely a matter of familiarity. Britain seems frightening to you because you have never been there. Besides, I doubt that you will ever see one of our warriors painted blue and driving his chariot in battle." Then she laughed at the startled look on Zenobia's face.

"Your warriors paint themselves blue?"

"Indeed they do," Dagian said, chuckling.

"Why?"

"Because, my dear, our warriors believe that if they fall in battle, their enemies may strip them only of their possessions, but never of their dignity as long as they are painted blue."

Zenobia thought a moment, and then to Dagian's surprise she nodded her head, and said thoughtfully, "Yes, I understand that."

What a strange thing, Dagian thought. I meant to tease her about our warriors, and instead I have calmed her fears. "Go back to sleep, Zenobia," she said. "We have a long journey ahead of us."

She slept again, awakening close to midday. Both Bab and Adria were with her now, and her soreness was almost gone. She stretched, yawning lazily, and Bab hurried over to the bed, her face concerned. "The lady Dagian has told me of your ordeal, my baby! Curse the Romans! They are evil people!"

"My husband is a Roman, Bab."

434

"No, he is not!" was the quick reply. "Perhaps his father was, but Marcus Alexander Britainus is like his mother."

Zenobia laughed. "You have settled it in your mind, I can see. Very well, I shall not argue with you, old friend. However, I do wish to rise. Please see to my clothing."

While old Bab did as she was bid, Adria gently lifted the bed coverlet back, and helped Zenobia to get up. Her face flushed with embarrassment when she saw her mistress's body, and she turned away. Looking down, Zenobia gasped in shock. "Venus aid me!" she cried, for upon her breasts were distinct fingermarks, her lower torso was criss-crossed with narrow, raised red welts, and in a small table mirror she could see over her shoulder that her buttocks were badly bruised.

Turning around, Bab shrieked in horror and gaspingly clutched at her chest. "What have they done to you, my baby?!"

Zenobia was concerned less for herself than for the old lady who had so faithfully served her since childhood, and so she said, "It's all right, Bab. But do you know of some potion or unguent that will help me erase these bruises quickly?"

Diverted, the old woman thought a moment, and then said, "I will send one of the slaves to the apothecary's shop for what I need. Do not fear, my baby, I will have the mark of that beast gone as quickly as possible. What crassness to mark your lovely skin so! Why even the emperor never treated you thus!"

"No," Zenobia said, "he didn't," and she remembered Hostilius's remark about the difference in treatment among imperial captives.

Early in the afternoon they left the house of the Alexander family. They traveled to the barge landing by litter, the slaves and the servants walking along beside them. It was not a particularly large or impressive party, nothing that would attract attention. In addition to Adria, Bab, and Charmian, there were half a dozen Alexander family slaves. At the docks their papers were checked and approved by a centurion, for no one entered or exited the city without permission.

The barge was luxurious, but not overlarge. It had a sail that was now raised to catch the afternoon winds, and they began their trip downriver to the harbor at Portus.

The weather was fair and warm, but still they traveled, master and servants alike, in a state of nervous expectation. Neither Marcus nor Zenobia nor Dagian would feel entirely safe until they were at sea. When night fell slaves and family partook of a simple meal upon the open deck of the barge. It was a meal that they had supplied themselves, for the bargemaster was bound only to offer them passage and shelter to Portus.

When night fell the slaves settled themselves to sleep upon the open deck while the family and their personal servants sought shelter in the barge's cabin. There were but two bunks, and Dagian was settled in one, while Mavia and old Bab were put in the other.

Bab protested loudly. "No, no, my baby, it is not right that you sleep upon the floor while I rest in comfort."

"Peace, old woman!" Zenobia said. "Remember your years. In the last months you have been dragged from Palmyra to Rome, and now you undertake another long journey. I would have you comfortable so you will always be here to serve me. What, Bab, would I do without you?"

"I will be with you as long as the gods allow, and no longer," Bab said.

Marcus smiled warmly at the faithful old servant, and he put a kindly arm about her sturdy shoulders. "Britain will be lovelier, Bab, if your old bones do not ache. Sleep with Mavia, and argue no longer."

Bab looked adoringly up at him, a look that Zenobia had never seen her bestow before upon any man. "Yes, master," she said, "and I thank you for your kindness to me."

Adria and Charmian were settled, one beneath each bunk, and then Marcus and Zenobia returned outside to sit on the open deck. Above them, the warm spring night glistened with a million bright stars. The river gently caressed the flat bottom of the boat, and the wind teased at the loose tendrils of Zenobia's long, black hair as she faced downriver.

He stood behind her, his arms wrapped securely about her waist, drawing her firmly against him. For a long while they were silent, and she marveled that just his simple gesture of holding her could make her feel so marvelous, so loved, so cherished. She adored the hardness of his chest against her back, the softness of his breath against her hair.

"I am so glad that you love me," she said quietly.

He laughed softly. "At last we are together."

"Do not say it," she begged. "Not yet. Not until we have escaped the empire. Once we are free of Rome then I shall care not what happens as long as we are together, Marcus. I have loved you for so very long that I dare not believe in this happy ending quite yet."

"We are together, Zenobia, now and forever," he said with quiet assurance, "and we shall rebuild our lives on the edge of Britain, and rear our daughter in safety, and have a son to love and raise."

"I yet fear the motives of the gods," she said softly.

"Do not fear them, beloved, for you are their chosen, and have always been."

He turned her now, and his mouth touched hers with infinite gentleness, tasting as a bee tastes of precious nectar, caressing possessively, communicating his love of her, his need of her. With a sigh she returned the kiss, her lips parting for him, her arms wrapping about his neck to mold her lushness against his hardness. His tongue darted through her lips and about her mouth, touching with wildfire the tip and sides of her tongue, the roof of her mouth, the corners of her mouth. The kiss deepened, growing more ardent, more possessive, stoking the passionate fires burning deep within them both. Zenobia shuddered with surrender, but with the sudden realization of where they were Marcus very gently broke off the embrace, still holding her close to him.

She laughed weakly, and said low, "Never has any man ever driven me to such passion, my darling. If only there were a place upon this ship of yours where we might be alone. I do not think I can bear being parted from you for much longer."

He chuckled, and replied, "You are a most tempting morsel, and I long to ravish you with my love; but for now I think it best we seek the arms of Morpheus, and sleep."

Re-entering the cabin, he spread his large cape upon the floor, and they lay down to sleep.

Two hours after the dawn they arrived in the bustling harbor town of Portus, having passed from the Tiber River through the Claudian Canal. At the dock they were met by the Alexander family retainers, and litters that carried them down to the waterfront where Marcus's ship awaited them.

It was a magnificent vessel, its dark wood sides polished to a glistening red-brown sheen. The stern of the ship was beautifully carved with scenes of leaping porpoises, ocean nymphs gamboling amid the waves, and delicate whorled shells, all exquisitely gilded with gold. The deck was of well-rubbed light-colored oak. The four light-blue sails—a square mainsail, the two triangular sails called lateen sails above the mainsail, and the small square sail at the bow called the artemon—were of the finest canvas. The vessel was one hundred eighty feet in length, and forty-five feet in width.

There were two rudders, one on either side of the stern. The helmsmen stood upon a small elevated deck that had on it the upper half of a swan, painted quite realistically and hollowed so that it might serve as a shelter for the captain of the vessel or one of the helmsmen when he was not at his steering oar.

On the main deck was the master's cabin, made up of two rooms, the larger front room an airy and light place where they would eat. Behind the main cabin and beneath the steering deck was set a smaller inside cabin, where Marcus and Zenobia would sleep in privacy.

Below decks was the enormous cargo hold and a place for the crew to sleep. Also below the decks would be all of the Alexander household slaves, but it would not be overly crowded, for the cargo space would be only half full with all the family's goods.

The merchantman, called a corbitae, was a round ship. It was sturdy and reliable, but could easily be caught by a faster bireme or trireme, Roman warships, which were not only sail-powered, but oar-powered. It was therefore important that the Alexander family cause no attention to be drawn to them. The captain had been ordered to file a course for Cyprus with the authorities, and only when they were under way would Marcus order that course changed. The fewer people involved in his secret the better.

Little Mavia was delighted with the ship, and promptly told everyone so. "What is it called, Mama?" she demanded of Zenobia, who turned to Marcus for help.

"It is called the *Sea Nymph*, my daughter," he answered her.

"I am not your daughter, am I?" Mavia asked innocently.

Marcus lifted the child up into his arms, and looked into the blue eyes so like his own. Gently he brushed the chestnut hair, also like his. "You are my own true child, and I love you," he answered her simply.

Mavia put her arms about his neck and kissed him upon the cheek. "I have always wanted a father," she said. "I am glad you are my papa."

It was as simple as that. From that time on, Mavia, the Princess of Palmyra, disappeared into the mists of time. There was only Mavia, the daughter of Marcus Alexander Britainus, and for Mavia, it was as if he had always been there. Although until this moment she had never called him Father, she would, when she grew older, never remember *not* having called him Father.

Zenobia's eyes were bright with unshed tears. "Thank you," she said to her husband, and Marcus understood.

"It was the right time," he told her.

Then, together, they went aboard the *Sea Nymph* to be warmly greeted by Captain Paulus. Charmian took Mavia off to see the ship, and the others settled themselves while Zenobia and Marcus spoke with the captain.

"The next tide is two hours after midday, sir," the captain said. "With your permission we can sail then."

"Is there a reason to stay longer, my love?" Marcus asked.

"No," she replied. "I am willing to sail this day."

"So be it then!" Marcus looked to the captain, who nodded his agreement.

"We've all our supplies aboard, and plenty of fresh water, sir. If you, my lady, need any extras you would be wise to purchase them now. I can have one of my men escort you to the harbor shops."

"I do not think that I lack for anything," Zenobia replied, "but I shall call my servants and visit the shops you suggest. Mayhap in the looking we will see something we need. Your escort will be most welcome."

Zenobia sought out Dagian and Adria, and the three women spent the next hour shopping in the company of two brawny sailors. As they returned to the *Sea Nymph* Zenobia's heart lurched as she saw a familiar figure standing upon the deck with her husband. The three women climbed the gangway, and while Adria hurried to store away their few purchases Dagian and Zenobia came forward to meet Marcus and his guest.

"Gaius Cicero, it is good to see you," Dagian said cordially.

The tribune bowed from the waist, and replied, "And as always, Lady Dagian, it is good to see you. You are well?"

"I am. How is Clodia? And your children?"

"They thrive."

There was a short awkward silence, and then Dagian said, "Come, Zenobia, let us see to Mavia."

"No." Marcus looked to his wife. "You go, Mother. I would like Zenobia to stay here with us for a few moments. You will keep Mavia occupied for us."

Dagian withdrew, and Zenobia looked at the two men. "Well," she said, "what is it? I can tell that all is not right."

439

"I have an order for your return to Rome, Majesty."

"Never!"

Both men were startled by the vehemence in her reply, and in an effort to calm her Marcus put a hand on her arm, but she shook it off angrily.

"I would die before I would return to Rome, Gaius Cicero. I am tired of wars, and I am tired of politics! My only wish now is to live my life in peace. If I cannot then take your sword and kill me, for I will not return to Rome!" She looked to her husband. "Have you told him?"

Marcus shook his head.

"Tell him!" she commanded.

"Tell me what?" Gaius Cicero looked puzzled.

"Zenobia and I have been married for two months now, Gaius. We have witnesses—my mother and Zenobia's two freedwomen."

"By the gods," the tribune said in a low voice, "you are leaving Italy!"

"We are."

"I cannot let you, Marcus. The senate must be informed of Queen Zenobia's marriage to you. They will, of course, set the marriage aside, for with a mate the queen becomes dangerous once more to Rome. I'm sorry, but I cannot let you go." He looked honestly regretful.

"You owe me!" Zenobia snarled, and suddenly she was once again all queen. She drew herself up to her full height, and looking Gaius Cicero directly in the eye, her gaze was proud. He remembered the first time he had seen her standing in all her queenly array atop the walls of Palmyra, defying the mighty Roman Empire. "I warned you of Aurelian's impending fall so that your wife need not mourn *your* death, so that your children both born and unborn would not lose their father. Gaius Cicero, I gave you your life! Now give me mine!"

"Majesty, if it were my decision I would wish you Neptune's own luck wherever you went. But it is not my decision. I am only a servant of the empire, but I am a good servant. I will not betray my people."

"We do not ask you to betray Rome, Gaius," Marcus said quietly. "Zenobia and I have nothing to do with Rome. We are nothing more but a man and his wife trying to begin anew amid the ruins of our old lives. Palmyra is gone. It will never again arise from the destruction that Rome inflicted upon it. Its young king lives in exile with his family, its younger prince is lost in time. There is no longer a Queen of Palmyra, there is only Zenobia, the wife of Marcus Alexander, the mother, the woman. Let her go, Gaius.''

During his impassioned speech Zenobia found herself pressing close to her husband. They were at last a family, she and Marcus and Mavia. This time when he put his arm around her, she melted back into the embrace with pride, for she was proud to be his wife.

Gaius Cicero looked at them, and knew in that instant that they would not be separated. He knew that they would die first, or that his old friend, Marcus Alexander Britainus, would even set their long friendship aside and slit his throat before he would let Gaius take her back to Rome. He didn't know why the senate had changed their minds, but, he reasoned, how important could it be? Aurelian's execution was a certainty, and Zenobia was fleeing the empire. He could see that she posed no danger.

"I came ahead of my soldiers," he said. "There is no one to know that I saw you. Who will contradict me when I say that your ship had already sailed when I reached Portus?''

"Thank you, my friend," Marcus said gratefully.

"What course do you set?"

"Cyprus," came the answer.

Gaius Cicero's face said that he did not believe for a minute that Cyprus was actually their destination. "I have no order to follow you," he said. "I shall ascertain your destination from the harbor master and return to Rome with my information." Then he smiled at them. "May the gods speed your journey, my friends, and bring you to safety.''

The two men clasped arms in the old Roman fashion, then Gaius Cicero turned abruptly and left the ship, walking away into the bustle upon the dock.

Marcus turned and spoke to a nearby sailor. "Is everyone aboard?''

"Yes, sir!" was the reply.

"Then take the gangway up," the ship's owner commanded. Giving Zenobia a quick kiss on the forehead, he hurried off to find Captain Paulus. The captain was on the helmsman's deck. "I have ordered the gangway drawn up," Marcus told him. "Is not the tide turning now?''

"Yes, sir," was the reply. "I am just now giving orders to get underway.''

"Change your course," Marcus said.

441

"Change my course? For where, sir?"

"For Massalia, Captain Paulus."

"If we are to catch this tide, sir, there is no time for me to inform the harbor master."

"That is indeed unfortunate, Captain Paulus," Marcus said thoughtfully, "for I do want to depart now."

"What harm can it do, sir," the captain replied. "We are only transporting our new owner, and his family, and their goods and chattel. It can be of little import to the mighty Roman Empire." So saying, the captain began to give orders, and the ship slowly got underway, taking its place amid the vessels catching this tide.

Marcus Alexander Britainus returned to the main deck below, and stood with Zenobia at the rail, watching the activity of the harbor as *Sea Nymph*'s sails caught the afternoon wind and began to move gradually out into the open sea.

"I remember," he said, and he caught at her hand, "the day that we arrived here from Britain those long years ago. How different it was from my homeland. I never loved Rome the way I love Britain, nor did I love Rome the way I loved Palmyra." He sighed. "I wonder," he said, "if I shall still love Britain. It can be a harsh place, Zenobia. You are not used to chill weather, and Britain can be cold."

"You have told me that the climate is mild on the island where we shall make our home. You have told me that palm trees grow on our island. Palms cannot exist in a harsh climate. As long as the palms thrive, then so shall I, my love."

They had cleared the harbor, and as the *Sea Nymph* swept into the open sea Zenobia felt a small thrill of excitement. Strangely, the sea did not frighten her, child of the desert that she was. She found it very much like the desert, vast and rolling and ever-changing. It seemed to go on forever, and in the days ahead she found that she could stand at the rail for hours, her eyes seeking, searching, ever watching, for what she knew not.

It had been early spring when they left Portus, and now they would shortly be reaching Massilia, the great and ancient port in that part of Caesar's Gaul known as Narbonensis. Here, the Alexander family would leave their ship and journey up through Gaul, using the roads traveled for centuries by the tin caravans. On the north coast of Gaul they would once again meet up with *Sea Nymph* and cross the channel to Britain. Because of the dangers of sea travel Marcus had preferred his family to travel by land where safe routes existed. The slaves would remain with the ship; but Zenobia and Dagian's personal servants, Mavia's nurse, and Severus would travel with the family.

At Massilia there was no undue activity about the docks, nor any interest shown in the *Sea Nymph* or her passengers. Marcus breathed a deep sigh of relief, though he realized that if Gaius Cicero had returned to Rome with the information that they had sailed for Cyprus, there would be a pursuit ordered in that direction. When their pursuers discovered no trace of them, the search would probably be ordered in the direction of Britain; but by then the trail would be cold, and they would be where Rome could not reach.

They left *Sea Nymph,* and traveled easily and quickly up from the coast bordering the Mediterranean to the coast on the channel that faced Britain.

The weather was pleasant, and they traveled amid the beauty of Gaul with its flower-filled fields and its great forests of oak. It was the forests with their soaring trees and dappled sunlight that made Zenobia nervous. She had never seen such vast expanses of trees, and she did not like being shut off from her sun. The nights they spent in the forests were most frightening to her, and she lay hollow-eyed and wide awake against Marcus, who slept unconcerned by her side. Every hoot of an owl, every unexplained rustle (and the long night seemed full of them) set her heart beating quicker. Zenobia welcomed their arrival at the coast where *Sea Nymph* waited to ferry them across to Britain.

They sailed from Gaul on an evening tide. By morning they would be in Britain. Zenobia dozed fitfully that night, her entire body attuned to the dawn, and when it came she rose from her place and wrapped herself in a long cloak before leaving the cabin. There was no wind, and the sky was white. *Sea Nymph* bobbed gently amid the clouds of fog, the only sound the rhythmic splash of the sea against the sides of the ship.

Then, as they sky began to grow a clear blue and the mists were driven away by the rising wind, she saw ahead of her a large island, its white cliffs rising out of the sea. Behind her she heard a step so familiar she didn't even bother to turn. "What is it, Marcus?"

"It is the island of Vectis, and just beyond it is Portus Adurni, where we shall land."

"What makes the cliffs so white?"

"They are made of chalk," he said.

"Interesting," she replied, then added, "Will Vaba and his family be awaiting us in Portus Adurni?"

"No," he said quietly.

"Are they already upon our island, or are they to come after us?"

He sighed. "They are not coming at all, beloved."

"Not coming?" She turned and looked up at him. "Why are they not coming, Marcus?"

"Because Vaba chooses not to come. Cyrene is not the grandest place in the Roman world, but he prefers to remain there with Flavia and their daughter. He has found contentment."

Quick tears sprang to her eyes. "He is rejecting me, Marcus. He is rejecting his own mother! He has never forgiven me for Palmyra, and I doubt he ever will. My children are gone, and I am alone."

"Your children are all alive, although they choose to live their own lives, beloved. Demi was found amid the ruins of the city, and has been nursed back to health by your brothers. He chooses to remain with the Bedawi. So the sons of Odenathus have survived despite all, and we have our daughter! The gods have taken away with one hand, it is true, but they have also given with the other."

She cried then, weeping against his chest until her sorrow was finally purged. Then, sniffing loudly, she looked up at him. With a loving smile he kissed her on her nose, and she had to laugh softly, for it was the sort of thing a mischievous little boy would have done. "I love you," he said, "and we are about to begin a new life. Put the past behind you, Zenobia. Only today and tomorrow matter."

"Yes, she said, "you are right, Marcus, and yet I cannot help but be sad. They were only little boys the last time I looked, and now suddenly they are grown men and they do not need me any longer."

"I need you," he answered her, "and our daughter needs you, and the son you will give me needs you!"

"I know, Marcus, but let me mourn my loss without guilt. Sometimes a woman needs time to mourn such a loss. I shall not die of grief, never fear."

Sea Nymph sailed past Vectis, and around the island's headland into the harbor of Portus Adurni. Compared to the great harbors she had seen, this one was tiny, and yet it was a main port of entry for Roman Britain. Around them on the deck great activity was taking place as the ship's sailors prepared for landing.

"Look!" Marcus pointed. "There is my brother, Aulus, come to meet us!"

"*Your brother?* How did he know we were coming?"

"*Sea Nymph* arrived on the Gaulish coast before we did. Before we left the ship at Massilia I had instructed Captain Paulus that he was to send a messenger ahead to Britain as soon as he reached Gaul. That is why Aulus is here." He turned back to the rail and, grinning, shouted, "Aulus! You are getting fat!"

"And you are graying like an old man!" came back the laughing reply.

The ropes from the ship were thrown shoreward and made fast. The gangway was lowered, and Aulus Alexander Britainus rushed aboard to embrace his brother. There were tears in his blue eyes, although, to his older brother's amusement, he quickly brushed them aside. Still, Marcus was touched. "Praise the gods you are safe!" Aulus said. "And our mother?"

"I have brought her to safety also," Marcus replied.

The two broke apart and stood for a moment staring delightedly at each other. Then Aulus's eyes swung about to light upon Zenobia, and he boldly assessed her. She stared back as coolly. Finally Aulus grinned in a boyish, impudent fashion.

"Is this Zenobia?" he demanded.

Marcus chuckled. "Yes, you overgrown roughneck, this is Zenobia, my wife. Zenobia, this is my charming but rude younger brother, Aulus."

"Hail, brother!" Zenobia said, and then she mischievously embraced him, kissing him on both cheeks and pressing her beautiful bosom against his chest.

As her heady hyacinth scent rose up to assail him Aulus felt a quick stab of desire, and he gasped in surprise. Both Marcus and Zenobia laughed. "Whew!" chuckled the younger Alexander. "I surrender, sister. You are more woman than I'm prepared to deal with, and I bow to my brother's ability."

"As well you should," Zenobia teased him, and then she turned to her husband. "I will go and fetch Dagian. She will want to see this reprobate, I am sure."

Aulus and Marcus both watched her go, and with a grin Aulus congratulated his older brother. "By the gods, she is a beauty! You'll get a host of sons on her, brother!"

"Perhaps if we are fortunate, Aulus, but I will not endanger her life to insure my immortality. Zenobia and I are no longer children, though we be newly married. We already have a child, and if Mavia is all we ever have then I shall be satisfied."

"But Zenobia's daughter is the child of her late husband. That does not count."

"Zenobia's daughter is mine, brother."

Aulus still did not understand, but then he saw the little girl exiting the main cabin of the ship, running toward them.

"Papa! Is this Britain? Are we here?"

Marcus swept her up in his arms, and Aulus gaped at the two heads so alike in color, the matching blue eyes, and the child's nose and jaw, so like his and Marcus's. "Mavia, this is your Uncle Aulus," Marcus said matter-of-factly.

Mavia held out her arms to Aulus, and, charmed, he lifted her from her father's grasp into his own. She kissed him sweetly. "How do you do, Uncle Aulus."

"I do very well, little Mavia," he said.

"Do you have a little girl like me?" she asked him.

"Indeed I do! Today you will start your journey to Salinae, where we have a fine villa. You have lots of little cousins awaiting your arrival, Mavia, and I promise you a very good time."

Mavia clapped her hands gleefully. "Do you hear that, Papa! I have cousins who wait to play with me! I have never had any cousins before. I shall like this Britain! I know I shall!"

Aulus put her down, and she ran off, re-entering the cabin as Zenobia exited it.

"Your mother will be here shortly," Zenobia said.

"What news of the emperor?" Marcus demanded.

"Which emperor? Aurelian is dead, assassinated outside of Byzantium. Tacitus reigns."

"The old senator?"

"Yes. The army asked the senate to appoint him, as it could not agree upon a candidate."

"Has there been any outcry over the disappearance of the queen?"

"None. I have not even heard she was missing. The Empress Ulpia, however, died, they say, at the very hour of Aurelian's death."

"Faithful Ulpia," Zenobia said. "She will serve him as well in death as she did in life."

"You are sure, Aulus? You are sure that there has been no mention of Zenobia at all?"

"None that I have heard, Marcus, and I am privy to accurate information."

"We are safe then?" Zenobia queried him.

"Perhaps, beloved, but nonetheless I will take no chances." He touched her face in an affectionate gesture, and then turned back to his brother. "Aulus, I wish to purchase from you the island off the southern coast that grandfather's concubine brought him as her dowry."

"It is yours, brother, but I will not take your gold. It is my wedding gift to you. What will you do with it?"

"We will live there, Aulus. There I believe Zenobia and I will be safe from any pursuit."

"Yes," Aulus agreed, "you will be safe, and I will help see to that. With the luck of the gods we will have plenty of time to prepare. First, however, you must come to Salinae so that Zenobia may meet the rest of the family."

"I had thought to go immediately to the island," Marcus said.

"With that *Roman* ship of yours, and its *Roman* crew? No, brother, I think not. When it returns to Rome, all the captain and crew can say is that you were brought to Portus Adurni. Past here they will be able to tell the authorities nothing. This land of ours may be an island, but it is a large island. *Our* own people will get you to your island, Marcus."

"*Aulus!*" Dagian hurried up to her son and kissed him. "Did I not tell you it was not my fate to die in a foreign land? I am home after all these years! I can scarcely believe it! Tell me how fares Eada and my grandchildren?"

He returned the kiss, and smilingly told her, "Both my wife and the children are all well. If you are ready, Mother, we shall begin our journey to Salinae."

Dagian nodded happily and turned to Marcus, Zenobia, and Mavia. "We are going home, my children," she said, and they were all unable to contain their joy.

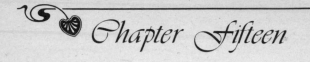

Chapter Fifteen

Portus Adurni had not been particularly impressive, being more a village in size, though it had its baths and temple to Jupiter. The streets were hardened dirt and, Zenobia imagined, in winter a sea of mud. Although Rome's influence was evident in the soldiers and the more prosperous citizens who affected Roman garb, these were outnumbered by tall, black-haired, light-eyed and fair-skinned men and women wearing their own colorful dress, including leg coverings for the men. She had stared openly, and was stared at in return.

Aulus Alexander Britainus had arranged that his brother's entire family be transported by wagons the hundred fifteen miles from Portus Adurni to his villa outside the small town of Salinae. Salinae was located in a beautiful river valley surrounded by gentle hills near the border of the Ordovices tribesmen in Wales. Even the slaves rode in the wagons, for the Alexander brothers wanted quickly to put as much distance between themselves and the coast as possible. The farther away they moved from the coast the less strong the Roman influence—and government.

Zenobia insisted upon being given her own horse. She reveled in this freedom, the first she had had since Aurelian had taken her prisoner at Palmyra. The countryside was like nothing she had ever seen before. "It is so *green*," she remarked several times almost to no one, and the brothers grinned over her head at each other.

She had always believed Palmyra the fairest thing upon the earth, but this green land with its orchards of pink and white blossoms, its fields of wild white daisies and purple yarrow, its rushing streams of clear water; it was all too much. The fields seemed to go on forever in their lushness; the hills rolled gently down to the valleys. Zenobia was falling more in love with the glorious countryside as each mile passed. Nonetheless she noticed a subtle change in her brother-in-law. The closer they came to the village of Salinae where the Alexander villa was located,

448

the less Roman he became, the trappings of the empire falling away from him easily. The morning of the day they were to arrive he appeared in a riding costume of a medium-blue knee-length tunica embroidered in gold thread around its lower edge and the long sleeves; deeper blue braccos, cross-gartered with bronze studded straps; and a dark-blue cloak fastened at the shoulder by a fibula.

"By the gods," Marcus drawled, amused, "you're affecting a Briton's dress, little brother."

"No, Marcus, I was affecting Roman dress in order to have easy access to the waterfront in Portus Adurni. I dress like a Briton because I am a Briton. My wife is a Briton, my children are British, and I live in Britain. I have never been a perfumed Roman."

"Our father was Roman," Marcus said in a tense voice.

"Our mother was not," came the reply.

"You reject Rome, Aulus?"

"I do. We do not need the Romans here in Britain."

Zenobia sighed. She might have been in Palmyra, and it might have been she who spoke, not Aulus. The Romans seemed to bring nothing but dissension with them. "Nothing changes," she said quietly.

They turned to look at her, and Marcus realized what she was thinking. "It will not be like Palmyra," he reassured her. "This is my brother's way of being his own man."

"Your brother is very much his own man," Dagian said. "He did not want to tell you, Marcus, but we are so near to Salinae that now I must. Aulus is chief of the Salinae Dobunni. He was elected by the tribe when his uncles were killed in a fight with at the Ordovices. It was just before he came to Rome at the time of your father's death. Your cousins had not the leadership ability, and in fact it was they who put him forth to be elected."

"So the elder brother, landless and now without power, must look to his younger sibling for succor," Marcus said. Suddenly he laughed, seeing humor in the situation. "You had best let me retire to the island, Aulus. If I decide to stay at Salinae I shall overcome you and rule the Dobunni myself. Can you see me, my hair long, twin mustaches drooping mournfully, my body painted blue, leading a screaming charge into a legion?"

Aulus laughed back, imagining the picture his elegant elder brother had painted. "I shall indeed give you the island, brother. You are far too civilized to be Britainized!"

449

"Briton or Roman, Aulus, I care not. All I wish now is to live in peace with Zenobia and our child. I have had enough of wars and intrigues!"

Aulus was sympathetic to his brother's wishes. His own life had been strangely easy, he realized now that he looked back with more objectivity than he had ever had. He had known from the moment he had met Eada that she was the woman for him, and they were today the proud parents of six sons and two daughters.

Aulus Alexander Britainus felt an enormous burst of love for his older brother and his sister-in-law. They deserved peace, and they deserved happiness. He was going to try to see that they got both.

They had long passed through Corinium and Glevum, and now the houses of the village of Salinae came into view. It was a pretty place, its white houses having red-tiled roofs, each building or group of buildings walled in from the street. There was a market in the center of the town, but it was a small place and there were no public baths or temples in evidence. As they entered the village Zenobia could hear the cry being taken up, "The master is home! The master comes!"

They rode beneath a tall, roofed gatehouse and into a pleasant courtyard. From the open portico of the house came a tall and lovely woman in a pale-blue tunic dress, her long yellow braids bound up at the back of her head, upon which rested a sheer white linen cloth held in place by a plain gold fillet. Aulus was off his horse in a minute to sweep the woman into his arms and place a resounding kiss upon her lips.

Laughingly she chided him, but her light-blue eyes were soft with love. "For shame, my lord, and before our guests!"

Marcus dismounted and carefully lifted Zenobia down from her horse. Drawing her forward, he said to the blond woman, "Eada, I am your brother-in-law, Marcus, and this is my wife, Zenobia."

"You are most welcome to Britain, brother and sister, and to our home!" was the cordial reply as Eada came shyly forward and kissed them both on the cheeks.

Dagian now stepped forward and stared at Eada. Eada stared back, and then the two women embraced. They had never before met, but they knew in an instant that they would be friends; and Dagian knew that her old age would be a safe and pleasant one in this young woman's house. "Where are the children?" Dagian begged.

From the portico eight youngsters came forth, and Eada, the love and pride shining from her eyes, proudly introduced her children to their grandmother. "My eldest son, Graf-ere. He has seventeen summers; and this is Leof-el, who is fifteen; and Aelf-raed, thirteen; and his next brother, Ban-brigge, eleven. They are the four eldest, Mother Dagian."

Dagian hugged each of the boys, admiring their healthy good looks. All were blue-eyed, but three were dark-haired like their father, while Leof-el was a blond like his mother.

Eada continued her introductions. "Here are my daughters." She drew forth two pretty blond girls, their long hair in two neat plaits on either side of their heads. "This is Erwina, who is nine, and her sister, Fearn, seven."

Dagian knelt and, holding out her arms, embraced her two newly found granddaughters, who shyly kissed her in return. "Mavia? Where is my little Mavia?" Dagian asked.

Mavia stepped from her hiding place behind her father, and came before Dagian. "Yes, Grandmother?"

"Dearest child, these are your cousins, Erwina and Fearn. I know you shall have good times together!"

The three little girls looked at one another, and finally Erwina spoke. "I have a pony," she said with the importance of the eldest.

"I have a kitten," little Fearn piped. Then the two sisters looked to their cousin.

"I am a princess," Mavia said, settling the matter.

The sisters' blue eyes grew round with wonder. "You are?" Erwina said. "*A real princess?*"

"Of course," Mavia replied. "There are no other kind. Take me to see your pony, cousin! My papa will give me a pony too, and we shall ride together."

Marcus chuckled indulgently, but Zenobia was mortified. "She must not do that, and you must not encourage her, Marcus! Palmyra is gone, and Mavia is just a child."

Eada laughed, and tucked her arm companionably through her new sister-in-law's. "She is clinging to the past because this is all so strange and new to her. It cannot have been easy for her, either. She will soon forget she was once a princess, and she will be running barefoot in the fields with her cousins. Come now and meet my two youngest."

A sturdy apple-cheeked nursemaid came forward holding by the hands two tow-headed little boys with mischievous and twinkling dark-blue eyes.

"These two scamps are Gal, who has managed to reach five, and his baby brother, Tam-tun, who is now three."

Dagian bent to kiss the littlest boys, but tears flooded Zenobia's eyes as she remembered her sons, now lost to her. Marcus put his arms about her, and she wept softly into his chest as he soothed her gently. "We will have our own sons," he said.

"I am past thirty," she sobbed. "Oh, why did I not wed with you years ago?!"

"Because you were stubborn, and proud, and Queen of Palmyra, beloved. You had so much responsibility, my darling. You could face nothing more, and how were we to know that it would end this way?"

"How old are you, Zenobia?" Eada asked, and when Zenobia told her Eada laughed. "Tam-tun was born when I was only a year younger than you are now, and I suspect that I am breeding again with another child. It is not as if you have never had a child. Come on now," she said briskly, "and I will take you to your room."

The interior of the house was like nothing Zenobia had ever seen. They entered into a vast hall with three fireplaces, the floors of stone. On either side of the main fireplace were corridors, leading to a bath on one side, and the kitchen wing on the other. Off the entry of the house, which was located before the main hall, were staircases leading up to the sleeping quarters. Zenobia and Marcus were led to a large, airy, comfortable room, which was to be theirs during their stay with Aulus and his wife. Mavia was somewhere with her cousins, probably already running barefooted, thought her mother.

In the days to come Zenobia began to learn a way of life that was quite different from the life she had led as the Queen of Palmyra; nor was it like that of the proper Roman wife whom Marcus liked to tease her about. If it resembled anything it was somewhat similar to her childhood within her father's tribe. Aulus and his family were very close, and that closeness extended to the members of the Salinae Dobunni tribe of whom he was chieftain. He looked after those who could not look after themselves, settled their arguments, approved marriages between families, kept the peace, and administered the law. It was not always easy, although Aulus was a popular leader. His loyalty was clearly to Britain, for he had long ago cut his ties to Rome. Britain, however, was a large land peopled by many tribes, some more civilized than others, and it was necessary to be constantly vigilant.

Zenobia still felt pursued. She could not escape the feeling that the Roman authorities were not about to let an important imperial captive simply walk away. As much as she enjoyed being with Aulus's family, she was anxious to gain the safety of their island, for instinct told her that she would have no peace until they were there. One afternoon she and Marcus rode out across the vast estate owned by Aulus, stopping to dismount upon a little hill. About them spikes of purple lavender scented the air. They sat upon the ground, the sun warming their backs, and looked out over the valley below, the river winding its way across the green landscape.

"When will we go to the island?" she asked him.

"Soon, beloved. I want to go on ahead of you, and see what must be done to make it habitable."

"You have paid your brother for it?"

"He did not want the gold, but I made him take it. I could not feel the island was really mine if I did not buy it. I wanted no charity from Aulus."

"The rivalry is still there, isn't it?"

"Yes. And so it shall always be. I cannot forget it, and neither can Aulus. We are better friends when we each have our own territory."

"I shall be glad when we have our own home at last," she answered him. "Eada is kind, but it is her house . . . and the walls are thinner than I would wish. Last night when you slept I could hear Graf-ere and Leof-el with a servant girl in the room next door to ours. One of them, and I am not sure which, grunted like a boar in rut when atop the girl."

"So that is why you have been so reluctant, and so restrained," he chuckled.

"If I could hear them, Marcus, then surely they could hear us!"

"There is no one to hear us now," he said slowly, and then he ran a finger down her arm.

"*Here?*"

"And now," he said softly, and then he reached up, took down her dark hair, and began to undo the braids. "I far prefer your beautiful hair loose and flowing, as you have worn it in the past." His fingers threaded themselves through the waves, undoing them, spreading the hair like a dark silken mantle over her shoulders.

She felt a surge of joyous pleasure at his sensuous action, and rising to her feet, she loosened the girdle at the waist of

her tunic dress and drew the gown and its undergarment off,
letting them fall into the sweet-smelling grass. She stood tall
and proud, her beautiful golden body with its softly blowing
black hair swirling about her. The air caressed her body, and it
felt good. "When and where you are Gaius, I then and there
am Gaia," she said, repeating her wedding vow to him.

Marcus looked up at his golden wife outlined against the
blue sky, and said, "Oh, Zenobia, how very much I love you!"
Then he stood, quickly disrobed, and pulled her into his strong
arms. Her hands caressed his back gently as he drew her against
him. They stood, bodies pressed tightly against one another,
for several long moments, and then he lowered his head to kiss
her.

It was a deep kiss, a passionate kiss; a kiss that demanded
and gave no quarter. His mouth bruised hers, but she kissed
him back fiercely, her heart soaring wildly as the passion of his
lips and the warmth of his hard body communicated to her
their intense need of each other. Her hands ran down his long,
smooth back to cup his buttocks, to fondle them, to feel the
hard muscles within them.

He groaned, shifting against her, murmuring lover's thoughts
against her lips. "Beloved! My beautiful beloved! The gods,
how I want you! How I long to possess you—and be possessed
by you!"

Her hands slid back up his frame to tangle themselves within
his chestnut hair. She held his head with her hands, and pressed
feathery kisses across his face. "I love you," she said. "I think
I always have from the moment that we met in the desert
outside of Palmyra!" Then her mouth found his again, and they
kissed once more, hungrily, eagerly, greedily. Like bumblebees
seeking the sweetest nectar from a rose, they drank of each
other's mouths.

His big hands sat firmly upon her hips, and now he began to
draw her down to the sweet grass. The earth was warm beneath
her back as she drew his head to her glorious breasts. "Love
me, my Marcus," she said low. "Love me as you have always
loved me!" And then she lay quiet, her head thrown back.

He leaned over her, tenderly looking deep into her silvery
eyes as they mirrored back his love of her, and then he kissed
her gently, fleetingly upon the lips before moving slowly from
the corner of her mouth to the soft hollow beneath her ear, just
above her jaw. He lingered there for a few moments, enjoying
the sweet perfume of her fragrance and the tiny pulse that leapt

beneath his lips. Moving lower, he slipped along the side of her neck and down to her rounded shoulder, which seemed to him to be begging to be nibbled. Gently he nipped the firm flesh before returning to her throat, which beckoned him onward to the deep valley between her breasts.

One of his arms cradled her with tenderness, while his other hand moved to caress her breasts, trembling at the silky fineness of her skin. He had touched her this way a thousand thousand times, and yet it was as if this were the first. His touch brought a little cry of pleasure, which excited him greatly. Swiftly bending, he captured a trembling nipple and sucked deeply upon it while his hand kneaded her breast. For several long and wonderful minutes he gave all his attention to her one breast, and then he moved on to the other lest it feel neglected. Zenobia now began to writhe slowly beneath her husband's expert lovemaking, her excitement rising fast now.

Finally he lay his head upon her belly, and his fingers began a delicate teasing of her Venus mount, stroking, probing tenderly between the plumpness of her nether lips; finding the sweet, hidden bud of her womanhood; taunting it with a clever finger; bringing his dark head down to taste of her honeyed sweetness, coaxing the bud into blossom. She shuddered forcefully, and he swung a leg over her, mounting her gently.

She reached out to caress his manhood, her long fingers brushing him, exciting him with her very touch. Softly she cupped the pouch of his sex in her hands, her warmth communicating itself to him as she lightly fondled him. Then she guided him into her waiting body, sighing as he buried his lance to the very hilt. She wrapped her legs around him, allowing him to go farther, rejoicing in his skill as he began to find the rhythm.

For a moment her eyes focused upon the blue sky above her, and then Zenobia began to soar with the glorious pleasures he was unleashing throughout her body. She became one with the sky, floating free above the troubled earth. She became one with him, and they were invincible! Her cry startled the horses, who snorted and danced about the tree to which they were tethered. Her nails raked down his back, making thin bloody weals in the flesh, and he reveled in the sharpness, groaning his delight as his seed overflowed her parched and throbbing womb. Her hot sheath clutched at him, drawing the last drop from him, and then he fell exhausted upon her chest, their wild hearts matching beat for beat.

They both lay semiconscious for some minutes, and then he rolled off her and pulled her into his arms in a bear hug. "If I had died then, beloved, it would have been a glorious death."

"I thought I *had* died," she murmured back.

They lay a few minutes longer, the warm sun and the breeze lightly brushing their skin, and then he said, "We will have to go back, Zenobia, although I should far prefer to remain in this outdoor bedchamber of ours."

"It is the first time I have felt relaxed since we arrived in Britain," she answered him. "Please, Marcus, do not leave me when you go to our island. I should prefer to live roughly than to be without you."

"I don't want to leave you, beloved, but how can I take you when I do not know what I am going to find?"

"Then go tomorrow! Go tomorrow, and return quickly to me, for I cannot even bear the thought of being separated from you!"

They rose from their bed of sweet grass amid the lavender spikes and quickly redressed.

Together they rode back toward the villa of Aulus Alexander. They were almost there when a Dobunni tribesman stepped from behind a tree along the path. "Marcus Alexander Britainus," he called. "Do not go back to the villa! The Romans are there, and they seek you and your wife! You are to come with me to a place of safety."

"Mavia!" Zenobia's face paled. "I cannot leave her!"

"The little one will be safe," the tribesman replied, but Zenobia was adamant.

"I must get my child," she said. "I will not leave her!"

Marcus reached out, and put a steadying hand on his wife. "Who are these Romans?" he asked the tribesman. "Are they from Rome, or are they from Corinium?"

"Corinium," came the prompt reply.

"Listen to me, Zenobia. I think you can get safely into the villa to Mavia. If the soldiers leave, then we will leave almost as quickly. If they stay, then we will have to get you both out of the villa; but I know that you will not rest easy without Mavia, and I can trust the woman who led Palmyra's legions not to get caught."

She nodded, dismounted her horse, and began to walk toward the village. She turned once, blowing him a kiss, then continued on her way.

"What if they catch her?" asked the tribesman.

"They won't."

Using a garden gate, Zenobia slipped into the grounds and entered the house. "Are you mad?" Aulus's voice hissed in her ear.

"Are there any among them who know me?" she demanded of him.

"No, but you risk everything by coming back!"

"Did you think I would leave my child?" Zenobia's voice was fierce.

"Who is this, Aulus Alexander Britainus? You said that all of your household were present." The speaker was a plump young man, obviously new to Britain.

"I do apologize, Centurion, but I had forgotten this serving wench. She is but newly acquired. I bought her at the last captive's market." Aulus cuffed Zenobia about the head. "And where have you been this time, dog? Not at your duties, I'll wager!"

The centurion was less interested now, but still sought answers. "Where is she from? She does not look British."

"She is from Ierne, the island nation to the west of Britain. She was brought back from a raid," Aulus answered. "I think she is a bit simple-minded, for she has a tendency to wander. Go to your mistress, wench, and don't let me catch you out again! Probably in the stables humping the men," he grumbled, and the centurion laughed, his interest in Zenobia completely gone.

"She's a bit too long in the tooth for me," he said. "I like 'em young, around eleven or twelve."

Zenobia hurried to stand beside Dagian, her head lowered in a servile attitude. "What has happened?" she whispered.

"They arrived about an hour ago," Dagian whispered back. "Wait, and I will tell you."

The family was finally dismissed and permitted to go about its business. Zenobia hurried upstairs with Dagian, and almost at once the older woman began to speak. "They came without warning. It seems a trireme returning from Massilia reported seeing *Sea Nymph* docked there, and it was quickly ascertained that you had fled to Britain, although they did send to Cyprus and Capri both in case you were being clever with them. Finding *Sea Nymph* at Portus Adurni confirmed the trireme's sighting. The ship was seized." Dagian caught her breath. "Why did you come back? Where is Marcus?"

457

"I could not leave Mavia, and he is with the Dobunni. I am safe. They have no idea what Zenobia, the Queen of Palmyra, looks like. Are they going to stay?"

"I am not certain, but I do know that this centurion is not very bright. All he knows is that he is looking for Marcus and you. He has no idea that I just arrived here several weeks ago."

"They are not staying." Eada came through the door and into Dagian's room. "Oh, Zenobia, how you frightened me! When I saw you come into the room, my heart went into my mouth. Why did you not stay away? You might have been caught!"

"I was in no danger of being caught," Zenobia soothed her sister-in-law. "I could not leave my child to seek safety. Mavia is our most precious possession."

"They are coming back," Eada said. "They feel sure that you are in this area, although Aulus has denied seeing you. They are returning to Corinium for more soldiers, and then they are coming back to search the whole area around Salinae."

"How long will that give us?" Zenobia asked Eada.

"They cannot return to Corinium until tommorow, and it will take them all day to get back. Then they must come back with more soldiers. I think you will probably have three days."

A mischievous smile lit Zenobia's face. "We shall leave before them," she said, "and since we will be riding, we shall be through the town of Corinium before them. While they are retracing their steps to seek us, we shall be going in the opposite direction!"

Eada began to laugh softly. "What a marvelous strategist you are, sister! Is it true that in your own land you were a great general?"

"I led my armies," Zenobia admitted modestly.

"Marcus says she was indeed a great general," Dagian said.

"I well believe it," Eada replied, and then she asked Zenobia anxiously, "You will forgive Aulus for cuffing you, won't you?"

Now Zenobia laughed. "I think my brother has missed his calling," she said. "He would make a marvelous actor! Humping the men in the stables, indeed!"

"There was really no need for Aulus to be quite so crude," Dagian chided.

"No, no," Zenobia defended Aulus. "It was that marvelous touch that convinced the centurion that I was naught but a blowsy and stupid slave woman. It was quite clever of him."

That night, Aulus was forced to offer the hospitality of his table to the centurion and to the legionnaires in his courtyard. Zenobia and Mavia kept to their bedroom, safe and out of sight. Mavia was nervous as she had not been since Palmyra, and at one point she began to cry. Zenobia soothed her child, making a game out of what they would do later. "We are going to sneak out of Uncle Aulus's villa just the way Mama snuck out of Palmyra to seek help from the Persians," Zenobia said.

"But the Romans caught you!" Mavia wailed.

"Only because Papa wasn't with us, Mavia," her mother said.

"Where is Papa?" the child demanded.

"With the Dobunni. They will help us to reach our island."

"The Romans will not catch us?" Mavia sniffed. "We will not have to live with the emperor again?"

"No, my darling, the Romans will not catch us, and we will never again see the emperor. I promise you, Mavia!" and Zenobia hugged her small daughter tightly.

"Always on the run, always fleeing," Bab muttered as she packed their things. "I hope that eventually before I die we will be given some measure of peace again!"

Adria bowed her head, smiling at the old woman's grumbling. They all knew that Bab, now in her late seventies, thrived on the excitement that seemed constantly to surround her mistress.

"Be patient with me, old woman," Zenobia said. "Surely this must be the last time I am forced to flee. Once we have gained the safety of our island home, then they will never find me again."

"I certainly hope so! If your dear mother were alive it would have broken her heart to see how those Romans have hounded you."

The clothing and personal effects necessary for a journey were packed carefully by Adria in a small trunk. Everything else was packed by Bab in the trunks for shipping later.

The centurion had been plied with excellent wine, and now with the aid of a light sleeping draught slipped into his last cup, he lay snoring noisily in a guest chamber. He did not hear the family as they slipped one by one into Zenobia's chamber to bid her farewell. Erwina and Fearn brought their cousin Mavia a small gray and white kitten as a farewell gift.

"She is called Blossom because she loves to smell the flowers," lisped Fearn.

Mavia, hugging Blossom to her chest, thanked her cousins and promised to visit again one day.

"You must travel quickly now," Eada said, "but when we can send your things along safely, I will include many rootings and cuttings from my gardens for you." Her blue eyes filled with tears. "I wish you weren't going, Zenobia! I shall miss you."

"I have never had a sister," Zenobia said slowly. "I am fortunate that you are now mine. How can I ever thank you for your hospitality? If I were still a queen in my own land . . . but I am not. I have nothing I can give you except my love, Eada."

The two women embraced warmly, and then with a teary look at Zenobia, Eada left her. "She will never forget you," Dagian said. "She is a simple chief's daughter who has never in her entire life been farther than Corinium. You have brought the world into her life."

"She brought kindness into mine," Zenobia returned. "She opened her home and her heart to us. I can never forget that, Dagian, for it went beyond the bounds of hospitality." She looked searchingly at her mother-in-law. "Are you sure that you want to remain here? Once we have settled ourselves you are most welcome to come to us. Both Marcus and I love you, and Mavia is going to be lost without you."

"No, my child, I shall be content here."

"At least come for the winters. Eada tells me that the winters here can be harsh, and upon the island it will be mild."

"Perhaps for the winters," Dagian said, and then she enfolded Zenobia in a loving embrace. "Be happy, dearest daughter, for you have made my son happy! I could love you for that alone. We shall meet again." Then she kissed Zenobia tenderly, and hurried from the room.

Aulus came to get them. "You'll be leaving through the garden gate, and there's little likelihood of your encountering the Romans. There'll be a Dobunni to guide you to Marcus, and then you're safely on your way."

"Thank you a thousand times, Aulus. Without you I don't know what we would have done. The Romans came so quickly. I thought we had more time."

"You survived without me," Aulus muttered, embarrassed, for he was a simple man.

She kissed his rough cheek, and then before he might protest, said, "Let us go, brother! Bab, Charmian, Adria, Mavia! Come along!"

Old Severus was to go with them also, and he was waiting in the garden by the street gate for them. Dressed in dark cloaks to camouflage themselves, the six set off through the gate and down the street. At the corner they were joined by a barely distinguishable tribesman who stepped from the darkness to lead them. Silently they followed him, their eyes upon his dark shape as they traveled through the village and out into the open fields.

A fine moon had now risen to silver the landscape and show them the way. Finally they entered a small wood, where in a clearing Marcus awaited them. Thankfully he embraced his wife and daughter.

"Praise the gods you are safe!"

"They never saw Mavia, and Aulus told them I was a captive slave from Ierne. It was simple, my darling. Tell me now how we get to where we are going?"

"We will travel to Glevum, and be through it by morning; but we shall be able to bypass Corinium entirely, for they have built a new road in the last five years between Glevum and Aquae Sulis."

"Then we do not have to worry about a large Roman garrison!" She was relieved.

He continued. "From Aquae Sulis we go to Lindinis and finally the last really important Roman settlement in Britain, Isca Dumnoniorum. Aulus has sent a message to the high chieftain of the Dumnonii. They will take us the rest of the way to the coast, where a ship awaits us. From here to there we travel in safety under the protection of the warriors of the Dobunni." He smiled down at her. "You are safe, beloved! You are safe now and forever!" And looking up into his moon-lit eyes, Zenobia, the Queen of Palmyra knew that he spoke the truth.

"Then lead on, my husband," she said quietly, "and take me home."

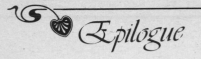

Epilogue

The island sat like a small green jewel in the bright blue sea. The mainland had suffered a bitter winter, but here the flowers had already bloomed and the air was mild and gentle. When they arrived there had been no habitable building upon the island, only the bleak and crude ruins of some past civilization; but there was a fine harbor and several freshwater springs and ponds. There were wild goats, and small game, and a host of birds.

Marcus had given Aulus a goodly supply of gold in order that his brother might barter and negotiate for him with the tribes, for Marcus did not think himself capable in this instance. Whatever Aulus had done he had done right, for the very day they landed upon the island another ship, this one bearing men and supplies, arrived. At once the building of a house had begun. Using the sand from a local beach, the builders began to mix concrete, and within days a large two-story house with walls fifteen inches thick had risen on the cliffs above the harbor. The inner facing of the house was of stone, the outer facing of fine white limestone that gave the building a smooth, hard, white finish. The roof tiles were red.

The house had been designed very much like Aulus's home, with an entry that had staircases on either side, and beyond, a large hall. There were wings on each side of the main fireplace, one containing the baths, the other the kitchens and servants' quarters. The second story of the house contained six large bedchambers, all looking out upon the sea. Between the wings of the house was a lovely sheltered garden where the family would sit in the evening and on warmer winter days. Beyond the garden wall stretched a long building whose lower story housed the farm animals they had imported to the island, and whose upper story housed the farm slaves. The entire area was enclosed by a wall, although Marcus did not expect to have to repel invaders.

Slaves had been imported to the island, strong men for the

462

farm, and young women for the house and the gardens. Some of the slaves had had children, and Marcus had purchased them also, for Mavia was apt to be lonely without friends her age. In Rome, old Senator Tacitus was already gone, having caught a chill in the fourth month of his reign. He had been replaced by his much younger brother, who was head of the Praetorian. The younger Tacitus had, in his turn, succumbed to poison, and now less than eighteen months after Aurelian's assassination a third emperor sat upon the shaky imperial throne.

The new emperor was Marcus Aurelius Probus, the son of one Dalmatius, a country gardener by profession. He was a distinguished military leader who had served under both Valerian and Aurelian. How long he would last was, of course, a moot point, Zenobia thought as she nursed her infant son on a late summer's afternoon. At least Roman interest in them seemed to be dying down, although Aulus had written that twice the Romans had returned seeking them, the last time in a midnight raid that had frightened everyone half to death.

Dagian had come to the island to be with Zenobia for the birth, bringing with her an old herbal woman of the Dobunni. The birth had been incredibly easy, but the herbal woman had advised Zenobia against having future children. "You are no longer a girl, and your life has taken its toll upon your health. I can help you to regain your health, but another child will kill you."

"But Eada is older than I, and she continues to have her babies and thrive," Zenobia protested.

"The lady Eada is of this land, and she has never stopped having children in all her married life. How many years are between your daughter and the son you have just borne? Too many! Do not fear, lady. This boy will thrive, and go on to father you many grandsons! I shall give you something to use so you will not conceive again, yet your husband's pleasure will not be spoiled."

"Listen to her," Dagian said, seeing the unhappy look in Zenobia's eyes. "She has never been wrong."

Zenobia had finally agreed, although reluctantly, for she had hoped to give her husband several sons despite the fact she was in her late thirties now. Still, Marcus had not been disappointed that they would have no more children. Rather, he had been delighted that she had given him another child at all.

They had named the boy Lucius, for his grandfather. Now the child was six months old, and his mother was beginning to be as restless as his father was. They had been on the island well over a year now, and Zenobia was well rested. She was no longer fearful of capture. She was bored. She loved her children, but she had been born to rule, and now that she had no kingdom she found herself at loose ends.

Wandering about the house one afternoon, she discovered Marcus in his library, hovering over some maps. Drawn to join him, she saw that the map was marked Ierne. "Isn't that the island kingdom to the west of Britain?" she asked.

"Yes."

"Are there Romans there?"

"No, not to my knowledge."

"What is there?"

"I do not know, beloved." He looked up, and she could see in his eyes the same longing he could see in hers.

"When do we go?" she asked.

"*We?*"

"You do not believe that I shall stay here like a good Roman wife while you go exploring?"

"What of the children?"

"It's a marvelous excuse for us to keep your mother with us. As for Lucius, my milk is not plentiful. There is, however, among the slave women one who has just had a still birth, and her milk is. Let me give her Lucius to nurse." She caught his hands in hers. "We were separated for too long, Marcus, for me to let you go from me now; yet I cannot deny you the opportunity. I am restless, and bored too. Our island may be a safe haven, but there is little for me to do."

"It could be dangerous, beloved."

"Oh, I hope so!" Her face was alight with the anticipation of a child who looks forward to some special treat.

"You will never be a Roman wife," he said with mock despair, but his blue eyes shone with his love for her, a love that would live on forever.

"No, Marcus, I shall never be a Roman wife though I live to be as old a woman as Bab." Her silvery eyes laughed up at him, sympathizing with him, loving him back.

"Then," he said slowly, "there is nothing for it but we go exploring; and perhaps we shall find another kingdom for you to rule over, beloved."

"No," she replied. "I have ruled Palmyra, the greatest city in the East, perhaps on this earth. There will be no other earthly kingdoms for me. I shall be happy to be with you, to rule within the kingdom of your heart.''

His hands rested lightly upon her shoulders, and looking down at her, he said again the words that had first won her to him. ''I have loved you from the beginnings of time, and I shall love you long after our memories have faded from this earth.''

Zenobia's heart swelled within her chest. It swelled until she thought it might break with the happiness she felt permeating her entire being. As Marcus lowered his head to capture her lips in a tender yet passionate kiss, her last rational thought before she gave herself up to him was that no matter what happened now she was whole in body and spirit once again. The world lay before them. A wonderful new adventure was just over the horizon. It would be all right now, for she had Marcus Alexander Britainus for all eternity. She was still the beloved of the gods, though in the end they would have the last word! It is enough, Zenobia thought. It is more than enough!

Author's Note

Zenobia is the sixth of my heroines. Like two of her fair predecessors, Cyra Hafise and Adora, she actually existed. Researching women in past centuries is not always easy. The farther back you travel in time, the less you are apt to find. Few women have come down to us through the centuries who were not simply some famous man's wife, mistress, or mother.

Yet there is a good deal of information available about Zenobia, though she lived in the third century after Christ. Most interesting is the fact that I could find nothing derogatory about this fascinating female who for a time held off the might of the invincible Roman Empire. She is hailed in song and story as beautiful, wise, educated, compassionate, and a great leader. The most unkind word I read regarding her was "ambitious."

Before disappearing from the pages of history Zenobia was actually pensioned off by the Roman government. An unusual end for so formidable a foe. I think she was quite a lady, and if you agree, I hope you will write to me at P.O. Box 765, Southold, N.Y. 11971. As busy as I am, I always find time to answer my mail. I'll be waiting to hear from you.

—Bertrice Small

About the Author

Bertrice Small is the best-selling author of *The Kadin, Love Wild and Fair, Adora, Skye O'Malley,* and *Unconquered*. She lives in the oldest English settlement in the State of New York, a small village on the eastern end of Long Island. She is called "Sunny" by her friends, and "Lust's Leading Lady" by her fans; but her son insists that to him, she's just plain "Mom."

Mrs. Small works at an antique desk in a light-filled pink, green, and white studio overlooking her old-fashioned rose and flower garden. It is furnished in what she describes as a mixture of office modern, and Turkish harem. Mrs. Small's only companions as she writes creating her handsome rogues, dashing renegades, and beautiful vixens are her typewriter, Rebecca, and her large black and white cat, Ditto.